THE FOUR-GATED CITY

This is the best of Doris Lessing. Like her previous works, capped by the genius of **THE GOLDEN NOTEBOOK**, it is social chronicle, autobiography and reportage. Like nothing that has been written before, **THE FOUR-GATED CITY** defines and dramatizes the world we spend our lives in.

The city of the title is London—but you will know the people and the life from your own experience. The story begins quietly twenty years ago, and ends with inevitable apocalypse twenty years hence. Here is a major writer at the height of her powers, writing about reality and defying all categories of fiction in her unique, disquieting style.

In four previous novels, set in Africa and looking back to the past, to the violent heritage that shaped our social and psychological present, Doris Lessing has explored the end of an epoch. Now, in this immense visionary novel, she carries her protagonist, Martha Quest, to London and the world, into the present and the future. The power of her vision, its very shock and anguish, should prove liberating for the generation she defines as the Children of Violence.

THE CHILDREN OF VIOLENCE . . .

Martha Quest, familiar to Doris Lessing's readers as a rebellious young girl, increasingly at odds with the white colony she grew up in, searching, through political involvement, sexual experience and commitment to others, for a world she can justify to herself. In **THE FOUR-GATED CITY** she reaches her maturity, looks back on the causes she has believed in, and experiences the insanity of others as the century moves to its ironic, inevitable end.

Mark Coldridge, Martha's employer and lover, whose insane wife lives in the basement with a mad woman she befriended in the asylum.

The children, relatives, neighbors and friends who are the traumatized inheritors of this violent world; mothers, mistresses, daughters and wives; lovers, psychiatrists, Communists and witches—all live together in **THE FOUR-GATED CITY.** The essential nature of each is unique, they are real human beings who grow old yet remain unchanged in certain ways—they learn and relearn things again and again, and they stumble, pick themselves up, and rush toward the end of their lives.

These are the Children of Violence—subjects and readers of

THE FOUR-GATED CITY

THE FOUR-GATED CITY is:

"Extraordinary"

—Commonweal

"Clairvoyant"

—Christian Science Monitor

"Powerful"

—The Houston Post

"Staggering"

—The New York Times

"Absorbing"

—Cleveland Plain Dealer

"Superbly horrific"

—Newsweek

"Valuable new perception"

—Atlantic Monthly

"Provocative"

—Publishers' Weekly

"Chilling"

—Newsday

"Laudable"

—The New Yorker

"Brave"

—The New Leader

"Impressively frightening"

—Chicago Tribune

The Four-Gated City
Doris Lessing

BANTAM BOOKS · TORONTO · NEW YORK · LONDON

*This low-priced Bantam Book
has been completely reset in a type face
designed for easy reading, and was printed
from new plates. It contains the complete
text of the original hard-cover edition.*
NOT ONE WORD HAS BEEN OMITTED.

THE FOUR-GATED CITY
*A Bantam Book / published by arrangement with
Alfred A. Knopf, Inc.*

PRINTING HISTORY
Knopf edition published May 1969

Bantam edition / November 1970

2nd printing .. November 1972	5th printing ...... February 1976
3rd printing .. November 1973	6th printing .. September 1978
4th printing .... March 1975	7th printing .... February 1980

*Bantam Books are published by Bantam Books, Inc. Its trade-
mark, consisting of the words "Bantam Books" and the por-
trayal of a bantam, is Registered in U.S. Patent and Trademark
Office and other countries. Marca Registrada. Bantam
Books, Inc., 666 Fifth Avenue, New York, New York 10019.*

PRINTED IN THE UNITED STATES OF AMERICA

0 9 8 7

DEDICATION

Once upon a time there was a fool who was sent to buy flour and salt. He took a dish to carry his purchases.

"Make sure," said the man who sent him, "not to mix the two things—I want them separate."

When the shopkeeper had filled the dish with flour and was measuring out the salt, the fool said: "Do not mix it with the flour; here, I will show you where to put it."

And he inverted the dish, to provide, from its up-turned bottom, a surface upon which the salt could be laid

The flour, of course, fell to the floor.

But the salt was safe.

When the fool got back to the man who had sent him, he said: "Here is the salt."

"Very well," said the other man, "but where is the flour?"

"It should be here," said the fool, turning the dish over.

As soon as he did that, the salt fell to the ground, and the flour, of course, was seen to be gone.

A dervish teaching story, from
THE WAY OF THE SUFI
by Idries Shab

THE FOUR-GATED CITY

PART ONE

In its being and its meaning, this coast represents not merely an uneasy equilibrium of land and water masses; it is eloquent of a continuing change now actually in progress, a change being brought about by the life processes of living things. Perhaps the sense of this comes most clearly to one standing on a bridge between the Keys, looking out over miles of water, dotted with mangrove-covered islands to the horizon. This may seem a dreamy land, steeped in its past. But under the bridge a green mangrove seedling floats, long and slender, one end already beginning to show the development of roots, beginning to reach down through the water, ready to grasp and to root firmly in any muddy shoal that may lie across its path. Over the years the mangroves bridge the water gaps between the islands; they extend the mainland; they create new islands. And the currents that stream under the bridge, carrying the mangrove seedling, are one with the currents that carry plankton to the coral animals building the offshore reef, creating a wall of rocklike solidity, a wall that one day may be added to the mainland. So this coast is built.

THE EDGE OF THE SEA, RACHEL CARSON

One

In front of Martha was grimed glass, its lower part covered with grimed muslin. The open door showed an oblong of browny-grey air swimming with globules of wet. The shop fronts opposite were no particular colour. The lettering on the shops, once black, brown, gold, white, was now shades of dull brown. The lettering on the upper part of the glass of this room said *Joe's Fish and Chips* in reverse, and was flaking like stale chocolate. She sat by a rectangle of pinkish oilcloth where sugar had spilled, and onto it, orange tea, making a gritty smear in which someone had doodled part of a name: Daisy Flet ... Her cup was thick whitey-grey, cracked. The teaspoon was a whitish plastic, so much used that the elastic brittleness natural to it had gone into an erosion of hair lines, so that it was like a kind of sponge. When she had drunk half the tea, a smear of grease appeared halfway down the inside of the cup: a thumb mark. How hard had some hand—attached to Iris, to Jimmy?—gripped the cup to leave a smear which even after immersion in strong orange tea had left a thumbprint good enough for the police. Across the room, by another pinkish rectangle, sat Joe's mother, Iris, a small fattish smeared woman. She was half asleep, cat-napping. She wore an overall washed so often it had gone a greyish yellow. A tired soured smell came from her. The small fattish pale man behind the counter where the tea urn dominated was not Joe, who had gone off to the war and had never returned home, having married a woman and her café in Birmingham. He was Jimmy, Joe's mother's partner. Jimmy wished to marry Iris, but she did not want to marry again. Once was enough, she said. Meanwhile they lived together and proposed to continue to live together. Although both were now "resting," this being a slack time in the café, and had announced, as if they were turning a notice on a door to say CLOSED, that they were resting, both observed Martha. Or rather, their interest, what was alert of it, was focussed on what she would do next, but they were

3

too good-mannered to let this appear. About an hour before she had asked if she might use the telephone. She had not yet done so. From time to time the two exchanged remarks with each other, as thickly indifferent as words coming out of sleep, sleep-mutters; but yet it was open to Martha to join in if she wished, to comment on weather and the state of Jimmy's health, neither very good. Today he had a pain in his stomach. Really they wanted to be told, or to find out, why the telephone call was so important that Martha could not make it and be done. The air of the small steamy box which was the café vibrated with interest, tact, curiosity, sympathy—friendship, in short; all the pressures which for a blissful few weeks since Martha had been in England, rather London, she had been freed from.

For a few weeks she had been anonymous, unnoticed—free. Never before in her life had she known this freedom. Living in a small town anywhere means preserving one's self behind a mask. Coming to a big city for those who have never known one means first of all, before anything else, and the more surprising if one has not expected it, that freedom: all the pressures are off, no one cares, no need for the mask. For weeks then, without boundaries, without definition, like a balloon drifting and bobbing, nothing had been expected of her.

But since she had taken the room upstairs over the café, had been accepted into the extraordinary kindness and delicacy of this couple, she had made a discovery: "Matty" was reborn. And after how many years of disuse? "Matty" now was rather amusing, outspoken, competently incompetent, free from convention, free to say what other people did not say: yet always conscious of, and making a burnt offering of, these qualities. "Matty" gained freedom from whatever other people must conform to not so much by ignoring it but, when the point was reached when conformity might be expected, by gaining exemption in an act of deliberate clumsiness—like a parody, paying homage as a parody does to its parent-action. An obsequiousness, in fact, an obeisance. Exactly so, she understood, had the jester gained exemption with his bladder and his bells. Just so had the slave humiliated himself to flatter his master: as she had seen a frightened African labourer clown before her father. And so, it seems, certain occupants of recent concentration camps, valuing life above dignity, had made themselves mock those points of honour, self-respect, which had previously been the focus points of their beings, to buy exemption from the camp commanders. Between "Matty" and such sad buffoons, the difference was one of degree. Somewhere early in her childhood, on that farm on the highveld, "Matty" had been created by her as an act of survival. But why? In order to prevent herself from being—what? She could not remember. But during the last few years before leaving "home" (now not where she was, England, previously "home," of a sort, but that town she had left) "Matty" had not existed, there had not been a need for her. Martha had forgotten "Matty," and it was painful to give her houseroom again. But here she was, just as if she had not been in abeyance for years, ready at the touch of a button to chatter, exclaim, behave with attractive outrageousness, behave like a foolish but lovable puppy. In this house. With Jimmy and Iris. (Not with Stella down the river, not at all.) Here. Why? For some days now Martha had been shut inside this person, it was "Martha" who intruded, walked into "Matty," not the other way about. Why? She was also, today, shut inside clothes that dressed, she felt, someone neither Martha, nor "Matty."

For the weeks of her being in London the sun had shone. Strange enough that she could now see it like this. In a country where the sun is always so evident, forceful, present; clouds, storms, rain briefly disguise the dominating, controlling presence of the sun; one does not say "Today the sun shone," for it always does. But after a few weeks in England, she could say "The sun shone today" and only by putting herself back on that other soil felt the truth that the sun never stopped shining. Even in the middle of the night, the sun blazed out, held it in its blaze all planets and the earth and the moon, the earth having merely turned away its face, on its journey around away from light and back.

All the warnings of the seasoned about the hideousness of the English climate had for those weeks, while the sun shone, seemed like the croakings of the envious, or like those exaggerated tales created by the experienced to terrify greenhorns. The sun had shone, day in and day out, not with the splendid golden explosiveness of Africa, but had shone, regularly, from a blue high sky; not as deeply, as solemnly, as brazenly blue as the skies she had been bred under—but blue, and hot and almost cloudless. Martha had worn the brief bright dresses of that other wardrobe, which she had almost left behind altogether. She had worn brown bare arms, brown legs, and hair still burnt a rough gold from the other sun. Just as if she had not left home and its free-and-easiness forever, she had been carried by that current of people, that tide, which always flows in and out of London through the homeowners, the rate-payers, the settled: people visiting, holidaying, people wondering if they should settle, people looking for their ancestors and their roots, the students, the travellers, the drifters, the tasters, the derelicts and the nonconformists who must have a big city to hide themselves in because no small one can tolerate them. From room to room, cheap hotel to hotel, a bed in the flat of a man whose name she could not remember though she remembered him with warmth, nights spent walking with men and women as enjoyably vagrant and as footloose as she, nights with Jack—so she had lived, for hot blue sunny weeks, and now, suddenly, two days ago, the skies had descended in a greyish-brown ooze of wet, and Martha wore a thick skirt, a sweater, stockings, and black coat given to her before she left by Mrs. Van der Bylt out of (so Martha accepted it) concern because of Martha's refusal to believe just how terrible the English climate was. But really the old woman was giving Martha much more than a coat when she had handed the young woman, who was about to leave, the thick black matronly garment which now hung over the back of a wood chair painted greasy daffodil colour in Joe's café.

She had put it there an hour ago. She ought to get up and say to Jimmy and to Joe's mother, Iris: "I'll be back in a few minutes. I want to go for a walk." *Ought.* She *ought* to make this statement, put on the coat, go out, walk for the sake of clearing her head into decisions, come back, telephone and then act on what she had decided. Ah yes, but to do what one *ought*—and then there was the enemy "Matty" so very much stronger than she would have been prepared to believe.

Martha stood up, and at once two pairs of eyes, both pale blue, surfaced with noncommitting goodwill, but inwardly hungry for sensation, fastened themselves on her. Martha said, putting on the heavy black coat which had encased Mrs. Van through several Zambesian winters: "I am going for a short walk." At once the two bodies subtly froze: disappointment. Then, suspicion. Of course, and quite rightly: had not "Matty" been here for weeks now, the freakishly "charming" visitor from such different worlds, had not she even worked behind the counter to earn the rent for her room upstairs, and always half the buffoon, at least the willing-to-be-teased, self-confessedly inefficient if full of goodwill, always offering honesty about what she was doing, to these so gently avid hosts? They were now in the right to feel that she shut them out, rejected them, by saying, coldly—so they must feel it—"I am going for a walk." That would not do, now, after letting them have "Matty" for so long. "It's nice to tell other people your troubles," Iris had said, waiting to hear Martha's—invented, or at least exaggerated, to please her.

Martha now said, with a small rueful laugh: "It's all too much for me, I need a good think," and as she pushed back her chair she banged her leg and said, in a half groan, "Oh damn it!"

"Oh, mind your nylons, dear," said Joe's mother, softening at once, and even exchanging palliated glances with Jimmy as he leaned forward, smiling, to watch Martha rub her leg.

Martha continued to rub it, gasping with pain-infused laughter, until she was able to make her escape to the door, the fee having been paid, passing the telephone on the counter which, if she were to do as she *ought*, she would have used before this.

Defeated, she went out. The dirty sky pressed down over the long street which one way led to South London, and the other to the river and the City. Terraces of two- and three-storey houses, all unpainted since before the war, all brownish, yellowish, greyish, despondent. Damp. Martha stood outside the café where *Joe's Fish and Chips* was outlined by the hearse-dark of blackout material: Iris and Jimmy had not got around to taking it down. The shops which were the ground level of the long street mostly had dull black visible; and some windows of the upper rooms showed black above or beside the faded cretonnes and chintzes. The war had been over five years. The street itself was empty. Traffic had been diverted because of a great crater from which protruded the top halves of men attending to gas, or telephone, or electric cables. A great gaping jagged hole. Not war damage; but according to Iris ever since the bomb had dropped a couple of hundred yards down the road, the gas mains had been leaking into the earth, and the road was always being dug up, as now. The crater was roped off, and had red-eyed lanterns resting about its lip. Martha stood at its edge and watched a dozen or so men at work. One of them was a black man. He wore a whitish cotton singlet. The bottoms of his trousers were torn. He was a tall spindly fellow and his face was set into the no-expression of a man doing an unliked job of work—as were the faces of his white fellows. Muscles moved in rhythm under grey skin, under black skin. The muscles were great fruity lumps moving between the dull grimed skin and the bones. There was no body among them that might have been chosen to represent the human form in its aspect of beauty, since all were in some way deformed; and there was no face that did not carry marks of strain, weariness, or illness. All life, all health, the immediately recognisable spontaneity of energy was in the muscles. Spades and picks tore into a dull heavy damp soil. It was a yellowish soil. In it was embedded a system of clay pipes, iron pipes, knotted cables. No roots. No trees in this street. Not one tree: therefore, no roots. Martha had never before seen soil that was dead, that had no roots. How long had this street been built? Iris thought about two hundred years, but she didn't know. For two hundred years this soil had held no life at all? How long did roots live under a crust of air-excluding tarmac? There was a smell of gas from the crater, like the smell of decay, yet it had a mineral tang, not far off the stale smell of a mineshaft a couple of hours after blasting.

Martha went on towards the river, passing shop fronts, each one the face of a low oblong room like Joe's café: haberdasher, grocer, chemist, greengrocer, hardware, fishmonger, then all over again, chemist, grocer, hardware, grocer, laundry, a pub. All over London: millions of little shops, each one the ground floor of an old house. On either side of her the terraces: damp. Stained with damp. Under her feet, a damp concrete. Fitting down over the street, a low hat of grey sky.

The surface of water, moving, rippling, rearing, crashing, is what we see when we say "Sea" or "River" or "Lake." Standing in the water at waist or thigh level a skin of light separates wet from air. If one were to wade through earth in Africa, around one's legs roots: tree roots, thick, buried branches; then sharper thinner vines from bushes, shrubs, then a thick clutch of grass roots—a mat of working life. Walking to one's waist in an English lane, roots, such a thick mass of roots—tree and shrub and bush and grass. But walking here, it would be through heavy unaired rootless soil, where electricity and telephone and gas tubes ran and knotted and twined.

Now the place where the bomb had fallen. That was how they spoke of it: "The bomb." Their bomb, out of the thousands that had fallen on London. About three acres lay flat, bared of building, almost—it was a half-job; the place had neither been cleared nor left. It was as if some great thumb had come down and rubbed out buildings, carelessly: and then the owner of the thumb had blown away bits of debris and rubble, but carelessly. All the loose rubble had gone, or been piled up against walls, or the fence; but pits of water marked old basements, and sharp bits of wall jutted, and a heap of girders rusted. The ground floor of a house stood, shacked over with iron, in the middle, and a single wall reared high up from it, intact, with fireplaces one above another. The place had a fence and a sign which said under crossbones and skull: DANGER. NO CHILDREN. Behind the ruin of the house a group of children squatted, spinning marbles off their thumbs across yellow earth. Seeing a woman in black outside the fence, they froze, betrayed like animals by their moving alerted eyes. Then they melted out of sight into walls, rubble. The door to this bomb site was a tall metal grille and it was held shut by a bolt or baulk of timber. This was about ten feet long and so thick that if her arms had been twice as long they could not have met around it. This object had been a tree. For some days now Martha had been pausing by it, trying to make it out. Because it was hard to imagine it as a tree. Its surface was not smooth: if it had ever been planed, that smooth skin had been worn away long ago. It was splintered, eaten, beaten, battered. Touching it was not touching wood, but nearer to water-eaten stone. It was almost spongy. Damp had swollen and filled every fibre. Wood had meant a hand on a trunk under which sap ran; wood had meant the smell of bark; wood had been the smell of oiled surfaces where grain showed patterns. Wood had never meant a great baulk of greyish-brown substance that smelled of wet, of damp, of rot, and of the gas which must have soaked everything in this street since everything smelled of it.

Iris had said that "they" had pulled this great beam out of the river at some point: she remembered that they had. It had come in useful for a decade, having been used as a base for a stair into an area before the bomb had destroyed house, area and stair, though not the timber itself. So it was used to keep the gate shut against children. That was what it was meant to do, at least; though looking through the grille, it could be seen that the other side of the bomb site, a parallel street, had no fence at all, was open; had, merely, a sign with a skull and crossbones.

In the hulk of timber was a cleft, more like a crack in rock than a split in wood. Moss grew in it. Salt lay seamed in finer cracks, salt from the salty, tide-washed river. Iris said the timber was probably part of a ship once. She said a piece of wood that size must have been part of an old ship when ships were wood not metal: for what else could they have used a beam so enormous? Half a dozen men had been

9

needed to lay it propped where it was now—she had watched them doing it.

Iris, Joe's mother, knew about this timber, about the houses which had been bombed, about the people who had lived in the houses, and the people who now lived in the houses of the part of the street which stood intact: some of them were from this site of rubble and dust and mud. She knew everything about this area, half a dozen streets for about half a mile or a mile of their length; and she knew it all in such detail that when with her, Martha walked in a double vision, as if she were two people: herself and Iris, one eye stating, denying, warding off the total hideousness of the whole area, the other, with Iris, knowing it in love. With Iris, one moved here, in state of love, if love is the delicate but total acknowledgement of what is. Passing a patch of bared wall where the bricks showed a crumbling smear of mushroom colour, Iris was able to say: Mrs. Black painted this wall in 1938, it was ever such a nice pink. Or, looking up at a lit window, the curtains drawn across under the black smear of the blackout material which someone had not got around to taking down: Molly Smith bought those curtains down at the market the first year of the war, before things got so scarce. Or, walking around a block in the pavement, she muttered that the workmen never seemed to be able to get that piece in square, she always stubbed her foot against it. Iris, Joe's mother, had lived in this street since she was born. Put her brain together with the other million brains, women's brains, that recorded in such tiny loving anxious detail the histories of window sills, skins of paint, replaced curtains and salvaged baulks of timber, there would be a recording instrument, a sort of six-dimensional map which included the histories and lives and loves of people, London—a section map in depth. This is where London exists, in the minds of people who have lived in such and such a street since they were born, and passing a baulk of timber remember, smiling, how it came rolling up out of the Thames on that Thursday afternoon it was raining, to lie on a pavement until it became the spine of a stairway—and then the bomb fell.

Martha walked on to the river, still invisible, though she saw the ponderous buildings across it which was the City. She had to walk across the river, walk into a decision: not loiter and dally until she found herself back at the café with a joke that was the currency of false pleading: she had caught herself thinking, I'll go back to the café and take off this coat before I ... The coat was too hot. Mrs. Van had had it during the war, that is, when skirts were knee-high and shoulders thick. Pulled tight around Martha it gave her the tight waist of that year's fashion and came halfway down her calves—the fashion. But the folds which had once snugged Mrs. Van's large bosom pouted over Martha's, and the sleeves came to her knuckles. She must buy a new coat. But she had no money. There were five pounds left. Which was why decisions were imminent and responsibility inevitable. She must make that telephone call today: she was to telephone Marjorie's sister Phoebe.

A telephone box stood ahead. It had been, would be again, a military scarlet: now it was a pinky-orange with a bloom of damp on the paint. But it was a colour—Martha went into it. She opened the coat, propped the door of the telephone box with her foot and breathed the cool wet air in relief. Marjorie's sister's number was in her bag. She did not look for it. Instead she told herself that while Marjorie's sister and what she stood for could wait, Joe's mother and Jimmy could not. If she did not do something now, in four or five days' time of this enjoyable lazy drifting on her inclination through London, saying every hour: I should ring the café, she would do no such thing, but simply turn up, and at the last moment and when she had to, for her suitcase. Which would really be letting them down. Though of course, ringing up now, half an hour after leaving when she could have said what she had to say, was letting them down. It seemed that letting them down was inevitable. Why? Had she made promises, offered what she had not given? She was *not* "Matty"! Could they have been so kind to Martha, had she not offered them "Matty"? It was too late now to know. She dialled the café and Jimmy answered. People had come in for tea and margarined buns since she had left: slack time was over, she could hear voices and activity. "This is Martha, Jimmy." "Oh, is that you, love?" "Yes." *Now, you will not make a joke of it.* She wrestled with the need to exclaim, laughing, that she had been just taken with a whim, a folly, an urge, mad Matty, oh dear, what a fool she was . . . "Jimmy, I've decided to leave." A silence. "Well, if it's like that, love." "I'm going to take a job next week." Through these two and their friends she had been offered three jobs, not to mention Iris's cousin, Stanley, as a possible husband. He said nothing. "I'll come and pick my case up soon." "Half a tick then, I'll call Iris." A clatter and a long pause. The voices went on. It was jolly in the café; people coming in knew each other, knew Iris and Jimmy. They had shared, many of them, their childhoods, their lives:

they had shared, most of them, the war. And they had opened their hearts to her. Iris now said: "Is that you, love?" "Iris, if you want to let your room, go ahead." Now that room was not easy to let, being a tiny box over the café, always noisy, and smelling always of frying-fat, the steamy tea, the fish: Iris knew Martha knew letting that room was not the point. "Are you all right, love," she asked, anxious. "Look, Iris . . ." No, no, she would not play for false advantage. "I'll come and get my suitcase sometime soon." "As you like, then: Well, if you're late coming in tonight, give us a shout." "I'll pick it up in a couple of days, Iris." And now the moment of real hurt, betrayal, the end. Martha was proposing to wander off "with nothing but what she stood up in" to take her chances for the night, and possibly other nights. And she had said it without remembering even to soften it. Martha could do that. Iris could not. No law said Iris could not: "Matty" had made a joke of travelling with her life in a suitcase: two changes of underwear, two dresses and a couple of skirts and sweaters and some papers. Even "Matty" had been careful of saying too much of how she had washed around London on this tide or that. Sometimes Iris said: "I must go up to the West End one of these days and have a look around now the war is done." She had not been "to the West End," two miles away and half an hour's bus ride, since V.E. Day. She, limpet on her rock, had known that Martha had drifted and eddied around this city which she would never visit, never know, but it had not been forced on her, that knowledge, as Martha had done by saying so finally: "I'll pick up my case sometime soon." And now off Martha went, from them, Iris and Jimmy, as casually as she had come, by chance flopping down in the café for a cup of tea, her legs having collapsed from hours of walking. Now, Martha, standing in the telephone box, a third of a mile from Iris, feeling the wires buzz with uncomprehending hurt, fought her last and final battle, swore she would not make up some funny story about freebooting around London, she would not buy forgiveness. "You'll come for your case, then?" "Yes, I'm not sure when, though." Silence. "Iris, I'm sorry," said Martha, sudden, sincere and desperate. "That's all right, love," said Iris, cool.

What would be the words used to sentence her? She did not know, and it did not matter: what people actually said in that café was the least of what they were able to convey. But she had done it, she had not clowned or apologised in the wrong way. She had done it, if she had done it badly. And

Iris would be slowly replacing the receiver, pushing the telephone back into its niche, and saying to whoever was there that afternoon, in one of her repertoire of tones which made her sparse vocabulary so rich an instrument: "That was our young lady. She's off." "She's off, is she?" And that would be that.

Well, that was one door shut behind her; which proved that she would find the strength of mind to shut the others. Martha retied the coat, while tears ran down her face, cool on hot. She went on, crying, to the river. A ginger-moustached cloth-capped man passed, with a sideways furtive look that became knowing, diagnosing exploitable weakness. She frowned at him, and wiped the tears off—he went on his way. A moment later a young head came out of yet another hole in the ground where repairs were being made to subterranean London and a young voice said: "Cheer up, love."

"I don't see why I should," said Martha, and he leaped up out of his hole. Martha smiled, friendly. He was tall and gangly, raw in bone and finish. Using a yardstick discovered since she had come to England, she mentally fitted him into the uniform of an officer of the R.A.F. Impossible. Impossible even if he hadn't spoken and revealed his status in his voice? Impossible. She fitted him into the uniform of an aircraftsman—yes.

Ever since she had come, she had used memories of the two nations which had descended on Zambesia at the beginning of the war to fit men into their appropriate class. She had not been wrong often—what was it? Not only bad feeding: this one had deprivation bred into him; it was something in the way of standing, the gestures, the eyes. And as for him, if he hadn't spoken and shown she was from abroad and therefore outside his system of tabus, he would not have climbed up out of his hole. He had rather raffish blue eyes; and a come-and-get-me-smile evolved for such occasions. But all that was put on, he was a gentle and serious soul. "Come and have a cuppa?" he suggested, chancing it. Nearly Martha said: "Yes, I'd like to," but—couldn't, having decided on the end to such enjoyable chances. "I'd like to but I can't," she said, straight. He looked carefully into her face, placing her according to some rules of his own. Liking each other they stood, about to part forever. Then he said, "Right then, another time," and he nipped back into the earth.

"Ta ta," he said, picking up his shovel.

"Bye," said Martha, walking on.

Now, in front of her, the river. For Martha, the river was

13

still the point of reference in the chaos of London. Lost several times a day, she made for the river.

A few days after her arrival in London she had been wandering among the wharfs and the docks, three, four miles lower down the South Bank, in a world of black greasy hulls, dark landing stages, dark warehouses, grey dirty water, gulls, and the smell of driven salt, when she had come on a landing stage where a mushroom shape of rusting iron held thick coils of rope which tethered a flat barge that had a lorry on it. On this she sat, until an official came from a shed and said she should not be there. She was about to leave when to her came Stella, a gipsy of a woman in a striped grey apron, with greying black hair falling in wisps over a sallow face which was all shrewd black eyes. This woman had been watching her through the windows of her house twenty yards away. Martha, in green linen, sandals and sunburn, had tickled the imagination of this watchdog of her clan, and she asked her to tea; and, nosing out inside a few minutes that Martha was ready to stay anywhere she was welcome, let her a room over her parlour.

Stella was the wife, mother and daughter of dockers; and in her kitchen Martha drank tea, ate chips and bacon and fried bread several times a day and listened to the talk of a race every moment of whose lives had to do with the landing and unloading of ships. They talked about the war and about the government—and about the war. They were fiercely and bitterly working-class, class-conscious, and trade-union. Labour Party? That remained to be seen, they did not trust government and almost five years of a Labour government had done nothing to win the trust of these people who trusted nothing. In that kitchen Martha suppressed any knowledge she might ever have had about politics; for she knew how amateur it would sound among these warriors for whom politics, in its defensive and bread-and-butter aspect, was breath. Besides, they, rather Stella, were not interested in Martha's interest in England. Stella took Martha to her bosom because of an unfed longing for travel and experience which was titillated every moment by the river, by the ships that swung past her windows, by the talk of foreign countries. She said herself that her blood must run from some visiting sailor from a Southern place, Spanish she thought, Portuguese?—so strong a fancy did she have for those parts. And she read: all her life she had nosed out books, comics, magazines which might have a story or an article about the sea. Her sons and her husband teased her, there'd be no room for them soon, they said; she had old trunks crammed with sea-treasure. If there was a film about the sea, she went, might see the same film through a dozen times if it had ships or sails or mutinies or pirates; and when there was someone to go with her, visited the naval museum at Greenwich where she knew all the sailing ships, their histories and the men who had captained them. Well: so Stella wanted Martha to talk about foreignness; and Martha, feeling that nothing in her experience could match up to such an appetite for the marvellous, made a discovery: that it was enough to say, The sun shines so, the moon does thus, people get up at such an hour, eat so and so, believe such and such—and it was enough. Because it was different. Martha's so-ordinary experience was magicked by Stella's hunger into wonders, and when her money had run so low she said she must get a job, Stella got for her a job in a pub, for she could not bear to lose her. The pub was Stella's brother's wife's pub and it was a couple of hundred yards inland. So they talked of territory not immediately on the Thames's banks. For a couple of weeks then, Martha had lived inside the area which was policed invisibly by the spirit of Stella, and under her protection. For instance, walking to work in the bar one evening, a group of men coming from loading a ship started the usual whistles and catcalls and Stella emerged from some kitchen where she was visiting, put her hands on her hips, and shouted across the street that this was Martha, her friend, and if they knew what was good for them ... and a man who felt that Martha might make a suitable wife approached Stella, as if Stella were Martha's mother, to ask if she would approve the match.

It was not until Martha left Stella, left the water's edge, and had got to know the café people, that she was able to compare and ask questions. For instance, why had "Matty" never once come to life with Stella and her clan? Admittedly another imposed personality had, the hip-swinging sexually gallant girl—or rather, had until Stella rescued her from the necessity of it. And again, why had she not felt bad about leaving Stella, though Stella had not wanted her to leave? She had not let her down, as she was letting the café people down. And then there was Stella herself, the matriarchical boss of her knot of streets, among the body-proud, work-proud men who earned their wages by physical strength and who judged everyone by strength and their capacity for work —was Stella the only Boadicea among the masculine communities of the river's edges? And then, there was this business of "the working classes," of "socialism," which, before she had crossed the river, had not been what interested Martha.

The newspapers never stopped, not for a moment, informing the nation and the world that Britain, in the grip of red-handed socialists, was being ruined, was being turned into a place of serfs without individuality or initiative and rotted by ease—in the tone of some pamphleteer at work while heads rolled under the guillotine. So irrelevant were these newspapers to anything she found she could not believe that anyone read them seriously, nor that anyone could be paid enough to write them. For what she had found on the other side of the river, let alone in the streets around the café and around the docks, was something not far off conditions described in books about the thirties. What had changed, that the public-opinion men (who presumably believed what they wrote) could so write? Were Stella and her people poor? Very. They were better off, they said; but their demands were small and had not grown larger. Were Iris and Jimmy poor, though they owned their café on mortgage and ate well? Very: they expected so little. These were all people who had no right to expect much. Had the editors and journalists never met Iris and Jimmy and Stella, did they know nothing of what they could find out by getting onto a bus, crossing the river, and living for a week or so with Stella or with Iris? It seemed not. It was not credible—but no. But to read the newspapers, absorb the tone of the editorialising of that time—it was unreal, afflicted her with a sense of dislocation. And this was her real preoccupation, what absorbed her: this was a country absorbed in myth, doped and dozing and dreaming, because if there was one common fact or factor underlying everything else, it was that nothing was as it was described—as if a spirit of rhetoric (because of the war?) had infected everything, made it impossible for any fact to be seen straight. Nor would she, had she not by chance crossed the river some weeks before (during one of the looping bus rides she had taken around, across, through, and over London—by the simple device of getting on buses and staying on them till they returned to their starting points), and stayed with first Stella and then Iris, now be able to pick up a newspaper or listen to the radio without feeling as if she were in the middle of the Russian revolution, or something not far from it in cataclysmic thoroughness. She would not have been able to hold on to the simple fact that, in essence, nothing much had changed in this country—you had only to listen to the people in the docks and in the café to know it hadn't. Which was why more than any other person it must be Phoebe, Marjorie's sister, that she should telephone—when? Today. Yes.

The tide was out. Gulls squawked in their sea voices over the low marsh of water between smelling mud banks in search, not of fish in these polluted waters, but of refuse. White preened wings balanced over diluted chemical, between grey cement walls that held such a weight of building. And it was so ugly, so ugly: what race was this that filled their river with garbage and excrement and let it run smelling so evilly between the buildings that crystallised their pride, their history? Except—she could not say that now, she was here, one of them; and to stay. It was time she crossed the river. But it was hard to leave it. But she must leave it. She came so often to lean with elbows on damp concrete looking down at ebbing or racing or swelling or lurking waters because here she was able to feel most strongly—what she had been before she had left "home" to come "home." In a street full of strangers, on the top of a bus in a part of London all barren little houses and smoking chimneys—who was she? Martha? Certainly not "Matty." She became lightheaded, empty, sometimes dizzy. But by the river, looking down at the moving water, she was connected still with—a feeling of being herself. She was able to see herself as if from a hundred yards up, a tiny coloured blob, among other blobs, on top of a bus, or in a street. Today she could see herself, a black blob, in Mrs. Van's coat, a small black blob beside a long grey parapet. A tiny entity among swarms—then down, back inside herself, to stand, arms on damp concrete: this was what she was, a taste or flavour of existence without a name. Who remembered. Who noted. And not much more.

A stranger last week had said: "What's your name?" Her mind, dizzying, Martha had said: "Phyllis Jones." For an afternoon and an evening she had been Phyllis Jones, with an imaginary history of wartime work in Bristol. And just as it was enough to offer to Stella phrases like "The sun is overhead at midday" to evoke for her all the stimulation of a new country, so now it did not matter she had never been to Bristol, even when talking about it to a man who knew it well. Enough to say: Ships, terraces, and Yes, I know so and so, I've been to so and so. In such a conversation she was just as much Phyllis Jones as she was Martha with Stella. People filled in for you, out of what they wanted, needed, from—not you, not you at all, but from their own needs. Phyllis Jones, a young widow with a small boy, an object of great interest and compassion to Leslie Haddon, a clerk from Bristol, a man uncomfortably married and in search of a "congenial female companion," spoke through Martha's mouth for some hours, until, pleading maternal duties and an inviolable memory of her dead husband, she left him in the pub. And left Phyllis Jones. And—interesting, this—a week later, when another stranger had said "What's your name?" she had nearly offered Phyllis Jones, but it was the wrong name. This person, a woman on a train, was wrong for Phyllis Jones, did not evoke her. So Martha had been someone called Alice Harris instead. Why not?

For a while at least. What difference did it make to her, the sense of identity, like a silent statement "I am here," if she were called Phyllis or Alice, or Martha or Matty; or if her history were this or that? But for a while only. Because she knew that ringing up Phoebe was not only because now she must earn money, and become responsible to her fellow human beings. Something (a sense of self-preservation?) could not tolerate much longer her walking and riding and talking the time away under this name or that, this disguise or that; calling strange identities into being with a switch of clothes or a change of voice—until one felt like an empty space without boundaries and it did not matter what name one gave a stranger who asked: What is your name? Who are you?

Martha crossed the river, left it, moved among streets that looked as if they had just survived an earthquake, and came to the rubble of damage left by the bomb that had fallen on St. Paul's. To Iris, "where the bomb fell across the river." She had been to visit the scene the day after. So had Stella and some of her men. City workers emerged everywhere from doorways, hurried off to buses and tubes. This day was ending—and where was she going to sleep tonight? Another telephone box, orangy-pink and faded, stood ahead. She went into it, to ring Phoebe. Soon, on the pile of telephone books, there were bits of paper with telephone numbers on them, Phoebe's among them. And the café's number. If she rang there now, saying, even as Martha, "I'm coming back tonight," Jimmy or Iris would say: "You're coming back then, are you?" And she would walk in, and, after a moment to judge whether she brought pain with her, a snub, they would smile. Extraordinarily kind they were; kindness was stronger than their anxious need to hold, to keep. Iris felt for Martha, or rather Martha's experience that enabled her to drop into the life of Joe's café like a migrating bird, exactly the same emotion as she felt for a baulk of timber hauled up out of the tides of the river or a yard of curtain material got off the ration, or teaspoons found among rubble after a bomb had dropped. Which was not to denigrate what she felt: not at all. Martha had been something extra, something given, something unearned—as the children playing on the bomb site had come running into the café with an old metal meat dish found under some broken bricks, used now for the week's meat ration at Sunday midday. Treasure. And Martha to Stella was a heady wind from countries she would never visit.

Henry Matheson's number, on a bus ticket: she had also to telephone Henry. She could sleep at Jack's—that is, she could if he didn't have another girl there, which was likely. She should ring Henry. Not wanting to ring Henry was quite a different reluctance from not wanting to ring Marjorie's sister. Henry Matheson was a relation of Mrs. Maynard. Mr. Maynard had arrived to say goodbye to Martha at the station when she left, not oblivious to the fact that Martha did not want to say goodbye, or even to see him, but not caring. He was in the grip of that need with which Martha had become only too familiar seeing it at work in so many different people: it was to make sure that Martha did not escape from him, or rather, from what he represented. His wife's cousins the Mathesons would be only too delighted to see her, said he, formidably present for a half hour before the train steamed out of the station from which she, at last, after having seen so many people leave there for adventures in England, was leaving. Clearly her manner had not indicated strongly enough that she would be delighted to see the cousins, so Henry Matheson had been at the boat train to meet her. Martha felt no obligation to be grateful to the Maynards, who were not kind; but did feel she must at least be polite to Henry, who was. Henry, altogether charming, and delightful, had hovered, the eye of the Maynards, in the background of those weeks; and Martha had bought him off by offering—not Matty, too crude a persona for him—but a slaphappy freebooting adventuress, cousin of "Matty," who, she thought, was close enough to his secret fantasies about himself (he was the essence of conformity) to keep him quiet. She did not want letters from Henry to the Maynards of a kind which would cause Mrs. Maynard to telephone her mother in the mountains near the Zambesi: "About that gal of yours, it would appear that . . ."

The thing was, Henry had offered her a job in his firm: he

was a lawyer, and she had legal experience. But she had refused it. Typical of anyone anywhere near the Maynards, thought Martha, that it had not been enough to refuse the job once: somewhere Henry was so convinced of his generosity and Martha's luck that he could not believe she would be foolish enough to refuse it—must believe she was too green to known how good a job it was. Jobs as good as that one were short, she knew. The only way to convince him was to take another.

She rang Jack. "Jack, this is Martha." "Oh Martha, just a moment . . ." So he was not alone. She waited. Outside the glass-apertured box in which Martha stood, people jostled, heads down, under their low weeping sky. Like cattle rushing forward into the dip on the farm: it was the same blind impelled movement. On a barrow at the corner fruit. Apples, mostly. A pile of waxy-green apples with rain on them. And, crowning a pile of apples, a single bunch of grapes, displayed proudly on a wad of fibre. A single bunch of green grapes. In Cape Town grapes had dripped, dangled, overflowed, from barrows, carts, shops, a wealth of grapes, from which one bunch had flown overseas to land on this cart by the rubble near St. Paul's. As she held the receiver and watched, a woman picked up the bunch, decided it was too expensive, replaced it, and a single grape rolled down off the cart onto the pavement, lying like a pale green jewel among trampling feet. The salesboy, who had been looking desperate, dived for the grape, retrieved it, and with a quick look, wiped it on a bit of newspaper and then was about to put it back on the crown of grapes when a small child buttoned into a hooded raincoat stared at the grapes from eye level. He had probably never seen grapes at all. The youth pressed the grape into the child's mouth. Smiles: from young mama to youth, from mama urging child to smile, at last, from child to youth: thank you. Apples were bought and the child went off on mama's hand, looking back at the bunch of translucent wet green grapes. "Martha, I'm so glad you telephoned, man, but where have you been?" He was South African, but his accent had been fined down by much war-travelling. "Jack, I haven't got anywhere to sleep tonight?" A pause for calculations. "Just a tick, Martha, I must just . . ." Again the other end of the phone had gone silent, but receptive: Martha could hear voices off somewhere, Jack's, a girl's. Jack was telling a story of some kind to the girl who was there. Or the truth, who knew? He came back. "It's like this, Martha, I'm going to have to work till midnight." She laughed. Then, so did he.

"Midnight would suit me fine." "See you, Martha." "See you, Jack."

If she did not now ring Henry, she would take a bus to Bayswater and spend the evening drifting in and out of the pubs with the other visitors, migrants, freebooters. They would talk about England. That is, for a lot of the time, about Henry Matheson and what he stood for; and Iris and Stella and what they stood for. Someone would have a newspaper that jittered about the advent of red socialism in Britain, and how the working classes grew fat and luxurious, and how the upper classes dwindled into poverty. The aliens would look at the newspaper and talk about Iris and Stella, whom it appeared literate natives did not meet.

She rang Henry's office. He was, said the telephone girl, just about to leave. This girl's voice was a careful London suburban (Martha could already "place" it) and was exactly why she, Martha, if she accepted that job, would be working, not where she dealt with people on the telephone, but in an office where her merits would be of benefit to her fellow-workers and not, or at least not immediately, the public.

Henry came to the telephone. "But my dear Martha, where have you been? I was just about to send out a search party!" She laughed; convivial buccaneer with secrets she was prepared to share; and calculated whether she would be able to get away with just saying, even if for the third time: *Henry, I've decided I don't want that job.* "Henry, I was phoning to say I've done some serious thinking and thanks ever so much, I don't think I'll take the job." A pause. The two "wrong" phrases carefully planted into this arrangement of words to emphasise what Henry must find so hard to take in her were doing their work. "Well, Martha ... if you're sure, but we would be so pleased to have you." "Yes, I'm sure ..." and now she made a mistake, from nervousness. "I've been working, as a matter of fact"—too late to think of a satisfactory lie, she had to go on—"in a pub." Silence. "How very enterprising of you. You did promise to *ring*, Martha. Look, how about a bite and a sup. Have you time?"

"Yes, I'd love to."

"How about Baxter's. Do you know it?" This meant, as Martha knew perfectly well, Are you properly dressed for it?"

"Of course, how should I not know? It's in all those novels about the twenties."

"Is it? Dear me. How very well read you are—so much better than I am. Well then, if you get there before I do, tell old Bertie—he's the head man, you know—that you're supping with me."

"I'll do that. In about an hour?"

"Yes, we can have a drink first and you can tell me all your adventures."

It was now raining hard: a dirty rain. Martha would have stayed in the box, but a girl was knocking on the door. Martha opened it. The girl had a wet headscarf and a thick damp mackintosh. Beneath this disguise she was a pretty dapple-cheeked English girl. "Did you want to get out of the rain, or to telephone?" A short offended laugh. "Actually, to telephone." "In that case, I'll leave." Another, but an appeased, laugh. She watched Martha, wary, offering her smile like a shield. These were people totally on the defensive. The war? Their nature? But Martha was so clearly an outsider, breaking the rules with a smile in an alien accent, that had she persisted, talked, broken barriers, the girl would have enjoyed it, would have been grateful to have the defences broken, but also resenting, also wary, like an animal accepting overtures but ready to bite at a clumsy movement.

It was pouring. Martha went into a cigarette shop. The woman behind the counter raised eyes to Martha's face and then looked at Martha's feet. Water dripped from Mrs. Van's coat to the floor, which was already smeared and wet.

And now Martha—although it meant she would have instantly to leave the shop and go out into the rain—asked: "Can I have a dozen boxes of matches?"

Sullen: "You can have one box."

"Oh, I'd like a dozen. Half a dozen?"

"There's been a war on, you know."

Martha had asked for three boxes of matches in a kiosk during her first week. Since then, she had made a point of asking for a dozen, in kiosks in every area of London.

"There's been a war on, you know."

And with what hostility, what resentment. And what personal satisfaction.

"I'm sorry, I was forgetting."

"I suppose some people can."

Martha got one box of matches in return for her tuppence, and smiled into a frozenly angry face. But the face said she must leave, must get soaked in punishment for her heartless indifference to the sufferings of her nation.

Martha left. A bus looked as if it might have room. She jumped on, and the conductor said: "Hold on then, love." She smiled, he smiled. Disproportionate relief! She had discovered swapping notes with other aliens in pubs, that it was not only she who had to fight paranoia, so many invisible rules there were to break, rules invisible to those who lived by them, that was the point. Warming herself at the conductor's smile, the journey was made up Fleet Street, invisible behind cold rain, past Trafalgar Square, where lions loomed in a cold grey stream, and up to Piccadilly Circus, where the conductor sent her on her way with smiles, a wink, and an injunction to look after herself and enjoy her holiday.

It was with Henry that she had first seen this place, on a clear gold evening, the sky awash with colour. She looked at the haphazard insignificance of it, and the babyish statue, and began to laugh.

"My dear Martha?"

"This," she tried to explain, "is the hub of the Empire."

For him a part of London one passed through, he attempted her vision, and smiled his failure: "Isn't that rather more your problem than it is ours?"

"But Henry, that's so much the point, can't you see?" For this exchange seemed to sum up hours of their failure to meet on any sort of understanding; during which nagged the half-memory of a previous failure—what, who, when? Yes, as a child, when her mother had laid down this attitude, this dogmatism, this "It's right, it's wrong," and Martha, reacting, had examined, criticised, taken a stand, brought back a stand to the challenger—who had lost interest, was no longer there, had even forgotten.

"Well, it's quite a jolly little place, isn't it?" he enquired, uncomfortably facing her—but only just.

"Well, I suppose it's the war again," she said at last, "all that myth-making, all that shouting, the *words*—but you can't say things like 'jolly little place.'"

"You're a romantic," he said, sour.

"Ah, but you're having it both ways, always—having it both ways, sliding out ..." She had, for a moment, been unable to conceal a real swell of painful feeling, all kinds of half-buried, half-childish, myth-bred emotions were being dragged to the surface: words having such power! Piccadilly Circus, Eros, Hub, Centre, London, England ... each tapped underground rivers where the Lord only knew what fabulous creatures swam! She tried to hide pain, Henry not being a person who knew how to share it.

She supposed she did hide it, for in a moment he was urging her into a pub, buying her drinks, talking about the war, and radiating relief that nothing was to be asked of him.

"You know, Henry, after one's been a week here, one simply wants to put one's arms around you—oh no, not you personally."

"Oh dear, I was rather hoping ..." said he, laughing with relief that he would have to suffer no such demonstration. He had even involuntarily glanced around to see if there was anyone near that he knew.

"No, the whole island, all of you."

"Oh but why! Do tell me!"

"If I could, you see, there'd be no need to feel that."

The exterior of Baxter's was in no way more distinguished than that of Joe's. A modest brown door had *Baxter's* on it—just the word, nothing more. There was a window completely covered by white muslin that needed washing. Martha stood outside for a moment, holding this delicious moment known only to newcomers in a city: behind this door, which was just like so many others, *what will there be?* A Southern courtyard with a lemon tree beside a fountain and a masked Negro lute-player asleep? A man with a red blanket slung across his shoulder stands by a black mule? A pale girl in sprigged muslin goes upstairs with a candle in her hand? Two old men in embroidered skullcaps play chess beside a fire? Why not? Since what actually does appear is so improbable. Last week she had opened a door by mistake on a staircase in Bayswater and a woman in a tight black waspwaisted corset, pearls lolling between great naked breasts, stood by a cage made of gold wire the size of a four-poster bed, in which were a dozen or so brilliantly fringed and tinted birds. Martha said: "I'm sorry." The woman said: "If you are looking for Mr. Pelham, he's in Venice this week."

She went in. A man in shabby dinner clothes and sleekeddown dandruffy hair came forward, already disapproving. Through his eyes she saw a young woman with damp hair, a damp coat, and a stretched smile. For Martha was suddenly bloody-minded, because of this man's automatic bad manners, though she knew they were the stuff of his life and what he earned his wages for. A subordinate man, a waiter, came to stand by the first, the headwaiter. Together they surveyed her with a cold skill that cracked her into speaking first. "I am meeting Mr. Matheson," she said, awkward. The two conferred, in a long silence and a swift glance. The first man turned away, to other business; and the second, having not said a word, took her, without going through the main room, to a table which was turned to one side. He pulled out a chair in which she would face a wall. He had not asked her to take off her coat. She did so, shrugging it on to the back of her chair. A lean, elderly man, whose whole life had been dedicated to the service of such minutiae, he again flicked his eyes fast over her and again with an arrogance of bad manners that astounded her, so naked did it seem to her. Her sweater and skirt were adequate. But wrong? Why? She did not know, but he did. He left her to wait.

The place was still half full, since it was early for dinner. The people were middle-aged, or gave an appearance of being so. She saw, glancing with difficulty backwards, that there were two young people, but their youth was damped into the staid middle-aged air of the atmosphere. They, and the waiters, fitted into the décor, which was designed according to unwritten invisible rules to fit them. The place was muted, dingy, rather dark; and no single object had any sort of charm or beauty, but had been chosen for its ability to melt into this scene. And the people had no sort of charm or flair. Yet, looking closely, things were expensive: money had been spent and obviously since the war, to keep the restaurant exactly as it had always been: in an expensive shabbiness, dowdiness. The girl—the only one present apart from Martha—wore a black crepey dress. It was ugly. Martha recognised this dress because before leaving "home" Marjorie had told her what she would need: she gave her a list of clothes she would need, not for utility or warmth, but for occasions. "A uniform!" Martha had exclaimed. This dress was part of that uniform, relating to no standard of charm or sexuality; doing nothing for the girl who wore it: it was a black dress worn with pearls, and it had a cousinship with the restaurant, its furnishings, and the people in it, who, when you looked, were good-looking, even well built, certainly well fed and easy. But, now, Martha could see perfectly well why her clothes, every bit as expensive, and certainly more attractive, that is, if clothes are to be judged by what they can do for the appearance of who wears them, would not do, and why the black dress did: she was not in the right uniform.

The point was, not a word of what she thought could be told to Henry; he would not understand it; but when she met Jack tonight, she would only need to mention the girl's dress, her pretty artless face and hair, the dull-flowering wallpaper, the men's emphatic faces—and he would laugh and understand. And Jack would understand perfectly well when she said—though she would not need to say—"The trouble is, you have to choose a slot to fit yourself to, you have to narrow yourself down for this stratum or that." Yet although the essence of Henry's relation to her was that she should choose the right slot, find the right stratum, he would not understand her if she said that: he'd be embarrassed, irritated, if she said it.

Yes, because Jack had chosen a life that freed him, he would understand all this: but he could not understand her other preoccupation, and the trouble was, the only person she had so far met who did was Marjorie's sister—Phoebe.

Henry came in. Silent communications had already taken place between him and the headwaiter, because his face was prepared whimsically to accept her unsuitability for this restaurant. And all this because the weather had changed! A month ago, in another expensive dingy restaurant, she had been wearing, because of the heat, a slip-dress in black linen, and had been perfectly comfortable—though much better dressed than anyone else in the restaurant, because they were overdressed, being people who could not dress for the sun. Henry had been showing her off: slightly embarrassed, since her simplicity was challenging; and partly because, when the sun shines in England, a license comes into power with it.

He sat down. "My dear Martha, how very well you look."

"I know that my hair is wet: but I was not asked if I wanted to use the ladies—if they've got one at all."

This challenge caused him to send her a quick thoughtful look, before he looked past her head at some brown varnished wood and said: "I remember, about two years ago, my Aunt Maynard sent me a protégée—from Cape Town I think she was. She was very combative, you know."

"My problem is, what part of Rome is one going to choose to combat?"

"Hmmm," he said.

"And I had no idea Aunt Maynard's fief extended as far as Cape Town."

"Oh, one of those places."

Martha sat checking herself like an engine: had she eaten, had she slept, was she overtired—no, no, yes: because her flare of anger was really so very strong. That aspect of "Matty" which was brought into being by Henry was pure childish aggression. If she chose and was in control enough not to be aggressive or show hostility, then "Matty" was bumbling, charming—apologetic by implication. She preferred aggression: it was a step better than the infant clown.

Henry was looking past Martha at a man who had just

come in. He was like Henry; all open good looks, charm, assurance. He smiled at Henry, and was about to come forward, but Henry smiled differently, and the man sat down behind a menu sheet across the room.

"Your partner?"

His look was very quick now: "Yes."

"You had asked him to look me over, but you find I'm not look-overable at the moment, so you've radared him that you'd rather he didn't?"

"He was going to eat here in any case—why shouldn't I want him to meet you?"

"Ah, but why not now?"

Here came the waiter with the card, which he held before Martha. She ordered some pâté and the fish, but Henry said: "If you'll take my advice, the coquille is excellent. Not, of course, that their pâté isn't." Here he offered a small humorous grimace to the grey old waiter, who accepted it.

"Of course," she said, and changed her order.

She asked for a dry sherry. The wine waiter brought a bottle of semisweet sherry, because in such places a lady would be expected to drink sweet sherry. Henry was given an Amontillado.

She drank hers. He drank his.

"Martha, have you heard from your mother?"

Martha noted how this ancient goad to rage now had no effect on her at all: by putting several thousands of miles of sea between her and her mother she was saved? Hmmm—possibly.

"No, but I expect I shall?"

"You said you thought of taking a job?"

"I had one in a pub down by the docks."

"Ever such a lark of course—but not for long surely?"

"I've also been offered the job as a secretary in a firm which hires out lorries." In one of the lorries Iris's cousin worked: the man she had intended for Martha.

He waited. She would not help him.

"You'd be living—near your work?"

Almost she said: Why not? But lost interest. What was the use?

Here came the scallop shells filled with lumps of cod covered with a cheese-coloured white sauce. That this was a restaurant where people eat, not to eat well, but to eat conformably she had understood from what she had seen on the plates near her; and she knew that when she tasted the

27

fish it would be rather worse than she had been eating at Joe's, with Iris and Jimmy.

"It's very nice," she said hastily, to Henry's enquiring eyebrows.

"Delicious," he affirmed, so that she could make a note of what was admirable.

She could fault, even as a housewife, a dozen points on this table: the bread rolls were not fresh; the tablecloth only just clean; the parsley on the fish was limp; the peppermill was nearly empty; the roses sagged; everything was second-rate. But Henry did not care, he was at home, cosy with his kind.

Claustrophobia filled her like a fever; and she took herself in hand: Be quiet, steady—you'll be out of it for good when this meal is over.

"I really do see," he prompted, "what fun it must be, sl— experimenting, for a time."

"Ah, but you see, one has to be brought up in this country to be able to see it as slumming."

He had coloured.

"Now look Henry—you're right. I couldn't for long stay in those jobs—but for exactly the same reason that I couldn't take yours, that's what you ought to be able to see. Can't you really understand that?"

"Well, frankly, no."

On the chair by him a folded evening newspaper; and even from where she was, she could see, peering over, that the headlines and editorials were to do with the red, socialist, classless etc. Britain.

They had finished their fish. Henry had ordered some blanquette of veal for both of them. It wasn't bad. The wine, however, was very good indeed, marvellous; and Martha was drinking it, although she knew that drinking it might lead to an exchange every word of which she could recite even before it happened. She smiled, offered him scraps of traveller's tales from the strange land across the river, to which he listened, with the air of a potential traveller choosing possible landscapes for adventure.

At last he said: "If it's a question of your being a restless sort of person, that you'd want to move on after a year or two, I think we do rather expect that from our staff. The war has unsettled people, including me, I'm afraid."

"No, it's not a question of being restless."

Determined that the tedious exchange, imminent, would not take place, she reached for her wine glass—and knocked it over. The waiter being away, she dabbed at the stain with her napkin. Then the imp took over.

"I'd like another serviette," she said.

Henry called to the waiter with his eyes.

"If you could bring another napkin," he said.

Martha suddenly laughed. He frowned incomprehension.

"I don't know why it is," he said, "but I do know that girls are so much cleverer than men at ... picking things up. You could, you know, if you tried. For instance, we had a girl in our office. She was only ... her father was under me during the war, a very good type of man ... well, she came to us as a typist and inside a year she had picked up ... now you really can hardly tell her from ... she takes over on the switchboard, for instance ... for some reason men don't do it so well, they aren't so adaptable. But if you listened to how other people talk, you could learn very easily ... that sort of thing."

The gaps in this homily—which had been delivered half with irritation that he was being forced to verbalise his position even partially, half with a genuine concern for her future, for which, the Lord knew why, he felt himself responsible—she now filled in, summing them all up.

"I could learn to *pass*," she said.

He sat back in his chair, his handsome fair well-bred face all dark with annoyance.

It was not the slightest use. But the imp had control.

"Henry, if I told you that this meal we are eating is going to cost you over five pounds, in spite of the fact you are supposed to be restricting yourself because of the war—and that the people I've been with don't spend that on food in a week—and then ask you to look at that newspaper ... oh, I don't know, what *is* the use!"

"Very poor, are they?" he said quickly.

"Very. But that isn't the point."

He leaned back. "Well, aren't we all, these days?"

"I should have said not."

"You weren't here during the war," he said emotionally.

"I've learned that after that, there's nothing to be said."

"You must see, Martha, that it's going to take time to get this poor old country on its feet again."

"Of course."

"God knows we're poor—but what more do you people want? You've got your Labour government in. They're not my thing, far from it, I'm more of a Liberal I suppose, though I vote Tory, but they're in, they're doing a job—

you've got your socialism. Of course there are people who think that five years of Labour Party has ruined this country. I'm not one of those, but there is no class left in this country. What do you want?"

"But Henry—well, I really don't know, how can you say—or believe . . . Henry, if those people I've been with—if they turned up here at this restaurant, they wouldn't be admitted . . ." He froze, attacked, undermined: here was precisely where he could not think or look, therefore it was in bad taste. "Not that they would turn up of course, they know better. After all, I wouldn't have been admitted, probably. They'd have said the place was full. It was only because I gave your name."

"If they did turn up, I for one'd be only too proud—the salt of the earth. We learned that in the war."

"Not to mention the other war."

There now was rolled towards them the sweets trolley. Henry chose for her and for him, a trifle, though it had another name. Throughout the restaurant, people were eating nursery puddings, under French names.

"I really don't know what it is you people want," he said pettishly.

"To have things called by their proper names, that's all. Did you ever actually meet your Uncle Maynard?"

"No, well of course, he was rather the black sheep, so one gathers."

"Justice Maynard? Well, I've been remembering something he said to me. Ten years ago, more. He said that he couldn't stick England because no one called a spade a spade. So now he administers law and order in the colonies, where one can. I've only just recently understood what he was talking about."

"Hypocrites," said Henry quickly. "Of course, they've always called us that."

"No, no, if you were hypocrites that would be something. A hypocrite is somebody who maintains a virtuous position knowing it to be false. You all seem to me to be—you're drugged, you're hypnotised, you don't seem to be able to see facts when they're in front of you. You're the victim of a lot of slogans."

Here the wine waiter offered the lady a sweet liqueur and Henry brandy. The lady insisted on asking for brandy: the wine waiter offered Henry a look of commiseration, so far had complicity grown between them. But Henry frowned at him and told him to bring brandy. Martha and the brandy changed the note or current: Henry was able to let slide away any chance there was of their meeting on at least the possibility of there being something in what she said; Martha, gay buccaneer, adventuress, warmed by wine, enabled him to wave over his partner. There arrived at the table John Higham, as charming and as handsome as he, his face presented towards Martha in a look almost transparently eager to taste this phenomenon, who was outside the rules of ordinary politeness—for he examined her openly, boldly, exactly as the dockers, before being made to know by Stella that she was, temporarily, one of their women, were able to call across a street: Hello darling. She had been outside their circle of humanity. Martha was outside John Higham's. For a moment the two men sat, united, opposite Martha, eyeing her. It was ugly: behind them, the waiter, and behind him the headwaiter; very ugly. And again, she never would be able to explain why; they would not know what she meant. They were savages, masters and servants both.

"Martha will have none of us, I'm afraid," said Henry, insolent, but smiling.

"I'm sorry," said John Higham.

"I simply cannot imagine, apart of course from the Maynards asking you to keep an eye on me, what you want me for?"

They even exchanged glances here, as if she were not able to see that glances were being exchanged—as if they were invisible. Extraordinary, extraordinary people: Iris and Jimmy, Stella and her men, had more delicacy, more consciousness of themselves.

"You underestimate yourself," said John Higham. "You've done legal work, haven't you. You've got experience. And I don't know why it is, but while there are hundreds of girls on the market, there aren't very many . . . experienced ones."

"It isn't that we mind our girls getting married—far from it. We welcome it, they tend to stay," said Henry.

"And a large part of our practice is out of this country— we've been doing a lot of work with refugees for instance. Tidying up after the war—that sort of thing. And we really do need someone with—a wider experience than most English girls have."

Now Martha had to be silent. This last point reached her. And, besides, she was exactly in the same position here as she had been, still was, with Iris and Jimmy. She had promised, or had seemed to promise, without knowing she was doing it, more than she had ever meant. She had never, not for one moment, considered working for Henry, had said, in every way she knew: No, no, no. Yet both men now expected her to say yes: were in fact counting on her. A manner which was assumed as mask, a defence, appearing to be a half flirtatious consideration of possibilities, had been felt as so much more? Or was it that being in a situation at all, being involved with people, was a promise of more? That was more like it, that was the truth: oh, yes, there was something intolerable, unforgivable, about the drifters, the testers, the samplers, she was only just beginning to see it. But it was unjust, unfair! She had been in this country for not much more than a quarter of a year, had seen it as time out of responsibility. She was not going to be allowed to taste and drift and knock about. The genuine feeling of betrayal shown by her friends of Joe's café (though not by Stella of the docks—why not?), and the expectation shown by Henry and John, proved that she must have made promises implicitly; she, Martha, had something in her which forbade her to drift and visit and slide out. Other people might: she could not. Otherwise why, after such a very short time out of responsibility—what was four months after all?—were the nets closing in? Which was how she felt it. The net had been set from the moment she saw Henry's politely charming face outside the Customs when she arrived. It was probably, though she did not want to recognise this, that her temperament shared more than she liked with Marjorie and with Marjorie's sister Phoebe—an earnestness, a readiness to be involved and implicated—and that temperament was in itself a promise, made promises and offered.

She could be weak and say something like: I'll think it over. But she must not. And she must not buy forgiveness with "Matty." With a great effort, she said (abruptly, and without grace, but she said it straight), "Look. Please believe me. I'm not taking the job. Thank you very much—but I don't want it."

"What have you got lined up instead?" asked John Higham. He was annoyed.

"She's thinking of being a barmaid," said Henry with a laugh to indicate, not that she would not, but that she was only too capable of it.

"Really, are you?" said John Higham. "Of course, it is a way of—getting round?" he enquired. "One does see that."

"The thing is," said Martha, again furious, trying not to be, "I wouldn't see the job as you do—as something extraordinary. You simply don't understand—all of you, you talk of the people you call the working class as if they were ... people from the moon. Not that you use words like 'the working class' of course— Oh, I don't know," she concluded, in real despair. "One can't even talk about it with you."

Glances were again exchanged between Henry and John, and again as if she were not present. "Well," said John, "that is precisely why we are so keen to have you—you see a great many of the people we deal with have had a rather rough time, and one does need someone to handle them who knows what they are talking about."

"Perhaps," said Martha, "having had *a rough time* as a refugee would include rather more than would be covered by having *experience* as a barmaid?"

She was now really angry, really discouraged. Even frightened. After all, such people ran this country, no matter what the papers said. And, when you came anywhere near the Maynards and their kind, this is what happened. It was like talking to—well, the blind, people blinkered from birth. Which is what they were. What was the point of ... one simply had to get out of their way.

The waiter was bringing the bill. The restaurant was full now, it was about ten o'clock, and had more than ever the atmosphere of a family, of people who were at one with each other. And they were off guard now; with a licensed childishness about them, as if, threatened outside, here they found refuge. Across the room, a man with a heightened colour and a rakish look flicked bread pellets to a girl in a fluffy pink sweater, who flicked them back, giggling, while waiters watched indulgently.

The bill was for six pounds.

"Where are you going, can we lift you?"

"Thank you, I'd like to walk."

Henry pushed back his chair. The waiter had three people by him who wanted this table. Getting out and away fast, which is what she wanted, was easy for her.

She walked down Oxford Street; that is, at eye level goods confined behind lit glass moved past her: above were dark weights of masonry. The goods, clothes mostly, were as bad and as tasteless as everything else. This is the greatest city in the world, she kept saying, loitering, but not obviously so, among people window-shopping. The biggest city, the biggest, and this one of the streets whose name I've been brought up on, like Piccadilly Circus. The labels of these shops are covetable, sewn on clothes—there was not one object or article she would have cared to own. Of course, there had been a war on. Of course, even five years after such a war, buildings and streets must be propped and shored and patched and unpainted, and cloth must be thinned and impoverished. Of course. But even a yard of war-impoverished cloth can be woven with more sense or art. Good Lord, she found herself thinking, for the thousandth time, what kind of a race is this that chooses, inevitably and invariably, or so it seemed, the ugly, the graceless? Well here she was and to stay.

The shops ended and sky opened above the trees of Hyde Park. Now here was something different, oh yes, when it came to trees and gardens, then everything was as it ought to be. She walked down the pavements at the Bayswater Road, with the park on one side, balances and patterns of leaf dramatically green where the street lights held them, retreating into mysterious shadow beyond, with the lit moving sky over them. On her right hand, the great ponderous houses that stood so assertively on damp soil. Great ugly grey houses. They were boarded up or empty or in makeshift use; no longer houses; all in a condition of transformation towards being hotels. And unpainted. Ugly. Even in this changing racing wild light, ugly. But she was under the trees that edged the pavement, and they seemed like an extension of the trees of the park, so that it was as if the traffic that poured down the street was riding through softly lit trees which ended here; the grey cliff of buildings on her right being the start of the city. There were now few people. There had begun, from the moment she had left Oxford Street and the shops, that heightened wary atmosphere which meant she must walk careful of her eyes, because in this stretch of the Bayswater Road, men prowled after women. Invisible boundaries, invisibly marked territories—just as, across the river a boundary could be marked by an old hulk of timber with river salt in its seams, so that one side of it was the riverbank, the other a landlubber's country, here the corner of a street or the hour of a day could say: Here a certain kind of order ends. Martha now walked fast, protected by the thick ugliness of Mrs. Van's coat; but she was a "young woman," category "young woman"—yes, she must remember that she was, and that along these pavements, a category of being, "man," prowled beside or behind her. That was what she must be for a few minutes, not Martha or Matty, only "young woman." A man veered up beside her, muttered an anxious aggressive invitation and dropped behind when she presented to him her aloof lifted profile. He fell back, muttering words she was meant to hear. The greatest city in the world . . . if only I could understand that it's a question of trying to see things steadily all the time, then perhaps I *could* understand it. Martha's daytime brain had become detached, wary, watchful, on guard—to protect another part of it which had just started to wake, to listen, because of the fast walk through the moving lit streets. And when this happened (and she never knew when it would) nothing mattered but to protect, to keep the irrelevant at bay. It was this business of having to divide off, make boundaries—it was such a strain. Jimmy and Iris's café, the bombed streets, the river city where Stella was, this hunters' street, the great stained damp houses where Henry Matheson's and John Higham's parents and grandparents might have lived, one family to a house: even to begin to understand it was—but one's daytime brain was slotted, compartmented, pigeon-holed. . . .

Now she slowed, almost stopped in surprise at a cool hard getaway look from a young woman who stood with her back to a hedge. Of course, she had passed another invisible boundary. From here until past Queensway, the pavements were lined with prostitutes, standing singly or in pairs, dozens of them, along the pavements. But Martha was freer here than she had been in that other territory she had only just left, whose boundary was simply a bisecting street. She was protected precisely by the line of girls for sale, who knew she wasn't one of their trade union and because of their hostile warning faces that said go away, you shouldn't be here, kept her safe from being accosted. Three kinds of animal here. The women, standing with their backs to the hedges, on sale. The ordinary traffic of the pavement—but a slight traffic, mostly couples hurrying past the marketplace, keeping close under the lights, looking embarrassed, as if they were here by a mistake, yet glancing furtively at the buying and bargaining. The customers, men of all ages, walking slowly past the women, or standing under the trees smoking, making choices. And across the street, policemen, spaced out with twenty or thirty yards between each couple, not looking directly at the haggling and dealing, but observing it sideways to make sure that it went on without incident. Martha walked more slowly than she had had to walk in the part of the street she had left. All the way down the street, by lit airy trees, they stood. Although it lightly drizzled, they wore summer dresses, bare-necked, bare-shouldered; and high thick sandals with bared insteps; and sometimes they held a jaunty umbrella. But there was no elegance here either. They weren't well dressed. They shared the national disposition towards gracelessness. There has been a war on. Suppose one of these men who was making up for the starvation of the war (like Jack, still obsessed by it) approached one of the girls saying: I'd like you to wear ... whatever was his fantasy, would she snap back: There's been a war on, you know? Yes, very probably.... Martha found herself imagining rooms where furniture, curtains, objects had charm, had flair, and a girl with charm, flair, undressed slowly to show off wittily charming underclothes—a man's fantasy? Perhaps in all this city it was only these girls' rooms where there was anything attractive, gay, rightly made? Well, not from the way they were dressed as they stood on the pavement.

She had left the street of prostitutes behind. She was getting towards Notting Hill. And now, although she had headed this way with an intention to loiter and look, to spend time until midnight when she might safely reach Jack's, she had to brace herself before turning off the main road into an area which was worse than anything. The little streets across the river had never been other than small and thin and poor. The "West End" was a market only, with what was full-fed and comfortable in it hidden from the pavements. The enormous piles along the Bayswater Road had been and would be again a climate of money. But the streets from here to the canal were depressing and lowering: irredeemable by fantasy. She waited for glimpses of a scene created by light out of the dark that pressed houses into the soil, houses that were cracked and leaning and dirty and wet, streets and streets and streets of them, and among them, the boarded-up spaces full of rubble or water-filled craters, or damp earth cleared for rebuilding. She was walking along a long low street with dark trees along it, and low pools of yellowish light at intervals, consciouslessly bracing herself against depression, which she understood that in fact the part of her mind whose intimations she courted had spread, was swallowing the rest: she was on the verge of a sensation—no, wrong word, but what words were right?—a state then, that had been in fact the surprise of her being in London, its real gift to her. She had learned that if she walked long enough, slept lightly enough to be conscious of her dreams, ate at random, was struck by new experience throughout the day, then her whole self cleared, lightened, she became alive and light and aware.

Her practical self checked her physical condition: the

meal in the restaurant was the first proper meal for days; the wine the first alcohol for weeks; she had scarcely slept last night, because of the noise from the café downstairs, which closed at midnight and started again at about five. And she had been walking and alert all day. The conditions were right, then. First, before the lit space, a terror: but slight, nothing that could overwhelm, less fear than the reluctance to acknowledge her condition of being so alien, of walking always as a watchful critic. This was loneliness? Yes, she supposed so. But, if so, what else had she ever known? So that was a gift too: people said "loneliness" speaking of an ultimate dread; and she had once said "loneliness" meaning a blow of fate that might make her alone among her fellow creatures, something that in the future might claim her. But no, since she had been in London, she had been alone, and had learned that she had never been anything else in her life. Far from being an enemy, it was her friend. This was the best thing she had known, to walk down streets interminably, to walk through mornings and afternoons and evenings, alone, not knowing where she was unless she walked beside the river; sometimes walking so long she did not even know what part of London she was in, her feet tired, but conscious of strength in their tiredness, her head cool, watchful, alert, waiting for the coming of the visitor, silence. And her heart . . . well, that was the point, it was always her heart that first fought off the pain of not belonging here, not belonging anywhere, and then, resisted, told to be quiet, it quietened and stilled. Her heart as it were came to heel; and after that, the current of her ordinary thought switched off. Her body was a machine, reliable and safe for walking; her heart and daytime mind were quiet.

This then was what she had discovered, had been given rather; and was so reluctant to give up. This was why she did not want to choose this slot or that, this or that job, this or that person, to become a tactful assistant to Henry and John Higham; or an addition to the people across the river. If only she could go on like this, walking forever through the interminable damp hostile streets of this doomed city, all cracked and thinned and darkened by war—if only she could stay, here, in this area of herself she had found. . . . Her mind was swinging slowly from light to dark, dark to light. Into it came impressions: a tree, an intensely variegated mass of light; a brick wall picked out in a flood of glowing orange by a slant of light from a window; a face that looked out briefly from behind glass before a curtain twitched across. Her mind was a soft dark empty space. That was what she was. "Matty" was an intolerably tedious personage she could think of only with exhausted nausea and fear that she might ever again be afflicted by her. "Martha"—well, ordinary Martha too had moved away, could be looked at: she did well enough, was not important. As for "Hesse," it was a name acquired like a bracelet from a man who had it in his possession to be given to a woman in front of lawyers at the time of the signing of the marriage contract. But who then was she, behind the banalities of the day? A young woman? No, nothing but a soft dark receptive intelligence, that was all. And if she tried—but not too hard, a quick flash of effort, a light probe into a possibility, she could move back in time, annulling time, for the moment of the effort, and stand in another country, on another soil. Walking down damp-smelling pavements under the wet London sky in the summer of five years after the war, she was (but really became, as if nothing had intervened) Martha Quest, a young girl sitting under the tree from where she could see a great hot landscape and a sky full of birds and clouds. But really, not in imagination—there she sat. Or she was the Martha who had pushed a small child under leafy avenues with the smell of roses coming off town gardens. But really, there she was: *she* was, nothing to do with Martha, or any other name she might have had attached to her, nothing to do with what she looked like, how she had been shaped. And if she were able to go on walking, as she was now, day after day, night after night, down this street, up that, past houses, houses, houses, passing them always, with their shuttered and curtained eyes behind which a dull light hid, if she were able only to do that . . .

And now, into the quiet, came something she had forgotten—one always did forget. She had forgotten what could happen when the dark deepened and one thought it would remain, being so strong. It was as if behind the soft space was a maniac ready to dance inwards with idiotic words and phrases. Words and phrases and fragments of music were niggling at the back of her mind somewhere. But she had really forgotten that this idiot was there, who accompanied the gift of the quiet swinging dark, and whose words did not seem to mean anything. They came out of dark, floated for a while on the space and went on into dark. Then the words of songs and tunes—yes, of course, during the past few weeks she had become familiar with this phase, or stage. First, the quiet empty space, behind which stood an observing presence. Then, into the quiet space, behind it, an enemy, a jiggling fool or idiot. Humiliating! Absurd! Again and again she had won, with such difficulty, the quiet; and then encountered this silliness. She had resisted it. Again and again she had descended from the quiet because of this silly enemy. Tonight, she did not resist: she was too tired. And besides, she was remembering that she had made a discovery, found a new thought—rather a thought had floated in with the silly words and bits of music: that somewhere in one's mind was a wavelength, a band where music jigged and niggled, with or without words; it was simply a question of tuning in and listening. And she had made the discovery, and then forgotten it, that the words, or tunes, were not all at random: they reflected a state or an emotion. Because the words of the songs, or the phrases, had a relevance: one could learn from them, if one did not shy off, indignant, annoyed, because of the banality, (the silliness, the jumble of this band of sound just behind (beside?) the empty space. For, as Martha had told the wavelength, or the station, before tonight (and had forgotten that she had), you have a very poor sense of humour, you have no taste at all. For instance, a couple of weeks before, walking by the river, first achieving the quiet, then reaching, or being afflicted by, the band of sound, she had discovered that far from not caring about having no money, and reaching the end of what she had, she was worried, frightened in fact, because the tune that jigged there was "the best things in life are free" over and over and over again, like a sardonic, squalling baby, grinding into her daytime consciousness that she must stop now, must look for work, must get back a condition of earning money. And because night after night she had reached this place, and been informed over and over again by this appallingly frivolous and silly voice that she was in fact scared stiff, she had taken the decision to put her life into responsibility, to leave the drifting and floating. So why resent the method if the information was of use? How did she want useful information to be given? In crashing chords no doubt, or with trumpets? That particular part of her brain did not work like that, and if she resented it, shied off, fled away, made a decision to descend, resisted, she also lost information she needed. The most interesting discoverings were made through banalities. Now, jiggling away there on the edge of the empty space, was the announcement that she was tired and wanted to go home. True: but her feet had been telling her that loudly for more than an hour. It was not her feet, her body that were tired—but another part of herself: she understood that in fact she was under great strain, and in a flash of foreseeing realised the plunge into inert exhaustion that would follow this height. But who, what, was tired, that she needed to be told she was? She walked on; in a few minutes she would be at Jack's house. That is, she would be if she did not take a great loop through surrounding streets; she did not want to get to Jack's place yet, no matter what price she would have to pay for being, as she was now, at a height in herself. When she got to Jack's, well, that would be a very different place in herself again; and once in it—but suddenly she understood that there was only one person she knew in London, who could allow her to go on living as she was now, rootless, untied, free. That was Jack. No pressures there. And she understood just why he lived as he did. She had "understood" it before; but she understood it differently now that she was in that area of the human mind that Jack also inhabited. Yes. But in that case, why did she shy so strongly away from Jack, from what he stood for—or at least, she did with a good part of herself. That part whose name was Self-preservation. She knew that. *He was paying too high a price* for what he got. She knew that. What was the price? The jiggling wavelength was telling her: Jack fell down and broke his crown, Jack fell down and broke . . .

Yes. He could not go on as he was now, he'd fall. And so would she if she did not move out of this high stretch of herself. Ah, but not yet, please not yet; she could spend time with him, in his area, just a short time, before moving on to responsibility? Responsibility, that is, to the normal, the usual—she had debts to pay, that was it. One could not move on before all debts were paid, the accounts made up. Terror struck, thinking of the debts she did have to pay: Caroline invaded her mind, the two men she had married so absurdly—her mother. Debts. They had to be paid. A great descent down, down, was before her. Then a wave would lift her up again (when?) to where she was now, on a height, and from where she could glimpse other perspectives. The tune said: Mother, must I go on dancing? Infuriating, ridiculous, banal, this had recently entered her listening mind as soon as she reached the boundary in it. Always. Mother, must I go on dancing? Yes, she knew only too well she had to go on dancing. She knew it, both now, when she was inside the empty space, away from ordinary living; and inside ordinary living, when the space seemed a very far country.

She knew what she had to do—ring up Marjorie's sister Phoebe. She could not stay with Jack, even for as short a time as he would be able to live as he did before he fell down and broke his crown. The words "Be Careful" were printed in black jagged letters across the empty space. She looked at them, as they faded in a fall of stars, like fireworks dropping through a dark night sky. Perhaps she should warn Jack? That thought, the housewife's thought, told her she was sinking, she was coming down. After all, she could not maintain it for long, could not stay where the air was cool and where it was ridiculous to think: I must warn Jack. Who am I to warn Jack? Responsibilities and commitments, she was sinking towards them, fast ... She had to go on dancing ... BUT NOT YET. With an effort, she shook, tightened, forced herself up, up through the quiet space and into the wavelength where, now it was not resisted but accepted, it crashed around her inner ears in a din of appalling sound, music, voices, screaming, the sounds of war—and, through it ... Even as she understood that she had reached, through acceptance, through not being afraid of or irritated by the silliness and jumble of this area, a state of quiet and distance as far removed from the state of quiet known up till now as that state was from the humdrum of ordinary life, she was already sinking away from it. Sinking, she said, Remember, remember, don't let it go, remember it's there, please, please, don't forget, you forget all the time, hold on to that even when ... But once with Jack it would be hard to remember. She was sinking fast down, down: ahead there was a telephone box, a sentinel at the end of the street near a pub, now darkened. Yes, but remember the space you discovered today. It was gone, gone quite, not even a memory, and she sunk down out of reach of the place where words, bits of music, juggled and jangled and informed. And even the calm place below (beside?) was going, it was a memory, a memory that was going. The thing was, memory was not possible. One could not remember. The knowledge of a certain condition belonged to one, when one was inside it. That was memory. No use to say: remember the lit space and its marvellous brother, the turn of the spiral above it when one had gone through the band of noise. Because, having left them behind, having sunk away, one was in a place with its own memories, its own knowledge. You could, perhaps, during the long day of work, responsibility, people, noise, have a flash of reminder: *These places exist,* but that was because the day had lifted you towards them, like a wave, for just a brief moment; you could think *I can reach it again* when you were near it, not otherwise. Because for some reason the walls of the place you were in now had become thinned, and light came in from the other. That was why people did not remember. They could not. You remembered X with X, Y with Y. It was as simple as that: I must please please remember ... She had reached the telephone box. A tall box under a tree which had black railings around it. She was going past. Why had she wanted to telephone now, this moment? It already seemed ridiculous that she had wanted to, decided to. But an urgency shook her: if you don't ring Marjorie now, commit yourself, you'll stay with Jack. Why on earth shouldn't I stay with Jack? Has he ever indicated, even for a moment, that she should stay with him? Never. Ring Marjorie's sister. Oh, don't be so pompous and absurd. Tomorrow will do. *Ring her now.* When you see Jack, you won't remember at all why you have to ring Marjorie's sister. Mother, must I go dancing? Yes, my darling daughter.... Martha had walked past the telephone box: she had walked past it fast, to get it behind her. It was as if hands took hold of her and turned her around. In the telephone box she rang Phoebe, whose voice came out of a world of tedious and ridiculous duties and responsibilities: it was nearly midnight and Phoebe was working on a report. Yes, Martha would meet her tomorrow. Tomorrow lunchtime? Mother, must I go on dancing? Tomorrow evening, Phoebe? Can't you make lunch, said Phoebe, cross, saying with her voice that Martha had nothing to do with her time and should be prepared to fit herself in busy and responsible Phoebe's life. Yes, I'll meet you for lunch. Very well then, lunch at one, Martha. Phoebe rang off: she had another two hours of paperwork to get through before she could go to bed. Mother, must I go on dancing?

Martha went on, to Jack's place.

Two

The street ran low and dark between dark terraces that were
set back behind hedges. There was no light in the houses and
the street light outside Jack's house made a pool of yellowish
haze about its hooded shaft. Between it and the next blur of
yellowish haze a hundred yards down was dark. The street
was up, and a small red eye showed the edge of a crater.
Behind the terrace was a canal, unused by commerce, where
children swam. From its dirty waters that received old
chairs, refuse, unwanted litters of kittens, mattresses, rose
into the air of this area a foul clinging smell that no wind
ever seemed strong enough to lift away. Behind the small
hedge, near the front door, was a heap of brick and rubble
from inside the house. A cat sat on the rubble, its eyes
gleaming green at Martha, who put out a hand. But the cat
slunk away. Looking up at the second floor, a chink of light
showed at the window, so perhaps behind other walls of this
black street, people were awake to tend a baby, or to make
love, or to read.

Martha knocked, gently, and at once the front door
opened inwards into a hall where a dull light showed bare
boards, flaking walls, a cracking ceiling. There was an awful
smell of damp, of rotting wood. A young man stared at
Martha. A thin body like a coathanger held a dark blue
dressing gown from which lanky white legs protruded below,
and a thin neck and a thin wild face above. He had black
shock-hair, and black eyes.

"I saw you through the shutter."

"Thanks, is Jack in?"

He laughed, but without sound, shaking his shoulders to
mark that he laughed, watching for her reaction from anxiously serious eyes. She smiled, turning her face so that the
heavy ceiling light could show her smile.

"They come and go," he said.

Martha now felt afraid for the first time this night of

walking alone through dark streets. She went slowly towards the stairs, feeling how he followed her, close.

"Mind you, I've known worse places. During the war." He was right up against her back.

"Are you a friend of Jack's?"

"I live here, don't I?"

On the bottom stair she turned to offer him her smile; he stood grinning, his face on the level of hers.

"I'll show you my place." He tugged, grinning, at the sleeve of Mrs. Van's coat; Martha followed him into a room off the hall, which had once been a reception room. It was long, high, with the remains of some fine mouldings in the ceiling. The windows were shuttered; but there was a crack, and against the crack was set a chair: an observation post. There was a camp bed, with dingy blankets, and against the wall a painter's ladder, with hooks up the sides that held shirts, a jacket, and two pairs of shoes tied by their laces. There was a candle in a bottle near the camp bed; and by it, a mess of comics.

"They lived under the rubble in Germany," he said.

"So I read."

"I was there."

Now she looked at him, understanding his wildly grinning face, his staring eyes, his perpetual soundless laugh; it was quite simple, he was crazy.

"In Poland they lived in the sewers."

"You were there too?" she asked politely.

He laughed, shaking his shoulders, and his black eyes narrowed into a frenzy of suspicion. "I didn't say so, did I?"

"No."

"I was. In the sewers. I fought."

Martha now found that she was not only afraid, but tired. Her legs were stones under her. Her head was heavy. A very long way was she now from the light easy-walking creature of only half an hour ago, whose head was like a lighthouse or a radio set. She thought: I must remember, I must, I must; but stood back, as the young man came a step nearer, grinning and staring. His hands had come out to grasp—not her, but her wandering attention. They were young, thin, sad hands, rather grubby.

"If you are interested in other things, then I'm very very sorry," he said. "Very!"

"The thing is, I'm rather late."

"The other one left at eleven eleven. I let her out. It is now one nineteen precisely."

"In that case, I really must go up, Jack'll be waiting."

She smiled and turned and went out, feeling him immediately behind her, and his grin somewhere just behind her head. But she walked steadily up the stairs, saying as she turned into the landing: "Thanks for showing me your place."

"It's all you need. With bell, book and candle. The church across the canal has a bell. Do you know it?"

"I've heard it. Good night."

She stood in a breathing dark, in front of her a door that had light behind it, while below she heard him shuffle back into his place. Martha knocked softly on the door. There was no answer. What she stepped into was a quiet room with fresh white walls, a glossy dark floor with rugs on it, and candles burning on the handsome mantelpiece. And it was warm: the heaters glimmered. On a large bed under the window, Jack lay sleeping. He was naked under a blanket, and was on his back, his cheek on his hand as if he were thinking. As he almost might be: he was lightly, alertly asleep. Martha slid off her shoes and into a chair to rest a moment; if she had not sat down then, she would have fallen; she was thinking, What nonsense, if I'd had to walk another five miles I would, and not been tired till the end of them. Now she sat; for a moment half conscious. Her back was to the shutter that kept off the smells from the canal below. Above this floor, a floor was empty: rooms that had been open to the sky for a year, receiving wet and wind and snow, and letting the wet seep down, of course, to the white fresh ceiling she now stared at. It had been, Jack said, flaking and cracked, and crumbling and soaked a dark mouldy brown. Then Jack had mended the roof to keep the weather out, and removed the rubble. Below this floor was another, dry, unaffected by the war, but empty, unpainted for years and smelling of mice or rats. Below that, the room in which the young crazy man had made his camp. But on the side of the hall opposite him, a large empty room, beautiful, but the shell of its inside was flaking and falling away. And under the whole tall house, a basement which had had water in it for years. Then, when Jack had drained it, it had damp rubble and old boards. Now it was empty, slowly drying out, he hoped; but sending through the entire house an odour of old damp. But this room was all clean: the old blackout curtains had been left, to add to the theme of black and white. There were Jack's pictures on the walls. Not many: enough, as he had said, to show he was a

45

painter. And there was an easel and some painting things in a corner. The pictures were mostly abstract, and mostly black and white or grey or brown. Some of them had been made out of queer materials—bits of sack glued onto board; brick rubble mixed with paint smeared on board; paint mixed with sand. Jack had become a painter because at the end of the war he had not wanted to go back to a settled life. He needed a label. What was more respectable than to be a painter: in Jack a cycle had come around to an ironic end. Perhaps even ten years before he would have had to fool himself that he was a painter, in order to live the life he wanted under that label. But the war had taught him that there wasn't time for anything but essentials, he said. In the war he had learned that you must take what you wanted and then fight for it. If you were an artist you could get away with anything. You should either be very rich or an artist or a criminal. He had acquired some canvas and an easel and some paints, and had bought a lot of old pictures from a junkshop which he kept stacked about the walls for the sake of their atmosphere. He did a few days' work with sand, rubble, bits of sack and some glue and some paint, and behold, he was an artist, with a label he could use on passports and forms.

In 1947, a sailor discharged from the purposes of war, he had been walking down this street in which he had found a room, and had seen this house, then a wreck, a ruin, a shell, with a collapsed roof. He had gone into the open door and to the top of the house. He had spent a day in the house, not really making plans or decisions, but it seemed they had been made without his knowing about it, for the next thing he knew was, he had gone out and brought back a bucket, a scrubbing brush, and soap. With the roof still open above him, he had cleared rubble and scrubbed until he felt rain on his back and realised the roof ought to be mended. He mended the roof. He was just finishing it when Garibaldi Vasallo the Maltese had come in. He was a large swarthy man who looked as if he ought to have gold rings in his ears. But he wore a striped businessman's suit.

"What are you doing, son?"

"Mending the roof," said Jack.

"It's my house, do you know that?"

"Well I'm living in it, aren't I?"

Garibaldi Vasallo went down to the water-filled basement, inspected every floorboard and inch of plaster in the decaying place, and returned to under the roof, having decided to buy it. Previously he had decided it was in too bad a state to buy, like all the bomb-shaken houses of this terrace. But he watched Jack at work for a few minutes and said: "You'll have to leave."

"You can't do that, I'm a protected tenant."

"How's that?"

"I live here."

"Since when?"

"Have a cigarette."

Jack came down from the roof and sat cross-legged on the damp floorboards, and Garibaldi Vasallo sat opposite him and they smoked and discussed the war. Garibaldi Vasallo had been in the Merchant Navy. Jack had been in a mine-sweeper. If Jack had been in a minesweeper throughout the war, then he could not have been living in this house as he continued to claim that he had. He continued to make this claim, affably, while he talked of his minesweeping years with Garibaldi Vasallo, who for his part continued to say that this was his house. And so it went on for some hours, and then Garibaldi went off to buy the house. It cost him £450. He bought two others at the same time for £500 each. Then, lacking further capital for the time being, made it his business to sniff out possible other buyers (very few, the terrace being in such dilapidation), letting them know that "the blacks were moving in." He now had no money at all. He dropped over to watch Jack's work on the top floor of the house, and began work himself on the roof of one of his other houses. Meanwhile Jack had brought in his belongings, at that stage a camp bed (now being used by the mad youth downstairs) and a candle in a bottle. He had about £1,000 from the war. So far he had spent none of it, and mending the roof had cost nothing, since he had borrowed tools and used available materials from nearby bombed houses. Now he cleaned and painted the second floor, and in the evenings Mr. Garibaldi Vasallo dropped in to see what Jack was doing and how he did it. For while being in the navy was a fine training in inventiveness and small skills, he knew nothing about building, and building had been one of the ways Jack had earned a living. When this floor was all painted out and clean, Jack bought a large bed, a chair, a chest of drawers and some rugs at a street market. Total cost, five pounds. Jack was now at home. But there was no electricity in the place and no plumbing. He used candles and went to the public bathhouse and the lavatory at the old cinema at the corner, in payment for which he mended cracked windows for the proprietor.

Now Garibaldi asked Jack if he'd like to go into business: for Jack had seen that he knew about the £1,000. Garibaldi was desperate for even half that amount, a quarter: he could buy another bomb-damaged house, or do one up good enough to sell at double what he had paid for it; the thought of £1,000 made Garibaldi desperate.

"Yes, well," said Jack, "but I think I'm happy as I am."

And now Garibaldi stood in the middle of the newly black-painted floor, a stout Mediterranean man with hot Mediterranean eyes, and went off into a great storm of rage while Jack laughed and scraped old varnish off a chest of drawers. Laughing, Jack stormed and raged back, while the fat speculator threatened. At last Garibaldi shouted out what he had meant to ask, shrewdly, and as a probe: "And there isn't any electricity here, it's illegal."

"True, the whole place needs rewiring," said Jack.

"And the plumbing is disgusting, no one but an animal would live in a house without plumbing."

Jack then offered to do the wiring and some plumbing, the minimum, for a half-share in the house, for £225. At which Garibaldi raged and stormed again, and said that the house had already appreciated, it was worth double by now; and Jack shouting and laughing said that was only because he, Jack, had repaired it. Garibaldi went off, shouting to the front door, but was silent outside it: already too many of the people in the street knew about him, watched him, meant him harm.

Next time he came in, Jack had seen him through the window, and was at work on the wiring.

"You give me £500," said Garibaldi.

"£225," said Jack.

After some weeks this agreement was come to but it took another six months to get Garibaldi to the lawyers, of whom he was deadly afraid. "Oh, don't worry," said Jack, insisting on a respectable lawyer, with real offices, in the West End. "You're all right with me. You're nothing but a dirty little dago and a crook, but I'm a gentleman and they'll know I'm all right."

Which was how Jack had become half-owner of this great shattered house which now had some plumbing and some electricity, and where one floor, this one, was the kind of place Martha could enter and feel . . .

Yes, but that was an uncomfortable point. Down in Stella's territory, or with Iris, or walking through streets she did not know, she was skinned, scaled, vulnerable, an alien, always fighting in herself that inner shrinking which was the result of surroundings that did not know her, until, fought, it became the strength which set free. She had only to walk in here, to be greeted by skins of white, of black paint, and instantly she was at home. She was very definitely Martha: the dullness, the inertia, of being at home took over. And very far was she from the open-pored receptive being who hadn't a name. People like her, for some reason, in this time, made rooms that were clean and bare and white: in them they felt at home, were safe and unchallenged. *But she did not want to feel like this*—in that case why had she rung Phoebe?

Jack still lay asleep. He breathed lightly but steadily: probably deeper asleep than she had thought. Well, of course, he'd spent the earlier part of the evening making love with the girl who had been let out at eleven eleven. She should take off her clothes, very quietly, and get quietly under the blanket with him and sleep. Ah, but she was so tired, she would descend into a gulf of sleep and she did not want that. Sooner or later, she would have to. She stood up to take off her coat, and that small movement made Jack open his eyes. His head was turned towards her, but she wondered what he saw in the soft light of the candles: his face was hostile. "Who . . . ?" he began, and sat up, shaking his head free of sleep.

"Martha. Hell, man—but . . ." She had taken off Mrs. Van's coat, and now he smiled. "You looked like an old woman." He came over, naked, and putting two hands on her shoulders stared into her face. "Hell, Martha, but that gave me a scare." Now he kissed her cheek as if tasting it, and laid his face against hers. "Martha," he said, and went off to the spirit stove he used for cooking. "I'll make some cocoa, hell you look tired, Martha."

She stripped off her clothes, fast, knowing that by doing it she put herself farthest from what she had been, walking alert and alone in the streets. She sat on the foot of the bed, back in that area of herself where she was not much more than a warm easy body. She looked at Jack, his back turned, a tall, a very thin young man, very white, with brown forearms like long gloves, and brown hair falling straight: he wore his hair rather long. When he turned with two mugs of cocoa, he came smiling across to the bed, stepping in big bounding strides, and sat close, smiling into her face. He was

altogether delighted. "You've been walking again, I can see."
"Yes." "God man, Martha, I do envy you, I do, when you
first come to London, the whole place is yours, I don't know
how to explain it, I remember that, I think of it often, but
now I'm a householder and that's the end of that. I'm sorry.
But believe you me, I like to think of you doing it."

"Not for long," said Martha.

"No. You go to a new place and for a while it's fine, and
then it gets you. You should move on then."

"You're not going to!"

"But I tell you, Martha, when I saw that old woman
sitting in that chair, it gave me a scare, I thought, who's
that old woman in my room?"

"Then that's why it's over for me," said Martha, "I've got
to get a job so I can get a coat so you don't think I'm an old
woman."

They were sitting so their knees touched: prickles of
electricity ran from one to another, while they smiled, drinking cocoa, and looking with pleasure into each other's faces.
Now, after a questioning look, which she answered, to find
out if it was time, he looked, smiling at her centre, so that it
livened and became the centre of herself. Slowly he let the
pressure of his eyes go up to her stomach, then wait, then to
one breast, and wait, then to the other—her breasts lifted
and tightened, and he laughed. Now she looked, smiling, at
his genitals: they tightened and began to lift. She put out a
hand to touch him; he touched her; then they joined these
hands, so that current ran through them, through knees and
hands. Now, set together in rising rhythm, they could sit and
talk, or be silent, for a half hour, an hour, or through the
night, and everything they said, or their silences, would flow
up into the moment when they began to make love. If they
touched too soon, then it was too strong, set a too urgent
current. The looking, slow and pleasurable, was like the
perfect meshing of the right gears.

"I haven't seen you for so long, Martha—what is it, it
seems weeks? And I've been thinking about you."

This "I've been thinking about you" was true: he thought,
deliberately, about his girls, maintaining that in this way he
kept them connected to him. But he said it because of a
necessity he felt to keep, hold, reassure, be reassured. He
meant, *In spite of the other girls, I think of you.* "What have
you been doing, Martha?"

"I've discovered that I've got to get a job."

But this went past him. Women had jobs, but for him that

was not important. Women got jobs to buy clothes, to make themselves pretty for him, for themselves, for their men. It did not matter what jobs they had. What lives they had outside this room, he did not care, provided they came back. He wasn't serious, not really!

"I was thinking a lot about how it was the last time: I swear it, Martha, that with you there's something I haven't with the others."

She was delighted. If he said it, it was true; but it didn't matter: he felt like saying it.

"Who was the girl who was let out at eleven eleven?" She said this deliberately, in order to see if she would feel jealous. All kinds of emotions she had considered hers had retreated during the last few weeks. For instance, Henry motioning her mother: in the past, what resentment, what fear had flared up, taken hold. But now, it didn't touch her. And a slight pang of jealousy faded at once: they were emotions without force behind them like jets of water without pressure.

"He's a bit crazy, Martha. He's got a thing about time. He's got a chart: he marks every day off in hours and crosses off every hour."

And now, his face hardened and clenched: for he above all had time riding him. Suddenly he lifted her hand and pressed it tight to his eyes: she could feel the round pressure of his eyeball against the ball of her thumb.

"Is that why he's here?"

"Yes, you're right, I hadn't thought of that, but that's why. I was saying to myself it was because—well, for one thing it tests Vasallo. And for another, if the police pick him up again he'll be back in the loony bin."

He sat quiet, eyes shut, holding her hand so tight the bones hurt. He was sitting inside his living breathing body, assuring himself of it. Jack had done four years in the minesweeper and had been in continual danger. He had been sunk twice. Once he had spent twelve hours in the water. What he had been left with was an awe of the flesh. The existence of his body now was a miracle: he never ceased to feel it. Time bled away from him in every pulse beat. Thomas had had that too.

She was thinking of Thomas. Again? With Jack, she found herself thinking of Thomas. She did not think of her two husbands, Knowell and Hesse, she thought of Thomas.

Thomas Stern. Thomas. Who was Thomas that she had to go on thinking of him?

Thomas was a soldier. Thomas was a gardener. Thomas was a tradesman. He was the husband of his wife and the father of his little daughter. He was an exile, Thomas Stern, Polish Jew from Sochaczen, tossed out of Europe and into Africa by a movement of war. When they put his name on documents to make him part of the Medical Corps, Zambesia, they wrote: Thomas Stern, Pole, *alien*. When the Germans killed his family in the Warsaw Ghetto, they might have written (did they keep records?) "Sarah Stern, Abraham Stern, Hagar Stern, Reuben Stern, Deborah Stern, Aaron Stern . . ." Thomas was the son and the brother of these dead people. Thomas was a man who killed another man deliberately because he had gone mad and chosen to believe in revenge for revenge's sake. Thomas was a man who had chosen to live with some particularly "backward" Africans on the edge of the Zambesi River in a tract of land now covered feet deep by the waters of the Kariba Dam. These Africans (now dispersed to other areas chosen by the white man and dead as a tribe) had thought of Thomas Stern: A crazy white man with a good heart who lives with us and who sits in his hut scribbling words on paper. Martha had thought of Thomas who was her lover and not her husband: "With this man I am always at home." Martha Quest (then Martha Knowell, then Martha Hesse) had thought, still thought of Thomas.

Thomas had lived inside his body as if it were an always dissolving reforming shell or shape with many different names and times. At the end, Thomas's way of living, or being, had wrenched his body from large blond solidity into a lean dark bitterness of purpose. Thomas's flesh breathed time and death; but his mind and his memory moved along another line parallel to it.

That was why she had been with Thomas.

That's why she was with Jack.

I couldn't be with a man who hadn't got it: time moving in one's breath. I suppose once you've entered into some kind of knowledge, then you can't go back on it. . . .

Suddenly she saw something: All Jack's girls had it. Of course, that was how he chose them, while he thought he was choosing a smile or the promise of a body.

"What's she like, this new one?"

"She's lovely, a little fair thing, whitey-gold all over, her hair, skin, everything. She sits on my bed like a little whitey-gold statue. I wish you could see her."

"Well, who knows, perhaps I will."

A couple of weeks ago Martha had been sitting as they were now when a girl walked in. She was tall and fair, with solemn brown eyes. She wore an elegant camel coat, in spite of the heat, and had long silk-covered English legs. She had seen the two of them as she came in and turned around slowly to close the door to give herself time to know what she wanted to do. Then her face came back into view with a smile on it, and she advanced smiling to the bed. Martha, introduced, nodded and smiled. Jack said: "Joanna, come and join us."

"Not altogether, if you don't mind," said Joanna, with a short amused laugh. Composed, she pulled up a hard chair and sat quite close. The three smiled at each other.

"I was passing," she said; at which Jack and Martha laughed, and then, after a while, she laughed too, for this was not an area where she could possibly have been passing.

"I wanted to set eyes on one of the others," she said, gruff and abrupt, making a confession with difficulty.

"Well, here I am."

Joanna gave Martha a slow once-over.

"You're very pretty," she said.

"I'm sure that I'd think the same of you!"

Meanwhile Jack sat, not at all embarrassed, or amused, or annoyed. He was pleased and interested. He was never amused, never ironic, never felt a shock of improbability. He was delighted, pleased—or so unhappy he could not move but lay face down on his bed suffering till a weight lifted off him.

"Shall I make you some cocoa?" he asked.

She shook her head, smiling.

"The thing is, Jack, either we both have to get dressed, or Joanna has to get undressed."

"Yes, of course," said Joanna in her brisk fair English way.

Jack wanted Joanna to get undressed. Afterwards he had said to Martha, the tears positively drowning his eyes: "If she had trusted me so much—if she had taken her clothes off—then I swear, I'd have been so happy, I can't make you feel how happy I'd have been. But not yet. She will, though. I am sure she will."

He left it to them, the two women, to decide when to trust him. Martha began to dress. That had been during the heat wave, and she had put on, but not too fast, while they watched, bra, pants, slip and a narrow blue linen dress. Joanna had admired the dress. Then Jack had got dressed and they had all gone out to eat lunch at the Indian restaurant.

Joanna was engaged to a second cousin who had been in the Guards and who had a big house in the country. She intended to marry him although he had not done more than kiss her aggressively when taking her home after the theatre once. He had been rather drunk. She came to Jack, once or twice a week, to make love. She was not young: that is, she was not a girl, for she had the war behind her. From the war she had got one thing, a need for security. The security was the cousin. Jack was for her.

"I was too close to it in the war," she had said to Martha, not feeling that she needed to explain. "And love doesn't last, does it?"

"Love may not last, but sex does," said Jack, when Martha reported what Joanna had said. And he rang up Joanna in the country to say the same to her. "I'll be here, always," he said. "Remember that."

For Joanna "it" was poverty. This was the edge she was afraid of.

For Jack? He had spent the whole war, he said, dreaming about women. And so here he was, receiving girls, one, two, three a day, making love for hours every day. And he painted. For instance he had painted a picture while Garibaldi watched him. He was only serious about sex.

But *he's* not serious, thought Martha. He can't spend the rest of his life ... but why shouldn't he? Why on earth not? Considering the way most people did spend their lives.

The boy downstairs was mad. About time? Death. And Jack was mad. About women. Death. Joanna was mad: she proposed to spend her life with a man she didn't much like because she was afraid of—poverty? And she, Martha—but she would be lunching with Phoebe tomorrow. In a few hours, now.

"If I asked her to meet you, would you come?"

"Would she?"

"If she actually met you ... if I could get her to do that ... when women are jealous, I've discovered, they aren't when they've actually met the girl they've been thinking all those thoughts about. But men don't realise that, do they?"

That's only because you aren't serious, Jack. We don't take you seriously. Why not?

"You're tired, aren't you, Martha?"

"I was very, not now."

He looked at her again: centre, breasts, back down to her

54

thighs, back up to her eyes—smiling. But the smile dimmed. "You're not with me, you're not . . ." He nearly touched her breasts, but withdrew his hand and enclosed hers again with it. "Martha I won't mind if you say yes—but have you been with another man?"

"No—really not!"

"Because if that's it, tell me, and we'll try something else. I've noticed with my girls, when they've been with a man, even their husband, this one doesn't work—something gets switched off. Then you just have to start again, you have to have a good ordinary fuck to make the contact again. But that's not as good as when you can let it slowly build up like this . . ." He was in a fever of anxiety, as he leaned forward, explaining to her, comrade in the fields of love: his expertise was all urgency; he looked as if something might be taken away from him, had been taken away. Did he know that she had thought: I won't be coming back again?

"This little one tonight, Jane, she was with a man this afternoon, and I was sitting with her like this, and she said to me, all wide-eyed and wanting to know: Jack, I don't feel for you the way I did last Thursday, what's wrong with me. I don't want you to touch me."

"She'd been making love?"

"Yes. All afternoon."

She laughed; then so did he, to keep her company.

"But not me, I haven't."

"Well then, we'll wait until it's right."

"Who is she—Jane?"

"She's English—a sweet gentle wide-eyed little English girl. You know."

"Indeed yes, there was one in the restaurant I was in tonight. She was so pretty. And she wore that black dress, that uniform, you know it? The little crepe dress. With an awful brooch. Just *there,* you know—the whole thing, so wrong, so ugly, so nastily *smart* . . ."

"Yes, yes, yes," he said, delighted, laughing.

"There was no relationship between that dress and that girl. And then another came in. They knew each other. And she had a black little dress with a little square of white neck. Like plump little teddy bears. Everyone was playing nurseries. It was an upper-middle-class restaurant—I'm coming on, I can tell the difference. And I looked at those girls and they broke my heart, and I thought: Well, at least I can tell Jack, he'll understand."

"To hell with it, Martha, you're sad, I don't like that."

She rested on his smooth naked shoulder. But it was not a shoulder for comfort, not a body for support: it was a body for love. She rested against him, for his sake. On the arm that did not hold her, but lay on his knee, she saw the fine gold hairs stand up, each in a pucker of flesh. Then his body, an instrument more sensitive than any she had known, shivered. Then she knew why: it had started to rain, to rain heavily, and the roof was sounding with it. The house was an empty shell reverberating to the rain: his thin lithe body was alert and anxious, like an animal's, and he put back his head and sniffed, like an animal when there is rain or smoke on the wind. They rolled over, together, and lay side by side, both shivering in the warm room because of the booming rain, looking at each other. Now as he looked, and she looked, began the ceremony for whose sake he had put all the passion of his life into women: for here was where he fought with time, wrestled with it, held it, understood it; here the gates were held.

The two bodies lay face to face, held loose together by arms, and legs; one long and white, all narrow bone and muscle, one solidly fleshed; these two separate organisms were connected by a steady interchanging gaze, eye to eye. Now he waited for her fingers to touch and annul the long scar on his neck. Diving off a ship that slanted into the water, he had slid past, under the heave of a wave, something jagged which had ripped away from his shoulder, a flap of flesh. This, while treading water and holding on to a floating baulk of timber, he had found drifting in the water, with a hand numbed by the loss of blood, and thought it was weed or debris, to be pushed away. "Think of it, Martha— there I was, holding on with one hand. I told that hand hold on, hold on there man, that's what I said to it, and then I swear I forgot that hand, I didn't think of it again, it just went on holding on without my thinking of it again. And the other hand kept coming on a bit of weed or something. It irritated me, and then I looked and there was a sort of flap lying in the water. Like a bit of filleted fish. There was my shoulder, the shoulder bones. I was looking at white bone with some gristle on it and I thought: that's like a bone a dog's been at and left, and then I realised; it's my shoulder bone. And the bit of weed or something was the flesh of my shoulder. It was nothing—skin with some red blood vessels inside—hell, but I'd never known before how thin I was, it scared me. That's why I eat so much, I eat and eat, because of that flap of skin. I made the swimming hand bend up and hold the flap down on my neck, and pressed down to stop the blood all going into the sea. The funny thing was, I had no feeling in that hand, but I made it do what I wanted. And the hand which was holding on to the bit of timber, that held on too, but it was numb—dead. That's where I learned about the body, you can make it do what you want, and it's where I first learned about sex. That's funny isn't it. You can tell your body what to do and it does it. There I was for a whole day, watching the sun go right across the sky and down, and the water was red all around me. Sometimes I passed out and then I came to myself and there was the sun, filling the sky, everything hot and glittering, and I thought I was dead already, because there was no sensation in my body anywhere. Then I thought of sharks, coming for us, because all the sea was full of red. But there was so much meat in the sea that day I suppose they didn't need me. And when I was picked up they had to force my arm back away from holding my shoulder flesh in place: it was bent and set hard in a crook."

This scar was a long white weal that slanted down into the armpit. Martha stroked it with her fingers while he remembered that afternoon in a sea full of rubbish and the dead and the dying; she stroked and thought of it with him. Then he, having kissed the fingers that held the memory, contained it, ran his fingers along the minute marks on her groin and upper thighs made by pregnancy, tiny silver marks on white skin, and she thought of a small baby, any baby born to any woman, and its absolute perfection. That is why women cry when their children fall for the first time and scar a knee or an elbow: that perfect body, with not a mark on it, well, now it is claimed by the world—that is the moment when a woman cedes her child away from her, to time. She thought of Caroline, the perfect little female body that had issued from her body which now held and always would the scars of pregnancy, and it was hard to tell whether she was Martha, or her mother who had given birth to her, or Caroline, who would give birth; and meanwhile Jack touched and understood the scars, lifting his head to look at them, and on his face was the awe of his love of the flesh and his terror at what ate it. She lay and watched the strong bony boy's face with the boy's brown eyes just above hers, and the face dissolved into time: his hard straight mouth and the eyes were those of the little tyrant his father; his nose, his falling brown hair, his mother's, the frightened farm girl's; and when he smiled, letting his head fall back on the pillow beside hers, she slid down her hand to the back of thighs which under the pads of her fingers were grooved and marred, and his brown eyes narrowed into a tension of memory. He was the son of a farmer in the Orange Free State, a small poor farmer with a large family: two sons, a cowed wife, and three daughters whom he adored and terrorised, and (so Jack claimed) had raped, just once, all three of them. The marks he had left on Jack and the other boy were across the backs of their thighs. He whipped them with his leather thong all through their childhood, and the moment Jack got free of him was when he went to the local Indian store and bought a pair of long khaki trousers: man's trousers. He was twelve, and he had to roll up the bottoms more than a foot. Then he had gone to the verandah where his father was sitting at sundown with his silent wife, and had stood there—a man. And when the father had stood up, anger swelling in the veins of his neck, Jack had picked up a big stone from the earth outside the house, and had stood there, stone poised at shoulder level ready to throw. Not one word had been said. There he had stood, a thin child in a man's long trousers that hid the scarred backs of his thighs forever from his father; the setting sun was hot on his back and made a long shadow right across the sand to the brick verandah where the man his father stood up to go inside and fetch his whip. But he stopped, because as he moved, the stone in the boy's hand moved while the narrowed brown eyes (replicas of his own) took aim. The man had sat down. He had not beaten the older son again, but went on beating the younger. He did this until Jack took the eleven-year-old into the local store and with money he had stolen from the tobacco bag hidden under his father's mattress bought him a pair of man's trousers. The two boys had confronted the father together. And again, not a word. Never a word spoken while the two boys stood side by side at evening looking in at the verandah where their parents sat drinking coffee. The mother had gone indoors, unable to stand it: and four females had stood in the room behind, watching the scene outside, too afraid even to cry.

A year later Jack left the farm early one morning when the sun was coming up over the edges of the sand, taking with him money he had stolen from under the mattress. He boarded the train to Port Elizabeth. "And there I suddenly understood, Martha—I was *mad*. I'd been mad all my life, ever since I could remember being a little kicker. I had spent every moment of my life hating my father. I stood on the edge of the sea, and that was something, the sea, for the first time. I had hardly known the sea existed. No one ever mentioned it, not really. God it makes you want to cry, man, sometimes it does make me cry, all the little kickers black and white all over the Fatherland, and they've never seen the sea, and Port Elizabeth and Cape Town and Durban and Johannesburg are the big cities. I stood throwing stones at the sea and crying. Because I'd understood—my father was nothing. It made me feel like nothing. All my life spent hating a poor little tyrant on a few morgen of poor soil, and he'd never known anything else. I knew I had to beat hating him. I knew if I went back to the farm I'd be finished, I'd kill him, I knew I would. I had spent most of my childhood working out ways how to kill the old man. So I said I was eighteen and got a job on the docks. But the hatred—it's there. It comes back into me when I don't expect it. It's my enemy. I can't hate that poor little nothing of a backveld farmer, how can I, what am I hating? But I do ... I can't help it."

So Martha stroked the backs of his thighs, following with her fingers marks made by an oxide whip held by a little tyrant now dead and lying under a thorn tree under the red sand, while Jack closed his eyes, and let hatred rise in him so that he could hold it and control it. He lay trembling with the force of his hatred, his lashes pressed hard against his cheek, until, with a gasp, the tension held, he opened his eyes and her smiled into her face.

Her face which was—whose? For her eyes were her father's, and her mouth too; and her nose and the shape of her face and even where the lines showed how they would fall, and a mole, her mother's. Yet it was Martha who lay now, endowed with these features which were not hers at all, merely from stock, the storehouse of the race, and smiled at Jack? Who smiled? Who smiled back, who, what, when Martha smiled at Jack, Jack at Martha, in these shapes of flesh that had come together as if a sculptor had flung noses, eyes, hands, mouths together? And was it Jack then, who bent her head back so that he could see where the thirty years of her life were written into the soft place just under her chin? Just there and nowhere else on her body did the wear of time show. He touched with soft fingers the soft crinkling place, and kissed it, tears in his eyes because of the anguish of time eating. Jack comforted Martha. Martha took comfort from Jack.

And now, the ritual was complete. They lay, taut with

power held and controlled. Ready. But if things had not gone right, if the hatred had built up and exploded, as sometimes it did, so that he gasped and jumped away from her, to beat his fists on the wall, swearing and crying and trembling; if he had gone white and cold remembering the terror of his being in the sea with his blood leaking away; if she had let herself go away from him into the anonymity of an ancient femaleness, something indifferent to men, even hostile, self-sufficiently female; if she had let herself go into the great indifference of sorrow, thinking how soon her body would sag down over her bones in a gutter of flesh, so that what delight there could be now was not worth the making of it, since it so soon would be in the past—if they went away from each other off a finely achieved and held point, then Jack would kiss her, jump up and say: Well, that's not right, it's not working this time—and make them both cocoa. This achievement of control which was so hard could not tolerate a second best, or a falling away: sex that was an explosion of force, or a weakening of it, was not possible, or too damaging to let happen.

"Martha, do you know what I've discovered—making love? I understood what hating is. You say all your life *I hate, I love*. But then you discover hatred is a sort of wavelength you can tune into. After all, it's always there, hatred is simply part of the world, like one of the colours of the rainbow. You can go into it, as if it were a *place*. Well, right at the beginning when I was using sex to beat me hating my father, then I suddenly understood. If you can get beyond *I hate*—then you find, *there is hatred, always there*. You can say, I am going into hatred now, it's just a force. That's all, it's not anything, not good or bad, you go into it. But man!—you have to come out again fast, it's too too strong, it's too dangerous. But it's like a thousand volts of electricity. And sex. Well, Martha, I don't have to tell you. But that's what I discovered. Do you know what I mean?"

Listening to him, listening to his words, had not been any use to her at first: since it had not been something she had discovered for herself. But, listening to him, she thought back; but no man apart from Thomas had been relevant. Making love with Thomas—that had been sometimes the "thousand volts," but that had shattered, they had not been able to stand it; they had sometimes broken away from each other and sat talking, hardly touching, or even had not met for a couple of days. Somewhere there, Martha and Thomas had stumbled onto something, near some knowledge, but had not been able to use it, benefit.

But some instinct, or some accident of experience, a coming into knowledge, had made this man, Jack, an embodiment of something she had not ever experienced, nor had she imagined existed. She had come near it, merely, but failed to understand. Sex, with Jack, was never an explosive, or the simple satisfying of a need; or rather, if that is what it became, because of tiredness, or failure of control, then it *was* a failure, and he shrugged his shoulders and waited for and prepared for the next time. Sex was the slow building up, over hour after hour, from the moment of meeting the woman he was to make love with, a power, a force, which, when held and controlled, took both up and over and away from any ordinary consciousness into—an area where no words could be of use.

Now, this night, with the rain still enclosing the empty softly drumming house, in this long white room with the candles burning down low, the two bodies on the bed lay in a state of high relaxed control, and Martha, looking at his face, the country boy's face, knew from its absorbed concentration that now they could go on, reach for the next stage: tonight there was no need to confess failure, make sex for the sake of satisfaction, break off for a new attempt. He joined with her and they lay still, sensing and aware of the different rhythms at work in their bodies, the pulse of the blood—blood washing back and forth; the breath, and its movement; the two movements at first out of tune with each other, till they adjusted themselves and became one, first in each separate body and then across the boundaries of separate flesh, the two bodies together. Then, slow, slow, a building up till a different rhythm, a high fine beat of nerves, took over, took control. All the time quite still, not a movement, but lying absolutely still, in a high alert tension, eyes closed, while the separate rhythms emphasized their separateness with a high strong emphasis, till they flowed into higher more powerful rhythm. So that the first movement of body in body was not a willed one, from his side or from hers, but came from, was impelled by, was on, the rhythm of blood-beat and breath. Eyes closed, listening, almost, to their bodies, slow. And now Martha distinguished, through the high tension of the superior rhythm, the different centres of her body—and through hers, Jack's. Sex: sensation pulsing on the currents of blood and breath. Heartbeat—heart: separate. Heart with its emotion, "love," but

61

isolated and looked at like this, a small thing, a pulse of little feeling, like an animal impulse towards another, a warmth. Sex, heart, the currents of the automatic body were one now, together: and above these, her brain, cool and alert, watching and marking. Body, a surge like the sea, but the mind above, not yet swung up, absorbed into the whole. And then mind dimmed and went, and Martha was swung up and away: and as she went she thought, trying to hold a flash of it before it did go: Good God, yes, I had forgotten, why is it we don't remember, with Jack there's this special place; nothing to do with Jack the person, he's the instrument that knows how to reach it—but you can't "remember" it. Yes, exactly like walking down the street in a high vibrating place: you can't "remember" it—it's the same place ... Her mind cleared, emptied, little thoughts like small trains darting across a vast landscape went by. An empty dark mind: pictures were flashing across her eyes, in front of her eyelids, extraordinary scenes, or perhaps ordinary ones made extraordinary by the solemn intensity and emphasis of their presentation to her, places she had not been to, faces she had never seen, gardens, rivers, the flash of a city she had never been in, then voices came into the empty dark place where her mind was. The vibration shifted and heightened; all her body was in a fine high vibration like a wire at very high tension. As she shifted up into this other state, she saw in front of her eyelids a picture of a man and a woman, walking in a high place under a blue sky holding children by the hand, and with them all kinds of wild animals, but they were not wild at all: a lion, a leopard, a tiger, deer, lambs, all as tame as housepets, walking with the man and the woman and the lovely children, and she wanted to cry out with loss; but it was a loss there was no focus to, there was no holding it. And then, out of the pain of loss, came another picture accompanied by a shift of mood or place: she saw a large layered house, not foreign or out of another climate, but London, it had a London feel to it, and it was full of children, not children, half-grown people, and their faces as they turned them towards her were tortured and hurt, and she saw herself, a middle-aged woman, thickened and slowed, with the face of a middle-aged woman. An anxious face, a face set to endure, to hold on—there was such pain in this vision, such hurt, and she heard herself crying: she had dropped back fast through layers of herself to find Jack holding her, the movements of their love-making stopped.

Martha, Martha, Martha. Wake up, Martha, what is it, you are crying—come back, what's wrong?

He was holding her as if she were a child in a nightmare, comforting her. She was back in herself, with the man comforting her, in a room where it was now dark: the candles had burned right down; and beyond the lowered blackout curtain a greying of light—morning.

"Oh God, Jack, it was like a nightmare," she wept in his arms.

"What, tell me, what was it?"

"Do you see pictures, Jack? Do you hear voices?"

"I see scenes sometimes—do you mean the pictures like scenes from a film?"

"Yes, but, oh my God, Jack, this time it really was awful."

"Tell me then, tell me, tell me . . ."

But the house had gone with its load of half-grown children and the woman who was reponsible for it, for them. She could not "remember" it: she only knew it had been there, because of the fearful sadness that filled her now.

"I don't know. It's all gone. And it was silly . . ." She sat up, Jack with her, she was back in her daytime self and it was silly. She was soaked with her tears. All her face and her breasts were wet with tears.

"I'm sorry," she said.

"You gave me such a scare, Martha. I was right away, and then I heard you crying, and I wondered, Who's that crying? And then it came to me, Yes, it must be Martha. So I brought us down again."

They sat side by side on the crumpled hot bed. Behind the blackout curtains, the light was already stronger: the sun must be up over the roofs and treetops of London.

"Look, Martha, you were terribly tired last night, you were upset. Perhaps this was really just a time for us both to come and then off to sleep. Shall I make you come properly Martha and then we'll sleep a bit?"

"Oh Jack, I feel so sad, there was something awful, but I've just remembered, there was something lovely as well: A lovely picture, like the golden age, men and women and animals and children all together walking along. I want to cry."

When she woke up, he was making coffee at the spirit stove. He stood naked with his back to her. A tall thin man—a body. A woman lying on the bed, a body.

She knew from the alert concentration with which he

turned with the cups in his hands that he was adjusting the tension that now lay slack between them for a new curve upwards. It was about seven in the morning. She had five hours before meeting Phoebe for lunch. They sat by each other, and slowly, without talking, let the wheel carry them up and over. This time, when her mind finally clicked off, went beyond the pictures and the voices, she did not retain any memory of it; was aware again only as she made the slow descent. The different rhythms disengaged and she entered normality: which was, she understood now, a condition of disparateness. She had never really seen before how the separate parts of herself went on, working individually, by themselves, not joining: that was the condition of being "normal" as we understand it. Breath flows on, blood beats on, separately from each other; my sex lives on there, responding, or not; my heart feels this and that, and my mind up here goes working on, quite different from the heart; yet when the real high place of sex is reached, everything moves together, it is just that moment when everything does move together that makes the gears shift up. Yet people regarded sex as the drainer, the emptier, instead of the maker of energy. They did not know. But why was it that people didn't know? There was a knowledge that was no part of our culture, hinted at merely, you could come across references. Or you stumble on it. Like Jack, who said to a hand numbed by loss of blood and cold: Hold on, and it held on because it had been given orders, for twelve hours. A moment of extremity in war had taught Jack a simple law about his own body. Supposing he had not had that chance, could Jack have become one of the men who regard sex as a kind of currency to be measured out? Well, whatever Jack could have been, it had to be an extreme, that was certain. Jack could as easily have been a sex-hating bigot, he could have been as violently afraid of sex as he now passionately pursued the knowledge of its laws, of its control and understanding. He would have been violent and extreme whatever course he had taken—or been set on, by the accidents of his experience.

But now, Jack and Martha, having made love for hours, came to themselves light and easy, and as if they had been washed through and through by currents of energy. She felt as if she had been connected to a dynamo, the centre of her life. But Jack could not be the centre of her life—he would not be the centre of any woman's life. *Why not?* And as she came around again to this warning thought, she opened her eyes smiling, to hide that she was thinking it. They lay there washed up side by side, smiling and delighted and rested.

At half past twelve she rang Phoebe to say she could not make lunch that day; it would have to be tomorrow; and heard Phoebe's gruff but businesslike reproaches knowing that she had earned them. And he rang Joanna to say that he could not see her today, but he would love to see her tomorrow. "You see, Joanna, Martha's here, and we don't want to stop yet." The conversation went on, amiable and brotherly on his side; but Martha could not make out from the tones of Joanna's voice what she was feeling: she probably didn't know herself.

"She'll come tomorrow," said Jack with satisfaction.

They began to dress, so as to go out and eat. "You are an extraordinary man," she said; and he kissed her gratefully. But she was thinking: Then, why don't we take you seriously? But this thought, when with him she was initiated into so much knowledge about the capacities of her own body, kept her silent and pondering; while he was silent, because he was so hungry he felt almost crazy with it. Hunger hit Jack like a mania, a fever: when he had to eat it was, he said, as if he were being eaten alive by a nestful of ants. He cut a hunk of bread and gnawed it, feeding hunger, while she finished dressing and thought: Is it because for Jack it is an end in itself, is that it? But she could not go on with this—for what ought to be an end then? She had gone way out past any buoys, lighthouses, or charted points in her knowledge of herself: and that meant that moments of criticism must be resisted, they would probably be nervous reactions, that was all.

They walked out into the ugly street, where now workmen clustered around a crater in the road, and went up the channel between flaking dingy houses which was Rogers Street in the daytime, until they came to a new Indian restaurant about a mile away, spent an hour or so eating a great deal, for they were both very hungry, and then strolled back to his house again. They hardly spoke. They had reached a condition that made speaking irrelevant. Yet for her it was not a contented silence. For now, as she and Jack returned to his room for another afternoon and night of making love, she began to feel bad about letting Phoebe down; she ought to have gone to lunch! All this was a delaying, a putting-off of something she had to do. She could spend weeks in Jack's country and still at the end of it she must go to Phoebe and whatever it was she represented. If she had gone to lunch with Phoebe then she would not now be facing with Jack—but what? Why was she so uneasy. Tired? No; flat? no—this condition of light well-being was not anywhere near that. But anguish lay somewhere just beneath the surface and threatened to well up: it was the pain that had accompanied the scene of the London house and the sad children. There had been the lovely picture of the golden age, the golden man, the woman and their children and animals; but the joy that had accompanied that was not as strong as the pain that came with the other. Oh, if she wasn't careful she was going to cry and cry—and that wouldn't do, not this afternoon when she had to be so strong. A decision or something of the kind lay ahead, she could feel it.

Back in the white and black room, new candles were lit. They were quite alone in the big house. The room was stark and bare now, the bed had a brown blanket stretched over it. There was only one chair; so Martha and Jack sat on a rug by the bed, leaning against it. He seemed nervous. "What's the matter, Martha?"

"I don't think I'm going to be a good partner for you today. Perhaps you should have let Joanna come."

"Joanna's gone off racing with her cricketer. What's the matter? I can see there is something wrong. Perhaps it's my fault. I've had a thought in my mind all this time and I didn't tell you. If you're with a woman and you are holding some thought back, then it breaks the contact. That's why you keep going away from me."

"Perhaps." But Martha had in her mind a hundred thoughts she could not share with Jack. He really was a boy, after all. He sat there, his strong face above his brown sweater, brown eyes anxious, intense; a boy, with a boy's fear that he's not strong enough to keep what he holds. He was nearly thirty-five. Yet she could have believed him to be twenty-five. Meeting him somewhere for the first time, she would have thought: A strong, simple boy, rather naive. That's what she had thought, allowing herself to be picked up by him on the underground. Everything he knew was in his body: it never reached his face, which was stiff with the fear that she would not accept the thought he wanted to share with her. With Thomas they had not set out to "share" thoughts. With Jack, you set up a simple communion of the flesh, and then your mind went off by itself—that was all right, what was wrong with it? If she couldn't have Thomas . . . Do you know what you've done, said Martha to herself in despair: I've become one of those women that

66

used to frighten me! I've got a dead man. Like my mother. Like Mrs. Talbot. Like Maisie. I say to myself "Thomas" as if that were the end of it! What does it mean? I say "Thomas" and—play with Jack! Except you can't possibly use the word "play," for anyone as desperately singleminded as Jack. All right then—imagine Jack dead, would I then be saying "Oh Jack!" and playing with someone else? No. I took Thomas seriously. I don't take Jack seriously. Why? It doesn't matter why.

"Martha, I don't know how to tell you what I've been thinking. I don't know how you'll take it. Why don't you come and live here. No, don't say no, think about it—there's the floor under this one. You could live there. The wiring's done, and the plumbing and the telephone's in."

"You mean, live with you? But how?"

"Well why not?" he muttered, already rejected, sullen. "You ask it as if—you don't trust me, that's it, that's what I was afraid of."

"But what would Garibaldi Vasallo make of it?"—trying to joke.

"What could he say? You don't understand. I've got the whiphand. He didn't want to give me a half-share of this house at all. But he did—I made him. Besides, he knows I know how he operates, with all his dirty tricks."

"Blackmail?"

His face darkened, clenched; was ugly. "Blackmail! That's a word you use for decent people, not a dirty little dago."

"I hate that word." She was discouraged: all her energy had leaked away; she wished now that she could wrap a blanket around her head, like an African, and turn her face to the wall and sleep. "When I left home I really thought I'd be free of the race thing. Isn't that funny? There's no end to our being stupid. One's always making up daydreams about places somewhere else. But since I've been here—things are just as ugly as they are back home, but people don't know it, it's all hidden. And now you start talking about dagos."

"That's not racialism! That's just—accurate. That's what he is, a nasty little dago. A crook. You deal with crooks in their own coin. If he plays me up, I'll go to the police with what I know about him. I'm not taking anything from him that isn't fair. By the time I've finished with this house it will be a real house, and it'll have cost him nothing. If he'd paid a builder, it would have cost hundreds—he knows that. So why is what I'm doing wrong? This house is my house. When

I came into it that day and saw it and started work on it I knew it was mine. It's my house because I've worked on it."

Every word of this being true, why did Martha feel uneasy: the intensity Jack put into his plea, exactly as if it were a false case, was that it? "Why didn't you simply go and buy it? He bought it for £500. You've got £1,000 tucked away."

"No, I'm not going to waste that. It's my future. I've got to have that money. And this is my house. I'm in my rights if I say you can come and live here."

"But Jack—you'll live up here on this floor, and I'll live on the floor beneath?"

And now he was crying: the fearful intensity of his need was wringing his body, making tears spill from his brown eyes. "What's wrong with that? You don't trust me Martha!"

"Look, Jack, you must see it's one thing coming here—by appointment, to make love—but surely you wouldn't want me or any woman just beneath you? What the eye doesn't see, the heart doesn't grieve over!"

"Oh, I hate that. I hate that attitude. That's what I mean by not trusting me. I'd not tell lies to any girls who came here. I don't tell lies. Well, not unless I've got to—only if there's a girl who wouldn't come to me if I didn't—they'd know that you lived here."

"A sort of senior wife?"

"Well, what's wrong with that? You don't want to get married do you? I mean not really married?"

"No. I don't think I do." She nearly asked: "And what about children?" But the nightmare vision of the house with the children and herself in it came back, and she shivered.

"You're cold, Martha. I'll start the heaters." He got up, glad to be able to take his tears away; and she was glad to have the pressure further away for a few moments.

He knelt by the paraffin heaters, first one, and then the other. His back was to her. From the set of his shoulders she knew something important was coming: what had gone before was not after all what mattered; the tears, the apprehension were for what he was about to say now.

"There's something else, Martha. I can't say it easily, though. Give me a minute. There—we'll be warm. Listen, Martha—oh hell, man, I'm afraid of saying because I don't want you to take it wrong. But would you like to have a baby? I mean, let me give you a baby?"

And now she was silent because she was shocked. That she ought to be, if not flattered, at least warmed, she knew. But he had taken flight somewhere away from any kind of reality she understood. Because this was the point. *His* point. She had not expected it.

"Why not, Martha? You could bring the baby up here. You could get some sort of job. Some job or other."

"Babies need fathers," said Martha, her voice coming dry despite herself. His body froze, was set in a tension of anger, his back was still turned to her.

"I could kill you for that, Martha." It came out between teeth clenched in anger. She remained still. He came back to the bed and sat on it, close, looking right into her face from a face that had gone a bluey-white. His eyes were small and black.

"I'm sorry," she said. "But it isn't only me, is it? You'd like to give all your girls babies, wouldn't you? That's it, isn't it?"

"Yes."

"Put cuckoos in nests?"

"Yes."

Now they were hating each other. But as he brought his face up against hers, black with hate, a wave of anguish swept from him to her: she refused to give way, to soften, and he flung himself face down on the bed, arms outstretched, stiff, in agony. So she had seen him before. This was the shape his black moods set him in, rigid; and how he might lie for hours, without moving.

"Listen, Jack. When I left my little girl, Caroline, do you know what I was thinking? I thought, I'm setting you free, I thought, I'm setting you free . . ."

"Well all right, I'm not talking about mothers, a child needs a mother, that's what I'm saying, isn't it? But fathers, no, I won't inflict myself on any child. I won't. I couldn't. I'm scared—scared, of my old man, I tell you, that's what scares me. I don't suppose he thought when he put me into my mother that he'd hate me, and then my brother, and have to screw my sisters."

"I had a sort of silent pact with that child," Martha went on. "As if she were the only person who understood why I was doing it. I was setting her free. From *me*. From the family."

"Yes, yes, yes," came from the bed. "It's true."

"No, it was so terribly not true. I was mad."

"You were right, Martha. Don't go back on it now."

"I was mad. So how can I say to you now: You're mad. I know how you feel. But it was such nonsense, when I think of it now . . ." And Martha began to cry, but silently, so that he wouldn't turn around again. "All of us lot, we were Communists, we felt the same . . ."

"Everyone was a Communist," came the muffled angry voice from the bed. "What's that got to do with? I was one, for a time in the war. It was all that stuff about the Atlantic Charter—it turned us up, we were reds, what of it?"

"Oh, sometimes I think Communism, for people who weren't in Communist countries, it was a kind of litmus paper, a holdall—you took from it what you wanted. But for us it went without saying that the family was a dreadful tyranny, a doomed institution, a kind of a mechanism for destroying everyone. And so . . ." Martha was crying uncontrollably, but trying to make the roughness in her voice sound like deliberate "humour": "And so we abolished the family. In our minds. And when the war was over and there was Communism everywhere, the family would be abolished. You know—by decree. Clause 25 of a new Magna Carta. 'We decree the family at an end.' And then there would be the golden age, no family, no neurosis. Because the family was the source of neurosis. The father would be a stud and the mother an incubator, and the children handed at birth to an institution: for their own good, you understand, to save them from the inevitability of their corruption. All perfectly simple. We were all corrupted and ruined, we knew that, but the children would be saved." Now her voice cracked, and she wept, loudly and violently. He did not move. He lay in his face-down position, listening.

When she had stopped, he said: "You were right."

"We were not right. Isn't it funny? Do you know how many people have become Communists simply because of that: because Communism would do away with the family? But Communism has done no such thing, it's done the opposite."

"I want you to have my baby. And I want Joanna to marry her Guardsman and I'll give her a baby. She can tell him, I don't care. I wouldn't mind in his place: what does it matter who puts a baby into a woman? And I want the little Jane to have a baby. We can get married if she likes. And I want Nancy and Joan and Melinda to have my babies. I'll see them, I'll give them presents. But I won't be a father. I wouldn't do that to any human being."

There was now a very long silence. Martha cried a little, feebly, out of helplessness. He lay silent, his face hidden. On the black of the curtains rough edges of light. Outside this

70

long black-and-white room where small candles burned was an afternoon blazing with sunlight. Briefly: when she looked again, the glow behind the black had faded. She had once felt something that was wrong so violently! She had acted from the feeling—what point now in saying what she ought to have done? She would probably do the same again, in the same position. So what did it matter what one felt? Or believed? It was action that mattered. And now Jack felt this so strongly that if she wished, she could have a baby: and if he later felt, "I was wrong then, my feelings were wrong"— what difference would that make? There would be the child.

At last she said: "There isn't any family I've ever seen that doesn't seem to me all wrong. But what right have I to feel like that? Where do I get the idea from that something better is possible? I keep thinking and thinking about it— why? Perhaps it's always like this, it has always been like that? Ugly. But that's how I do see things. I used to worry and nag at myself: there's something wrong with me that I do see what's going on as ugly. As if I were the only person awake and everyone else in a kind of bad dream, but they couldn't see that they were. That's how I felt on the ship coming over—you know, pleasure. Several hundred people 'living it up,' 'whooping it up'—enjoying themselves. Of course, you know ships from a different angle, you've worked on them, that's different. But that voyage—it was like being in a nightmare. People who had saved up money. From all over Africa. Just for that trip—years of saving. Pleasure—eating three times a day like pigs, no, five times a day, getting drunk, always just a little drunk, just to make things tolerable. Flirting, sex for titillation. There wasn't one person on that boat—except for one girl. And she was ill. She was coming to England for treatment. We used to sit by ourselves and watch. They called us spoilsports. It was like watching a lot of people who had been hypnotised."

From Jack nothing. He might be asleep. She went on: "For some reason, I've had that all my life. What's the use of thinking there must be something wrong with me? One's got to stand by what one is, how one sees things. What else can you do? And I've had the other thing too, the mirror of it: all my life I've believed that somewhere, sometime, it wasn't like that, it needn't be like this. But why should I? Last night again—the nightmare. But at the same time, the marvellous family walking with their friendly animals. The golden age. Why? But I've been thinking, Jack. What's the use of imagining impossibly marvellous ways of living, they

aren't anywhere near us, are they? You've got to accept . . .
parents have no choice but to be the world for their children. And if the world is ugly and bad for that time, then
parents have to take that burden on themselves, they are
ugly and bad too." She started crying again. This time it was
hysteria: it would be easy for her now to switch over into
being "Matty," then to make fun of herself, apologise . . .
"Matty" had always been an aspect of hysteria. She steadied
herself to finish: "Babies are born into this, what there is. A
baby is born with infinite possibilities for being good. But
there's no escaping it, it's like having to go down into a pit, a
terrible dark blind pit, and then you fight your way up and
out: and your parents are part of it, of what you fight out
of. The mistake is, to think there is a way of not having to
fight your way out. Everyone has to. And if you don't, then
it's too bad, no one's going to cry for you, it's no loss, only
to yourself, it's up to you . . ." Hysteria arose again in a great
wave: she was trembling, shaking with it. She was saying
what she really believed and it was to a man who was
asleep. She laughed and she cried, trembling. At last she
stopped. Silence. Jack had turned his head: his face was
visible. He was listening, with his eyes closed. The hand that
lay stretched out was in a tight fist and it trembled.

"I'm sorry," she said, sober. "I know you hate—fuss."
Jack did not say anything. "But in a way it's a compliment. I
could have chosen not to be hysterical. But I've discovered
something, Jack. About hysteria. It can be a sort of—re-
hearsal." She was thinking of last night, walking. She could
not "remember" the lit alive space, though she knew it
had been there; but she could remember the approach to it:
something giggly, silly, over-receptive—hysterical. "When
you get to a new place in yourself, when you are going to
break into something new, then it sometimes is presented to
you like that: giggling and tears and hysteria. It's things you'll
understand properly one day—being tested out. First you
have to accept them like that, silly and giggly . . . Jack?" She
knelt close up to him. "Jack?" She had to stop herself
saying: "Are you angry?" like a little girl—like "Matty."

"I've been listening," he said. "And do you know what I
was thinking? Is this just Martha's way of being a woman, of
getting her own way over being married and having a child.
But I can see it wasn't that." He sat up. He looked beat:
pale, ill, and under his eyes, dark bruises. "I'm sorry, but I
didn't follow what you were saying. It didn't mean anything
to me. I know you mean it for yourself and that's good

enough for me." He got off the bed. He was shivering. "Martha, I'm so hungry I've got to eat."

They had been to eat very late at midday; and it was not yet six in the evening. "I was lying on the bed, feeling all my bones. Sometimes when I lie still like that, I'm a skeleton: I can't feel the flesh anywhere, just bones. I've got to get some flesh on me."

They went back to the Indian restaurant, through late-afternoon streets. A meagre sunlight; people rushing back from work along the ugly street. In the restaurant, the Indian who had served them their lunch was still on duty. He was from Calcutta, had been sent for by an uncle who owned another, much smarter, restaurant, in Earl's Court. This was a new, small restaurant, the bottom floor of an old house. The Indian from Calcutta, working for a pittance in a cold foreign country to escape from his family's poverty, welcomed them with white-teethed affability, and for the second time that day, served them with enormous quantities of food. Then they returned to Jack's house. They were both sad and low, and gentle with each other. When they went in, the door was open into the room where the grinning boy lived. He was sitting with his back to the wall, cross-legged, playing patience with a candle alight beside him. He nodded and grinned and waved. They nodded, leaving his smile behind to fade on the dark stuffy air of the stairs.

They lay on the bed with their arms around each other.

"You won't come and live here, Martha?"

"No. I can't, Jack."

"I knew you wouldn't. I suppose that's why I was afraid to bring it up—I didn't want to hear you say no."

"Somebody else will, I expect."

"Yes. But I would have liked it if you could have trusted me." He was nearly crying again.

"Have you ever thought—we make decisions all the time: but how? It's always in reference to—we make them in obedience to something we don't know anything about?"

"No. *I* make decisions."

"Ah, you're master of your fate."

But one did not tease Jack, he could not be teased.

"Don't laugh at me, Martha!"

"I'm not. But looking back, we think we've made decisions —it's something else that makes them."

"Ah, Martha," he said suddenly, rough: "You're not coming back to me, you aren't going to stay with me!"

"I didn't say that."

"No? I don't know why, but that's what I thought you were saying."

"No."

"You've got to believe I want you to. I know what you're thinking—you're a woman! He's got so many girls, he doesn't care. But it's not true. I'm not promiscuous, I don't like changing and having new girls. I want girls who'll always come back, the same girls. I'm very faithful, Martha, you've got to believe me."

Soon he fell asleep. She was not sleepy. She lay holding his body, the long thin cage of bones, over which such a light shelter of flesh lay breathing. She felt how he was alert, ready to wake at a sound or a touch, even though he seemed to be deeply asleep. She would have got up and dressed and gone, if she could have done it without waking him. But she knew he would start up if she so much as slid her arm away from beneath his head. Her hand lay on his back, feeling the bones branch off from the central column of bone. Past his shoulder she looked into the recess where the window was that had to be kept shuttered because of the odours from the canal. Beneath that window, a scene of littered back garden, unkempt hedges, rubbish bins, a slope of dirty soil to a low weed-grown canal. On a hot afternoon during the vanished heat wave, she had sat in the window watching children brown from six weeks of that sun dive and swim like water rats among the weeds. From time to time a woman shrieked from a window: Tommy! Annie! Where are you? You're not to swim in that water! The children cowered in the water, looking up at the windows. The woman knew that the children were in the water, and that there was no way of stopping them: they had swum there themselves when they were sleek brown rats among water weeds.

The candle on the floor near this window sunk, shook wildly and went out. The man in Martha's arms slept, his face, a boy's face, tear-marked, a few inches from hers. The candles on the mantelpiece burned for a while longer. Then the room was a pit of dark. Then Martha herself dropped into the pit. She dreamed. That picture, or vision, she had seen behind her eyes of the house with the sad children, came again but now it was not a sharp image, a "still," or a series of "stills"; but a long moving dream. A large London house—but not this one. There was traffic outside it, but also the presence of trees. Full of people. Children. Half-grown children. Sad. It was a sad, sad dream. But not a nightmare: no fear came with it, Martha was in the dream, she was responsible for the children. She was worried, anxious: but she held the fort, she manned defences.

They woke very early, having slept so early. It was just light—about five. Jack cooked them breakfast on his spirit stove. Then she kissed him and left. The door off the hall was still open, and in the low grey light, the mad youth lay asleep on the floor beside the candle that had burned itself out. Outside, a young morning, with a low wet sun. With luck, it would be a fine day. Martha set off towards Iris and Jimmy across the river, locked inside Mrs. Van's coat.

Three

She rode high in a red bus over streets tinted by damp sunlight, crossed a strongly ebbing river with gulls at eye level—flashing white wings, seen through dull glass—and descended to earth or street level as Big Ben said it was seven. But it would not do to reach Joe's café before eight. That household had two starts to its day, one at about five, when Iris, Jimmy still asleep, rose to feed cornflakes, toast, scrambled powdered egg and tea to some young lorry drivers from a lodging house down the street whose landlady would not feed them so early; another at nine, when the side of the card that said OPEN was turned in invitation to the pavement. With the apprentice lorry drivers were a couple of older men, among them Iris's cousin Stanley, whom she had fancied for Martha; and some charwomen, their early office-cleaning over, who dropped in for a cup of tea before going home to feed breakfast to their families. Between five and eight that café was a scene of bustling steaming animation, of intimacy. If Martha were to go in now, unexpected, after two unexplained nights, she could only do so as "Matty." And she was damned if she would. *If I get taken over by her, then I'll have her riding me for the rest of the day and I won't have her around when I'm lunching with Phoebe.*

Early sun flashed on a thousand windows and on the gull's wings. The great buildings on either side of the river stood waiting, empty; and a thousand windows flashed back the sun. Not empty: for at this hour an army of women were at work with their vacuum cleaners, making them hum and vibrate like beehives. They stopped to gossip along corridors where soon, but not for two hours yet, men still fighting for another few minutes' sleep in suburban bedrooms ten, fifteen, twenty miles away would come hurrying in, Good morning, good morning, good morning, diverging into rooms where the wastepaper baskets had been emptied. In they'd flow, to be flung out again by the sound of Big Ben striking five, as thousands of telephones went silent, all at once. Martha dawdled, lost her way in a mesh of little streets, and hit the street of the café a hundred yards down from the bombed site. Turning right, she greeted the slab or hulk of timber. In the less than two days since she had seen it, a minute yellow flower had emerged from a crevice. That great salty, sour, more-stone-than-wood monument had put out a coronet of green leaves and a flower. A small wind tugged at it, but the flower held firm, its roots being well dug in. Martha peered through a wire door that had the death's head and NO CHILDREN on it, and saw the lock was loose in its socket. She pushed and went in. Deserted: too early for the children. But no, a small girl wearing an ancient black jersey over a white dress that looked as if it had been starched for a party sat on a brick in the dust. She kept still. "Good morning," said Martha cheerfully, and the child's eyes concentrated in terror. Then she fled, jumping like a cat over a far wall into safety away from the woman in the black coat. If this were a ruined city, a poisoned city, what would the excavators a hundred years later deduce from what they saw here? Facing Martha, the surface of a jagged wall, three stories of it, rose up sharp from the low edges of rubble. There were three fireplaces, one above another. Each level of wall was tinted a different colour, as if by moss or lichen: wallpaper soaked and dried, soaked and dried, again and again. Pale green. Above that, pinkish shaggy brown. Above that dim yellow. Coming closer, it could be seen, where a long strip had been torn away off the green, that beneath was a darker green. Martha got up onto an edge of wall and slid her fingernails under the edge of paper. A thick sog of paper: layers of it, now stuck together. Once each had been a loving and loved skin for the walls, which held the lives of people. But they were fused together, like a kind of felt. Martha pulled. A lump came away. Picking at the layers, she counted thirteen. Thirteen times had a man stood on trestles, or perhaps a table (these were small cheaply

76

built houses, with low ceilings, and probably the kitchen table would have been high enough), and stretched new clean paper over the stains and dirts of the layer beneath. Thirteen times had a wife or children said, Yes, that's very nice, I like that, Dad; or had said, No, we chose wrong. The two papers at the very bottom were rather beautiful, judging from the inch or so she had to look at: they got progressively uglier as the decades slid by. The one at the top was hideous, must have been an acid green, with a bad jangling pattern. In the middle was a rather pretty sprigged pattern, like a Victorian young lady's morning dress. . . . Voices from the street. Precisely as the little girl had done, Martha froze: authority! She ought not to be here. She sneaked down off the wall, pushing the wad of coagulated paper into Mrs. Van's pocket; and hid behind a heap of bricks until it seemed safe to go out into the street.

Against the dim muslin that screened the café, shapes of bodies; the lively intimacy of the early-morning session shed warmth onto the pavement. She was too early after all. Martha went around into the side street where, this house being on a corner, was a side door into a yard. The door was of slats of wood held with two crossbars. It had been painted once, for there was crumbling greenish pigment in the cracks. But now it was a greyish colour. "From before the war," Iris had said. When Iris said something was from before the war, this meant, something that would have been replaced, or mended or painted, if there had not been a war. She would not, for instance, have said that the wall, which was a single yellow brick's thickness surmounted at the height of a tall man's head by a litter of broken glass, was from before the war. Martha unlatched the door and was in—a neat, tended garden. Hidden behind these street fronts, tucked in among wastes of brick and cement, were gallant little gardens. This one, the size of a large room, had a pear tree, an old wooden bench recently painted a new bright green by Jimmy, and an ancient rose that ambled over the back of the house. It was in full pink bloom and it scented all the air. In the corner of this patch of garden was a privy: the house did not have an indoor lavatory. It was like a little sentry box, and to it went a flagged path with musky plants growing in crevices. Beyond the window into the kitchen, Iris sat, at a table framed by pink roses. When she had finished with the early-morning stint, she took what she said was a bit of a kip: she slumped in a tortoise condition, her hand stretched towards a flagon of tea, her eyes open, but

77

not really seeing anything. Meanwhile Jimmy had got up and had taken over the café. He was not in the kitchen now. Martha pushed open the back door and was received by a sleepy stare from the surface of Iris's eyes. Then she said vaguely, "Oh, it's you." Martha sat down, and Iris gestured towards a brown teapot and yawned. "We've used your ration," she said. "You didn't come, did you?" Martha poured tea. Iris smiled: but she resented being made to wake up.

The kitchen was small. Along one wall was apparatus for the café: the frying machine for the fish and the chips; and an electric stove which Jimmy had filched from the ruins down the road after the bomb had fallen. There was also an old-fashioned wood stove, which was used as a cupboard, or larder.

"So you're off?" said Iris.

"Yes. I've come to get my things."

"They're ready. And I've put your ration book and your coupons on your case. Upstairs."

"Thank you, Iris."

"Stanley's next door, if you want to see him." Martha had not wanted to see Stanley, evidence of her bad heart though this undoubtedly was; and Iris's tone said that see him she ought, even if Stanley did not particularly want to see her. But now, since it was clearly up to her to go through and make her presence known to the man whom Iris had decided would suit her as a husband, Martha actually got as far as the door before rebelling. Why should she? Whatever debts she would leave behind her, Stanley was not one of them. She sat down again, in silence. The two women confronted each other: Martha determined not to apologise, plead guilty, or evade; Iris now awake, exuding a stubborn determination to suffer betrayal.

"I don't think Stanley and I are suited," said Martha.

"Well, I suppose one of these days he'll make his bed," said Iris, full of grievance.

"Yes, but not with me," said Martha.

Iris measured herself a small sour glimmer in reply to this invitation to laugh; and then, against her will, laughed out, and slammed her hand palm down on the table.

She continued to laugh, laughter ebbing from her like water: it was like crying.

"Ah," she said, "but a man's a man, and when the war's out of his blood, he'll settle well enough."

According to Iris, Stanley had been uprooted by war;

which was why he had chosen the lorry run to Birmingham five days a week, and spent weekends doing labouring work— he couldn't rest. Martha thought it was nothing to do with the war, it was his nature. And she knew, though Iris did not (for she and Stanley had come to an understanding, had made a pact against matchmakers), that there was a woman in Birmingham with whom he spent nights. He did not want to marry. Certainly not Martha. Though he had liked her well enough to suggest a job as secretary to the firm he worked for.

Iris now got up, defying Martha, or, more likely, asserting her right to choose her cousin a wife, and called through the hatch: "She's here!"

She sat down again, saying to Martha, "You'll want to say good-bye, won't you then?"

In a moment Stanley came in. He was about forty, a lean narrow slouching man with hard blue eyes.

"I'm due to be off," Stanley said generally. "My mate's already at the bus. So you've got yourself a job then, have you?" He did not look at Martha, but at his cousin: and towards her a warning, or a resentment, was directed. Not at Martha: he was a fair man and proud of it.

"Yes, I think so," said Martha.

"You're all right then," said Iris, hostile.

"See you sometime," said Stanley, and, on his way out, turned to give her a good warm smile, snubbing Iris with a cool nod.

"He's a case," said Iris, grieving. "There was a girl at the laundry who fancied him, but not him, no."

"How do you know he hasn't got a girl of his own already?"

"Well, if he'd do a thing like that!" said Iris bitterly, highlighting for Martha some area of family grievance, bonds, or bondage, that she'd never now, with the time left, be able to understand. Tears were in Iris's weak blue eyes, and she stirred her tea savagely.

In came Jimmy, wearing a striped apron, full of a contained reproach.

"So you don't want that job, then?"

"She's got a job," said Iris, "up West."

"Up West is it?"

"I don't know yet," said Martha.

"Then you don't need any job we can get you, do you then?" He took a big scrubbing brush and went back into the café, saying, "Want some breakfast, help yourself if you do."

On the shelf over the old wood stove were set out the week's rations. Each person's separately: that week's four ounces of butter, three times; the bacon and two eggs each; on a big dish. And tea. Martha's had gone.

Iris watched Martha out of a practised interest in the unfairness of the world, to see if she would take eggs, butter, bacon. Martha did not like the butter anyway: a hard salty grease. But Iris had a large china bowl of dripping, the aromatic distillation of a dozen Sunday dinners.

"Oh, you're back to my dripping?" said Iris, friendly again; and she smiled as Martha fried bread in the delicious crumbling scented fat, for herself, for Iris, and they sat eating and drinking tea while the sound of Jimmy's scrubbing brush went on next door.

He did not come back in: he was not going to forgive her. Martha said goodbye to Iris; was invited to drop in when she felt inclined; and she went upstairs while Iris joined Jimmy in the café.

In the minute room which was already cleaned and impersonal, over the café, her case stood ready for her near the door, with the ration book on it. She took out a summer dress, bundled Mrs. Van's coat and the sweater and skirt into the case; and prepared for the summer day which it was fairly doubtful that the day would remain. She left through the little rose-scented garden.

It was ten in the morning. In the great buildings along the river that administered London, men and their secretaries arrived for work. In three hours, the feeling of the city had changed. The great market that was London had opened: a dispersed, scattered, diversified market, so that in every street was a corner, a block, a centre, where it seemed as if wealth had swum together just here, to offer congealed money, furs, carpets, silver, gold, robes, but like icebergs, only a fraction of them visible in a sign or the name of a banker, or the glass case full of embroideries, or luscious furs; for above all, it was a sense of hidden wealth: and walking over the damp grey pavements it was to feel that under one's feet stretched invisible warehouses of luxury and richness and beauty—miles of them, caverns of them. And, to the dealers and merchants who owned them, it was not important to sell, or to display, or to offer. A secret city. A hidden city. And, if instead of walking past doors, show-cases, the proffered sample, one pushed open a door, passed the rather inferior items for sale, or challenged an inner door, which only needed to be pushed, for so little did the owners expect temerity on the part of docile customers that there was no doorkeeper—suddenly, hey presto! a great descending stairway to the underground city beneath London where were stored for miles and miles the most fabulous carpets and tapestries and silks in the world.

Martha ought to buy something to wear. Imagining she had a hundred pounds to spend, she stalked clothes up and down the rich streets in Knightsbridge. But if she had had a hundred pounds, she would not have been able to spend a penny of it. The point was, she understood at last, that she did not know for whom, for what, she was dressing. If she had stayed in the streets across the river with Jimmy, Iris, and Stanley, with Stella and her clan, there would have been no problem: the working girls had a style and a dash of their own. But it was only necessary to imagine wearing, with Henry, what they wore, to see its impossibility: a tight skirt, a shirt, a sweater: no, no, onto his face would come the look that meant that here was something attractive, and licensed—outside his codes. Was he aware of it? Probably not. Or, she could choose the uniform of a lady: plenty of these, unmistakable, in shops that sold nothing else. But she did not "fancy," as Iris would say, that particular uniform. What then? For there were streets full of clothes, "utility" from the war, hideous and dull and tasteless. For whom? Who were the men, the women, who deliberately sat down, and onto drawing boards sketched such clothes?

No, not if she had a thousand pounds to spend was there anything to buy—until she knew what she was going to have to be. Her suitcase in her hand, she dawdled, wasting time until it was one o'clock and time for Phoebe.

The restaurant off the Strand was a lower-level version of Baxter's; a large room dotted with small tables each with four Windsor chairs. There were dull floral curtains, and wallpaper of a pinkish floral design. The standard to which both related was the same; somewhere behind both was a country house, or a large farmhouse: the country, at any rate, with centuries of a certain kind of taste behind it. If Fanny's and Baxter's had to do without paint or new curtains for fifty years, they would still present themselves to the world with impermeable self-esteem. The menu of Fanny's offered the same kind of food, but plainer, without sauces, and much cheaper.

When Phoebe arrived, she nodded at the waiter, who

knew her; she had inspected Martha thoroughly before even sitting down, though from different standards than Henry's. Martha's failure to ring up immediately she had arrived in London, and then her unreliability, had confirmed, if not frivolity, at least a more fortunate experience, than hers, Phoebe's. Martha's appearance underlined it. Phoebe wore a skirt and a rather dull jersey, and pearls. Martha wore a linen sleeveless dress on a day which was only by courtesy a summer's day: and her appearance paid no homage at all to service. Also, her suitcase stood by the chair, after so many weeks in London. Before Phoebe had even sat down, she had made it clear that Martha was a disappointment. She ordered, while Martha followed suit: chicken soup, tinned; boiled fish in an egg sauce; steamed jam pudding. There was a stain on the tablecloth.

"And how are you finding London?"

This, since it was Phoebe who asked it, was a serious question. Martha deliberated. To whom in the world could she say what she had found in London? Jack—perhaps. A little. And now, because it was Phoebe who sat there, opposite, the past weeks changed their aspect and presented "London" to Martha as a series, containing dockland Stella, the café and Iris; Jack; Henry; and the people in the streets and pubs. Fragments. This was a country where people could not communicate across the dark that separated them. She opened her mouth to say: I am thinking a good deal about class ... and shut it again, though Phoebe had seen her about to speak and still waited. It was nothing to do with class. In Africa, as a white, she was so and so; and if she had been black, must be such and such. There was something in the human mind that separated, and divided. She sat, looking at the soup in front of her, thinking: If I eat, if I start this routine of meals, sleep, order, the fine edge on which I'm living now is going to be dulled and lost. For the insight of knowledge she now held, of the nature of separation, of division (for any number of different sets of words would serve to state it, none being of any real use) was clear and keen—she understood, sitting there, while the soup sent a fine steam of appetite up to her nostrils, understood *really* (but in a new way, was in the grip of a vision), how human beings could be separated so absolutely by a slight difference in the texture of their living that they could not talk to each other, must be wary, or enemies.

Phoebe waited. She had never travelled out of England. Martha was a traveller. She wanted to know.

Class? Phoebe was dedicated to its abolition, presumably, as a stalwart of the Labour Party.

Martha picked up her spoon and started on the soup. "I think a great deal about food, for one thing," she temporised: feeling strongly that Phoebe deserved better than that.

Phoebe, let down, said, on a fine edge of rebuke: "Not very surprising, in the circumstances."

The war having appeared in the wings of their meeting, it moved off again: Martha felt guilty. She had heard that Phoebe had had a bad time during the war. Her husband had been mostly away, except for leaves when the two little girls were conceived. The marriage had broken up. One of the little girls had been very ill. Phoebe had held a job in a government office, had fire-watched, had looked after the children, had been ill herself. One could not imagine Phoebe as anything less than admirable. Martha kept quiet.

"I have just the right job for you," announced Phoebe at last, since Martha the traveller was silent. She was making a good many things plain in this one announcement. She was left-wing Labour: but not so left that she did not regard some well-known left-wingers, her ex-husband for one, as "extreme." She was bound, by her position, to regard all Communists with a greater hatred and suspicion than she would a Tory. Her sister Marjorie was—from her point of view—a Communist; she was dangerous, dogmatic, wrongheaded. But this was the role that Marjorie had always played for elder sister Phoebe. Martha was a friend of Marjorie's. But Mrs. Van der Bylt in correspondence, in constant touch with a dozen of the organisations which Phoebe committed or secretaried or manned, had written offering Martha as a valuable recruit for the cause. Which meant that Martha's degree of redness had been defined as tolerable—not only personally, as what Mrs. Van and presumably Phoebe could stand, as people; but what others might be expected to stand. In an inflammable time. Not altogether complimentary, that: Martha was not altogether sure she liked being so safe. Besides, whatever else she had learned in London, she was sure of one thing: anything her Communist friends had told her of the poverty of the working people, of the blind selfishness of the middle classes (she hadn't met the aristocracy, irrelevant, probably), was true. More than true. If she were going to have to be political, Communism was nearer her mark than "Labour" in its various degrees. Yet for days now she had been coming towards Phoebe, and knowing quite well that in doing so she was choosing her future. Her immediate future, at least. Well, one thing was certain. She was bound to be in a false position of one kind or another. That couldn't be avoided. To what extent?

"What kind of a job, Phoebe?"

"We are going to start an organisation for freeing the colonies, that sort of thing. A society or organisation here, with liaisons with the progressive movements there. And we need a secretary."

"I see."

Martha considered Phoebe's "we." She was not in a position to define it.

"A fairly broadly based thing."

"I see. Anyone who would support the objectives?"

Phoebe hesitated, coloured, gave Martha an acute but wary glance, and lowered her gaze to her soup. "There would have to be limits. You know, *of course*, that Communists are proscribed in the Labour Party—and other organisations?"

"Yes, of course," said Martha, bland out of irritation. The irritation was unreasonable. Phoebe was doing her duty. As she, Martha, would do in her position.

Phoebe now waited for Martha to say clearly where she stood. Martha was damned if she would—besides, she didn't know herself. Mrs. Van's recommendations were going to have to do.

Phoebe, annoyed, spooned in soup. Martha did the same.

"We do need someone with real experience of the colonies—someone who knows the conditions, experience with the natives."

"For a start you can't use that word any longer—natives."

"Oh! No? Well there you are, that's why one needs . . ."

"But I don't think I want to do that sort of job."

"Well of course the money wouldn't be very good," said Phoebe, making it clear that in her eyes this was no reason to refuse any job. "But there would be compensations." She meant, the society of people like herself; the interest of the work; above all, knowing oneself to be of use—exactly as Martha would in her position.

"The thing is, I don't want to be in that atmosphere. When I came to England, it was to get out of it."

And now Phoebe was bound to be disappointed in Martha. For one thing—why had she wasted her, Phoebe's, time? What other kind of job did she expect?

"I see," she said, tightening her lips, and looking for the

waiter to take away her soup and bring the fish. She was busy, had no more time to waste.

If Marjorie had sat there, she would have cried out, all emotion and affectionate indignation: Well, Matty, if you're going to take that line! If you're going to be like that! Well then!

But Phoebe was not Marjorie. And Martha was not Matty, was refusing "Matty" entrance. In order not to be Matty she had to be cool, brisk—hard. As hard as Phoebe.

Martha now ate gluey fish in silence, thinking of Phoebe, of Marjorie. For this was the real experience of the meal, what she would take away from it. Phoebe was physically like Marjorie. Coming on Phoebe suddenly, without warning, Martha would have embraced her, lovable and absurd Marjorie, the younger sister. She had known Marjorie for how long? Over ten years! They had seen each other nearly every day. Marjorie had appeared, before the war, in the colony, an "immigrant"—a girl from England. The people who worked with her all had the same attitude to her—an affection, almost an amusement. "Marjorie" they had said, meaning her quality of charm, desperate enthusiasm, earnestness. But what had they known? Only this: Marjorie the younger sister. And an arrangement of eyes, nose, hair, pretty English skin. Here they were in front of Martha now, as Phoebe.

What had made Marjorie was this: a doctor in a country town in England with bookish tastes and an interest in politics had brought up two daughters, his wife having died when they were children. They were very alike: pretty fair lively English girls. Phoebe, the elder, was bossy and downright with Marjorie, the girl five years her junior. Eventually Marjorie had escaped from Phoebe, had had to, to gain herself. *But:* sitting opposite Phoebe, who spoke in Marjorie's voice, who was so like Marjorie: how could one not wonder: Who was Marjorie? She was not her voice; not her face; not her body; not her eyes or her hair. Her manner then? But Marjorie's breathless defensive, agitated charm— that was all younger-sister. So had she won breathing space from Phoebe through their childhood. Marjorie was just— the younger sister? Of course not.

But who, what? Martha had no idea.

Martha sat opposite the brisk, pretty, efficient Englishwoman who was Phoebe, consciously preventing herself from talking to Marjorie. She was ashamed. She had never known Marjorie. As always, she had been lazy, unimaginative: she had never done more than talk to the younger sister. Well, if she wasn't careful, she wouldn't do more than talk to the older sister! For that manner was so strong in Phoebe, it was hard to imagine one could get past it.

"Of course, I'd be prepared to advise," said Martha.

"There are always plenty of people ready to do *that*," said Phoebe at once; then, seeing that she contradicted herself, looked irritated, and suddenly very tired. "We do need help," she said.

"Phoebe, have you felt *caged*, shut inside an atmosphere?"

"Well, frankly, *yes*," said Phoebe, meaning the war again.

"No, I didn't mean the war," said Martha, clumsily, for Phoebe's reproach was so strong.

"I can't imagine myself not working for what I believe in—frankly, I can't."

"Does one actually have to work in some organisation! Well, I can see why you are annoyed. You're not an employment agency! I don't know why I imagined—"

Phoebe's glance at the words "employment agency" betrayed that that was exactly what she had been thinking.

"Well, I do always seem to know of jobs that need filling ... let me see then."

"I suppose what it come to—I've had enough of organised politics for the time being."

Phoebe was silent for some time. Martha knew why. Without Mrs. Van's recommendations, Phoebe would have set her down as one of the people whose reforming energies had come out of passionate identification with Russia, the pure and the perfect; just another red with a broken heart, a weak red, a neurotic, a washout. But Mrs. Van had said differently. Therefore Phoebe sat, eating jammy sponge with a teaspoon, her eyebrows drawn together. She looked so like Marjorie that Martha experienced a variety of awe, or panic. It seemed inconceivable that she could not say: Marjorie! and that the person opposite would not respond out of ten years of—friendship?

"Mrs. Van der Bylt said you had done research—that kind of thing?"

"Yes. Tell me, Phoebe, do you and Marjorie ever write to each other?"

"We are neither of us very good correspondents. How is she? She's had another baby, she said. That's four now?"

In her voice the shadow of a pain, something personal. "And I've never met her husband of course."

"He's a nice man. A quiet kind of man. He's a civil servant."

"So she said," said Phoebe, making it clear what she thought of civil servants: reminding Martha that she herself had married a crusading firebrand from the left. She lifted her face and smiled at Martha, who felt as she had that morning with Iris and her Stanley: an area of family emotion had been highlit, touched on.

Suppose I said to her: Your sister's a very unhappy woman. She's bored with her nice reliable husband. She has children out of a compulsion. She's living in a permanent nervous breakdown.

No, of course she could not say this. This woman did not understand despair—or rather the admission of it. And besides, such information, if it were not diagnosed (and it would be) as a symptom of Martha's own identification with the neurotic weakness of this world, would be confirmation of the younger sister's always expected failure.

"Is it a success—that sort of thing?"

"Well, yes; I think the four small children are a bit of a handful at the moment."

"I don't see that. After all, you have plenty of servants out there, don't you?" She snapped this out, her face in high colour, and said everything about her own life, which was doing a hard poorly paid job, and being responsible, and bringing up two small girls without a father—without help, without servants.

"I think I know something for you," said Phoebe, pushing aside the personal, while her face still flamed red, and her fingers clutched her purse. "There's my brother-in-law. My *ex*-brother-in-law. He wants some help. He's a writer. Of a kind, of course. It's a hobby really. He's got some sort of a business or other."

"What sort of a writer?"

A silence. Phoebe took a mouthful of weak coffee, while Martha registered an old atmosphere: oh yes, she had been here before, and very much so. "He did get a book published." Another sip. "It got quite good reviews." One could see that the good reviews were not only a surprise, but a disappointment. She disliked the man, or disliked the book? No, the atmosphere was so strong that Martha waited for the next phrase with confidence. "I haven't any time for books that aren't about something real, have you?"

So Marjorie might have said; or Anton. Among a selection of similar phrases, she could also have used: I'm not interested in ivory-tower writing. No, that would probably be too literary a choice of words for Phoebe.

Martha tried: "What was it about?"

"Oh, just personal emotions."

"Well, I need a job."

Here Phoebe looked, lips tight, at Martha's suitcase.

"Where have you left your luggage?"

Almost Martha let Matty say for her, humorous, deprecating, charming: All I've got in the world!

"That's my luggage."

"You must be a very efficient packer," said Phoebe, making a virtue of poor material.

"What sort of help does he want? What's the job?"

"Oh, I don't know—he's always running about, you know, he's got so many irons in the fire. He lives rather near here, actually. I was thinking, we could drop in if you've time?"

"Yes. Good."

"Dropping in," so much not what Martha had experienced of London—that is, the London where people actually lived in houses, had organised lives, as distinct from the wanderers and campers—meant that Phoebe had a special relation with this man?

"I'll telephone," said Phoebe.

One didn't "drop in" without telephoning first.

Phoebe went across to the waiter, conferred, and disappeared into a door marked "Private." She came back to say: "Mark says we can come round. He'll be free at two thirty for an hour."

Yes, that was more like it: one was free by appointment for an hour. What made the difference? Of course, servants! With servants, plentiful and cheap, one could drop in, drop by, stay for meals, develop large casual acquaintanceships.

Around the corner meant Bloomsbury.

Martha's arms were both wrenched by the suitcase to a condition of permanent ache. She suggested a taxi. Phoebe never used taxis. They went by bus.

The house was not part of one of the famous squares, but nearly so: from the front door, it seemed as if the trees and plants of the square claimed the house. Tall, narrow, formal, it was like the houses of the squares; and the whole neighbourhood, now that the different shades of "white" chosen by their owners before the war had dimmed into an unremarkable but uniform grey, had the unity of its original design: houses, terraces, grassy squares full of old trees. Here, in short, one thought of the beauty of London, not of its ugliness. Standing in the hall of the house, which had Persian rugs on a dark floor, and a minimum of old furniture, Martha knew that for the first time in her life she was in a setting where, if she chose to stay, there would be no doubt at all of how she ought to behave, to dress. She had always resisted such a setting, or the thought of it. If she took this job, then it must be for a very short time. She felt attacked by the house—claimed. Besides, she was out of place. And so, she noted, was Phoebe, who was dowdy, seemed clumsy, where she, Martha, was strident.

A man came down the stairs, half seen until he turned on a light. He was dark, and of middle height; but he was strongly built, and his face strongly featured, so that he gave, at once, an impression of force and of height. A presence: a strong one. But then he spoke, and what came over was anxiety, worry, even annoyance.

"How very good of you ... let me ..." Here he took Phoebe's coat over his arm, and Martha's suitcase from her hand. "Now let me see. Really, Phoebe, it is so very kind of you to take so much trouble." He was giving them no more than the courtesy he felt that he should. Either something had happened since Phoebe had telephoned half an hour before, or he had taken a dislike to Martha on sight. At which Martha reacted—and saw herself doing it—with the childish: All right then, I don't think much of you either! For she didn't. The colonial in her named his politeness insincerity, since he was so clearly angry about something; and the worry that he radiated was alerting her nerves for flight. She wondered how quickly she could make excuses, while Phoebe reclaimed her coat, saying she had work to do and must leave at once.

"No, do stay, do, Phoebe," he almost cried, his face anguished in his effort to smile. "Let me see now, where ..." He opened a door off the hall, displaying a drawing room. "I'm sure Margaret wouldn't mind my using ..."

Martha understood that she was about to be interviewed, by a man who had no taste, either for her, or for interviews, she could not decide which, and he was trying to decide on an appropriate place for it.

"I'm very sorry," said Phoebe, reproving his lack of faith in her busy-ness. "Let me know how things go," she said to Martha. "Because if you and Mark don't suit each other, then I'm sure there's plenty of work that needs to be done." She went.

Martha and Mark Coldridge stood in the hall, left to their own decisions.

"You aren't the young lady from Birmingham?"

"No, should I be?"

"Oh, well then ..." He held the door open and she entered the long, subdued, beautiful room which looked as if no one had been in it for months.

"For some weeks now Phoebe has been urging me onto some protégée of hers from Birmingham. Labour Party or something."

He was looking at her more closely. She stood, to be inspected; examining him. But all she felt was: Here are claims. Not only from him, the man, very strong ones, though she did not know how to define them; but from the house, the furniture—even this area of London.

"Look," said Martha, almost becoming Matty in her desperation to escape. "There's been a mistake. You're in a false position. I'm so sorry—I'll leave." And she was on her way to the door.

"No. Wait. We'll go upstairs," he said, thus making it clear that Margaret's room, whoever Margaret was, had been chosen probably to put off, or intimidate, the young lady from Birmingham, or Phoebe; at any rate, the room was seen as a kind of no-man's land or defensive area. She followed him upstairs to a small room on the first floor, which being full of books and papers and comfortable clutter, made it easier for Martha to sit down.

"Who are you, then?"

She replied, giving him minimum information, resisting impulses to reply as she had done to other strangers, I'm Patty Jones, I'm Joan Baker, I'm the mother of twins or the sister of a sailor who ...

"And what kind of job did Phoebe say it was? What are you expecting?"

This, so far away from the suavity which was one of his inbuilt attributes, indicated so much anxiety, defensiveness, that again she was on the point of running away. She examined his face before replying: a dark, strong, well-featured face. Handsome? As handsome as it did: it was all clenched up with watchful tension.

"You needed some sort of help with a book, but I don't really think ..."

"I see." He was more relaxed. He smiled. "Well, but don't go. Because I do."

"What sort of help?"

And now a look which, if he had not been a man to whom such devices were foreign, if he had been anybody else, Martha would have said was cunning. No: but here was something hidden, tucked away.

"Well. I've a deadline—that's the word they use for it. And I've got to . . ." He let all that drift away. Sitting halfway onto a writing table, his legs held up, as if they rested on a stool, or a chair—but they rested on air, he looked at her as if around a corner. Everything was out of scale, disproportionate—discordant. Martha understood she was repelled, not by him, whom she could say she liked; but by a situation. There was one. Anything here, in this house, she understood, would be the absolute opposite of everything she had hoped to find.

She rallied and said firmly: "I am looking for a job for a limited period. I don't want to be tied down to anything. And I did hope, regular hours."

His face had remained steady during the first condition, but it definitely darkened at her last.

"Oh, very reasonable of course. But I was rather hoping . . . you see, I work irregularly myself. Mostly at nights. I've got an office to go to in the day . . ."

Here there was a commotion outside, as of an entrance being set or arranged; then a firm knock, and then, before Mark could say anything, there came in a lady, holding a small boy by the hand.

"Ah," said Mark, hopelessly. He got off the desk. To the small boy he said: "Well, old chap?" and the child, a round, dark, very pale boy with extraordinarily defensive dark eyes pathetically smiled. He looked around for somewhere appropriate to sit, and sat, while the woman watched to see if he did it right.

"This is my mother," said Mark. "Margaret Patten. And this is my son. Francis. And this is Mrs. Hesse."

Martha felt that she knew the lady only too well; since she was large, light, buoyant, and seemed much younger than she must be to be this man's mother. She wore an ample flowered silk dress and carried gloves, which she now laid down on Mark's desk and, without looking at them, patted and fitted into a finger-matching pair one above the other, as if they still lay on a display counter, or as if she wished they did. Meanwhile she took in a variety of physical facts about Martha, age, dress, presence, style, and could be heard thinking loudly: Hesse? German? A German name? She's not German, no. But she's not English either . . .

Mark looked increasingly annoyed.

"Well, I do so hope that you've found someone at last,"

she announced. "Won't you sit down?" she said to the child, who had got up, to come closer to his father. He sat again, promptly, his feet side by side, watching the hostile grown-up world from which, so those eyes said so terribly clearly, he could expect nothing that wasn't painful. Martha found her heart was aching. That little boy, Francis, was unbearably painful. Meanwhile, Mrs. Patten was most frankly summing her up; while her son Mark watched her do it and resented it.

"Mrs. Hesse has only just this moment arrived and we have not agreed about anything at all."

"Oh," said Margaret Patten, smiling at Martha across her son, as if behind his back.

"In fact we are engaged in a sort of mutual interview."

"Oh well then, we must leave you to it, mustn't we, Francis?" She held out her hand and Francis instantly rose to grasp it.

"If she does stay," said Mrs. Patten, "it's lucky the big room will be empty for a bit—that is, if dear Sally can bear to keep away!"

He said nothing. Martha said nothing. She was angry for a variety of reasons: mostly pressures from the past, and strong ones. She resented Mrs. Patten on her own account and on Mark's. And on the child's. Francis now offered his father a smile, which Mark returned: like prisoners of fate they were, condoling briefly before inevitable parting. Then Mrs. Patten removed him from the room.

There was a pause while Mark recovered himself. Then: "She's left her gloves, damn it." He picked them up and carried them to the door where he saw them into his mother's hand. Goodbyes were said again. He came back.

"It's like this," he said. "My wife's in a mental hospital." He paused, not looking at her, while it sank in. "My mother's had the brunt of Francis for quite a bit and she feels that if there were a woman in the house, it would make it easier—during school holidays, for instance."

There was so much information here that Martha remained silent, digesting it, while he waited for her. And as she thought it out, she saw before her eyes the child's face as he turned to leave: it was a long, curious, hopeful look.

Oh no, said Martha to herself. Oh no, no, no!

At last she looked at Mark and waited and he said: "But you mustn't think that if you did work for me—for a while—you'd be in any way responsible for Francis, or that you'd have to live here."

"Who does live here?"

"A good question," he said, laughing at last. "Yes. Well I should have told you before. The thing is, it's often hard to know. Well, I do, basically. And my wife—when she's well. . . ." A long pause. "That's not likely to be . . . she's not very . . . it doesn't look as if she'll be home for some time. Or if she is, she's not . . . My mother has the use of the room you saw downstairs. She somtimes likes to entertain in town. And there are the rooms upstairs. They all seem to belong to someone. Or did. We are a large family. We were."

"I see."

"Yes, I supposed that you had." This was an appeal as well as an apology. Martha felt as if she were being swept fast over an edge, and by her own emotions; for the first time since she came to London, she was unfree. She wanted to run out of the house—anywhere. She was extraordinarily upset. So was he.

"The job itself," he said at last, "is pretty straightforward. But you see, my difficulty is, I've got to have someone who isn't going to be upset by—tricky situations."

She saw very clearly. Martha was thinking: she had no money left. If she were to go to a hotel or find a room she must ask Mark Coldridge for an advance on salary (not yet mentioned). The room upstairs (who was Sally?) would be a godsend, until she could find a place of her own. But that would mean landing herself even deeper in this terrible involving situation which had already involved her: the child's face haunted her. Why had she been so stupid as to leave herself without any money? To work here, living somewhere else—that would be safe enough, probably. (Would it?) She could borrow money. Who? Jack. She must ask Jack.

"Can I think it over," she said; and he said, cold with disappointment, interpreting it, as she almost meant, as a polite refusal: "Of course, you're quite right."

"It's not that I don't like the idea of working with you . . . it's just that . . ."

"I do understand."

And that moment could have been the end of it: she might have walked away and been free. But she said, unable to prevent herself: "Oh, I'm so sorry, I am really so desperately sorry."

"Look, you could either live—anywhere, where you please. Or here. But there's nearly always someone else here. It wouldn't be a question of being alone with me. Sally's so often here. Sally's my brother's wife. But in either case it wouldn't have to be a question of hours you didn't like. But I'd pay you twelve pounds a week, whether you lived in or out."

His tone was saying that this was generous—and indeed it was; much more than the market rate.

Martha got up. So much emotion was now swilling around the room that she couldn't stand it. "I'll let you know before today's out. Will that do?"

His face was suddenly alive: friendly, delighted.

"Oh good, good," he said, "I do so hope ... but I don't want to put any pressure on you. And you mustn't mind—you see, for some weeks now, I've been beset by Phoebe's choices, and most of the time they are so very definitely not mine."

"She's very forceful, certainly."

Smiling over Phoebe's so useful force, they went down the stairs, while Martha remembered how people had smiled over Marjorie: a different smile. Odd: one could never smile, for Phoebe, the smile one used for Marjorie!

Martha left him, resisting his suggestion that she should leave the suitcase and pick it up later.

Where could she go while she made a decision?

Where was there for her to go, but Jack's? And now, walking down through the lovely square, where the summery trees waved their branches in a cool air, she was free of that house, of that man, of that haunted child. She would go to Jack's and ask if she could, after all, live in the floor beneath his. Just for the time at least. She went to the telephone to ring Jack.

When he heard it was Martha, the voice of his first impulse was a rise into a warm relief: "Oh, Martha, I'm so happy—I really did think I'd never hear from you again. I don't know why I did." Then a pause, and the judicious voice, low, of his present situation. Joanna was with him. He offered Martha this fact, waiting for her to see that Joanna, put off twice for Martha, had earned the preference now. Martha saw it. "Look, Jack, can you lend me some money? I need about ten pounds. Five would do." And now a very long pause. At last: "Well, Martha, you see, I don't keep money here." He was silent, waiting for her to think of another resource. Martha found herself taken over by the thought: Of course, he's so mean ... and with such violence that she discarded the judgement. All the same, he did keep money there: like the old farmers of his tradition, in a bag under the mattress. Quite a lot of it. Then she understood that this demand for money meant in fact that she didn't want to be in the rooms beneath him, she wanted to go to a hotel: she was asking Jack for money to escape from any pressure he might put on her. And he felt it: he was feeling it.

"Perhaps Joanna could lend me some money?" said Martha; urgent, her voice on a high pitch of desperation.

"Wait a minute, Martha."

Martha stood in the telephone box, watching the people pass outside: it was the rush hour again, and the sky held the dark of imminent rain. She was in a panic. Funk. This was a danger point in her life: she was being taken over. Had been taken over? Jack's voice, again measured: "If you come over now, Martha, then we could talk about it, hey?"

"Good. Thank you. Thank Joanna."

"Are you coming by taxi, or walking?"

"Bus."

"See you."

He had been asking: How long have we, Joanna and I, got before you come? All the talents for minute organisation of a talented housewife went into the organisation of his women.... Martha was raging with spite against him. She had known before that Jack was careful about money—if that was the word for it. But she had judged him generously: he was guarding the £1,000 that were his freedom. Never before had she felt dislike or repulsion for him or his way of life. Now she felt both. And also for the household she had been in that afternoon—a parcel of sickly neurotics, and Phoebe a humorless bigot.... Hatred burned through her veins. She had to stop it—had to, must ... she boarded a bus headed west, in a jostle of people who smelled sour with sweat this muggy afternoon. She was tired. The weeks of not sleeping, not eating enough, the restless walking, had caught up: she was ready to collapse finally into tears. She wished she could be in a dark room and pull covers up over her. The bus was charging down the Bayswater Road. A couple of nights ago, here Martha had walked, light and easy and alert. That was the night when, walking, she had understood ... but she could not remember now what it was she had understood. And she had a violent reaction against that too—posturing around, she thought; making yourself important, imagining all kinds of great truths when all it was really ... well of course if you're going to not-sleep and not-eat properly and then make love for hours and hours · with a bloody ... She saw herself, a young woman in a matron's

95

black coat, walking through the dark dirty streets with an idiotic smile on her face; but somewhere at the back of her mind the thought held: it was here, it was here, it *was*—just because you can't get anywhere near it now, that doesn't mean to say it doesn't exist. She got off the bus, her legs weak, and almost staggered with the heavy case past the canal where children splashed in a dull sunlight. She arrived at Jack's door to lean against it, breathing deeply, to recover herself. In the street men in singlets dug up the street, standing to their waists in a greasy yellow earth.

The door was opened, before she had rung, by the grinning youth: he had been watching through the panes.

"There's one up there already," he said, delighted.

"Yes, I know. Thanks." She went past, hearing his idiot's chuckle. Good Lord, she couldn't possibly live in this house with an idiot and a . . . Jack came smiling down the stairs to meet her. And at the sight of him her revulsion dissolved into simple affection. Everything she had felt was the result of exhaustion and was not to be trusted. A young man in sloppy blue trousers and a heavy blue pullover chosen to disguise the thinness which was his shame and his terror, he took her case, and pulled her close inside the circle of bone that was his arm. He kissed her and said: "Hey there, Martha, what's up?"

She shook her head, nearly crying, and went before him into the black-and-white room where Joanna sat, dressed, on the chair near the window. Either she had not undressed, or she had dressed for Martha. She wore her perfect clothes: a beige well-hung skirt, beige pullover, long legs in silk, not nylon, and highly polished low brown shoes. Her camel-hair coat was folded over the back of another chair. She looked as neat and shiny as a newly washed child. Smiling, she nodded at Martha. "Would you like to lie down?" Still held inside the bony circlet, she was being urged towards the bed.

"No. I don't want to sleep—not yet."

There was only one decent chair, and Joanna was on it. She got up and sat on the bed, and Martha took the chair. Jack turned his back to make coffee on the spirit stove: he was leaving it to them, to the two women, to define the situation, to handle it.

"Was the job no good?" he enquired, as neither spoke.

And suddenly Matty exploded through Martha's mouth in a storm of half-giggling tears. "Oh yes, it's just my style. Just up my street . . ." Her voice rose in a wail of laughter. "You'd be surprised, it's tailor-made for me. I tell you, it's been sitting there waiting for me for years—everything as sick and neurotic and hopeless as you can imagine ... and a dominating mama over all, and a wife in a mental hospital, and a man just sitting waiting for some sucker like me to cope with everything."

Jack's blue back was still bent over his cups and spoons: he was alertly waiting. And behind the cool little face of Joanna's upbringing was dislike and upset. And the cool Martha, who watched the giggling tearful Matty with as much detachment as either Jack or Joanna, knew that it was Jack who would earn Joanna's dislike of this situation, not Martha. This thought pulled her together. She sniffed, wiped her hands across her eyes and cheeks, for she had no handkerchief, and sat silent, recovering.

"There's plenty of jobs in London," commented Jack, turning with three filled mugs—black, black, coffee. On the farms of his tradition, great black cauldrons stood always simmering on the back of wood stoves, with coffee grounds in them inches deep, coffee being added daily to make a brew which depth-charged the nervous system at first sip. This black liquid in the cup Martha held would be too much in her present state. She sat holding the cup.

"Anyone who wants to live in London ..." said Joanna. "What for? Why don't you live in the country? You can live there like a human being."

"Joanna can lend you some money, Martha. A fiver?"

"Yes," said Joanna. "But if I were you I'd get onto the first train out of London."

"But you look all in, man—why don't you lie down on the bed and sleep a little. Joanna and I can go out for some supper—Joanna?"

"I've got to go," said Joanna, sipping her thick black coffee and watching Martha.

Martha thought: Neither of them *heard* what I said. Joanna dislikes Jack now because she's been subjected to my being hysterical, and Jack is feeling: Martha's upset.

Jack now lowered himself to the floor. First he put his cup down on it, and then felt the floor, as it were greeted earth: the way an African villager might touch the earth with one hand, assessing it, before squatting down. Jack squatted, his hand flat on the floor beside him. Martha thought: If he and I were alone, we would make love, and what I said, what I felt, would be answered with how he made love. This seemed to her an extraordinary discovery.

"What sort of work do you want?" said Joanna.

97

"It's not the work as such I care about. But I do know exactly what I want." For she did. In the last few minutes, something had happened, a balance had shifted. She knew.

"I want," said Martha, "to live in such a way that I don't just—turn into a hypnotised animal."

Jack, smiling with affectionate hope that he would soon know what Martha was so excited about, kept his palm flat on the floor—earth; but Joanna was saying with abrupt hostility: "Oh no. I had quite enough of all that during the war."

"What do you mean?" asked Jack, turning the antennae of his sensitivity towards Joanna.

"I know what I mean. And I've had enough of it. I simply won't have any more," said Joanna.

"It was on the boat. I understood on the boat," said Martha.

"Martha didn't like the trip over," Jack explained to Joanna. "But all the same, Martha, it must have been all right, just sitting there with your girl friend and watching everyone. When I came back as a passenger it was the same ..." Now he was talking like a host, soothing Martha's smarts away. "But I spent all my time in the gym. I wasn't going to mix myself up."

"Ah, but I did, I did, and that's the point."

"You said you sat with that sick girl and watched—it's always awful, a lot of people crammed together, just animals."

"No." Martha was in the grip of a necessity to explain, even to claim an ally in Joanna, and in the face of Joanna's hostile negation of her, Martha's, vital discovery. "Before I left ... home? I used to dream about the sea. All the time. It was an obsession. When I got off the train at Cape Town, I thought, The sea, but we were put straight onto the boat, and the sea was harbour water full of ships. And the boat— I swear everything was designed to make you forget the sea was anywhere near. And if you stood at night on the deck and looked at it, or walked around the deck, someone would say, Moongazing! Or: I've got to get my weight down too. You know ... hundreds of people, some of them had been waiting the whole war for this trip. There was this girl. She was sick. Dying I think. A blood disease. She was a pale thin girl—sickly. We teamed up. But she didn't accept me. I was healthy, you see. I kept catching her eye on me, sceptical and hostile—like you sometimes, Joanna."

"I wasn't aware of it."

"Yes. Yes. Where was I, yes. We two were a challenge to the men, not joining in. She thought that's why I was doing it. Well, and perhaps—or put it around the other way, it was that that dragged me back in again, so perhaps she was right. In a way. But all the time she was polite, and rather cynical, watching to see how long I'd stick it out with her, instead of joining with the others."

Joanna said: "You should have locked yourself in your cabin." She said it fierce and angry.

"I was sharing a cabin with four others. Not everyone can afford private cabins—oh, damn it, that's childish."

"Yes, it is," said Joanna.

"I know how Martha feels," said Jack. "There's been times in my life I could have killed you for your money. And that's the truth. There were times in Port Elizabeth I used to look at the rich tourists and I tell you, if I could have killed you safely I would."

"But I wasn't there," said Joanna, almost amused.

"On that boat I used to think that for millions of people I was a rich person. All over Africa, there are people who know that a trip on a passenger boat is heaven—always beyond them. Imagine that. Because I'd only been on the boat a couple of days and I realised that really everyone was hating it. I used to wake early and watch the other three women wake up—lying half asleep, not wanting to wake up, then groaning awake and reaching for cigarettes. Bodies on bunks, wishing they could sleep all day, but the day had started. The whole ship full of groaning people not really wanting to get up, and shaved and washed and dressed. And the holiday clothes. The women had spent months or fortunes on those clothes, just for that trip. Then breakfast. Everyone eating enormous meaty breakfasts, making jokes about greed. They didn't want to eat it, but they had to, because it was there and they had paid for it. The stewards running around after us like a lot of nursemaids, and people making jokes, you know, about the stewards earning so little. The one thing South Africans, all of us from down there, understand—it's making jokes defensively and throwing money at people. After breakfast, people making jokes as they went down to the lavatories. And an hour later, around came the stewards with soup. And everyone had soup. Then the real drinking started: at last they could begin to drug themselves. They were knocked over the head already by all that food, but now the alcohol. And then lunch: two hours of food, everyone eating and eating and drinking. And then down to sleep. Thank God they could get rid of two hours of being alive in sleep. But some of them were running around in the sun playing games and making jokes about keeping their weight down. And then tea. People coming up from their bunks in different clothes. Tea and masses of cakes. And then dark came and the sexing it up and the drinking. All over the boat, people sexing it up and not liking their partners much because what they were doing didn't come up to the months and months of fantasies about the trip. And music coming out of every pore of the ship. Everyone on the boat but the crew drugged with food and drink and sex. And then bed. But going to bed very fast, either because you were sexing it up with someone or because you were a bit drunk. Back to the pyjamas and the nightdresses. Back to oblivion—thank God."

"Well?" said Joanna, in a fine steady anger. Her eyes shone, her cheeks glowed very pink.

"I spent my time in the gym," said Jack.

"Yes. But it was like a—I can't explain. Everything was just like ordinary life, only more so. It was a nightmare, sitting with that girl. Her name was Lily Maxwell and she came from one of the mining suburbs outside Johannesburg. I swear we were the only two people among the passengers who weren't—hypnotised. We sat and watched. But for me, it was a new feeling, and for her—she had lived with it for a long time. She was dying. I think so, anyway. She was sitting looking at living people. She was quite alone, all the time, you see. And I was with her, but she was waiting for me to crack. Cynically. She knew I would. She sat very quietly, watching me looking at the men, and the men looking at me. So then that was it. It took four days. A nice farmer from the Orange Free State. Oh everything very civilised and in order. And I was permanently heavy and dead and gone with food, alcohol and sex."

"I don't see the point of that," said Joanna.

"Oh yes, you do," said Martha rudely. "I know you do. But I wasn't quite lost, because all the time I was hanging on to just one thought: that I was drugged and hypnotised and that I didn't have to be. And above all that I mustn't be afraid of being—obvious."

"Well it is, isn't it?" said Joanna. She got up. She wanted to leave.

"Yes. But what then? Quite so. I want to be sunk in the obvious. It seems to me that there's a sort of giant conspiracy, and it's all our fault. There are people who know quite

100

well that they are drugged and asleep, but there's a weapon against that—you mustn't be obvious. It's a cliché. Oh, I know perfectly well that there's nothing new in what I said, but I *felt* it new then and I feel it now. But I'm not going to be laughed out of it by people who are afraid of words like cliché, or obvious, or banal. I learned that before. Funny, where was it? Who? Somebody—I've forgotten. We keep learning things and then forgetting them and so we have to learn them again."

"You just want to be a bohemian," said Joanna. "To be different. Well, I watched all that during the war."

"No. The opposite. I remember finding out some time before—that that is what learning is. You suddenly understand something you've understood all your life, but in a new way. But there's a pressure on us all the time to go on to something that seems new because there are new words attached to it. But I want to take words as ordinary as bread. Or life. Or death. Clichés. I want to have my nose rubbed in clichés."

Joanna was swinging her shoulder bag over her handsome camel coat. She wanted to leave. Jack was standing near her, watching her. He was afraid he had lost her. Martha thought that he probably had. He had not "heard" what she had said. Not with his mind. But Martha knew that with his body he could have answered her. And that understanding, really a new one, that there were people who simply did not operate or function through their minds, was as if Jack had stepped towards her from dark to light. She knew that if they had been free to make love now, it would be in a different way, because Jack had caught, sensed, felt, what she had said. But if he were now asked to put into words what Martha had said, he would answer: Martha's tired, she's upset. People were really so very different from each other. She was always forgetting it. Jack's way of experiencing the world, and hers, they did not touch. Except when they made love. He understood, and communicated, through the body.

A ring from downstairs. Jack's face had for one second the look of someone caught out: both women saw it, and even exchanged small ironic glances, so strong is the force of custom. Because neither really felt it. Jack went running downstairs, and they were alone.

Joanna said: "I know what you are saying, but what's the point of all that? There's nothing we can do, is there? So what's the use?"

Voices on the stairs in energetic exchange and Jack entered first, saying: "It's Jane!" with a look of appeal at them both. Now Martha and Joanna asked each other silently if both knew about Jane: both did. And they knew the rules of the game said they should leave. They nodded at Jack, who went out, and came back with a pretty little blonde thing who, however, had the stormy sparkling reddened look of a baby who has been crying enjoyably from temper. Some grief of love had struck her into a splendidly tempestuous need, and she hardly saw Jack's two women visitors who stood ready to leave.

They left together, side by side, and were let out by the crazy youth who grinned his congratulations that they were in such numerous and desirable company.

The two walked down streets where Joanna would never have set foot if it had not been for Jack. Her clean, impeccable country clothes made a space all around her.

"I think I'll take the train home," remarked Joanna. "I've had enough of interesting experiences for the time being." She was still very hostile.

"Are you coming to Jack again?" For it seemed to Martha that Joanna would not.

"I don't know. It's not what I bargained for. I simply don't want things to be all—interesting and dramatic."

"I'm sorry for my part of it, then."

"It's partly my fault. I shouldn't have come in that time—curiosity. It serves me right."

Deepening her accent, making her manner frank and easy, because the colonial could ask personal questions a fellow Englander could not, Martha enquired, risking a snub: "Will you go on sleeping with Jack after you are married?"

"I expect so. Perhaps. I don't see why not." This with a short gruff laugh. "But not if I'm going to get involved in ... I'm not interested in Jack as a person."

Martha risked it and said: "You talk about Jack as men talk about prostitutes."

"Really? I don't think I've ever discussed prostitution with a man. Well, what's wrong with it? I hate sex," she went on coolly. "I mean, I can't stand all the fuss and bother. During the war, there was nothing but sex and people being desperate for each other. But I like being satisfied, I suppose."

And now Martha had to be silent, because being satisfied, was not how she was able to think about sex with Jack. Joanna said: "We're just animals, that's all. Why pretend anything different? Jack satisfies me. It's simple and quick and it's all over with. That's what I like."

"I see."

"Well," said she, with her short gruff laugh, "you're not going to tell me you love him or something piffling like that, are you?"

"Certainly not," said Martha, laughing equally. The question then was: Did Jack say to himself, I give Joanna satisfaction, short and simple and quick, because that's what she wants, and I give Martha—whatever were the words he used for it. Or did he respond simply out of his marvellous sure instinct?

They had reached the bus stop. They stood together in the half-light of the summer evening. "Anyway," said Joanna, "that's that. I want to get married, have children, and lots of money and never have to think again about—all that. And if you'd been here during the war you'd know. It seems to me that a lot of people who weren't in the war, like Jack and you, you are trying to be part of it, you felt you missed something."

"Jack wasn't in the war? He was minesweeping, didn't you know? He was sunk."

"Oh yes, but I didn't mean that. I mean, being here, in England. That was different."

"I see."

Here the bus arrived. Joanna smiled cool and formal at Martha, and stepped quietly onto the bus, from where she remarked: "I expect we may meet again one of these days." The bus went off. Martha now remembered that all of them, Jack, Joanna and herself, had forgotten the money that she needed. Quite right: money was not what she had gone to Jack's for. But she now had about two pounds. She could go to a cheap hotel, the suitcase being her passport, and ring up Mark in the morning to make an appointment to confirm terms, in the English manner.

But she was too tired. Besides, she remembered those moments when they had understood each other—oh yes, only too well, and thought: what's the point? I know perfectly well I'm going to move in. She went to a telephone box. It was about nine o'clock.

When Martha arrived, the house seemed to have nobody in it. Then at last he came down the stairs. He was working, he said. He supposed that Martha would rather wait until tomorrow before starting work, otherwise he'd be only too pleased . . . but she was too tired for anything but bed. He

103

carried her suitcase up to the second floor, and into a large quiet room. He had made the bed. Or somebody had. He left her saying that the kitchen was downstairs if she wanted to make herself coffee in the night—as he often did.

She closed her eyes on a room whose presence was so strong, so confident, that she was saying as she went to sleep: I'll stay for just a while, just a short time. A couple of months ...

Four

She was rising towards light, through layers of sleep, fighting against being sucked down again by the backwash. Light was on her eyelids. She opened them. The room was full of pure brittle sunlight. The black branches of the tree across the street held a glitter of water. A cold black tree, framed by domestic curtains, grey and pink: a tree on a stage. A white counterpane dazzled. On the white, near the window, the black cat sat in the sunlight, washing its face. On the opposite corner, a black fly cleaned its head with its arms. Cat and fly used the same movements. Cautious, so as to frighten neither, Martha reached out for a brush, sat up, brushed her hair. Behind her, a shadow on the white wall attended to its head. Fly, cat, woman, their images were shaped in no-light. The cat's shadow was a steady movement of dark on white. On the side of the fly away from the window a small darkening, but the movement of the fly's working forelegs was not visible. If she were fly-size, would she then be able to observe the working shadow from those energetic hairy arms? The cat was watching its moving shadow as it cleaned its face with its paw. Was the fly looking at its shadow at it cleaned itself?

Sunlight in London brought an emphasis: shadow. For the most part a day was clear sunless light, like water, that contained objects: houses, trees, a stone, people. But in hot countries, everything was underlined, everything had its image. The light was draining away off the counterpane back through the window. The cat jet-black in sunlight, now showed the variations of colour in its fur. It was dark brown, with a gloss of black, and it had white hairs on its chin. The fly seemed weightless. The white wall behind Martha showed its need for repainting. The black tree stood sodden; it had lost its glitter. And the sky was grey.

There was no need to get up. Not for hours yet, if she felt like staying in bed. While every moment of her attention was claimed by Mark, her employer, from lunchtime onwards, which was when he returned from his factory, often until two, three, in the morning, he would not have her working in the morning: he said it lessened his guilt. Nor would he have her doing anything about the house, which badly needed it. This morning, for instance, she knew that there were no eggs, no butter, and that the plumber should be summoned to the water taps. But she could do none of these things. This was part, not of protecting Martha, but of protecting Mark against his family.

She thought: Well, I'm leaving so soon anyway. If I broke the rules just for one day? For that matter, if I spent the two weeks before I leave just getting everything fixed up, would it matter? The housewife in her yearned to do it. She had not told Mark that she was leaving. He knew she wanted to. To leave just before Christmas! That was heartless—yet she intended to, she had to, she must ... Good Lord, she cried to herself, had been exhorting herself for weeks now, there is no reason in the world why you should feel guilty. None. It's not rational. It's not your responsibility, it never was.

Mark was hoping, though of course he would never say so, that she would stay until after Christmas. Because of Francis. If Martha stayed, then the child could come for the holidays. Possibly they would let Lynda out of the hospital. There would be a sort of a Christmas, enough to use the word to Francis. Otherwise, Mark would take Francis to his mother, which he most passionately did not want to do.

I've got to go I must. Now. Or I'll never be able to leave this.

This, particularly, was the room, which had become, in the last six months, her home. The moment of greatest pleasure in every day was waking in it, beneath the window, which framed the tree whose leaves she had seen stand in solid leaf, then thin, then fall. It was a sycamore tree. The cat slept on her bed. Which was how she saw it: but the cat always slept on that bed, he did not care who was in it. The cat saw the bed and room as his. When she left, the cat would sleep just there, on the corner of the bed nearest the window; would wash itself, just there, watching its shadow or the birds in the tree; would roll over on its back in sunlight, a black plush cat, all purring warmth.

A terrible pang—real pain. Oh no, she must go, and fast, Christmas or no Christmas, particularly as a good part of her fear of going was that London had no more space in it for her now, that it had had months ago, when she had arrived. She did have some money now, though, thanks to Mark—over £200. She never seemed to have anything to spend her salary on. She would leave—in the next few days, take a room, or a small flat, and risk her chances with all the other waifs and strays of London who had no family at Christmas. Waifs and strays! Once she could not have thought of herself like that—oh no, she had got soft, and badly so, it was time to move on, even though she would never live in such a room again. The whole house was like it, of a piece, a totality: yet no one could set out to create a house like it. It had grown like this, after being furnished by Mark's grandmother at the end of the last century by what Martha would have called when she first came "antiques." Nor was this room assertive or bullying as she had first thought: on the contrary, it was quiet, it had tact, it served. But it certainly absorbed. Money? For weeks when first here she had moved around the room, the house, like a cat, feeling for corners, and essences, and odours and memories, trying to isolate just that quality which no other place she had ever been in had had. Solidity? Every object, surface, chair, piece of material, or stuff or paper had—solidity. Strength. Nothing could crack, fray, fall apart. A chair might break, but if so it would be put together as a surgeon does a body. The curtains had a weight in your hands. The carpet and the rugs lay thick on the boards of the floor which were beautiful enough to lie bare. if there were not so many rugs and carpets. Nothing in this house believed in the possibility of destruction. Imagine being brought up in such a house, to be the child of it. . . . A child's voice sounded across the passage. It was Sally's little boy. Martha had the room Sally used, when she came to stay, but Sally, here for a few nights, had not thought it worth dispossessing Martha from it. She was in James's room, used as a spare room because James was dead.

The door opened and Paul wriggled in, smiling shyly. The cat jumped down to wind around his legs and the fly buzzed away. He was five, or six, a small lively dark boy all charm and warmth.

"Paul!" came his mother's peremptory voice: "Paul, you are *not* to worry Martha!"

Paul grinned at Martha and sidled to the bed, glancing at the door where his mother was due to appear. And now Sally's beautiful dark head showed around the door. She gave a great dramatic sigh of "Oh!" at the sight of the disobedient child; and then she curled herself into an armchair. She was in a striped purple-and-yellow silk dressing gown. Her hair hung down on either side of her small apricot-tinted face in black braids. Her soft black eyes shone. She was, as the family never said, but never ceased to make evident, Jewish. That is, if put down anywhere near the Mediterranean, she would seem at home. In this room she seemed almost perversely an exotic. Now she put out a small hand towards the child, who ran to her, climbed on her lap, and cuddled. She sniffed him, with pleasure. Wound together, they breathed contentment. Almost, she licked him like an animal with her cub.

"I'm going to make breakfast," she announced.

"I don't eat breakfast."

"Well then, some tea?" She wanted company downstairs.

"I don't get up yet," said Martha. This was partly to obey Mark: he feared Sally's encroachment even more than he did his mother's. "And besides, I like this time of the day here."

"Ah yes, the room," cried Sally. "When I came into it, after *there*, you understand?" Martha understood. And Sally knew that she did. They shared the knowledge of outsiders. Sally had been Sarah Koenig ten years ago, when she was a refugee from Germany. This being the kind of family which served, had civic responsibility, and took on burdens—at its height, it had been that above all—naturally they put up refugees. Sarah had come, with half a dozen other refugees, from Europe. Here she had met Colin, Mark's brother; and here she had married him.

"Are you going to stay here for Christmas?" she asked, going straight to the point as always. "I want to know. Because Mark could come to stay with us. With Francis. That would be nice for Paul." Here she squeezed Paul, with a chiding pouting downwards glance, to make him agree. He buried his face in her silken bosom.

Mark said that Francis and Paul did not get on. Mark would never go for Christmas to his brother Colin—not because he didn't like Colin, but because of Sally. She did not seem to know this, or if she did, conducted her life from standards which made it irrelevant. For one thing, when she had married Colin, she married the family—she had no family of her own. In terms of Anton's grim definition, her Jewishness was absolute: she had no relatives alive. So this was her family, the Coldridges. Therefore she loved them and they must love her. They did not dislike her so much as that they were pleased when she was somewhere else. Nor would any one of them have said that it was a pity Colin had married her—particularly as not only Colin, but Mark too had made a marriage that was so palpably a pity. But they were upset by her. Which Martha could understand: she was upset by Sally, who always lived inside her own emotional climate with apparently never a suspicion that there might be others.

She said: "And a family Christmas would be good, I have told him, instead of all this nonsense about spies! Politics and Communism—nonsense!"

Colin was a physicist. He worked at Cambridge on something to do with the bomb. The man he worked under had been arrested and charged with spying. Colin was naturally under suspicion. The family was behaving as if this was—well, not far from a joke. Of course, if one lived in such houses, filled with such furniture, knowing "everybody" in England, then spying was—a joke. Or rather, the idea that they could be suspected of it. Colin was a Communist, they said: though from the words Mark used of him Martha could recognise nothing of Communism as she had experienced it, but then of course she knew nothing about England. She found it disagreeable that they talked about his Communism as a kind of eccentricity, but tolerable because it was his, a Coldridge's—as if he stammered, or bred pythons. They had a big family's possessiveness to it, everyone had their funny ways, their traits, and that was Colin's. This was not true of Mark, who loved his brother and was with him against the family. The two brothers were isolated in this: and Sally-Sarah was excluded, and suffered and had been complaining Mark hated her. There she sat in the great warm chair, a colourful little beauty with her pretty little boy, all warm tactlessness, warm claims, warm insistence, a challenge to the Coldridges, who had seemed never to do much more about her than to insist on calling her "Sally." Well, if she was tactless, they were intolerable, arrogant: when she made a scene that they "had stolen her name from her" they had only laughed; and her husband still called her Sally.

And it was all Martha could do not to call her, sometimes, Stella, she was so like that other warm-shored beauty
of ten years before who, however, had been transformed by
matrimony and right living into a pillar of good works and
righteousness.

And in due time, Sally-Sarah too would become a handsome and portly matron?

Meanwhile she suffered, and everyone in the family had to
suffer with her.

"Is Colin worried?"

"No, not he," said Sally-Sarah scornfully. "Not he. I keep
telling him, Darling, you are mad. Why Communism? Communism for the English? They know nothing at all. Isn't that
so? You agree with me?"

"Yes," said Martha.

"Yes. It is so. Playing. Little games. I tell him, You're like
a little boy."

Colin, Mark's elder brother, the eldest son now that James
was dead, killed in the war, was a solid, serious, painstaking
man. Dedicated. According to his brother Mark, the only
serious member of the family, meaning by this, a singlemind-
edness; meaning, too, a criticism of his own many-sidedness.
Colin, devoted to science, was devoted to Communism because for him Communism meant internationalism, meant
the sharing of science. Colin had decided that science was his
destiny at the age of eleven and had thought of nothing else,
ever since. Except, perhaps occasionally, for Sally-Sarah? He
could not have relished being told he was a little boy playing
games.

"I tell him, Colin, if you knew anything about what
politics can do—like I do, oh yes I do, Martha, believe me,
do you believe me? . . ." Since she was not likely to go on
until Martha had said she did, Martha said she did, and
Sally-Sarah then continued: "But if you did, Colin, I say,
then you would not play with fire."

She was crying. Curled in the great chair, a small dark
girl wept, her face all frail white terror. And in her arms her
son, unhappy now and crying too, sucking his thumb like a
baby.

"Mark says it will be all right," said Martha. "After all,
they must have cleared Colin by now, or they would have
arrested him too."

"Mark. What does he know! What? He's a literary man.
And he plays with his electric machines. They are always

109

playing, these people. The police often do not arrest until later. Meanwhile they watch and lay traps."

"Well, but I don't think . . ."

"You think! What do you think? I *know*. You're like them all, it doesn't happen here. Yes! But it is happening here, isn't it? They are looking for traitors in the civil service—a purge. It happens now. They dismiss people from shops if they might be a Communist. And in the B.B.C.—no Communists."

"Yes, I know, but I don't think it's as bad as . . ."

"Bad? What do you know! You talk like them. People losing jobs for politics. I know that. A purge in the civil service. I know that. A purge among the teachers. I know that. You think it makes it different to call it by another name? No. It is no different. It is the same. People are afraid. I know that too, I know it."

She buried her face in her child's hair and shook with sobs. The little boy was weeping noisily.

"I'll make you some breakfast," Martha said.

"No. I don't want breakfast. I want nothing, only that at last there is an end to . . . but no, there is no end to it. Never. But thank you, Martha." She got up and carried the child out of the room.

Doors slammed. Drawers slammed, a few moments later her voice chided the child, as they descended to the kitchen on the ground floor. From her bed Martha followed the progress of breakfast being made: well, let's hope that Mark was at the factory today and not being disturbed by it.

I shall tell Mark that I'm leaving. Today. I don't want to be involved in all this . . . She meant, this atmosphere of threat, insecurity, and illness. Who would have thought that coming to this house meant—having her nose rubbed in it! Yes, but that wasn't what she had meant, when she had demanded from life that she must have her nose rubbed in it. Something new, surely, not what she had lived through already, was what she ought to be doing? Why was she here at all? If you start something, get on a wavelength of something, then there's no getting off, getting free, unless you've learned everything there is to be learned—have had your nose rubbed in it? There was something really terrifyingly creepy about the fact that the job heard about from Phoebe at a lunch designed to hook her into quite another job had led her here, back into what she already knew so very very well. No, she would leave, probably in about a week, certainly before Christmas, and approach Phoebe for a job. She might very well take that secretary's job in "the thing for the liberation of the colonies." If politics were inescapable, and they seemed to be, then let her at least be practical, on the simplest day-to-day level. Besides, hearing the English—and that included people like Phoebe, well-informed as she was—talk about African politics was enough to tell her how very useful she could be. She felt as Sally-Sarah must feel when listening to the people of these islands talk about invasion, or the loss of national identity. There was no substitute for experience. Put Phoebe in Africa, in what she called "a progressive movement," and in five minutes she'd be suspected as any enemy not because of her opinions, but because of—the tone of her voice. And as for Sally-Sarah's terrible knowledge, nowhere in London, not even in suspicious dockland, or in the poor streets, or among the waifs and strays, had she met one person who understood, as Sally-Sarah understood, insecurity. These people still lived inside the shadow of their war, they were still rationed, their buildings were still thinned or ruinous, men had been killed, men had not come back from fighting: but that face which Sally-Sarah lifted from the chair where she sat clutching her child as if she were the child and he some kind of shield or support, that frail terrorised face with the great dark eyes—well, Britain did not understand that face. And Sally-Sarah was quite right; anything, anything at all that made it possible, was a mistake. There ought to be one country in the world without that experience. This house should be treasured because in it such experience was inconceivable. Yet it was from this house that Colin had come, at this moment under threat of being considered a spy. And Mark's identification with his brother was a drive to understand, to participate?

Mark was the one among the four brothers to have had an unconventional education. Their father, Henry, had been a conservative member of Parliament: he was conservative by tradition, it was in the blood, as Mark emphasized, to make Martha understand that there were two kinds of Tory, those like his father constitutionally incapable of understanding that the country could be run by anybody else; and the Tories by intellectual conviction, whom Mark found intolerable. But he had loved and admired his father. The four sons had been brought up here in this house, and in a house in the country, sold at the father's death because of duties. This house belonged to the sons. Margaret Coldridge had then married for love (Mark claimed she had not loved his father, but had been married off to him) Oscar Enroyde, a financier; and for the four years the marriage lasted Margaret had inhabited the world of international money which it seemed had been an unpleasant surprise to her. Not because she disapproved of it, but because she was indefatigably English, and was hardly ever able to be in England. The sons, being educated, were for the most part in England, while their mother was mostly in America. She described her second marriage's breakup as: "I couldn't stand dear Oscar's friends." Mark said his mother was fundamentally a hostess, and one of a certain kind: she needed to attract, then domineer, guests. Married to Oscar Enroyde, she had found her guest list already established, and she spent most of her energies heading people off one of the world's very rich men. And besides, she was a woman of multifarious talents, none of them now useful. If a chair, for instance, was broken, she knew just that one little man, in Kent, who understood that kind of chair, and she liked to take it herself, and exchange talk with minute professionalism about the chair's history, condition and needs. She hated being waited on.

During the war James was killed. There was a daughter, Elizabeth, now absorbed into the wife's second marriage. This girl, about fourteen now, sometimes came to stay.

After the war Margaret married again—improbably, to everyone but Mark. Her third husband was an amiable country gentleman, an amateur of the arts, vaguely a publisher, who served on a sort of semi-official body to do with the arts. He adored Margaret. Oscar Enroyde had not adored Margaret. She had adored him. Now Margaret entertained a good deal. Mark said his mother had an infallible instinct, unrecognised even by herself, for what was the next thing, what was in the air, and this marriage proved that the arts would soon be fashionable—unlikely as this seemed in grey, colourless, restricted postwar Britain. Mark neither liked nor disliked this husband, John Patten, but he violently disliked him in his role of the arts. This was a tension between son and a mother who wished that Mark, now that he was a "writer," not only potential but published, would attend her weekend parties or at least an occasional dinner table. If Mark had to go down for Christmas, he would hate it. But he would go, because of his concern for the child, for Francis's Christmas. Yes, but that was not Martha's affair. Unless the mere fact that she was here, had arrived here by what seemed such a slight chance, made it her affair? Had she ever, by any hint or lapse of behaviour, made it seem likely (to Mark, to Margaret) that she felt it was her affair? Yesterday Margaret had telephoned, apparently about some set of spare curtains, but really to find out if Martha intended to be there for Christmas. It appeared from her tone, gaily casual, that she both wished that Martha would not be there, so that Mark would be available for a Boxing Day party, and wished that Martha would be there looking after Francis, because there would be no other children at the Pattens, and she, Margaret, was afraid the little boy would be lonely among so many adults. Margaret had not mentioned Lynda, so much in both her and Martha's thoughts. She had, however, said she hoped that supplies would be laid in for Christmas because if she, Martha, did not attend to it, who would?

Martha now decided that she would get up. Downstairs was quiet. Sally-Sarah would have gone out shopping. Margaret was right, she, Martha, should arrange for food and supplies before she left: not to do so was positively neurotic. Today, however, she would be careful not to notice the absence of butter and eggs.

For the first week of her being here Mark had been stubbornly resistant to her doing any housekeeping at all. But when she had understood the situation, and said that she did, they had established a defensive pact against the whole family.

Which wished that Mark would divorce his wife Lynda and marry again. Not, of course, Martha, equably unsuitable. But Martha in the house, housekeeping, being kind to the little boy, was a kind of bridge from Mark's previous condition of total womanlessness to the possibility of a new marriage. Because before this he had always refused to have any sort of woman around at all, even a secretary. For he was married to Lynda. The house was ready for her return. She was only temporarily away, temporarily in the hands of the doctors. She would—perhaps not soon—return to a house kept empty and waiting for her and to a child waiting for his mother.

This had been going on for three, four years.

Francis had been sent to a boarding school, though Mark did not approve of boarding schools; and spent an orphan's life with his grandmother, who found the little boy a burden; with Sally-Sarah and Paul (Colin was always working, he was seldom at home); with the other brother's family, Arthur's—Arthur was Phoebe's ex-husband, now remarried. And sometimes he stayed with Phoebe. Sometimes he was alone with Mark in this house.

There were photographs of Lynda in his room and in Mark's room. Lynda's clothes hung in Mark's cupboards. It was all wrong—the family were right. It had that stamp of excessiveness, of unreality, which—indicated a passion. Indicated, in short, the growing point, that focus in a person's life which so few people are ever equipped to see, and which is why lives remain, even to the nearest and dearest, so often dark, obscure; lit only by these flashes of what seems an unhealthy-gleaming light: a passion. But if Martha were the family she would do the same, feel the same, and try every way, fair or foul, to make Mark see that he could not spend the rest of his life as if he were married to Lynda. Who, it was clear, was unmarriageable. The family were right about that. Lynda had never been a wife, never been a mother. She could not be. Mark ought never to have made her either—so said the family. And here it was that a close secret nerve ached and nagged in Martha: she had not met Lynda, save through improbably beautiful photographs, but she knew her, oh yes, very well, though she and Martha were not alike, and could not be, since Martha was not "ill" and in the hands of the doctors. But for a large variety of reasons, Lynda Coldridge, who was in a very expensive mental hospital because she could not stand being Mark's wife, and Francis's mother, came too close to Martha. Which was why Martha had to leave this house, and soon.

She went down to the kitchen. A note on the table said in green pencil: "Martha! No eggs! No butter! The left tap is leaking! I shall bring back food when I come. Love. Sarah." She submitted (for what alternative did she have?) to being Sally in this family, but she always signed herself Sarah.

There was a letter on the table. A child's hand. It was from that nasty school—a cold, heartless military camp of a school.

Dear Martha, How are you? I am very well. I need football boots. I don't like football. But I do like cricket. I hope you will be there for Christmas. With sincere greetings, Francis. P.S. Please tell Daddy about the boots. Last time he got the wrong size. I want a chemistry set for Christmas. A real one, not a baby's one, please tell Granny I want a real one. With sincere greetings, Francis. See you at Christmas, what a hope, ha ha!

Now Mark came into the room in his dressing gown. He seemed annoyed: he had been disturbed by Sally-Sarah? He looked at the note on the table: eggs, butter, tap. He was helplessly annoyed.

"I'll have coffee," he said. "No, I'll make it."

Martha handed him his son's note. When he had read it she said: "I'll stay for Christmas. But I must go afterwards." They looked at each other.

"It would be good of you to stay," he said, appealing, and hating himself for it.

"No. I want to. But Mark, after Christmas I've got to go."

"Of course. You are absolutely right. Absolutely."

Six weeks later, on a bitter day, Martha was dressed in layers of sweaters, clearing and arranging the basement. This was for the housekeeper that Mark had at last agreed he should have. The business of the basement had been going on since Christmas, a groundbass to so many apparently pre-eminent themes, apparently a minor thing, an annoyance, a question of organisation merely. In fact she could see now that it had been the most important, it was the one theme that had possibilities of development, of movement: a growing point in this stagnant mess. Before Christmas she had gone to Mark's study, late, braving his reluctance ever to be confronted, and pointed out that a housekeeper would give him all the advantages of a Martha, and none of the disadvantages. He did not want to see it. He liked her, he said: how was he to know he would like this housekeeper?— He wouldn't until he had engaged her!

He did not want a strange person!—Yes, but she, Martha, had been strange until she arrived.

Where was she to live, this housekeeper?—Why, where Martha lived of course, why not?

Yes, but—There was the basement, why not use that? It was simply a question of . . .

Yes, yes, yes . . . he muttered, he would. But first he must just . . .

He had been unable to stand any more. Martha could see that, and went down to survey the basement. It had been used as an overflow depot for years, both from upstairs, and from the house in the country, when that was sold. It was stacked with furniture, carpets, pictures. Some of it had to be sold. Mark could not bear, he said, to see the furniture of his childhood carted off to salerooms; but there was no help for it. He came briefly down, indicated the pieces that were valuable and should be kept, and for the rest a dealer had come and taken things away. And now Martha was to arrange the place as she pleased, since they were not to know the taste of the future housekeeper, who would be getting a luxury flat when she came. The walls had been done for damp; cupboards had been put in; a bathroom and a kitchen were ready—almost, since although they were employing a firm which charged high prices for efficiency, it was impossible to get anything done well. Meanwhile, since workmen were in, workmen might as well attend to the rest of the house. As Martha was leaving, had actually put down a deposit on a flat, she felt free to take the house in hand. Which was in a dreadful state beneath its surface of order. If it hadn't been built to stand attrition, it would have been a slum, Mark having done no more than engage in a holding operation—his phrase—since Lynda's illness. Workmen dug everywhere into floors and walls and filled the place with the smell of new colour. The roof was mended—or would be; these things took time. Carpets and curtains were cleaned—patience, there had been a war on. Martha dealt with men and their employers, while the people whose home this was were clutched in such fearful anxiety, and it seemed to her that yet again she had walked onto that stage where two or three different types of plays were running together, for it did not seem possible that such discordant events could be sharing a texture of time or place, except in a dreamlike capacity to change into something else, like the flamingoes into croquet sticks. Margaret, for instance, took to storming in, rather regally, in order to drop well-chosen words about if-a-thing's-worth-doing-at-all-it-is-worth-doing-well, like a white housewife to her black "boy," while the workman so addressed would put on the act of a humble yet self-respecting servant deferring to his better. Then Margaret would depart. Martha was a foreigner, and not a member of the British ruling classes, and besides she knew one of the useful languages, the dialect of trades-unionism, and therefore the workmen did not bother to put a show on for her. Not one of them was prepared to do a minute's more work than he had to, or do it better than he could get away with, for the most basic of reasons: he would get nothing out of it if he did, while the people who employed him were interested only in making money, which it was their business to do. And besides, there had been a war on. There wasn't one job these men did that wouldn't have to be done again and very soon, so badly was it done and so poor the materials. There were frightful but good-natured battles of wills, since both sides knew the limits of such battles, and Martha cajoled and argued and bargained and made small gains. Meanwhile newspapers flooded into the house which trumpeted the destruction of Britain by socialism (internal, the Labour Party) and by Communism (external), as manifested by people like Colin Coldridge's colleague, working for Russia.

Meanwhile, Mark, spending his days for the most part with his brother, or in his factory, since he could not endure to see his home under attack, spent his nights talking to Martha in his study, mostly about his childhood and about Lynda. He was not a person who found it easy to talk, she discovered; but it had been easier since Christmas, which had laid so much open.

Christmas had been dreadful. First, Lynda, allowed home by her doctors on condition she was returned to them the moment she showed signs of strain. Then, Francis home from his school—to spend Christmas with his father and mother. So he had been told by his housemaster. "I'd like that," he said, or quoted, cautiously, in his way of testing out phrases, words, used by others about his situation. "I must be careful," he went on, his wide painful eyes fixed on Martha's face so that she could confirm or deny: "My mother isn't very well, you see. I mustn't upset her."

An awful school. A couple of hundred little boys, guarded by men. "The little ones" (Francis's description of the boys younger than himself) had a matron, but "the big ones" had men. They all slept in dormitories, were made to play games, were bullied by those older than themselves, exactly as these institutions have been described, mostly by their victims, for decades. It all went on, as things do, out of the inertia of what is in existence. Francis wore a tight grey flannel suit, with a tie and a collar; he was obsessed with his shoelaces, which were always getting themselves untied, and his brown wide eyes were always on the alert, for fear he might be doing something he should not.

Three days before Christmas Sally telephoned to ask if she could come with her child for the holiday, her husband being "impossible, Martha! He's as stubborn as a horse. I'm not going to stay where I'm not wanted!" His impossibility, apparently, was that he would not talk to his wife about what preoccupied him. He was spending all his waking time with his superiors, being cross-examined about his possible links with international espionage, and his relationship with his friend and superior, now awaiting trial. The police were making visits too. He would not talk to his wife; but he came to London to talk to Mark. The brothers had spent all afternoon together; and then Martha joined them for dinner and the evening. Colin announced almost immediately that he was "not a Communist but a Marxist."

Martha kept sounding notes to which he could not help responding if—he were not trying to hide something? Were not a man numbed by terror? How to account for this lack of resonance? Unless, of course, he was not a Communist and never had been one? But she had not before met this type of person who, because he admires a certain Communist country, or a Communist achievement, or to annoy Aunt Authority, will call himself, herself, a Communist or a Marxist without ever going near the Communist Party. They are pretty common at times when the heat is off and to admire Communism not dangerous—during the war, for instance, or during the later fifties and the sixties. But this kind of platonic admiration, at the height of the Cold War, was quixotic or simply—crazy. Unless to be a Coldridge absolved one from the necessity for caution, which is what Martha was beginning to believe.

For Colin did not seem to be frightened in the least. Of course, in Mark's calm, storm-excluding study, it was hard to believe in danger. Nor did he seem to want to conceal anything. On the contrary, he talked all evening about his principal, now awaiting trial, whom he had visited frequently, obviously despising (or ignorant of?) the danger of doing this, and in spite of the entreaties of his wife, who had begged and wept. The man was his friend, he had said; just as Mark was to say later: Colin is my brother.

It was, obviously, a relief to get away from his wife—not that he said so, of course. But Sally-Sarah was present throughout the evening, in silences and looks exchanged by the two men; and afterwards Martha saw that it was on this evening that they had decided, without actually saying so, that she must be here for Christmas.

When she came, she spent her time in James's room, with her child, weeping or sleeping. The little boy came downstairs from time to time, his face still wan from hours of tears, to say: "Mummy's asleep." When Martha went up with tea, coffee, she found Sally-Sarah curled up under an eiderdown, thumb in her mouth, like a child, but not asleep. She stared at the wall, or traced out the pattern on the wallpaper with a finger. "I wish I was dead," she said to Martha. "I do. I wish I was dead."

Lynda arrived on Christmas Eve. The photographs said she was beautiful. Martha knew, too, that she would have beautiful clothes, because the bills for her clothes were enormous: one of the points of self-respect, return towards normality, was that she must always be perfectly dressed. Mark willingly paid the bills.

Lynda arrived in Margaret's chauffeured car, and stepped into her home like a visitor. She smiled, cool, at her husband, and was about to smile, cool, at her son, when she reminded herself, and kissed the child's cheek, murmuring: "Darling!" as he froze in pain and embarrassment. She was tall, very thin, with a face strained by the effort of not being "upset." She smiled steadily, while great grey eyes stared out of brownish hollows. But she was staring inward at the place where she kept her balance. She was enveloped in a great pale fur coat. Her hands, long and white and lovely, ended in nails bitten to the quick: there were rusty stains around the cuticle. Her hair, just done, was a soft gleaming gold: all her health seemed to be in her hair. At once she asked to be taken to her room—to wash, she said; but she stayed there all evening.

The room had been a problem. Since this Christmas occasion was designed, primarily, for Francis, for normality; and since mothers and fathers shared a room, or at least should appear to share one, Lynda was put into the married room, Mark's own, on the first floor. But Mark had a bed put into the dressing room, because, as he told Martha, curt, giving necessary information, Lynda could not stand having him near her. It would be necessary, if she were not to be upset, that the door between bedroom and dressing room could be locked. They had to have a new lock made.

The Christmas Eve dinner was eaten by Mark, silent, but smiling a determination to present normality to his son; Sally-Sarah, miserable, and making no attempt to hide it; her son, near tears; Francis, his wide anxious eyes on his father's face; and Martha. During the meal, Paul had climbed onto his mother's lap and the two had sat enwrapping each other, her cheek on his head. Francis watched: he was looking at a mother and her little boy. After dinner he shook his father's hand good night. Later still, Martha heard him crying. His room was next to hers. She went in to comfort him. He held his breath, held back tears, while she put her arms around him. He would not respond. As she shut the door she heard the great burst of breath and tears and *Go away and leave me alone.* Christmas dinner was the same, a kind of endurance test. Lynda sat at the foot of the table, serving the food cooked by Martha: her son watched her. Colin, exhorted by his wife that "It was the least he could do," came for

119

just that meal, and sat grimly through it, while Sally-Sarah kept her great dark eyes on him in tearful reproach, and spoke reproach to him through his son. He left the moment it was finished.

"We've got that over, thank God," said Mark to Martha, as he helped her clear uneaten food into the refrigerators.

There was another week of getting it over, spent by Martha for the most part with workmen, and in the basement with dealers. Meanwhile the family suffered in separate rooms of the house and Martha felt the ridiculousness of furniture, leaking roofs and plumbing. It felt almost as if an underground guerrilla war went on, the fabric of the house as battleground, while amiably incompetent men came and went, carpets vanished and appeared, the sounds of banging and hammering shook walls and floors. She invited Mark to inspect the future housekeeper's flat; but he left it to her. Lynda should not know about the basement, the sale of the furniture, he said. Yet one afternoon, when Martha was in the basement with a dealer, Lynda had appeared in her pale furs, and was competent about values and prices: seeing her thus, Martha found it hard to believe she was ill. This would be a nice flat, Lynda had said; she wouldn't mind living in it herself. She had retired up the stairs with the remark that Martha must not tell Mark that she, Lynda, had been doing this. "I don't think he'd like it," she said. "He doesn't, you know."

One afternoon Lynda spent with her son. They sat in "Margaret's room," the drawing room, on a big sofa. She asked him questions, gentle, detached, about his school. She was answered by a child who measured everything he said against the minutest signs, the tiniest reactions, of his mother's face; as if a word, a phrase, from him could harm or "upset" her. And indeed, at the end of this interview—for that was what it seemed—Lynda announced, suddenly, she felt ill and must lie down, and Francis sat alone, near a Christmas tree with coloured bulbs alight on it. Mark and Martha, across the passage in the dining room, heard muffled crying.

Mark burst out: "I can't stand it, it's a mistake—we've got to get her back to the hospital. Or is this better than nothing?"

"Perhaps it is. I suppose so."

"Are you sure?"

"No, of course I'm not sure!" And now Martha wept, or nearly did, understanding exactly how Francis must feel: one did not weep, show strain, with people who were so palpably suffering much more than she could.

"I'm sorry," pleaded Mark: she must not cry, he was saying silently. "But there's no way of doing anything right, is that the point?"

"I don't know. I suppose so. Isn't this better than not having a mother at all?"

"Or a wife?" said Mark. "But that isn't what you think is it?"

"It doesn't matter what I think."

"It isn't what *they* think!"

"I know that!"

"My mother hasn't been near us. It'd make her happy if Lynda was committed."

"Probably."

"Oh all right, all right—you're leaving. I keep forgetting."

Unfairly, outrageously (she felt), this was all ironical reproach. So, doing what she could, where so little could be done, she continued with taps, cupboards, floorboards.

Every night she heard Francis crying. She would creep to the door, open it—try to force herself to go in, in another attempt at comfort ... where there could be no comfort. Once he felt her there and sat up: "Who's that?" he said. Martha knew he hoped it was his mother.

"It's Martha. Are you all right?"

"Perfectly all right, thank you very much." And he laid himself down, silent, to endure: exactly as he would in that dormitory of his where he would not be able to cry without being overheard by a couple of dozen little boys.

A couple of nights before Lynda was due to leave, Martha, unable to stand the sound of the muffled weeping from the next room, went down to the kitchen to make coffee. It was about three in the morning. Lynda sat at the big kitchen table, with a spread of cards in front of her. In a little heap to one side of the cards were some pills. Lynda wore an old-fashioned high-necked nightdress, all lace and tucks and frills. She saw Martha and ignored her, went on playing cards, humming a small sad tune to herself. Martha made some coffee and sat down at the other end of the table. Lynda had not been to the hairdresser during the last week, and her hair hung in lank, colourless strands. She seemed all great staring eyes and skull. The illness, or the pills she took so many of, made her sweat a lot: she smelled sour. Nowhere in this sick creature could Martha find the competent woman who had assisted her in planning the basement.

She drank coffee, silently, while Lynda sat swaying and humming.

"You're going, you think," she remarked.

"Yes. In March."

"No you're not," said Lynda, rude as a child. Now she peered into her cards, and said: "It's coming out!" Angry, she pushed the cards together—apparently her own internal rules would be broken if the patience came out.

"Have you got a cigarette?" she now demanded.

Martha handed her a packet. Lynda took one, then scooped out three more with a bland sly smile and laid them side by side, near the pills.

"If I take these now, I shall have to go back to the hospital tomorrow, not the day after, because I won't have enough pills," she explained. Smiling, challenging Martha, or some authority, she separated a couple of pills from the heap, a small yellow one and a big yellow one.

"I know what you're thinking," she announced, looking up and smiling at Martha—direct now, personal, charming. Oh yes, one could see how beautiful she was or could be. "Well, you're right. But what's the use of being right?"

Martha said nothing.

Lynda pushed the two pills back into the heap. "I'll stay over the other day. But what for?" She put her head into her hands, and sat swaying and humming. A pause. "No," she said, violently, and sat up. "It's not true, I couldn't come out and *try*. How could I?"

Martha said nothing.

Lynda was now leaning forward and peering into Martha's face, as if listening.

"Why can't you accept it? Some people are just no good. Useless! No good. Not for ordinary life. I keep telling you. I told Mark when he married me. I told him. Why do you want to make everyone like yourselves? I know what I know!"

Martha said nothing and drank coffee. The big kitchen was like a ruin. Curtains, taken down to be washed, were bundled on top of a stepladder. Floorboards had been taken up and pipes lay exposed near the wall. The tiles behind the sink had been ripped away; but the man had forgotten to put them back—he would have to be telephoned in the morning. Last morning he had arrived at eight o'clock to be paid: putting the tiles back was not his job, he had said, but somebody else's. The argument had woken Mark. Mark's dressing room was over the kitchen. Was Mark awake over their heads now?

"Mark's asleep," said Lynda. "When Mark's asleep he sleeps. I am happy when he's asleep; then I know I'm not tormenting him. Sometimes I want to kill him, because if he was dead then I'd know he wasn't unhappy because of me. Do you see? When I came down to the kitchen now I went to look at him. I like looking at him when he's asleep. When I was married to him, I used to wake up at night so that I could see him asleep."

"You are married to him now," said Martha.

"There's no need to say anything," said Lynda. "You said that because you thought you ought. If I were asleep now, you wouldn't have to say anything, would you? That's why I like sleeping. I wish I could sleep all my life. But they won't give me enough pills. I tell them, all right, if you won't let me have what I know, why can't I sleep? What's the difference between being kept silly, because they keep you silly, you see, and being asleep? I'm no use to anyone, so I might as well be asleep. You see," she said, once again offering her intimate, enchanting smile, all of her there for a moment, "I'd kill myself, but I'm afraid. After all, we don't know, do we? It might be worse there than it is here. You don't believe in God, do you?"

"It's a word," said Martha.

"Yes, but the devil is a word too. I know there's a devil. He talks to me."

One of Lynda's symptoms was, she heard voices. But the doctors had told Mark that this symptom had abated. Which was why Lynda was allowed out for Christmas.

Now Lynda screwed up her face, so that she suddenly looked like a malevolent old witch, and leaned forward to peer at Martha.

"Don't tell them I said so. I keep quiet about what I know. I have to, you see." She sat swaying back and forth, back and forth. Then: "That's freedom, isn't it? Everyone has a bit of freedom, a little space . . ." She traced a small circle on the wood of the table, about an inch in diameter. She looked down, peered close. "That wood is nice, isn't it? I chose that table, did Mark tell you? I got it off a street market in Guildford. It cost ten shillings. An old kitchen table, yes, like the one we had at home. It was in the kitchen. The servants ate off it. Nicer than ours. The grain of this wood—look." Martha came nearer to look at whorls of hard grain around which the soft fleshy part of the wood had been worn or scrubbed away. They looked at the cross-cut of a spiral that had once been a growing point in the wood. Lynda sat tracing it with her finger—contented. "That is freedom," she said. "That's mine. It's all they let me have. They wouldn't let me keep that if they knew how to take it away. But if I say to them: I don't hear voices, you've cured me, the voices have gone ... they can't prove anything. That's my freedom. But I suppose they'll develop machines—they always do, you know. They won't be able to stand that, that amount of freedom. So they'll make a machine and clamp it to our heads and they'll be able to say: You're lying, we can measure the shape of the voices on this machine. What are you trying to hide? What do you hear? ..." She swayed, swayed back and forth, in an increasingly rapid rhythm. "But they haven't made that machine yet. I'm still free. I know what I know. You do believe me, don't you?"

"Yes," said Martha.

Threatening, Lynda leaned forward, ready to hit or to strike; her white grubby hand was clenched around an imaginary knife. "Yes, but what do you believe, Martha?"

Her eyes shifted past Martha to the door behind. Martha turned. Mark stood in the door. He looked weary and frightened.

She cackled: "Look at him. He wants me in prison. He doesn't want me to have my freedom. He wants me cured."

"Lynda," he said, desperate—and all wrong. A man, a husband, all warm and responsible, he said: "Lynda, this is Mark!"

At this pressure on her she smiled, became evasive, went inside herself and stood up. Her hand went out to the pills. She was smiling like a disobedient schoolgirl. She pretended to put the pills in her mouth, then let her hand drop and stood shaking with laughter. "You've persuaded me," she said to Martha. "You're right." She now carefully, neatly, soberly, filled a glass with water, swallowed two pills, and put the rest into a cup, with the cigarettes. This she held before her, and went out of the kitchen, carrying the cup with the pills and the cigarettes as if it were a candle. In her old-fashioned frilly nightdress, she looked like a good child going up to bed.

Mark went after her, giving Martha a hasty good night.

Lynda stayed over an extra day, but Francis did not see her again. He was taken off by his grandmother in the big chauffeured car for the other week of his holidays. He took with him a chemistry set, a proper grown-up one, from Martha; a football from his father; and a great heap of toys from his mother, ordered by her on the telephone from Harrods.

Before Lynda went back to hospital, she made another visit to the basement. Martha found her there, telling a workman who was about to put in a cupboard that he was using the wrong kind of wood. If he had any pride in his work, she was saying, he would refuse to use the wood supplied by the foreman, which anyone could see was going to warp inside a year, because it hadn't been properly seasoned. The workman was saying yes, he knew that, but he was only being paid to do the job, it wasn't for him to reason why.

Martha took over the altercation from Lynda; tackled the foreman, who said it was not his fault if the firm chose to do a bad job, then the owners of the firm, who said it was the fault of the workman. As a result of this, and many similar battles, the basement, by the end of January, was at least within sight of being occupiable. Who was going to live in this basement? What the situation needed was some kind of sensible "body"—a young one rather than an old one; but Martha could not see Mark choosing such a one. Phoebe, he said, was sure to come up with somebody: Martha could give Phoebe a ring perhaps?

Martha did no such thing. For, now the flat was ready (well, nearly) and Martha's departure only four weeks off, she was concerned to see that the woman who did come would be good for Francis. Because if one thing was essential, it was to see that Francis left that school of his. He would not be able to do this if there were not the right kind of woman in the house. The housekeeper should be a good deal more than a housekeeper. The flat must be properly tenanted. Martha was imagining how Francis, returning from his sensible, human day school, would come down to this flat to the woman who would live here, for talk, supper, homework—warmth. It was simply a question of getting Mark to see . . .

She faced Mark with it. Or tried to. He countered with being busy, with needing his attention for his work, with irritation, with embarrassment—than finally, in a great burst of explanation, the first time he had been able to say this to anyone, apparently, of how all his childhood he had felt different from other people and he did not want to inflict discomfort on his son.

As has been said, he was the only one of the four not educated normally for his class. The other three boys had gone to public school and university. Mark had been odd man out, a silent, watchful, uncomfortable child—this by nature; and Margaret, currently under the influence of friends who were educational reformers, had sent him to Neill's school. Not for long: it was too extreme, she had decided. Mark remembered enjoying the school, but finding it painful, adjusting that world to his own, when he went for holidays. Margaret had then sent him to a "progressive" school, based on Neill's lines, but less "extreme." There Mark had found his two worlds more easily aligned; but he was still cut off from his brothers; who thought him and his school—any kind of school but their own being beyond the pale—odd, a challenge to them. He tended to go for his holidays, when he could, to school friends. He was seldom at home. Then his father died, the country house was sold, and Margaret married her financier. Mark spent holidays in America. It was there that he had got to know his brother Colin, and the two had become friends. Mark had not gone to university. His education, his experience, had put him at an angle to his class. Now he said he did not want this for Francis, who already had too much to bear.

And he turned his back, picked up a book, and stood looking at the book, his taut back saying simultaneously that he wished Martha to go on, but proposed to resist what she said. She braced herself, and went on, there being no way of bringing up fraught subjects with Mark without barging in, breaking in, battering. Never had she known a man so armoured, so defensive. As pain-laden subjects came near him, his dark face, whose predominant expression was, in fact, one of dogged enquiry, a need to know, to find out, closed up, his mouth tightened, and he turned away.

To his back Martha cried out: "But Mark, what sort of logic or common sense is it! Let alone any decent ordinary humanity! You say you are pleased you weren't sent to a public school, you say being sent to America was the best thing that happened to you—you carry on about the upper classes like a socialist in Hyde Park—and now you are sending Francis through that mill. What for?"

His back still turned, he said: "They have some kind of a strength. I haven't got it. I want him to have it."

"What strength? Who has it?"

"Oh ... some of them. Oh I dare say it's a kind of

narrowness. They're blinkered. If you like. But it is strength. One's got to have something."

His dead brother (and Mark was the last person, as his writing proved, to see a death in war as arbitrary, unconnected with what a person was) has been, when war broke out, on the point of throwing up his job, or jobs, as chairman of companies, to go farming in Kenya. Hardly an evidence of unconformity to his own type, but his reason for wanting to do this was that England was no longer a place to bring children up in, people cared for nothing but making money. The second brother was Colin. Then Mark. Then Arthur, left-winger and regarded by the Coldridge family as not much better than a street agitator.

"Well, all right then," said Mark. His back was still firmly turned to her. "Take Arthur. He talks red revolution all right. But put him beside that Communist Party scum and you see the difference."

"What scum?"

"I wouldn't trust that lot further than I could kick them. But Arthur—well, if he says a thing, you know that's it. You understand? You can trust him."

And now Martha could not reply: he was saying that Arthur was a gentleman.

Unable to reply, she sat down, and waited. As usual, it was long after midnight, and the street outside was quiet. This room was quiet. It had two focuses, or areas of interest. One was the desk with piles of notes, notebooks, a typewriter. The other was a table on which stood all kinds of models, and prototypes, stacks of diagrams and blueprints, to do with the machines made in the factory. Mark's business, started by him after the war, manufactured electronic devices used in hospitals, in medical work generally. He worked with a man called Jimmy Wood. The money made on one or two regular lines was used by them in experimenting and inventing and paying for how the two men seemed to spend most of their time: sitting in the office in the factory talking their way to new ideas.

At last Mark did turn around. It was with an effort. And when he sat down, facing her, he had to make himself.

"I suppose I'm inconsistent?"

"I just keep thinking of Francis crying half the night."

"He's never going to have the ordinary thing, a mother, that kind of thing? So he could have the other thing to hold on to?"

"You couldn't compromise?" she suggested, humorous

through necessity. "I mean, do you have to choose a school that's like a caricature? Aren't there any that aren't like that?"

"My brothers went there."

"Then that's all right then, isn't it?"

"Margaret's on your side. She wanted me to send him to my old place."

"Why didn't you?"

Now he hastily got up and went to the window, to examine the curtains. They had been cleaned. Last time he had made that movement, to evade an emotional point, he had muttered; "They need cleaning." Then he had turned to say: "I have a talent for tragic love affairs." For he had had a couple of hopeless passions before Lynda.

The reason why Mark did not want Francis to go to his own school, the compromise progressive school where, after all, he had been happy, was that in his own mind he was a failure: or so, Martha worked out, was likely. Mark felt he had let his educators down; exactly as he might have felt, had he gone to Eton like his older brother James, if he had embezzled funds. His school was dedicated to emotional balance and maturity—etc. Well, he had not made that grade. If he sent Francis there, Francis would go as the son of a failure: it seemed that Mark felt something like this.

But that talk did bear fruit; for Mark went to see his mother, who came to see Martha. The meeting took place in "Margaret's room"; and Margaret sat on the edge of one of her pretty chairs with her gloves in her hand, and smiled at Martha.

"But you've been so good for Mark. What a pity you have to go off like this!"

"I dare say. But I do have to."

"Of course. What did you say you had to do? I forget."

To withstand this kind of accomplished insolence it was necessary to have had the kind of education Mark was now providing for Francis. To withstand it gracefully, that is. Ungracefully, Martha held out.

"What is Mark writing at the moment?"

"You should ask him."

"Has he done any work since you've been here?"

"But he always does work hard."

"I meant, a new book. Anyone can play about with those electric toys."

"I don't think he sees them like that."

"Hmmm. Well. I do hope you're not going to go off when

he's in the middle of something. People will be asking if that book was just a flash in the pan."

Knowing very well that her silence now must look like a kind of sulk, Martha kept silent.

"Very well then. Let's see what you've been doing with the basement."

Martha was very pleased to see Margaret in the basement flat. For even when it was polished, dusted and arranged, it did not look at all like the rest of the house. It was charming; it was comfortable—and it had no life in it. For rooms to look like those upstairs, it was necessary that a person, after feeling (for months perhaps) that there was something wrong with that chair, that table, should move it two inches, just *there*, where it would catch the light, just *so*, or stand in an exact relation to a rug, a cornice. Martha half expected that Margaret's being in the flat, walking around it, would supply its missing quality.

But Margaret said: "Yes, very nice. It needs to be lived in." And went upstairs again.

Before leaving she said: "Do see that he's not left in too much of a muddle, there's a good girl."

These words, so much more offensive than others she had used, were in fact the most appealing: of such importance is a tone of voice. But they missed the point of what Mark in fact needed from a "secretary"; what his relationship to his work was; and what Martha could contribute to it.

When Martha first came to be his "secretary" and waited for typing work, something of that sort, she found that they were sitting in his study, talking. It took time for her to understand that he was trying to define his own attitudes through other people's—hers, since here she was. Nor did she easily understand how hard it was for him to talk. He prompted and prodded her into words, listened, came back with comments, though sometimes not for days. Partly, this was a way of talking about his life: it seemed he had never had people to talk to. Not at school? Well, yes, but he had had no close friends. Not since? Well, there had been Colin. And of course there had been Lynda and others. "But one doesn't talk to the people one is in love with, does one?" All this Martha found hard, her experience, as good as a dozen universities, having been in the talking shops of socialism.

Mark had asked Martha to read his novel; and it was typical of him that he had not expected her to have read it and to have thought about it. He had, he said, just reread it himself.

This novel, a short one, had been published in 1948. But it had been written in 1946, while Mark was waiting to be demobilised with the occupation forces in Austria. The book had been, as they say, widely noticed. This was because, Mark said, giving the fact without emphasis, he was a Coldridge. Exploring this (unfair! she judged it, in the face of his amusement that she should) it became clear that the literary editors, the reviewers, the people who ran the arts in England at that time, had been at school, or at university with—not Mark, but his brothers, and "knew" Margaret, or at least all knew each other. No literature-fed person comes from outside Britain without expecting to find some marvellous free marketplace of the arts, internationally fed, high-minded, maintained by disinterested devotees drawn from wherever they can be found. All that excellence, the high standards—surely they were not maintained by Tom and Dick and Harry who had gone to school with Mark's brothers and who "knew" Margaret? Well, why not? Mark demanded, when he finally saw that what he took for granted, she took with incredulity. Why not? If it works?

Mark had sent the manuscript from Austria, to Jack, a friend of Colin's, once a guest of Margaret's: he was now the partner in a publishing firm.

He had taken it for granted that the book would be "noticed"; would not vanish, scarcely mentioned, as do half of the novels published in Britain. No, what troubled him was the note, or tone of the reviews: cold, disliking, even hostile. He did not understand the reason for it.

"I suppose they were hedging their bets," he said, scornful. "They never condemn a dark horse—a cowardly lot!"

One reviewer complained that the book had been written as if the war had been over a hundred years, instead of in its miserable aftermath. It was fatalistic, they said. It was pessimistic, it was deterministic. It had no compassion and it was cold.

"It's because you aren't indignant. You aren't shocked."

"What about?"

"Look at the writing that's come out of this war—there isn't much of it as yet, of course. And that's pretty unforgivable in itself—getting a novel out before the guns have even stopped firing. Positively callous!"

"I didn't have anything to do. None of us did."

"But in what has been written, there's a note—protest. Disgust."

"I don't see protest. Things happen."

"And the novels from the First World War. Elegies for lost paradises, or anger."

"Well what's the point of still feeling like that?"

"But you ought to be able to see why other people are offended!"

The novel's attitude was as if humanity (the earth and its people) were a variety of living organism, a body, and war was a boil breaking out on it—and could be expected to break out. It was written out of the attitude, implicit, not described, that war was bound to happen, that nothing could have prevented it, and that forms of war would erupt again. This was not at all the atmosphere of the late forties when governments, politicians, and the press talked, not only as if war, the next one, was preventable, but as if the actions they were engaged in would prevent it.

But Mark saw the activities of press, politicians, and generals as the dust games of children. As he had thrown away in a couple of paragraphs, as being too obvious to need more, throughout the thirties the coming war had been organised, planned for, expected; the nations had intrigued and aligned and deployed and bargained—but the salient fact of that war, the one which had shaped it, no one had foreseen, which was that Bolshevik Russia would be fighting alongside Britain and America. This although the powerful energies of the most powerful groups in our nation and in America had been working in the opposite direction. No need even to develop that: it was so obvious. It had not mattered what they planned, since human beings were the prisoners of events. Yet, the moment the war had worked its way to its end, as a disease runs its course, governments, generals, newspapers, again started making plans, authoritative statements, and prognostications, proving that they were incapable of seeing the most obvious fact when it was in front of their noses. They were not to be taken seriously.

And Mark could not see that this attitude, at that time, was likely to offend. For him it was all self-evident. And Martha, explaining, came to represent that naivety, that inability to draw conclusions from obvious facts, that he found so hard to understand.

Meanwhile, Martha was making a discovery—unexpected. "Matty" was being summoned back into existence. "Matty" had not been in evidence in this house, she had made no appearance. Another person had: and it took time to see that this was merely an aspect of the hydra, Matty. This was—at first Martha christened her "the Communist" but had to widen it to "the Defender," since it was a mask shared, for instance, by Marjorie's sister Phoebe. This person got shrill, exclamatory, didactic, hectoring, and went off at a word into long speeches. "I'm not interested in speeches!" Mark had said, early on in his relationship with this orator. Martha had not been aware she made speeches. Between the clumsy self-denigrating clown and the Defender was a link: Martha was beginning to see it. She had plenty of opportunity for study of it, since the novel stung the Defender into such lively existence.

At Mark's statement that in a hundred years' time (if anyone was alive in a hundred years' time) people would not describe the Second World War as people did in 1950—the year that had just started—Martha said: "Well, of course not."

But they would not judge it as a victory of good over evil, they would not see Hitler's armies as worse than those they fought. They would say, only: War expressed itself thus and thus in the years between 1939 and 1945. Moralising was never more than the justification of willing belligerents.

But here Martha suffered. Mark had, during the last year of the war, seen one of the concentration camps opened— just as Thomas's friend had done, writing Thomas a letter which had been the cause of Thomas's subsequent development. Or so it had seemed.

"What am I supposed to say?" Mark enquired. "Those bloody Huns? Or what?"

"Well what do you say?" demanded Martha.

"If I go on and say something about Russia, we'll swap atrocities. I can't stand that conversation! You say, Gas chambers. I say, Collectivisation of the peasants. You say, Master race. I say, Purges. You say, Freedom. I say freedom. What is the point?"

At which the Defender, night after night, had argued, quoted figures, emphasised, while he sat listening. "So there's no progress, it doesn't matter what attitudes one takes up, one might just as well have fought for Hitler?"

"If one is going to draw up a balance sheet of atrocities— of course."

"What then?"

"That's all."

"Ah no, I've been here before. When? I must have been twenty—not much more. Nothing mattered, a tale told by an idiot. That was a man called Mr. Maynard."

"We've got some second cousins called Maynard. Was he from Wiltshire?"

"*I don't know.* But I do know fighting him was the best thing I ever did."

"Fighting," said Mark with distaste.

"Well then, if that's true why bother about Colin?"

But here it was Mark turned away, fiddled with drawers, pencils, the lamp switch, became angry, bitter. Watching her own enemy personalities at war, she was easier able to see his.

One, that cool observer who was able to see events as they might appear a hundred years from now. Always? Mark had gone through that war able to see it like that? Hmmm—possibly.

And, at the mention of his brother, a cold angry man, the brother to the Defender.

"Progress," muttered this angry man—hardly to Martha, more to himself, a conversation with himself possibly, of the kind one has alone, when other people are asleep. "That's not my thing. I don't care about it. If things do improve, then it's not because one nation fancies itself better or more humane than another. That's a farce—it always was. The way people see themselves—that's for children. Look what's going on now! The Cold War! What a phrase. What kind of thinking is it? The tune changes, from one year to the next—well why not, it always does—but am I expected to take it seriously? Is Colin? Colin's stand is that he was an ally of the Soviet Union for years and during all that time he was fighting to share scientific information—they all were, the scientists . . ."

"Because the governments of this country and America were doing everything not to share it, because they hated being allied to Russia."

"Granted. Of course. But the same went for the Russians. But Colin is a scientist. He's not a politico. He stands for the internationalism of science. So, the tune has changed and suddenly he's a traitor. Well, I stand by my brother."

"Well, it's childish to be upset about words like 'traitor.' "

"Upset! I'm scared stiff. I never thought that would be possible—in this country. As far as I can see Colin isn't scared. As far as he is concerned it's all perfectly clear—they are in the right and that's that." By "they" Mark meant Colin and his superior, the man now awaiting trial. "They say America wants to start a war with Russia. America wants to destroy Russia. Before Russia gets the atom bomb.

Well, of course, America wants to destroy Russia, you've only to read the newspapers. Colin says, it's about Communism. I think, nations need to go to war. If it wasn't Russia it would be another country. But if *they* were able to supply Russia with information about the bomb, so they could make one, Russia would get equal with America, and then America would be afraid to start a war."

"Is that what Colin says he's been doing? Because if so you should keep quiet about it."

"No, it's not what he says he has done. It's what he says is logical. It's his point of view. He's entitled to it."

"All the same, you'd better keep quiet."

"Why? This is my country. Or I used to think so. But what scares me is—that I'm scared stiff. I think words like 'traitor' and 'treason' and all that stuff are childish. Rubbish. They've never been anything but stuff to scare the populace into behaving. Suddenly I'm scared. I read the newspapers from the States—well, they're always going in for pogroms over there, it's part of their thing. But it's starting here. I read our newspapers and see the word 'traitor' in big black letters and I realise I'm cold—literally cold with fright. What about you?"

"Yes." He had never asked her if she would, in Colin's position, hand over information about the bomb to the Russians. He talked around it, and about, coming back to this point where he looked at her, as if waiting for her to clarify where she stood. She had been frightened to: reading the newspapers, which she did, every morning, for hours, left her without courage.

"What it amounts to is, thank God, thank anything you like, that I'm not in Colin's position, believing that it is my duty to give Russia information. I don't think I'd have that much guts."

"Yes. That's about it. There but for the grace of . . . but he's my brother. I'll back him through anything." And, saying this, he was all bitter, locked determination.

Another person came into existence when his mother entered the house. Again a man who turned away—but, Martha judged, some years younger. When Margaret, having telephoned—she never arrived unannounced, because, as she would announce loudly, one ought not to drop into one's grown-up children's houses without warning—emerged from her car, for lunch, tea, or dinner, Mark who had not been able to work before she came, seemed to shrink and grow younger. He was rude to her, or abrupt. She, these days, came to discuss Colin—who was always too busy to see her, she complained. And Mark would say: "I don't know. I have no idea. Well, then, why don't you ask him?" Meanwhile he watched her, with a helpless fascinated look, as if here was force which no act or word of his could propitiate. He behaved, in fact, as if he were about fifteen, a boy newly defending his manhood against his family.

And Margaret complained to Martha that Mark was as stubborn as a mule, as close as a clam. No, she had no intention of putting Martha in any false positions, but that reviewer had put his finger on it—dear Bertie. Martha knew Bertie Worth perhaps? No? He used to visit the old house before it was sold. But Bertie had said in the *Times* that Mark had no moral sense. He lacked a feeling for essential values. And she departed, emphatically.

To return, less emphatically, indeed, with a curious evasiveness, to say she had just the right person to live in the basement. She was a Mrs. Ashe, the widow of a Major Ashe, ex-Indian Army. It turned out she was nearly seventy and difficult. The right person to run that house, to give Francis what he needed? Put thus, Margaret cried out that she was really such a dear old thing. She looked quite extraordinarily guilty. She's up to something—again, Mark said. What?

Margaret retired. Temporarily. Telephone calls and visits pursued the cause of Mrs. Ashe. Why? There was something odd about it, something wrong. They could not define it. Particularly as everything, the texture of life itself, seemed wrong, ugly, with so much hinted at and hidden—waiting to explode. Yes, they were waiting. They were sitting time out. Or, Mark was: Martha only until she must leave.

Before she left, she could at least try and do something about Mark's finances: he asked her to "make suggestions." Mark's father had left money, but not much. The upkeep of this house, which belonged jointly to the three brothers, was paid by Mark, who lived in it. He spent nothing on himself, but Lynda and Francis cost a great deal. And so did Martha and her salary, as she pointed out. But that would not be for long.

The publisher who had been a friend of the family had signed with Mark a contract that conceded nothing to friendship. There had been an advance of £150 and he had earned not much more than that on the war novel before it had stopped selling. He had contracted for three more books on the same terms. A ridiculous contract, which he should not have signed. But he had no agent. A second novel had been begun and abandoned: he had ideas for others. He said he was not particularly interested in writing another book. He was not a writer, he said. He supposed, one day, he would write another book.

The factory made money on the machines for hospitals. It could make more. But Mark said he was not interested in the business from that point of view. If he could not use the profits for what he called "having fun with new ideas" then he wouldn't bother with the factory at all.

If he were able to sell the war novel in America?

An American agent arrived to see Mark, who received her in his study. She was a woman of about thirty-five, well turned out, full of professional friendliness. For her benefit (indeed, one could do no less), Mark offered "the writer" and "the writer's secretary"—Martha.

Miss Sayers sat at ease, conducting with relaxed efficiency this interview which was only one, after all, in a tour of British writers. She said she liked Mark's novel, for what it *was,* but that kind of thing, the protest novel, was dated.

She saw his novel as a protest novel?

War was not a good thing, and therefore a novel about war was a protest novel—her mind seemed to work in this way. Or perhaps she had not read it? At least she was able to use with familiarity the name of the chief character.

Perhaps she was one of the people who don't know how to read. Very few do, after all.

However that was, she explained that the war novel was hard to sell in her country at that time. But she was interested in Mark's second. That was why she was here: she would be so very privileged to think she could handle Mark's second book which she was sure would be an advance on his first. And what was his new book about?

"Life," said Mark, bland, intending to be rude.

"Well," she cried, gaily, "of course, it is bound to be."

But if Mark could give her some idea, she would then be in a position to . . .

"You are an agent, you say?"

"Yes, that is so. And I think you'll find one of the best known."

"I see. Well perhaps it would be better to wait until the book is finished? Otherwise I might find myself altering it in the hope that you might handle it?"

"Well, now, Mark, I really wouldn't like you to think that I'd be capable of putting any pressure at *all* on my authors, but it is true that I feel myself a friend to my authors, I do like to think they take my advice."

"And what might that be?"

Here she began a short lecture, frowning, like a teacher concerned to remember words from notes made. It was a lecture given, that was clear, many times already.

What Mark should understand, said she, was that only second-rate writers dealt with social conditions, or politics, or concerned themselves in any way at all with public affairs or . . .

"Oh I don't know . . . there was Tolstoy, and Balzac, and Dickens, and . . ."

Her face glazed, at the effort of associating these names, "classics" (she had read them?), with her subject.

"All that kind of thing," she insisted with authority. "The real great artist creates truth and beauty from within himself, he deals with the eternal truths . . ." And so on.

It took about fifteen minutes. Mark and Martha listened, in silence, fascinated, to the opinion currently in vogue in America, being put so trippingly in this alien tongue.

Finally she asked if Mark would be prepared to sign a document giving her first refusal of his new book, when finished. She was not prepared to pay anything for this: his return would be, that he had an agent and a friend.

She left, having asked if she could use the telephone: she needed to check if her interview with her next author, a young man from Wales about whom she asked if it were true that he was the finest poet (in Mark's opinion) since Auden, was still viable.

This visit raised interesting questions.

One was: If Mark's novel had been published now, instead of 1948, what reception would it have got? Two, three years, had changed the climate completely. "Out" was humanitarianism, warmth, protest, anger. What was "in" was the point of view put by the able Miss Sayers. Why? Very simple indeed. The "Cold War" was spreading, had already spread, from politics to the arts. Any attitude remotely associated with "Communism" was suspect, indeed dangerous. Few intellectuals had not been associated with the left, in some form of it, during the thirties and the forties. Precisely these intellectuals were now running, in one way and another, the arts. Tom, Dick and Harry, they were now peddling, for all they were worth, a point of view summed up by the slogan "the ivory tower." This was admirable, subtle, adult, good, and above all, artistic. Its opposite was crude, childish, bad, inartistic.

In America a period of political reaction can be foretold as much when publishers and agents and editors, those most sensitive of barometers, talk about Art in capital letters as when panels of psychoanalysts issue statements that political rebellion on the part of the youth is a sign of emotional immaturity. In Britain hard times are on the way when there are rashes of articles on Jane Austen and Flaubert. "Jane Austen vs. Thomas Hardy"; "Flaubert the Master, Zola the Journalist."

"Besides Sappho, Jane Austen and Firbank, who could be deemed fit inhabitants of that ivory tower which . . ."

If the war novel had been published now, it would have fitted neatly inside the ivory tower.

It might even have made some money?

As things were, Mark had an overdraft of £1,000, his bank manager protesting; and large unpaid bills for Lynda's hospital and Francis's school.

Something ought to be done.

Not knowing what, they talked. To good effect, so it turned out.

On a crucial evening they were in his study. It was after twelve. The curtains were drawn in a cold and sodden night. The light was low. Mark, wearing slacks and sweater, lay on his couch—in his place. Martha sat at the desk—hers. They were drinking brandy, were a little tipsy, felt safe for the time, the sense of threat shut out. This was, after all, a warm, gay room. Once it had been a warm and gay house. Mark, seen thus, could be imagined as a warm, easily responsive young man. Even now his face was relaxed, and was smiling as he teased Martha.

"Well, how do you want to live, then? Everything you say, all the time, implies there is another way to live. Did you know that?"

"There isn't, then? Everything has to go on and on, as it does? Nothing better is possible?"

"Very well, then. But you haven't said, you know."

"I don't want to have to split myself up. That's all . . ." He maintained a quizzical smile. "Yes. Any sort of life I've been offered in London—I'd have had to put half of myself into cold storage. Pretend part of me didn't exist."

"And here?"

And now it was necessary to evade, sidestep. Because it was fantastic he could ask at all: a measure of how much of

138

himself was shut away, or, more accurately, put into cold storage with Lynda.

It would not have been necessary to have this conversation with Thomas: she could not prevent herself thinking this.

Several times, late, after one of these evenings of talk and friendship, sex had approached—of course. But not straightforwardly, honestly. Slightly tight, they would have got into bed, enjoyed themselves or not, and in the morning, there would have been a note of apology, even of embarrassment. The point being, that it, love-making, would be because they were a man and a woman sometimes alone in this house. Well, that would have been right with some men. But not with Mark. He did not see this—rather, feel it.

One evening, before Christmas, she had telephoned Jack. A voice she did not know said that Jack was in hospital somewhere in the north. He had trouble with his lungs. No, he did not want his address known. He did not want letters forwarded. Of course not: Jack, all his pride in his body, would not wish to do anything but crawl into a dark hidden place, until it got better.

"Well," he said, and again with the unfair reproach: "You're going off. You're right."

"I'm not what's needed here!"

"Yes, but what is! Oh, very well—I don't want to ... So you're going off to find ... Do you know what it is you're really wanting, Martha?"

And he proceeded to tell her. She was seeking, without knowing it, for the mythical city, the one which appeared in legends and in fables and fairy stories, and (here he laughed at her, but affectionately) it was a hierarchic city, which is why she refused even to consider it. He proceeded to describe it, as clearly as if he had lived there; and she, laughing affectionately at him, who knew this archetypal city so well yet said he believed in nothing but a recurring destruction and disorder, joined him in a long, detailed, fantastic reconstruction which, by the time they had finished, was as good as a blueprint to build.

Great roads approached the city, from north and south, east and west. When they had fairly entered it, they divided it into arcs, making a circling street, inside which were smaller ones: a web of arcs intersected by streets running in to a centre. All these streets were wide, paved with stone, lined by trees. The centre was planted with trees and had buildings in the trees. These were schools and libraries and marketplaces, but their functions were not overdefined. People might teach in the market; and in what looked like a temple, or a place of worship, goods could be bought or bartered for. Carpets for instance, or jewellery, or poems. There was no central building to the city, yet the people maintained that somewhere in it was such a lode-place or nodal point—under the city perhaps; perhaps in some small not apparently significant room in one of the libraries, or off a market. Or it could have been that the common talk about this room was another way of putting their belief that there existed people, in this city, who formed a kind of centre, almost a variety of powerhouse, who had no particular function or title, but who kept it in existence. The city had been planned as a whole once, long ago: had been built as a whole. It had not grown into existence, haphazard, as we are accustomed to think of cities doing. Every house in it had been planned, and who would live in each house. Every person in the city had a function and a place: but there was nothing static about this society: people could move out and up and into other functions, if they wished to. It was a gardened city. A great number of the inhabitants spent their lives in the gardens, and the fountains and parks. Even the trees and plants were known for their properties and qualities and grown exactly, in a relation to other plants, and to people and buildings; and it was among the gardeners, so the stories went, that could be found, if only one could recognise them, most of the hidden people who protected and fed the city.

"And all this," said Mark, stating his position, "went on for thousands of years—until, one day, there was an accident, something as senseless and stupid as an earthquake which swallowed the city, or a meteor from space."

"Oh no," said Martha, stating her position, "around that city, just like all the cities we know, like Johannesburg for instance, grew up a shadow city of poverty and beastliness. A shanty town. Around that marvellous ordered city, another one of hungry and dirty and short-lived people. And one day the people of the outer city overran the inner one, and destroyed it."

Next day Mark did not go to the factory. He sat in his study, and by evening had produced a short story, a sketch merely, of this city. It was for Martha. He was excited by it and so was she. They thought it should be longer. He took back the pages, and went to work.

The second version was quite long—longer than a short

story. In the first version sudden dust storms had buried the city. In the second, outside the central gardened city rose the encircling shadow city of people who looked enviously in at the privileged one. They always talked of attacking it. But they were afraid to—they didn't know why. Centuries passed. The outer city was growing rich and strong. It was even built on the plan of the inner city, in emulation of it. It had gardens and fountains and—a temple, with a hierarchy of priests. But the outer city was not like the inner one, no matter how often or loudly it claimed it was. Inside was harmony, order—joy. Outside people fought for power and money and recognition, there were soldiers, and a constant growing and overthrowing of dynasties based on the army. Then, one of the ruling families wanting an advantage over the others, sent envoys into the centre, asking to buy their secret. But the reply came back that the secret could not be sold, or taken: it could only be earned, or accepted as a gift. The rulers of the outer city were angry: they did not understand this answer. They overran the inner city, killing everyone. They looked for the hidden people, of whom the legends had reached the outer city. They could not find them. When the sacking of the city was complete, a story started, they said among the soldiers, that someone had indeed found an octagonal white room under a library. Something about this room, no one could say what, had made an impression. They tore down the room, pulled up the floor—but there was nothing there. It was empty.

Now the new rulers announced that everything would go on as before: this was the magical city, it was open to everyone. They were going to run it, with their priests and their soldiers.

But of course, they hadn't the secret, and now the old city of the legend became exactly as the outer city had been. But it was from this time that the city in fact reached history—before that it had not been known, except to the people who lived in it and around it. Now it reached a great climax of fame and power; and it spread out into a kingdom and then an empire, which attacked other cities and countries. It had a fine literature, and an art of its own, and was envied for its richness and achievements. And a whole branch of its learning was to do with the history, based on legends which persisted, of the old lost city; and this particular aspect of its culture was in the hands of a priesthood.

In this version the original city was built in a desert, in North Africa perhaps, or in Asia. Nothing but hundreds of miles of sand under a blazing sun. Then the oases became more frequent. Then, starting in the desert, so that the great roads running inwards began, literally, in sand, was the city.

Travellers coming in from the desert found it hard to say when the exact moment was when their feet found the right road. Then trees appeared, on either side; then in the distance, the first houses of the city. For leagues of that dusty travelling, a silent yellow sand, and then the white city, with its sharp black shadow and its shaded gardens, and over it, a blue sky where birds wheeled, into which rose domes and spires and the sounds of voices.

Mark was pleased with the second version, and Martha began to type it. Then he asked her to stop. He wanted to do more work on it. It turned out that he planned to turn it into a kind of novel: something much more worked out, detailed. But she was leaving in less than a fortnight.

She heard that the flat on which she had paid a deposit was not ready. It was in a big new block of flats built on a bombed area near Notting Hill Gate. It was not going to be ready for at least another month.

Francis was going to be home for a half-term. It would be nice if Martha could be there.

Martha suggested that she stay on another month. It was agreed that at the end of March, she would leave.

Meanwhile it was still February. There wasn't very much for her to do. She wrote some business letters, dealt with accounts, kept the house, put linen and cutlery and so on into the basement. A great deal of her time was spent in her room, with the black cat whose attitude so clearly was, as he arched his back under her hand, and settled at the foot of her bed, that she was a visitor, in this, his home.

She was waiting again! Always waiting for something!— So she discovered herself muttering crossly.

On the whole it seemed that her job was to protect Mark— from journalists, from people ringing up on this or that pretext, from anybody who didn't understand the pressure Mark was under.

Which was why she protested when Margaret rang up to say she planned an election party: an election was due in a couple of weeks.

Martha said: "I don't think Mark would feel up to it," and stopped herself from saying: "But don't tell him I said so."

"I dare say," said Margaret, "but I do feel that we ought to try and behave normally, don't you?"

142

Which left Martha to think it over that in this family behaving normally meant holding election parties, for it appeared that Margaret always had them. Then why didn't she hold a party in her own home? As Mark demanded, angrily, when told of the plan. But Margaret felt it would be nicer to have it in London, where people could drop in and out on their way to and from election stations, voting stations, parties at hotels, etc. etc. But this was not the real reason. She had bought a television set, a new toy, and it was not working well in Sussex, for some reason. She proposed to watch the election on television in Mark's house.

This was to be the first real television election.

Margaret arrived with the set and an engineer to instal it. Mark was in Cambridge.

Martha stayed in her room, listening to Margaret's loud and capable voice giving instructions to the engineer. Then she watched the man depart along the pavement below her window. She braced herself, for she knew what was going to happen.

There were steps on the stairs—firm steps. Then a knock on the door—a confident knock. In came Margaret, smiling. The trouble was, Martha rather liked her, once she had got past that enemy the capable middle-aged matron coping with everything by sheer force of long experience.

Oh how hard it is to be a middle-aged woman, who has to stand in for everyone's difficult mother, and who has to take (and return) looks from younger women examining their futures, exactly as one used to do oneself, and who are thinking, *What a short time I've got left*. Oh how tiresome (and how tiring!) to be the target for such complicated emotions, none of which has anything to do with oneself.

Margaret sat on the foot of the bed before remembering that she ought to ask Martha if she could. Remembering too late, she decided to say nothing. But she looked defiant as she stroked the old cat. "Poor old Starkie," she said. "Well, you look pleased with yourself. Really, you are a spoiled beast."

Martha had sat herself on a chair across the room.

"Where's Mark?" demanded Margaret.

"He's in Cambridge."

"He always did this, you know—he gets himself involved."

She was talking as if Colin, her son, were less of a son than Mark?

Continuing, she said: "After all, if Colin is going to insist on being silly, then he shouldn't expect one to—why should be stand up for that man? What's-his-name? He was only working with him, wasn't he?" Here she waited to see if Martha could tell her anything. Martha couldn't. "And of course, Mark has to get into a high horse over it. He always did. Mark's stubborn. So's Colin. In different ways. And of course there's Arthur—he's not likely to be a spy for Russia, that's something, when he hates them so much. So one is thankful for small mercies."

Margaret had once been a fine-boned graceful English beauty like Lynda. She was now a tall, handsome, grey-eyed woman with elegant hands. Martha watched the subtlety of the hands as they caressed the cat. The cat started to purr loudly. Margaret picked the animal up and put her ear to it, like a child, to listen to the purring. But the cat didn't like being picked up, and stopped purring.

"What do you feel about Mark?" demanded Margaret.

And now Martha could not help laughing—out of annoyance, really. Also, she supposed, from affection. Margaret smiled a strained readiness to be told why Martha laughed. She put the cat down; it rolled over and began purring. Margaret stroked the cat. She had tears in her eyes.

The tears were very weakening. "Listen, Margaret. There's just one thing that none of you seem able to see. Mark loves Lynda. I do understand why you all—but there it is."

"But it's ridiculous. It always has been. And before Lynda there was an American, a cousin of Oscar's. Hopeless—a hopeless girl. And she cared nothing about Mark, and he ran around after her like a little dog."

"Well haven't you ever loved anyone ridiculous and hopeless?"

The cat had moved off, and sat licking its ruffled fur to rights.

The grey look Martha now got from Margaret held irritation. Martha recognised it easily as that emotion one feels when another hasn't seen that truth obvious to oneself.

"Yes, I have. I was in love with Oscar. I adored him. But one has to live, you know—one *has* to. I *do* know. I could have stayed married to Oscar. But I don't like—suffering, I suppose. I hate it. Some people enjoy being treated badly. I wasn't Oscar's first wife and I won't be his last—by a long chalk. I'm told the woman he's going to marry is getting the treatment. Just as I did. Look, Martha dear—I really *must*—haven't you any influence at all with Mark?"

The tears poured out, and, as Martha could see, were

unchecked because Margaret had noticed Martha was influenced by tears. Martha was now very angry. Months of resentment came pouring out.

"I know you are much older than me, and ever so experienced, and you've always been able to do exactly as you like. But you seem to me like a little girl. You can't always have your own way. You always have had it, haven't you? You can't stop people doing things just because you think it's not good for them."

Margaret stared at Martha, not so much surprised as wary. Then she turned away her wet face and dabbed at it. Martha looked at a reassuring calm back. Martha had even more strongly the feeling that she was an instrument being played upon. When that face was turned to her again, what look would be placed upon it?

No, she was being unfair. Probably Margaret was acting out of instinct—if that made it any better!

Once again, Martha was sitting in the presence of a strong elderly woman, herself a seethe of conflicting emotions, which she could not control. Sometime she was going to have to learn to control them.

Margaret turned to her a quiet sobered face.

"I don't agree with you," she said. "If someone's doing something that's simply *silly*, you try and stop them. I wish you'd try and stop Mark. He ought to leave the country for a bit. He could take Francis. He might fall in love with someone that's some use."

Martha laughed in resentment. "You can't see that he could never do it? It's not the kind of thing he could do?"

"No. I wish you'd try."

"No. I've got no right—one hasn't. Not unless you get right into something and—get your hands dirty too. Only if you fight."

"And you won't?"

"Why should I? It's not my mess!"

"You want to get married again, I suppose?"

"Oh for goodness sake!" Martha was becoming incoherent. "I don't want to get married for the sake of it! You talk like a—fortuneteller or something."

"Oh! I don't see why? Why not, if that's what you want?"

"Well, one doesn't say, I want to get married, and then go out looking—isn't that what you meant?"

Margaret was almost smiling: she was humouring Martha.

Who now stood up, confronting Margaret. Who stood up, ready to leave. The women were furious with each other.

"If Mark divorced Lynda, it wouldn't make any difference. He'd either go pining after Lynda, or he'd be in love with someone else ridiculous and hopeless. Or you'd think she was. Can't you see that?"

"Well no," drawled Margaret. "Frankly, I don't. But I must bow to your superior wisdom."

At the door she said: "The man's got the television to work. It'll be rather fun, watching it on television." She laughed, and apparently genuinely. She was looking forward to the evening. "In the old days, when I had an election party I had to be careful to keep the left and the right apart—now it's the left and the left. I suppose Colin wouldn't come—he can't, with the case just starting?"

"I don't know."

"Oh well, if you just lump people into a room, they'll have to behave. But I must say, if Colin's coming, then it will be tricky with Phoebe and Arthur and Arthur's wife. I really can't imagine why they hate the bolshies so much when they've got precisely the same aims. If they had their way, this country'd be as bad as Russia—it's not so far off as it is."

With this, she went downstairs again, to arrange drinks and food for her party.

By evening the big room, which Martha had only seen as asleep and shrouded in invisible dust sheets, was full of flowers, and it had a buffet at one end, the television set at the other. Now it presented itself, discreetly festive, as a setting for parties. People started coming early, the attraction being the television set, as much as the election. Most had not got one, or refused to get one, or might get one if this one seemed satisfactory. The set was, in short, the focus of the party, almost its chief guest. Margaret was the only person who adored it. Most people seemed apprehensive: in fact one could more or less work out someone's political bias from the attitude he took towards television.

By ten or so there must have been fifty people in the room in an atmosphere rather like a sweepstake, or the races—and although outside this room, which imposed a truce, they stood for violent antagonisms. Bets were being made, victories and defeats were cheered or booed, everything went on in the greatest good humour.

The Tories were represented by Margaret herself, and by a man who made an appearance early, a formally good-mannered quiet man who was taken down by Margaret to see the basement. Another tenant for it who she thought would be suitable? The man, Mr. Hilary Marsh, was easily overlooked and not remarked much by Martha: afterwards she wished she had paid more attention. There was also strongly present the spirit of Margaret's first husband; and for her sake even opponents hoped that the Conservative who now held his seat would continue to hold it: he did. The Conservative people held the view that five years of Labour government had ruined the country by the introduction of red and ruinous socialism, but the electors (they hoped this evening) would see their mistake and where their ingratitude towards their natural governors had led them, and reintroduce the Conservatives.

That section of the Labour Party which actually held the reins—a couple of Ministers were present—was represented by Margaret's present husband, John, a pleasant man, without much force but with nothing to dislike about him either. He was smilingly attentive to the guests (Margaret's rather than his, one could not help feeling) and kept the television set working. There was something about him damped down, held back, kept in check—whatever he was, there was a slight uneasiness, hard to put your finger on. Martha felt it: he presented to her the surface of an extraordinary control, while he asked the politest kind of question about Mark's well-being, about Colin. She was pleased when he moved on.

These, the Labour incumbents, held the view that the country had been in such a bad condition after the war, and particularly after years of Tory rule, that they could not have been expected to do better than they had: and that most of their election pledges had remained unfulfilled through no fault of theirs. "The country" (a phrase that resounded all evening) would understand this and return them to power with a larger majority than before.

The Labour left was represented by Phoebe, by Phoebe's ex-husband Arthur, and by his present wife, Mary. Phoebe arrived early with her little girls, pretty blonde creatures excited by being up late for the first time in their lives. His wife came early with the two children from the new family. Phoebe and Mary, who were great friends, and had been for many years, together greeted Arthur, who arrived late with a great mass of supporters. He had kept his seat in South London, with a reduced majority. They were all very excited, and he was a hero that evening. Martha wondered if yet again she would be faced with a shape of flesh like one already known (Mark, Colin, the picture of their dead father) whose spirit was yet utterly different; but Arthur did not look like his brothers, or his father. He was a vigorous-looking man, with an open face, blue eyes open to enquiry, a rocky, rugged craggy man. An agitator. An orator. A troublemaker. His half hour's visit did in fact cause some tension in the general well-being, and people seemed pleased when he left, taking with him his wife, his children; and his previous wife and her children. These, the Labour left, all believed that a Labour government in power after such a war and after years of Tory misrule needed to be what it was accused of being by people like Margaret and practically the entire press—vigorously socialist. They despised the larger part of the party they belonged to for cowardice, pusillanimity, for being unsocialist. They believed, however, that the electorate would vote back the Labour Party, because of the existence, in the Labour Party, of people like Arthur, who might yet force it to be what it should be.

Mark was not there. Colin was not there. Invisibly and very strongly present that night was "Communism"—a threat. Everyone knew that Mark was with his brother and that his brother was in bad trouble. People either asked sympathetically after them, or—mostly—did not mention them at all.

If Mark and Colin represented Communism, then they represented the view that the Labour Party had always been, would always be, could never be anything else but, a function of capitalism, the force, or trend, in the British nation which made capitalism work, saved it, bolstered it—and could be no more than that even if the Labour Party were composed entirely of Arthurs. (Who, of course, hated the Communists, local and international, with a bitter passion.) The Labour Party had got in because, capitalism (the Tories) being in a jam after the war, it was the right time for it to get in. It had fulfilled none of its election pledges because it could not possibly do so—only a Communist government was in a position to change anything radically. And here presented itself an interesting paradox, or political anomaly. For a century at least Communism had defined socialist non-Communism as bound to fulfil this function; the fatalism, the determinism, which is so oddly rooted in that revolutionary party's heritage must have it that Labour, or social democracy, by its nature could do no more than what capitalism would allow it do. Q.E.D. Why, then, so much abuse, the gutter criticism, the emotionalism—why such a crying out against that inevitably behaving and conditioned

148

function, the Labour Party? One might almost believe it a form of love, or of hope; as if, rooted right there, at the heart of an "inevitability," of something determined, there had always been, in fact, half a hope that perhaps, after all—the Labour Party could be socialist.

Among the guests there was also, but not for long (politics bored him, he said) Jimmy Wood, Mark's partner. He was a short fair man. Wispy. He had soft baby's hair on his overlarge head. He had a carefully kept, almost scared smile. He moved about, with a glass of whisky in his hand, listening, and looking, always on the edge of a group, always with his half-smile. He did not look at the television set, only at the other guests, and as if he were a stranger doomed to be one. He talked briefly to Martha, smiling, or rather grinning, and clutching his glass. He wore strong spectacles. Behind them were small strained-looking eyes. Mark said he was a variety of scientific genius.

Half though the evening Mark called from Cambridge to say that Martha should get James's room ready for Sally: she was coming back with him. Paul too.

Martha therefore was away from the party for some time. When she returned, they were saying that even if Labour did get back, it must be with a reduced majority. Margaret and some Tory friends who had come in from a nearby hotel drank to the defeat of the reds (Labour). Those "reds" near them drank an opposition toast—everything was very jolly. Mark had sounded harried, even rather frightened. Jimmy Wood went, on hearing that Mark would not be there for at least two hours. Mark said that Jimmy and he talked—days at a time. Mark said Jimmy was a lonely man; and so little given to talking about personal affairs he did not know to this day if he were married.

In the room were two new people. Young men. One was Graham Patten, John's son by a former marriage. He had a friend with him. Both were in their last year at Oxford. They stood on the side of the noisy scene and despised it. They were also at pains to despise television. Politics were unfashionable among the undergraduates of Britain at that time: Graham and Andrew thought politics were derisory. Dandyism was fashionable: they wore embroidered waistcoats and would not surrender their cloaks, one black lined with scarlet, one scarlet lined with leopard skin. They both maintained supercilious smiles, until someone, unable to stand their frustration, went up to them, when they delivered themselves of a great many observations on a large variety

149

of subjects. They were a bit better when they got drunk, if not very endearing.

Margaret was heard to apologise for them: they would grow out of it, she said.

Mark had told Martha that he would take Sally and the child straight up to the room. She listened for him to come in, and went quietly out into the hall when he did. But Margaret was there seeing some guests out. Afterwards Martha kept the clearest picture of their brief scene.

At the door were a group of noisily tipsy people on their way back to the hotel where they proposed to celebrate Labour's so greatly reduced majority. Margaret was saying "Goodbye! Goodbye!" to them; but she was watching Mark, who stood on the stairs with Sally-Sarah, who had Paul in her arms. By Margaret was Hilary Marsh, observing them all—a quietly smiling, unnoticed man. Sally-Sarah looked ill. The little boy had his thumb in his mouth and stared over his mother's shoulder with large blank shocked eyes. The two were wrapped in a travelling rug Mark had taken from the car. In this cheerful din (the noise from the big room was shattering, when one listened to it from outside) they had the look of refugees, of people in flight.

Mark summoned Martha with his eyes. She went to Sally-Sarah while Margaret came forward saying: "Sally! Is Colin here? What's the matter?"

Martha led the two up and away from Margaret and her party, while Mark stayed. Sally-Sarah was quite passive. She was trembling. In the big bedroom on the second floor, she stood until Martha suggested she might sit; and sat, staring until Martha said she might like to get into bed. Martha took the child and undressed him. Sally-Sarah was undressing herself like an automaton. Offered tea, coffee, milk, she did not hear. Martha put Sally-Sarah and Paul in the same bed.

When she left them, Sally-Sarah had not said one word.

Downstairs the big room was emptying fast, because of Mark's presence. He stood with his back to a wall, grave, anxious, looking past the two undergraduates who stood in front of him. It was now clear why they had come to this party: to meet the writer. It appeared that some tutor or teacher had said that Mark's novel was influenced by Kierkegaard. Andrew had his clever young face, now rather flushed by drink, close to Mark's, and he was unloading a series of observations: he did not agree with the tutor, it seemed. He was explaining to Mark why the novel was to be compared with Stendhal's *The Red and the Black*. Mark was

150

not listening. Close to this group Hilary Marsh stood, observing. Martha went forward to rescue Mark. She listened while the two young men, unwillingly accepting her as substitute, continued their ingenious literary game, their eyes not on her, but past her, on Mark. Hilary Marsh was expressing concern to Mark about his brother Colin. After a few moments Mark said: "Yes. Yes. Excuse me . . ." and went out of the room.

It now occurred to the two young men that Mark might be upset about his brother Colin, whose name had been all over the newspapers that day. Colin's principal, the man with whom he had worked for years, had been sentenced to fourteen years in prison for giving scientific information to the Russians. When Martha left the party finally they were being witty about spies to Hilary Marsh, who, it seemed, was quite prepared to listen to them.

Upstairs Martha found Mark in Sally-Sarah's room. She was not asleep. She was curled up in bed, like a child, her child asleep beside her. Her eyes were shocked.

She said, "Thank you. Thank you. You are very kind. Thank you. Thank you."

Mark and Martha left her.

"I'll tell you in the morning," said Mark. "I must get rid of . . ." He went downstairs.

Next day Mark stayed in his room. Sally stayed in her room. Martha kept buying newspapers. Late that afternoon it was announced that Colin Coldridge son of—etc., etc., brother of the writer Mark Coldridge, and of Arthur Coldridge the well-known left-wing member of Parliament—had fled the country, presumably to Russia, leaving behind him his wife and his son.

Martha took this newspaper to Mark. "Did you know?" she asked.

"I knew he was going to."

"Are we to look after Sally?"

"I don't know. I suppose so."

"Didn't he say anything about her?"

"I didn't see him yesterday. I couldn't get hold of him. I had a telephone call from him in the hotel. He was in a call box. All he said was, that he would be away from a time. He rang off."

Sally-Sarah came down to supper with her little boy. She wore her purple-and-gold-striped dressing gown. On the whole she seemed composed. The telephone rang continuously from Mark's study, but they were not answering it. Outside the house, newspapermen stood in groups. They did not tell Sally-Sarah this, but after supper she went to a window and looked out at the group of men in their raincoats, with their cameras and their notebooks.

She then asked Mark and Martha if they would look after Paul for a day. She wanted to go back to Cambridge to fetch some things. They dissuaded her: she must not go by herself, they said. She appeared to agree. Late that night going up to see if she needed anything, they found she had slipped out of the house, though it was hard to see how she had done it without alerting the newspapermen.

In the morning Martha got Paul up and told him stories. His mother had gone back to fetch something; his father had gone for some work somewhere. Paul was not concerned about his father: he had seen so little of him. He asked once or twice about his mother, but on the whole played quite happily.

When Sally did not come back by lunchtime, Mark telephoned the flat in Cambridge. There was no reply. Shortly afterwards, as Mark was preparing to go to Cambridge to find her, the police telephoned. Sally-Sarah had gone to the flat, and gassed herself. She had left no message—nothing.

And now, though there was no need at all to say it, Mark said: "You can't go, Martha. I don't see how you can?"

"No," she said.

"I don't think Colin intends to come back. He never *said* anything—not directly. But I understand some things I didn't at the time."

Martha rang up the estate agent to say she would not be taking the flat, now nearly ready. The churlish gracelessness that was the spirit of the time spoke through him as he said: "Well, if you don't want the flat, there are plenty that do. You do realise your deposit isn't returnable?"

Life frayed into a series of little copings-with; dealings with; details, details, journalists; newspapers; telephone calls; threatening letters.

Paul had to be looked after, Francis had to be told—something. What?

One thing became clear at once. Mark was going to be isolated. By refusing to condemn his brother, or inform, or to "co-operate" with the police (very insistent they were that he should) he was tarred with Colin—a traitor.

Margaret rang up. Having enquired about Paul she then started talking about the flat downstairs. Mark said his mother must have become unhinged by the crisis. She wanted Mrs. Ashe, the widow from India, to live in the flat. She wanted this, apparently, so much, that she was prepared to bring Mrs. Ashe herself, and settle her in. She went on ringing up about Mrs. Ashe and the basement until Mark lost his temper.

She then wrote a letter about Mrs. Ashe. It was an extraordinary letter, entreaty, threat, apology—Martha was ready to agree that Margaret was temporarily off-balance.

But they did not have time to worry about Margaret.

Mark said: "I think it's going to be a bad time."

It was already a bad time, all muddle and misery and suspicion and doubt.

PART TWO

However, the Man Without Qualities was now thinking. From this the conclusion may be drawn that it was at least partly not a personal matter. What then was it? The world going in and out, aspects of the world falling into shape inside a head.... Nothing in the least important had occurred to him. After he had been dealing with water by way of example, nothing else occurred to him but that water is something three times as great as land, even if one takes into account only what everyone recognises as water—rivers, seas, lakes, and springs. It was long believed to be akin to air. The great Newton believed this, and most of his ideas are nevertheless still quite up to date. In the Greek view the world and life originated from water. It was a god, Okeanos. Later water sprites, elves, mermaids and nymphs were invented. Temples and oracles were founded on its banks and shores. But were not the cathedrals of Hildesheim, Paderborn and Bremen built over springs?—and here these cathedrals were to this day. And was not water still used for baptism? And were there not water lovers and apostles of nature cures whose souls had a touch of peculiarly sepulchral health? So there was somewhere in the world something like a blurred spot, or grass trodden flat. And of course the Man Without Qualities also had modern knowledge somewhere in his consciousness, whether he happened to be thinking about it or not. And there now was water, a colourless liquid, blue only in dense layers, odourless and tasteless (as one had repeated in school so often that one could never forget it again) although physiologically it also included bacteria, vegetable matter, air, iron, calcium sulphate and calcium bicarbonate, and this archetype of all liquids was, physically speaking, fundamentally not a liquid at all but, according to circumstances, a solid body, a liquid or a gas. Ultimately the whole thing dissolved into systems of formulae that were all somehow connected with each other, and in the whole wide world there were only a few dozen people who thought alike about even as simple a thing as water; all the rest talked about it in languages that were at home somewhere between today and several thousands of years ago. So it must be said that if a man just starts thinking a bit he gets into what one might call pretty disorderly company.

THE MAN WITHOUT QUALITIES, ROBERT MUSIL

One

A bad time is announced by an event. A woman gasses herself because her will to survive is exhausted. This event is different in quality from previous events. It is surprising. But it should not have been surprising. It could have been foreseen. One's imagination had been working at half-pressure ... Martha had been here before.

When a bad time starts, it is as if on a smooth green lawn a toad appears; as if a clear river suddenly floats down a corpse. Before the appearance of the toad, the corpse, one could not imagine the lawn as anything but delightful, the river as fresh. But lawns can always admit toads, and rivers corpses ... Martha had been here before.

When Sally said she was going back to her flat for a day or so, leaving her little boy, that was so unlike her, so improbable, that if Martha had been alert, she would have—but what? Called the police? The doctors? There was no set of words which Martha could imagine herself using. "Sally, you're not thinking of . . . ? Oh, please don't!—You'll feel better in a few days ... Lie down for a little and we'll get you a sedative. Sally, you're a coward! How *can* you think of ... And what about your little boy, he won't be able to live without you . . ."

(People are infinitely expendable, feel themselves to be, or feel themselves to be *now*.)

"Sally, we'll lock you up until you come to your senses!"

Sally had gone back to her flat to become Sarah. What had she really felt when the family which had taken her in had done so only under the passport of Sally? "They've always called me Sally," she said, once, exchanging with Martha a look which the family itself could not be expected to understand. If she had refused to be Sally, had insisted on remaining Sarah, would she then have had to make the journey alone to her empty home where she could turn on the gas?

Before that double event, Colin's departure, Sally's death, the quality of life was different; seemed almost, looking back

on it, as—no, not happiness. Happiness, unhappiness, these
were not words that could be used anywhere near this family,
every member of which held the potentiality for—disaster?
But that had been true before the double event. How then
had it been possible for Martha to feel that "the holding
operation" could in fact hold off what had been so loudly
heralded? Something had been bound to give. Yet to look
back from the day after Sally's death, to even the day before
it, it was as if a bomb had gone off.

So a war begins. Into a peacetime life comes an announcement, a threat. A bomb drops somewhere, potential traitors
are whisked off quietly to prison. And for some time, days,
months, a year perhaps, life has a peacetime quality, into
which warlike events intrude. But when a war has been going
on for a long time, life is all war, every event has the quality
of war, nothing of peace remains. Events and the life in
which they are embedded have the same quality. But since it
is not possible that events are not part of the life they occur
in—it is not possible that a bomb should explode into a
texture of life foreign to it—all that means is that one has
not understood, one has not been watching.

And, the bomb having exploded, the heralding (or so it
seems) event having occurred, even then the mind tries to
isolate, to make harmless. It was Martha's concern, and
Mark's, to try and minimise the double event, as if they felt
it to be an isolated thing, without results, as if it had had no
causes. Or at least, that was what it seemed they felt; for
with the little boy Paul playing upstairs, his mother dead, his
father gone, they were discussing how to soften and make
harmless. "How to break it"—as Mark put it.

Paul was going to be six next week. He had plans for his
birthday. His mother had talked of a party. Some sort of a
party there must be.

"Is my mother going to be here?" asked Paul.

"I expect so," said Mark, and turned away from the child's
acutely fearful black eyes. Paul had never been separated
from his mother, not even for one day. And now his uncle
said: "I expect so," Paul became very gay, manic. He rushed
all over the big house, bouncing on the beds, teasing the cat,
standing to look out of all the windows, one after another.
Through one of them, he would see his mother come. He
turned, saw Mark and Martha watching him; and pulled the
heavy curtains so that he was hidden from them. He took
the black cat to bed with him, where he hugged and kissed the
beast, which suffered it. But he did not like Martha touching

him, nor Mark. Particularly not Mark. He was not used to contact with a man; his father having been kindly, but concerned (he had even said so) to make up for the emotionalism of the unfortunate Sally-Sarah by being cordial but restrained.

Mark and Martha were prisoners in the house, because the reporters patrolled outside. Paul asked to go for a walk. He did not say that he hoped to catch a glimpse of his mother in the streets. He was told that no one was going for walks. Through the windows he saw men trying to peer in; and asked who they were. He tried to slip out of the back door, but found a smiling man on the doorstep, who frightened him. He stood outside the study door, listening to Martha answering the telephone. No, Mr. Coldridge was not in; no, he could not come to the telephone; no there was no comment about Mr. Coldridge's brother.

"Is Mr. Coldridge's brother my daddy?" he enquired.

The exchange was asked to alter the number. This was done; and for a couple of days there was peace. But then a reporter got the new number from Jimmy Wood at the factory. Jimmy Wood had been asked not to give it. In explanation he said that the man sounded "as if he really wanted it." The number was changed again. Jimmy was again asked not to give it. But he did: he thought, explained, that the man asking for it was an electronics expert. After all, he had said he was. Jimmy's part through the long siege was simply—not ever to understand it. Mark asked Jimmy to come to the house, so it could all be explained to him. He must be careful of the journalists, he was told. He arrived at the front door, and was enclosed by a group of news-hungry men. To them, smiling, he told everything he knew. Not much, not more than Mark knew; but affable and willing, he chatted, and entered the house, still smiling. But then, he always smiled. Some time in his life he had decided that life must be faced with this smile, and he never switched it off. A defence? An explanation? Who knew? But this small, wispy man with his great head covered in baby hair—smiled, as if he could not help it. They said to him: Please be careful, please don't expose us, please don't talk to the press, and he smiled. Almost at once he began talking about affairs at the factory. It seemed he could not see the necessity for all this fuss.

But he agreed, not so much impatiently, as with tolerance, not to give the telephone number to anyone at all.

For a while, then, it was quiet. But Margaret telephoned

from her country home. She had not been near them since the election party. She was concerned about Francis. "You ought to get him back home," she said. "He must be having a dreadful time at that beastly school."

"But it would be worse here with the journalists."

"You think so? I don't know. Mark could get rid of them, easily, if he wanted to."

"Yes, but I don't think he'd want to do that."

"You ought to make him."

"Perhaps you'd like to talk to him?"

"No. No. I really haven't got any more patience with . . . Have you let the basement?"

"The basement!"

"Mrs. Ashe still wants it."

"But Margaret, for God's sake . . ."

Margaret had sounded embarrassed, about the basement. Now she hurried on: "But he always was so wrong-headed. Always."

"I think you ought to be discussing that with him."

"Well, yes, but—and don't forget about Mrs. Ashe, I must really ring off, I'm really very . . ." She rang off.

This was so odd, struck such a discordant note, that Martha was unable to think about it, forgot to tell Mark.

It was Mark who took the next call from his mother.

Margaret had telephoned Francis's school, and the head-master said Francis was all right. As far as he knew the news had not reached the school. "But he's such a fool," Margaret said. "I asked him if he banned the newspapers there and he said, he was sure his boys understood the meaning of *esprit de corps*."

"Perhaps you could take Francis for a week or two?"

"Oh, I don't know—anyway, I'm off to America next week."

"You could take him until then, couldn't you?"

"I don't really think . . ."

She then went on to talk about Mrs. Ashe.

Mark said he really hadn't time to worry about being a landlord, and rang off. It was so extraordinary of Margaret that Mark, like Martha, let it slide.

Paul had listened to this from outside the study door.

"Why should Francis go and live with his granny?" he asked.

"She's your granny too."

"No. She isn't. She doesn't like my mummy."

"Well, it would only be for a little time."

She tried to pick him up. He was a heap of heavy limbs. The black frightened eyes, already lit by cunning, held Martha's face, while he held himself rigid in her arms. She put him down.

"I don't want Francis's granny to come to my party."

"She's not coming."

His birthday was the day after the next.

"I want my party, I want my party," he sobbed, from the floor. He was saying, I want my mother.

Next morning, Martha put on a headscarf, and Mrs. Van's old coat, and got out of the house by eight in the morning, by the back door. Only two journalists had arrived, and they were at the front of the house. She went across London to Harrods, and bought a cake and presents for the party. When she arrived at the back door, it looked unoccupied. But before she could get in, a man ran up.

"Who are you?" he demanded.

"I work for Mr. Coldridge. I do the cleaning."

She had the key in the door, but she was gripped by her other arm which clutched parcels.

His face was alive with suspicion, but also with the delights of the chase.

"What's going on in there?"

"I don't know. I'm just the cleaner."

The clothes were right, but her voice was not. His face was hard, self-righteous. He was a man seeking to unmask evil. He took five pounds from his pocket. He hesitated. Five pounds was more than enough for a charwoman, but not for a friend or mistress or fellow-conspirator of Mark Coldridge. Hesitating, he lost his force of purpose; Martha slipped her arm away, and shot indoors, scattering parcels onto the floor of the kitchen. Through the back window his face appeared, in an angry teethbared scowl. Framed thus, emphasised, it was almost—yes, funny. He looked like a bad actor in a melodrama: my prey has escaped.

One of the aspects of a bad time, before one has entered into its spirit, is that everything has a feel of parody, or burlesque. Martha stood in the kitchen, looking at the ugly, threatening face, and had to suppress laughter. Nervous laughter, certainly, and when he shook his fist at her, it was ugly and she was afraid. That evening, among the pile of newspapers that came from the newsagent, brought past the reporters by the newsagent's boy, was one which carried a story about a mysterious woman, who had entry to Mr. Coldridge's house, and who would not give her name.

Next day was the birthday. In the morning Paul was given presents, which he opened, Mark and Martha watching. He tore through them, throwing them aside, one after another: he was looking for evidences of his mother. He had not mentioned his mother for some days. Clearly the birthday had become for him the talisman which could produce his mother. The presents had not, but there was still the party.

After breakfast he went to Mark's study and stood by the desk watching Mark pretending to work. By now they were waiting for him to ask: Where is my mother, so that they could tell him the truth. Which they should have done before. But the right time had gone past, and they did not know what to do. Everything was wrong, the "party" absurd, the presents a mistake.

But now they did not know how not to have the party.

Martha laid a party-spread on the table in the dining room. But Paul demanded that it should be in the kitchen. Nothing came in the front door, only sheaves of newspapers, falling through the letter slot. But the back door could admit. It was through the back door that he expected his mother.

Martha spread out the cake, with its six candles on the kitchen table, and some biscuits and little cakes. While Martha moved about in these pathetic preparations, Paul stood just inside the kitchen door, watching them. Mark, trying to engage Paul's attention, played with a wooden train on the floor. From time to time the two grown-up people exchanged glances of helplessness, and of shame, because things could have been allowed to reach this point.

There was a heavy knock on the back door; and the little boy, crying "There she is! There's my mummy!" rushed to open it. Two men stood there. One was the journalist of yesterday, looking angrily sullen. The other was a large smiling man.

"Where's my mummy?" shouted Paul.

The two looked at each other, then studied Martha, arranging cakes, and Mark, playing trains.

The large man said: "Take it easy, son, take it easy. Your mummy's not coming, you know."

"Why not, why not?" screamed Paul, and flung himself down. Lying face down, he banged his head hard on the floor while his face exploded tears.

"Is this Colin Coldridge's boy?" asked the sullen man, bending to examine him for describable details.

Mark now scrambled up off his knees, and advanced on the journalists. Yesterday's man was suspiciously angry. The large man was smiling, ingratiating. The child continued to bang his head, crying noisily. Mark, with his eyes wide, his mouth open, his face white, appeared comic.

"Take it easy," said the large man again, and backed away, in a parody of fear: he was making fun of Mark.

The self-righteous man was now making mental notes about the kitchen. Having done this, he returned his attention to Paul, who was writhing at his feet, and said accusingly: "Why didn't you tell the boy about his mother?"

At which Paul shot off the floor and grasped his uncle around the knees, so violently that Mark staggered and leaned sideways to catch hold of a chair back. "Tell me what?" screamed Paul. "Where's my mummy?"

"Your mummy's . . ." The journalist stopped, unable to say "dead" to the child's face.

With a mutter of inarticulate disgust, he backed out of the door. The goodfellow, smiling deprecatingly, said· "Here's my card." He laid a piece of card on the table by the cake. *Miles Tangin. The Daily*——— "If you'd cooperate, Mr. Coldridge," he suggested, "then it would be better."

"I'll complain to your editor," said Mark over Paul's head. The child was sobbing noisily, and gripping Mark's knees, so that Mark had to hold himself upright with one hand on the chair back while with the other he tried to soothe Paul.

"You do that," said the first man, all contemptuous bitterness.

The two went out together.

Mark carried the sobbing child up to bed.

In bed he was quieter, whimpering a little, while he watched them both. He was waiting.

"Where is my mummy?" he asked at last.

Martha said: "She's dead, Paul."

Paul took it. It was a fact which marched with the events of the last week.

"And is my daddy dead too?"

"No," said Mark, with emphasis. But both he and Martha knew that of course he would not believe them. They had been lying to him: they were probably lying again.

"He's away," said Martha. "He'll come back."

Paul said nothing. He lay staring at them, with his black untrusting eyes. Then he turned his face to the wall, and shut them out. They stayed with him. Hour after hour passed. He was not asleep. He kept dropping off, but he whimpered in his sleep, and this woke him. It was nearly morning when at last he fell into a deep sleep.

Their days were now spent with Paul, the child who could not trust them. He had gone silent, evasive, listless. He spent hours curled in a chair in the kitchen, sucking his thumb. He usually did not answer when Martha or Mark spoke to him. This did not look as if he were trying to be a baby again, wanting to be fed; but as if he really could not take in the existence of food, of mealtimes. He would sit listening, or apparently listening, if they read to him or told him stories. He sat quietly for the children's programmes on the radio. Put to bed, he slept. When he looked out of the back windows, the front windows, and saw the groups of reporters waiting there, he examined them, then looked at Mark or Martha for explanations. It seemed he was afraid to ask questions. But they wouldn't have known how to answer.

In the evenings the two sat in Mark's study. Mark's white face had acquired a staring masklike look; as if wide-eyed at the incredible, the impossible. He did not believe what was happening. This was because he was Mark Coldridge, to whom such things could not happen.

Yet he was also Mark Coldridge who had written that book about war which came from the heart of an understanding of how such things happened—must happen. Martha was waiting to talk to the man who had written that book: but he was not there.

Mark was saying things like: "We must get Paul to school so that he can get over it." Or: "When it's blown over, I'll take Francis and Paul for a holiday somewhere."

He was still talking in terms of a situation normal enough to blow over. He could not bear to see that a deep harm had been done; and that they, or at least he, must expect the results of it, and that the results were for life.

But how could Martha blame Mark when she caught herself thinking several times a day: Before Sally killed herself, before Colin went away—the double event which her nerves, geared to laziness, still felt as a watershed. And it was as much her fault as Mark's that Paul had not been told the truth (as much truth as could be told to a child of six) so that now he trusted no one; it was as much her fault that the affair had been handled so that the truth had come through journalists scavenging for news.

And what was the use of feeling guilt, blaming herself and Mark, when they still did not know how to act, still sat night after night in the quiet book-lined study, with a decanter of old brandy on the desk, and when they did act, absurdity or

164

worse came of it. For they had lost a sense of the ordinary machinery of life.

One afternoon they had watched through the windows a couple of press men rummaging through their dustbins in search of incriminating documents.

One of them was Miles Tangin. Mark telephoned the editor to protest, could not get through, left a message that he would like to be rung back, was rung back by—Miles Tangin. The telephone number then had to be changed again.

Martha suggested that he should ask the police to guard front and back entrance, to keep the journalists off.

Mark was furious. "I'm not being guarded by police in my own house in my own country because of a lot of . . . I'll get Margaret to tell the editor what's going on. She must know him."

He rang his mother's home in the country. It was only when it had been ringing for some minutes that they realised it was after two in the morning. After a long wait, John came to the telephone. He was polite, of course. Mark spoke to the colourless husband of his mother, a man whom he despised, though of course, he had never been anything less than polite to him. Martha sat on an old brown sofa, feeling velvet rub soft under her fingers. She was watching Mark clutch the telephone as if the machine itself could come up with sense, or protection. In the last couple of weeks he had lost over a stone. His clothes were hanging on him. His fingers were stained with nicotine to the knuckles. He looked half crazy.

John said that Margaret was asleep after a hard day. The press had been out to the house, and the telephone was never silent.

"I want to speak to her," said Mark.

"I'll tell her in the morning that you rang."

"Then tell her to get hold of those editors and call off their dogs," said Mark.

A short affronted laugh.

"Perhaps if you were prepared to make some sort of announcement to the press?" suggested Margaret's husband.

"What announcement would you suggest?"

Another short laugh. "As things stand, your mother, my wife, is the mother of a man who has escaped behind the Iron Curtain, suspected of being a spy, and of another who refuses to disassociate himself from him."

"But he happens to be my brother," said Mark. Again, he

sounded incredulous. It was precisely here: what he could not believe was happening, or could happen—to him.

"But what can they expect me to do?" he asked Martha again. And he listened with his wide fascinated look as if this time he might understand what previously he had failed to understand.

She said, again: "They expect you to make a public announcement that you repudiate your brother and all his works. And to make a public affirmation of loyalty to this country."

"But good God," he said softly, "I mean—but they can't— but this is *this* country, it's not . . . I mean, the Americans or the Russians or people like that, but not . . ."

He was looking at her with dislike.

"Don't tell me that's what you think I should do! He's my brother," he insisted. As if it were she who was his enemy.

"You keep asking me what they want."

His eyes were hot and dark with refusal. He sat locked in himself. Then he understood he was making an enemy of an ally, smiled, though stiffly, and poured her a brandy.

"I'm sorry," he said.

Next morning Margaret rang. It was very early. Mark was half asleep. He came up to Martha's room to say that he thought his mother had gone mad. She had telephoned about the basement and about Mrs. Ashe.

They could not understand it. Martha said that this was perhaps Margaret's way of preserving normality. She was probably right: to worry about letting basements was better than what they were all doing. It was even reassuring of her.

As they spoke, the telephone rang again. Mark went to it. Mark did not come back, so Martha went down to him. He was sitting, looking very white, by the telephone.

Margaret's second call was hysterical. She had shouted that Mark was ruining her life. The very least he could do was to have Mrs. Ashe. On being asked please, to explain Mrs. Ashe, Margaret had muttered, after a silence, something about Hilary Marsh—restoring confidence in that quarter. And at last it had all become clear to Mark, but so suddenly that he had simply put down the receiver.

Hilary Marsh, the correct unnoticed gentleman from the election party, had been Margaret's friend for many years. He was in the Foreign Office. Weeks ago he had been to Margaret, to ask what she knew about her son Colin's connections. Margaret knew nothing. She had said that Mark did, but Mark would never talk to her, he was always so wrongheaded, always had been. Hilary Marsh had suggested that it might be a good idea if a very old friend of his, Mrs. Ashe, lived in the basement. She was a sensible sort of woman, and could keep an eye on Mark for both of them.

Mark having digested this, he rang back his mother to ask how she proposed to explain this attempt to spy on him. She said, cold: "You have no right to talk to me about spying!" Then, as he remained silent, she had screamed: "You've ruined my life. You've ruined John's career!" And had rung off.

It turned out that John Patten, in his capacity as representative of British Culture, had been going on a lecture tour to America. But the Americans had not been happy about this, since he was the husband of the woman who had given birth to Colin Coldridge. They had made unofficial and tactful representations to the body who employed John Coldridge. This body had been excessively apologetic and had quite understood America's feelings in the matter. After a long committee meeting, someone had suggested that it would be better if nothing were made public, but that the lecture tour on Contemporary British Literature might be postponed. Everyone agreed. The chairman telephoned John Patten while the meeting was still in progress. He asked them to wait while he thought it over—which would only take a few minutes. He asked Margaret what she thought. Margaret rang her old friend Hilary Marsh, who thought this procedure would be best for everyone concerned.

Mark offered these facts to Martha; sat waiting for her to explain them. He looked extremely ill. He was trembling. He kept dropping his cigarettes. The gap between what a Coldridge believed was possible and what was happening had widened to the point that he was in a kind of collapse. Martha suggested he should go back to bed and stay there that day. He went.

It was time to get Paul up. He was sitting cross-legged on his pillow, waiting for her. He said: "Am I going to live here now?"

"Yes, I think so."

"I don't want to."

"I'm afraid you'll have to, Paul." This was almost cool: her mind was with Mark, so near a breakdown. It was not a tone anyone had used with Paul before.

He gave her a very long thoughtful stare. Then he got out of bed. Sally's child had not been good at dressing himself.

He dressed himself, slowly but competently, while she sat and watched.

"Now we'll have breakfast," she said. Obedient, he came down to the kitchen. He sat, obedient, while she cooked. He was looking at the window, which showed nothing. Martha went to see if the attendant journalists were there. But no, only a box of groceries left on the step by the delivery people.

She was about to open the door to fetch them in when Paul said: "I want to go for a walk."

"We can't go for walks yet," said Martha.

"You don't want them to tell me my daddy is dead," he said. Then he pushed the plate of eggs off the table, laughed as it crashed, and ran upstairs crying to his bedroom.

Martha opened the door to get in the groceries, and found Miles Tangin there.

"Good morning," he said affably.

She tried to shut the door, but his foot was in it.

"Nothing new to tell me?" he enquired.

"Nothing."

"May I ask who you are?"

"Certainly, I'm working for Mr. Coldridge."

"Living here?" he enquired. There were two expressions on his face, superimposed, as it were. At any rate, he managed to convey simultaneously a camaraderie of understanding for her situation—he was a man of the world, after all!—and the salaciousness with which he proposed to tell the story to the public.

"What's your name?"

"Find out. It'll give you something to do."

"Come, come," he said. "You're not in any position to use that tone, you know."

He was now propped against the doorframe, holding the door open. He was looking past her at the mess of broken eggs and bits of china on the floor.

"His wife's in a loony bin, I hear?"

She remembered that on the stove was the frying-pan, with hot fat in it. She fetched the frying pan and stood facing him.

"In your face if you don't get out," she said.

"Temper, temper, temper!" he said softly. He was arranging on his face the smile that says: I admire a woman of spirit. Then, seeing she meant it, he looked ugly. She came nearer, with the pan poised.

"Tell me," she said, "while you've been chasing this juicy story, have you ever thought of that child?"

168

And now a great wash of sentiment: the blond, goodfellow's face was all soft and sad. "But I'm only doing my job," he said. "But I can tell you, that poor little chap keeps me awake at nights."

"And I shall do mine if you don't get out."

He went, and she locked the door.

That evening the Coldridge story acquired a new element, in a piece by Miles Tangin. The previously mentioned sinister female figure now appeared as some sort of watchdog or guardian of Mark Coldridge. There were links, hinted at, with the Soviet embassy. She had a foreign accent. She was under orders of silence. For some days, the vigilance of the reporters was redoubled: it had shown signs of slacking off. Martha had to be careful to move around the house so that she could not be seen from the windows.

Upstairs in one room Paul lay on his bed, playing with the cat. She brought food to him there. And in another room, Mark lay in the dark, smoking and thinking. After a while he got up, went down to the study and very carefully read all the newspapers from the start of the affair until the present time. There were several weeks of them; and they included the serious newspapers, the popular press, and the high-class magazines that were studying the subject of treason in depth, and in articles that had a very high intellectual tone.

When he had done this, Mark said that he had finally understood the meaning of the old saying that the last refuge of a scoundrel was patriotism.

He sounded rather cool about it. He was still ill though, or at least looked ill. But he was in possession of himself. And he had made a decision. He was going down to the country, to stay with his old nurse, who had looked after himself and Colin, and he would take Paul with him.

"And what about Francis, it's going to be holidays again in a month?"

"He can come to Nanny Butts too—it'll be quiet there. And perhaps things will have blown over."

When he and Paul were ready, suitcases packed, he said: "I'm afraid you'll have to be a decoy."

Martha put on a coat, made herself seem indifferent, and walked openly out of the front door. A group of men waiting there at first seemed stunned. At her impertinence, at daring them? At any rate, she had gone several yards before they chased after her. One of them offered her £100 for the story. She smiled. He put it up to £200. She smiled again. She went around the corner and into a café. They all came in with her. She kept them there, discussing the possible sale of her revelations about the Coldridge household, until she judged Mark and Paul had got well away. Then she walked back to the front door. The car had gone. Mark Coldridge had gone. "Nice work," said one of them, laughing. But others, professionally hating, scowled and muttered, like parodies of journalists in a bad film, or in a comedy.

Inside the house was now only Martha. She went openly in and out, smiling politely at two hopeful journalists who remained. Then at one. But he went too. Then, peace, until Miles Tangin knocked at the front door and asked to be admitted. He had a proposition, he said. She was angry. He was affable. His manner was that of a wronged man concerned to give explanations. There was a genuine reproach for her lack of understanding. She should have retired to sharpen her anger, and set it on guard. But she let him in. Curiosity had a lot to do with it. Curious, she sat listening while he offered her £1,000 for the story of Mark's mistress. He accepted her refusal with the remark that everyone had their price, but that the story was not worth more. He seemed to expect that she would feel belittled by this; he even made a consoling remark: If Mark had a larger reputation, then more than one thousand pounds would have been forthcoming. Of course, if there were any justice, his reputation would be larger. It turned out that he admired Mark for having written the best novel for his money—Miles Tangin's—since *All Quiet on the Western Front*. If he, Miles Tangin, were a critic, that would be put right. But for his sins, he was a journalist. Only for the time being: he was writing a novel. He also admired Mark for (he hoped Martha would not take this amiss) his taste. The house must be empty, if Mark was away? He did not think Martha ought to take it like that, all was fair in love and war. Anyway, he'd be making the suggestion again later: she was his cup of tea, all right. Meanwhile he was busy, he was off to the country to find Mark Coldridge.

"There's a lot of Britain," said Martha.

"No, dear, there isn't. When one of these upper-class types goes to ground he's at an old teacher's, or nanny. I know how their minds work."

He left, affable.

She telephoned Mark, to warn him. But a journalist had already appeared at Nanny Butts's cottage. Mark was coming back to London.

He came that evening. He had been to his old school, explained the situation to the headmaster, and Paul was already installed.

And now, said Mark, they are welcome to me. He dictated a short piece for the press saying that he stood wholeheartedly behind his brother in whatever action he had seen fit to take. Asked if he was a Communist, he said he was, if that made him one.

And now, silence.

Mark was in his study. He stayed there. What sort of a state he was in, she did not know. His manner was cold, abrupt, but agitated.

She was in her room trying to see what was likely to happen next, trying not to be taken by surprise by events. The immediate facts were that Francis would be home soon, after what must be an awful time; Mark had been writing the usual weekly letters, but had not mentioned the sensational news which every paper had carried for weeks: Francis must surely have seen the newspapers. Paul, in a state of shock, had been dumped in a school which, "progressive" or not, was still a boarding school. Mark, as far as she could see, was in a state of shock. He certainly wasn't dealing with the problem, now pressing, of finance.

The bills for Lynda's hospital were unpaid. There was Francis's school—very expensive—and there would now be Paul's school. Ideally, Mark ought to find, in the next month, a couple of thousand pounds. He could not find so many shillings.

The factory? But she did not like to interfere with something she understood nothing about. Then Jimmy Wood arrived one afternoon to see Mark. Mark's door was locked. Martha therefore talked to Jimmy.

Or she tried to. They were in the kitchen, and they drank tea and ate cake—everything that was normal and reassuring. There he sat, smiling, as usual. And there she sat, opposite him, trying to understand him. She had seen that he was a human being constructed on a different model from most, but this did not help. Making contact with Jimmy, or trying to, one understood how one meshed with others. They were angry, they were pleased, they were sad, they were shocked. They might be several things in the course of an afternoon, but at any given moment one talked to an angry man, a frightened man, etc.; one contacted a state, an emotion. But Jimmy Wood? There he sat, smiling, while he heartily ate cake and asked for more, and even got up to

171

refill the kettle and put it on the ring. All this went on, the activity of a man enjoying his tea. He had come to this house because he wanted to say something. Mark not being available he was saying it to Martha. But what? He was disturbed about something. His movements were those of an agitated man. His eyes were hidden behind the great spectacles and his mouth, a thin, pink, curved mouth, smiled.

He was upset by Mark calling himself a Communist? Martha tried this note—but no. There was no resonance. Yes, that was what was throwing her off balance: where other people resounded, he did not. He wanted to leave the factory and find work elsewhere. But he said this without emotion: it was a fact that emerged after an hour or so. Why? He talked about two contracts that had not been renewed. Did he know why? He thought it was because of the "fuss about Mark in the papers." But that was not his point. Did he think the factory was going to have to shut down? No, not necessarily. They could coast along for months, even a year or so. But there was a job that would suit him in a factory in Wales. Martha suggested that Mark would be upset if he, Jimmy, left. They had worked together for years. From what she could make out of the mask-face, this embarrassed Jimmy. She pressed on: "He's very fond of you." She was faced by the great baby-head and the round glinting spectacles, and the pink smiling mouth. She felt extremely uncomfortable. He poured himself more tea, and energetically dotted up loose currants on the end of a wetted forefinger. Martha sat, going back in her mind over the various points that had come up. Not politics—no. To him, the greatest of irrelevancies. Not money—the business would survive temporary difficulties. At random she said: "I expect Mark will be back at work in a few days. Perhaps sooner." And now, just as if Jimmy had not said he would leave, he began talking about a machine he and Mark had planned to start making. It was as if she touched a switch, which had caused him to work again. From his remarks, all random, even disconnected, a picture emerged of Mark and him, spending days at a time in the office at the factory, with blueprints and scientific papers and their own imaginations— talking. Was it that, some sort of machine himself (or so she could not help feeling), he needed this, had been deprived of it, had felt deprived of something, but he did not know what—and now, knowing that this need to talk would at some time in the near future be met, was prepared to go on as before? At any rate, after three hours or so he left, smiling, with the remark that the foreman had said he'd like to see Mark sometime, to give him assurance that he and the men thought he had been shockingly treated: they were going to stand by him.

Martha wrote on a piece of paper: "I don't understand your Jimmy Wood. But he says the foreman wants to stand by you. I think Jimmy will leave if you don't go and talk to him soon." This she pushed under the door of the study.

The financial problems had not been solved.

One thing could be done at once: which was to let the basement.

Martha pushed another note under the door saying that Mark must at once write to Lynda's hospital asking for time to pay: the last account had been peremptory.

Mark telephoned. The doctor suggested that perhaps Mrs. Coldridge might come home for the weekend: she had a plan for her future which would involve Mark's cooperation, and which might help Mark financially. For his part, said Dr. Lamb, he was prepared to say Lynda was better. Not cured, but better.

Lynda came home for the weekend. She was like a guest. Mark came out of his study and was like a host. She said she wanted to leave the hospital, and live in the basement. No, she was not well enough to be by herself, but she could share it with a friend from the hospital. She said with a laugh that she did not think Mark would like her friend, who was called Dorothy. Sometimes she didn't like her either. But they got on.

Mark said he would of course do anything she wanted.

A moment later she took up her little box of pills and went up to bed.

Later, when Martha was ready for bed, her sense of things that were waiting to be said was strong enough to send her down to the kitchen. There sat Lynda in her dressing gown with a spread of cards in front of her.

"If I came to live here," said Lynda, continuing the conversation, "it wouldn't cost so much, would it? Oh—I don't mean, I want to be Mark's wife, I couldn't be that. But if I were here in the house, then it would be better, wouldn't it? Then they couldn't say you were taking him away from me."

"Why, are people saying that?"

"They are bound to be saying something, aren't they?"

"I suppose so. We've been too busy about this other thing."

"Oh, politics. Oh well, I don't care about that. That's just

173

nothing at all. But Dorothy's got some money of her own. She could pay some rent. It would help, wouldn't it?"

She shuffled the cards, humming cheerfully for a time. "Of course, there's Francis. But he hasn't a mother anyway. I thought it would be better to have me in the house, than not at all—for what he has to say to his friends, I mean."

More shuffling of cards, more humming.

"And about clothes. I've all that money for clothes in my bank account. You must make him take it. That's what he wants you see—that I shall be beautiful all the time."

"Yes, but I don't think he'd take it."

"I wouldn't mind if he divorced me. I know that would be best really. But he wouldn't ever divorce me, I know that."

"No, he wouldn't."

"I don't care about all that—all that's not what I care about."

And now she looked, very close, at Martha, studied her. She leaned forward, her chin in her hand, looking. As if she were trying to find out something? Was it that she wanted to know if Martha could guess what she did care about? She looked disappointed, she even sighed, and made a small pettish gesture of disappointment as she returned to the cards.

"You can go to bed, if you like," she said. "I'm all right by myself, you know."

That was on the Friday. Next morning early Paul's new headmaster telephoned to say that he would consider it a good thing if the child came home for the weekend: he and the staff thought it might help him.

His name was Edwards. He sounded very competent. He sounded in control. Martha felt that he and the staff would have every reason not to feel in control, with Paul in the state he was. She felt he might well have been entitled to say more than "Paul seems rather confused."

Paul was put on the train at the village station fifty miles away, and was met by Mark. When Paul got out of the car, a pale, spiky, black-eyed waif, he was already in the uniform of a progressive school—jeans and sweater. He came into the drawing room where Lynda sat, like a visitor in her pale fur coat, smoking and guarding her little box of pills.

She studied Paul, for a while, while he wriggled about in a chair opposite her. Then she smiled at him, her wide, beautiful smile. He, slowly, smiled back, a rather tentative offering. Slowly he approached Lynda, sidled around her, then tried to climb on her lap. But she held him off.

"I don't like being touched," she said. "But you can sit here." She indicated the patch of sofa beside her. He sat close, snuggling, as he would have done with his mother. But Lynda, at the touch, shrank from him. He felt it, and moved away, examining her face as a guide to how far he must go. Side by side they sat, a space between them.

Martha and Mark were busy with tea things. This ought probably not to happen at all. But then nothing of this ought to be happening.

"Why don't you like being touched?"

"Because I am ill."

"My mother liked it."

"But I'm not like your mother."

"She's dead."

"She killed herself," said Lynda.

"Why did she?"

"Some people don't like living."

"Didn't she like me?"

"Very much, " said Lynda.

"I don't think she liked me. Or she wouldn't have killed herself."

"That doesn't follow."

"Yes it does."

Lynda had moved where she sat, so that she was looking at Paul with a direct, cool smile. And he was leaning forward, gazing up into her truth-telling face.

"Didn't my daddy like living?"

"You say that because you think he is dead."

"Yes, he's dead."

"No, I don't think he's dead."

"He is! He is! I know he is!"

Tears were imminent, but Lynda made no attempt to stop them.

"No. Perhaps he is, but we don't think so. And he may come back."

"He won't come back, because he doesn't like me."

"You are making yourself much too important," said the sick woman to the desperate child. "Your daddy had work to do. It was important. If he went away it wasn't because of you and your mother."

"Did my mother kill herself because he went away?"

"No. He went away and she killed herself—the two things at the same time."

"How did she kill herself."

"She made herself stop breathing."

"Could I?"

"Yes, it you wanted to."

"Do you want to?"

"Sometimes."

"Are you going to?"

"No."

"Why aren't you?"

"Because every time I think I will, then I decide to stay alive and see what happens next. It is interesting."

He gave a scared laugh, and snuggled closer. His hand, meeting hers, felt hers go away. He put his two hands carefully onto his knees.

"At the school, the other children have mothers and fathers for the holidays."

"Well, you haven't."

"Why haven't I?"

"I've told you."

They observed that his face had gone red, and his mouth was pinched up.

Lynda slapped him. "Stop it. You don't die by holding your breath."

"I shall if I want."

"Anyway, it's silly. You're unhappy now. But later you might be happy, who knows?"

"Am I unhappy?"

"Yes, you're very unhappy."

"I don't want to be."

"I dare say. But you are."

She smiled, and got up. At the tea tray she took up a cup of tea, and sugared it. She went towards the door, with the cup.

"Why are you going? Can I come too?"

"No. I can't be with people for long. I'm ill, you see."

"What sort of ill?"

And now a bad, twisted moment, a jar. "I have to be careful. I have to be on guard," she said, "so that's why I'm ill." He had rushed to her, stood near, looking up. She bent down and widened her eyes at him, smiling secretly, straight into his face: "I know things, you see. They don't like it."

He looked afraid, shrank. The small boy stood, pathetic, staring up at the tall woman. And she felt that she had made a mistake. Her smile faded. She looked sick and anxious.

But he needed her too badly to be afraid of her. Before she got out of the door, he was after her. Careful not to touch, he stood as close as he could get.

"Lynda. Lynda. Are you my mother now?"

"No. You have no mother."

"Are you Francis's mother?"

"Yes. No. I suppose so. Not really. I'm not much good at being that kind of person. Some people aren't."

He drooped away, his finger in his mouth.

"But Paul, I'm your friend. Do you want that?"

He nodded, merely, not looking at her. Then he gave her a scared glance, and saw her wonderful smile. He smiled, slowly.

She went to her room. Later that day, Paul went to her, was admitted. He was there for about half an hour. They did not know what was said or felt; but Paul was cheerful through his supper, and he asked Mark to tell him a story. When that was over, he said he would like to go back to the school next morning.

Mark took him back in the car. When he arrived back at the house he found Lynda establishing herself in the basement.

He telephoned the hospital.

Mark said to her: "They say you've made a remarkable recovery."

He was watching Lynda and Martha arrange the bed for Lynda. What he was really saying was: You still might get quite better and be my wife again.

But Lynda smiled at him and said: "What awful fools they are. What fools! Well, thank God, they are." She laughed, was scornful. She continued to smile, scornfully, during the evening, but muttered once or twice: "But I must be careful though."

She did not feel able to stay alone in the basement. Martha moved down, and slept in the living room for a couple of nights. But then Dorothy, Lynda's friend, came to live with her. She was a Mrs. Quentin, but it seemed that her husband was living with another woman somewhere in Ireland. She was a large, dark, slow-moving woman, anxiously watchful of the impression she might be making, with a tendency to make jocular remarks. She had a large quantity of jackdaw possessions, which she set out all over the flat before even unpacking her clothes. She was not the person either Mark or Martha could associate easily with Lynda.

But Lynda was pleased to have her there, did not mind the embroidered velvet hearts, the magazine covers tacked to the walls, the dolls; did not mind her friend's possessiveness. It seemed that she liked Dorothy telling her to do this, and to do that; liked it when Dorothy said to Mark: "I think it's time Lynda went to bed now."

Mark did not like it. There was a moment when Lynda, being ordered to take her pills by Dorothy, looked across at Mark's hostile face and openly laughed. It was in a kind of triumph.

Lynda wanted Dorothy here as a protection against Mark, against having to be Mark's wife.

When Mark, or Martha, descended to the basement to offer help, or their company, the two women became a defensive unit, which excluded everybody. They exchanged private jokes, and made references to the hospital. There was something about them of two schoolgirls engaged in a world-hating friendship.

In short, having Lynda back in the basement, with a friend who had money and would pay some rent, would make a difference to the finances of the household; but not to much else.

Two

The bad time had been going on for—but one of the qualities of a bad time is that it seems endless. Certainly everything that happened, the events, had long ago ceased to stand out as unpleasant incidents, or harbingers. The texture of life was all heaviness, nastiness, fear. When she tried to put her mind back into places, times, when things had been normal (but what did she mean by that?) she could not. Her memory was imprisoned by now. And when she tried to look forward, because after all this was going to change, since everything changed, she could see nothing ahead but a worsening. The poisoned river would plunge down, yes, explode over a fall of rocks—but not into any quiet place. There was probably going to be war again. Yet that she could think like this at all meant she had learned nothing at all from the war so recently finished. A war *was* going on, at that moment, in yet another place no one had heard of before there was a war. Korea. A nasty war. If she were a Korean she would not now be saying: There is going to be a war. And if she were in America—well, from there England would seem all sun and sanity. In America she would have certainly lost her job, would probably be in prison. She would be wanting to emigrate, that is, if she could get a passport, which was doubtful. To a liberal country like England. Which so many Americans were finding such a refuge.

But they were not in houses like this one.

There was nothing to stop Martha leaving. She had only to pack her cases and go. Well, why didn't she? She couldn't—any more than she could not have come here in the first place. Besides, where was she to go to? For instance, several times she had been to Mark's old nurse's home in the country, to visit Francis, or to take him there, or to bring him back home. That house, in its old village, with its quiet people, was England, as one had always imagined it. Except that ten miles away was a war place where new atomic weapons were being developed, in secret; and forty miles away in another direction was a factory for the manufacture of gasses and poisons for use in war. Mary Butts and Harold Butts gardened, grew vegetables, kept chickens, made presents of fresh eggs and flowers to Francis to take back to the big city London: which they disliked, it was too noisy, they said. They were a couple in their fifties. Harold Butts had always been a gardener; for many years with Margaret. Mary Butts had always been a children's nurse. They had served the Coldridges while they worked, and served them still in their retirement. They were infinitely kind and good people. To Martha, a friend of young Mark's, they were kind, and they asked her to stay. In a little cottage bedroom that smelled all through the summer of the flowers Harold Butts grew, Martha lay and thought, Yes, this is England, this was what they meant when they said England. This is what my father meant: he grew up in a place like this. The Buttses never mentioned the death factories so close to them. For one thing, England is not a small country for those who have never left it, and ten miles, forty miles, are large distances. For another, these were people who did not understand ... what? Harold Butts had fought in the First World War. In France. But horror, anarchy, happened in other countries, not in England.

If Martha had lived in that cottage, she could not have forgotten those factories. Lying awake in a flower-scented bedroom, the Buttses gently asleep past one wall, and Francis asleep past another, she was made to think of the difference between herself and them. Being what she was, it would make no difference if she stayed with the Buttses, found work in the pretty village. She might as well go back to the house in London. The Buttses were a refuge, reminders that sanity could exist. Nastiness simply bounced off them. Very early in the bad time, they had been visited by a man called Mr. Bartlett. They had been distressed by the visit. Mary Butts had written a letter to Mark: "He seemed a nice enough gentleman, but Mr. Butts thought it was not his place to ask questions about you behind your back. Mr. Butts said to him, you should be asking Mr. Coldridge such things. He said it to him straight. Our love to little Francis. Yours respectfully, Mary Butts."

Before this letter reached Mark, he had already been visited by Mr. Bartlett, who used the ordinary forms of social life to arrive for tea in the drawing room. He said he had been an old friend of James's, the dead brother. Mark offering tea, and cake, talked to a man who had known James at Cambridge. He had also visited Margaret. He was an old chum of Margaret's—well, who was not? Ottery Bartlett talked of recent meetings with Margaret; and Mark, who was not by nature a suspicious man, waited for him to come to the point. He was interested in literature perhaps? Needed help with a book he had written? Mr. Bartlett talked about Colin. They discussed pleasantly, for some time, the gap between the way Colin was being seen, as a spy, and the way Colin saw what he had done (if he had), which was a proper exchange of scientific information between colleagues. Teatime passed into a drinks time, which soon was dinnertime. Martha cooked and served an informal kind of dinner, and was present. She was preoccupied with other things, and did not think about Mr. Bartlett except that it was nice for Mark that at least one of the old friends of the family was prepared to visit him. For Mark was obviously touched by it: his warmth with Mr. Bartlett told Martha how much he had been feeling his isolation. During dinner they talked about Sally-Sarah and Mark's relation to Paul. Mr. Bartlett was sympathetic about Lynda—he had known her, long ago; and was sympathetically interested in Martha's presence in the house. After dinner Martha left the two men with their brandy. Late that night Mark burst into her room, when she was nearly in bed, demanding that she must come down to the study at once. It had just dawned on him: it had just made sense. He, Mark, was the most incredible fool: a hundred times during the afternoon and evening he could

180

have seen what Ottery Bartlett was, if he had been awake. He now needed Martha to retrace the conversation with him. He had gone past ordinary anger into a state of sick quivering rage where he kept bursting into inarticulate exclamation and protests. They could not follow any train of thought. They could not discuss anything that night: Mark drank himself silly. What was upsetting Mark worst was that the man had used James, the family, to come here.

Next day came the letter from Nanny Butts, and fresh anger. When this cooled, they were able to discuss what had happened.

The man was probably from the Foreign Office, but could be from any one of the six or so secret services that operate in Britain. He had mentioned Hilary Marsh once, but that proved nothing. Anyway, it was not important. They (who?) thought that Mark knew where his brother was. If not, that he was at least in contact with him. And that he was probably a secret member of the Communist Party. If so, he might drop useful information about the Communist Party. (And if he had been he certainly would have done, so incredibly obtuse Mark had been for the whole of an afternoon and an evening.) Finally, Mark, if handled right, might be prepared to become an agent for Britain, whether a member of the Communist Party or not. This last point was not reached by Mark and Martha for some days. But, going over and over the talk of that day, they could put their fingers on a dozen moments where it had been reached—very delicately of course, only hinted at.

"A spy!" said Mark. "Me! A spy!"

And so, Martha could see, Colin had probably reacted, when with his version of Ottery Bartlett: What! Me! Colin Coldridge! A spy!

And, for some hours, Mark went over and over, back and around that incredible fact: Hilary Marsh, Ottery Bartlett, were gentlemen. Yet they were prepared to do such work. He could not believe it. He certainly did not understand it.

It was this incident that sent him off into another week of silent misery in his study, with bottle after bottle of cognac. And it was that incident, the visit of Ottery Bartlett, that had given birth to a new personality. Before that, he had been Mark Coldridge as Martha had first known him—under stress, of course, miserable, out of his depth, but himself.

There is a certain kind of Englishman who, on learning that his country (like every other) employs spies; or (like every other) taps telephones, opens letters and keeps dossiers on its citizens; or (like every other) employs policemen who take bribes, beat up suspects, plant information, etc.—has a nervous breakdown. In extreme cases, such a man goes into a monastery, or suffers a sudden conversion to whatever is available.

An Englishman of this type has of course been the subject of amused and indeed affectionate speculation among other countries for generations. Though sometimes not so amused, or affectionate.

During the course of that week, Martha went into the study, where Mark, red-eyed, and half drunk, was walking up and down and around and around, to tell him the following story which had once come her way.

Sometime in the course of the Second World War, a certain member of a certain British Secret Service had been instructed to go to (let us say) Istanbul to find out the probable intentions of the Russians in regard to something or other. The place where he would most likely get this information, he was told, was the bed of the wife of a British official. She had proved in the past a mine of information, being indiscreet as well as beautiful. Besides, she could never resist a Russian. The hero of this anecdote departed to the city in question in pursuance of duty, but did not return when expected. He was summoned. Back in London, interviewed by his principals, he confessed that he had learned nothing. Yes, the lady was beginning to attract him, he said. But he found her morals distasteful, and besides he had known her husband for years.

Mark did not find this amusing. "He was quite right," he said. And went back to his brandy, his anger—and his illness. He was having migraines, for the first time in his life.

Martha returned to her consideration of Mark's character. When Hilary Marsh had come to the election party, he had done so using old friendship—to be a spy. Mark had been angry, but more with his mother than with Hilary Marsh. When Hilary Marsh had used his mother and old friendship to try and instal the widow Ashe in Mark's basement, to spy on Mark—Mark had been angry. But it had taken the actual visit of Ottery Bartlett, using old friendship, to Mark's house, to make him more than angry.

Supposing Ottery Bartlett had not come, had not been to see the Buttsses, would Mark have remained Mark, talking sardonically about "the comrades," whom he couldn't trust further than he could kick them? Very likely.

After a week or so of being ill, and semi-drunk, he rang up

a man who had been a friend of his brother Colin, a Communist. He went to see him, for a long weekend. The weekend after, Freddie Postings came to stay, and several of his friends spent Sunday afternoon and evening in Mark's study. Martha was not present. She was being treated with cool friendliness. Mark had suffered a conversion, sudden and dramatic, and Martha was able to follow it through its rapid stages, since it was identical as far as she could see with the one she had undergone ten years before. As if scales had fallen from his eyes, Mark was looking at defects in his own country that previously he had not noticed, minimised, or thought could not exist. His previous self he was regarding as hypocritical, or wilfully blind and certainly as callous to the sufferings of others. He had a new viewpoint, a new vocabulary, new friends. He was undergoing in his own person, through his own experience, that process which can affect nations or parties, or people, when everything that is good in oneself is identified with a cause, and everything bad identified with the enemy. But the interesting thing about Mark's conversion was that this was not the time to see the cause as perfect; nor, judging from the little Martha saw of the half dozen or so men and women now visiting the house, were they the kind of Communists likely so to see it. Yet Mark was, when they met over breakfast, over conversations about Lynda or the children, using language identical with hers of ten years ago. He had walked into a personality (or, if you like, a state of mind) and he was inhabiting it.

And, just as if he had never protested to Martha that he could not stand political oversimplifications, or the taking of sides, as if he had never written the novel in which what was represented by Hilary Marsh and Ottery Bartlett was taken for granted—he had become the Defender. Martha saw that this aspect of herself, already weakened when she came to this house, then brought briefly to life in discussions with Mark, had been taken over by him. She looked, when she looked at him, at herself of the past: hot-eyed, angry, violent, unable to listen.

They had changed roles.

During the time, some months, when Mark was in this condition, she was, minimally, his secretary; she kept the house; she tried, inadequately, to befriend the children; and was able to save the novel about the city in the desert from being destroyed.

He wanted to tear it up. He could not understand how he had written such "ivory-tower rubbish."

Martha went over the manuscript. He had achieved a final version before the Defender had come into the picture. It was a cool, detached account, like a history, of the existence of the city, and the principles on which it was run; and of the alien envious growth outside which eventually overran it, destroyed it, and set up the debased copy of what had been destroyed. This needed some minor tidying up, nothing very much. But recently the Defender had been making some additions. They were rough, and wild and emotional, written in snatches, and inserted into the typed pages in the form of handwritten additions. He had taken episodes from the story and enlarged them, giving certain characters a psychological depth. "I tried to put some life into the damned thing," said he to Martha, "the damned thing didn't have any guts." The trouble was, "life," not to mention "guts," had no place in that story, or at least not in this form. Reading the story, with its recent additions, was like watching a battle between two personalities, one trying to take over another.

She said this to Mark and he said: "I'm not interested in subjective criticism." This phrase meant nothing, in this context; it was a phrase in use around left-wing circles at this time: by Phoebe as much as, let's say, Stalin.

Now Martha remembered that other old manuscript, or heap of ant-eaten notes she had brought to England because she could not think of anything else to do with it. It had been lying in a suitcase in the loft. She took it down, and laid it beside the manuscript of "A City in the Desert." Thomas's last testament. Mark's book. And what was interesting was this: the insertions into the original manuscript made by Mark, the clumsy hot emotionalism of them, were the same in "feel" as a good part of Thomas's writing. They had come from the same place, the same wavelength. Somewhere, those two extraordinarily different people, Mark, Thomas, inhabited the same place, made contact there. A small place perhaps: because the sardonic anger, the nihilism, that was Thomas's strongest trait, was not in Mark. Mark's insertions, which were going to have to be thrown out, because of fidelity to a whole, were in scrawled red ink. Thomas's additions and riders, in red pencil. From here, this place, Thomas had gone down into madness and to death. Mark? Well, this was one kind of a descent, of an entering in. To write books like "A City in the Desert," or the war book, cool, abstract, detached: one had to earn that; one had to be that kind of person. Mark was not. Not yet, at least. Probably, next, he would write a clumsy raw kind of book. When people open up a new area in themselves, start doing something new, then it must be clumsy and raw, like a baby trying to walk. . . . Here a nerve of memory sounded: she had thought this before, when? Or something like it. Jack; she was reminded of Jack. She had been walking somewhere—to Jack? She had understood once before that the new, an opening up, had to be through a region of chaos, of conflict. There was no other way of doing it.

She said to Mark that unless he specifically forbade her to send the manuscript to the publishers, she would do so, having removed the clumsy additions first.

He did not, merely muttered that he supposed it was no worse than most, and so she sent it off. She had expected him not to want to be involved in the business of proofs, details of publication, etc.; but he did this work himself, and apparently with interest. Certainly, with the furious energy that he brought to everything through the bad time. For months, he scarcely slept. He was up every morning by five, to read and study. He was appallingly ignorant, he said: he knew nothing. He studied economics and that kind of history which is still unofficial history, that is to say, still vital—not yet taught, or quoted or represented by a school of academic thought. His study was full of books by journalists, the novels that are reportage, newspapers, statistics arranged from a certain point of view, and those documents, usually badly cyclostyled or typed, put out by political groups whose viewpoints are not popular. And, as Martha had done a decade before, he was acquiring a grasp of recent history which was the shadow, or reverse side of what was taught—what had been taught, even, at his own school, "progressive" as it was.

At the same time, during the hours while everyone else was still asleep, he was trying to find a subject to write a new novel about—one that he could approve of. "I want to write about something real!" he said, fierce, to Martha. With antagonism: for she was the enemy within the gates who was responsible for the "unreal" book *A City in the Desert*, the proofs of which he was correcting with such energy. With Martha, the enemy, he discussed possible subjects. He was thinking about a novel which had Mary and Harold Butts as a theme. For he was seeing them as victims of the oppressing Coldridges. But after a weekend with the Buttses and his son Francis, he came back saying there was no point in writing about such damned feudalistic rubbish: this was an industrial country. He was spending his mornings at the factory with Jimmy, partly in the talk which was the oil for Jimmy's inventive genius, but also in considering his employees. He was convinced that he had never considered them before. One morning he had the foreman and the six workmen who had been with him since the business started, and thanked them for their class solidarity. Jimmy, recounting this tale to Martha, in his smiling way, did so, as she could see, not so much because he wanted to be enlightened, but because he wanted to be reassured. For him, Mark's new preoccupation was a waste of time; and anyway, Mark's speech had not been correctly understood: the support given to him by the foreman and the men was not because of his socialist allegiances, but because they liked Mark. Mark saw this—and with regret: feudalism again, he said. He spent hours walking around the streets near the factory, which was a slummy area in North London. It was not that he hadn't seen them before; not that he had not recognised the existence of poverty; he hadn't imagined it, hadn't felt part of it. He did now, and for a while thought of a novel set in those grim streets. His new friends, however, discouraged him by pointing out that such novels, produced by the hundred in and near the socialist parties, were exactly what that current in the Communist movement which they represented was trying to get away from: the proletarian novel was dead. Mark, in the grip of early conviction when everything was new, argued against them. He even wrote a couple of chapters. The purest logic said he should. The *and, and, and; therefore, therefore, therefore; a, b, c, d,* of Communist logic is always irrefutable because while that particular Person, Personality, absorbs, to shoot out, facts, figures, convictions, like a machine, its substance is in fact all emotion. And timeless, within the bounds, let's say, of 1917 and—but we don't yet know its end. Half a dozen decades of impassioned socialist polemicising about Art went for nothing: click, click, click, went the machine, oiled by anger, therefore, therefore, therefore—out comes the Proletarian Novel.

Out came two chapters of Mark's working-class novel, called *Working Hands.* Neither the new friends nor Martha had to tell him they were appalling. And, late at night, after the friends had gone, he came to Martha, ready to talk still, to talk until morning if she were ready to stay up. But while he was driven direct from that source of emotional power which is all pure, perfect conviction, Martha was all lethargy. The bad time for her was a slump into exhaustion. She slept too long, she ate too much, she was all heaviness and division: and watched Mark as if she were watching her own young self. And came to realise something she had not before: her memory had gone cloudy. Only ten years ago—and what was ten years? But it was as if her past had become fused with Mark's present. Almost; or as if Mark was herself, or she Mark. Saying to herself: Yes, I did that, I thought that, I read that book too, I used exactly that vocabulary—she was not able to put herself back there, in that place in herself where she had been; for that place was inhabited by Mark.

In Mark, now, there were at least half a dozen different people, all operating apparently with perfect efficiency, side by side, and not recognising the existence of the others. But the Defender did not, after all, prevent him from talking to the enemy Martha, even taking her advice. It did not prevent him visiting Harold and Mary Butts, where he behaved as he always had: feudally. It did not prevent him talking for hours every day with Jimmy, in the way Jimmy needed, the humorous, fanciful, creative play which resulted, extraordinarily, in the models of this or that machine which littered Mark's study. Nor was he less patiently Lynda's potential or past husband, in cold storage though that person was. Yet neurosis, mental trouble of any kind, was by definition, at that time, in the Communist Party, reactionary and bourgeois.

And he tried, patiently, clumsily, indeed, pathetically, to be Francis's father, even while he said to Martha, in language she knew she had used, that the family was doomed.

He tried, too, to be a father to Paul: but Paul would have none of him. The child came home for holidays, and spent his time with Lynda, his friend. Two years of being an orphan had changed Paul into a lively, aggressive, self-contained little boy who was clever at school, but, as the school reports said, "made inadequate social relationships." He certainly had no relationship with Mark: it really was as if Mark did not exist for him. Mark would offer visits to the zoo, walks in the park, a story: Paul did not seem to hear him. Mark said that sometimes he felt as if he were invisible. For it was not rudeness. Paul looked through him, or said to Martha: "Can I go down to Lynda now?"

When Paul was at home, the house was open, the door to the basement always ajar. Never when he was not: then the basement became a separate, almost secret establishment.

But Francis was a different matter. His mother was "at home"—and not in a mental hospital, which was helpful at his school, as Lynda had said. But he did not bring his friends home.

The very first holidays after Paul's mother's death, Francis came home after a bad time at school. He had changed. Previously silent, serious, watchful, he had suddenly become— something Martha recognised, with pain. He was the clown. In a reaction to what had been brutal teasing, if not worse, his father being a traitor and his uncle under a cloud; accused of being a Communist, a Red, a Commy: he clowned being one. He had joked; adopted, jokingly, Communist phrases which he had got out of the papers. Well, there was the mechanism, for Martha to see: yet in herself she could not remember what had created "Matty." "Matty" had joked, claimed exemption by clumsiness, made fun of herself; Francis joked, guyed, bought himself off by a boisterous clownishness. In this condition, he visited his mother and the watchful friend of his mother, in the basement. He was noisy; he racketed about the basement: he badly tired the two sick women.

Then came the time, and very soon, when he returned home to find his father's friends all Communists. They were not figures of fun, but people. His clowning Communism stuttered and failed. There were wild scenes of rage, temper, hysteria. It was after that period of holidays that the school reported his work was suddenly very bad, he was at the bottom of the class. Not being a "progressive" school, they said he was lazy and bad-mannered. His father ought to give him a talking-to. Mark went to the school to talk to Francis, but the child was locked in a silent hostility, very polite, saying Yes Sir, No Sir.

When the time came around again for holidays, Francis said he wanted to spend them with Nanny Butts. Since then, that was where he always went. Mark visited him there, returning to say painfully to Martha: "He's like me—I could never bear coming home either."

At the Buttses', Francis was able to be the clown, without conflict: his school personality and his holiday personality were one. Nanny Butts was not upset. She wrote: "Francis is a very cheerful little boy, always having his fun. It's a blessing, when you think of his poor mother."

But once, when Martha was down in the village, for she was to take Francis back to school, there was a glimpse of another Francis.

It was late evening, summer, and time for Francis to go to bed. Martha went out, through the cottage garden, into the long field beyond, which sloped down to a stream. Francis was walking up towards her, with a little girl. He was still a short stocky boy, his black head on the level of the frothy white of the half-ripe oats. He held the little girl's hand, and was bending towards her with the gentle protectiveness an adult uses towards a child. A path led through a birch wood to a half-seen cottage. Francis led the child to the path, and there she ran away home, looking back to wave at Francis. He stood to wave at her, smiling. The smile faded. He turned, and walked slowly along the edge of the field, serious, thoughtful, running one hand along the feathery tops of the oats. Then he saw Martha waiting there. A moment when you could see the mechanism work: a startled defensiveness, then the smile fitting down onto the face. Francis raced up to Martha, hilarious, grinning, and as he reached her, shouted: "Supper, jolly good!" and cartwheeled up through the garden into the cottage.

In between Paul's visits, when the door to the basement was shut, the two upstairs had learned not to go down, unless asked. It was Lynda who telephoned from one part of the house to the other, to ask if they would like a cup of coffee. And she never asked Mark by himself. This meant, when you thought about it, that she must be watching through the windows to see how people came in and out. Also, when you thought about it, that the invitation was the result of some conflict with Dorothy. For on these occasions Dorothy would sit silent, rather apart, watching. And Lynda would slide her small defiant guilty looks, like a girl who has won a victory over her parents. Mark was polite to Dorothy. It was not that he wished her ill, or even wished her away: if Lynda wanted her there, then that is what Lynda should have. But there was no connection between himself and Dorothy: he was courteous to his wife's friend. The emotional reality of Dorothy and Lynda, whatever that was, was not real for him. He was Lynda's husband, tenderly protective, attentive to Lynda. The four of them would sit for an hour or so in the extraordinary room, which now had an incongruity built into its very substance. The beautiful furniture, every piece of which was a museum keeper's dream, the rugs, Lynda's small belongings, a favourite lamp from her own home, books— this one world, Lynda's. But every inch of the walls, every surface, was crammed with Dorothy: a magpie schoolgirl who had crushes on Royalty and film stars. The curtains were always drawn: they lived in artificial light. There was a low stuffy smell of sickness and drugs. The four sat drinking coffee, and Mark talked to Lynda, while Martha tried to talk to Dorothy; who, however, never took her sad anxious gaze off Lynda.

A tension that was all anxiety slowly built and built. Lynda smoked furiously, scattering ash. Then Mark would jump up, and say: "How about drawing the curtains for a bit?"

"Yes, yes," Lynda would most eagerly assent, but with a hasty glance towards Dorothy, to reassure her that they would soon be alone again.

Mark drew back the curtains, and let in the cold day. There sat two ill women, exposed, smiling their fortitude.

Lynda's fur coat, her handbag, a scarf, dark glasses, lay at random on chairs.

"Lynda, wouldn't it be better if . . ."

"Yes," she said eagerly, "Yes, Mark." And she hung up the coat in the hall, and rushed off the other items into the bedroom, which, glimpsed through the open door, was a total disorder. She shut the door on the mess and sat smiling pathetically. By now they longed for him to leave.

Once, after they left, they heard how the two women started a violent quarrel before they had even got up the stairs. Then, weeping. Whose? They could not make out.

But Mark did not give up. For a while he asked them up to dinner once or twice a week. On these nights his new friends did not come, and Martha and he took trouble over the food.

There sat Lynda and Dorothy, with their handbags near them, on their best behaviour.

Mark remained a husband. All of his best qualities, qualities he had not known until then he possessed, had gone into Lynda, when he discovered he had married a sick woman: for months, then years, while Lynda fell to pieces, he had used a loving strength which (and this was the point) he simply could not believe she did not need now. But she had not been able to stand it then; and she could not stand it now.

At the end of one of these dinner parties she said, suddenly, in a low fierce voice, but smiling still, so afraid was she of her own violence: "Leave me alone, Mark. You're killing me."

And she ran off down to the basement in tears, Dorothy lumbering after her.

Throughout all of this were incidents of a different kind: but there had to be three or four of them before they were seen as a pattern.

Dorothy had taken over the management of the flat, though Mark and Martha had offered to run it with the house. Dorothy was, or had been, an efficient woman. During the war she had managed a factory that made parts of bombs: she had had about forty women working under her. Becoming normal, for Dorothy, meant once more learning to be competent. It was she who got in a charwoman, ordered food, sometimes went shopping—managed. Then something went wrong, a little thing, like a tap, or the telephone. Dorothy contacted the machinery of the outside world. A week or so later, Martha would find one of the women carrying water downstairs in a bucket, or coming up to use the telephone. When the affair finally came into her hands, or Mark's, Dorothy would supply a piece of paper on which was written something like this:

"FRIDAY EVENING: Lynda said the tap was dripping. I rang five plumbers. Three didn't answer. This *in spite of the fact* they advertised to ring after six. The fourth said he would come at nine. He never came at all. The fifth said he would come on Saturday morning at ten. SATURDAY MORNING: We waited for the plumber. When he had not turned up by twelve, I went out shopping. Lynda went to sleep. The man came while I was out. I telephoned him that afternoon. There was no reply. SATURDAY EVENING: I telephoned him. His wife answered. She said it was the weekend. Her husband did not work over the weekends. She suggested I ring Mr. Black of Canonbury. His wife said he worked at weekends. I left a message. SUNDAY MORNING: I rang Mr. Black. He was out. His wife said she would try to get him to come in the afternoon. I stayed up, instead of going to sleep. SUNDAY AFTERNOON: Mr. Black telephoned. He said if it wasn't urgent he would come on Monday. I told him off. I told him if he was so slack he wouldn't be any good as a workman. MONDAY MORNING: I telephoned the first plumber. His wife said he would come that afternoon. MONDAY AFTERNOON: He did not come. By then the tap was leaking badly. I turned off the main.

"The question is: are we in a position to sue for loss of time and damage and inconvenience? When he turned up *at last* on Wednesday afternoon, *he had the nerve* to say he was going to send in an account for the first visit (see under Saturday morning) so I told him where he got off."

This, or something like it, happened fairly often, as it does in every household. Dorothy was always in the right. Each time she got herself into a state of furious, helpless irritation which ended in her having to go to bed, where Lynda nursed her.

Mark dealt with each new crisis, and this brought him into

contact with Lynda for several days, while Dorothy was ill. The reason why Dorothy would never until some situation was desperate—no water, no gas, no electricity—come for help upstairs, was that it meant bringing in Mark, or Mark's deputy, Martha. It meant that she, Dorothy, had failed Lynda. It meant a collapse into inadequacy in a dark bedroom, and oblivion in drugs.

Mark and Lynda, with Dorothy asleep in her bedroom, achieved some hours of companionship, even gaiety.

The telephone, or tap, restored to normal, Lynda went back to the basement and the door was locked.

Mark made a visit to Martha's room. When he did this it meant something of importance, something he found hard to talk about; which, perhaps, he had been working himself up to talk about all that day, or even several days.

She had been sitting in the dark, looking out of the window at the ragged sycamore tree, thinned by late autumn. The knock on the door was abrupt, but soft.

"Do you mind if I come in?" He switched on the light, and saw, as he always did, a succession of rooms in this one, back to where young children played in it, he among them.

He took hold of the present, where a woman in a red housecoat, with untidy hair, sat by a dark window, looking out, a cat asleep beside her.

The cat woke, stalked across to him, looked up into his face, and miaowed. He sat down, the cat on his knee. He was in his dressing gown. They were like an old married couple, or a brother and sister.

This thought passed from her to him, and he said: "This is no sort of life for you."

"Or for you."

"Don't you ever think of marrying?"

"Yes. Sometimes." The worry on his face was to do with her: not what he had come about. "People have been saying I'm after you?"

He coloured up at once, changed position: the cat jumped down, annoyed.

"Yes. Do you mind?"

"No. Yes, a little. Not much."

"It was stupid of me. I'd forgotten completely that—well, what with everything else . . ."

"You shouldn't let yourself listen to them." As she spoke she knew she was saying more: Why are you letting yourself be influenced. He heard this, gave her an acute look, acknowledging it. In a different mood he might have become the Defender. But not tonight. He was Lynda's husband.

"I want to ask you something. I get so involved in—I know I'm not seeing something. It's Lynda. Why do I upset her so much? Do you know?"

"You always ask too much of her."

"But how is she ever going to get well if ... I mean, what was the point of her coming home at all?"

She could not bring herself to say what she was thinking.

"You mean, it was just to get out of the hospital? I mean, it couldn't just have been that—I am here, after all!"

"She didn't have much choice."

"She could have gone off and shared a flat with that ... what was to stop her?"

"I don't know."

"She came *here,* where *I* am."

"And Francis."

"He's never here. She never sees him."

"Perhaps she wants to. I don't know, Mark. How should I know?"

"Do you think they are Lesbians?" He found it difficult to say this. He had gone white now, was all dark hot eyes in a white face. One mask, or look, does for several different emotions. So Mark looked when contemplating his mother's connivance with Hilary Marsh, or the affair of Ottery Bartlett. That was anger. This was misery.

"I don't know. A bit, perhaps. I've never known any. But I shouldn't imagine that's the point. It's probably more that they make allowances for each other."

"A dreadful woman, dreadful, dreadful."

"Well ... I don't know."

"You wouldn't choose to share your life with her!"

"Well, no. But I'm not ill."

Lynda had been diagnosed by a large variety of doctors: there had been a large variety of diagnoses. She was depressed; she was a manic depressive; she was paranoid; she was schizophrenic. Most frequently, the last. Also, in another division, or classification, she was neurotic; she was psychotic. Most frequently, the latter.

"They said she was better. Well, I don't see it."

"She is managing out of the hospital."

"Yes, but ... when we were married, it never came easily to her—sex, I mean. It wasn't that—I mean, she's normal enough. What's normal? But how do I know? It's not as if I had had all that experience when we were married. It's not as if I can make vast comparisons. But I remember it striking me always, it was as if being able to sleep with me was a proof to herself—do you understand?"

"How can I? One could say that of lots of people these days. Sex is a kind of yardstick, one's got to succeed. Were you her first lover?"

"Yes. Well, yes, I am sure I was. But sometimes it was like making love to a drowning person."

"She wanted to be saved?"

"Yes. Yes! Exactly that!" He was excited because she saw it. "Sometimes I thought, my God, am I murdering this woman! Did you hear that, when she said, Mark you're killing me."

"Yes, but that . . ."

"No. That meant something. It made sense. She used to say, Save me Mark, save me! Well, I had a jolly good try!"

"Yes."

"And now what? What is one supposed to do? Just let her—drown?"

He sat, white, stiff, his eyes full of tears.

With this man one could not easily use the ancient balm of arms, warmth, easy comfort. She pulled a chair near his, took his hand, held it. The tears ran down his face.

"Mark, listen. She's not going to be your wife. She's not ever going to be. Sometime, you've got to see it."

"You mean, I should look for another wife? Oh, I've had plenty of that sort of advice recently, I assure you. They've even said I should marry you!"

"Well, God knows I'm not one to say that one should marry for the sake of being married. But Mark, you've got to give up Lynda. I mean, you've got to stop waiting for her to be different."

"If I can't have her, I don't want anybody."

"All right. Then you'll have nobody."

"But why? The other afternoon, when that dreadful woman was not there, it was as if—it was like when we were first married." After a time, when she did not say anything, his taut hand went loose in hers, and he stood up. The look he gave her was hurt: she had not helped him, not said what he wanted to hear.

Next day, he asked Lynda if she would go away with him for a weekend, to stay at Mary and Harold Buttses'. She had always loved Nanny Butts.

"Yes, yes, of course," said Lynda. "I'd love to. What a lovely idea."

194

They were to leave by car on Friday afternoon. In the morning there were voices shouting in anger from the basement, screams that wailed off into tears. Objects crashed against walls, doors slammed.

Mark packed a suitcase, he went downstairs at the time he had appointed, to fetch his wife. Lynda was sitting on her bed in a dressing gown, with a desperate trembling smile that was directed generally, not at Mark, but at life. Dorothy sat knitting in the other room. She was making a tea cosy, of purple and red wool. Lynda's clothes were on the floor, in a heap beside the suitcase.

Then Lynda stood up, still smiling, walked out of the bedroom, and went up the stairs, with her husband following her. In Mark's bedroom, on the table by his bed, stood a photograph of a radiant young beauty who smiled back at the soiled, ill, sour-smelling Lynda.

The sick woman ground her teeth with rage, picked up the photograph, looked at it with hatred, then flung it down to break into a mess of glass and wood. Then she went into the study. On a long table against one wall stood Jimmy's models of possible electronic machines. One of them was a development of existing machines that could chart the human brain in terms of electric impulses. These machines she systematically smashed. Then she went downstairs again, locking the door into the basement behind her.

Late that night Martha, on her way up to bed, saw the study door open. Mark was sitting by his desk, and the face he lifted was the white black-eyed mask.

"Martha, will you get rid of that—picture? I can't."

She went to the bedroom, swept up the glass and the bits of frame, and took up the photograph of young Lynda: undamaged. It was hard to tear up that beautiful face, but she tore it up, and disposed of it all in the rubbish bin.

As she passed the study for the second time, Mark called her in.

"I'm going to see if I can find my brother," he said.

This could have been foreseen: if she had been awake? Possibly. It was a shock. She sat down, opposite his challenger's face, to challenge him.

"You can't."

"I'm going to."

"What did you have in mind? That you'd turn up in Moscow and say, Where is my brother?"

"Yes."

"But he might be anywhere—not necessarily Russia. And you wouldn't get a visa."

"I know people during the war who got in and out of Nazi Germany. My brother James did once. He was on some sort of secret mission."

"Your brother James was working for a secret service?"

"Well, that was the war. A lot of people did."

"If you get killed then Francis won't have a father. And what will happen to Paul?"

The white face and the black bitter eyes seemed all there was of him. Then a switch turned somewhere, and he went red, and he said: "Capitalist propaganda. You're an ex-Communist. That's how you are bound to talk."

"Never mind about Communism and capitalism for the moment. But if you go bouncing about behind the Iron Curtain being a nuisance, you'll find yourself in jug. Or worse."

A sneer. The Communist sneer. Indistinguishable of course from a sneer of any kind. But melodramatic, improbable. Particularly on this face, in this quiet study, in this house. And in Radlett Street, Bloomsbury, London.

"Or don't you read the newspapers?"

"Well, really," he said, with a laughing sneer.

"All right then, ask the comrades—you just ask them if you can go to an embassy and say: I want to get a visa to let me travel to Russia so I can find my brother who has defected East because . . ."

"Because he's a spy? He's not a spy. I tell you it's not possible."

"You've just said your brother James was."

"That's *not* . . . if you can't tell the difference, then . . ."

"Probably what happened was Colin got a visit from somebody like Hilary Marsh and he got into a panic."

"Colin is not the kind to scare easily."

"Then he was a fool not to be scared. You were scared. So was I. I'm scared now."

"I've got a lot of time for you, Martha, you know that. But when you start talking like the gutter press, then I'm sorry."

"Have you actually asked any of the comrades about it? Why don't you?"

"I shall. Good night." And he dismissed the enemy.

She remained the enemy for some weeks. Night after night, he asked his friends in, or went to their homes. She was not introduced to them: they met on the stairs with nods and smiles. Then, as a result of Mark's inquiries, Patty Samuels came to the house, on a proper, formal interview, to see Mark. They were together for an hour or more. Martha enquired what the advice had been.

Mark said, briefly, that "on the whole it was considered inadvisable." Then, with an apologetic laugh and glance: "What a warhorse!"

But he had liked her, or had been intrigued by her. She came again, became one of the people who dropped in, by herself, or with others, in the evenings. She was a lively vital woman in her early thirties, and a veteran of the party, absolutely unlike anyone Mark had ever met, but like dozens Martha had met—and like what she herself had been for a brief period.

Patty was the opposite, in every way, of Lynda.

And this time, Martha was able to foresee what would happen.

While Mark developed an affair with Patty, Lynda, in the basement, had a relapse, a falling back. For a time it was touch and go whether she would have to go back to hospital.

Dorothy came up to Martha, a few days after the incident of the photograph, to ask if Martha would come down to see Lynda, who was asking for her.

Lynda was in bed, crying hysterically that she was no good, she was useless, she had ruined Mark, and she didn't understand why Mark didn't kill her. She wished Mark had killed her. If Mark did not kill her, she would kill herself.

Martha wanted to call in Dr. Lamb, whom, after all, both women visited regularly, for drugs and for advice. But Dorothy, weeping, begged Martha not to do this. Dr. Lamb would send Lynda back to the hospital; they would both have to go back to the hospital. Lynda added her tears and pleas to Dorothy's. Why, then, had Lynda asked for Martha to come down?

Then Martha saw that she was Mark's deputy. Lynda could not face Mark himself. But she could say to Martha what she was afraid of saying to Mark. Lynda did not mean to kill herself. These bitter tears and self-reproaches were a way of announcing to Mark, through Martha, and to Dorothy, and perhaps to herself, her sorrow at not being able to be Mark's wife, and her intention of refusing to be. It was also a reproach to Mark: look you are making me ill by asking so much of me. Mark, hearing that Lynda was ill, appeared in the basement, but Lynda shrieked at him to go away. He went.

Lynda wept that she was a beast and unfit to live: but there was relief in it. Mark did not, for a while, go near the basement. But Martha was admitted, and reported to him.

For some weeks Lynda remained low, and weepy. Nothing, it seemed, could break her misery. Then Paul came home for a month's holiday, and he made her better.

Lynda and Paul together—it was charming, delightful; they were like two children. Dorothy watched, indulgent: Lynda's mother, she now became Paul's as well. For Lynda still could not bear being touched. So Paul sat on Dorothy's large steamy sad lap, and was hugged and given sweets. With Lynda, he played. Martha made excuses to go down and watch. She was seeing Sally-Sarah again. Yes, there she was, in her child, a bright exuberant vivid creature, all charm and peremptory emotional demand, who cuddled up to Dorothy, and flung his arms around Martha's neck, and sat very quiet, by Lynda's side, his hands in his lap, while he smiled and listened to her fantastic stories.

But that was in the basement. In the rest of the house, Paul was a cool, shrewd, clever little boy ("too clever by half!" as one teacher had let drop) whom no one would dare to touch or pet or fondle.

Then, the holidays ended and Paul went back to school, and Lynda remained well.

There was a new balance in the house. Upstairs Mark was absorbed in his developing affair with Patty Samuels. It seemed that he no longer expected anything from Lynda. He saw very little of Martha, and did not speak at all about the search for his brother.

In the basement the two sick women were trying to expand their lives, to become like ordinary people. Dorothy now started to go out of the flat, which she had not wanted to do before. She shopped, sometimes went to the cinema, talked of getting a job. But Lynda did not leave the flat. They had visitors, women for the most part. When this happened Lynda made an effort to dress, and to be beautiful again. Once they invited Martha down. It turned out to be a séance. A couple of men and half a dozen women had arrived. In the heavy curtained room, with its air that smelled of drugs and anxiety, the lights were turned low and a woman called Mrs. Mellendip invoked the spirits: successfully, as far as some of those present were concerned. After that, Martha tried not to go down unless the two were alone. Otherwise it was an atmosphere of inordinate tea-drinking, palm-reading, fortunetelling. They would sit through entire afternoons and evenings laying the cards again and again and again for guidance on matters like buying a new handbag or having a hairdo. They worked out the horoscopes of themselves, their friends, their doctors, and public persons. Mrs. Mellendip earned her living by doing horoscopes, but did not charge Lynda or Dorothy. Without being asked, she did Martha's. It turned out to be more of a character reading, and was very shrewd indeed. Martha said it was, but that she had not learned anything about herself she did not already know. To which Mrs. Mellendip, a large forceful handsome woman in her middle fifties, returned: "Well, dear, I could tell you more if you knew it." Which remark was very much the note, or tone, of these gatherings. For when the tea leaves or the cards confirmed what a person already knew, this was not a sign of failure, but of success, and added to Mrs. Mellendip's confidence in herself, and her powers.

Martha told Lynda she did not care for her new friends, which Lynda accepted, in her way of tolerating the unenlightened. Thereafter she would telephone Martha to say: "Have you time for a visit to the condemned cell?"—or some such joke.

Martha was much alone, in the doldrums, her life becalmed. She was doing her job: that was all. The house was running, the children's lives organised, Mark's affairs attended to. But what was she really doing? What ought she to be doing? She did not know. She sat in her room and watched the structure of the sycamore tree disappear in spring green. Spring moved futilely in her veins. She watched. She was a person who watched other people in a turmoil of living. Could that be true? When Mark, or Lynda, or even Mrs. Mellendip looked at her, did they see a woman who watched and waited—passive?

For what? For the bad time to be over? It was like waiting for the end of the war. Worse: war was easier, it had a form, one knew what one was supposed to be feeling, even if one didn't conform to it. The last war, after all, had been easy: one's head and one's heart had moved together. By and large and for better or for worse, she, and everyone she knew, had been able to identify with their country, with their side: and now, with all the slogans and the speeches and the propaganda in perspective, all the accounts done, they could still say, Yes, we were right, fascism was worse than anything.

But now? If a new war started now, spreading out from Korea: if, to use the political shorthand of the time, "America dropped the bomb on Russia before Russia could develop the bomb"—then what would she feel? No use to sit here thinking. *It won't happen*, because it might very well, and it was now that she should decide what to do. To decide that meant deciding or deciphering what she felt. This country would be allied with America, that could be assumed. She could not support America; she could not support Communism. She would have to support one or the other. No matter what form the war took this time (and it wouldn't be remotely like the last, but probably all slow spreading poisons and panic and hysteria and terror at the unknown), she would have to be a traitor, not only from the point of view of society—her country; and the point of view of her "side," socialism; but from her own. Because there would be no middle place. Well then, she would be a patriot and a coward, rather than a traitor and a coward . . . She was immensely tired. A lethargy like an invisible poison filled her. Sitting through the darkening evenings, she looked out into the street, at the lively tree, and she began to think of death, of suicide. If the war started, that is what she would do, kill herself.

Thoughts of death slowly filled the room. When she came into it, it was to enter a region where death waited. While spring slowly crammed London with flowers and greenery, she allowed herself to be taken over . . . and then, one afternoon when she had been down to see Lynda, she thought how strange it was; a few weeks ago it was in the basement that people, or rather Lynda, talked of death, of suicide, of killing. Now, no outside circumstance changed, the basement was alive again, and futures were possible and talked about: even if they were no more than a new dress or that Dr. Lamb's horoscope promised he would be in a good mood for next week's monthly visit. Death had moved up to Martha's room on the second floor.

It seemed as if her capacity to think this, see this, had the power to shift the fog in the room, start a fresh current.

She was able to move outside the listless woman who sat hour after hour looking through a window.

She had a glimpse into a view of life where the house and people in it could be seen as a whole, making a whole. It was not a glimpse or insight which could be easily brought down into an ordinary air: it came late at night, and afterwards Martha remembered that the phrase "Having something in common" had had, for the time the condition lasted, a real meaning. They, in this house, had something in common, made up something . . .

Mark and the comrades, all furious energy and defence;

Lynda and her Dorothy in the twilight of their basement; Martha, all passivity; the two sad children, who were the pasts and the futures of the adult people: but an onlooker, someone looking into this house as if it were a box whose lid could be taken off, would be struck by a curious fact. Martha, defeated by the house, by the currents of personality in it, was the one person in it who had no reason at all to be suffering, to be weighed down: yet she was the only person who (at that time, during that particular spring) was weighed down, was suffering, who thought of death.

Martha was suddenly, not easily, but after effort, able to look down into the house, achieve that viewpoint. As she did so, the heavy atmosphere of death in her room cleared, thinned, and went.

There she was, in her room, empty, at peace. She watched other people developing their lives. And she? In every life there is a curve of growth, or a falling away from it; there is a central pressure, like sap forcing up a trunk, along a branch, into last year's wood, and there, from a dead-looking eye, or knot, it bursts again in a new branch, in a shape that is inevitable but known only to itself until it becomes visible. Yet here she sat, watching the sap pressing up in other people, feeling none in herself.

One of the observers, or critics, who might be imagined looking down through that roof, would say: a man. This is a young woman, and she wants a man. Martha had been here for nearly three years now, and she had put aside thoughts of a man, of marriage, and even, for the most of the time, sex. She had been dormant.

Now she was invaded by sex. One had only to think: A man, I need a man, and sex invades in its battalions. Mark? She wanted Mark? She had only to think this, and she did. Yet she had not. She found herself, all at once, jealous of Patty Samuels. Then, soon, furiously, self-pityingly jealous of Lynda who had kept Mark's love for years *without having done anything to deserve it*. This last, for a time, did not strike her as absurd. She was possessed. Waves of vicious emotion washed in and out of her.

The room, a few weeks before, fogged by the listlessness of a drift to death, was now all sexual fantasy, anger, hatred.

On the stairs she passed men on their way to and from Mark's study. She looked at men: sex. This one? That one? She nodded a greeting to Patty Samuels and hated her. She was unable to go down to the basement: she hated Lynda.

In this condition she telephoned, again, the house by the canal. Jack answered. He said he would love to see Martha.

In this condition she made the trip across London to visit a memory.

The terrace of houses, since she had been here before, had been partly done up. Some houses were still corpses, with leprous faces, others were clean and had jolly coloured doors. In Jack's house, she entered a hall which was carpeted, and softly lit. The door into the room where the mad youth had camped was open. It was now somebody's drawing room, a pleasant room with sofas and chairs and books. A young woman carried a baby out of this room, and with a smile, disappeared into the room on the other side of the hall.

Martha, already half sober, ascended the stairs. Jack's door was opened by a plump blonde girl who said, in a low voice: "Come in—you're Martha? He's asleep."

The studio room had not changed. Jack was propped up in the bed, and there was an atmosphere of illness. The blonde girl returned to her chair by the bed. Jack opened his eyes and said: "Hello, Martha," and began coughing. The coughing roused him. He tried to sit up, failed, collapsed back, and lay holding Martha's hand, and the blonde girl's. He had lit wild eyes, a feverish glow on the bones of his face; was very thin.

Martha stayed for a time, until he went back to sleep.

In the hall, as Martha left, the blonde girl, Betty, said that Jack had insisted on leaving the sanatorium, against the advice of the doctors, and that she was nursing him. But she was persuading him to go back there: if he would only stick it out in the sanatorium, he would be cured, they said. But Jack was very worried about leaving the house: Mr. Vasallo, a not very nice man, took unfair advantage—Martha was an old friend, please would she come again?

Martha, cured, left that house and returned home.

But she was not cured of anger, of hatred.

A few weeks ago, she had sat watching Lynda and Dorothy, pursuing their fortunetelling, their astrology; and Mark and Patty Samuels, with their Communism. She had watched, interested, as if there was no more to be said than: Well, that's what they are doing, that's how they are.

Now, she found herself in the grip of violent distaste for the preoccupations of the basement; and disgust for Mark and his politics.

Even a few weeks ago, she had been reading the

newspapers that flooded into the house from left, right, and centre; observing a process of interlocking, inter-reacting currents. Now she read the right-wing press as if every word had been written by herself; and it was not only with fear, but with hatred that she read the papers of the left. She was able only to maintain enough objectivity to recognise the depth of the fear. She was being threatened with another conversion. She could see that. But seeing it was not enough to shift it, to chase away the disgust. A phrase used by Mark, from the Communist jargon, or an insensitively jolly competence observed on Patty's face, flooded her with an angry irritation.

Yet, while she was in this condition, a set of phrases or sentences from the armoury of the right which objectivised precisely what she was feeling, so that she could see the crude ugliness of it, was enough to switch her over—not to any position where she could include, hold, tolerate, understand—but to an extreme leftism, just as if she had never left there.

For some days she kept switching from one viewpoint to the other; one day she was violently "anti-communist"—and self-righteously so. The next, she was a pure, dedicated, self-righteous Communist. The two states had no connection at all—apparently.

In this condition she had a dream which, while she could not clearly remember it, woke her with a warning. She was muttering: "If I let myself do this, I'll have to live through it again, I'll be made to do it again." She went back to sleep and woke in a clear morning, summer outside, the sky all sunlight and fresh white clouds, knowing that she had made a shift in her sleep. She knew, as if someone had told her so, that if she now allowed herself to hate Mark, to hate Patty Samuels, to hate the comrades, she would be doing worse than hating a younger self. She would be threatened with more than "Having to do it all over again." Inside her would be lying in wait what she hated, to emerge in ogreish disguises she could not now imagine. And this would be the same if she returned to being a Communist. Shapes of hatred much larger than she could envisage waited like the shadows on a nursery wall for fear to fill and move them.

But, knowing what she had to do, she could not do it. The energy it needed, the effort: she could not find it. Brought again and again by herself to that point in her where she had to untie knots of violent emotions, she shied away, baulked. No, no, no: she could not.

For days she was locked in that condition which is called a

sulk, turning herself to that point in her where she had to untie knots of violent emotions, she shied away, baulked. No, no, no: she could not.

For days she was locked in that condition which is called a sulk, turning herself away, saying no, no.

Then, one night, she had a dream of Patty Samuels, who was also her younger self. Patty approached her smiling. But Martha turned angrily away. Patty Samuels, multiplied into an army, in the shape of a nation which was all sinister threatening power, encompassed Martha, threatened her with death. This was a nightmare and it woke Martha completely. She sat in the dark room whose walls had the shadow of the tree moving on them, shadows on a shadow, and she listened to the dream. She could not sleep. The moon rose. Light came into the room and the tree's shadow dissolved. Over the earth's shoulder the moon was catching light from the sun. A quietness came into the room, with the vision of the little world, one half bathed in moonlight, the other in sunlight.

Next day, meeting Patty Samuels in the kitchen, she was able to smile at her younger self. A stiffness went from her face; muscles went loose all over her body that she had not known were knotted.

Patty Samuels wore a brisk blue skirt and white shirt, and had a pile of papers in a suitcase. She was cool with Martha, then, after a hesitation, warmed. Because, as Martha saw, Patty felt that Martha had changed. In the kitchen, observing each other, Patty made coffee, Martha made coffee, and neither was in a hurry to leave. Soon they sat drinking coffee at the table, allowing goodwill to do its work.

Patty had at first met Martha with the hard shell of contempt that went with the words "ex-Communist that has sold out." She had once muttered, so Martha could hear: "Well of course people leave when the heat's turned on . . ."

Patty Samuels had become a Communist when she was twenty, at the time of the Spanish Civil War. Her life had been spent organising. She had been a secretary, or assistant, to Communist officials, had been an official herself, though on an unimportant level. She was now "doing Culture." She used the phrase now with irony; five years before she would have regarded irony as treachery. A great part of her time was spent wrestling with Soviet and other East European countries in order to get their ideas of efficiency over visas for delegations, and so forth, to coincide with hers. This was a task which had reduced the strongest to nervous breakdown; and Patty, a strong woman, was showing strain. Also, by the nature of things she was bound to know a great many of the people in Russia, and in other Communist countries who had disappeared into prison or were dead; and most of her friends in Britain and in America were under suspicion, passportless, or in one sort of trouble or another.

The relation between herself and Martha was a curious one, based on the closest of understandings born of shared experience—yet full of antagonism. For there was no person more hated, vilified, and distrusted by the comrades, at that particular time, than someone like Martha.

What Patty Samuels wanted, Martha realised, had been wanting for a long time, was to talk about Mark. They did not talk about Mark during this first reconnaissance over the coffee cups, but as their cautious friendship developed, Patty began to talk, and obsessively, about Mark, his friends, his way of life.

She suspected, of course, that Martha was in love with Mark. "All's fair in love and war," she said, once, accepting a rivalry as natural. But she was much more worried about Lynda, whom she had not yet met; it was some time before Lynda entered their conversations.

She did not understand Mark. "These upper-class types?" she would say, or enquire; or "People like him?" or "These political demivierges!"

The affair was in bad difficulties.

"Do you know what I sometimes think, Martha? I do believe that Mark thinks that one of these days in the extremes of passion I'm going to divulge the truth about his brother—he keeps coming back to it. I keep saying I don't know anything, I mean, why should he think that I should? He simply doesn't know the score. . . ."

Knowing the score: the painful phrase at that time, for the grim realities of Communism, which was so shortly to become absorbed into that other phrase: "Stalinism." Soon, trusting Martha, the enemy, she began discussing, or rather suggesting at, or talking around, what was going on inside Communism. A great deal did not need to be said: there being no substitute for experience. Martha, for the most part, listened: for the most part, when with one's younger self, one listens; one hears, bouncing off oneself, one's young voice. Painful. But not to be rejected, or repudiated, without asking for bad trouble.

Very painful, for both of them, these times when they drank coffee, or Patty came up to Martha's room.

Patty was in the grip of an aspect of herself she had not known existed, and which she feared and despised.

Mark was the enemy: he was a capitalist, member of an old upper-class family, and an intellectual, to cap it all. Yet she was fascinated by all this, and knew it. She would have been delighted to be introduced to this world. But even she, who had every reason to understand, from her own experience, the realities of isolation, did not understand how cut off Mark was from his own kind. She believed that Mark was deliberately excluding her from his real life, his friends. Once she asked: "Tell me, is Mark mean with housekeeping money? I mean, is he careful?" She did not at all see that her attraction for him was—her world, which she was tired of, had grown out of. The fact that for years she had lived in bed-sitting rooms, eaten badly if at all, in cafés, and cheap restaurants; had not taken holidays, had worked like a horse for so little money; was, in short, dedicated, seemed to Mark not romantic, but admirable. He admired her. He enjoyed tasting this life for which he knew he had no capacity. He liked to turn up at her shabby room near King's Cross, late at night, to find her still at work for her cause. And he did not see, as Martha did, that she was due to break. He thought the reason she did not want to discuss "the Party" with him was because of secretiveness, possibly even because she was concealing facts about his brother. But the truth was, for her he was a relief from the monotony of her life and work.

Underneath all that jolly competence was a very tired woman. And a frightened one. After all, she was getting on for thirty-five. She had been married and divorced, but that was some time ago. She had had some affairs. She wanted children. She was beginning to see that Mark would never marry her.

And now she brought up Lynda. "Surely he ought to divorce her?" she kept saying.

One day she met Lynda, who had come up for something. She saw a very thin, untidy woman, with strained wide eyes, in a dress that looked as if it had been slept in.

The encounter changed Patty.

"You say he loves her?" she enquired, in a way which was characteristic of her at that time, troubled but determined to know.

"Yes, I think he does."

"Well, that's not my idea of love. I mean, what's the point of being in love with someone who can't ever give you anything?" She looked scared, hearing herself say this: for she had announced an intention, and knew it. She laughed, at last. "I'm not getting any younger, am I?" and, finally: "I mean, love ought to be a partnership."

The affair did not come to any dramatic end. For one thing, it was embedded in Mark's social life: the people who came to visit him were her friends; when he went to their homes, she was often there.

Three

The bad time continued. It was expressed in a number of separate events, or processes, in this or that part of the world, whose common quality was horror—and a senseless horror. To listen, to read, to watch the news of any one of these events was to submit oneself to incredulity: this barbarism, this savagery, was simply not possible. And, everywhere in this country, in the world, people like oneself sat reading, looking, watching, in precisely the same condition: this is not possible; it can't be happening; it's all so monstrously silly that I can't believe it . . . The war in Korea was at the height of its danger for the world, the propaganda on both sides had reached a point where no one sensible could believe a word of it, and for months it looked as if nothing could stop America using "the bomb" there. In America the hysteria had grown till that great nation looked from outside like a dog driven mad by an infestation of fleas, snapping and biting at its own flesh; and a man called Joe McCarthy, who had no qualities at all, save one, the capacity to terrorise other people, was able to do as he liked. Throughout Africa various countries fought in various ways against the white man, but in Kenya there was a full-scale war, both sides (as in Korea) fighting with a maximum of nastiness and lies.

In the Communist countries things went from bad to worse. In South America—but first things first; whole continents, let alone countries, have to be overlooked when the future of the human race balances on what seems to be needlepoints somewhere in Korea, Berlin, Vietnam . . . As for Kenya, it was ugly, it was a turning point and a crossroads (etc., etc.) for Africa, but it was not of vital importance. No world war was likely to start there. It affected, nastily, the atmosphere in Britain, which was already craven and corrupted because of breathing the poisoned winds from across the Atlantic. It affected, for instance, Arthur Coldridge and his ex-wife Phoebe.

When Martha became a friend of Patty Samuels and ceased to be a traitor and an enemy, she was admitted, through her, to the group of comrades, who met nightly in Mark's house, or in a café or a pub. She was admitted to—talk, discussion, debate. It was a long time since she had been in an unconstituted committee. She was joining it, as she immediately saw, as it was about to disintegrate. For two, three years, it had been a tight defensive little group: Mark; Patty Samuels; Freddie Postings, a physicist and friend of Colin; Gerald Smith, a Marxist historian from a provincial university; Bob Hasty, an economist; one or two others. Mark was the only non-Communist. Of these, not one would be a Communist in two, three years. Meanwhile, they were under violent fire from their own side, which they criticised—but never publicly, since everyone else did that; and submitted to the subtle, creeping, crooked pressures that characterised the time, from outside. For instance, Freddie Postings, due for advancement in his job, had not been given it—had been transferred to work he was not interested in and where he could not advance, because as his superior had told him one night when drunk, of his past association with Colin. Gerald Smith had lost his wife into a mental hospital: she had been unable to stand the social isolation of being his wife, an isolation which was never explained, put into words, defended: just slowly deepened, till she cracked. Bob Hasty—but, one way and another, it was the same for all of them. In America they would be defending themselves before committees, would be deciding whether or not to betray friends and associates: here nothing of the sort was asked of them, they were just having a very bad time. This group was where they were able to relax, where they created the energy to go on, where there was a breathable air. But what was this air? Remarkably enough, if it was one part faith in humanity, it was two parts pure nihilism, a kind of painful, despairing, angry denial of faith; as if, threatened from outside both from friends and enemies by bad faith and destruction, they had to create the same qualities here, in a homeopathic dosage. It was the nihilism of Thomas's last testament. Here it was. Here? Why? Sometimes Martha felt as if Thomas had walked in, a thin bitter man, burned nearly black by his river-valley sun, and was leaning by the door, smiling: he had been drawn by the atmosphere, so much his own.

But it did not last for long. Jimmy Wood took to dropping in. Even a few months ago this would have been impossible: his politics, or rather his lack of them, would have excluded him. But things were breaking up: here was Martha, an enemy, here was Jimmy. Why did he come? For a while people talked and talked, of Korea and America and freedom; of Stalin and freedom; of Kenya and war and freedom; of Berlin and Russia and freedom. He was bored, sat smiling his baby smile, waited. As soon as he could, he came in with his own passion—no, that word could never be used of Jimmy Wood. His interest, then. He came to this house, it began to become evident, because Mark was not often enough at the factory. Mark was not talking enough to Jimmy. Jimmy was here to get his allowance of fuel: which was talk. Probably he was quite unconscious why he came, but could not help coming; and if Mark had not given it to him off he would go. Until Martha saw this, she did not really see it—to use the way of speech current in the basement. Nor did she see it at once. For a while, there was Jimmy, inexplicably, even embarrassingly, a rather silent but smiling visitor, among people who talked, or ingested politics. He turned his face, or rather his spectacles, towards one speaker after another, until Mark started to talk. Then in dodged Jimmy, suddenly all attention and energy, like a sheepdog in a flock of sheep. He was isolating Mark, bringing him out towards himself. And, in a moment, it would be Jimmy and Mark talking—not necessarily about scientific matters, not at all. It could be anything, even politics. Then, while the others listened, silenced by the little man's extraordinary detachment from them, for it was really as if they did not exist, as if only Mark existed, the talk was swung towards something close to factory matters. Soon, Freddie Postings, the physicist, came in. Politics were being pushed aside; the talk was of physics; but not for long, not so that Mark could not stay in it. It did not matter what the subject of the talk was, Martha saw; it mattered that Mark was in an exchange of talk with Jimmy. Jimmy had probably quite unconsciously manoeuvred the subject of the talk so as to gain Mark's maximum participation in it. That is what he needed. It is what he came for. It is what he got. Why? He was no stronger, no more intelligent, no more well informed than anybody else. Jimmy dominated the group, the unconstituted committee. Jimmy destroyed it. He did this by dominating it. He continued to dominate even when Phoebe and Arthur came.

Their coming was extraordinary: indeed, until it happened, impossible. For two, three years, the brothers had been so opposed that they had communicated through brief business letters, if at all. Arthur, Phoebe, that section of the Labour Party they belonged to, were busy, like everyone else, crusading against Communism. Then, when the war began in Kenya, Arthur and Phoebe were of that small number of people in Britain who supported the African side and agitated for Britain to withdraw. They became increasingly unpopular.

They continued to hate Communism, but this seemed irrelevant when a large newspaper was running a campaign against the Coldridge family, den of traitors, spies, and destroyers of Britain. "How long will the authorities allow these enemies within our gates . . ." "The Coldridge family continues its work of undermining those liberties which . . ."

This being not the first time Mark had dealt with newspaper suggestions that he should be locked up, he revived previous plans, which this time included Arthur and Phoebe. True that Arthur was a member of Parliament, and true that Phoebe's work in her various organisations was above-board and open to anybody's inspection. Whatever divided them, they knew one simple thing: that in times of public hysteria anything was possible. Whole nations went mad overnight. It had happened in Stalin's Russia. It had happened in Germany. It had happened in the England of the First World War. It was happening now in the States. The tiniest turn of the screw one way or the other, and anybody could be locked up, lose their jobs, be put into prison, interned. Or, possibly, killed.

It was just here, when the bad time was in fact ending, or soon to end, that it reached its climax of nastiness. It was a question of living from day to day, trying to make plans for possibilities they could only guess at. They were a group of isolated individuals, with very little in common, forced together because of danger: their differences became sharper because of the tension. Phoebe seemed in a permanent state of near hysteria; she snapped and was rude and unpleasant. Mark was sullen and withdrawn. Martha was listless. Arthur, aggressive by temperament, was luckiest, but he fell into a depression—unusual for him.

The question was, Who was there to look after the children if they were all locked up?

210

Not Martha, as vulnerable as anybody. Not Lynda, since she might at any moment crack up again. Margaret was on speaking terms with neither Arthur nor Mark: that is, if the phrase was taken literally. She wrote them letters, appealing for their better judgment: the blacks in Kenya were all filthy savages—she enclosed various articles about Mau Mau; Mark was destroying democracy. On the evidence of past behaviour one could assume she would support their being locked up, if she did not actually organise it.

Eventually Mary and Harold Butts were asked if they would come and live in the house and look after Paul and Francis, keep an eye on Lynda and Dorothy. This they agreed to do, with equanimity, even when the responsibility stretched to taking on all Arthur's children as well, and possibly Phoebe's.

In the unconstituted committee the discussion of politics had become impossible, now that Arthur and Phoebe were so often there, and so very hostile to Communism. Discussion about politics is, after all, only possible when people agree, or have at least something in common. They all agreed about Africa, about Kenya. They agreed about . . . a large number of matters, but not about what had constituted this group's chief reason for existence in the first place. The meetings became fewer, then stopped.

Mark spent more time with Arthur: the brothers had always liked each other. His children came to play with Paul. So did Phoebe's little girls. There was a holiday down at Nanny Butts's with all the children, seven of them, and Mark and Martha and Phoebe and Arthur and his wife. Patty did not see Mark for two weeks: she wasn't feeling well, she said. She had been called in by superiors in the party and talked to about her political line—unsatisfactory, they said it was. She had not been openly threatened with expulsion, but she had to think out her position, what she was going to do. At Nanny Butts's final arrangements were made for looking after the children in the event of their entire complement of adults vanishing into prison or internment. When Arthur Coldridge was driving to the house, one night, the car was stopped and a couple of men in masks told him that if he didn't "Lay off the whites in Kenya and forget the blacks" they would see to it he had a nasty accident. He reported this to the police; his garage was blown up, but there was no way of proving who had done it. The atmosphere was worsening—could it get worse? Even down in the village, there was a feeling of being under siege. They stayed

211

in the cottage, tried not to go out into the garden, because there always seemed to be people staring over the hedges. Nanny Butts got some poison-pen letters; the children found their village friends were unable to play with them.

Then things began to shift. The change began for Mark with the publication of *A City in the Desert*. On the whole he had ignored this, for he still did not know whether he regretted writing it or not. The reviews were pretty good. The literary world was still in its stance of "nonengagement," it was still claiming all virtue for the interior of the ivory tower. *A City in the Desert* fulfilled every requirement of this mood. It did not deal with anything controversial, or political, or social. It could be put aside safely as allegorical, and above all, it could not possibly be approved of by the Communists. It was a safe book to praise and it was praised, although Mark had been described as a Communist for four years now.

The point was, in this small incestuous world where everyone had known Mark, or Margaret, or Mark's brothers, where everyone knew, and so very thoroughly, what "the score" was (how not, since everyone had been red, or pink?), they knew that there would come a time when Mark, just as they had, would see the light and repudiate Communism. *A City in the Desert* was taken as a proof of a change of heart: no Communist could possibly have written it.

Patty Samuels, for instance, regarded it as shockingly reactionary. The affair was finally breaking up: the appearance of this novel and the good reviews hastened the process.

Not that this meant Mark saw less of her: he was seeing more. She was having a breakdown. Stalin had died, the Communist world was in chaos, and Patty in chaos with it. The trouble was, nervous breakdowns were not considered possible for progressive people. Socialist circles were not admitting the possibility that mental troubles existed, or were only just beginning to, and Patty's illness was being claimed as purely physical: her doctor was a Communist Party member. She had had headaches, and her heart gave her trouble: when Mark suggested that she might be under stress, she snapped, "Thanks, who are you calling neurotic." She wrote him an emotional and abusive letter about *A City* in which she said among other things he was a cowardly rat, and talked about ships that sank or did not sink and could be patched up, etc. He was very concerned about her. Mark had gone to Patty, seeing her a representative of a sane and dedicated life. Now, for the second time, he found he had a

212

woman in breakdown on his hands. Once again, it called out the best in him. Martha saw him as he must have been with Lynda when she was first ill: he was all gentleness and strength. But he was very unhappy. Not because of Patty—for him, that was all over. Nor, at the moment, because of Lynda, who maintained a kind of balance.

No, it was because he did not understand what was happening. To say he was becoming an anti-Communist was impossible. For one thing, that would have meant betraying his brother: so he saw it, or rather, felt it. But he had, at a very emotional time, met a group of people who had been calm, judicious, unhysterical. Now they were in fervours of doubt, conflict, emotionalism, and over Stalin, whom Mark had never seen as more than a useful kind of warlord, "rather like Churchill." Mark had never been more of a Coldridge than over Stalin. Such people had to be, he supposed; "One had to have politicians." But, putting forward such views, in such language, to people separating rapidly into Stalinists and anti-Stalinists, proved more than ever, if it needed proving, that he, Mark, had never known the score.

But he had not changed, he felt: he, his views, were the same. Yet, suddenly, having been ostracised for four years, he was being invited to dinner parties. The telephone, silent for so long a time, had come to life, with old friends ringing up as if nothing whatever had happened. The intellectual weeklies asked him for articles and reviews. Vast sums of money were offered for his "confessions" about the Communist Party by, among others, Miles Tangin, who had changed his newspaper but not his attitude that he, Miles Tangin, had no connection with what he wrote. The newspaper was the *Evening X* instead of the *Daily Y*, but both were running articles headed "I worked for Stalin" or "Fifteen Years in the Communist Hell," being the public breast-beating not of the people who had been in Communist hells, but who had been members of the Communist Party in Britain. The letter in which Miles offered Mark £500 for his confessions included a request to be introduced to Harry Pollitt (presumed to be a close friend of Mark's) because "I hear he is a decent sort of chap."

Mark seemed to be feeling, not so much that people were inconsistent—they could be expected to be—but that they had no sense of honour. He had not used this word for some time. He was using it again. He was using it as if nothing whatsoever had happened.

In short, his diversion from himself into Communism was

over. He had had a dose of Communism. Some people can fall in love often and violently, but it doesn't affect them. When it's over they haven't changed. Similarly, some people get doses of this or that kind of politics or religion: but it doesn't really affect them.

Mark was not changed: it had never gone deep. It was very likely only the fact that his brother was presumably a Communist that stopped him from saying again that you couldn't trust a Communist further than you could kick him.

Instead he said that there was no honour left in public life.

In which case, Martha wondered, why did he spend so much time with Jimmy? She had once said to Mark that if someone came to Jimmy and asked him to design an improved instrument of torture, he would at once do so, the ethical aspects of the thing being dismissed with that vaguely embarrassed grimace which he offered to Mark's political and personal problems. Mark said yes, yes, very likely, he was like that. Mark did not, then, expect "honour" from Jimmy. But he did from Miles Tangin?

They discussed this: discussing honour and politics in this way, they resumed their evening sessions in the study. They drank brandy, smoked, were together a great deal. Patty had gone off to visit a sister in Essex, that flat country; the sea winds, the marshes, the birds, were all considered likely to do good to her heart and to her headaches.

"Thank God for you," said Mark to Martha, "you are always so calm."

Mark, then, had always seen Martha as calm? But he chose a moment to use the word which turned a spotlight on what a calm could mean.

Some weeks before the publication of *A City in the Desert*, that is, before Mark's return to public respectability, Martha had had a letter from Mrs. Quest, announcing her intention to come to England. Well, why not? Nothing could be more natural. Putting down that letter, Martha understood she was shaking from head to foot, calm. She sat there, the letter in her hand, calm. But she trembled. A week later, when a second letter arrived announcing a date, Martha understood she had been in bed, not getting up at all except for the nightly sessions with Mark—for a week. She had not been able to get up. She lay in a half-dark, in a kind of half-sleep, like a thing waterlogged. Yet she could not say she was unhappy. She was calm. But she could not get out of bed.

A third letter. The arrival was a few weeks off. This letter had to be read carefully. It began, My darling girl, and ended Your loving mother. In between, were pages of reproof, reproach, hatred. Martha had always got letters like these from her mother. For years and years—when had they started? But she could not remember. She did not read them. Or rather, she had learned a technique for reading them, skimming over them fast, to extract necessary facts, but insulated against pain. In her room was a suitcase full of letters from Mrs. Quest, beginning My darling girl, and ending Your loving mother. Martha wrote letters to her mother once a week, like a schoolgirl, saying nothing that was not polite, even affectionate.

Now she forced herself to read four years of letters. It took days. She was ill—but very calm. Martha now had to tell Mark something; and so said that she had flu. He was kind: he was always kind, but particularly so when he had a sick woman on his hands. Martha searched his face for signs that he might feel she was going the way of Lynda, of Patty, but if he felt it he did not say it. He brought hot-water bottles and oranges and aspirin and sat with her in her dark room. He told stories, anecdotes. Martha vaguely listened. They concerned a brother and sister, called Rachel and Aaron. It seemed as if she had known them. Then she understood that Mark was in the process of talking his way into a new book, conceived by his affair with Patty. But Patty had become fused with Sally-Sarah. Mark was tormented by guilt over Sally-Sarah. If he, Mark, had not been so obtuse, she would not have had to kill herself. Mark was taking onto himself a burden of guilt about the fate of the Jews in the last war. There was Patty, there was Sally-Sarah, there was also, though Martha did not see immediately that this was why his tales were half familiar, Thomas. Mark had found the ant-laced heap of manuscript and was using it in the creation of his brother and sister, Jews from Poland ... how odd to lie here and hear Mark's voice tell of Aaron, a Jewish boy from Poland, who was also Thomas. Rachel and Aaron were dark, lithe, vital, handsome creatures, children of a corn dealer in a village near the German border. Aaron was once beaten by his father so hard he couldn't sit down for a week because he refused to go to school: the teacher was no good, he said, the teacher didn't even know any Latin.... What was Thomas's voice like? Martha could not remember. She could hear Mark's, she could see Aaron, that flashing rebellious lad. What had Thomas really looked like? He didn't look at all like Aaron, no: he had been large and blond and blue-eyed.

For a time, at least. There had been two Thomases, one of them alien to her, a sombre bitter man—as Aaron might have become if he hadn't died in the concentration camp?

Whole areas of Martha's life had slipped away. She lay, half listening to Mark, trying to remember the simplest things. Her childhood had gone, except for small bright isolated events. For instance, she had once sat under a tree and looked across the veld and imagined a city shining there in the scrub. An ideal city, full of fountains and flowers. Like Mark's city. Perhaps the same city: but both, after all, were imagined. What had that stretch of country looked like? She could not remember, the blue mountains on the horizon stood up high into a cool blue sky, and they were streaked with snow. What had the house been like? It had gone. A shabby old grass-thatched house on a hill: but she could not see it. And inside? All gone. Even her bedroom, which had once been her place, her refuge, and where she had known every brushmark on the wall, and how the separate strands of grass had glistened when the lamps were brought in. And after that, she had been married. She had lived in different places with Douglas Knowell. She had had a large house. She had had a daughter. Caroline had been a pretty, small girl. She was now—what? Twelve? But that wasn't possible. And that long period, or it seemed so at the time—when she had been such an active busy Communist and then an active and busy social person—what was left of it all? Anton. She could not remember the rooms where she had lived with Anton. Thomas. She could not remember his voice, could not hear it. What came back from Thomas was—the strong smell of fresh wet greenery, growth, a sound of strong rain hitting dust, the sun on a drenched tree.

Her father's long illness; her mother—ah yes, here it was, and she knew it. She had been blocking off the pain, and had blocked off half of her life with it. Her memory had gone. Well, almost. But in a few weeks, Mrs. Quest would arrive in this house, to this life Martha was living now, and as usual not one thing about it could be revealed to her, because she would be so upset. It was perfectly clear from the letters which Martha was forcing herself to read that Mrs. Quest planned to live in London, and with Martha. This is what she had been dreaming about. But what had she allowed herself to remember of Martha that she could believe in it? For one thing, she had seized on the address: she knew the area very well. Her father had often taken her to the British Museum when she was a girl. She thought she remembered the house:

that big white one on the corner with the balconies painted such a pretty green? Martha was the secretary of an author. Was he well known? Mrs. Quest did not seem to know the name. Well, perhaps Martha could find her a room near by, though of course old ladies did not take up much room, and she hoped she knew how to make herself useful.

Mrs. Quest planned to live in this house, as Martha's mother, and to participate in some kind of imagined life. Bloomsbury. For Mrs. Quest this did not mean literature, she would not have that kind of association. It meant trips to the British Museum. She had written that she could help Martha with her work—she had learned to type. This, of course, drove knives into Martha: particularly because her mother could have no idea of the pathos of it. Mrs. Quest had got a secondhand typewriter on one of the rare trips into town, and on the farm among the mountains had sat learning to type so that Martha would make her welcome. She had not been getting on with her son and her daughter-in-law. That this, after all, was a common enough thing did not seem to strike the old lady: it was the fault of the modern generation (she could not bring herself to say that it was the fault of her son and his wife), and though the children were delightful, they were badly brought up. Of course, having four children wasn't really sensible, not when the farm wasn't doing too well, but of course Jonathan and Martha had never listened to advice. They even talked of having a fifth. She only hoped that the tobacco prices ... And so on.

The letters were coming faster, sometimes two and three by a single mail. Details, details, details: of the trip, which was being organised to the last hairnet and reel of cotton; and of a London forty years before, which existed in Mrs. Quest's mind to be communicated in letters about tram routes and the kinds of elastic sold in Harrods. Would Martha ring up the Army and Navy Stores and ask them if they still had a certain type of flannel, and if so, would Martha buy a yard and a half of it ... Anxiety. Mrs. Quest was in a fever of anxiety, for while she kept saying that she did expect things to have changed, she was trying to arrange in her mind, before she came, that they had not. Mrs. Quest was about to visit the London of before the First World War, and her daughter who had a nice job as the secretary of an author.

It was the first time that she saw a look on Mark's face of a patient apprehension that got Martha out of bed. She had been in it for a month, reading, rereading letters. But reading them exactly as one puts one's hand into hot water to test it. In with the hand—quick, no, it's too hot, withdraw it; a pause: in again ... no, no, I can't bear it. Don't be a coward, go on, stick it out. So the letters got themselves read, and one evening Martha realised Mark had been sitting there talking, and she had not heard one word. And so he sat, regarding her, his face all pain.

Martha went down to the basement to ask Lynda for advice.

The two women had been living there now for nearly four years. Dorothy had a job. Rather, she had had a succession of them, for her nagging perfectionism drove one employer after another mad. She worked for half the day. The other half she cleaned the flat and made dolls and tea cosies and cushion covers. As for Lynda, she never got up till about twelve, and sometimes she did not get properly dressed for days, unless there were visitors. She moved vaguely about, smoking, cooking a little, laying out the cards, making tea for Mrs. Mellendip and her cronies, reading astrological magazines.

Martha sat down opposite Lynda and her spread of cards and said: "I think I am having a breakdown."

"Oh yes?" said Lynda.

"My mother's coming."

"God, yes!" said Lynda, emphatically. The words, years before, had carried fervour. But the emotion had burned out.

"What shall I do?"

"If you're having one, you are."

"But I can't have one, if she's here. I could otherwise."

"That's the point, isn't it."

"I must do something."

"You had better keep out of their hands," said Lynda. "That's my advice."

"But don't they help—psychiatrists?"

Lynda smiled, watching Martha from large eyes surrounded by bruised flesh. "Well," she said.

Martha, for the first time, burst into floods of hysterical tears. "I've got to do something, I've got to."

Lynda made no attempt to get up, comfort Martha, stop her crying. For years, so her face and pose said, had she watched people crying, screaming, cracking: one watched.

She laid the cards, and after some minutes made a cup of tea. Martha's head lay among the litter of the playing cards: she felt she could never move.

"What about Mark?" said Martha. "I can't inflict this on Mark."

"Poor old Mark," said Lynda. "He does have a bad time."

Martha went back upstairs to bed. Later, Mrs. Mellendip ascended the stairs to visit her. She was wearing a very correct red suit, and carried a large black handbag. Her hair was grey, and cut short and neat. She looked like a business-woman. Her manner was all brisk kindly authority.

She had worked out the prognostications of the stars for the forthcoming visit. Things could not be expected to go well, but it would be a help if she knew Mrs. Quest's birthdate: there might be helpful aspects there. Martha was in for a bad time. But there were elements in her chart which showed that it was up to Martha to make use of it. Some-times charts showed nothing but unrelieved disaster; and on such occasions Mrs. Mellendip advised people to take a trip or a holiday—get right away. But there were bad times which were also good: that is, held the potential for good, a change, a deepening of experience, if properly used. There-fore, she was not advising Martha to go away, but to stay where she was and live through it. . . . Martha had not asked for Mrs. Mellendip's advice at all. She lay silent in her half-dark, listening to the sensible voice. Which continued. The advice was just the sort which she, Martha, would be giving if she sat in that chair, and Mrs. Mellendip lay helpless on the bed. Though one could not imagine Mrs. Mellendip as helpless or ill.

She told Mrs. Mellendip that she had not thought of running away. A small pause. "There's nothing wrong with running, if you know you can't do any good by staying."

This maxim carried an extraordinary authority.

Martha's problems would be solved, her present weakness would vanish, all was well. Martha was full of confidence.

Full of confidence, she sat up, ready to take life on; and lay down again, with the thought that if Mrs. Mellendip had said: All's well that ends well; or even: A bird in the hand is worth two in the bush, with that same smiling authority, Martha would have felt as much strengthened.

Mrs. Mellendip was a person with reserves of strength, and this strength she was able to inject into the people around her.

Martha lay and regarded her old antagonist, the competent middle-aged woman. Here she was again, Martha, a poor confused helpless creature, watching, with envy, Mrs. Mellendip, who was so strong. And calm. Calm. Mark said Martha was calm.

It occurred to Martha that she, Martha, was after all—what? Nearly thirty-five. For other people now, she was that creature, all confidence and strength. It was impossible, but almost certainly true. Time, dear time, had brought her here, to lie on this bed, a small girl, inwardly weeping Mama, Mama, why are you so cold, so unkind, regarding the admirable calm of Mrs. Mellendip with envy: but, when she got up out of that bed to resume her role in the household it wouldn't matter a tuppenny damn whether it was she or Mrs. Mellendip who said: Time heals all; or: You can't have your cake and eat it.

Mrs. Mellendip sometimes lay, a small girl, on a bed in a darkened room, all helpless envy of the strong?

Panic flooded Martha. She understood that it was because she did not want to think of Mrs. Mellendip as anything but infallible. If she didn't get herself out of this, inside a month she would be one of the group of people who floated in and out of the basement, telling cards and swirling tea dregs around the bottoms of teacups. A strange movement that, the quick circular jerk of the hand, to separate tea leaves and liquid; exactly the same as that used by a man panning ground rock for gold: a kind of wriggling jerk, and the liquid carried off the light useless dust, leaving the heavy, possibly gold-carrying sediment on the bottom. Over it, one bent and peered, peered at a smudge of tea leaves, a smear of wet grit that glittered.

"Mrs. Mellendip . . ." she began.

"Why don't you call me Rosa?"

Well, why didn't she? She had been meeting Mrs. Mellendip around the place for months and months. Rosa Mellendip smiled, a little drily, as she waited for Martha to answer.

The answer was of course that she didn't want to be associated with her. It was cowardice. God forbid that one's rational friends should ever . . . at the idea, she was all embarrassed shame.

"Rosa" she said, "I'll think it over. It's very nice of you to come up."

She said it badly, without confidence, apology imminent for in fact asking her to leave. She said it *almost* as if begging for forgiveness. However, she hadn't given a nervous laugh or made a squirming puppylike gesture. She hadn't been Matty. It did rather look as if for the rest of her life she could expect, when in any weakened or lowered state, that "Matty" would appear absolutely unchanged, the same as she had been at nine years old, a miserably apologetic clown ... here she was now, standing by the bed, called back by the powerfully self-confident Rosa.

Rosa got up, smiling. Smiling, she stood looking out of the window at the tree. Then she nodded, smiled, and went.

Martha felt disproportionate relief, as if a threat had gone. Which was a danger in itself. The basement flat, its occupants, were isolating themselves in her mind, as if it was a territory full of alien people from whom she had to protect herself, with whom she could have no connection. What was happening in fact was exactly the same process as when some months ago she watched "Communism," meaning Patty, Mark and their friends, becoming separated from herself, becoming alien so that for two pins she could have become a hater. For two pins now she could switch into an enemy of the shadow world of the basement. She could watch the mechanisms at work in her mind, see how Rosa Mellendip became surrounded by a light first ridiculous, then menacing. She became something to be destroyed, like a witch in the Middle Ages. Sweep it under the carpet! Sweep it out of sight! Save poor Lynda, save poor Dorothy, save all the weak-minded fools from the power-loving fateful woman ...

What an extraordinary household this was, after all, this entity, containing such a variety of attitudes, positions! A whole. People in any sort of communion, link, connection, make up a whole. (She was feeling that again, as she had before, in a heightened, meaningful way, as if a different set of senses operated in her to enable her to *feel,* even if briefly, the connection between them all.) Mrs. Mellendip, who was capable of saying: Dorothy, you should be careful all day on Thursday, you are going to be accident-prone. And the comrades, who . . . yes, but that pole, or opposition point, had shifted, was dissolving.

Mark regarded Rosa Mellendip as ridiculous. For her, and her influence over Lynda, he had a sort of snort of offended amusement, that was also disgust. What pressure, what small switch could change that uneasy amusement into the person who could light the faggots, set up the gallows? Looking into the movement of her own mind, Martha could say: A very small pressure, a very easy switch. There was Jimmy Wood. But here Martha failed. Even to think of Jimmy made her uneasy and she did not know why; and to imagine him and Rosa Mellendip together was simply to give up: one simply had to shrug one's shoulders. Jimmy Wood would have to wait, she must get herself on her feet, get herself working again. And not through Rosa Mellendip—simply because it would be so easy for her, Martha, to become a person who wouldn't step outside the door on Wednesday, if the stars threw the wrong sort of shadow.

Martha got up, dressed; before she had finished she knew what she was going to do. She put on a coat, took up a couple of very large shopping baskets, and departed to those streets of London whose facades are showcases for the millions of books they contain.

Somewhere in Martha's life it had been instilled into her, or she knew by instinct, that one should never read anything until one wanted to, learn anything until one needed it. She was in for another of the short intensive periods of reading during which she extracted an essence, a pith, got necessary information, and no more. She was looking for books which would tell her about that area of knowledge referred to in the house in Radlett Street as "Dr. Lamb." She knew nothing, had read nothing. Yet, so much was it "in the air" that she knew roughly the right books, the right authors to ask for. The two great exemplars, forming as they did the two faces or poles of the science, or art, were easy. "Freud" and "Jung" were easy. She sniffed and nosed and smelled her way in the country in between and returned at nightfall with her baskets full, and dozens more books on order. These books were now spread out over her room, and she settled down with them. Mark came in at night, saw her there, sat for a while to watch, or comment, and was relieved. Because she was up and doing *something:* what she was doing was another matter. A man who had spent so many hundreds of pounds on hospitals and on Dr. Lamb to cure poor Lynda was not likely to be anything but dubious. But Martha was normal: his friend was back to ordinary life, and so he was relieved.

Martha, her stomach a pit of terror because of what was approaching, behaved normally, and was astounded that she could. To reassure Mark, she cooked some rather good meals; they even went out once or twice to restaurants; she bought some dresses and had her hair done. In the mirror she saw a solid competent-looking woman with a fresh light make-up and hair that gleamed an attractive dark gold. The dark eyes, made-up, seemed unchanged.

Meanwhile, she read. She read. She read. She searched and sampled and dipped and extracted what she needed. She emerged from this equivalent of a university course with one essential fact. That these practitioners of a science, or an art, agreed about absolutely nothing.

A hundred years ago, or something like that, this way of looking at the human being had not existed. A human being was what he seemed. Then, hey presto! into being had sprung the great exemplars, and a human being was an iceberg. But, a century later, now, a large variety of emphatic people had very emphatic opinions about which they argued inexhaustibly in print and at conferences all over Europe and America. Not over Russia and China, however: where this view of things was suspect.

Well then, it was into no cage of dogma that Martha was going to allow herself to be led; because by definition there were no grounds for dogma.

She went down to the basement again, to see Lynda, not caring whether her cronies were there or not. Lynda sat smoking on her bed. In the living room, Dorothy wound dark blue wool while a grey little man held his hands apart to support wool. Meanwhile, he gazed at Dorothy, whom he wished to marry. Dorothy concentrated on the wool, ignoring him.

Martha sat by Lynda on the bed.

She said: "What is Dr. Lamb like as a person?"

"Oh, they are all the same!"

"They can't be!"

"Well, that's one of their points, you see: it shouldn't matter what they are like as people."

"But that's ridiculous."

"I shouldn't if I were you."

"I could stop if it were no good."

Here Lynda gave Martha a rather sour look: amusement gone bad. "You get hooked in," she said.

"What would you do, then?" asked Martha.

And now Lynda made one of her very sharp switches; one moment, she was a listless tired-looking woman, smiling or not, polite, normal, or more or less so; the next she was near-virago. She jerked herself up, her great eyes dilated and stared.

"Me? I'm a nothing-but!" she said.

This phrase was part of the jargon of the basement. Affectionately, or angrily, or spitefully, Dorothy would call Lynda, Lynda would call Dorothy, "a nothing-but." Sometimes, hysterically, Lynda screamed that she was "a nothing-but," and had to be left alone.

A "nothing-but" could not be asked for anything.

"That's what they want," said Lynda, between clenched teeth. "That's what they aim for: to make you a nothing-but."

"I don't understand."

"You will then!"

And Lynda flung herself back on the bed, and turned her face away in a sharp dismissing movement, her chin averted, as if the turned chin were a kind of closed door, excluding Martha. Her eyes stared, over the chin, at the wall—blank. Martha must go.

Next door Martha sat by Dorothy and her attentive would-be husband. Dorothy now stacked balls of blue wool into a raffia basket, made by herself.

"What does this nothing-but mean?" asked Martha.

"Oh it's just a joke we have," said Dorothy.

"Please tell me."

Dorothy gave a theatrically peremptory look at her swain, who stood up apologetically, and with an apologetic nod and smile, shambled away.

"He gets on my nerves," said Dorothy. "I keep telling him, You get on my nerves, but he just keeps coming back for more."

He must have heard this, or part of it—he had not got further than the hall. But he put his head in, and said fretfully: "I'll see you tomorrow, Dorothy. You are a naughty girl, you know!" She shrugged, magnificently, eyes proud; he withdrew his mouselike head.

"Marry!" said Dorothy. "I mean, what would happen to Lynda for a start?"

"This nothing-but," said Martha.

"Oh, well, it's not much, it's just a joke we had in the hospital. You know, it's that point when they get all pleased because they can say: "You're nothing but—whatever it is. They've taken weeks and weeks to get to that point, you know, and it's, You're nothing but Electra. You know, that girl who killed her mother?"

Martha said, "Yes," and Dorothy nodded. It was a placid domestic sort of nod. Now the man had gone, all drama had ebbed. A large, sad soft woman sat sorting balls of wool, chatting ordinarily as if it were eggs and butter and bread she was concerned with.

"It's nothing-but you want to sleep with your father. Nothing-but your brother. Nothing-but, nothing-but, nothing-but ..." This sounded like a croon or counting-rhyme. "I'm nothing-but a depression."

"What is Lynda?"

"Well, Lynda's always more tricky, you see." This was with pride: Dorothy was proud of Lynda's complexities. "Sometimes Lynda's one thing, and sometimes she's another. But that isn't the point. Whatever nothing-but you are, at the time, that's it, you see, until there's another nothing-but. Lynda was nothing-but Cassandra the last time I heard, but who knows by now?"

Martha telephoned Dr. Lamb for an appointment. The secretary enquired after Mrs. Coldridge: Martha said it was for herself. An appointment was made for two weeks away. Martha observed, with interest, that she was resentful because it could not be tomorrow. Martha having laid awake all night deciding to make this great step, then of course Dr. Lamb should be available the moment she had decided. Towards her rushed crisis and misery—her mother's visit; Dr. Lamb was irresponsible, if not callous: there was no time to waste.

Two weeks. She set herself not to go back to bed, and not to worry Mark. The calmest of confidence was offered to him, and he accepted it with relief. She marvelled at her ability to do it. Meanwhile, not to waste time, she sat in the chair, not on the bed, which might drag her like a quicksand into its depths, and tried to resurrect her lost past. Every day more of it was slipping away. Sometimes she felt like a person who wakes up in a strange city, not knowing who he, she, is. There she sat, herself. Her name was Martha, a convenient label to attach to her sense of herself. Sometimes she got up and looked into the mirror, in an urgency of need to see a reflection of that presence called, for no particular reason, Martha. In the mirror was a pleasant-faced woman whose name was Martha. She had dark eyes. She smiled, or frowned. Once, bringing to the mirror a mood of seething anxiety, she saw a dishevelled panic-struck creature biting its nails. She watched this creature, who was in an agony of fear. *Who* watched? She sat in the chair. Outside the elegant tall window with its graceful frame and panes, a tree. Nothing was more extraordinary and marvellous than that tree, a being waving its green limbs from a grey surface. Beneath the surface was a structure of roots whose shape had a correspondence with the shape and spread of its branches. This curious being that stood opposite the window was a kind of conduit for the underground rivers of London, which rushed up its trunk, diffusing outwards through a hundred branches to disperse into the air and stream upwards, to join the damp cloud cover of the London sky. She felt she had never seen a tree before. The word "tree" was alien to the being on the pavement. Tree, tree, she kept saying, as she said Martha, Martha, feeling the irrelevance of these syllables, which usurped the reality of the living structure. And, as if she had not lived in this room now, for four years, everything in it seemed extraordinary, and new, and when the old black cat rose, arching its back, from the white spread, the delight of that movement was felt in Martha's back.

She went down to the basement to see Lynda: there was no one else who could understand her.

"Lynda, do you know who you are?"

"Me," said Lynda.

"Do you see that when you look in the mirror?"

"No. Not often. Sometimes."

"When?"

"Oh, I don't know. There are times, you know."

"Are you always someone who watches yourself?"

"Sometimes more, sometimes less."

Lynda was sitting on her bed, in a white frilled negligée, doing her toenails, giving this process all her attention.

She now waggled her toes, which had bright pink shell-shapes on their ends. She laughed with delight, looking at Martha, who saw exactly what she meant by it, and laughed with her.

"All the same," said Lynda, "you'd better be careful, you mustn't tell them that."

"What?"

"About the two people. Sometimes you are more the one that watches, and sometimes that one gets far off and you are more the one who is watched. But they look out for that, you see, and when you make a mistake and say it, then that proves it. You're a schiz."

"Nothing-but?"

"Well, that depends. That's what I was for a long time with a doctor when Dr. Lamb was in America, but Dr. Lamb has other ideas. But you shouldn't tell them, you see, you should be on guard. It's very difficult, though, because they trap you."

"The point is, if that's what I am now, that's what I've always been. But now more than before."

"Well, if they trap you into saying it, then you'd better say it's the other way around: it's less than it was. Because the way they see it, it'll mean you're better and not worse."

Martha understood that for years she had been listening, half listening, to talk in the basement which she had thought was too crazy to take as more than pitiable. Now she was understanding it—or a lot of it. She was even learning the language. Several of the visitors to the basement had been in mental hospitals, or were under some sort of treatment. One of them was Dorothy's would-be husband, the grey little man who seemed all loving, pleading, doglike eyes. He was schizo-pherenic, they said: or at least, was so off and on. Sometimes when he felt bad, he went around to his doctor, and was readmitted for a few weeks. He was given a great many pills, got better, and left the hospital.

For years, all her life, the world of mental illness, and the doctors who dealt with it, had been alien. Not even frighten-ing: it was too distant from her. Looking back, she was able to think, of people: a friend, the husband of a friend, someone's mother, who had a "a breakdown" of some kind. But she hadn't thought about it. Fear? She had been afraid? No. Because, from the moment it was said: So-and-so is mentally ill, so-and-so is having a breakdown, then it no long-er concerned her: the words, the labels, had removed them from her, whisked them out of her experience. Yet all her life she had lived in atmospheres of strain, stress, neurosis, which were freely admitted, freely discussed. People were neurotic. People said they were neurotic. Other people said people were neurotic. Once upon a time, it had been said of people, So-and-so's unkind, or bad-tempered, or intolerant, or a bully. Now, they were neurotic. Yet, between this climate, the ordinary air in which one had always lived, and that other, where people were under psychiatrists, had been an absolute separation.

Yet, now, suddenly, because she was experiencing it, she felt as if she had been blind. For, suddenly, far from mental illness (as distinct from neurosis) being something that hap-pened somewhere else, it was all around her: and, which was odder, had been all around her for a long time. Not only Lynda and Dorothy, there were their friends, formerly thought of as people who had unfortunate leanings towards Rosa Mellendip. Martha remembered that Gerald Smith, one of the comrades (he had already become an ex-comrade), had a wife in a mental hospital. She enquired of Mark what was the matter with the wife. She, Martha, had not met her: Mark had. Mark said merely that she seemed a nice enough girl, a bit harassed. What was wrong with her? She had been depressed; but she had been given shock treatment, and was,

227

they thought, a bit better. Gerald said she might be coming home soon, but in the meantime they were trying more shock treatment. There was Patty Samuels, from whom Martha got desperately jolly letters from Essex: Patty wanted to know, of course, about Mark, and Martha told her. Patty had said in one of the recent letters that she thought that perhaps she was a bit screwy, "I'd better admit it, and be done with it." She was going to a psychiatrist in Norwich. And, coincidentally, there was Mavis Wood: it turned out that Jimmy had been married since he was twenty. Mavis Wood was unhappy about her marriage. She had been to see her mother and her two married sisters, who had asked her if Jimmy was a good provider—the mother; if he fulfilled his marital duties—one sister; if he was kind to the children—the other sister. Mavis had said yes, to all three; and was left plunged in guilt. Clearly, it was all her fault that she was miserable. Pressed by Mark to say what she felt was wrong, she could only weep that sometimes she thought Jimmy wasn't all there, but of course it must be her fault if Mark said that he was.

Mark brought this to Martha, who said that of course Jimmy wasn't all there: though God only knew what part of him wasn't. Mark, who continued Jimmy's devoted admirer, said that geniuses were notoriously difficult to live with, and anyway Mavis was obviously not very bright. Poor Mavis had, last week, started screaming, and had continued to scream for two solid days, while Jimmy bobbed and smiled around the house, asking her what was the matter. Mavis had gone into hospital, and the two children were being looked after by one of the sisters—the one who had asked if he was kind to the children. Jimmy, said Mark, must be very upset, but he didn't have time to be, luckily: there was so much to do in the factory, and anyway it turned out that he had taken to writing. He was writing space fiction: that was what it was called, though Mark couldn't see why "space," but he supposed one word did as well as another.

There were only two days to go before the appointment with Dr. Lamb. The letters from Mrs. Quest were now arriving in batches, every day. Martha forced herself to read them. Even the act of reaching out her hand to pick up a letter, and ripping open the envelope, started up in Martha, as if buttons had been pressed, or sluice gates opened, two violent but opposing emotions. One was pity, strong, searing, unbearable. The other was a wild need to run—anywhere. Under the bedclothes if there was nowhere to run. Therefore she sat and raged useless rebellion. Against what? A poor,

228

lonely old woman whose life had never given her anything she wanted, or never for long. But, and this was the point, as she sat and raged, she was able to revive a part of her past that had got lost. She remembered herself as the violent, aggressive adolescent, who had reached out on all sides to grab up anything at all as a weapon in the fight for survival: her own body manipulated into a challenging attractiveness, clothes, ideas, thoughts, books, people, anything. That person she had certainly been, and was now, as she read the pathetic, heartbreaking letters. And, as she sat being that adolescent girl, she remembered that even then there had been that other person, the silent watcher, the witness. Nothing else was permanent. She returned to the mirror and remembered the face of that girl: she saw it again, a shadow behind the face she saw now, two faces, the present face and one of the faces of the past. They were connected by the eyes.

Then something happened which seemed impossibly cruel. Dr. Lamb's secretary telephoned to say that Dr. Lamb was ill, he had very bad flu. They would make a provisional appointment for two weeks ahead.

Martha collapsed. She crawled back under the covers. Her mother was going to arrive before she could grab hold of that baulk of floating timber in an angry sea, Dr. Lamb. She was abandoned, defenceless, and Dr. Lamb was cruel, he was letting her down. (But a part of her watched these so predictable reactions, described so graphically in the books she had recently read.) Watching, she smiled; reacting, she wallowed and panicked and wept.

A letter came from Mrs. Quest saying that she had postponed her sailing date for a couple of months. She was staying with friends in Cape Town. At the time Martha grabbed at just this one fact: she was saved. Later, reading this letter, she saw that Mrs. Quest, as terrified of this visit as Martha, had put it off to give herself time to face the pain which she knew (somewhere or other inside her) was coming. But Mrs. Quest had not admitted to herself that this was what she was doing. The hidden fear of pain, the foreknowledge of it, twisted and became a flood of reproaches against Martha, who was unkind and uncaring: why had she not answered the last two letters? And she had said nothing about the vests which Mrs. Quest asked her to buy. Well, it was perfectly plain to see that Mrs. Quest would have to get them herself, though surely it had not been too much to hope ...

The ordeal was postponed: but it was on its way. Dr.

Lamb, the cruel betrayer, might betray again. And Martha lay in the dark, not moving.

Later she believed that this double postponement was the luckiest thing that had ever hapened to her. If it had not happened, if Dr. Lamb had not had flu, and Martha had gone to him unprepared, without learning anything of what she could do for herself—well, she believed she would have been lost. Perhaps. Perhaps not. And perhaps there's no such thing as luck, as there's no such thing as coincidence.

But as things were, Dr. Lamb did not get back to his work for a month, and Mrs. Quest stayed on with her friend in Cape Town, where the oak trees reminded her of England, and the slopes of the mountains were covered with vineyards, and where she could see the ships coming in and out of Cape Town harbour from her bedroom windows high above the slopes of the lower town.

Martha crawled out of bed. She sat looking at the tree. Once she had lain above rough boards through which rose the smell of freshly watered earth: the boughs of a tree showed through a high square of window, carrying loads of wet, smelling of wet, carrying sun-scented air. She tried to put herself back into that other small high room, see the boughs of that other tree: what she saw was this one, the sycamore. She tried. Two shapes of tree fought in her mind's eye, and the sycamore dissolved into a tree glowing orange under an African sun. It went, dissolved back into the sycamore. She fought. She was in the loft, or rather was in a warm compost of scents, wet growth, soaking dust, tree-air, roses. The loft took shape. Into the loft climbed Thomas, a strong brown man with farmer's hands. She held it. She held Thomas. Holding Thomas, using his strong presence as guide, she moved out of the loft, into the café with its smell of the army, and hot fat, and floor polish. She let the great room and its eating people come back, with Athen, with Solly and Joss and Jasmine; holding them, she moved up into the avenues and the gardened house where her mother . . . and now pain came in a hot sear, and it all collapsed. Spent, she lay, everything she had got back gone again. Slowly, she sat up, took up a thread, a fragment, a scrap: sunlight on a wall, a voice, a smile, and worked again to the point where she had to enter the house where plants stood on sunny verandah walls, and where Mrs. Quest . . . she held it. As one puts a hand into hot water, withdraws it, puts it back, gingerly, holds it there, withdraws it—so she worked. The house in the avenues had come back, and she walked into the room which smelled of drugs and faeces and saw her father's white face on a pillow. Soon her mother came in, and she watched her fill a glass with pink medicine, and go frowning to the bedside, heard her voice: "Alfred, I should take this now if I were you, you had all that chicken for supper."

Then she collapsed, lay unable to move, to feel, to think. But what she had excavated, remained. Small self-contained landscapes, lit with pain, remained. She was able to move in and out of them. She went back then to the house on a hill in the veld. Nothing remained of it. Of the farm, nothing remained but a hot sunlight, a glitter of stars. On starlit nights they had sat out in deck chairs and watched the stars, watched the fires burn in chains of red light over the hills. She sat there again. The roughness of canvas. An owl. The lamplight fell on a slope of stony soil. A strong scent of verbena—her mother stood, outlined by light from the door, saying in a cheerful indoors voice: "Time for bed, it's late." Pain came, swallowed everything; back went Martha, patiently, to a scent of flowers, an owl hooting, the smell of her father's pipe. Soon she moved into the house. Room by room she created it, or rather, holding on to a detail, a cushion, the grain of a curtain, light on a strand of thatch, she allowed the rest to come back. Slowly. It was very slow. It was very painful. It was completely exhausting. Her stomach clenched and hurt. She fought. *Who* fought? She could sit on a chair, or rather feel herself held on soft support, and look at a tree, or rather a brownish-grey thing that stuck out of the pavement and became a green mass, which was made up of a thousand little pieces of green—look, feel, as empty as a pool. Who? Into the pool came a word, sycamore. Came, chair. Into the pool came scents, sounds, voices, pictures. When scents, sounds, pictures, words, went, she remained. Who? If one day she found herself memoryless in a new city, and they said, What's your name, she might say, let's see, Rosalind Macintosh. Or Montague Jones. Why not? The sense of herself which stayed had no sex. Suppose shutting her eyes, holding that sense, that presence, she imagined herself into the body of a man? Why not. An elderly man, large-framed, broad, with guttering flesh, blue-eyed, a slow ruminative man, with a history behind him of work and women and children. Why not? Or a young man, Aaron, Rachel's brother, a lithe sparkling boy. Or even, letting the sense of herself go into a different shape, a horse, a small white horse. She saw it; into it she fitted herself, saw the world on either side of her head in two outstretching expanses of grass, bushes. Who are you then? Why, me, of course, who else, horse, woman, man, or tree, a glittering faceted individuality of breathing green, here is the sense of me, nameless, recognisable only to me. Who, what?

This being moved in and out of the house on the kopje, every detail of every room clear, sharp, visible. But, let this person become Martha—she was swallowed in a wash of hot pain. Right then, fight it.

She fought. The house was back, the country around the house was back, she was able to sit in imagination under the tree and look across the valley as it had been, a low scrubby valley, with its varying tints of green and red and brown. But there were great gaps in her memory. There were still months, even years, where she could say nothing but: I was in these in these and these rooms, these streets; at that time were these people around me. She worked, laying hold of a detail, a cushion, a flower, a voice, the light on the lenses of a pair of spectacles. White shoes; small white shoes, a child's; a small girl with a pink dress and shining black curls. She turned her face toward Martha, a small, rather sharp face, watchful. Her smile was strained. Martha reached towards the smile, saw it dissolve in tears: Martha heard herself crying. She wept, while a small girl wept with her, Mama, Mama, why are you so cold, so unkind, why did you never love me?

Day after day, Martha loafed about, lay about, sat about the room in Radlett Street; performed what duties were necessary adequately, "Would you like some dinner cooked tonight, Mark? Very well, what time?" Mark and Martha sat on either side of a dinner table, and chatted. He did not like, was uneasy about, her forthcoming visit to Dr. Lamb.

"I don't really see what they can do for you, these people, but if you say you . . ."

Dr. Lamb could do nothing for the person, or being who was there always; the sense, only, of existence. But he could, he *must* do something for Martha.

Somewhere a long way back, beyond where she could reach with memory, an angry fighting resentful Martha had been born. It was a result of a battle against pity. Pity, a long time ago, had been an enemy. Pity could have destroyed.

What Dr. Lamb must do for her was to give her back pity, the strength to hold it, and not be destroyed by it. She must be able, when her mother came, to pity her, to love her, to cherish her, and not be destroyed.

Dr. Lamb turned out to be a middle-aged man, wearing a good dark suit. He had a strong guarded face. On inspection

232

it became clear the armoured look was due to spectacles. His quick instinct for what his visitors felt was shown by how he removed them, at the moment Martha discovered she was looking at the spectacles as at a defence she couldn't penetrate. A rather nice-looking man; the eyes, thoughtful, shrewd, quick; the mouth firm, held to contain humour in its right times and places. At conferences, reports of which she had studied, Dr. Lamb showed a nice dry style of wit. An altogether likeable man. She looked at him. She heard what Lynda had said of him; what Dorothy had said; what Mark had said. "Not a bad sort of chap, I suppose." Lynda had once screamed that he was a devil.

He was a round man: round face, round head, rounding body, and the hands that go with it, sensible and confident hands. He sat in a black leather chair, his back at an angle to the window, so that its light would fall full on his visitors. The room was entirely functional. Square, white, it had a desk, a neat black leather couch, with a tartan rug folded at its foot, a couple of leather armchairs. There was no object in this room that connected with Dr. Lamb as a person, except, perhaps, the rug. For the kind of room that Dr. Lamb would choose, as a person, was not this room. When he put on that suit in the mornings, he put on his profession; when he came into this room, he entered the impersonal. Yet, if one could only see them, this room's air must be saturated, crammed, with painful and violent emotions: years, probably, of anguish and terror were concentrated in it. The walls must be sodden, vibrating with them. Emotions. But not Dr. Lamb's.

Sitting there, while Dr. Lamb waited, courteously, for her to speak, she had, all at once, such an extraordinarily strong sense, of this proceeding, this process, that she was struck into silence by it. Hundreds and thousands of people, millions of them, came into this room, or others like it, to Dr. Lamb, or people like him, their lives having run out into dry sand. A hundred years ago, what had they done? A hundred years hence, what would they do? In such a short space of time, this phenomenon had come into existence, Dr. Lamb, who, because of several years spent taking degrees in universities and in medical schools, could sit there adjudicating, could say, This is wrong with Martha, that is wrong; *was prepared to take the responsibility* for the results of what he decided; was unmoved whether Lynda screamed that he was a devil, or that Mark said he was a decent chap. Society had willed it. Had suffered it, then: Martha, too, who was prepared to come several days a week for goodness knows how many years, and to spend every penny that she had in the bank. If he beat his wife, or was cold to his children: if he was an arrogant man, or a humble man—it was all the same. Like a character in a play who wore a mask which said "I am Wisdom," it did not matter what he was personally. If Martha decided, on the evidence on which she conducted her life outside this bleak room, that Dr. Lamb was lacking in insight, or was arrogant, then in this room, this decision could mean only that she fought, resisted, her own higher self, as represented by Dr. Lamb. For any emotions in this room, any attitudes, beliefs, were hers, never his. Dr. Lamb might choose to sit absolutely silent for months or years; or, to give advice and direct (according to his persuasion)—but as far as he was concerned, and society too, as long as Martha reacted against him in awe or in criticism it was her own best development that she thwarted.

Yet outside this room, he might go off to a meeting of fellow practitioners where they would disagree; or might write papers for medical journals which contradicted other papers; or might not love his children, so that they became the patients of other men or women wearing masks that said: Wisdom. Truth.

Well, what was she doing here then?

Because she had nowhere else to go.

He shifted his position in his chair, and spoke. About Lynda, first, and about Mark, then about Dorothy. This was to find out if his treatment of the two sick women might have to be adapted because of Martha; or if Martha was here because of either of them.

As he talked, she noted that her attitudes to Dr. Lamb became less and less objective, took on Lynda's and Dorothy's: she was seeing him as powerful, to be placated. With this, came resentment. By the time they had gone around to her, she noted that she was even sitting in a position which said: I am resentful, I fear you. He watched her, missing nothing.

Asking why she had come to him, she put forward the view of his profession, as she had been seeing it, only a few minutes before, and enquired if, with this attitude, he believed anything could be done for her. Now, while she had toned down, softened, out of sheer politeness, what she had been thinking, it came out aggressively enough. He listened with blandness, as if the situation she had described, extraordinary from any point of view, could have nothing to do with him.

He enquired if there was an immediate problem which brought her here.

She said it was that her mother was about to pay her a visit. Her problem was that what her intelligence said had no effect at all on her emotions. The first said that her mother deserved, at last, a pair of loving arms and someone to comfort her until she died. Her emotions put her into bed with the covers over her head, made her a creature without will or energy ... well, of course, that had not been entirely true. But here she remembered Lynda's warning and was able to keep quiet.

"Hmmmm," commented Dr. Lamb.

Here he glanced at his clock, prominently in evidence. She was astounded to find that over half an hour had passed. She had another quarter of an hour.

Here Dr. Lamb made a series of statements, all of them to do with his particular school of thought's approach to the human soul, with which she was bound to disagree. But of course he knew she was bound to disagree: watching, while tides of anger arose, she saw that he was choosing precisely what he said. Extremely angry, she countered what he had said with her own position. With five minutes to go, she had talked herself into rejection of everything Dr. Lamb stood for. At which he reasonably said that in that case he did not think he could help her. She reacted in a flood of being rejected, refused, turned out, which caused her to beg for another appointment at the very earliest moment. Tomorrow?

Alas no, Dr. Lamb was so busy: but in two days' time perhaps?

She left. In the taxi she noted two things. One, she was exhausted. The sudden burst of anger, so skilfully evoked by him, had drained her. She was emotionless. Second: He had not at any point not known exactly what he was doing; nor had there been any point when she had not watched what he was doing, and understood it.

She went home to bed. She had planned for that evening some hard work, on recovering more of her past. But she did not have the energy. For weeks she had had the energy, for this hardest of all effort, had had it even when busy, worried, or *almost* incapacitated by the thought: She's coming, she's coming.

Yet tonight, not. Yet she knew, absolutely, without any

doubt at all, that this "work" was more important than anything, more important than anything Dr. Lamb or anybody else could do. Yet she was committed to return to Dr. Lamb.

She remained listless, merely a person who, at such and such a time, would return to Dr. Lamb. She was not able to work on her past. Indeed, the person who had been able seemed further away.

During that hour, she talked. That was the process, the patient talked and talked, the doctor listened. The process made sense. She could understand it, not only theoretically, but out of experience. One talked, one did this or that: finally, one "heard" for the first time what one's life had been saying over and over again, in various ways, for years. One hadn't heard before, because one had had nothing to "hear" with. Living was simply a process of developing different "ears," senses, with which one "heard," experienced, what one couldn't before.

Dr. Lamb, then, embodied that growing principle in life which fed one, developed one, so that one had "ears" where one hadn't before?

She talked. She was emotionless. She had had no emotions since she had sat there last, two days before. When she left it was as if nothing had happened. Well, no, that was not quite true: for she had gone there—that had happened. And this process, submitting oneself to Dr. Lamb, seemed to annul the other, the work prompted by the silent watcher.

On the third occasion, she knew from the moment she sat down that Dr. Lamb was trying something different from what he had done yesterday. With great skill, playing her like a fish, he brought her again and again to points where she would be angry. Watching, she avoided, fought, backed away, because more than anything else she dreaded the exhaustion that would follow. Then she cracked as she was bound to: she wept, she screamed, she shouted. He remained bland, unmoved. She crawled home, like a fly on sticky paper, and crept into bed. Now, the idea that she had once had the energy to sit in a chair and fight with her own mind, her own memory, seemed utterly ludicrous. She knew she ought not to go back to Dr. Lamb. If her own self, her own self-preservation, was being destroyed, then that was more important than anything, and she should stand by that.

"Ah," she remembered Lynda saying, "but you get sucked in."

She rang Lynda downstairs, and asked her to come up and

236

see her. Lynda came, in a pink dressing gown that as always seemed very faintly soiled. In her hand she carried the small jewelled box, a present from Mark, in which she kept her pills.

Lynda sat in the chair. The cat, purring, jumped on her lap. Martha lay in bed, watching Lynda.

"I want to ask you something."

"Yes?" Lynda observed Martha, from her distance, shrewd, rather sour perhaps.

"When you talked with the doctors, had psychotherapy, did it do anything for you at all?"

"Well, you learn things about yourself, I suppose."

She did not go on. When she used that tone of voice, Martha knew, it meant that one was being stupid. Lynda had come up here, she was sitting there, she was quite prepared to talk—but Martha must ask the right questions.

"What does he do for you now, then? When you go and see him?"

"They give me pills now."

A silence. Impasse. Lynda crooned at the cat. After a decent interval, she got up to go.

At the door she said: "If I were you, don't take the pills, I mean, if they give you pills, don't take them. Whatever you do."

She left. Martha lay and thought that these two women lived on pills, their lives were regulated by pills, and their visits to the doctors where they got prescriptions for more pills.

Of course, Lynda was paranoid: one of the doctors she had been to had said so.

Next day she said to Dr. Lamb: "Would you mind telling me what my diagnosis is? What's wrong with me?"

"Certainly, Mrs. Hesse," he said instantly, announcing it with the willingness to come clean that was the policy of his particular sect; "You're manic-depressive, with schizoid tendencies."

Now Martha suppressed a joke which she would have made had Dorothy not used it continually: "If that's depression, then when's the mania?"

One of Lynda's diagnoses (not by Dr. Lamb but by another doctor) had been that she was manic-depressive with schizoid tendencies.

"Dr. Lamb, what is schizoid?"

"Well now, that's quite a question!"

"Well, just a rough working definition?"

"It doesn't mean that you are two people."

"Doesn't it?"

"That's a layman's view of it."

"It would have nothing to do, for instance, with that part of me that watches all the time?"

She said this, deliberately, daring danger, listening to Lynda's warning. She had to say it: this process, sitting here, opposite the silent listener, in this case Dr. Lamb, forced you to say it, say everything. She knew now that it made no difference what resolutions she might make outside this room, not to say this and that, to be this and that: he played her like a fish. The antidote was cunning. That was Lynda's weapon. It was not Martha's. Cunning was the weapon of the desperate. Martha, then, was not desperate?

He had picked up her fear at once, for he now said, heartily reassuring: "Well, if it did, what of it?"

He waited for her to go on.

Deciding she would not go on, she went on: "Dr. Lamb, what words would you use to describe that, how would you put it?"

A hesitation. Now he laughed. "I'd rather you told me, Mrs. Hesse."

Martha listened to the bells of warning for a moment and said: "The best part of me. The only part that is real—that's permanent, anyway."

"Ah," he said, affably. "I see."

He waited. It was as if gages had been flung down, the ground marked out.

She waited.

Her interview came to an end while they sat silent.

She went back home, feeling that she had betrayed herself.

She was lying on the floor, face down, the lights out, when she saw, not six inches from her face, a shoe with a foot in it. She turned over. Mark sat in the chair, the cat on his knee, watching her.

"Well," he said.

Then as was bound to happen, for the third time in his life Mark found a woman clinging to him, "Save me, save me," and again he became the all-strong, all-consoling.

A man's body: that country she had not been in for—four years was it?

Of course they should have done this years ago, right from the beginning. What fools they had been! (For, in this country, where the ordinary rules of life are put aside, one says such things, pretends that the long sad affair with Patty

238

Samuels had not been as inevitable as this was, since both belonged inside the laws of growth.)

The room was outside pain. It vibrated with shared intimacy, trust, happiness, love.

Except that somewhere in Martha sat the person who watched and waited. Oh God, if only she could kill that person, send her, it, him, away, make it be silent, be able just once again to vanish entirely into this place of smooth warm bodies whose language was more beautiful and more intelligent than any other . . .

"Mark, is there somebody in you who always watches what goes on, who is always apart?"

And now, a sudden tension in the loving body. After a time: "No."

"Lynda said something like that, did she?"

"Yes, I believe she did."

So, quick, make love again, cover it all over, this moment when ordinary life came in again; forget it, quick.

"Martha, tell me—have you always had it—the other person?"

"Yes. And more and more."

He comforted her. He was infinitely kind and strong.

"Tell me, Mark, when you were a boy, were you ever with Margaret when she was ill—something like that?"

"I don't think my mother has ever been ill in her life."

"Or unhappy?"

"In one of my interviews with your Dr. Lamb he was suggesting something of the kind."

Dr. Lamb having entered, he was not likely to go away again.

"I told him that if what he suggested was true, I thought it wasn't important. The thing is, they grasp hold of something, and then they make it everything."

"Yes."

"He was right, in a way. I went with her on a holiday to Scotland. I suppose one could say she was ill. My father had just died. I thought she was desperately unhappy. I suppose she was. But she was already in love with Oscar. I hated her for it—I half knew it. Looking back, I see that she spent those holidays with me as a sort of an apology. She let me look after her. I was never so happy in my life. Then at the end of the holidays she told me she was going to marry Oscar. I felt as if I'd been made a fool of. I admitted all this to Lamb. . . ."

"Funny, isn't it, one automatically talks of *admitting*—as if he had the right . . ."

"I said to him, Very well. I was able to look after Lynda because something happened to me that time with my mother. As far as she was concerned, she was paying off a debt to one of her sons. If she thought of it at all: she's not introspective. But for me, during that time, I learned I was not a little boy any longer. I looked after everything—herself, and me—everything, for three months."

Lynda; then Patty; now me, thought Martha.

He said: "There was Patty. I was able to help her. I know I can help you. If he wants to make it a mechanism, that's his affair. But everything is, if you want to look at it like that. That's the trouble with these people: they think it's enough to say you behave like that because when you were six and a half or sixteen and a half, you did that. My answer to them is: And so what? And certain types of people set themselves up as judge and jury. Good luck to them."

The only thing is, thought Martha, you've never found yourself in bed with the bedclothes pulled over your head for weeks at a time, unable to get up.

He said: "Who is Dr. Lamb? He's been in my life for, let's see, it must be getting on for ten years. If you are treated by him, he'll be in it a lot longer. One of these days I'll be getting a pleasant little letter from him, do I feel inclined to go along and have a little talk about Martha. I'll trot along. We'll chat about Lynda and Martha. Lynda can't live without him. But when all is said and done, who is he? He's a decent enough chap, I suppose."

For a week she did not go near Dr. Lamb: she was safe with Mark, nothing existed outside the landscape she inhabited with him.

Then a date on a calendar three weeks away sent her back.

She talked. She talked about the mechanisms.

He said at last: "If you are in the mechanism, then that's what you are." It was calculated: she could feel him calculating.

"No. If I were in the grip of the mechanism one hundred per cent, that is not all I would be."

"What would you be?"

Martha, having again made a decision not to mention the silent watcher, to protect her deepest self, said, with aggression: "I'd be the person who watches."

He let this pass: it was extraordinary how, sitting here,

alert, alive, all senses functioning, she could feel the lightning movements of his—mind? No, all of him, in this work he brought in all of him, a sensing whole: formidable. He said, deliberately: "You are sleeping with Mark now, just when your mother is coming. It's for only one reason. You're saying to your mother: 'Look, I'm a big girl now.' "

She laughed: out of surprise that he had chosen this, a much lesser provocation, than he could have done. For a second he looked put out because she laughed.

"Of course. I know that. I can explain this bit of the mechanism as well as you can. My mother was a woman who hated her own sexuality and she hated mine too. She wanted me to be a boy always—before I was born. She knew I was going to be a boy. She had a boy's name for me. My way of fighting her was—to be a clown." (Martha, saying this, realised that after all, saying something made one understand it differently.) "She was always making fun of me because I wasn't good at the boy's things. My brother was always beating me. But I never once said, which is what I should have said: I'm a girl, why should I be good at boy's things? No, I did them, but I did them badly and laughed at myself. I clowned, and she laughed at me. It was a way of protecting myself. I know that. When at last I became a girl, and I spent years and years longing for the moment when I would have breasts and be a woman, I was able to defy her at last. I made myself beautiful clothes, and every man I had, for a long time, was a weapon against her. Do you suppose I don't know that?"

He waited. She was not going on.

"What *don't* you know then?" he enquired, with irony—calculated.

"It's a question of *how* one knows it," she said, waiting for him to meet her here on this, the furthest point she had reached in her life.

He sat intuiting for the right provocative words. He wanted to provoke. He wanted to . . . a word came into her mind. It was "explode." Yes. He wanted an explosion. The word had a weight of meaning. She did not have time to examine it now.

"I think you are proud of your knowing—you are proud of that more than anything. It's your intelligence you are proud of. You are still fighting your mother with that—the masculine intelligence."

He waited, all alert, watching.

Anger flared: was held.

"I didn't learn that out of books. I experienced it. Is what you know from experience, the masculine intelligence?"

"Yes! Yes! Yes!" he said, deliberate, cold, watching.

"My first weapon was my sexuality. My second was—what I got out of books?"

He sat, alert, his mind nosing about among what he knew of her—for the right words. He was all alive, alert, watchful attack. She, all alert, watchful defence.

The time was running out. At the same moment, they thought it, and he glanced, deliberate, at the clock. Five minutes. He was casting about for the trigger to set off the explosion. Her mind racing, she checked up possible triggers he might use. At all cost, whatever happened, she wasn't going to explode—*she needed the energy.*

"You said, I think, that this person, the observer in you, could be masculine?"

"Oh, easily. Or anything. A horse . . ." As she said this, she thought a horse, masculine. What's a tree? She did not say, "Tree," but impelled by this extraordinary need to placate, the betrayer in her, she said instead, grasping up a phrase from the armoury of masculine words, "Or an express train . . . do you know why I said that? I was sitting in my room thinking, my mother's visit rushes towards me like an express train. Masculine. Dr. Lamb would like that. No, I don't think of myself as an express train—the phrase got into the wrong place, because I said horse, and I knew you'd think, Ha! masculine. An empty pool if you like. That's round. Feminine . . ."

She waited. In he came, under her guard.

"And of course, the other reason you are sleeping with Mark is because you are saying to me, I don't find you attractive, Dr. Lamb, I have another man."

Martha snapped into rage. She saw red. "Rubbish!" she snapped, while she clutched to the thought that around her the air had been red—for a flash of time. No metaphor at all. A wave of hot scarlet with sparks in it that had faded into ordinary air: but the fade itself, the time of it, had a quality about it as if it belonged to another measurement or wavelength of time. But now she was drained. She had exploded. He was looking at the clock. The interview was over. He had done what he had intended to do.

She sat, thinking: making notes of what she must remember and try to understand afterwards.

He smiled gently: "You are not a woman," he said, "who is likely to admit easily that she is attracted to a man."

This was right off any point. It simply was not true. But she was suddenly understanding something: she was grabbing at a comprehension as it fled past. It was this: *It did not matter what he said nearly so much as the time he chose to do it.*

She said: "That isn't true. I am easily attracted to men. And if you weren't my doctor, I could easily be attracted to you. In fact I am. It's not the point."

He smiled with a calculated, as it were retrospective, sarcasm. No need now for the triggers: today's work had been done. She had exploded. He was merely keeping the weapons oiled for next time. Some time in the future, at the next session perhaps, *but at the right moment,* he would say: You are not a woman who will easily admit she is attracted to a man: and she would explode into anger. Or—but almost anything would do. You are a woman who is overanxious to admit that she is attracted to a man: why? *It was all a question of timing: the whole process was built on it.*

She went home, preoccupied.

To Mark. To bed. To love. To happiness. At this time she was a woman who couldn't stand not being in bed. Yet for four years sex had been an appetite she had chosen not to feed. Except when, for a brief period, she suffered violent desire for Mark because of that mechanism, jealousy for Patty Samuels. She might easily never have gone to bed with Mark, just as she would never go to bed with Dr. Lamb. If she went to bed with Dr. Lamb, they would enter, effortlessly, the marvellous country of love; as may any man or woman "on the same wavelength." She had seen red. She had had an extraordinary experience. It hadn't seemed extraordinary at all. It was necessary now to say: Don't forget it, don't take it for granted—you must think about it.

There were a great many other things to think about.

Mrs. Quest kept putting off, or threatening to put off, or promising to make, her visit. Each letter was as if written in reply to one of Martha's which had put off, or rejected, or invited. But Martha continued to write, every two or three days, the same letter: Your room is ready and I am waiting for your visit.

In a pretty house on the slopes above Cape Town an old lady was engaged in a fight with a cold rejecting hating demon to which she gave the name Martha.

Martha was being treated by Dr. Lamb. But she was not seeing Dr. Lamb. In theory, she was going three times a week. In practice, she kept postponing appointments. It was a simple question of psychological economy, the medium of exchange being energy. She wanted to see Dr. Lamb, she lived hour by hour in a curve of expectation towards the next, but cancelled appointment. Because when it came to the point, she could not face the collapse into lethargy which must follow Dr. Lamb's making her angry so that she exploded. She had too much to do.

For one thing there was Mark. For another, there was his work. The publishers had asked: Where was his next book? Mark returned a joke, that he was a once-in-five-years novelist. But this would not do. Publishing was changing. Literature, like everything else, is an industry. A book comes out, a "name" is promoted; reviewers go into action; a few months later, that book is processed, done. Where is the next? Well, Mark was working on the story of Rachel and Aaron. When was it going to be finished? Put like that, Mark had to face that it wasn't going to be finished. It was being written to himself, perhaps to Martha, or to the dead Sally-Sarah. To Thomas?

The question was more, perhaps, was it written by Mark? Certainly the admirers of the war novel, or of *A City,* would never think so. If Mark had wanted to write a book all blood, sweat and tears, well, this was it. It had good bits in it. To make it a good book, one would have to remove all the parts that were emotional, violent, protesting. He could make a separate book of them perhaps? He had written two books? A novel and a play? The emotional parts were written mostly in dialogue. Interesting, that, if you thought of it: Mark, plunging into anger, and the rest of the emotions so remarkably absent from his usual kind of work, then had had to separate himself into characters who might easily walk on and off a stage—the directions were already here.

MIRIAM (*speaking slowly, haltingly: she is very frightened*): "But Aaron, if they catch you, they'll kill you ..." (Miriam was Aaron's mother.)

And so on.

Thinking about it, talking about it, they spread sheets of typescript all over the floors, the desk, the bed in which they spent so much time.

The publisher, Terence Boles, was insistent: "But Mark, you have to keep your name before the public!" He was humorous, but he meant it. Was there not something else Mark had that could be published? There was something lying in a drawer?

As it happened, there was. Long ago, before the war, when

he was a boy, Mark had written a series of stories, or sketches, about his mother's house in the country, where she had entertained politicians, writers, relations. The sketches were about the people who had been guests. They were mostly fanciful, since Mark had so seldom been home; were created, built up, out of things his brothers had said: for the most part what Colin had said. Colin had found the proceedings for the most part humorous. Colin had had a great sense of humour in those days—Mark remembered this with surprise: one had not, for many years, associated Colin with a sense of humour, or even of enjoyment. It must have been the war that had changed him. These stories were not so much immature, as thin. It seemed that Mark's persona, the writer, the person in him who wrote, had never been "young," had been born an old man. It was not the view of an adolescent boy, but of a humorous mature observer, part Colin, but mostly Mark.

Well, these sketches, formed into a book, might very well do. Nothing startling, but adequate. A holding operation; something to keep the machine fed while Mark considered what he should do next. While he considered, he continued to do what he enjoyed, which was to let that remarkable manuscript proliferate, in which two dead people fed the existences of the two soon-to-be-murdered brother and sister, Miriam's children.

Martha polished up the sketches. She got ready her mother's room. She and Mark made love, remained inside a tender and charming fantasy life where there was no responsibility, no time.

From which Martha woke one morning with the knowledge that in two days from now her mother would arrive.

She ran to the telephone to confirm an appointment with Dr. Lamb.

She travelled towards him through the hot and noisy traffic of a summer's day, thinking that he was going to make her "explode." Why? Why was the antidote to her lethargies to make her explode? In all those innumerable books she had by now read, she could not remember it being stated that way. There was the word "catharsis." Hmmm. What was that? An explosion. In the old plays, the old theatre, that was what they did? Pity and terror—one was forced to live through it, one exploded, one came out at peace? What was the result of years and years of this process, during which, several times a week, one was exploded, and so skilfully, by Dr. Lamb? A continual repetition of the same skilful process, the explosion of certain energies. Bad energies? Bang, bang, up go terror, fear, anger, resentment, in a surge of energy. *Red*. Pity, too. What colour was pity? It didn't matter—bang! Up goes pity, bang, bang. And bang go love, warmth, compassion? Years and years of it, for some people.

While chatting to Terence Boles, about the book, he had remarked that his wife was finishing an analysis that week. At the time she had not been listening, had been thinking about the new book, "The Way of a Tory Hostess." What an extraordinary phrase that was: finishing an analysis. Terence had let it drop quite casually: he had not found it extraordinary. "My cost of living is going to drop sharply this week," he said, humorously. "My wife's finishing her analysis."

At some point, after years of being exploded by Dr. Lamb, one stepped forth, a developed human being, "finished."

She was sitting in the leather chair opposite Dr. Lamb, who, as she could see with one part of her mind, wanted to talk about her sleeping with Mark, and her wishing to sleep with him, Dr. Lamb. She was thinking what it could mean, what they, Dr. Lamb, could possibly mean when they said "finishing an analysis," when she heard Dr. Lamb say: "I think you'll see it more clearly when you've finished."

"I'm sorry, I wasn't listening. What did you say?"

"I said, when you've finished your analysis, Mrs. Hesse, you'll see it in proportion."

"What made you say that then?"

He looked humorous.

Dr. Lamb had never mentioned finishing an analysis before.

She had never before thought of finishing an analysis.

Some weeks ago, she had been sitting here, and the air of the room had flashed scarlet. She had "seen red" but literally. The blaze of scarlet had faded slowly as her anger had faded.

"I put it to you, Mrs. Hesse, that you are feeling guilty because you've been sleeping with Mark. You have been breaking your appointments with me at the last moment because you've been afraid I'm going to punish you for it."

She considered this.

"How could you punish me?"

The time was up. She made an appointment for a week later, because her mother was coming, and she could be quite sure her time would not be her own. She went home.

Four

An old lady sat in a flower-crammed balcony high above the breathing sea. Behind her was the famous mountain. She had looked at it, admired it, been taken up it, had made a great many exclamations about it, and about the magnificent views. Milly was infinitely kind, dragging her about all over the peninsula, to look at views. Milly had suggested a second trip up the mountain: Mrs. Quest's refusal was pettish. She had believed she had been polite, half believed this was what she had wanted, being dragged about . . . good Lord, had she actually used that word? Been impolite? Certainly, she hadn't meant to be querulous: her own voice had shocked her. First she had seen the look on Milly's face, then, wondering at its cause, heard her own voice. Surely she hadn't been . . . apologetic, flurried, she redoubled her exclamations. It was dreadful! Milly, who worked so hard, had given up many plans of her own, Mrs. Quest was sure of that, to visit oak forests and vineyards and beauty spots of all kinds.

But Milly was a young woman who was really, truly kind, unlike others who—here Mrs. Quest's mind went dark briefly, refusing to specify who was not kind.

Milly was silent, thoughtful, then suggested that May should herself ask to be driven, when she felt like it. "Please, my dear, I really would like you to please yourself."

The phrase almost touched off another charge of rage: when had she ever pleased herself? When had she not sacrificed herself for others? But she was learning not to use those words, no matter how often she thought them. When she did, that look appeared on people's faces which . . . People? Her children. Her own children, for whom she had . . .

Old people, servants, children, slaves, all those who aren't in control of their own lives, watch faces for minute signs in eyes, gestures, lips, as weather-watchers examine the skies. It seemed to Mrs. Quest that for years now she had been covertly watching her son's face, his wife's face, for that look.

247

For a long time she had not been able to put a name to it, for the truth was so impossible. How was it that the sacrifice of her own life led to—embarrassment. As if she were an ill-mannered little girl, or a dog who had to be patted and fed but who embarrassed by tactless remarks or by jumping up to bark and lick.

Milly did not look embarrassed, though perhaps she might be hurt, or thinking. Why did she not say so before?

Well, why hadn't Mrs. Quest said so before? For Milly *was* so kind, unlike . . . Milly was *really* kind. She never made one feel as if . . . Mrs. Quest did not want to remember how she had been feeling. She did not want to think that Milly, a young woman every bit as busy, as responsible, as her own children, had time for *real* kindness, whereas they . . . She did not want to think about the last few years on the high dry hilly farm horizoned by mountains. She had had enough of mountains, peaks, rocks, dryness and the winds that shrank one's flesh till one felt all dried skin on old bones.

Mrs. Quest sat among flowers hundreds of feet above the sea. It seemed that if she leaned foward, she might dip her hand into it, or even pick up a toy ship, or simply float off, like a sea bird, over the crisping, bounding or solid surfaces of water to play like the wind, on moving blue, or green or grey.

She had always loved the sea. She was that member of the family who loved the sea. "What I really enjoy is a good sea voyage." As a child, holidays on the Isle of Wight, trips around Cowes, journeys across the Channel or to Ireland; small boons for a sea lover, which she had always been, knowing that, in spite of her circumscription, she was born, like the real sea people, for sailing ships, merchant ships, seaports, sea islands, sea winds, tangy and alien shores and the men who chart them. To her, the sea meant what deserts mean to the desert lover, or mountains to those madmen (or so they seem to those who do not love mountains) who choose to die absurdly on peaks among storms and avalanches.

This being so, how was it that she had spent thirty years, more, on the highveld, thousands of feet up and away from the sea, where the only reminders of sea were the sound of wind in long grass, or a mackerel sky at sundown?

For, as she sat expanding and breathing in the salt air, she was forced to think that one could say, every day of one's life, that one loved the sea, but could forget, except in the falseness of nostalgia, what the sea could be.

248

How was it possible for a sea creature so to organise her life that she hadn't been near it? What had happened?

Simply, what had happened was that she had married Mr. Quest; and therefore had she spent her life as a farmer's wife on the highveld, instead of as a sailor's wife near some port.

An old lady with grown-up children and five grandchildren sat thinking: Perhaps I made a mistake, I should have married . . .

She thought it defiantly; she had a right to the thought, hadn't she? After all, it had depended on her, on her choice—hadn't it? Yet there was something about the thought itself that made her mind go suddenly dark, as if it fainted, refused to go on. More and more these days, her mind kept coming up against places where it jibbed, shied away, seized up: or she'd find herself giving a small sharp laugh, like a stifled snort; then she'd glance quickly around to see if anyone had heard. But no, for hours of every day, she was alone in the flat, could talk to herself if she wished. And she did. Why not? Didn't everyone? Her son's wife might give her *that look* but she talked to herself too: but then she was a young woman who, when caught talking to herself, could make a joke of it, even claim it, as part of an attraction. But if an old woman talked to herself, they gave you that look.

Here she was alone every morning, till lunchtime, when Milly's little boy came in from his nursery school and the coloured girl came to clean and be nursemaid. In the afternoons Mrs. Quest became a helpful old lady—what else was she alive for, if not to help others? But in the mornings—what was she then?

Sometimes, sea bird, sailor's wife, sailor, she sneaked in off the balcony to look into the mirror and saw a timid, defiant old face with its wind-shrivelled flesh, but her mind went dark, it kept going dark: she returned to the balcony, where she sat wrestling with something concealed, something she could not meet, did not know how to meet—sets of facts, or of emotions, kept jangling together, but could not merge, they did not fit.

And old lady, sitting alone, thinking of children, grandchildren, may say to herself, Well, you needn't have been in existence, any of you! I might have married Johnnie, or Freddie, or Paul. And where would you have been then?

It had been up to her, forty-odd years ago, to say, I choose you, or you, or you . . . and because of that choice, such and such children, new people in the world, had come into being; but if she had made another choice, they would have been

249

different. But she could not begin to imagine Jonothan or Martha as different. They were inevitable. The fact that she could see only too clearly the embarrassed look either would give her if she had suggested such an idea proved how ridiculous it was. But if that *was* ridiculous, where had been her choice? It was here lay the impossibility, the incongruity, the heart of something terrible . . . as if she, May Quest, were nothing, a nullity, a channel merely.

. As if in a romantic novel, or a fairy story, she saw herself, wayward beauty, flirting with this one or that one, then bestowing herself: I, your despised mother, gave myself to your father, your grandfather—your existence is the result of my choice.

Such thoughts elderly ladies have, while they pass the marmalade or darn the socks—and watch, fearfully, like servants or infants, the faces of their powerful children, who imagine, God bless them, that they are in control of their own lives. (Mrs. Quest, sitting on the balcony, heard herself titter, and looked around sharply—it was all right, she was alone.)

Thirty or forty years ago, I, a courted and desired young woman, chose . . .

Though of course she had not been beautiful. She had been plain. They had always said: You are the plain one. "What a pity she is so plain." Plain Jane they had called her, in fun; and she had taken it like a good sort. She had been forced to be a good sort. *Why had she been plain?* After all, she had had a beautiful mother. A thought came to life here which she remembered having before, oh, but so very long ago— when? She had been a young girl? She had looked in mirrors, tied her hair this way and that, bit her lips to make them red: they had laughed at her, teased her. *Perhaps she had never been plain at all?* This thought, appalling in its implications, came near consciousness, was refused admittance, as it had been shut out before, but knocked again. . . .

Mrs. Quest, who never moved without her photographs, dug into her trunk, opened an album from her girlhood. A serious round-faced girl, with her hair pulled back and tied with a ribbon, stared back at her. Plain. *Why, plain?* As if a mask or a veil were drawn off the young face, she saw her, poor plain Jane, as a good-looking girl. If she had been able to paint and powder, the way everyone did now, or arrange her hair differently without being laughed at, she wouldn't have been plain at all! And she had had a good figure—they had always conceded her that. And of course she had always carried herself well, unlike these girls nowadays who slouched about anyhow. Who slouched? Martha? Jonothan's wife? Milly? Slouching, lolling, painting and powdering, lazy flibberty-gibbets, who ragtimed and tea-danced and cocktailed and were definitely no better than they ought to be, a frieze of irresponsible and dutiless girls unrolled before the old lady's eyes—and vanished, like the ugly veil over her own photograph. She ought to do something about the way she spoke, perhaps? Was that what made people embarrassed? But was it right to criticise an old woman because her slang was out of date? Was it kind? What was in a word, after all! And why go on punishing her, hadn't they all done enough, with that miserable girlhood behind her—plain Jane. She hadn't been plain. She had been pretty. More, perhaps, if anyone had ever been kind enough to help, or encourage. Rage spurted and boiled, an awful anger that seemed beneath everything she did, like an underswell in the sea, ready to leap up and overwhelm at a word or a look.

Besides, even if she had been plain, that didn't mean plenty of men hadn't seen her as a good wife. There was the young naval doctor, dead in the old war. He had never "spoken," but everyone knew what he felt for her. For years his photograph had stood on her dressing table—where was it? Where had she put it? Surely she hadn't lost it?

But why that photograph, why not others? It was as if she had been allowed one photograph, one alternative love: an allowance made by her family: Mummy might have married the poor doctor killed in the First World War. Her lost love. Poor Mummy's dead love, a memory, an official memory, the family's memory which she had permitted to become hers. Why had she? Why had she allowed herself to be plain Jane? Why had she married ... Why, why, why, why! It was all nonsense, starting with that sad good sort of a schoolgirl. There had been half a dozen men, at the time she got married, who wanted to marry her. They were patients; men wanted to marry their nurses. Men *did* marry their nurses. Her husband had married her. Handsome Captain Quest had married his plain nurse. What of the others? Odd that she had so completely discounted them as possible husbands, which they had been after all. They had proposed, or allowed to be understood that they would if she gave them a chance. But she had not considered them—why not? She had considered marrying the naval doctor; had married the soldier who became a farmer. But she had not only not married the others, but had not even thought of them as husbands. Yet they were every bit as good as the doctor or the soldier. Yes, of course, she had loved. Twice. Love. An old lady, who had been using the word "love" with confidence for decades, looked at it, and her mouth had the thin peaked look of the mouth of an unloved little girl, or the wife of a man who had married his mother. Love, she thought, love—her mind went dark. If that was love, then it had taken her to a hard sad life on first one farm, with her husband, than to another, with a son, hundreds of miles away and up from her real love, the sea.

Sometime, after these long lazy mornings, when it was as if the sea had invaded her, filled her with a soft, blue murmuring peace, and she returned indoors, to play with the little boy, and to help the coloured girl, Marie, she thought: If I had been able to live like this, been myself, would I have been good and kind, as I am now, instead of turning into a . . .

Had she had a choice, ever? If her choice of a husband had been no choice at all—as the solid finality of her children, her grandchildren proved, then what choice had she ever had? Of course it was different for all these flighty girls now, they did as they liked, look at Martha, it was certain she was pleasing herself, as she always had, selfish, inconsiderate, immoral . . . Mrs. Quest's head ached, she felt sick. These days, girls *did* choose, they were free: but in her young time, girls had that brief moment before they were married, when plain Jane was courted, was free to choose a husband, could say, Yes, no, I want this one and not that one, before she became a mother, and a nurse, and had no choice but to sacrifice herself.

She must be careful never to use that word when she was with Martha: she'd be lucky to get away with embarrassment! No, probably some cold, hard argument—unkindness. An awful kind of common sense, a logic. Like Jonothan's. Every word was a trap, one had to watch every syllable as it came out.

Yet in the evenings here with Milly, she spoke as she felt. Milly liked her. Milly was pleased to have her here, with a husband away. Milly reminded her very much of a school friend she once had. She had timidly said so, and Milly had not minded: old ladies seldom meet new faces, new people. Milly, the daughter of an old friend, with her pale little face, her seriousness, her tendency to headache and lassitude, was *very* like Rosemary. Milly, who had asked her to stay for a week while waiting for her boat to sail, had, exactly as

Rosemary once would have, asked her to stay as long as she liked, "to make herself at home." Milly's husband was a journalist, and he was attending some international occasion in America. Milly had a job teaching at the university. The little boy, Mrs. Quest thought, missed his parents, although the coloured girl was quite good. Why did Milly have to work at all?—but she must stop criticising, it was not her business.

Bringing it up, delicately, with Milly, Mrs. Quest heard that there was a previous wife in Johannesburg, and she was paid alimony. Milly's salary was necessary to help out. Did Milly mind? Mrs. Quest wondered—but she must not pry. Bringing it up, she found Milly ready to discuss, to be comically dry about it all. With Milly she could talk like a human being, but not with . . .

On the other farm she hadn't talked to anyone for years.

By the time the old lady arrived there, there were two small children and another on the way. Both Jonothan and Bessie worked very hard. The farm was a new one. The house was large. There was a great deal for Mrs. Quest to do. "If there is one thing I know about," said she to herself, and to them, "it's how hard a farmer's wife does work!" She busied herself with the children, and was sure Bessie did not mind. When the baby was born, Bessie added to her other duties, the business of looking after the dairy herd. Mrs. Quest thought this wrong: quite enough to be a mother and a farmer's wife. But Bessie was stubborn. She was pregnant again very soon, and at suggestions it was too soon, said the pregnancy was "planned." The young couple had planned four children, as they had planned to buy this remote raw farm, and build a large stone house on it.

It was all too much, they did too much, they were both worn out, looked pale, were on their feet from six in the morning to nine at night, and then of course there were broken nights with the children.

The whole thing was absurd: Mrs. Quest brooded and grieved and lay awake at night herself, for fear she might miss a baby crying, and not get to it before it woke her son or his wife. Then there was the first of the big rows. Bessie had snapped out one breakfast time; Mrs. Quest had defended herself; the young husband, looking impatient, had stayed away from the farm work (thus making Mrs. Quest feel guilty) to calm the two women. The "row" went on all morning: afterwards Mrs. Quest could only see the faces of those two, sitting opposite her, irritable, weary—embarrassed. They kept saying: "You must try and understand that everyone doesn't see life as you do." And "Yes, but you see, we don't agree with you." We! The word "we" used of that unit, her son and his wife, cut her every time she heard it. She had complained that "they discussed her behind her back," and that "Jonothan always takes her side."

Afterwards she stayed in her room for days, full of that grieving concern for others which she had always called "love." But, also, a nerve of justice had been struck. What they had said was true. Underneath everything she felt, was this: that they ought not to be here on this farm at all. She even felt it as a kind of betrayal.

Throughout the Quest tenancy of that other farm, there had been one consistent note struck. "Getting off the farm; when we get off the farm; getting away from all this." But young Jonothan, once free from the army, had headed straight back not to the same farm, but to one much worse: it had not been "opened up," it was nothing but hundreds of acres of—nothing. Among mountains. At one point Mrs. Quest had produced figures to prove that with the same amount of money (small, but of course they started on loans like everyone else) they could have bought a developed farm nearer town. At which they had looked—embarrassed. They liked this farm. This is what they liked. And they did not mind borrowing money. They did not have to build a great stone house with far too many rooms, when a smaller one would have done. Stone costs nothing, they said.

Why start a dairy herd, up here: there wasn't another for miles? That was the point, they said. Why build a dozen tobacco barns when a couple would have done, to start with, anyway? Jonothan evaded, conciliated, Mrs. Quest understood what he was not saying: that he was determined not to be like his father, happily, or at any rate dreamily, content to muddle along hoping for good things another year. The young couple felt themselves pioneers. Mrs. Quest was watching the birth of a really large farm, and a large family. Well, she muttered at last, if they want to kill themselves in the process I suppose it's their affair.

There started another phase, after that row. Mrs. Quest was avoiding Bessie. Bessie avoided her. The old lady heard, with closed critical lips, that they were employing a couple of black children to act as nurses to the white children: she continued to believe that black flesh should not contact white. She said nothing, though it nearly killed her. She then started a flower garden: the couple hadn't time for it. If there was one thing she understood, it was gardens. She planted, on a rocky hillside that looked across a vale to the mountains, a garden that became, very soon, all roses, bougainvillaea, jacarandahs, cypress, jasmine, plumbago, and lilies. Then she started a vegetable garden. These under control, and a new windmill being installed, she suggested adding ducks to the chickens. She was already running the chickens. Then she asked if Bessie would like her to supervise the dairy herd. She expected a rebuff but Bessie agreed at once. Had she been waiting for the old lady to suggest it? This started a new nasty suspicion: had Bessie gone out of the house to do farm work in the first place just to get away from her, her mother-in-law?

She did not know. She thought it was so. At any rate, Bessie spent more time in the house, which is where she ought to be, and Mrs. Quest, an old lady of sixty-five, then sixty-six, then sixty-seven—goodness, she would soon be seventy—rose at six, with relish, made herself a snack of breakfast, got out of the way of the family, and was off around her gardens, and livestock while the sun was still new.

She worked. She worked. She had never worked so hard. And in the evenings, just as they did, she was off to bed by nine. Mrs. Quest hardly saw the children. Was Bessie keeping them away from her? They were always in the hands of those dirty black . . .

Sometimes at meals she studied Bessie's face, and thought: Why this girl, why this one particularly? Bessie was a short plump dark woman, with cheeks that had been rosy but now were pale. She had brown eyes—rather small, Mrs. Quest thought. She was all right, the old lady supposed. Sometimes, as their paths crossed in the day, Mrs. Quest would turn to watch, eyes narrowed under her great shady straw hat, a plump dark woman walk in her brisk determined way to pantry, or storeroom, and think: She's the wife of my son. Why this one? Mrs. Quest could not remember ever exchanging more than politenesses with her, they had never really talked, or opened to each other.

Mrs. Quest was lonely, as she had been before, on that other farm, with a husband who found his own thoughts more interesting than her company.

Lonely, she brooded, over the children, over the past. She worried over Martha, whose letters said nothing, and particularly nothing about getting married.

There was another row if you could use that word for the awful cold, brisk, conciliatory discussions, with the three of them paled by tension and anxiety. Logical—that is what Jonothan was, and his wife. For, when she complained that she was getting on for seventy, and that she worked all day, of coure she did not want to stop working, she wanted only to be loved and praised for working.

As a result of this, but not at once, there was a change. Shortly, Jonothan announced he was getting an assistant. He would like the assistant in the house: more convenient, he said. He suggested building the old lady her own house. She listened, bright-eyed, disbelieving. They were kicking her out! That was the truth, but of course, this cold logicality couldn't allow the truth.

They built her a two-roomed house with a large verandah, about a hundred yards from their own, turned towards the mountains, and with windows cut down almost to the floor, so that the rooms admitted mountains, mountains, everywhere you looked. She liked the house. She moved into it with a quiet grim smile, saying how much she did like it. No, she would prefer to do her own cooking; yes, she would sometimes come for family meals, perhaps on Sunday; no, of course she wouldn't be formal about it. Yes, she understood that the assistant would look after the dairy herd. Was she to be allowed to keep the chickens and the ducks? The outrageousness of this quiet question in view of her outburst about her exploitation—*I'm nothing but an unpaid servant*—did not strike her as such, because she had never meant it. She did not deserve, she knew, their look of furious exasperation.

They entreated, begged, implored her not to tire herself, and when she said she was quite capable of doing the ducks and chickens and the gardens, they sent to her, as personal assistant, Steven.

Steven was a child of twelve. His real name she never knew. He had been christened Steven by another farmer where he had been working before he came here. She said she did not want Steven; they did not argue, merely instructed Steven to stay with her. There followed an absurd and painful period when Mrs. Quest went about her chickens, ducks, gardens, with a set angry face, followed by Steven, who tried to help her and was snubbed every time he asked: "What shall I do, missus?"

Steven seemed to her a final insult. She lay awake at night raging and storming, talking to herself aloud, that at the end of her life she, May Quest was being put aside like an old dog with a black keeper, called Steven.

Two years later, when Mrs. Quest left to visit England, she

wept, and she knew it was not her son, or grandchildren, she wept for, but for Steven.

For weeks she saw him through a cloud of anger: she saw a young black face, always watching hers. He was a tall child, very thin, obviously undernourished. She began scolding him about washing himself; and made him eat bread and vegetables from her little kitchen. It had occurred to her that he was a child, that he was three hundred miles from his village, that he had no one but some kind of "brother" near him, and he was on a farm twenty miles away, and that she, May Quest, was the only human being with whom he had any sort of contact. He spent all his time with her—left at ten o'clock at night to go to the compound. When told he could go earlier, he replied, simply, that he preferred to stay with her, he had no "brothers" in the compound. He preferred to stay with a cross ugly old woman (Mrs. Quest had seen her face in the glass reflecting the thoughts she had over Steven) rather than be with his own people? She thought, at last, that he was twelve, alone, lonely. She began to talk with him. They sat on the little verandah, looking towards the mountains. She sat in a grass chair, very upright, knitting. The child sat on the edge of the verandah with his bare feet in the dust, tracing pictures in the dust with his forefinger, or tossing a pebble from one hand to the other. He talked about his village. He said he had a grandmother. He missed his grandmother. Mrs. Quest, being compared to an old black woman in a native village, felt a reminiscent surge of anger, but it carried no conviction. She found herself amused. She began to knit him a jersey: he possessed one pair of shorts, one singlet, and a blanket, that was all. Sometimes they sat quietly, perhaps watching how the four white children played under trees a couple of hundred yards away with the two black children watching them. Mrs. Quest asked if perhaps Steven would like to make friends with them? He said quickly that no, they were not from his tribe, they had no language in common but English. Anyway, he said, his brows knitting, "I like it with you missus." This hurt the old lady. She suffered that she had been so unkind. She was suffering more than that: she had been in the country for thirty years and she had never talked to a black person before—not like this, as she was now. She had not thought before of the hundreds of black people that had been on the old farm and were on this one, that they might not be able to talk to each other because they did not share a language, or that a child might be lonely and miss his old grandmother, or that a black person might be solitary by nature. For it was clear that Steven was. He had, he confided, always liked being by himself in the village. They had teased him about it. They had called him Go-by-himself. Mrs. Quest told Steven the story about the Cat Who Walked by Himself. He laughed, was delighted. Mrs. Quest, secretly, got hold of a copy of the Kipling tales so that she could refresh her memory of them, and told him others. In return, he told her tales from his village, and he sang her songs. When Mrs. Quest woke in the mornings, she lay smiling, waiting for when she would hear first his bare feet on the bricks of the verandah, the soft slur of the door over cement, the sounds of his movements in the kitchen, then see his bright face as he opened the door, very softly, to see if she was awake and he could bring in the tea. She hurried through bathing and dressing, to get back to the verandah, where she would sit with her friend and talk. He said one day: You have a black heart, missus, you are my mother. Mrs. Quest could not speak: she was crying. One morning, when she made an exclamation of pain as she moved her leg—her old arthritis was coming back—he leaped across with an exclamation and began rubbing her knee. She sat, suffering as waves of repugnance rose in her, then ebbed and went. A black child was rubbing her knee as, so he said, he had often rubbed his granny's legs for her, when they had pain in them. She could not bear to think of what she was feeling now, what she had left: she was having bad headaches, slept badly, was full of low grieving emotion that she knew was probably remorse.

When, one Sunday, she was lunching with the family and the new assistant, they asked if she liked Steven, or if she'd prefer another boy, she said no, he seemed a nice enough boy, she didn't mind him. And, speaking like this, she realised how far she had moved from the woman who would have said once, he was cheeky, he was dirty, he was—black. She was ashamed of her new friend, tried to keep a watch out for her son or his wife who might discover her telling Steven a story or talking to him. Once or twice they did: questions were asked. They said they hoped she was not spoiling him. She said, with appropriate severity, that she hoped she knew how to treat kaffirs after all this time. They made jokes that it was bad these days to say kaffirs, or munts, one should say Africans, those loud-mouthed politicians in town who spoiled the blacks said so. She remarked, for it seemed to her utterly irrelevant, that if they wanted, she would call them Africans. Wasn't she an African, after all this time? she enquired.

After nearly two years, a man passing through the compound brought a message from Steven's father: they wanted him back home, if he had earned enough for his tax. Steven assured the old lady that though he must go home, he would be back again.

"When?"

"Oh, perhaps they want me for the planting, it will be the rains soon."

"Will you come back after the planting?"

"Oh yes, yes, missus, I will come back."

Of course, blacks, kaffirs, Africans, have no sense of time. She knew she could not ask. She knew she must not—what right had she? And besides, she was alarmed at the distance she had moved from her old self, that she could grieve because a black boy was going back to his village. This alarm was switched into a grievance against her son and his wife: if only they weren't so cold, so unfeeling! *They had white hearts,* she found herself thinking. She thought how, with this child, it would be inconceivable to conduct one of the cold logical exchanges where there was no feeling, no heart, only a kind of word-fencing where no emotions could be admitted. She thought: Very well, they find me a tiresome old woman. Of course, it's natural. Well, why don't they tease me for it then, make a game of it, instead of this therefore and because and if and but. When I'm bad-tempered with Steve, he teases me, he jokes.

She thought that, with these black people, it was natural that an old woman was difficult, needed the tact that comes from the heart. Steven had talked of the old people who were cross, or a bit crazy, or even hit other people—they were old, his manner suggested; they were entitled, had a right, to be difficult. But Mrs. Quest was not, not with her own children.

She said that perhaps she might go to England to visit Martha. Yes, of course she would come back. She heard in her voice the same vague note that had been in Steven's: Yes, I'll come back after the rains. He was not coming back. Why should he? He was fourteen years old. On this farm, the pet, or servant, of an old white woman, he earned one pound a month, and—this was the point—saw nothing of the world. He said he wanted to go to a big town, a real town, like Salisbury. He had not ever seen a big white man's city. Of course. It was natural. But when Mrs. Quest returned to her little house, where she had been pensioned off, from England, she would be alone again. No, she would see if Martha ...

after all, time changed people . . . time had changed her, May Quest . . . she had been told by a black boy that she had a black heart! Let Martha put that in her pipe and smoke it!

Steven left one Sunday morning, with his blanket rolled up over his shoulder, and in it a jersey knitted by Mrs. Quest, and an old shirt of Jonothan's. His possessions. He was going to walk back home with some brothers who were going that way. He lingered, smiling, on the verandah. Mrs. Quest lingered, smiling. Then she said briskly: "Well, Steven, we will both have travelled a long way before we meet again . . ."

"Yes, missus, goodbye missus." He went off down the path into the trees and Mrs. Quest lay on her bed and wept.

Now, after Steven, there was Marie, the coloured girl. She brought the little boy from his nursery school, gave him lunch, and then cleaned the house while he took a nap. Then she prepared food, darned, made tea for Mrs. Quest. She was a brisk little thing, who looked about eighteen. She had two children, cared for by her mother while she worked. Mrs. Quest suspected them of being illegitimate. Marie was religious. Mrs. Quest, religious, found Marie's religion altogether too much of a good thing. Marie could not smoke, drink, go to pictures, dance or—Milly said yes, the children were illegitimate. Milly did not appear to be upset by this. She and her husband were liberals; they hated the Nationalists; they took it for granted that Mrs. Quest, like themselves, must regard *apartheid* as criminal. Marie, staying late to baby-sit, slept in a spare room, and she sat down to eat with them if she was there at mealtimes. Mrs. Quest thought: Well, it's all right for them, they don't understand our problems. Milly and her husband had been five years in the Cape, and proposed to return to England when they could. It was not that Mrs. Quest disliked Marie; on the contrary. She was a very good kind of girl, clean, and responsible with the child. Once when Mrs. Quest had a headache, Marie put her to bed in a dark room, and laid strips of cloth soaked in vinegar on her forehead. Marie talked a great deal about her own two children, about her mother, and about God, who rewarded patience in this vale of tears. Mrs. Quest, listening, thought that her own faith was less, but had once been like this. She remarked, with the quietly grim humour which she knew upset some people, though not Milly, who shared it, that she did so hope so, but there didn't seem to be much evidence of it. Marie sighed, smiled, said she would pray for Mrs. Quest. Spending her afternoons with Marie, the old lady thought of Steven, whom she would probably never see again, and reminded herself that in England she would be free of colour problems. She made a note never to discuss them with Martha: she really must remember not to.

Her pleasant intimacy with Milly ended when Milly's husband Bob returned from America. He was very clever, well informed, energetic. A short, spry, gingery man whose hands always seemed to be full of papers and newspapers, he seemed to Mrs. Quest to be not good enough for Milly. In the evenings, when he was not at his newspaper, he made a great many pronouncements about everything in the world, particularly America, which country he did not admire. He was opinionated about Africa, about the policy of her own country's government. Mrs. Quest tried very hard to be tactful, to say yes, and no; and not to disagree.

It was from him she learned that her daughter's employer, Mark Coldridge, was a well-known Communist writer. She was given a novel to read which she found cold, and intellectual. It described an ideal Communist city somewhere in the Middle East. But it was a very dishonest book, sly: it did not mention Communism. Discussing the novel with Bob, or rather listening to his opinions, she agreed with him: Communist propaganda was dangerous because it was so dishonest. No Communist city was like the one he described, nor had ever been. But naive people, or backward people (like the Africans), might very well read the book and believe it. Bob did not believe in censorship, but he did think some kinds of propaganda ought to be forbidden: this novel, for instance.

Was her daughter a Communist, he enquired? Mrs. Quest said she supposed she must be.

She remembered a letter from Martha in which she had said she was not. Mrs. Quest had a cardboard box with all Martha's letters in it. She spent one evening reading back through the letters, which said so very little, until she found the one she looked for, dated about two years back. The relevant sentences were: You know I'm not a Communist; don't you think it would be a good idea if we kept off politics.

But she was probably lying: they were sly.

Mrs. Quest shut away Martha's letters, feeling panicky, bewildered. She could not remember writing to Martha about politics at all. What had she written about? She had been writing a lot recently, of course, but that was only because she did not want to be a trouble when she arrived, she wanted to have things clearly understood.

The thought approached the borders of Mrs. Quest's consciousness that she was writing three, four letters a day to

Martha, from the balcony over the sea, and before she got up in the morning, and before she went to sleep at night. Well, wasn't that natural?

Of course one wrote letters when . . . her mind went dark.

And so, her mind dark, she wrote the letters, fast, flowing, not thinking, page after page, and sealed them without reading them. She posted them in batches, every morning after breakfast, with the vague thought: Well, that's taken care of.

She was glad when the time came to leave Cape Town. She was ready and packed two days before. On the day before, she felt bad, did not think she could get out of bed, all her body ached and her legs were like sticks. Milly had not gone to work that day; she stayed, quiet, concerned, affectionate, saying no more than that if Mrs. Quest did not leave by this boat, then there would be another in a couple of weeks' time. Mrs. Quest lay in bed and looked at the young woman's gentle, humorous little face; she knew that Milly had quarrelled with her husband because of her: she had heard the quarrel through thin walls. Then Bob came into the room and said that he was going to telephone the doctor. Milly was giving him looks that she seemed to imagine Mrs. Quest did not see: they thought she was stupid, did they? She announced, brisk, that there was no need for the doctor, she would be ready to leave when the time came.

Bob left the room, brisk. Milly kissed the old woman, and held her for a moment in her arms. "Poor old thing," she murmured, and Mrs. Quest, almost weeping with gratitude, said briskly that she was not at all a poor old thing! The two woman exchanged their grimly humorous understanding, in a long close look—then Mrs. Quest heard herself give a snort, or yelp of laughter.

Milly, nodding, as if to say: Yes, but it won't do, you know! There's my husband to consider!—went out of the room, to the bedroom, where a married altercation took place. Mrs. Quest listened to its sense, not to the words, which she could not quite catch.

Ah, she was thinking, these awful, opinionated dogmatic people: well, thank goodness she was leaving tomorrow.

That morning she was up before the light came, to sit on the balcony for the last time. The sun rose over a flat grey sea, painted it purple and green, painted the great ship that was to take Mrs. Quest to England, in candid paintbox colours. The sky reverberated with light. She sat in a brilliant world which tired her badly, and she looked at the sun and said to it: I won't be seeing you again, thank goodness!

As if an entirely different sun, friendly and modest, shone over England.

She was seen off by Milly, who gave her a bunch of flowers. In her cabin she found chocolates. She and two other old ladies settled themselves and their many belongings into the oversmall space. She went back to the deck which her fare entitled her to cover, to watch Cape Town slide away into smallness. She needed to say goodbye to her Africa, as she had needed to say goodbye to its sun. In a confusion of emptiness she was laying hold of licensed and appropriate thoughts: about time, which passed; about life, which was unexpected; about death, inevitable. She was pleased, supported by, the joyful bustle of the departure, by the flowers, the chocolates, a farewell telegram from her son. Checking up on these, and her thoughts, as she would have done the number of wreaths at a funeral, or soldiers at a ceremony, she was aware that behind the gestures and rituals that she was, as always, depending on, her mind lay bare, very quiet. Indeed, she seemed quite extraordinarily clear-headed: perhaps it was because she had got up so early. She took a chair as near the railings as she could get, among people who stampeded about like herds of cattle, hoping that some of the salt spray might reach to where she was. When she had come out all those years ago, had people rushed about like this, made noises, shouted, fought over stewards and places? If so, she had forgotten it.

Reminding herself that she must not get tired enough to be caught talking to herself, she sat on while the confusion settled, and routines became established. Then she descended to find out which part of this great machine she was to fit herself to. She did it with a grim private amusement: on this longed-for sea voyage, she, gallant wayfarer, was going to be an old lady among old ladies. She had forgotten it.

By the end of the first day it was as if these hundreds of people were obeying rules that had been posted up for them: for one thing they were sorted out into their age groups. Children ran about in their private world, not seeing the grown-up world, seeing only each other. The young people—and there seemed an incredible number of them—flirted and drank and played games together, seeing each other. Mrs. Quest found their behaviour disgusting, but she kept this to herself: she knew she was old-fashioned. There were the married couples, worried about their children. And these shaded off, shredded away into middle age, and then into old age, which was chiefly old women, with one or two old men. So

263

had the tables been arranged in the dining rooms, and so they all conformed.

Mrs. Quest, an old lady among old ladies, all of them widows (for women live much longer than men), sat in her deck chair, which had been placed well out of the wind. She would much rather have been in it. She had a rug over her knees, and she knitted something or other: they all knitted or sewed, and they watched others at play. When Mrs. Quest had said how much she loved a voyage, a good deal of what she loved was the games: she adored the atmosphere of organised jollity, the jokes, the teasing, the good-sportsmanship of it all. She always had . . . but had she, she wondered? Well, she had always been a good sort, of course. Now, a good sort, obeying, as she always had, she played whist and bridge. She played well. She loved whist and bridge. But she did not play all afternoon and evening, as some did, she played for an hour or so every afternoon, paid her dues, and went back to the deck. On the deck in the evenings everywhere were kissing couples. More than kissing, she suspected. She tried not to notice them and watched the stars overhead, and held the thought that there would be different stars in England. The old ladies remarked on the Southern Cross, that it would soon leave them, but Mrs. Quest found herself thinking that they were all, every one, from the cities, and what did they know about stars and the Cross—or about Africa? She had as little in common with them as with a woman who had never left England at all. Privately, she put her decades in Africa beside theirs and tried not to scorn them: she must not criticise so much, she really must not! They talked the talk of old ladies, and Mrs. Quest paid her dues. Here, one might have thought, was the only place where she might unload the weight of her husband's long last illness, and her thoughts about her children. But the old women, every one, carried their own loads. It was as if again, a notice board printed in invisible ink had been posted up: Thou shalt listen to your old sisters' complaints about life, as they will listen to yours.

Every one told her story, the others listening. But if Mrs. Quest were to tell truthfully, the long years of that dragging illness—why, it would last the voyage. And they had all had sons in the last war; and they all had children, grown-up, about whom they tended to be dishonest. Mrs. Quest was able to acquit herself well: she had her son, married satis-factorily, on his great farm in the mountains, with his four children. Mrs. Quest had four grandchildren—five. There

264

was Caroline. Mrs. Quest found comfort in the fact that, modern life being what it was, she was not the only one to have a daughter who had come to grief in the divorce courts. But she was the only one whose granddaughter was not being brought up by her mother. She slurred this over, rather, though Caroline could have been her favourite, such a decided, clever, well-brought-up girl she was, if rather alarming. The truth was, Caroline tended to patronise her old granny when she came in from the farm to take her out for the day.

The talk tired Mrs. Quest. She was really very tired. It must be the sea air. She rose late. She napped after lunch. She went to bed early. The noisy meals in the dining room, where the amount people ate seemed truly incredible, exhausted her. She sometimes stayed on deck and asked the deck steward to bring her a cup of soup.

He was a delightful young man, chosen either by the laws of his own temperament or by a percipient management to wait on old ladies. They all vied with each other, asking this youth who was like a fantasy ideal son (emasculated and in real life not to be tolerated for a moment, being always obedient, attentive and thoughtful) to bring them their favourite brands of chocolate or a rug or cushions. They followed him, sighing, with their eyes, as he whisked towards them with trays and cups, balancing on the balls of his feet to the sway of the ship, making a joke of his facility. Also, while they smiled and sighed, they might exchange glances: they knew perfectly well why it was this one, and not another, who waited on them. Did people think them fools?

That people should not think them foolish because of this disguise they wore, white hair, graveyard faces, unsightly bodies, was a preoccupation with them all: this was the root of their tetchiness, their bad humours. And it was with their own kind, among each other, that each stood on her dignity, fought politely over little points of precedence, made little claims of privilege. Who else would allow it?

The voyage was half over. The group tended to dissolve into couples. There was a Mrs. Foster who had spent some years on a farm when she was a young woman. Mrs. Quest was able to talk to her. They sat talking in the official language about time, life, death; but knowledge gave the barest phrases a depth which made it hard sometimes for them to meet each other's eyes. One old lady might say to another, as they watched the young people flirting, the young married couples with their children, all these smooth bright bodies: Yes, but they don't know, do they? It was like a curse, or a spell.

A group of old women in their jerseys, and their warm scarves, and their hair in nets, with their knitting and their careful exchange of phrases, shed their sorrowful glances on the young people who, glancing that way, might pause, grow silent for a moment, even remove themselves to another part of the ship.

Thirty years ago, on the journey out to Africa, Mrs. Quest had been one of them, a strong young woman with two small children, a handsome husband, and a nurse. Thirty years, she kept repeating, entitled to the words, to the idea—but it would not come to life. She could not make it mean anything. She knew if she said to one of the young women, Thirty years, what they would hear was the promise of an endlessness, full of possibility, like an open ticket for a gambling table. But when Mrs. Quest said Thirty years, thirty years, thirty years, she could not fill the words with more than what she felt after a bad night: she had dreamed a lot, she had dreamed of an exile, of heights, and dryness and mountains.

Mrs. Foster and she, choosing each other's company because they had something in common, in fact said very little. They sat silently in the shelter of companionship, watching the young—but guarding their eyes, as if what must come from them would be too baleful to bear.

Mrs. Quest kept running over the official words, phrases: Empire was one. (She tried to change it to Commonwealth, but it was not the same.) Duty was another. God, another. At the service on Sunday there had been fifty people present, out of all the hundreds on board. They were all too busy enjoying themselves. Mrs. Quest had always tried to do her duty. She went quietly over the Ten Commandments, and thought that she could honestly say her life had been regulated by them. Mrs. Foster was not religious: she, too, was alone, was off to visit old friends in England she had not seen for twenty years, because, as was clear to Mrs. Quest, her children did not want her. Mrs. Foster had not been to the service on Sunday. What difference did it all make? And she, Mrs. Quest, was a white settler (once a proud claim, not a stigma); a bloodsucker, an exploiter: Bob had as good as said she was. Her mind rattled with words, phrases, bits of prayer, and hymns, and remarks about life and death which all her life had fed her, supported her. But she was really very tired, very tired. She told herself that two years before she had been working as hard on the farm as her daughter-in-law or her son, and that two years could not have turned her into an old woman who was always tired and who needed to be waited on. But they had.

She had been forced to become an old woman: she had been forced to join this group of old hens with whom she had nothing in common; she was being made to play bridge and to sit out of the wind knitting and to sleep away time because she had nothing to do.

It seemed to Mrs. Quest that a word, a wave of the magic wand, and she would be a young matron again, all self-reliant competence—like that girl over there, a browned healthy young creature who played deck games all day, with her husband and a group of friends. She was a good sort, ready for anything. The old woman sat watching the young woman. She would make excuses to move her deck chair so as to keep Olive Prentiss in her sight. It seemed to her that there was an understanding between them, that although they had never exchanged a word, they felt for each other. The old lady waited for moments when the girl looked in her direction, waited for her to smile. She did once. Then, she said, "Good morning!" And the day after, she asked how Mrs. Quest was. Mrs. Quest imagined that Olive came and asked for her advice—"with all your experience . . ." Mrs. Quest told her not to put off having children too long: children were the only thing in life worth having.

One night Mrs. Quest stood on the deck by the rail watching her sea rushing past. It was dark, with a little light falling from a door. Olive Prentiss came out, alone, a few paces off. She looked harassed—guilty? She turned her back to the rail and looked up and down the deck. She did not see the old lady. She half squatted, put her hand under a brief white skirt, pulled out a little bloody swab and then tossed it over the rail into the sea. She stood up again, looked quickly about—and saw Mrs. Quest. Mrs. Quest was smothered with emotion. She called it, later, outrage; it was the carelessness of the girl that shocked. A couple of brief glances around, not seeing Mrs. Quest, who was so close (Am I invisible then? the old lady asked herself, furious), then the fast, practised half-squat and the disposal of the horrid object. Seeing Mrs. Quest, there was the briefest reaction of surprise. Then she smiled, and said, "Plenty of room in the sea." She lingered (out of *politeness,* Mrs. Quest saw, incredulously), smiled again, and went into the lounge.

Mrs. Quest seethed, raged, suffered. When she was a girl . . . but she could not, suddenly, bear to remember what now seemed like a long story of humiliation and furtiveness, great soaking bloody clouts that rubbed and smelled, and which one was always secretly washing, or concealing, or trying to burn; headaches and backaches and all kinds of necessary tact with obtuse brothers and fathers; and then her breasts, her first sprouting breasts, about which the family had made jokes and she had blushed—but of course, had been a good sort.

She went to bed early and felt ill. She pushed Olive Prentiss out of her mind, and with it the incident, and the memories it had brought up.

There's plenty of room in the sea, indeed!

Mrs. Quest, two days away from England, decided not to get up. She felt bad, she told Mrs. Foster, who came to visit her. Mrs. Foster was pleasant, tactful: much too tactful to suggest the doctor, or medicines.

A cabin maid fussed over her. A cabinmate, an old Mrs. Jones from Johannesburg, offered her own symptoms in exchange; Mrs. Quest was thinking, as she listened, that Mrs. Jones was only doing it to get some attention, there was nothing at all wrong with her.

She lay in her bunk, delighting in the sway and the grind of the ship under her, remembering how she had enjoyed that same sensation on the voyage out. She thought now, not of Martha, but of her girlhood, calling it "England." Through her mind ran phrases, words, her official memory: pain was approaching so fast, with the approach of Martha, that she had to return to old supports.

Say what you like, she had enjoyed herself when she was a girl: young people had clean fun in those days—not that one could use that phrase now, it was a joke, apparently! But there had been none of this nasty emphasis on sex all the time: that girl in the swimming pool the other day, you could see her breasts, at one point even her nipples had been visible as she pulled herself out of the pool—it wasn't nice for the crew; many of them were Coloured, it wasn't responsible. No, when she and her friends and her friends' brothers met for their musical evenings and their visits to the theatre, and concerts, there was none of that. And it wasn't as if any of them had had much money: no, in those days people knew how to make their own amusements. They played healthy games, and none of them were morbid. Not like young people now, who only cared for pleasure, they didn't believe in God, and the girls, nothing but flibbertygibbets, all make-up and drinking and sex ... but that was before the war, of course, before the old war ...

On the night before the ship docked at Tilbury, Mrs. Quest lay awake and tried not to talk aloud to herself. In the morning, one of the others said: "You didn't have a very good night, dear, did you?"

It wasn't nicely said—but never mind, thank goodness that awful voyage was over, that was done with: well, things don't always turn out the way you expect them to.

Before Martha saw her, Mrs. Quest had been watching Martha, first from the ship—someone had a pair of field glasses—and then from where she waited for her turn in the Customs. With Martha was a man and a small boy of about ten. Martha looked tired. With the man she seemed not to be communicating much, or at least, talking; but with the child she was laughing and animated: at one point was playing a kind of hide-and-seek around some piles of luggage. By the time Mrs. Quest joined Martha, the man and the child had disappeared.

They kissed.

"Didn't you have someone with you?" enquired Mrs. Quest.

"Yes. Mark came down with Paul—he promised to take Paul around the docks today."

Mark was the writer: who was Paul?

"Didn't I tell you?" asked Martha. "Paul is the nephew, you know."

Yes, Martha had told her: there had been facts, in letters. The child must then be the son of the Communist spy whom Bob had talked of so knowledgeably?

Mrs. Quest said, trying hard: "Then Mr. Coldridge is bringing up the child?"

Martha observed: "He is being brought up." It was rather grim; Mrs. Quest looked quickly at her; Martha was smiling, queerly: Mrs. Quest thought, That's like Milly! Wanting to meet Martha, to contact her here, she fumbled: "Well, it can't be easy, with that background."

Martha's smile faded. "No," she said.

They were in a taxi, Mrs. Quest's luggage filling every possible space.

Martha said, turning to her mother, again with the dryness, the humour, which made Mrs. Quest's spirits lift: "We thought it would be easier if we—you and I—were alone today, all things considered!" She waited, smiling straight into her mother's face.

Mrs. Quest, reaching, fumbling, desperate to match up to this opportunity, found words: "Who's *we?* she demanded.

Martha's paleness deepened, her mouth went tight.

Mrs. Quest, desperate, wanting to cry out: No, no, I didn't mean . . .

Martha said, "Mark. He's my employer, after all. I suppose," she added, with a sort of desperation of her own which at least hinted at the possibility of a return of the dry, cool, irony where Mrs. Quest had never thought she might be able to meet her daughter.

Afraid now, Mrs. Quest told herself to be silent. Later. Things would be all right later. Now, some demon had hold of her tongue, she had not meant to . . .

Martha said: "I asked the driver to go past St. Paul's. And then through Piccadilly Circus, and then past the Palace— But if you're too tired . . ."

Mrs. Quest heard this, like a child being offered sweets, when it has grown out of them. Martha meant well, she knew. And of course she longed to see St. Paul's and the rest.

Martha said, trying hard, as her mother could see: "It wasn't until I actually came that I saw what you had been talking about all these years."

And now Mrs. Quest heard herself let out a snort of laughter. "When were you last in St. Paul's or at the Changing of the Guard?"

Martha did not look at her; she looked away out of the window. Mrs. Quest was now as pale as her daughter. In silence they drove past St. Paul's. In Fleet Street, she said timidly: "Perhaps I am rather tired, perhaps . . ."

Martha leaned forward, knocked on the glass, and gave new directions.

Then she set herself, as her mother could see, to be polite. She asked a great many questions about her brother, about Bessie, the children, the farm, the voyage, and Mrs. Quest answered, in the same spirit. Martha did not mention Caroline. Mrs. Quest volunteered that she thought Caroline was well; she was clever; she always got very good reports from school. Martha said nothing.

Later she said, as if apologising for it: "Of course London must have changed a lot."

"It was bound to," said Mrs. Quest. Privately she thought it had not changed much; but probably Martha would be offended if she said so. All kinds of buildings were changed,

270

landmarks gone, but the essence of the place, what could change that—the heavy grey weight of it?

And when they passed the Museum, then nothing had changed, and Mrs. Quest for a moment forgot her daughter, remembered only how she had walked here as a girl with her father.

She was smiling when the taxi stopped outside the house. She stood on the pavement waiting, while Martha paid the driver. Then she understood that the taxi man and Martha were together dragging the luggage inside: there were no servants? She helped. Two large trunks, three large suitcases, and a dozen packages and bundles were stowed in the hall. "No, Mark will bring them up when he comes," Martha said. But, guilty, Mrs. Quest insisted on carrying up, Martha helping, all the weight that two women could manage, all but the two trunks. She was in a most charming bedroom on the third floor. Mrs. Quest suppressed the desire to say that all through her girlhood she had had the front bedroom on the third floor: she felt now as if she had come home. Martha was standing by a pile of objects on a table: obviously she wanted her mother to notice them. Mrs. Quest saw some flannel, a hotwater bottle, some safety pins, a lot of other things.

"I got them for you," said Martha.

Mrs. Quest had to think what she meant.

"Well, you needn't have bothered," she said. "I'm quite capable of shopping, I suppose."

She could have bitten her tongue off: but it was too late. Martha turned away, bright scarlet. When she came back, she was white, and would not meet her mother's imploring eyes.

"The bathroom is across the passage," she said hurriedly. "I'll go and make some tea . . ."

She almost ran out of the room, calling back: "I'll be in the kitchen, ground floor."

Mrs. Quest, walking around the room, to recover herself, noted that the room was everything, but really everything, she could have imagined. Later, she would relish it, but first

. . .

She hurried through washing and brushing her hair, she descended through the house, found the kitchen. It was a very fine kitchen, a kind of marriage between a Victorian kitchen with larders and storerooms off it, and modernity, with its devices and gadgets. Martha was lifting a tray off an enormous table—she led the way through the house, to a drawing room, which was, as Mrs. Quest could see, not much used.

"You needn't put yourself out for me," she said. "I don't want to be a nuisance."

"I thought you'd like this room," said Martha. "It's a lovely room. It doesn't seem to get used much, but when we do—".

It seemed that Martha enjoyed the chance to sit in it? Well then, she certainly must have changed!

Drinking tea, each eating small bits of cake to please the other, they exchanged information.

Later Martha said that Mark would not be back that day: he was driving Paul to his school, would go straight to his work in the morning: they would see him, probably, the following evening.

There was supper to get through: Mrs. Quest had decided she was very tired, she must sleep; tomorrow, she thought, they would get onto a better footing. They kissed good night, and then the old lady arranged her bedroom, her possessions, and, in bed, wrote a very long letter to her son, page after page, until, hearing a silence all around her, she looked at the clock and found it was three in the morning. She lay awake, admonishing her tongue not to betray her tomorrow.

Tomorrow she woke late, to find Martha infinitely at her disposal. They drove about London in taxis and on the tops of buses, seeing, they supposed, the same city, but Mrs. Quest, alert for moments like those of yesterday, which she had let slip, did not find them again. Martha appeared favourably disposed towards Harrods and Liberty's, and was prepared to spend as long as the old lady wished in both. Mrs. Quest, offered tea in a Fuller's, refused rather tartly: she was again feeling like a schoolchild being taken out for a treat. She went to bed very early: her head was aching.

She woke early, and descended to the kitchen to make herself tea. She was quiet, so as not to disturb. There she found Mark, dressed; pleasant, but preoccupied. He departed for his factory as Mrs. Coles, the charwoman, came in. Mrs. Coles sat down for a cup of tea. Mrs. Quest knew that things had changed in England; but at the end of half an hour, for which, after all, someone must be paying, when Mrs. Coles, an elderly lady complaining about food prices and her feet, seemed in no hurry to start work, Mrs. Quest said she was going up to do her own room out. Both Mrs. Coles and Martha exclaimed that she should do no such thing: but she left them, carrying dusters and a vacuum cleaner.

She did her room and the bathroom feeling criminal. Later Martha came up. Mrs. Quest could see she was ready with things to say. She sat down, fumbling for a cigarette, as Martha sat, and handed her one.

"You always did let yourself be exploited by servants," began Mrs. Quest, defiantly.

"Yes, well, that's not important. Look. You see, I want to say something."

Mrs. Quest put on a humorous expression.

"Yes. I don't know why it is, but we always do seem to—anyway. What I don't want to happen is that we should go through this—pretending—no, I don't mean that. I mean, you never did like what I am, how I am. But what's the use of . . . we could either put a good face on things, and be polite, all that kind of thing—but wouldn't it be better if we could try . . ."

Mrs. Quest, listening to this, was examining her daughter's face: every muscle, the implication of every tiny movement of eye, mouth, tense hands. She felt on the verge, at last, of discoveries. She was infinitely triumphant as her daughter sat there, in a defiant supplication.

"You see," said Martha, "I know this isn't exactly an orthodox household, but if you take it as it is, then . . ."

"Aren't you going to marry him then?" implored Mrs. Quest, and could have bitten her tongue off.

Martha laughed. She laughed despairingly, as if she had been bound to laugh, as if she were doomed to it.

Mrs. Quest said: "It's all very well!"

"Yes. I suppose so. But the point is, you see. . . ."

And now came the words which to Mrs. Quest were like a slap in the face, or a door closing. "You know, we don't all have the same ideas about life, do we?"

"No. But I have never said to *anybody* that we did!"

Silence. Martha got up, went to the window, looked out, and Mrs. Quest examined her back.

"Are you living with him, then?"

"Well—here I am. But no, I think, on the whole, that no I'm not."

"Because what his wife must be thinking I really can't . . ."

"I did tell you she was here, you know. She's downstairs. She's ill."

Mrs. Quest's mind raced: had she been told? If so, not in a way that one could take in.

Martha turned. "Anyway. I don't know why it is, we never seem to—"

Again Mrs. Quest felt triumph, a feeling of victory. This apology, which it seemed the girl was offering, was always the culminating moment of fantasies about Martha. At the same time, she was crying out: No, no, no, I don't want this, I only want to understand, at last.

She said sourly: "What is it you want to say?"

"Nothing in particular, I suppose. But Mark and I were talking. It would be easy to—make things easy, as it were. But that's what we've always done, isn't it? Wouldn't it be better if you tried to—accept me as I was?"

"What frightful sins are you concealing, then?" enquired Mrs. Quest, with the intention of humour.

"It's not . . ." Martha sat down and laughed again.

"Well, I don't know!" said Mrs. Quest.

"I don't know either!"

This was, genuinely, a moment of ironical contact, and they were both grateful for it. But Martha went down to do some work for Mark, and Mrs. Quest went down to the kitchen, where Mrs. Coles, whose feelings had been hurt, sulked and would not respond to invitations to gossip. For the old lady had been left with the feeling that the household concealed some monstrousness, or a hidden vice, which she might find out about if she tried.

Nothing happened for a couple of days. Then she was told that people were coming for dinner.

"Not a dinner party—it's informal."

There was something else meant here—what? Mrs. Quest wondered if Martha was worried that she would be wrongly dressed? Enquiring, she saw this was not the case: an afternoon dress would do nicely.

She approached the occasion with a defiant suspicion, and understood when she saw there were two black gentlemen in the drawing room, with sherry glasses in their hands, talking to Martha and to Mark. There was also quite a pretty woman who looked tired, called Phoebe, in some kind of relationship to Mark, and a gingery funny-looking man with such big spectacles you could see nothing else of his face. Mrs. Quest was annoyed that Martha thought she would not know how to behave. She demonstratively shook two black hands and enquired where the men came from. Both were from Kenya. She was about to say something about Mau Mau, but realised that it was at least possible that black men in this house were "on the side of" Mau Mau, which for some years now Mrs. Quest had been told represented every sort of evil. And so it turned out. Throughout a long dinner—cooked jointly, she discovered, by Mark and Martha—the old lady sat quietly, listening to talk which took it for granted that Mau Mau was in the right, and that her own views and the conduct of the British government disgusting. Towards the end of the dinner she decided that it would be simply cowardice not to say anything of where she stood, and she chose a pause in which to remark firmly that she did not mind being thought reactionary, but she hated Communism, which would be the ruin of Africa. At which first Phoebe, with a look of bitter meaning towards Mark, and then both Africans, who were bland but firm, said they entirely agreed with her.

Martha, she saw, was looking humorous, and Mark angry.

A violent discussion ensued, for which Mrs. Quest was afraid she could be blamed. There was very bad feeling here, she could see; Phoebe expressed sentiments with which Mrs. Quest was in agreement, while Mark, cold and authoritative, disagreed. A cold man, she thought, that awful logicality again: it went on to the end of the meal, and Mrs. Quest could not follow it. Her head was aching.

Back in the drawing room, the two black men discussed with Mark how best to get a book published which would put a view other than the official one on Kenya. Phoebe joined in. She seemed to be responsible for the Africans. Mrs. Quest could not stop herself thinking that Phoebe had never been in Africa and had no right to have such decided views about it. Mrs. Quest talked to Jimmy Wood, Mark's partner, but found him hard to follow: he kept making jokes and laughing, but Mrs. Quest did not understand what was so funny. Meanwhile Martha poured coffee on the other side of the room and was a silent observer: her mother had not before seen her in this role. Just as she was finding Jimmy Wood intolerable, Martha came over and began talking to both of them. Well, she was more tactful than she used to be, that was something! But Mrs. Quest did not understand the talk, which was about the deliberate creation, by some government, through science, of an inferior race whose job it was to do all the menial work of a society. She suspected Jimmy, and probably Martha, of in this way attacking her for her own views on race—which she had been careful not to express. Suddenly she found herself talking loudly, with glances across the room at the two Africans, about Steven, whom she had been remembering painfully all evening. It wasn't true, she kept saying, hot and defiant, that the black people hated the whites; why just before she left home she had had a little black boy called Steve who ... They listened, the Africans too, in silence. Mrs. Quest felt she had betrayed Steven; and anyway, she was not being understood. Her head was aching dreadfully now. Just as she was deciding it would be tactful to go up to bed, a tall fair woman came into the room. She was surely wearing a dressing gown? Though it was certainly very pretty. So was she. Mark was polite to her. Martha left Mrs. Quest to go across to offer coffee. There were introductions: Mrs. Coldridge sat down, took some coffee, talked a little to Martha, then put down her cup untouched, nodded, smiled and went out again, Mark politely going with her to the door.

Jimmy remarked, with a sort of giggle, that he wished it would take his wife like that: Mrs. Quest suddenly couldn't stand another moment of him. Whatever else Mark's wife might be, she was a lady. That was infinitely reassuring. But Jimmy! Mrs. Quest said to herself, angrily, that he was common, he was not a gentleman, he shouldn't be here—she said good night and went. Martha ran after her, to say she mustn't be upset by Jimmy; for her part it wasn't until she had met Jimmy that she had understood the phrase "a screw loose." Mrs. Quest could see that Martha meant well, but she was sore, and very upset, and could not respond as she knew she ought. She went to bed, and lay awake, saying—she was afraid it was aloud, she could hear her own voice talking—the things that she had not said during the meal.

Martha did not refer to what had happened next day.

A couple of days later she was asked if she would like to join "some people" to go to the theatre: Martha added hastily that Phoebe wouldn't be there. Mrs. Quest replied firmly that she had no objection at all to going to the theatre with Africans, if they were educated and clean. She wasn't all that behind the times.

She was careful to have a long rest that afternoon: she didn't want to be tired out again. The party consisted of Mark and Martha, Mrs. Quest, a young woman called Patty Samuels, a young man called Gerald Smith, and a girl, Mark's niece, Elizabeth. Mrs. Quest did not care who was there, provided it wasn't Jimmy Wood. Mrs. Quest liked Gerald Smith, who was definitely a gentleman—charming. Patty Samuels, whom Martha warned had been ill, did not seem ill, but was a jolly sort of a girl, if not a lady. Elizabeth was a lady, but never opened her mouth.

They were going to Shakespeare—a relief, one knew where one was.

It turned out that the little theatre was a Communist theatre, and well known for it. It was nearly empty. The play was *The Tempest* and it was in modern dress, and Caliban was an African. The programme said the play was a parable "if you like" about the oppression of the black man in Africa. There were references to Kenya. Mrs. Quest did not like it. She thought it was puerile, and in bad taste—but she was determined not to say so. Thank goodness they hadn't tampered with the language, that was something.

Afterwards they went back home, where there was a large supper. Mark had cooked it. Why hadn't Martha cooked it? Mark replied that Martha hadn't been feeling well, she had wanted to lie down. Mrs. Quest was very upset and hurt. Why hadn't she been asked to help? And what was the matter with Martha?

Nothing at all, said Martha, cross, but Mrs. Quest was not going to leave it at that: she'd get to the bottom of it later.

Meanwhile they all sat around the great kitchen table and tore the production of *The Tempest* they had just seen to pieces, saying everything that Mrs. Quest had been thinking: not that she would have used this clever-clever language. It appeared that this play, and the theatre, represented everything that was bad about the Communist attitude towards the arts. Sectarian. Dogmatic. Narrow. Lifeless. Mechanistic. Etc. It appeared that the charming young man Gerald was a Communist, and so was Patty, and that they both spent a large part of their time "fighting" to change the party line. Mrs. Quest had thought that anybody in the Communist Party who disagreed with it was shot. Later it turned out that neither Patty nor Gerald were Communists—they had stopped being. In which case why were they so violent about it all, and why had they gone to that awful theatre? But Patty said she had decided to work there, because it needed someone there who wasn't a dyed-in-the-wool reactionary. Mrs. Quest's head was aching again. She was thinking that it was a pity she hadn't said what she had thought earlier, instead of saying yes, very nice, very interesting. Honesty was after all the best policy; and she took an opportunity to say to Mark that she did not think his novel about that idealised city in Iraq or wherever it was was an honest picture of Communism. Mark said politely that he entirely agreed with her. Did that mean that he had seen the light about Communism too?

Mrs. Quest felt that she might have made another blunder, but could not put her finger on why—they were all talking about Africa, as if they knew anything about it! She soon went up to bed, where she tried to sleep. But she had slept all that afternoon, and decided instead to have it out with Martha about not asking her to help with the supper. And what was wrong with her? She went downstairs, and quietly opened the door to see if Martha was asleep. She saw the room was dark; and was about to withdraw when she noticed that two shapes were outlined against the window, and the glow of cigarettes showed Martha and Mark, side by side on the bottom of the bed. She withdrew, hoping she had not been seen.

Next day she said severely that she hoped next time Martha didn't feel well she would trust her mother enough to help her. Martha said she would.

Mrs. Quest thought she couldn't face another of those long confusing evenings again—not for a time at least. She started on a round of visits, for an evening, a day, a weekend, to old friends, with whom she had been exchanging letters for thirty years.

Once there had been a group of bright young people "with all their lives in front of them." They had had musical evenings and amateur theatricals and excursions to the theatre; they had studied for exams and flirted but had not married each other: they had all married rather late when they could afford it. That remarkable process which transforms any batch of nice ordinary middle-class youngsters into people who organise other people had done its work; they had all become civil servants, and sea captains and judges and matrons of hospitals. For the most part, out of England. Most had spent their working lives out of their own country in what they had called the Empire and in places like Japan and China. What was left of them now? A dozen or so old ladies living with relatives, or in flats that were parts of houses once their own. With these old ladies Mrs. Quest was at ease, and there were no problems of communication; and they exchanged throughout evenings and weekends the phrases of their own shorthand, while they caught up on the gossip of half a century. When one of them said that young people nowadays had no sense of responsibility, and that England was being ruined by all these foreigners, and that the lower orders (a phrase used freely among themselves though they would never dare use it to their children) were spoiled and showed no respect, each knew exactly what was meant. And, since no time was wasted on definitions and on seeing other people's points of view, they were able to exchange their real emotions, which was why they needed to meet. They felt a puzzled sorrow, a bewilderment: how was it that overnight (so they felt it) they had been transformed from people with responsibility and power into mendicants begging for the privilege of doing a granddaughter's shopping, or coaching a cousin's niece for their English O-levels?

Mrs. Quest felt about these visits as her own grandmother felt when she was able to take off her corsets after a dinner party, but all the time she was brooding, worrying: if Martha was ill, she needed help, and she, Mrs. Quest, was the person to help her. But for some reason she did not dare ask openly what was wrong with Martha. This business of illness—and had not her whole life been involved with it?—was not as simple as it seemed. As for Martha's being ill, Mrs. Quest had unpleasant memories that went back to her adolescence. The old lady could not quite remember the incident, the words, but lying awake at night rehearsing conversations that had taken place (might have taken place?), she heard herself saying: That's not true, you are always accusing me. How can I make you ill? Why should I want to make you ill? All I want is to look after you, what is my life for if it isn't to sacrifice it, for you . . .

She was able to help when Francis came home for two days at the beginning of his holidays. Everything about Francis was reassuring. The school had not changed at all: friends of her brother had gone there; she had visited there for sports days as a girl. Francis was very polite, clean, good-mannered, as a boy should be from a school with such a name. His room was a boy's room, with cricket bats, a silver cup for high-jumping; boys' books. She offered to take him to the zoo, but realised he was perhaps too old? He asked, polite, if she would take him to a Schoolboys' Exhibition at Earls Court. The trip wore her out, they must have walked miles, but she took him to tea, and was even able to "pull his leg" a little. He blushed and writhed and hung his head: so she remembered her brother's friends doing—even doing herself—when they were subjected to that process known as "ragging," or "being brought down a peg or two." Francis's scarlet-faced torments of embarrassment, his bare clean knees, made her yearn to put her arms around him.

Francis was to spend his holidays in the country—which seemed odd, particularly as his cousin Paul was coming home.

Martha said the two didn't get on.

Mrs. Quest remarked how sad it was: Martha replied with precisely that brand of grim humour which Mrs. Quest was always looking for in her, but always missed, that they were all stuck with that one, weren't they.

Mrs. Quest, trying to keep the moment, said, meaning to compliment, that Francis was really such a nice well-behaved litle boy. Martha said, "True, he's stuck with that too, poor boy."

Rage surged in Mrs. Quest and she snapped out that Paul, from what she had seen of him, was quite different, not at all like Francis.

She disliked Paul intensely, loud, shrill, intense, *Jewish*— but the word was censored before she could say it.

Was her disliking Paul so obvious, an embarrassment? For it was suggested she might go to the country with Francis. She went, bitter, and the fortnight she spent there was what she remembered aferwards as the best part of her trip to England. She spent her time with Harold Butts talking about flowers and plants: it was hard to say which of them knew more, loved more. And she talked to Mary Butts about the Coldridges.

Mrs. Butts was the essence of discretion, but Mrs. Quest learned enough to make her even more determined to help Martha. She even wondered if Martha had not been drugged by the Communists, or brain-washed in some way, as possibly Mark had been too.

She saw little of Francis during the fortnight: as a healthy boy should, he spent his time in the woods and the fields, and was silent at mealtimes.

When she returned to the house in Radlett Street, Paul had gone off to stay with schoolfriends. Because she, Mrs. Quest, was there?

But she did not mind. It was obvious Martha was not well, for she spent so much time in her room. Once or twice Mrs. Quest knocked but there was no reply: the door was locked. Mark was not at his factory, but locked in with Martha making love? Martha was pretending to be asleep? Martha had gone out and locked the door so as to prevent her mother examining her room?

Mrs. Quest examined the whole house and concluded that it was shockingly badly run: it was bound to be, for when she was a girl, such a house had needed a cook, two housemaids, and a cleaning woman. This one had Mrs. Coles—a shocking old slattern—and Martha. Mrs. Quest turned out the floor she was on, had the curtains cleaned, and the carpets done. She turned out the attics, in which she found much of interest in the way of clothes and papers and letters. Then, one day, when Martha was out, she found the door unlocked and went into Martha's room and examined it. Nothing to disturb except an indefinable aroma of secrecy, of things concealed. But Mrs. Quest took all the clothes out of a wardrobe and mended what needed to be mended. She took armfuls of clothes to the cleaners. She then gave the room a thorough turnout. No one said anything at all, though she waited for a reprimand. Then, forcing herself, she descended a floor and cleaned every inch of Mark's room and even Mark's study. Meanwhile Mrs. Coles did her usual minimum and remarked that if some people wanted to make work, they were welcome. This caused Mrs. Quest days of fury; she—as usual!—was forced to be a servant because servants would not work, and their employers spoiled them. Mrs. Coles gave notice. Mrs. Quest told Mark and Martha, defiantly, that there was no need to look for another charwoman: she, Mrs. Quest, would engage one. She hoped she knew how to engage a cleaning woman.

In the meantime she worked. She worked. From seven in the morning, for she was waking early, she cleaned and washed and scrubbed, avoiding Martha, who seemed very busy, or at least either locked herself in her room or was out of the house. She worked until after lunch, when she slept all afternoon, and, refusing all invitations from Mark and Martha for a dinner or an outing somewhere, visited friends in the evenings, or stayed in her room writing letters.

She once descended to the basement and spent a confusing afternoon with Mrs. Coldridge, who said that if she, Mrs. Quest, started cleaning it, she was afraid Dorothy would kill her. Later a woman called Mellendip told her fortune from a teacup. She prophesied a trip by air in the near future. She also saw (or so she claimed) gardens and mountains and roses among the dregs in her cup. The woman Mellendip (*definitely* not a lady, whatever else she might be!) also made some offensive remarks about old age, such as that it was a time for serenity and reflection and "the eating of stored honey." Or rather, the offensiveness of it only struck Mrs. Quest later: at the time she had felt they were having a nice talk. Mrs. Quest was twenty years older than Mrs. Mellendip —at least! She was old enough to be that lady's mother. Yet there she had sat, listening to impertinent advice from someone who would have done better to listen to her . . . she did not go again to the basement. For one thing, there was Dorothy, unbelievably common; and what that nice Mrs. Coldridge could see in her, she really couldn't . . .

Martha came up to her mother's room one evening during a letter-writing session, sat down, lit a cigarette, and said: "Mother, look, Mark can perfectly well afford charwomen, you know."

This declaration of war caused Mrs. Quest to burst into frightened and confused tears. Martha, after remaining quiet for a moment, looking very pale, put her arms around her mother, though Mrs. Quest could feel that it was not a "real" embrace. She said: "Please, you really must try and see ..." Mrs. Quest repeated that she just wanted to help, she wanted to be of use, what else was there for her in life? Soon Martha lit another cigarette and went downstairs again.

Mrs. Quest, weeping, wrote to her son. She was not feeling well. She was very tired. She was much too old to be on her knees scrubbing floors, and standing on ladders cleaning windows. A few days in bed was what she needed, she really didn't feel ...

Martha brought trays at mealtimes, but her mother jerked up from her pillows, looked guilty, scrambled into a dressing gown, insisted on going down to the kitchen to cook herself food. So she was neither ill, nor not ill; yet in bed she lay with arms and legs stretched out, unable to move them because of the arthritis.

In Dr. Lamb's room the dialogue, or monologue, or process which was the shadowy accompaniment to that which was unfolding itself in Radlett Street, came to a climax.

"You know that you have to tell her to go."

"Yes."

"Well then?"

"I can't. I can't."

"Why can't you?"

"She'll go anyway," Martha muttered.

"A sort of passive resistance, that's what you are doing?"

"If I did what you wanted, shouted and screamed at her—that's what you want me to do, isn't it?"

"You haven't, have you? Not ever in your life?"

"No. If I did that, it would be healthy, I would be saved?"

"Why don't you try it?"

"Who would I be shouting at? It would be like hitting a child."

"Excepting that she isn't, is she?"

"I keep looking at her face, that face, that awful miserable old face ..."

He was silent as this cycle came around again for what, the tenth time?

"What you say, what you keep saying, it's no good, it's no use—if it's intellectualising to wonder all the time, what's wrong with us all—because it's not just me. You fight your parents—everyone does—you have to do that. If you don't then you're sunk. So I didn't fight, not the right way. But that isn't the point. What is the fight? Who's fighting what? Why is it that we all of us have to get out from under awful parents who damage us? Because what are they? She's a pathetic old woman. All my friends, everyone I've known. It's taken for granted. And it's true—one has to. But was it always like this?" (Martha, listening to her own voice, knew it was like the voice of her mother, during one of those muttering monologues to which she listened, appalled, fascinated, helpless.) "Because there's another point, all the time: if either I or my brother said: Right, we give in, do run our lives for us, she'd never have another day's illness—she'd live till she was ninety or a hundred. But if I kick her out I sign her death warrant. I know that."

"So you feel guilty that you are murdering your mother?"

"No, I don't feel guilty. It's not my fault. If it were my fault that would be easy. Or if it were her fault. But I wish I didn't always know what's going to happen. It's like watching Paul and Francis—you know what's going to be eating them in twenty years' time. It's not their fault, it's not Lynda's fault, it's not Mark's fault . . ."

"But it's your fault?"

"No. You're on the wrong track, I tell you . . ."

"Am I?"

"Yes. If I wallowed around *mea culpa*, that would be a good mark? That's not intellectualising? No, that's easy enough. No. And if you say one shouldn't be asking the other questions, why? Was it always like this? What's gone wrong with us? Then you're wrong, you're wrong, what question is there to ask? Or are we just children, and not responsible at all, ever, for what we live in?"

"You need a historian perhaps, or a sociologist?" The sarcasm, carefully measured as always, no longer affected Martha.

"All right then—a different expert for every different type of question. But it's the same question always."

"Mrs. Hesse, what you want is for me to kick your mother out because you haven't the courage to do it."

"Yes, yes," muttered Martha. "I do. I know that. But what difference does it make who actually does it? Because she'll go anyway—she's not getting what she wants, so she'll have to go. . . . Will you see her?"

"I've already suggested that, I think. But you said no."

"I'll try to get her to come."

"If *you* can't do it, make yourself do it."

"She'll break her leg, something like that."

"There are hospitals."

"Hospitals and old-age homes. *What's wrong with us all?*"

"I have time at ten o'clock on Thursday."

Mark and Martha lay in each other's arms, in a cave of soft protective dark.

"If you like, I'll talk to her," said Mark, infinitely kind.

"It's my battle, it's not yours."

"Well, Martha, speaking as an onlooker . . ." Here they both laughed, helplessly, and then she began crying. "The fact is, that your mother's upstairs in one room, in one bed, and you are downstairs in another. If neither of you can break it, then I'm going to."

"No. No. Of course I must."

Martha sat in her room, remembering how a few weeks ago she had fought, fought for her own memory—such energy! Where was it now? She made herself go upstairs to her mother's room. She stood outside it. From inside came the old voice, in its painful monologue. She made herself open the door and go in. The voice went on.

Mrs. Quest lay, her painful arms stiff on the covers. Her eyes very bright with anger. "Filthy creatures," she was saying, or remarking. "Sex. That's all they think of. That's all they do. Well, I could live in this house too if I was ready to earn my living with my legs in the air."

"Mother," said Martha.

Mrs. Quest looked at her daughter—or rather, looked at her differently, for she had been looking at her while she delivered her monologue. "Oh, is that you?" she enquired cheerfully.

Martha said: "You don't mean a word of it—why do you say it?"

She stared at her mother, at the miserable old woman, trying to speak to the person in her who didn't mean one word of it.

Mrs. Quest began singing: "Lead, Kindly Light."

"I want you to see a friend of mine," said Martha.

"Who, dear?"

"His name is Dr. Lamb."

Here we go, thought Martha, one of these idiotic conversations—well, we've been having them ever since I can remember.

"I don't remember your mentioning a Dr. Lamb."

"Didn't I?"

"I've seen too many doctors. I'm afraid I'll have to live with it. After all, a lot of old people have arthritis."

A pause. Martha looked at the innocent frightened old face on the pillow.

"I don't think I want to, really."

"I think it might be a help."

"Well perhaps, if I'm well enough."

"I've ordered a taxi for half past nine tomorrow. I'll come up and help you dress."

"Very well, dear, if that's what you want."

Martha left. She leaned outside the door, too tired to move further. Almost, she collapsed where she stood, lay like a dog outside the door. Inside Mrs. Quest was singing: "Rock of Ages Cleft for Me." Then: "Filthy pigs. I'm expected to clean up after their mess, pigs. I'm nothing but a servant and she's a whore. Pig. Let me hide myself in Thee. They think I'm going to be their servant and do all their dirty work . . ."

When Martha came up next morning at nine, the voice was still talking. It continued as she went into the room, drew the curtains and said good morning. It went on, while Mrs. Quest looked through Martha as if she did not see her. "Whore," she said. "A decent woman shouldn't be under the same roof . . ."

"Mother, the taxi will be here soon."

"I don't really feel up to it," said Mrs. Quest brightly. "How are you today? Are you better?"

"I am quite well."

She fetched her mother's clothes and stood by the bed with them.

"I don't think I can move today," said Mrs. Quest, cowering under the clothes, holding them to her chin like a shield.

Martha stayed where she was. Suddenly Mrs. Quest flung back the covers, got up, and began to dress.

"It's a very nice day," she said.

"Yes, it is."

When she had dragged vests, bloomers, skirt, jersey over her ancient body, displayed carelessly, brutally to Martha, as if making a point, she clung suddenly to a wall and said she was in too much pain to go out.

"I'll help you," said Martha. She assisted her mother downstairs. Mrs. Quest clung to walls, banisters, the handles of doors, and crawled with two sticks into the taxi.

She came back that afternoon, walked up the steps and then up the stairs into her room, where she began packing. Martha went in, and Mrs. Quest said in a normal, almost jolly voice: "I've changed my ticket. I'm flying tomorrow."

"Aren't you going to be sorry to miss the sea voyage?"

"Oh I don't know. It's rather tiring—those big boats, they're not very nice."

She did not mention Dr. Lamb.

Martha telephoned Dr. Lamb, who said that he had been standing at his window waiting when the taxi drew up with the old lady in it. She had skipped out, paid the taxi man, with a haste which said how much she longed for the moment she could be face to face with Martha's friend. She ran up three flights of stairs, was met by Dr. Lamb at his door, and without saying more than "I am Martha's mother" ran into the room, sat down, and began to abuse Martha. She did not ask: "Who are you? What kind of a doctor are you?" She sat, and out of her flooded years and years and years of resentment, all focussed on Martha. Dr. Lamb had sat and listened. He had asked just one question: "If you two don't get on, perhaps it would be better if you weren't in the same house?"

"Oh she needn't think I'm going to stay there, just to be a servant," she had said, and continued with her complaint. At the end of an hour, reminded that someone else was waiting to see Dr. Lamb, she had not heard. Twice, thrice, she did not hear; and then, suddenly, she jumped up, said: "It was nice talking to you—it's not often Martha lets me meet one of her friends," had shaken Dr. Lamb's hand, and had run all the way downstairs again. She had walked rapidly away out of sight. Straight to the travel bureau? She did not say. It was not mentioned.

When the time came to drive her to the airport, Mrs. Quest refused to be driven: she wanted to leave at the air terminal—she did not wish to be a trouble.

They went to the air terminal in a taxi, both silent, avoiding each other's eyes, miserable, wishing to cry.

They chatted about small topics till the flight was called. Then, as she vanished from her daughter's life forever, Mrs. Quest gave a small tight smile, and said: "Well, I wonder what all that was about really?"

"Yes," said Martha. "So do I."

They kissed politely, exchanged looks of ironic desperation, smiled and parted.

Martha went back, into a collapse. She went to bed. She lay there, one day, two days, three days. She had an appointment with Dr. Lamb. She cancelled it. Then she cancelled another. She got out of bed and began testing her memory, prod, prod, was that still there? That incident intact? Yes, she had lost nothing of what she had gained in the long battle before Dr. Lamb. There was a great deal more she had to do: for instance, her mother's visit had gone into blackness, blank. She had to get it back. She went to Dr. Lamb, there was a violent explosion of emotion—she was back in bed. When she got out she knew she could no longer go to Dr. Lamb: it was economics, psychic economics; she needed energy. She wrote and told him she would not come back, thanked him for "doing what I suppose I went to you for." He replied that he was pleased to have been of use, and enclosed his account.

Martha began getting up very early in the mornings, to have an hour or so of quiet, so as to work on her memory, the salvage operation. She did not like leaving Mark, and he did not like waking to a bed cold beside him. But she told him she had to do it. Now, not seeing Dr. Lamb, it meant that the focus of her life was on the two hours in the early mornings, before breakfast with Mark; and then again in the evenings. She knew Mark had looked forward to her mother's departure, so they could return again to the evenings, closed in, sheltered, shut off from life, the curtains of love-making drawn around them. But she wanted her evenings, she had to have them. She was miraculously restored to energy again. She was able, again, to say: Today I will do this, and then do it. After dinner, she went to her room, and worked on her own mind, with her mind. The weeks of her mother's visit came back, each scene fought back into memory against lethargy, pain, reluctance. Afterwards she crawled into bed, worn out. Then Mark came in, to hold her and comfort her. She wanted this, very much. But also, she didn't want it: she had to stop being this helpless creature who clung and needed.

It was not that they ceased to be lovers: they were, but differently.

She knew that soon they would not be lovers. And he was hurt, deeply, where it mattered, not anywhere on the surface where it could be talked about. For the second time, or the third time, Mark had given everything that was good in him, all his strength and patience and warmth, to a woman who said, Save me, save me, and who then had—not been saved, or who had gone off to doctors, or at any rate, had not needed him.

They did not plan it or decide it, but soon it was at an end. Besides, there were the children, and Paul was a person from whom one could conceal nothing.

PART THREE

We can usefully think of air as an ocean in which we are submerged. Everywhere in this ocean currents swirl and eddy, torrents flow, masses as homogeneous as whales sink and rise travelling in the effort for equilibrium of hot and hot.

Air is a fluid mixture of gases and solids. 78% of it is gaseous nitrogen. It is nitrogen which is the principal food of plant life. Nitrogen is shocked into chemical existence by the action of lightning, and rain washes it down to the surface of the earth.

A lightning flash is only a spark which bridges cloud and earth or cloud and cloud. But in order for this spark to happen, one place must be negatively charged and the other positively charged.

Lightning is the parent of fire on our earth. It has its birth in clouds, which are water vapour suspended in air. This vapour falls in rain when drops can form about minute particles of dirt or solid matter. Thus, in a drama miles above our heads earth is host to rain which is suspended in air where fire is implicit in the separation of cloud and earth masses.

VARIOUS REMARKS ABOUT THE WEATHER
FROM SCHOOL TEXTBOOKS

One

1956, as everyone knows, was a climactic year, a watershed, a turning point, a crossroads; it has become one of the years one refers to: oh yes, that year, of course! As if years were pegs in a wall, on which one hangs a certain type of memory, or gives stars to, like hotels and restaurants. 1956 was a five-star year, classed with 1942: Stalingrad; or 1949: the birth of Communist China. Or—well, other parts of the world might look at it differently; or even other people in the same part. Harold Butts, for instance, tended to say things like: "That was the year the marjoram did so well"; and Iris across the river would say: "Let me see, that was the year we got that new bit of carpet in the front room." 1956 was particularly easy to see and to remember as extraordinary because of that one week when coincidentally the Hungarians rose against their Russian masters (impossible) and in Britain thousands of people made their ideas known about a view of Britain's role referred to as "Suez": unlikely, for no one had protested about anything for so long.

"Hungary"; "Suez"; violently juxtaposed, one of those moments when that other pattern briefly becomes visible, manifested in coincidence; as when, in the Underground, in a part of London you visit once in three years, you find sitting next to you a man not seen or even thought of for months. But you thought about him last night. Not odd at all, then, that there he is with his briefcase, in the next seat. "You live here, do you?" says he; "I don't think I've been in this part of London for let's see, four or five years." Or, those remarkable meetings that come under the heading of: "It's a small world, isn't it?" Or all those other hints and indications that the laws which operate have in fact nothing at all to do with, for instance, the way of thinking that gives 1956 five stars for importance, except that perhaps it is, just here, that we pay tribute to the other pattern, momentarily visible.

Subtract the words "Suez," "Hungary," with their associations of Communism, revisionism, imperialism, etc., etc., what there is left is ... that a great many people, in one way or another, said: No, enough, no more of that. And they milled about in open places in this city and that, with guns and hand grenades or without, shouting or silent, with policemen and troops in control or not, and, as a result of this activity then there followed that—but about what followed no two people are likely to agree. It was a year of protest and activity and lively disagreement, though, that is certain. So that now, looking back, the people who lived through it say, for the sake of speed and easy understanding: 1956, and what is conveyed is the idea of change, breaking up, clearing away, movement.

Yet the air had cleared well before 1956.

When a very bad time is over there is no moment when one can say: This is it, now it's finished. In an atmosphere where everything is slow, dark, sluggish, where every event is soaked in suspicion and dislike and fear, then suddenly there intrudes an event of a different quality. But one looks at it with distrust, distrust being one's element at the time, like being deep under filthy water. The river suddenly floats down flowers—but you wouldn't dream of touching them, they are probably poisoned, a trap.

Years later one says, No, no, it wasn't like that at all, that was the moment when ...

Apparently nothing very much changed in the house in Radlett Street. It had ceased to be so totally isolated when Phoebe and Arthur and Mary became visitors. They had come because they were under siege, disliked and feared in their own country, just as Mark was. And for some time, when they met, they exchanged news about the anonymous letters they got, or a visit from the police, or that Arthur was threatened with expulsion from his own party. They continued to discuss how their letters were being opened and their telephones tapped and how, "taking the matter up" with this body or that, nothing came of it but polite denials or statements that Britain, like any other state, had the right to protect itself from Trojan horses. And conversations with Phoebe, Arthur, Mary continued to be full of tricky places which had to be negotiated, just as conversations with Gerald Smith, Patty, Bob Hasty, visiting Radlett Street because there were still few places where they could visit with comfort, had to be handled carefully. Patty, although over her breakdown, was particularly complicated. She had switched into a happy-go-lucky anarchism which everyone found irritating, even though they did see a self-protecting mechanism at work. For any reminder that she had held (and only a few months before) the opinions she had in fact held might cause her to break into angry tears. The ex-Communists (for they had been expelled from, or had resigned from, the Communist Party) had been informed by the Mother of Communism that they were revisionists, and were now engaged in analysing their position in a way satisfying to themselves and honourable to the new term "revisionist." But they were not easy company, did not get on with that part of the left represented by Arthur and Phoebe, and were of no help to Mark, who was engaged in his own process of self-discovery—which once again was to spend hours talking to Martha in order to find out what it was he thought. Through all this Elizabeth, James's daughter, came often. For a long time it was hard to discover why: she said so little and did not seem fond of anyone. It turned out she was engaged in a late-adolescent battle with her conservative family. Once again it was salutary to discover how very little the storms of political life affected "ordinary people." Mark Coldridge, according to them, Elizabeth's family, country people from Norfolk, was a traitor. Recent shifts of the wind had not reached them: probably in a decade or so they might be surprised to learn that Mark was something else. Meanwhile, to visit Mark was to be the essence of defiant nonconformity. Elizabeth would wait patiently until Mark was alone, and then needle him slowly to get out of him remarks or definitions which she would take home to annoy her parents. In return she quoted to Mark what they said about him, mostly that he should be shot or deported. This went on for months and months: she was nearly thirty and had had one of the most expensive educations the country can provide.

They were delivered from Elizabeth by young Graham, transmogrified from a mannered undergraduate into a jazz musician. Or rather, he did not play himself or even, one suspected, particularly listen to jazz; it was that he had visited America at just the time that jazz was "taking", and there he had acquired a new vocabulary and set of attitudes. These were all to do with patient long-suffering, tolerance of other people's disabilities, loyalty to one's intimates, a contained despair: the qualities, in short, of a beleaguered minority, expressed in a highly stylised and formalised language. It sounded, in people who had no reason for the attributes of defence, like the romanticism of despair. Not since the days of *Werther* has there been so sentimental a cult. In Graham its acquisition was as if he continued to wear scarlet cloaks lined with leopard skin—for he was vigorous, energetic, confident, capable and with irons in a dozen fires. One of them was the film industry. He had written a script, according to a then acceptable formula, about a Russian Communist girl in love with a capitalist boy with a mutual passion for traditional jazz which they listened to in some bistro in Paris until ... (This plot was plentifully and variously used during the brief period of the break-up of the Cold War.) Graham's did not look as if it would become a film, but he thought that if his uncle's name was on it as co-writer, there would be a better chance for it. This aim he expressed to Mark with candour; perhaps more as if conferring a benefit. His whole upbringing had taught him that people would always be ready to assist him on his way; in fact, this is practically a definition of his education. In his new tongue, but with his old accent, he confessed that he was a little low on the artistic thing, but the ideas he had were fine, just fine, and if Mark could spare a few weeks—and besides it would be just fine to take a trip to Paris and choose the ground. He was not able to see that Mark's ideas were not his, because he was incapable of listening to anybody. For weeks he haunted Mark's house, waiting for Mark to announce that he was ready to start. But there he met Elizabeth, a kind of cousin, or niece, and she found his relaxed phrases about sex, drugs, race and so on more useful in her guerrilla war with her family than Mark's politics could ever be. Graham and Elizabeth floated out of the house on the wings of a love affair that was publicised in the papers and that caused a great many angry telephone calls from her father to Mark.

Meanwhile Mark had been going out, at first with reluctance, to a dinner party here, a party there. For him it was not at all enjoyable until he saw that the way he was seeing them, his hosts, his fellow-guests, was not at all as they saw themselves. His practised suspicion that there must be more to it all was—simply not useful. Or not useful now. What he had learned, that when you are in a tight spot you are lucky to have half a dozen friends, must be kept in reserve until, as it was bound to, it again became useful. Well, of course, it is no more than what "everyone" knows; since a thousand old saws, mottoes, bits of folk wisdom, proclaim this truth. Yes, but he had learned it. This new London that was coming into being after the long freeze, where everyone was so charming, so loving, so friendly, and so *very* tolerant, and where—so it seemed—everyone suffered from severe amnesia, it did well enough, it did for its purposes, none of them serious.

But, having learned not to take it seriously, he went more

often, and with more pleasure. He would return late at night from a party to drop into Martha's room with remarks about this and that person, or the food, or the clothes, as one does from parties.

The air had cleared, lifted, lightened, without there being any point where they could say it had. It was sometime early in the five-star year that Mark said to Martha over the breakfast table: "Good God, Martha, that was an awful time, wasn't it?"

Saying it put it in the past. They looked back at a bad time. They had got through it. Fear had moved away, somewhere else. Fear was no longer nakedly manifest in events—or not the events that affected them. Five years, six, had been endless to live through. But now they slid together in memory and became a phrase or a set of words, like a peg on a wall on which one hung certain memories.

At a dinner party someone might say: One day we'll find out just how close we were to war then. (A real war, not skirmishes like Korea, Kenya, Cyprus, Berlin.) Or: Thank God the Soviet Union has got the bomb at last, that gives us a breathing space. Or even: That's just American propaganda, you can't believe that. . . . In short, the most respectable people were making the kind of remark which as recently as the three starred years, 1954, 1955, had been treasonable, and had not been made out of the circles of the extreme left. Where, for the time being at least, had set in a distrust for the processes of any government anywhere—anarchy, in short; a bitter nihilism.

People had forgotten. Already? Was it possible? Margaret, for instance, just as in the old days, was dropping in and out of the house. That Mark tended to be ironical in manner she chose to put down to the fact that Lynda ("She always did!") had put Mark against her. "Why did she always hate me so much?" she cried, her fine eyes misting. Mark had waited for weeks after it became evident that Margaret again considered herself his mother, for some word of explanation if not apology. She did once remark that now that man Stalin was dead, perhaps people would be sensible again. The end of an epoch. A matter for pain? Incredulity? Roars, in the end, of laughter, bursting out between Martha and Mark at the breakfast table. Margaret had telephoned, a brisk call, the third in a week, to ask if Mark would like some plants for the house. Yes, he would be delighted, of course. He had put down the telephone, and looked at Martha, his face alive with the readiness for indignation, anger—anything. In the end he had flung himself down at the head of a table where *The Times* lay folded waiting for his attention, as it had for his father, and had roared with laughter. Martha joined him. They had laughed until they stopped, knowing they would cry if they didn't. The end of an epoch. But Mark had lost innocence, naivety—according to how one saw it. Had become—cynical, if that's a word you use.

Martha thought: He's become stripped, he's been flayed. For somewhere about this time an image became very real to her—born perhaps in a dream?—a stupid ignorant half-drunk cook, a solid ox of a woman, stands on two planted legs by a rather dirty kitchen table. In her hand she holds a bunch of root vegetables, just dragged out of the garden. She has a hand on one bulky hip. With the other she thrashes the bunch of roots against the table edge: dirt flies off. A turnip rolls under the table. The woman throws turnips, carrots, parsnips onto the table, and carelessly chops off the tops. A great boot cracks down on the fallen turnip. She looks. She hesitates, then picks up the bruised turnip, and into the soup pot it goes with the rest.

Mark was alone. The days of the self-constituted committee were over. All over London, indeed, all over Europe, new groupings, new societies, people talking, fresh versions of the unconstituted committees. But for Mark, this was no longer possible.

In his study he had put up two enormous maps of the world: this at random, and without, or so it seemed, knowing what he was going to do with them when he had them up. When Martha asked what they were for, he said, well, he thought perhaps it might be an idea to see what was really happening—you know, *really* happening.

One wall was soon devoted to atom bombs, hydrogen bombs, large bombs, small bombs (what one committee in the States had christened "kitten bombs") and the establishments which developed them, made them, and sold them. Soon the wall was covered with little red flags, such as his father might have used to mark the course of battles in various parts of the world. With black flags, on the same map, were marked the factories and laboratories which researched, made and sold, materials for germ warfare, chemical warfare, and drugs used in the control and manipulation of the brain. With yellow flags, on this map, were marked areas of air, soil and water contaminated by bomb blasts, fallout, the disposal of radioactive waste, concentrations of chemicals used for spraying crops, and oil discharged from ships. From collecting and studying material for the proper disposal of all these little markers, Mark soon learned how very little indeed was known by the men who used these various techniques. For instance, the movement of the air around our globe, which might carry poisons of different kinds into the lungs and flesh of humans and beasts, was not well understood. Therefore this map could never be anything more than approximate and rough: not only was information hard to get, guarded by officialdom, hidden—in a word, lied about—but the basis was ignorance.

The other wall had an almost metaphysical or medieval aspect. On it in varying colours were markers denoting War, Famine, Riots, Poverty, Prisons. These markers, like those on the opposing wall, steadily multiplied. On neither map was any attention paid to nationalisms or politics.

The study had in fact taken the place of the unconstituted committee. That it had was marked by the fact that various ex-members of the old committee, now all differently aligned, had protested that Mark was showing "subjectivity"—because the essence of the unconstituted committee anywhere is a readiness to manipulate and reclassify in terms of the national and the political. Maps with War, Poverty, Famine, etc., etc., like medieval Humours, are abhorrent to that way of thinking. Soon nobody, or rather, none of the old friends, was allowed into the study but Martha; and she was finding that most of her work consisted of studying and extracting information from reports, blueprints, newspapers, which enabled the maps to cluster their little coloured flags more thickly. Such work, once, a decade ago, she had done for Mrs. Van der Bylt, who had such information in filing cabinets under headings like Food Shortages.

It was not only the reaction of his so recent allies that told Mark he had become, overnight, a reactionary, but also the reception of his new book, dismissed by one reviewer like this: "These days who wants stories about Tory mums, even if they are well written? Mr. Coldridge should be told that in the thirties we were fighting fascism." The writer was just out of university, the brother of a friend of Graham Patten.

A pity, said Mark, that the book had not come out even two years before: it would have been right for the mandarin mood then prevailing. But things had changed. Gone were the days of the ivory tower, art for art's sake, and the rest. Progress was back in fashion.

At the same time, he had a play running, briefly, at the little theatre, the Red Cockerel, where Patty was working. It had been her idea. One evening he had been saying what a pity all that work on the doomed brother and sister, Aaron and Rachel, was wasted: it was a rotten book. A lot of it being in dialogue, he was prepared to see it as a play. Patty carried the mass of typescript off, and from it carved out, with the aid of a lively director, a play dealing with the events that led up to the resistance to the Nazis in the Warsaw Ghetto. But while the atmosphere in book-reviewing had changed, the theatre had not yet changed: not quite yet. Critics had not been near the Red Cockerel, except to patronise or sneer, for years. Mark's play was found by one or two critics who did go embarrassing, naive, and simpleminded. It was played to an audience of ten, twenty, thirty people: but then, their audiences were never bigger. The lively director, who had been producing some of the most interesting work in the British theatre, was used to it; Mark did not mind particularly; Patty minded very much—she remained a person who did, and must.

Meanwhile, an interesting development with *A City*. Throughout the Cold War, Mark had not been able to find a publisher in the States: publishers said with commendable frankness they would not publish a Communist. It was now published, and was taken up by the science-fiction addicts. Jimmy's novel, his first, came out at the same time. Mark began to spend time with science-fiction writers: of course such work was not then taken seriously in literary circles, but he found their way of looking at the world nearer to his own than any other.

In fact, Mark was extremely busy. So recently a man who never left his home except to go to the factory, a man entirely under siege, now he was never at home except for breakfast, which meal he and Martha took together. They both rose very early, for different reasons, and met in the kitchen. The basement was still asleep—would be asleep for some hours yet. The telephone was silent. It was an hour or so of gay and warm intimacy. Like a lovers' meeting. Except that they were not lovers now. They were more like an old married couple—so they joked.

There had been no moment when they had said: Now it's over. Yet it was over. Sometimes they slept together, from liking and good humour. Mark was having odd affairs: he might refer to them, casually, over breakfast. Martha had had an affair—it it was more out of curiosity than need: she wanted to find out what she was like now, as she explained to Mark. They agreed that affairs were all very well, but weren't much, after all. Yet they did not return to loving each other. It was latent between them: the possibility that they might again. Or that, if other things had not intervened, they might still be lovers. But neither of them were people who could say: *If only . . .* They had been stripped of that. Things having been as they had been; Mark, Martha, being as they were, then nothing else could have happened, and regrets were not in order. Mark might say: I must see to it that I don't let myself be a St. George again—his shorthand for what he hoped was an outgrown need to console and support. And she would say: Well, some women are unmarriageable. For now that she was out and about again, no longer under siege with Mark, there was not one man she could imagine herself married to, no man she wanted to marry. The fact was, she supposed, that in a way she was married to Mark. No joke that: it was a kind of truth.

They were split people, he with his Lynda, whom he would always love, and she with—what she had acquired during the last three, four years.

It seems that any battle must win more than the territory that is being fought over: she had done more than she had set out to do. It was as if she had pulled herself up, hand over hand, out of a hold full of old dirty water, a sour greyness. An interior experience had matched the exterior, the bad time. She was now able to say, simply: I've got it all back. Well, most of it. There were still blanked-out spots where, she knew, pain lay congealed too thickly to melt easily. But, she could walk easily in and out of that house, or place, or garden, or room, touch articles of furniture, sense the exact time of a year by the feel, the smell of sunlight or a quality of dry air. She could live again through this time, that time, when she wanted, so that, if she wanted, the past enveloped, seeped through, the present. Sitting at breakfast with Mark, she was able to sit at that other table, a child, with her father and mother, at breakfast; talking late at night with Mark, Thomas walked into the room and she could hear him say, Well Martha? Pain had become, not something which engulfed, but a landscape she could move into and out again. The hatreds and resentments were places or regions in her mind which she could visit, test—as one might dip a hand into water to see if it is too hot to bear.

But (and here was the point) all this fighting, the effort, had led her so much further than she had expected. On the lowest level, there was the machinery of it. If it is a question of survival, on a full day with a hundred letters to be dealt with and the children's food to be ordered, then one gets up an hour earlier. Impossible, you would have thought, to get up an hour earlier, so dulled and held and sleep-logged you are, at that time. But you do it, if you have to, and it's a question of survival. And if drinking brandy with your lover after dinner leaves you too dulled to work before sleeping you drink less brandy and eat less and even dismiss the lover, poor Mark, turned out of her heart for the sake of—survival. And if you find, as you sit fighting to dredge back that incident, sift out that emotion, that you are sitting knotted and tensed and your muscles hurt too much to let you concentrate, then you do exercises to release tension. Never had Martha said to herself, I must sleep less, I eat too much, I am physically flabby, I must not drink so much brandy in the evenings with Mark: but she had discovered, fighting against the dark, that she was sunk fathoms deep in sleep and lethargy and sloth and so—she had had to survive.

And had made discoveries. She had found doors she had not known existed. She had wrestled herself out of the dark because she had had to, and had entered places in herself she had not known were there.

She was like a woman with a secret, or one who is pregnant, but who hasn't yet told anyone she is pregnant. Yet she looked for people to talk to, people who would understand what she said. For it was certainly not possible that she was the only person to have made such discoveries. Where were they, then, the others? She went about listening, dropping a hint, a suggestion, waiting for an echo, but carefully, particularly with Mark, since above all she was still concerned that he would not have to think: First Lynda, and now Martha. No, she was looking for people who wouldn't think she was crazy.

Meanwhile she protected her life, so that she could be free for an hour before breakfast, so that she would not be too tired before she slept at night to "work," as she put it. For she knew very well that the Martha she had created during the last few years was fragile, and might easily again be lost into the dark.

Which was why she did not wish to look for a husband, though she could not explain this to Mark. She was now thirty-six—no, thirty-seven. If she didn't find a husband now she probably would not. But it was an abstract remark, almost a formal one, issued to her by convention, like "clothes suitable for one's age."

The truth was, she feared marriage, looking at it from

outside now, unable to believe that she had ever been in it. What an institution! What an absurd arrangement! Such remarks she made to herself, remarks issued to her, as it were, as suitable for use in her situation—the unmarried woman still of marriageable age. But to herself she was able to say precisely what she feared. It was the rebirth of the woman in love. If one is with a man, "in love," or in the condition of loving, then there comes to life that hungry, never-to-be-fed, never-at-peace woman who needs and wants and must have. That creature had come into existence with Mark. She could come into existence again. For the unappeasable hungers and the cravings are part, not of the casual affair, or of friendly sex, but of marriage and the "serious" love. God forbid.

It was poor Dorothy, of all people, who said it, put the words out into the air for her to look at. Dorothy had continued in one job after another, attracting various sad men, until she had come to rest in a large stationer's shop which she managed with a widower who decided he wanted to marry her. Dorothy for a time flirted with the idea of marriage. She treated him very badly, as it seemed that she had to, but he came again and again to the basement, could see, apparently, nothing at all wrong with Dorothy except that "she needed security." With him, she was coy, preemptory, an insulted queen—most upsetting to watch, since he was prepared to put up with it. To Martha she said, sensibly, with a sad humour: "When you get to the point when a man is a sort of *thing* for keeping you quiet—do you know what I mean? You know, you're in a bad mood, you just want to scream and throw cups, then you think, Oh for God's sake, why doesn't he sleep with me and shut me up . . . Well, what I think is, it's the end. I mean, who needs it?"

Well, quite so, when a woman has reached that point when she allies part of herself with the man who will feed that poor craving bitch in every woman, then enough, it's time to move on.

When it's a question of survival, sex the uncontrollable can be controlled. And therefore had Martha joined that band of women who have affairs because men have ceased to be explorations into known possibilities.

The possibilities had moved ground, were elsewhere—somewhere there must be people who could tell her, talk to her, explain.

Martha wandered over London, went to parties, looked, listened. The city had lost its grey shoddiness; that dirty, ruinous, war-soaked city she had arrived in, where the food was uneatable, the clothes hideous, the people with the manners of a beleaguered minority—it was gone. A fresh soft air moved through it, blowing colour onto houses, smiles onto faces, lifting and silvering the leaves on the trees. There were shops now that sold clothes one wanted to wear, clothes for enjoyment, for fun; there were coffee shops everywhere that sold coffee one could drink and where people sat and talked. She walked through this city and kept that other one in her mind, so that a long street of fashionably bright buildings had behind it, or in it, an avenue of nightmare squalor, a darkness and a lightness together, the light so precarious a skin on a weight of dark, for these sagging old carcasses had been dabbed, merely, with paint: there was a surface of freshness, hiding weights of shoddiness that threatened to crumble and lean, like the house in Radlett Street, with its white surfaces over a structure attacked by war and damp. And everywhere, a frenzy of rebuilding. Even walking in those squares that are synonyms for permanence, stability, was like moving through a slow earthquake. Somewhere in our minds there is an idea of a city. A City, rather! A solid, slow-moving thing, not far off that picture of a city presented by Mark, where streets ran north and south and east and west and known landmarks could be referred to through generations. But London heaved up and down, houses changed shape, collapsed, whole streets were vanishing into rubble, and arrow shapes in cement reached up into the clouds. Even the street surfaces were never level; they were always "up," being altered, dug into, pitted, while men rooted in them to find tangled pipes in wet earth, for it seemed as if the idea of a city or town as something slow-changing, almost permanent, belonged to the past when one had not needed so many pipes, cables, runnels, and types of machinery to keep it going. If time were slightly speeded up, then a city now must look like fountains of rubble cascading among great machines, while buildings momentarily form, change colour like vegetation, dissolve, re-form.

The old city was all movement. Exhilarating. Just the setting for the "affair" which one might discuss, pleasantly, with Mark at the breakfast table. Though there was no particular reason why one should have one at all, since she had proved that the hungers and the cravings belonged somewhere else.

They discussed these and similar matters exactly like

prisoners on parole meeting to exchange notes on benefits encountered out in the free world.

For neither believed that things would go on like this, easy, amiable, pleasant.

How could they? They never had in the past! So they must make the most of it, enjoy it while it was there; and she above all must use what time there was on "work," the silent hours by herself in her room.

The upheaval came not from Lynda, from whom they expected it; but from the children, who for so long had been people who came for holidays, or for weekends, but who did not actually live in the house.

Paul came home first.

If he were at an ordinary school, one could say that he had been expelled. But progressive schools do not expel children: this would be bad for their "image." Far more than ordinary schools, however, they "ask children to leave." Paul had been asked to leave before. He stole. He had been stealing (or pilfering, a smaller word) since he had been there. Trifles like sweets and socks and ties to begin with; then, as he grew, pens and bicycle pumps and small sums of money. Then he organised with some friends small thefts from the shops of the village near the school. At this point, two years before, there had been a great scene, Paul had been threatened with being asked to leave, and first Mark, then Martha, had gone down for a lot of interviews with staff and with Paul.

With Paul one had conversations of extreme frankness which, since no adult could for a moment forget his painful history, they felt as brutal. With Paul one was always in a position of having to be brutal.

He had been about nine when Martha had overheard a conversation between him and some friends of the same age. They had all been sitting on a grassy bank outside a window inside which she sat.

A small girl said: "Paul, you can't be friends with Marcia."

Paul said: "Why not, if I want to?"

Another small girl: "Your temperament isn't right for Marcia."

First small girl: "You're not compatible."

Paul: "You're jealous: you want me to be your friend."

Second girl: "Yes, that's true, Rosie, you do, but I don't. I don't want to be your friend, Paul. I've got my friend for this term."

Paul: "I don't want you or you. But I'm friends with Marcia."

First small girl: "It won't last, then."

Paul: "I didn't say I wanted it to last, did I? Nothing does."

This being the atmosphere in which he grew, the conversation between Paul and Martha on that occasion was straightforward.

Paul: "If I do steal, and I'm not admitting it, then I'm stealing love. Anyone could tell you that."

Martha: "That isn't how the shopkeepers see it."

Paul: "They've had a progressive school on their doorstep for years, so it's time they did then!"

Martha: "The headmaster says you must leave."

Paul: "I'm not going to leave. This is my school just as much as it is his school."

Martha: "I don't think he sees it like that."

Paul: "But that's what he is always saying."

Martha: "What he's saying now is, Stop stealing or leave."

Paul: "If no one ever loves me then I have to steal."

Martha: "Then I'm afraid you'll have to leave."

Paul: "He means it is my school as much as it is his school as long as I do what he wants."

Martha: "As long as you behave so he doesn't get into trouble with the Education Authorities."

Paul: "Why should I have to agree with the Education Authorities?"

Martha: "You can reform our educational system when you grow up."

Paul: "Lynda loves me. Nobody else does."

Martha: "Does she tell you to steal?"

Paul: "Give her my love. *All* of it."

Martha: "I shall. But Paul, you'd better think hard. You can stay here on one condition: that you don't steal again. It's up to you."

Paul (screaming): "It's not fair. It's not fair."

Martha: "Whoever said it was fair? What is? Goodbye. Better ring Mark tonight and say what you've decided."

That night he sent a telegram which read: I submit to blackmail. Love to Lynda. Paul.

For a couple of terms, exemplary behaviour, but his schoolwork was very bad—suddenly he was at the bottom of the class.

Mark said: "You're just sulking. What you are saying is, If I'm not allowed to steal, I'm not going to work."

Paul said: "I can work any time I want to, I don't have to when I don't."

Suddenly a telephone call from the school. Paul had organised a real robbery, with two friends, from a shop. He had stolen about £500 worth of goods. The robbery, according to the police, "might have been the work of a professional thief." What the children had stolen were things like tape recorders, cameras, record players: the school was flooded with them. They had been unable to sell them quietly, though they had tried.

And now Paul was being asked to leave. His two accomplices had already left, having been removed by angry parents.

Mark went down to fetch him in the car, but came back without Paul. He had refused to get into the car, had sat on his bed and sulked. He said he would not leave.

Martha went down. As she had done so many times before, she crossed the green playing fields, passed old houses converted into school buildings, saw the flights of brightly coloured children swooping and swerving in the gentle English air. A boy stopped, on seeing her, and said that Paul had sent a message: he was prepared to talk to her on such and such a bench. Martha made her way to a bench under an ash tree, from which there was a view of a field covered with small boys playing cricket, and waited. To her, then, came Paul, vividly sulking.

"You've got to leave, you know."

"I'm not going to."

There he sat, a thin, lithe, black-eyed boy, all his sulky charm smouldering. He wore the uniform of his age: jeans and a sweater.

"If you don't come home they'll make you."

"It's not my home."

"It's the one you've got."

"Suppose I don't want it?"

"Too bad. What are you going to do instead?"

"When I'm old enough, I'm going to run away."

"When you're old enough, you can."

"I shall go to my father in Moscow."

"If he is in Moscow."

"If he isn't dead, you mean."

"Perhaps he is. I don't know."

A long silence. He watched, as she did, the children playing cricket. He was good at it.

"You thought they weren't going to kick you out because they'd admire you for doing such a professional job."

This, a shot in the dark, told. He swung around towards her, hating her, eyes black and deadly.

"Well, isn't that true?"

"I'm not leaving."

"I don't suppose they'll call the police to take you away."

"It's my school, they can't."

"You knew they'd kick you out if you did it again."

And now the moment when one was defeated: he drooped, went limp and miserable. He had not known it; he had not believed it; it was not possible that this place, which was his real home, or so he saw it, could throw him out.

"If there weren't two other people involved, if the other two hadn't had to leave, I dare say it could have been patched up, but now it can't. It wouldn't be fair if you stayed, you must see that."

"Fair!" he exclaimed.

"Well, are you going to come with me? They can send your things on."

"No."

He got up and rushed off back to the main building, bounding like a deer in full flight. He was extraordinarily graceful. Passing another group of children, who greeted him, he greeted them, with a wild wave of a hand and a shout.

Martha returned home. Telephone calls to the school revealed that he was sitting on his bed, in silence, with some of the stolen loot packed in heaps around him. He was waiting. Presumably for the police. Headmaster and staff reasoned with him but he would not reply. He was putting the adult world in the position where they would have to carry him bodily to car or train. Possibly he was even waiting for the police to bring him home or take him to prison. Meanwhile, there he sat.

Meanwhile, Francis's school holidays were due. He had been at Eton for one year. He did not like it but he had chosen it.

For years, two or three days before his holidays he had telephoned: "Is Paul going to be there?"

"Yes, he is."

"Then I'm going to the Buttses."

Or: "No, he's with friends this holidays."

"I'll be on the eleven-twelve train."

It had never been discussed, brought out into the open,

ventilated. With Paul, one said everything. With Francis, one could say nothing, had to be careful, tactful, oblique. And Mark, who with Paul was easy and open, could not talk to his son at all.

Francis telephoned. He said: "Is it true that Paul has been expelled?"

"Yes, it is."

"Is he going to be at home then?"

"I suppose so. He'll be at day school from the look of it."

"He's a thief!"

"Yes, he is."

A long waiting silence. Suddenly Martha said, on an impulse: "Francis, I think you should come home."

He said nothing.

She said: "Please, Francis."

He said nothing. But he did not put down the receiver.

She said: "Francis, you've got to come home."

"In that case I've got to." But he sounded pleased. He had been waiting to be ordered?

He came, in a couple of days, and took possession of his room.

Mark hung about, looked helplessly at his son, and Francis was polite, and said yes, and no, till Mark went off.

Yet he was waiting.

Francis was now thirteen. He was a small adult, not a child. He looked like Mark. When they were in the same room, one saw Mark, and then his smaller copy, a dark round closed-in boy. He was not yet adolescent, had not yet shot into that stage of uneasy, half-poetic, half-mucky charm.

In the last five years he could not have spent more than half a dozen months in this, his home. When here, he had always been intolerably well behaved. He was being intolerably well behaved now. Martha remembered the small boy who had cried himself to sleep night after night after night. Did he remember it? Adults look at children and ask secretly: Do you remember? As if it matters that they remember the same things.

But he was here, though he had arrived in that lackey's dress of his which he had said embarrassed him.

Martha and he sat at the kitchen table. She poured tea and offered sandwiches and waited, as one had to, for the moment when he would give some sort of indication of what he wanted to be said.

307

At last she said: "It looks as if Paul will be living here—all the time."

He said nothing. Then, in a kind of a jeer, from the snobberies of his education: "A day school?"

"Yes. There's no law that says a boy has to go to boarding school."

When such triggered moments were over, he was himself, he had paid tribute to what he had been taught. Now he seemed to be thinking.

"Well, I supppose there are some good ones."

"I should be surprised if we can get him into a good one."

"I'm not going to be sorry for him," he muttered, miserable, flushing.

"Which means that you are?"

"Oh, he's all right, I suppose."

More silence, more tea, and he made himself some toast.

With his back turned he said: "Lynda will be pleased if Paul is here all the time?"

Now this was it, this was the moment. She said: "Has it never occurred to you that your mother has made a sort of favourite of Paul because she never sees you?"

This remark, had it been made to Paul, would have been no more than the stuff of the level he lived on, at his school. It was too straight for Francis.

He stood burning the toast, dropped it, then threw it into the wastebin and sat down. He had made himself sit down, instead of going out of the kitchen altogether. He was now pale with the effort of staying, and facing her.

She said: "She's your mother, not Paul's."

He gabbled, "Jolly bad show then, if that's it." But he was looking imploringly at her.

"Why don't you try?"

He got up and went out. She remained, discouraged. That had been no use, she decided. But in a moment he came back, having made himself come back. But he didn't sit down.

"But he's going to be here all the time!" he said.

"But it's not a question of a—competition. She's your mother. You're her son."

"That's all very well, isn't it?"

"And there's no reason why you should stay at Eton if you don't like it, is there?"

"I didn't say I wanted to leave."

"No. But you don't like it, do you?"

"I don't think one is meant to like it," he said seriously, wanting an answer.

"Well—why shouldn't one enjoy one's school? You're going to be there a long time yet, aren't you."

Now, after a moment when he might have gone out again, he turned himself about for her benefit, demonstrating his clothes, and their absurdity, with a seriousness that was masked by facetiousness.

"Are these funnier than any other clothes?" he enquired.

"If you like we'll find out about schools in London that are—appropriate."

She meant: not what you'd consider, after that prep school, and a small dose of Eton, eccentric. So he understood her.

"All right," he said.

"Why don't you take off that outfit now? It's the holidays, after all."

"Just the rig for a visit to Lynda, I thought." The facetiousness of this hurt them both, he gave a scared smile, and hurried out of the kitchen. A few minutes later she heard him come downstairs and go to the door to the basement. He knocked. Lynda called out, "Come in," and he went down.

A couple of hours later he came back to the kitchen, where Martha cooked supper.

He had changed for the visit, was wearing ordinary clothes, and he looked very tired.

"Was Lynda alone?"

"I wouldn't have stayed if that female had been there," he announced, making this point for the first time.

"Lynda needs her."

"Is my mother better than she was?"

"About the same, I think."

"*She's screwy*," he brought out, his eyes waiting to gather any crumb of information that Martha's face might offer: he did not expect anything at all from her words, so that avid gaze said.

"But that isn't all she is, Francis."

He was searching her face, leaning forward to do it.

"And she didn't choose to be."

"I can't help that, can I? If I had gone down in my uniform ... if Paul had gone down in that uniform ... Lynda would have thought it was funny, wouldn't she?"

"Lynda didn't like you in that uniform?"

"I don't think she likes it. But if Paul had it, they'd make a game of it."

"Yes, but then Paul isn't her son." She insisted on this; she leaned forward, offering her face to his gaze, to emphasise it.

"I think I make her worse," he said, very pale. It seemed that he felt sick. He went to the window for air.

"Well, why don't you try for a bit—give her a chance."

"All right," he said. "But just for the holidays."

For three weeks then, Francis tried. And so did Lynda. Francis did not like Dorothy; Lynda therefore asked Dorothy not to be there when Francis came down. This went so far as asking Dorothy to have engagements for the evening; to go for a walk, or to the cinema. There were frightful scenes between the women: they could be heard screaming at each other. There were the sounds of tears and of things breaking.

Francis would come up to Martha, and sit watching her face, as if the pressure of his misery would force her into a comment that could dissolve the knot, make it vanish.

"I think you'd be right to stick it out," said Martha.

"All right, I will."

When Mark came home, Francis stayed a little, transferring his acute wry gaze to the face which was so like his own, and, like his own, a guard against emotion. After a while he made an excuse to go to his room.

One evening, when Mark was not there, he came to Martha's room carrying a large book. This he spread out on a table, and he stood beside it, turning the pages. She went to stand by him. It was a book of blank pages in which there were press cuttings and his photographs.

He wanted her to look: she turned the pages to see.

"You subscribe to a press cutting service?"

"Yes."

"For how long?"

"Since it all started."

They began in 1949. Page after page of the great book was filled with what the newspapers had said about Mark, during the bad time. There was nothing there that wasn't painful: and for a small boy, reading about his father, it was not possible to imagine the cumulative effect of the thing. Martha was shocked—she was not able to take it all in at once. She sat down, lit a cigarette, and it was her turn to look helplessly at him, waiting for aid.

Meanwhile he stood turning the pages. He still wanted her to look. As she did not get up, he took the book to her, to spread it open in her lap, at the last filled pages, the reviews of the recent book, which he had pasted in under the heading: *The Way of a Tory Hostess.* Under that he had put a subheading: My Grandmother.

These reviews were those which said, for the most part, that Mark was out of tune with his times, reactionary, and so on.

"Has my father changed his mind?"

"What about, Francis?"

"About Communism?"

"I don't think his mind has changed—what he thinks. What he feels has, though."

He looked enquiringly at her.

"But he's not a Communist now?"

"He never was."

He took the book away, closed it tidily together, and sat on the foot of her bed, looking out at the tree. The old black cat, too large for a narrow lap, curled by him. The cat was the same age as Francis: taken into the household when he was born. It was Francis's cat. He stroked the cat with one hand, and looked forlorn.

"Your father loved his brother," said Martha.

"I don't understand it," said Francis flatly.

Martha now suffered that violent emotional surrender that is imposed when the young take possession of one's past— nullify it, if you like, or at least, jerk it out of the shape it has had.

She rejected: There is no reason at all why you should, and said mildly: "Mark is rather consistent really: he has always followed his own line—there's an emotional logic in it. What changes is the—zeitgeist, whatever word you want."

"Well, *yes*," he said, violently. "But it's just a bloody *joke*."

"It could very easily have not been a joke," she said, warning, out of her knowledge, the knowledge of her generation as to what is possible. But he looked at her vaguely, this not being remotely his point, and after a while, took up the book, *the case for the prosecution,* as Martha called it to herself in a sad private joke, and went out with it.

Next day, due to go back to his school, he said he wanted them to make a list of schools that were neither public schools, nor "aggressively" progressive.

He also said that he would be coming home for the holidays in the future. "I'll have to some time, I suppose," he said, in his forlorn way of outlining his position. "But I can't go to a day school. I can only take all this in small doses. It's too much of a good thing."

That he was able to talk like this, comparatively open, and straight, showed what the short period of the holidays had done in bringing him towards Paul's openness.

Francis, then, went back for his last term at Eton.

And Paul came home, since his school's holidays were starting. He had spent nearly a month, either sitting on his bed, or defying authority by stalking around the school as if he were entitled to, and going to meals. He had not gone to classes—but then, at that school children did not have to, though all did, except at moments of crisis like this; and he had insisted on going to the school church services, which were a kind of amalgam of a dozen different Christian sects conducted by a teacher. He had never gone near these religious exercises before, but during that month he had not missed one. The school was not likely to have failed to see his message to them. He came home, since the holidays began; and everyone was going home. He had not been expelled; and, although "asked to leave" could say that he had not left.

However, he was not going back; he knew that sooner or later he had to go to another school.

He was in a mood of violent, electric aggression. The school, his home, was no longer there for him: it had let him down, or so he felt it. And he had heard through the bush telegraph that link the young from school to school that Francis had been home for all the holidays, which he had not done once before.

As soon as he arrived, Paul went down to the basement to see Lynda. He found her in bed with a migraine. She was hardly able to speak. Paul understood it very well. He shrieked at her: "All right then, I hate you, I hate you too!" And he rushed back upstairs to lock himself in his room.

Lynda went on being ill. She was not more ill than she was very often: but Dorothy, who felt betrayed and sacrificed to Francis, would not help her. Previously, when Lynda was ill, Dorothy nursed her, suffered with her, sat by her: now Dorothy made a demonstration of having many things to do.

Lynda, for whom Francis's presence had been a torture of ineffective guilty love, and who had tried harder than she had ever done over anything in her life, had been longing for the moment when he would go back to his school. But she told Martha that she was happier than she had ever been.

312

She knew that because Francis was trying too, was no longer treating her and the basement as forbidden territory, "unclean, like lepers," she could learn to be with him, not to feel ill, not to be upset. Next holidays, she felt, things would be much better. Now she needed to rest.

And she did not have the energy for Paul. She was sacrificing Paul, her playmate, for her son; she was quite clear-minded about it. And when Paul, after remaining in his room for a couple of days, descending secretly at night to get food, retreating before he could be met and talked to, rushed down again to the basement to storm and entreat and accuse, she simply locked her bedroom door and pulled the covers over her head.

A few days after Paul came home, Lynda crept out of the house one morning, went to Dr. Lamb, and demanded to be put back into a hospital. If he didn't do this, she said, she thought she would probably kill Dorothy. She did not want to go back to the hospital she had been in before: she wanted to save Mark expense. An ordinary state hospital would do. She went straight to the hospital from Dr. Lamb's office; and Martha sent on some clothes. Dorothy was in a heap of misery in the basement, in a kind of breakdown of her own.

It became evident that it was Lynda who had supported Dorothy, not what they had imagined: that Dorothy kept Lynda together. At any rate, Dorothy, who had had a job, and kept her sad gentlemen dangling, and from time to time considered marrying her co-manager, now stayed in the basement, for the most part in bed.

Martha and Mark, descending to the basement, met, not a unit of two women guarding their precarious balances, but Dorothy, voluble, betrayed, vindictive.

All kinds of things were made clear. For one thing, drugs. In the last year Lynda had given up drugs. She had made a decision that if she couldn't do without them, there was no point in living. For living with the drugs the hospital gave her, the sleeping pills, the sedatives, the pep pills and the rest, meant that she was never "herself." "It is not that they are habit-forming, it is just that one can't do without them," explained Dorothy, in the sour humour that was the note of the basement when it was "well" as distinct from "ill" and violent. Giving them up, Lynda had slept badly, been frail and on edge: she had gone back to them, several times, and had again given them up. Into this battle had come Francis's determination to reclaim his mother and his home. Still

313

Lynda had not gone back to the chemicals. Then the conflict over Paul: she loved Paul, but had to betray him. Dorothy, betrayed, was urging her back on drugs. Dorothy could not do without them. At first she had aided Lynda, supported her: she, Dorothy, was not strong enough for this battle, but if Lynda could be . . . then, she switched, and Lynda found boxes of pills everywhere she went, put there by Dorothy, who knew her every weakness, the exact moments when she was most vulnerable. Dorothy was taking more drugs, larger doses. Living with Lynda inside a cocoon of drug-induced euphoria, or lethargy, was one thing, but quite another when Lynda was shrill, sleepless and jumpy. At any rate, drugs had been the battleground where their many accumulated differences had been fought out.

Dorothy did not want to stay without Lynda. She asked Dr. Lamb to send her to the same hospital; Dr. Lamb thought otherwise. For one thing, Lynda did not want it. Dorothy visited Lynda in the hospital, but Lynda, inside a drug-induced calm, would hardly speak to her.

Dorothy saw, or felt she did, that Lynda wished to be rid of her. She was convinced that the household wished to be rid of her.

From time to time she came up the stairs, in her dressing gown, and shouted, or remarked, or wheedled, according to her mood, saying that they all wished her to go.

They reassured her; but the truth was, of course, they did.

They were having to keep Paul away from her, and her away from Paul. She had been screaming at him that he was a "Jewish brat."

Paul said: "She's jealous because I live here and she doesn't."

But he was talking of a woman who had been a kind of mother to him, while Lynda had been playmate: his school had gone; Lynda had gone; now Dorothy called him names.

The young take precedence: if Dorothy was going to "upset" Paul, then . . .

About a month after Lynda went into hospital, Dorothy slashed her wrists, to an adequately alarming depth; and was taken off to another hospital, not Lynda's.

Meanwhile, a conversation with Paul.

The direction of this had in fact been indicated by Dorothy. Living with the mentally "upset" is a lesson in our own splits, discords, contradictions. No one was more intelligent about Paul than Dorothy, provided he was not in the same room. She had said: "What you've got to make him see is, he's not entitled to get away with it. Otherwise he's going to be ever so surprised to find himself in prison."

Martha: "When the term starts you've got to start school."

Paul: "I don't want to."

Martha: "It's the law."

Paul: "I shall stay here. I don't want to go to that school."

(Paul had been accepted by the local council school.)

Martha: "If you had listened to what we said, if you had believed it, you'd still be at your own school."

Paul: "If I promised not to do it again, would they take me?"

Martha: "No. It's too late."

Paul: "I don't want to go to school any more, why should I?"

Martha: "You've got to go to school for at least another three years. That's the law. I didn't make the law. Your uncle didn't make the law. The law is, you must go to school until you are fifteen. Are you listening, Paul?"

He wore a scarlet jersey and tight black pants. He sat huddled in a big chair under the kitchen window, on the defence, clutching the bars of the chair and looking over them at her.

Martha: "If you aren't listening then you are being as stupid as when you didn't listen about your school. We said exactly what would happen—but you didn't believe it. You'd better believe it now."

He was grinding his teeth and hating her: great forlorn black eyes stared at the cruel world, at Martha. But he was, she thought, listening.

Martha: "If you weren't in this house, if you weren't Mark's nephew, privileged, one of the privileged ones, it would be Borstal, police courts. But you are privileged. You've got some leeway. But not much. If you refuse to go to school, then you'll hang about here a little, and then the officials will start coming. The machinery will go into motion. Once it is in motion, then—you'd better think about it. For you it wouldn't be Borstal and children's officers. It would be psychiatrists and a school chosen because you are special. Well, if you want that, you can have it."

Paul sat twisted, gripping the bars of the chair with both hands, and his long look at her was both full of hate, and masked with cunning.

Once in the zoo Martha had seen a baboon, with its back to the people, squatting on the floor, rubbing something on the cement. Scrape, scrape, went the object it held. Mark joked: "He's sharpening a stone."

It was not a joke. The animal had got hold of a pebble from somewhere. How? Leaned down out of its cage to reach up a stone that had been thrown at it by a child, perhaps? At any rate, it had a pebble, and was trying to sharpen it. Sad, painful: it was a round smooth pebble. But it was the only thing the animal had. After some minutes of labour, it stood up, its back still turned to possible watching enemies and spies, and sawed with that very round, smooth pebble at the wire of its cage. It worked, and rubbed and tried and laboured. Then dejected, defeated, it sat down, having carefully hidden the pebble under some straw, and moved itself around to face the watching people: Martha, and Mark. The look in its eyes was the look in Paul's eyes now. What fantasies or plans of revenge, or hate, or escape did that poor baboon harbour, as it sat there, with its round pebble, its only weapon, only possession, pushed behind some straw?

Martha said: "Paul, the term starts in ten days. If you're sensible you'll be there at school on the first day. And in the meantime you'd better do some thinking: there's a limit to what your uncle can do. And don't let yourself be caught up in that machinery: there's a big impersonal machine out there—sensible people keep clear of it."

He remained silent, watching her. Then he slipped out of the chair and went up to his room.

There was a telephone call from Lynda: would Martha please come and see her? Previous messages had said that Lynda did not want to see either Mark or Martha.

The hospital was near a country town. Martha got onto a train, and travelled through the neat English countryside. Then off the train onto a bus; she travelled through nice suburban respectable England, little gardens, little houses, the families, Mummy, Daddy, and one, two, three children, all going to school, till they were fifteen—the underprivileged—or till twenty-three or so, if destined for university. On the outskirts of the little town, a birch wood, then a large long high red brick wall. She entered the wall through well-painted green iron gates, and was in something like a park, with trees, shrubs and flower beds among which were scattered all kinds of buildings, some large, some small, some like cottages, others like barracks, or prisons. For this mental hospital was huge, and catered for many thousands, from the very ill, in the barracky prison buildings, about whom the others joked—*Abandon hope all ye who enter here*—to the fortunate, like Lynda. Lynda was not in a cottage, but in a medium-sized block. It was approached through tidily arranged rosebeds, where some patients were working. They could be recognised as patients because of their slow-moving indifferent condition. Martha walked through clean glittering corridors, and rooms where people sat smoking, watching television, talking together, playing cards, in that unmistakable atmosphere of the mental hospital, where everything is in slow motion, movements, voices, air, sensations. Drugs. The smell of drugs. Drugged, slow people: as if they had entered a watery dream world, and moved there in a different dimension, hypnotised.

Lynda was in a ward, or room which had six other beds in it. It was very neat and bright. It had a mad tidiness about it. Each bed had a locker, and there was a chair for every other bed.

Lynda sat on her bed. She wore a greyish dressing gown, which was rather grubby. And her beautiful hands had bloodstains around the fingertips.

"Martha," she said at once, hurriedly, but with an effort, as if against the sluggishness of the drugs: "I've got to get out of here."

Martha sat on the chair near the bed. The bed was very high; a hospital bed. The chair was very low. She looked up at Lynda, whose face seemed somewhere up near the ceiling. She got out of the chair and climbed on the bed close to Lynda.

"But Lynda, you're not committed, are you?"

This was stupid. Too sensible. For some moments, entering this world, one was always too sensible. She had to adjust.

"They said they'd commit me, they'd lock me up—last time I was silly."

Martha knew, Lynda knew, that this was a threat merely, part of the game: naughty child, bad child, behave or else.

"What is Mark saying?" enquired Lynda, bringing her face close to Martha's: the lovely ill face, the great ill eyes were a few inches from Martha's. She moved back a little. So did Lynda, who exclaimed peevishly: "Everyone from outside is so ... you're all scared of landing up here yourself, that's why!"

She sat, trembling, angry.

"Mark would like to come and see you," said Martha.

317

Lynda trembled, turned away, looked for a box on her locker top, found a pill, swallowed it.

"I got violent," she said. "I do, sometimes. They give me injecfions and pills—then I fight and get violent. Then they say they'll put me in Abandon Hope. I keep asking them, Don't give me pills, I can do without them. But they do. You remember when you said about you getting your memory back, you couldn't have done that if you were drugged to the eyes, could you? No. I said to them, I've got a friend, she lost her memory, but she got it all back again. That goes to show, doesn't it? But they thought I was talking about myself. I'd forgotten, you've got to be careful about what you say. I expect it's in the dossier by now, that I've lost my memory."

"Lynda, why don't you just come home!"

"I know Mark doesn't want me home."

"That isn't true," said Martha, at once and with conviction.

Lynda, trembling, leaned forward to search Martha's face, her weight on her two hands. A nurse appeared. She was a young professional-looking woman. She drew a curtain across, and adjusted a blanket lying on the foot of a bed. She did not look at Lynda directly, nor at another young woman who sat dozing in a chair, but she had absorbed the atmosphere, whether Martha was "upsetting" Lynda, and she knew what she had to report to matron and to doctors. She went past, with a smile at Lynda's visitor, a nod at Lynda, and disappeared.

"This business of my losing my memory—the doctor goes on and on. They don't believe me now. The funny thing is, now I think: I can't remember that and that. Well, most people can't remember things. But I keep having to tell myself, it's quite normal if I can't remember this and that. I've got to get out of here ..." She started to cry. "I can't help crying, it's these bloody pills."

"Lynda, do you want to leave? To come home?"

Lynda sighed, relaxed, stopped crying.

"That's the point. Do you know why I came? I knew they'd drug me up to the eyeballs as soon as I came in. Then it would be their fault. Not my fault. That's why. But I discovered something. I've been off for a whole year. And I hadn't realised that I had improved—because I had, you know, really. I had forgotten what it was like not to be full of muck all the time. I kept thinking. What's the use, I might as well take them. But when I got back in here and I started in again then I realised how different I was. You don't have any *will,* you don't want anything, you just want to sit about. But now I'm scared. If I come home ... there's no point if I come home and go on taking pills. I might as well be here. Dorothy's not going to be there now, you know."

What it amounted to was, Lynda was saying she was going to be alone. She didn't want to be alone.

"You could come home and try to be—part of every-thing."

Lynda came to life, responded. This was the point.

"Yes, but Francis? What about Francis? It's all right for you and Mark, you're used to me."

"And Paul," said Martha.

"Yes."

"I think you should come home and try."

"Will you ask Mark first? I mean Mark might not . . ."

Lynda collapsed back on her bed and lay weeping, a handkerchief clenched in her fist, which was pressed to her cheek.

"Oh don't take any notice," she muttered. "I cry and cry, I don't know what for."

The nurse came back, smiled at Martha, and stood quietly by Lynda's bed.

"Mrs. Coldridge," she said, "would you like to get up now and come down for supper?"

"No," said Lynda.

"I think you should try. You've lost far too much weight, you know. You don't want us to have to give you insulin, do you?"

"Give me arsenic if you like," said Lynda.

"Now Mrs. Coldridge," said the nurse.

"Oh all right, I'll come in a minute."

The nurse lingered, left. Lynda sat up.

"Talk to Mark," she said. Sitting on the bed, she stripped off her gown. She was certainly very thin, her collarbones stuck out, her shoulders showed blades of bone. She leaned over, pulled a roll of pink out of her locker, drew it over her head, slid down to the floor with a bump, and unrolled the pink downwards onto her. It was, when pressed and looked after, a very pretty dress. Lynda stood, with rumpled pink hanging on her, running her grubby hand through lank hair.

"I'll get some food inside me," she muttered. "Talk to Mark."

Martha kissed her and left, through flower beds and shrubs and trees.

She went to see Dr. Lamb.

About a week before Dorothy slashed her wrists, Martha had seen, among the pictures that moved in her inner eye (very numerous these days), a scene of Dorothy, in a lacy black petticoat, that had a rip in the lace under the left arm, leaning over the basin in the downstairs bathroom. Martha saw this from the back, and slightly to one side. Dorothy turned, blood running from one wrist. In the hand whose wrist was running blood, she held a razor blade, and was sawing at the other. What impressed Martha about this was the care with which Dorothy did it. Her face, vindictive, was frowning with concentration. There was a smudge of blood on her cheekbone.

When Martha went down to the basement on the morning this scene took place (in life) because of the screams of the cleaning woman, Dorothy had fainted. She wore a black lace petticoat, ripped under the arm, and had blood on her face; and on both wrists.

This was by no means the first time this kind of thing had happened, but Martha was now brooding about possible responsibility. Should she have gone down to Dorothy and said: Excuse me, but you are going to slash your wrists, please don't! That is, unless you have already done it at some time? You will be wearing a black lace petticoat, etc.

Or she could have rung up Dr. Lamb: Dorothy is going to slash her wrists, she might have said. Oughtn't she be persuaded not to? Yes, I know she has taken overdoses in the past, but this time, it will be her wrists.

To Dorothy she might even have said, entering the persona of a Rosa Mellendip: Beware of a black lace petticoat that has a rip under one arm!

The thing was, she had a great reluctance to think about it at all: cowardice. She knew perfectly well it was cowardice; and she approached Dr. Lamb as it were with a sideways crab scuttle, trying to think out ways to ask questions and not expose herself. She was afraid of Dr. Lamb—of the machinery.

There was no one else to ask: that was the point. Very strange that, when you came to think of it. She was afraid of Dr. Lamb, and of the power that he had; yet, with a certain kind of question there was nobody in this complex and so-sophisticated society that she could ask.

There was nobody, ever, who could approach Dr. Lamb without a certain kind of tremor. When he spoke to law courts, or advised policemen, or sat in judgement about this sick person or that: when a mortally confused human being sat before him, what Dr. Lamb said was the truth. Very very strange, no matter how one looked at it.

Apart from Dr. Lamb's wife, or mistress, or child, or close friend, there was nobody who could approach him without this tremor, the slave's silent withdrawal behind defences.

As for the people who actually became Dr. Lamb's patients, and must submit to this or that treatment, they were all there as a result of force, or pressure, direct or subtle—that of society, their families, an ordinary doctor who was out of his depth. Dr. Lamb, whether benign, cruel, a secret lover of power, or a man gifted with insight, was always in a position of strength. Because it was he who knew—society had said he did—everything that could be known about the human soul. Or rather, while he would be the first to concede that his knowledge was merely provisional, this was not reflected in the way patients were treated.

This was the central, the key fact, about this great machinery of psychiatrists, psychoanalysts, psychologists, social workers, clinics, mental hospitals, which dealt with what they referred to as the mental health of the country. In any situation anywhere there is always a key fact, the essence. But it is usually every other fact, thousands of facts, that are seen, discussed, dealt with. The central fact is usually ignored, or not seen.

The central fact here was that nobody approached Dr. Lamb unless he had to. In approaching Dr. Lamb one approached power. It was hard to think of a power like it, in its inclusiveness, its arbitrariness, its freedom to behave as it wished, without checks from other places or powers.

There was in fact only one check: was Dr. Lamb by nature a man who had some kind of humility about this position he held, which was an almost unlimited power based on an admitted ignorance?

Dr. Lamb was not sitting in his chair; but at the end of the room where two small easy chairs were by the window. Martha had said on the telephone that this visit was not on her own account: he was showing tact, delicacy. This was going to be treated almost as a social occasion. In a few moments a small tray appeared with tea.

"I saw Lynda," said Martha. "I went to the hospital."

"Ah," said Dr. Lamb. "I tried to get her into another, but at such notice, there wasn't a choice."

He was apologising for the hospital.

"Would you say that Lynda was worse than she was?"

"Of course I'm not dealing with her personally. But I spoke to the doctor who is handling her, over the telephone, this morning." He took off his glasses, and laid them aside. He looked very tired.

"Of course you visited Mrs. Coldridge before, in the private hospital? You know, those enormous fees relatives pay, it's not for better treatment, on the contrary, it is often worse."

"I suppose they feel they are more in control of what goes on," said Martha. "If they are paying . . ."

He looked at her—acute, but he did not see her point. "Waste of money," he said. "Unless, of course, relatives just want to get rid of somebody and pay to have them kept comfortably—conscience money. But for someone really ill, I'd never advise it."

"Lynda wants to come home," said Martha.

"She asked to go in. She can leave when she wants. But if she is returning into the situation which, if you like, triggered her off, then. . ."

This was a question. He wanted to know what had triggered Lynda off. This meant the doctor who dealt with Lynda did not know; or that Dr. Lamb did not think much of that doctor; or that Dr. Lamb was trying to find out something about her, Martha

Martha said: "Lynda gave up the drugs about a year ago. That was one thing. And then, her son decided to—come closer. Two things. And then Dorothy—three things."

He looked at her. Then: "Her son decided?" Panic began to rise in Martha. She said: "Mark and I talked about it— well, for years we've been talking about it. You know—Paul and Francis. Francis is never at home because of Paul. Paul is going to be at home all the time. We thought . . ."

"It was Mark's idea?"

Guilt almost overwhelmed Martha: it was her fault. She fought it back.

"It was as much his *idea*—but it was I who suggested we should actually try to make Francis be at home more."

He remained silent.

"Well, was that the wrong thing to do?"

"Not if she can stand it."

"I think she would have stood it if she hadn't been fighting the drugs. And if Dorothy wasn't jealous."

Martha sat thinking: Within five minutes, I sit overwhelmed with guilt. Why? Should I be? Did he mean to make me? For two pins I'd rush out now and not say what I want to say. . . . She made herself sit quiet.

"About Dorothy, you'll have to deal with that when it arises. She's definitely not well enough to leave hospital at the moment. There's been another suicide attempt. About the drugs: when patients in Mrs. Coldridge's condition give up the pills, then they usually land back in hospital pretty fast."

"Well now, that's what I wanted to ask. Suppose Lynda had arrived in hospital and had not been given pills, what then?"

He said nothing: he looked enquiring.

"What I ask specifically is this: Do you know the effect on someone if for years and years—in Lynda's case, getting on for fifteen years—they are always full of some kind of drug?"

"I see."

He did.

There was a considerable silence. "Mrs. Hesse, I don't think there's a doctor in England who is satisfied with what he's got to work in. If we had ideal conditions then—but we haven't. In Mrs. Coldridge's case I can say definitely yes, she ought to take what we prescribe for her."

Dr. Lamb had withdrawn from responsibility, as of course he had the right to do.

Some years before, an act of Parliament had been passed, which had taken bars off windows, unlocked doors, made strait jackets and padded cells things of the past, created hospitals that were civilised. Well, not quite. Because, for this bit of legal well-wishing to work, it needed that a great deal of money should be spent on new buildings, doctors, nurses. This money was not being spent. (It was being spent on war, the central fact of our time which is taken for granted.)

Inside the dozens of mental hospitals scattered up and down the country, built like prisons, were many thousands of people who had been strait-jacketed, forcibly fed, kept in padded cells, beaten (in fact, the central fact, had had their wills broken), and were now derelict, "deteriorated." This was not Dr. Lamb's fault, who administered machinery he had not invented. Like the educators, and the ordinary doctor and—like everything else—he was part of a bit of machinery which was supposed to be working to a blueprint which in fact had never been put into operation, because there was never money for schools, hospitals, mental hospitals. The money was spent on war. Thousands and thousands of people all over the country could look forward only to death, they were

323

the victims and the casualties of the past. Meanwhile, all over the country, hundreds and thousands of people, more and more every day, were in conditions which Dr. Lamb wished were much better, but it was not his fault if they were not.

At this point Martha nearly left—out of cowardice.

She said: "I want to find out something. I'm trying to find out—you say Lynda is schizophrenic."

"Yes." He smiled. "You are not, Mrs. Hesse."

"Do you know what schizophrenia is?"

"No, but there are different theories. And we are treating it better than we did."

"Supposing I came to see you and said, I hear voices, would I be schizophrenic?"

He said easily: "It depends. What kind of voices?"

"And pictures, before my eyes?"

"A great many people see pictures before their eyes, usually before they go to sleep, and as they wake up. And hear voices."

"That's normal, not schizophrenic?"

"Quite normal."

"If I said to you . . ." Martha began, and changed it. "No, I *am* saying to you: I saw a scene, a vision if you like, of Dorothy slashing her wrists before she did it."

He remained where he was, not moving. But the muscles of his face tightened slightly: she knew it was a waste of time, because now what he said would be measured, would be diagnostic questions only.

"Have you ever heard of *déja vu?*"

"Yes. And read it up."

"Dorothy has made suicide attempts before," he said. "You knew that?"

"Yes. She has taken overdoses of pills, hasn't she?"

"Yes. She is a suicidal type."

"I saw something I was predisposed to see?"

"Yes. You imagined it."

"Dr. Lamb, what is imagination?"

He hesitated now, then gave her a charming gentle smile, almost teasing. "Mrs. Hesse, you aren't ill, I can assure you."

"Oh. You think I'm upset because of Lynda and Dorothy both landing back in hospital?"

"Are you sure you are not?"

"Well then . . . no, I want to go on. If someone sat here and said to you, Dr. Lamb, I hear voices—no, no, don't smile. I want to know, what would be the thing they said, they did, which would make you say 'schizophrenic' and not just, Oh well, everyone does that?"

"I'd ask them, do you imagine it? And the reply will be, No, I hear voices. Real ones. Like yours or mine, Mrs. Hesse." He emphasised this, meeting her eyes, half in enquiry, half to make it sink in.

"An imaginary voice, then, is fantasy—one sits and has a sort of daydream, that's imagination?"

"Yes."

"But a *real* voice, that's serious?"

"A typical reply will be: Everyone is talking about me, everyone is jeering at me. They want to kill me."

Martha suppressed: Perhaps they do! She said: "And what happens then?"

"We treat them."

"And then the voices and the pictures go away."

"That is the intention, yes."

"Dr. Lamb, if someone is hearing voices, seeing pictures, they must feel abnormal—different. People hate being different from other people. Don't you think that . . ."

He said: "It happens two, three times a week. The man who was here before you were, as a matter of fact. I say this: 'I know you hear voices. I know you do. You don't have to convince me of that. But I am a doctor, and a very great number of people sit there and say they hear voices. I tell you, you are deluded. We can treat the condition.' I assure you I don't, none of my colleagues would, try and make them feel different, or make it worse."

"You say, 'I know you hear voices, I know that, but you are deluded'?"

"Yes. Because they are," he insisted gently.

"Perhaps there are different kinds of voices?"

"Well yes, some say they hear voices in the air, or coming out of walls. Others say the voices are in their heads. Real voices. Like yours or mine."

"But the real criterion, the test is, whether this person says he *does* hear voices. If he says yes, he does, he doesn't imagine it, and you can't talk him out of it, then that's it, he's deluded?"

"Well, yes, that's about it."

"So if someone persists, he sticks it out, then he's likely to be classed as schizophrenic and treated as one. But if he says . . ."

"Mrs. Hesse," he said again, I do promise you, you can take my word for it, you're not a schizophrenic."

"Yes, but Dr. Lamb, supposing I insisted I had seen Dorothy's suicide exactly as it was, and I went on insisting, and you said no, I imagined it, and then I got angry and shouted at you, and went on shouting, and called you names, what would you call me then?"

"But you aren't shouting," he said. "You are entirely rational."

He was waiting, infinitely ready to be kind, to reassure, and if necessary to—give out pills.

She said: "Well, thank you. About Lynda—if she comes home, I think you can take it she will try and do without the drugs."

"Well, it's up to her, of course. But if I were you I'd try to persuade her. I don't think this spell in hospital has done her much good. She'll need time to get over it."

"Will you give instructions that she can leave?"

"Mrs. Hesse, all she has to do is to tell the doctor she wants to leave."

"I see. Well, thank you. Please send me the account. I came for my own curiosity."

"Very well. Look after yourself."

"Yes, I will."

"And how is your mother?"

"She's dead. She died less than a year after she went back."

He said humorously: "And that was your fault?"

"When you say it I can't help feeling it might be—but not when I think it over."

Lynda did not come home immediately. It appeared the hospital was very overcrowded, patients did not see doctors oftener than once a week, and one week was missed because a doctor was ill. In the end, Dr. Lamb intervened, and she came home. She was very thin indeed, low, inclined to weep and to blame herself for many faults, past and present.

Meanwhile Paul had gone to school. He went on the first day of term; and returned bitterly, violently complaining. After the freedom of the school he had left, he was going to find this one hard. He was in a class with forty other children, for one thing.

Suddenly Martha was very busy again. Suddenly there was no time for the sessions when she sat alone in her room. The early mornings were occupied with getting Paul up, fed and to school—an exhausting business, a fight all the way. And Lynda, alone, wanted company and a great deal of reassurance.

326

Martha began dreaming. Her nights became filled with fantastic, instinctive or routine dreams. It was as if something in Martha that needed to talk, to express, to speak, to advise, could use this channel or that—pictures, or voices, if she was able to sit quiet in her room, waiting, listening, and if not, was quite prepared to use dreams instead.

Two

A visit to Margaret Patten's house in the summer of 1958; not a dropping-in, a passing-by, a collecting of children, or of plants, but an event which had been built up to, expected, planned for, experienced painfully or at least vividly, and afterwards remembered. A visit typical of all such occasions in its quality of muddle, confusion, general irritation—for so things continued. It seemed impossible that they should not be all at cross purposes.

Margaret's invitation for the afternoon had been casual, and repeated in half a dozen telephone calls about something else. She had sounded increasingly guilty, but offhand. Mark had said: "She's up to something."

She was manipulating them. What did she want? For weeks now he had been trying to see her, but see her, as he put it, "properly." He had been trying to make his mother discuss her son, his brother, Colin. Mark had been back from Moscow for over two months: Margaret had not had time to do more than hear the most brief of accounts over the telephone and once as she hurried past to the theatre. She had not had time to talk about Colin, but she wanted Mark, Martha, as her accomplices in some plan of her own. The two needs—Mark's, Magraret's—were meshed somewhere?

A couple of years before, the Cold War having been officially declared as over—that is to say, referred to as being in the past in newspapers and on the television— Margaret had enquired of an old chum recently returned from the embassy in Moscow if anything was known about Colin. He said not. Enquiries had been made, on that kind of a level, but it was suggested he was dead. Then, a friend of Patty's, who had been to Moscow on some kind of delegation, said that another friend had mentioned a Mr. Coldridge, met at somebody's flat. Had Mark been in Moscow perhaps? Mark, then, after consultation with Patty, who after all continued to know the score, even if retrospectively, simply applied for a visa to the Soviet Union, as a writer. He got a visa without trouble. In Moscow he had asked his interpreter, an infinitely helpful young woman, if it would be possible for him to meet his brother; he spoke as if there could be no doubt at all that Moscow was where Colin must be. The interpreter, noncommittal, said she would make enquiries. After two days or so of ballet, the theatre, and excursions of various kinds, the interpreter had said that of course it would be perfectly in order for Mr. Coldridge to see his brother, it was only too natural, after so many years. His telephone number was so and so.

Mark telephoned, and heard his brother's voice reply. Colin had had no idea, apparently, that this was to happen, or so it seemed, for when he was told who it was, there was a short silence, and then: "How did you find me?" "I was given the number by Intourist," said Mark.

They met an hour later in Colin's flat, which was not half an hour's bus time from the hotel. It was a small, pleasant flat, in a new block which housed scientific workers. Furnished in an anonymous contemporary style, it could have been anywhere in the world. Colin was married to a charming Russian woman who taught ballet to children. She had a child from her previous marriage; her husband had been killed at Stalingrad. This boy was fifteen. There was also a little girl, the result of this marriage. Mark entered a family scene: was made very welcome.

Mark, in describing it to Martha, had used that grimly humorous tone which is the alternative to weeping—the tone of a generation. But this was not how he had felt at the time.

During the evening the children had been introduced to Uncle Mark from England. A great deal of very good food was eaten. Sally-Sarah's death was at last commented on: Mark was made to feel that suicide was a form of moral cowardice peculiar to capitalism, perhaps a lack of *esprit de corps*. Galina said several times that life was a precious gift; she really could not understand people who killed themselves. She sounded both prim and life-enhancing. Mark was irritated and ashamed of being: her tragically heroic life seemed to entitle her to anything. Priggishness was perhaps after all a sign of virtue, as antheaps in hot countries show that water lies for below. After all, the Victorian . . . it seems inevitable that revolution should evoke the Victorians. Colin asked after Paul, and suggested that the boy might visit them in Moscow. Mark continued to supply him with information about Paul; and at the end of the evening Colin ruffled through a great heap of gramophone records, and found some folksongs as a present for his son. Both Colin and Galina pressed Mark to visit them again, when he came back to Moscow. They drank several toasts, to friendship, and to peace. Mark had then gone back to the hotel room, where he had found himself swearing, and dashing about like a madman.

"I couldn't believe it. The whole of that evening was as if I'd walked onto the wrong stage, into the wrong play. There was nothing real about any of it. I began to believe that none of it had happened. I telephoned Colin. It was about four in the morning. I dare say I was over-emotional. I demanded to see him at once. He was cool. Then I thought I wasn't being tactful. Secret police—that sort of thing. But no, looking back, I think it was just very late to ring up. I demanded to see him alone. He said of course, he'd ask Galina and if she didn't mind he would be in the park next afternoon."

Mark had not gone to bed. He wondered, for the most part, why he had been given the telephone number. He was, perhaps, considered a spy himself? Fantasies of this nature occupied his mind for some hours, but at last he concluded that it was probably some kind of muddle. After all, most things were. In Britain, there were six, no seven, espionage organisations, for the most part engaged in spying on each other: the keynote of any operation one chanced to hear about was always muddle, but a farcical, painful, ridiculous muddle. The Soviet Union was increasingly prosperous, developed, stable; doubtless the spy organisations proliferated and competed there too. Perhaps some official had thought: Well, let's give him the number and then see what happens . . . Or even: His brother? Of course! Family ties . . . One could imagine, even, a humanistic smile.

All the same, it was that which stung Mark more than anything: the telephone number of his brother, printed neatly on some paper, given to him casually, as if nothing could be more ordinary. Every time it came back into his mind, he got worse-tempered, more emotional, and by the time he actually met his brother, he was in a fine state. But he saw at once that the more excited he was, the further that put him from Colin, who was even more matter-of-fact today than he had been yesterday.

In a park of Culture and Rest they strolled up and down eating ice cream. Mark wanted to ask a question, the key question. "Colin, why did you leave your own country? Were you frightened? Threatened? Guilty? And if you had to leave why didn't you come back later?"

Mark kept approaching the subject, then at the last moment skirting it. His feeling was that surely Colin must be expecting, waiting for, such questions. Yet he gave no sign of it. He seemed in an extremely good mood: he talked a great deal about Galina, with whom he was happy. He did not say in so many words that she was a nice change from Sally-Sarah, but that was what he meant. He talked about Galina's son, who had had difficulty in accepting him, Colin, as a father: he showed a good deal of sensible insight here. Time passed. He had said he must be off at about four; he intended to work late at his institute. At last Mark said something about Colin's leaving England. Colin seemed embarrassed, as if Mark were deliberately tactless. Mark came out with a direct question: Were you under pressure to leave, and if so, what pressure?

And now Colin started talking. He talked lengthily and logically till the time came for him to go to work, and say goodbye to his brother. What he was saying was a sort of abstract of the point of view in Communist circles of ten years back, and it was impersonal. His own emotions, attitudes did not appear at all.

So they parted.

All the way back on the aircraft Mark had wrestled with two sets of emotions, or viewpoints—he was trying to match the decade he had lived through inside the shadow of his brother's "escape to Communism" and his responsibility for Paul, with what he felt when he was actually with his brother, in whose life there appeared to be a gulf which made irrelevant anything that happened before. But he couldn't make the two attitudes, landscapes, come together.

Back in London, Martha and Mark discussed it, talked, argued, and finally ended with a set of facts, or sentences. Colin was a scientist. He had always been a scientist. Since he was a small boy with his first chemistry set, he had known what he was. Committing treachery, treason, he had acted as a scientist. In the Soviet Union he was—a scientist. No, not in as important a job as he might have expected in Britain, because—and he assumed that Mark must agree with him that it would not be reasonable to expect anything else—in the Soviet Union he would always be a security risk. If he understood nothing else, he knew the score, and in his case this meant that anywhere he was, he must be a security risk. But his life was science, and would continue to be. The ironical truth was that Colin was not interested in politics, and never had been. He said the capitalist part of the world was X, Y and Z, just as if he would have said the Communist world was Z, Y and X if he had stayed in Britain or gone to America. Whatever he was as a scientist, in politics he was a conformist.

Yet although Britain was corrupt and decadent, etc., etc., and his own family by definition its exemplar, he had said how nice it would be if his mother dropped over to see them: she'd like the Soviet Union.

Weeks after Mark's return Margaret had still not time to discuss it. It became evident that it would all slide away into the past, undiscussed, unfocussed, with nothing resolved.

Why not? Why shouldn't it? Because Mark could not bear it. Colin, his much-loved brother, the only person he had been close to in their youth, was lost to him, that was all finished. But he had set his heart on their mother facing— but what? Martha was unable to see what he expected from Margaret. I am guilty, please forgive me! she might cry, and then the past would be cancelled out . . . something like that, perhaps. Or Mark might confess: I made a mistake! Communism is an error! And then they would embrace.

The house happened to be situated about ten miles this side of the hospital in which Lynda had stayed a couple of years before. But, driving to Margaret's, it was hard to think: If I continued on this road then . . . Just as, visiting Lynda, she had not thought: I might drop off and see Margaret . . . To such an extent do destinations colour journeys.

The gates were discreet and set back from the main road, which was very busy, interrupted by towns and villages, but which showed glimpses of field and wood. This was the countryside, as experienced by those who do not turn in at those gates.

All over these islands are main roads full of traffic and villages and signs to towns and villages—the countryside. And set discreetly along them are gates, sometimes with a little caretaking lodge near by. Hidden there are—what, a thousand houses? Ten thousand? A magical kind of houses which must have something like aerial roots, for it is certain they feed on a different air to that breathed by ordinary houses. The breath of gardens, perhaps, of tamed forests ...

The drive to Margaret's house was half a mile through old trees. The house was an urbane white presence. It was Georgian, and had just been classed as a national monument. Mark approached it as the kind of place one lived in; Martha as a sort of inhabitable museum.

Beyond the house was a river. Between house and river, lawns. On the lawns were shrubs, cloud shadows, a tea table people, roses: a Sunday afternoon at Margaret Patten's.

But in the last three, four years, the guests had changed. One glance at the faces and the names attached to them— but no, whatever else she was, cynical she was not; nor, perhaps, even calculating. To be her kind of hostess, what is needed is passivity. Ten years ago, onto those lawns had been blown the editors, critics, pundits, writers of the Cold War; they were not gone, one or two could still be observed, in stances of experience, of maturity, their backs to the roses, but youth swamped the lawns, the new socialists. A single glance down past the house showed Graham Patten, Patty Cohen, and a crowd of people from her little theatre. For, in the past two years, the theatre had caught up with the rest: and nowhere could the change be so sharply observed as in this garden, for here were the actors, actresses, directors, from the two little socialist theatres which for years had been playing to empty houses and to patronising notices, and which were suddenly the stars of the theatre scene. Mark's play, for instance, revived because of the change of temperature, had been successful, enthusiastically reviewed by critics who analysed every reason for their change of front save one, the main one, and, transferred to the West End, had been running there for several months. Rachel and Aaron were talking to Graham Patten, and Mark, observing this scene unobserved, swerved off into the garden room with Martha. This room was chintzed and flower-potted and garlanded, and opened off into a morning room, now in shadow. Quietly they stood, side by side, watching the sunny grass and the moving people through panes of warmed glass. They looked at charming dark-eyed Rachel, at vibrantly handsome Aaron, the doomed brother and sister. But not doomed here, no, quite safe, for it seemed as if this scene, a summer afternoon in England, had always existed and always would, as if, any time of the year and in any season, one had simply to come to this glass wall and look through and there people moved smiling on deep grass beside roses.

Margaret was coming towards the house. She hadn't changed much. Her hair was dyed a dead-leaf colour, her skin was creamy, her eyes large, grey, thoughtful. She wore dark green cloth trousers and a shirt of orangy-yellow cotton. She, like everyone, was exceedingly ornamental. Seeing her, one became conscious of one's clothes—how very much things had changed, that one thought so much about clothes, wanted to look at them, touch them, could admire and envy. Martha hoped that her summer dress was all right: it had seemed so before leaving home; and Mark muttered that damn, he should have changed.

Margaret came. Now she was close, she looked tired and sad.

"Aren't you coming out?" she asked, already resentful.

"No."

"Aren't they friends of yours? Graham's here."

"He was with us last night, as a matter of fact."

She gave him an irritated look and sat down.

"So he said this morning. Then we can talk about it here."

Mark looked angry: believing her to mean that she was still so ashamed of Colin she wished to keep him a secret.

She said conversationally: "Graham says he knows a man who is writing a book about Colin—all that affair. Patty says she knows him too. He might come and ask me for material."

Mark had gone very white. A bad sign. She looked at him, puzzled.

"I really do think you might come out—after all, here's Rosie and Barney, and they are so fond of you."

Rosie and Barney were Aaron and Rachel.

"Delightful people," murmured Mark.

She gave him a look which was all a readiness to suffer exasperated patience. Last week she had exclaimed: "It's not as if they are the stuffy old lot, they are the new young exciting people."

She sat on an old cane chair by a stand full of pink and white variegated blooms.

Mark sat down on a wooden bench, his way of saying he was in a hurry. Martha, in a kind of compromise, sat by him, but accepted an offer of tea.

"How is Lynda?"

"She did think of coming, but then decided not."

"Francis wrote—he'll be home soon, he said."

"He is at home now. It's half-term."

Margaret sighed again: Francis would not be friends with his grandmother. She wanted them to say why he was not here this afternoon. They were determined not to say: they would either have to be rude, or tell lies.

"And Paul is very well," said Mark, to get it over with.

"Good, good . . . I could ask Graham to drop in and have a cup with us here," said Margaret.

"Well, actually, no time. I do have messages from Colin . . ."

"Yes?"

"He said, why didn't you go and visit him?"

"Well yes, I might," said Margaret, puzzled. Sitting quietly, enjoying this chance to rest, she let a hand with a cigarette in it trail by her side, as if in water: Mark, always difficult, was difficult again, she was feeling; and intended it to show.

"Galina, she is nice, is she?"

"Very," said Mark.

"Well, perhaps they might all come over for a holiday."

Mark was near explosion.

"I expect it might be dangerous to come here," said Martha.

"Oh I don't know," said Margaret.

"He'd be hanged, drawn, quartered—impeached," said Mark fiercely.

"Well, perhaps it would be better if he didn't come. A pity. We are having some Russians next week, as a matter of fact. We've been asked to put them up by the Council. Two writers, a ballet dancer and a newspaper editor." She was smiling with pleasure. Beyond Mark, and Martha, she looked towards the well-loaded lawns. Like every good hostess, or rather born hostess, she was almost certainly enjoying a vision, not of those people she actually saw there, but the ones she imagined for next week, or next year or—if one could only see who would be among those flower beds in ten years' time!

Mark sat rather hunched, staring at his mother. She removed her attention from guests, real and imaginary, and smiled at him. She could see he was writhing internally with every kind of anger, emotion, resentment. She really had no idea why. She wondered how to reintroduce *her* subject, Graham.

"Perhaps I'll pop over next year—after all, we have the address now."

"Why not?"

"What's he working at—not still bombs and so on, I hope?"

"I was careful not to ask him."

"Oh—I suppose not. Well, I don't know, we wouldn't understand what he said anyway, would we? And bombs are quite—well, compared to the other things everyone seems to be making, I suppose one should be pleased he's not making nerve gases or diseases or something."

"For all I know he is. Well ... I really do have to be getting back."

"But you've only just ..."

She rose as he did; they stood staring into each other's face, bitter, pained, and completely noncomprehending.

"I don't know why you ... all I know is, I'm to blame for everything as far as you are concerned," she said, in a low bitter tone. Her eyes glittered with tears.

"Oh, what's the point!" said Mark.

"It's not as if I haven't tried to see your point of view!"

"Why is it so very difficult? It's simply a question of loyalty. We have different ideas about loyalty."

"*Oh!*" she said, standing straight, ready for irony, for attack: but his fierceness outflanked her.

"Personal loyalty," said Mark.

"Oh well, I don't ..." Unexpectedly, she laughed. Almost, she went laughing out of the room, through the plant room, to her guests.

But Mark's face stopped her. "It's no good," she said. "It's not that I haven't thought about it. You say something like—my friend right or wrong, my brother right or wrong. Well, that's all very well, isn't it, except when something actually happens, and you are living with it—no, wait a minute, I want to have my say, I never have, have I? I'm simply a criminal, I'm in the wrong. But when Colin—did that, he wasn't thinking about me, was he? About his family? Not his wife—he never did think about Sally at all, nor about Paul. He simply went off on some moral high horse or other, to hell with everyone else, to hell with me too—and you, Mark, what sticks in my gullet is, you are so damned *moral* about everything. You're in the right. Well, why are you? Perhaps you were right and perhaps you weren't. But how do you know I wasn't right? But now when I come anywhere near you I feel ..."

She stood tall, laughing, bitter and reckless; opposite her was Mark, shrunken inside his old bitterness, his not-understanding—she was all colour and vivid emotion; he, cold and white. So he must have looked, in his hotel room in Moscow, waiting to see his brother, and after he had said goodbye to his brother. This, what they saw now, was the face of what he really felt, before transmuted into dryness, or irony, or patience.

"Anyway," said Margaret, "I was going to ask you to—oh but what's the use! I'll tread on your toes again I suppose, though I don't know why . . ." She nodded and smiled at Martha, gave a look at Mark as anguished as his at her, and went out over the grass to her guests.

"Come on," said Mark. "Unless you'd rather . . ." He nodded at the group.

"No," she said.

"You have a ridiculous life," he said. "Why shouldn't you . . . after all, it's quite enjoyable, this sort of thing, I suppose, people do enjoy it . . ."

Anywhere near Margaret, Mark began to suffer about Martha: he remembered other people's judgement and for a short time, a few moments, half a day, a week, would mutter and brood that he exploited Martha. For the most part both got on quite comfortably with what both had to do. She hoped now that his misery over his mother was not going to switch into misery over Martha.

"I don't care one way or the other," she said. "Anyway, Lynda's doing dinner and if there are masses of children again . . ."

Around the corner of the house, out of sight from the others, he kissed her. A kiss of old lovers, compounded like a liqueur of a hundred different flavours, the strongest of which today was anger: he ended it exclaiming: "Damn it, am I mad? Or is she?"

From the house came Patty Samuels, smiling, a handsome Jewish girl: still girl, although fortyish, since she had all the open readiness of one. She wore a short striped green-and-white dress, like a nightshirt, with frills at the bottom. Being large, she achieved a look of romping good health. Her smile was shrewd as she observed them both: became soft and confused as Mark kissed her too. The three of them stood close with far too much emotion loose and dangerous, while anger forked behind their smiling eyes.

"Oh Mark," said Patty, "you are always so complicated! Why can't you just play along? It would make her happy and it's such an odd thing to have a principle about."

"What? What has she said? What is it *now?*"

"Why did you say you wouldn't?"

"Wouldn't what?"

Graham Patten approached. He put his arm around Patty: one should always be seen to have one's arm around someone. He looked put out.

"Why did you change your mind, Mark?" he enquired.

"Look, I'm simply going home—I've absolutely no idea . . ."

"You didn't tell her you wouldn't be on the committee?"

"It wasn't discussed at all."

Graham, who had been cuddling and snuggling Patty, while she smilingly submitted, now let his arm drop—he had forgotten her. She quietly shook and trimmed herself back into shape, like a bird after an immersion, while he leaned forward and exclaimed dramatically:

"There does seem to be the most serious misunderstanding."

"There's nothing serious about it. I told you I'd sign the appeal and I will—my mother doesn't come into it."

The air became suspended on a moment of speculation. Patty and Graham exchanged the minutest of glances.

"But what is it?" said Mark wearily. "What? What can she possibly have got snarled up now?"

"If you're going back to London you can give me a lift," said Graham.

"No, we're going to drop in to some friends in Bone Hill."

"If it's the Mowbrays, do give them my love."

Mark went towards the car. Graham watched him. Patty not being near enough, he put his arm around Martha.

"I wonder if the Mowbrays would mind if I came too—I know her well, a lovely person."

Martha remained silent, so that he would understand Mark had been lying, and that he did not want Graham.

But at this stage in his life, Graham could not imagine being unwanted by anyone.

Another evening with him, possibly some of his friends, was imminent. Patty now tactfully went forward to Mark, who was already in the car, remarking: "I'll just get things cleared up with Mark, darling, and then . . ."

Tact was now all Patty's business. Officially she was the stage manager at the Royal Shilling. She spent all day and half the night smoothing the jostling orbits of a dozen budding stars, dealing with newspapers, dealing with Graham, the benevolent sun around whom people swung. The patience, the shrewdness she had learned during her long bad time now stood her in good stead. Success and appreciation had warmed her, prettied her, but underneath she was all competence. Graham had briefly had an affair with her, and now, watching her lean in at the car to talk to Mark, remembered he had heard she once had had an affair with Mark. Beside him was Martha, about whose relations with Mark people speculated.

Graham now amorously grazed about Martha's neck and ear, bending down to do it, for he was rather tall, while he put on the look of a young man envying an older man's success.

"Darling," he murmured, watching the car past Martha's forehead, "why do I never see you?"

This question had the stamp of the new style which was not yet christened "camp": it had not become self-conscious. Nor could it have, since the prevailing wind was all warm-heartedness and a tender concern for others. When someone murmured, Oh, you're so camp, it was not to pay homage to wit, or to outrageousness, a getting-away-with (as if, of the four aces with which one has just won the game the last has been slipped in from one's sleeve and everyone knows it but is too dazzled by dexterity to protest), but to a deliberate exposure of homosexuality in dress or voice which, with the political atmosphere as it was, could only be a variety of courageous protest.

Martha had to laugh; thus releasing them both from the embrace. For one thing, he had not left last night till after three. Rather, he had been thrown out crying: "But I hate going to bed early, I never do!" He had stayed, so he said, because of Phoebe's little girls: everyone was reading *Lolita* and he, like everyone, had been informed of a tendency which he claimed was his second most serious vice. Phoebe's little girls had read *Lolita* and were flattered. They had, however, gone off to bed at ten. He had rung early today to apologise for being rude: he said he had imagined he was being witty. The trouble was, the tone of this particular time was wrong for Graham, supposed to be one of its exemplars. He would be altogether more at home five, six years on; meanwhile, he was forced to see wit as the enemy of the heart—"an organ which has never been, alas, my strong point."

Over at the car, Mark was relaxed, smiling.

"She is marvellous," said Graham. "How does Patty do it? Everywhere she is, happy smiling faces ..."

338

She came over. "It's all right. Mark hadn't changed his mind at all. Margaret misunderstood."

"Oh good—in that case we can discuss it in the car." He hastened across to the car, while Patty and Martha, used to it, shrugged and submitted.

"I think Margaret is afraid John will have to go to prison," murmured Patty, in a warning. She meant: Calm Mark down, because Margaret is unreasonable.

"Is there a danger of it?"

"Yes. Kenny got six months last week."

They watched Graham get into the back seat. Mark, already scowling again, nodded at Martha to come.

She went in one direction, and Patty returned to the sunny lawn.

They drove back to London, nothing being said about the visit to the friends, Mowbrays or not, at Bone Hill.

Young Graham was being very active about the recent public drive against homosexuals. For this year it was not Communism, but homosexuality which was rotting the nation. The editors and the columnists roared and muttered and threatened and warned, week after week, and in this net, poor John Patten had been caught. He had been charged with soliciting in Green Park. A large committee was in existence, mostly as a result of Graham's efforts, and an appeal was in motion, and all kinds of public people involved. Mark had agreed last week to sign any appeal, but not to go on a committee, not his forte, he thought: it had not therefore crossed his mind that this could be what Margaret wanted him for today.

It now became apparent that Margaret felt that Mark must feel that there was no obligation for him to support *her* causes, when she had not supported his

She had returned to her guests with a murmur that Mark was always so difficult. They had understood this to mean he would not support the current "cause." This surprised no one. He was, they knew, reactionary.

For instance, when he was asked why he was not writing another play, after the success of *Rachel and Aaron*, he replied that he didn't have to, he had a private income. This was so much not the right note, that they were uncomfortable and had to cover up for him. Such a man might very well refuse to sign a petition on behalf of his stepfather.

Graham was not aware of Mark's moods. He was talking about poor Margaret, how upset she was: for one thing, she felt it was likely they would be asked (tactfully of course)

not to act as hosts to the expected Russians, even if John were not actually sent to prison. And she was expecting a houseful of Americans in a month's time, writers and poets.

He talked on, while Mark was silent, wondering if this was a retrospective reproach for previous curtailments of Margaret's social life. But on the whole it seemed not: Graham had forgotten, like everyone else.

And the "cause" was not at all why Graham was here, in the car: his life being once again at a turning point, he was coming to his uncle for advice.

His career in the film industry had not prospered long, but he felt his time had been well spent. A very great deal of good advice had been given by him to various rich but well-meaning men. If the fresh air now circulating through the other arts had not yet permeated British films, doubtless it soon would, and Graham Patten would deserve credit for it.

For a few months he had been at a loose end. Reviving, or making use of, his Oxford persona, he wrote a volume of essays called *Grey Nights* which were witty, urbane and erudite, but whose success made him uneasy; and meanwhile he employed his heart on the jazz scene, where he introduced a couple of American musicians and had an affair with an indigenous blues singer from Brixton.

Suddenly then, Hungary and Suez, in the five-starred year; though Suez had to claim him retrospectively, for he was in Budapest for the revolution. He had gone, as he later confessed, "on an impulse to experience the real thing." There he made some speeches "on behalf of the British Wellwisher," saw some people killed, and others let out of prison, and encountered other Englishmen, all from the universities, as romantic as he. These he found a distasteful mirror. Having watched one, very drunk, declaiming about world revolution from a barricade, while afterwards claiming that "he had been doing his bit for Balliol," he suffered a revulsion against amateurs. For some months he had travelled in East European countries and in Russia, mostly examining the theatre; and returned to London prepared to be a prophet of socialist realism, Brecht, contemporary humanism, and revisionism—the latter muted to the British scene. The thing was, others had done, were doing, the same thing, each believing himself to be a lone precursor. Half a dozen highly educated and influential young men with the tide behind them can do a great deal: he was one of the forces which had changed the stagnant landlocked theatre of the early fifties. But here was the point of his recurrent dilemma. What now? As he had said, was saying again: "I am not yet thirty, and I've already reached the top?"

It was no joke, for having compared himself to Max Beerbohm, and got every other conceivable side benefit from his situation, the fact remained, he had conquered London—what other peaks could there be? After that, it could only be all downhill.

Mark had suggested America: after all, it was at least three years since Graham had been there. Graham had returned to New York and was a great success. He had taken away jazz; he went back with Marxism, which had all the charm of novelty, for no one could remember hearing anything like it, their own Communists all having been silenced for years, either being in prison, or departed to take refuge in London, or dead from suicide, or in mental hospitals. In fact so far behind them was the age of Joe McCarthy, enormous numbers of people could not remember it, and were saying it never had happened. One thing was certain, no one would believe that it might happen again. As Graham said, bringing back the news of America's liberalism and love of freedom: "They are all such darling, kind, marvellous people—I tell you, Mark, I felt as safe there as I did when I went to Moscow."

But, having come back, what now? Keeping his had in, he arranged for a production of *The Tempest* which was, quite clearly, Shakespeare's message about the underprivileged: Caliban was an African, and the programme notes drew comparisons with South Africa. He did *Toad of Toad Hall*—a parable about the class society—for a theatre in Shaftesbury Avenue. Then—what? He needed a new field to conquer. Should it be television?

The problem was still unsolved when they reached Hammersmith Bridge, where a friend of Graham's lived who had promised to go on the committee. The ease with which this person had agreed reminded Graham of Mark's intransigence and he began pressuring Mark to join the committee. Mark said yes, provided he didn't have to go to committee meetings. Graham, new to politics, thought this was not workable.

Mark then developed his view, which was that on these occasions, when Britannia our mother is in a state of moral indignation, the less said the better.

"Well, really, you're not suggesting we should simply not do *anything*?"

"Not at all, you should do as much as possible, as quietly as possible. Because then it will all blow over—otherwise heads will roll, and scapegoats will have to be found."

"Blow over! The whole situation is disgraceful."

"I dare say. But when they're tired of homosexuality they'll start on something else, there's always got to be something."

Graham could not see this: there being no substitute for experience. He believed that if he argued long enough with Mark, Mark would be bound to change his mind, since he, Graham was obviously in the right, and Mark both pusillanimous and ill informed.

Still arguing, they arrived home to find Patty there: she had got a lift, and was waiting to see Mark and Graham.

The house seemed full of people of all ages: and music came from several sources. The kitchen and the drawing room being occupied, the four went into the empty dining room.

Patty was embarrassed: also, agitated.

These were public, or professional attributes: underneath she was angry, something quite different, because she had hoped to spend a pleasant evening at Margaret's, but had to come chasing into London to calm people down—as usual.

When she had arrived back among the guests with the news that Mark would sign the petition, and that Graham was to go into London with him, Margaret murmured, Well, that's all right.

She would have been happy to let it go, let things slide—but letting things slide was both her talent and her downfall: through not saying anything, allowing people to gather what they might, Mark was in a false position. She knew that, but could not quite see where it was her fault. She was in a false position too, most profoundly so, and any embarrassment Mark might be feeling was nothing to hers.

Discovering that her third, and she had hoped last, husband was, at least partially, homosexual, had caused her anguish—but apart from a dry word or two dropped to Patty, a great chum, she had not said much, save that "at my age, companionship is what counts." This was felt as a valuable lead by a great many women in need of one. But taking this stand was quite different from finding herself at the heart of a public battle on principle. She was annoyed with her stepson, but could not say so. Why did people always have to be on platforms, and making statements, and creating fusses? (Her attitude, in short, was rather like Mark's, only neither could see it.) She was desperately sorry for her

342

poor John, who had been away, staying with his aged mother, well out of the fuss and the limelight and the people who eddied around her, Margaret, so conscientiously on his side; but she did so wish everyone would find some other house to make a centre, or one of the centres, of protest. But she could not say so.

Now, she kept quiet while someone who had not realised that Mark Coldridge was Margaret Patten's son made some remarks about his living with two women, about heterosexuals being so much more immoral than homosexuals, etc., etc. This made her angry, and her head ached. For like many other people, while she was prepared to wish homosexuals every kind of happiness and success in their private pursuits, she wished this did not mean her supporting their claims to moral superiority. The same person went on to say that he was not surprised Mark Coldridge took this attitude; his novels showed him to be a natural reactionary; conservative, and indeed authoritarian.

At which Margaret snapped that was nonsense, Mark was a Communist "as she thought everyone knew."

No one knew; the new epoch had obliterated all others. The person who had spoken was enlightened in a whisper that he had been attacking her son; and her interjection was put down to natural annoyance.

After a silence, the subject was changed, and someone took Patty aside to say that Mark ought not to be associated with the committee, if he was a Communist—it would make things very tricky. In which case Patty said she ought not to be either, she was in the same position.

Embarrassment was now general. The atmosphere of the sunny afternoon was all darkened with annoyance, embarrassment and general doubt. Someone enquired—What was all this about anyway? Quite so, but it was too late to find out. The afternoon had gone wrong. Margaret made her headache public and guests began to leave.

Patty knew that these circles being as they are, feeding on gossip, talebearing and malice, Mark could expect a telephone call pretty soon, giving him an account of what had happened. In which case, tired of the whole business, he would probably back out. Patty knew what her job was: this was her job; what in fact she earned her large salary for.

She was going to be, as always, a lightning conductor, a kind of earth. Therefore did she stand in the dining room, privately angry, indeed, longing for bed and a nice read and

343

a glass of cold milk, but apparently full of public concern and feeling.

"It is too bad," said Graham, "I'm simply not going to stand for witch hunts of any kind. And if Mark has to stand down, I go too."

"Oh nonsense," said Mark, "for goodness sake have a sense of proportion."

The telephone rang. It was Margaret, wanting to tell Mark that he was not to believe "any stories about her"— no, she wouldn't go into details, but what he heard wouldn't be true, that was all.

She rang off. Mark said: "Look, three days ago, I told you, Graham, that I'd sign a petition. That's what I shall do. It's all perfectly simple."

"Oh, no really, it's too ..." Graham exclaimed and objected, while Patty did too, watching both to see how the matter balanced, and glancing at Martha from time to time so that Martha might add fuel, or damp it.

Patty knew that this kind of emotional blowup must run its course. Graham must use up an allowance of moral indignation about misdirected moral indignation, and Mark, a slow-burning stubborn man, must smother until Graham stopped, while Martha—"the silent sort, damn her!"— wouldn't be much help ... sometimes in the theatre, with a suitable female there, Patty could get such an incident over in a couple of minutes. For years Patty had been fulfilling this function without being conscious of what she did. Sometimes, knowing that outwardly she fizzed and exclaimed while inwardly she remained cool, she might have let out a self-parodying Jewish "Oi, oi, oi!" And when people had said she was hysterical, she had been humorously indignant: "What, me hysterical?" At some point, a mechanism had become clear to her: she could often direct it. But not with these two men, one so violent, so sentimental, one so slow to ignite.

Suddenly Martha put an end to it: she remarked, "In that case, if people are going to stand on principle, then I don't think Mark, or you or Margaret should be involved at all—you're all family and people working with you might be embarrassed ..." At which Graham exploded into a hundred expostulations about her absurdity—he was very rude. She then became silent; he, raging at a silent woman, could not stand it, and went charging at her, in what looked like an attack but turned into some effusive kisses: Oh God, Martha, I'm so terribly terribly *sorry*, I don't know *what* ...

It was over. Patty wondered, had Martha done it on purpose?

At any rate, she seemed to be employing tactics when she asked Graham to go into the kitchen to find out if Lynda wanted the table laid in here, and for how many, and asked Mark to see if Paul was all right.

The two women were left alone.

"God knows how you stand it," said Martha.

"It's the theatre, love, it's the theatre!"

"It's not the theatre—it's everything. However . . ."

Graham now passed the door, and put his head in to say that Lynda thought they'd eat in the kitchen.

Patty had pushed a chair back from the long formal table, and had sat, off guard a moment, smoking with her eyes shut. The room was hardly used, they all preferred the kitchen. Patty, a jolly fat child in her fashionable nursery dress, sat like a little girl in the heavy, grave, grown-up scene.

"Did you do all that on purpose?" asked Martha suddenly. "Did you?"

The little girl opened a pair of extraordinarily shrewd dark eyes, and winked at Martha. She shut them again. "Golly," said Martha. "I've just had a sort of—yes. *Of course.*"

"Of course," said Patty, flat. "But I tell you, it takes it out of one, it takes . . . do you think I could have a lie-down before supper—if you are asking me to supper. Please do. I couldn't face my lonely room tonight."

"What's happened to Eric?"

"Oh, you may ask."

In another mood, Patty would have discussed it: but the bare bones of her problem remained the same. She was too old for a "real marriage." Unless she wanted some old man, or an emotional cripple, she wouldn't get married at all; in the meantime she was on "the older woman roster—I suppose someone has to do it—it's a social function I suppose . . ." She had been making enquiries about adopting a child.

Martha sent her up to sleep in her room; and went to the living room.

There sat Graham deep in a big sofa, with the two girls on either side of him. He sat all held into himself, his two hands caught between his knees, chin lowered, eyes inflamed. Jill and Gwen, two fair, lustrous blue-eyed morsels were sitting by their witty uncle Graham, but gazing with passionate admiration at their cousin Francis, and his lovely

345

friend Nick Anderson, who had come with him from school. The two handsome boys, the lovely little girls, were engaged only with each other: outside their charmed circle, two Africans, Phoebe's friends, watched a London scene in polite curiosity, and Graham allowed it to be understood that he suffered torments of lust, for he might dandle, kiss and browse among the bosoms and cheeks of mature women as much as they liked, but here was his truth.

"Are you all right?" enquired Martha, looking at Graham, with every intention of mockery. And he raised his swollen eyes and muttered: "No, I'm not."

"Wouldn't you perhaps like to come and help me lay the table, Graham dear?"

"No."

"I take it you are staying to dinner?"

"Yes."

"I suppose Lynda knows?"

"Surely she must!"

Martha went to the kitchen, where Lynda was alone, cooking. She wore a dress, which meant that she intended to eat with them. She often cooked meals these days, but at the last moment escaped downstairs: many people upset her.

She looked much better. She had put on some weight. The battle of the drugs had not been entirely won, because she took sleeping pills sometimes, but then, as she said, so many people did. A year before she had cracked again, suddenly, over Mark's assumption that being better meant she was well—he had again suggested she could come back upstairs and be his wife. She had refused to go into a hospital, public or private, even though Dr. Lamb had promised she would not be given drugs: she did not trust him, she said. Privately she told Martha that also she did not trust herself: in an atmosphere where everyone took drugs, where one was expected to take them, she would. She could not stay in the basement, by herself, for she knew she was going to break things, and cry and scream. Paul was in the house now all the time; Francis was in and out from his new school; what was to be done? Suddenly everyone remembered Dorothy and talked about her—she was dead.

A suicide attempt had succeeded: they believed this had not been Dorothy's intention. Remembering Dorothy, always so kind when Lynda was "silly," Lynda got depressed, became worse. Martha looked about for a flat somewhere where Lynda could be silly in comfort. They found one, at enormous expense—Lynda found out how expensive it was, and began blaming herself for everything. A nurse went with Lynda to this flat, and rang up every evening to report on Mrs. Coldridge: a bit better today I think, no, on the whole not so well, I'm afraid ... Suddenly Lynda came home, asked them to dismiss the nurse and the flat, and announced she was all right. The nurse reported that she had been extremely quiet and well-behaved.

Quiet, trying very hard, Lynda had been ever since. The bad area of strain was—Lynda and Paul. Paul now hated Lynda shrilly and cruelly, which was one reason why she found it hard to come to meals. Lynda simply said that Paul was too much for her. She did not understand how badly he had been let down. She did not believe she was a person who had anything to give; she did not believe she had given Paul anything during that long long period when in fact she was his only friend. Withdrawing from him she could not be made to see that she was taking anything away.

When Francis came home for the holidays mother and son slowly built up a friendship. For they were like two very old friends who had been separated and were now allowed to be together. They were patient, tactful, considerate. For days, a week or so, a month, things would go well, then, suddenly, Lynda would be sitting stiffly, smiling too brightly, watching everything with a minute alertness, every gesture and smile and glance exposed overcarefully to everyone's inspection, while they felt their exposure to her; and then Francis would become very pale, and go off to his room. There, he cried. As he had done as a little boy, he cried now, and would descend, unashamed, to a meal with eyes that showed it. And Lynda, in her basement, cried.

Then, with the strain and the tension cried out, for both of them, they set themselves to try again.

In the two months since Mark had come back from Moscow, Paul had been—but words like "better" and "worse" seemed inapplicable. One of the experts consulted had said that the naughtier Paul was, the better: obedience, quietness, malleability, all these were bad. By this yardstick then, Paul was good, and Francis bad. Certainly Francis's extreme good behavior had always been upsetting—but could not this also be a form of self-protection, a guard behind which Francis quietly grew and prospered? But Francis's manner, his way of life, discouraged such questions, particularly when always and all the time there was Paul who took up so much time, so much emotional energy.

347

Judged by what he was demanding from the adults, he was much worse. He was abominable.

When Mark came back from Moscow he had for a time not mentioned the gramophone records—he felt ashamed, on his brother's behalf. Then Martha and he and Lynda sat trying to work out whether a present of gramophone records and a vague invitation to drop over to Moscow were better than nothing or the ultimate in cruelty. The discussion, the uncertainty, went on for some days. Whatever effect it all had on Paul remained doubtful, but for the three the incident highlit their condition at that time. Outside, everything was so jolly and easy and liberal, tides of happy warriors flowed in and out of the house, a friendly optimism was the atmosphere; yet this was a world in which they, at least, felt that it might very well be a better education to say: My dear Paul, you like everyone else are expendable, and you are lucky to get even a message from your father—after all, so many people's fathers are dead. And compared with nine-tenths of the world's population you have nothing whatsoever to complain about. . . . Instead, careful, insightful adults sat around, talking, planning, worrying about the balance and health of this tiny favoured few. Should one be thinking like this at all? Oh, very probably not. How was one to know? And, feeling themselves to be in an air, or on a wavelength, at any rate differently oriented to the world than as other people seemed to experience it, was it their responsibility to inflict this on Paul, or Francis? They should rather be protected? Even when one did not believe, not for one moment, that their future experience was likely to be protected, or anything but precarious and violent!

The records were put in brown paper, and concealed while they waited for Paul to ask a question—after all, he knew Mark had been in Moscow. But Paul said nothing.

At last Mark went up to Paul's room, where the television was now installed.

Paul had been watching a programme much too young for him, and had continued to watch it after he knew his uncle had come in.

"Paul, there's something I want to say . . ."

He had to repeat it, and then Paul turned off the programme.

"What is it?"

"I saw your father in Moscow."

Not a word from Paul. He stared at the blank television screen.

"He sent you these."

Mark put the records on a table, and Paul glanced at them, nodded, and turned on the television again.

But he had been playing the folksongs ever since.

The house throbbed with recorded emotion; until the others were forced to wonder if he was saying to them: This is what I feel.

He did not mention Mark's trip, or his father, or ask for any details of his father's new life.

His schoolwork, always erratic, plunged again, and there was a letter from his teacher.

When he first got to this new school, he allowed himself to be brilliant, for as long as it took to demonstrate that he could come first any time he liked. Then he lost interest. He continued to say that the moment he was legally able to leave school, he would.

Mark thought that he should be forced to stay, Lynda that he should be allowed to leave. Meanwhile, Martha fought him.

But he tried to avoid battles with Martha: he liked to fight with Lynda, who got upset, who might shout at him— and then he could feel ill treated.

Returning from any trip away from the house, Martha, Mark, would be met by Lynda's guilt—she had quarrelled with Paul again.

This afternoon she said: "Paul came down for a glass of milk." It sounded as if she were announcing crime.

"Was he rude again?"

"No. But I think I'll go downstairs for supper after all. I tell you, one of these days I'm going to hit him so hard . . ."

"Did he say anything about homework?"

"Oh Martha—who cares about homework! I never did any in my life!"

The kitchen was full of good warm smells. A cauldron of soup bubbles. A loaf of bread a yard long lay down the middle of the old table. Salad stood ready to mix. Mark often came in these days to say: This kitchen is like it used to be. . . . Though of course in those days they never ate in the kitchen. And Mark would stand, waiting, *not* looking at Lynda, to see if she would stay for the meal, re-create the family, sit at the end of the table, serve soup. And, *not* looking at Mark, so often she went away. But she cooked. She cooked well and carefully and enjoyed it.

"Did you say to Paul it didn't matter?"

"I always say to Paul it doesn't matter. That's what makes him angry."

"Yes, I know."

"But Martha, I don't know what it is—I simply want to—why do I dislike him so much now?"

Some months before, Lynda had been talking about an earlier time, when she had loved Paul, and Paul had spent so much time with her.

One afternoon there had been a violent quarrel between Dorothy and Lynda, with Paul there. Lynda and Paul had been in the bedroom, playing one of their fantastic games, words, music, silence, their images in the looking glasses, all going to make up some story no outsider could understand. Dorothy was shut out, as always, because she was too matter-of-fact, she spoiled it. This game had gone on too long, or she was in a bad mood, but she had called out through the door that Lynda was forgetting—she was nothing but a child.

Apparently, Lynda had said to one of Dr. Lamb's subsidiaries that if she was good for nothing else, she knew how to be with children. The doctor had said: "That's because you are a child yourself, you feel safe with children. They don't make any demands on you."

Lynda had argued that this was true, she knew it; but surely it was worth something? The doctor had suggested it was a form of regression, a way of refusing to grow up.

At any rate, for a time every descent of Paul to the cellar had called forth from Dorothy an attack on Lynda for being nothing-but-a-child.

She had never been able to feel easy and released with Paul after that—so she claimed now. She agreed she might be backdating a nearer emotion.

But in the evenings when Martha went down to visit, and Lynda talked about the children, she came back to this again and again—and stopped there. She fought with herself everywhere else but here, where it was as if there was a snarl or knot in her emotions. She hated Paul, and it was Dr. X's fault—she could not even remember the doctor's name.

"Martha, do you know what I think? You and Mark had better be careful, I swear one of these days you'll come back and find Paul and I have killed each other . . ." She lowered her voice, though her face was lit with vicious enjoyment, glancing at the half-open door, where, as everyone knew, Paul so often stood to eavesdrop. "And there's something else. I'd *love* it—and so would he. I'd like to kill him slowly, really nastily, you know. I never understood torture before, until Paul said to me, Lynda, you'd like to torture me, wouldn't you? And of course, he is right. I'd enjoy every bit. There's something about that sort of glossy soiled look he's got—you know, as if he had boils on his pretty bum, and he uses the pus to grease his hair? I'd like to suffocate him slowly with a pillow and watch him writhe, or throttle him, or ... And he feels exactly the same about me." In the middle of this, which she delivered fast, in a low smiling bright-eyed monologue, she went across to the door, quite unconsciously, and closed it, in case someone might hear— she was protecting them, anyone, probably Paul, from herself. "And do you know why? Oh it's all quite obvious when you come to think of it, it's because he's so damned unhappy. He's such a poor sick creature, crippled—like me. Nobody can stand us. No one. That's the truth, I tell you— what people really want to do is to blot us all out—the healthy would like to just take us all and ... there are so many of us, they can't ... sweep us all up and into the gas ovens, yes ..."

"Interesting when we come to define who is healthy," said Martha in a flat, almost bored voice, which was the right voice to use when Lynda took off like this. So she had learned.

Lynda came back to herself, and stood, rather flushed, breathing fast. "Well," she said, "but for all that, there's something in it, isn't there? Are you coming down to talk after supper?"

"If everyone goes off in time."

"Poor Martha," said Lynda with a vague callousness, and her marvellous gay smile. "But I know what you are thinking. You were thinking you ought to see that Graham didn't get up to mischief with Jill and Gwen. Well, why shouldn't he? Why shouldn't they all? And why shouldn't I torture Paul to death if ... why not ..."

She stopped as Francis came in with his friend Nick.

"Are you having supper with us, Lynda?" asked Francis.

"No—I don't think—not tonight ... good night, dear ..." She escaped. Francis, disappointed, made himself recover from it.

"I'm going to see Paul," said Martha. "Will you make sure there are enough places for everybody and tell them ..."

"I tell you something, Martha, if Paul's rude to Nicky again I'm going to beat him up."

"After me," said Nicky pleasantly.

He was a tall, light, graceful, English-looking boy, rather older than Francis, about seventeen. Never had anyone seen him angry, out of face, anything but calmly polite. However, as he talked of Paul his eyes narrowed in a quick relish of hate.

"Oh dear," said Martha, "everyone wants to beat up Paul this evening . . . Half an hour Francis, and we'll eat."

She went up the stairs, through a house separated with the people who inhabited it, into areas or climates, each with its own feel, or sense of individuality: Mark's rooms, unmistakable, even with one's eyes shut, even with sound shut off, because of their atmosphere of something closed in, enduring, stubborn; Francis's room, which was kept as it had been for years—a boy's room, with cricket bats and butterflies in cases; Martha's room, inside the sycamore's microclimate which acted like a roomstat, adjusting from outside the house rather than in, setting the flow of air, moisture, heat, light; then Paul's area—but even the flight of stairs that approached Paul's floor emanated electric storm, for here not even silence, or sleep, could be the quiet of peace. Even from the street, raising one's eyes, one expected that the apertures of the third floor would shoot out a baleful blue ray, was surprised to see a pair of neat and pretty windows, in the pattern of windows that opened the tall narrow house to the light.

On the flight that approached Paul's room, one waited a moment, took in breath and balanced . . . what an extraordinary business it is, being a middle-aged person in a family; like being a kind of special instrument sensitised to mood and need and state. For, approaching Paul, one needed this degree of attention; approaching Francis, that one; and for Lynda and for Mark, quite different switches or gauges set themselves going, but automatically. Not always automatically: on Paul's stairs one paused to take in breath and balance knowing exactly why one did it.

And, standing here, feeling herself (or rather, the surface of herself) to be a mass of fragments, or facets, or bits of mirror reflecting qualities embodied in other people, she looked at the ascending stairs, much narrower and steeper here than lower in the house, and at the edges of each stair, and noted that the carpet needed renewing. But it was not yet five years old . . . and the banisters of the stairs had had a bad-quality varnish put on, which had gone thick and gluey, and needed to be scraped off and renewed. And the paint of the walls had streaked. But this part of the house had been redecorated three years before.

All the house was like this, nothing obviously breaking or peeling, but everywhere was shoddiness and shabbiness, and—this was the point—there seemed to be no centre in the house, nothing to hold it together (as there had been once when it was a real family house?). It was all a mass of small separate things, surfaces, shapes, all needing different attention, different kinds of repair. This was the condition of being a middle-aged person, deputy in the centre of a house, the person who runs things, keeps things going, conducts a holding operation. It is a perpetual battle with details. Yet the house had been done up twice, thoroughly, since Martha had come into it—but still nothing was right, everything second-rate and shoddy. This was the real truth of what went on not only here but everywhere: everything declined and frayed and came to pieces in one's hands ... a mass of fragments, like a smashed mirror. She opened the door on a television din. Men fought all over the screen and guns blasted her ears. Paul saw her and turned the machine at once over to a small child's programme. He sat down again in his chair, with his back to her. He sulked, vividly and as it were professionally. He wore kingfisher colours, and his room, in extreme disorder, with small areas where objects and articles were displayed precisely, was all violent colour. Examined, the bones or frame of the room were plain, down-to-earth chairs, beds, cupboards. But the things he collected were always shining and brilliant. And he collected all the time, from school, from markets, in barter with friends—he seldom came home without some trinket or cushion or bit of silk.

"Paul, have you done your homework?"

"No, and I'm not going to."

This exchange, opening moves in a well-understood game, enabled them now to relax. Martha sat down. Paul gave her a look hostile only for form's sake. He leaned forward to turn up the sound.

The party hostess's voice, which is considered suitable for small children on television and on radio, interpreted the movements of some endearing little puppet animals.

"You're missing your Western," said Martha.

His sour smile, most unwilling, said: You score one! to Martha, and also: I hate you!

"Turn that thing off, then, I'm talking to you."

He pouted, then switched it off. He sighed exaggeratedly,

turned up his eyes to heaven, then bundled himself into a resigned heap, like a sad bird in his dark blue trousers and scarlet sweater. He stared at the floor, waiting.

In dealing with Paul, Martha had discovered, created rather, a forceful authoritarian who at first had dismayed, and now merely surprised her. The thing was, she did not believe in it—did not like this way of dealing with children, and could never believe that Paul did not see through her when she made use of this particular personality. Ordered, instructed, told, he would wriggle and sulk, but he obeyed—or often did, as if the game was real. One of the psychiatrists, now numerous, consulted about Paul, had said he needed authority. Mark had said: Stuff and nonsense! Which meant he did not choose to try it. Martha, at her wit's end with Paul, had attempted "authority," as if putting on a new coat. But she always felt as if she were acting in a charade, even when it worked. Which it did, if unpredictably.

There sat Paul, acting a long-suffering resentment. And there sat Martha, acting authority. She wanted to giggle. Catching his eye, she was unable to prevent a smile; he smiled back, a swift, beautiful amused smile, instantly suppressed. For it was outside the rules of this particular game.

Now Martha could either go on, risking a real horns-locked battle, or try coaxing, and teasing.

She was tired. She would have liked very much to go down to her room, lock the door and spend the evening alone. But being alone these days, it was a luxury, a boon, half an hour or an hour stolen where she could. The evening stretched in front of her: the long supper, where so many warring personalities had to be coaxed and balanced, and shielded; and then afterwards, with possibly Phoebe's girls and young Nicky staying the night—and then Lynda wanted to talk . . . and then, and then . . .

How very extraordinary it was, this being middle-aged, being the person who ran and managed and kept going . . . it was as if more than ever one was forced back into that place in oneself where one watched; whereas all around the silent watcher were a series of defences, or subsidiary creatures, on guard, always working, engaged with—and this was the point—earlier versions of oneself, for being with the young meant all the time reviving in oneself that scene, that mood, that state of being, since they never said anything one hadn't said oneself, or been oneself.

Except for Paul; because Martha could not remember this ever so dramatic creature, either in herself, or in people she had known ... there had been Stella of course. But she had been a young married woman. And then, of course, Paul's mother Sally-Sarah. But Martha had not herself been, as far as she could remember, anything like Paul; whereas nothing Francis could say, or Jill or Gwen, was a surprise to her.

"Well," said Paul, magnanimous, like a host, "I switched off the programme, didn't I?"

Martha settled for combat.

"Well, good. Now you can do your homework."

"I don't think I feel like it."

Now Paul most luxuriously stretched and yawned, reaching out two arms behind his head, and then bringing the back of one hand in a graceful movement against his mouth. Over the hand, black eyes drooped at Martha in a languor appropriate to not feeling like it. Almost, she applauded.

"There's half an hour before supper."

"You can't make me do homework."

"No, I can't. But I can see you don't eat any supper."

"I don't want any supper. I drank some milk."

"Oh well then— in that case, milk is all you will get."

Now Martha waited, amazed at the sheer nonsense of it all. If Paul intended to, he could descend the stairs while they all ate supper and he knew, as she did, that of course she would not make a scene in front of the others, and he could descend at any time when people were not in the kitchen, to take what he wanted from the refrigerator.

This was merely a ritual.

Silence. He swivelled himself away from her, so that she could observe him sitting chin on hand, staring into a fateful distance.

Then he suddenly jumped up and said: "O.K. For half an hour then."

He departed to his bedroom across the landing where, as Martha knew, he would probably do no homework, but might read. So what had been achieved in this bit of farce? Nothing?

She sat looking at the blank television screen. As far as she was concerned, the scene they had just played out was no more real than what they could see on that screen by turning on a switch.

She turned it on loudly: anyone wanting to know, Where is Martha, could be told: She's watching the news.

The middle-aged scheme, fight, negotiate for these small ten-minute intervals of privacy. She retreated from the machine, seeing its wired, knobbed, buttoned presence as an

355

alien being in this room which was eighteenth-century in spirit. Except of course for what Paul brought to it: but one could dispose of the glass of colour Paul had brought here by walking through from end to end, scooping up objects with both hands and simply depositing them out of the door— how very odd that was. Yet the room shouted Paul, Paul, Paul. Personality: Paul's personality, a dramatic sulk, a droop of great eyes, and a sheen over his rooms like light on a bird's wing. With Paul's personality one fought. Ridiculous battles, as far as she was concerned.

When a small baby looked straight at you, for the first time, its eyes having thrown off its milk-glaze, you looked into eyes that would stay the same for as long as it lived. Then the eyes might belong to an infant in a screaming tantrum, a hoyden, an obedient child, a day-dreaming pubescent, someone moonstruck by love—the point was, there was no cheating, no going around, the small baby, and the rest. Oneself, or Paul, had to be, for as long as it was necessary, screaming baby, sulking adolescent, then middle-aged woman, whose eighteen hours a day were filled with a million details, fragments, reflected off the faceted mirror that was one's personality, that responded all the time every second, to these past selves, past voices, temporary visitors. And it was not so silly, not so absurd after all, to insist on the right to feel, while one played these ridiculous games, Do your homework, Remember Lynda's ill, Be kind to Paul; that all the time one communicated with something else, that person who looked steadily, always the same, from eyes only temporarily glazed over with anger, sorrow, sulk ... Because, once the necessary allowance of sulk, or sorrow, or pain had been dealt out, then the reward was that in fact one did speak to the permanent person in Paul, or Francis, or anybody else.

If she didn't believe that, then it would not be possible for her to stay here, in this house, where the two problematical people Francis and Paul grew, partly under her care, partly her responsibility. For the rest of their experience, what life had dealt them, was so off-centre that there was no resting on normality, as ordinary people, families, could. (What ordinary families, people?)

Stripped: they were being stripped. They *had* been stripped, by their births, of everything an ordinary child (who, where?) could hold on to.

The conversations that went on—mostly implicit with Francis, candid, and indeed shocking, with Paul—were in themselves like a stage of growth that everyone had to go through (childhood, pubescence, etc.), because they had so much of the quality of unreality although, probably *because,* they dealt with the basics of morality.

With Paul above all one was made naked and disarmed, not only because of his history, but because, quite simply, he had no sense of right and wrong. When one had finished with the teachers and the headmasters and the psychiatrists, and all their various prescriptions, and descriptions, it was extremely simple: a moral sense had been left out of this make-up.

His extraordinary intelligence enabled him to pick up, very fast, like a monkey, what other people expected of one.

"I was stealing love, that's all," he had, not so long ago, said airily; and still might say.

But what gave it all its odd ring, its upsetting quality, was that it became a sort of dogma because it was something he had picked up, out of the air.

If a child stole, a child stole love, so he had read, or heard, or it was in the air of his old school, and now he would say it as other people might say, "Sunday is the seventh day of the week."

"I don't know who I am, you see, so I steal things which are a symbol of what I want to be."

And he would look almost hopefully, certainly puzzled, at Mark or Martha or whoever was around, to see if they agreed, if this was an acceptable formula.

Or: "I don't know who I am, and therefore I am always trying to define my boundaries?"

Behind all this, the reality: a sullen, angry bewilderment that his best, his brightest, was not accepted, not loved and appreciated. For his real skill, and his talents, went into—stealing, one form or another of it. At the new school for two years he hadn't staged any big coup or deal but everyone knew that he continually—no, not pilfered, too niggling a word, for Paul—but organised small thefts. He would not stoop to an act of kleptomania: he had been very indignant when someone had said he was a kleptomaniac, for he was perfectly in control of what he did, he said. But he would arrange for a half a dozen boys to swoop through a store and emerge with a hundred objects chosen beforehand, by Paul, with skilled care for their easy saleability. All the adults watched and waited, praying that he would not go too far, not be impelled over the edge into expulsion or disgrace before he became fifteen (in a couple of months now) and could legally leave school.

"Why don't you steal, Martha?"

"Because I'd get caught."

"That's because you'd do it so you had to get caught."

"Possibly."

"Yes. You could steal so you didn't get caught."

"Why should I?"

"Supposing you were starving, and you didn't have money, would you then?"

"I don't know. Probably."

"But I want you to think—you're just wriggling out of it."

"All right. But probably I'd get a job."

"Suppose you couldn't."

"Then I'd steal."

"Would you feel guilty?"

"Now listen to me, Paul, we've done this before—if you want me to say that Marks and Spencer or Selfridges aren't going to miss even a hundred pounds of goods, I'll say it. That isn't the point. The point is, I'd feel guilty. I've been brought up like that. I'm not interested in the morality of it. And you don't feel guilty. So what? But it doesn't matter how you feel or I feel, if we steal, we'll get put into prison."

"Not if you aren't caught."

"Most people are caught."

"No, Martha ..." And now he would lean forward, earnest, focussed on his point, almost absurdly dramatic in his intensity, because one could see that concentrated here was the energy of much thinking, brooding, resentment. He had to have an answer. "I want you to answer truthfully. Do you think it's wrong to steal?"

"It depends on who you steal from."

His face clenched, darkened, his fists clenched—he needed some moral statement from Martha, some final right or wrong. The game, the rules of bringing up children, demanded: Yes, that's right, no that's wrong.

She couldn't do it.

"You must know, Martha. Either it's right or it's wrong."

"I don't think it's either right or wrong at all. It depends entirely on the circumstances. Everything always depends on the circumstances."

Bitter eyes followed her—betrayed.

"Why don't you go and ask someone who'll give you a black and a white, if a black and a white is what you want? You know what I'll say!"

358

A flush, then a conscious look, then a slow smile, like a counter in the game he played, You're up one or I'm up one: "You're bringing me up, though, aren't you?"

"Partly."

"So if I turn out badly, it's your fault."

Nonsense. Oh, if that's what you want—welfare workers and psychiatrists and prison officers, they'll say, poor Paul, he's had a hard life, poor poor Paul. But I'm not going to say it. *And you won't say it either . . .*"

At which point there came a brief flash of what made it all worthwhile—only for a flash, a moment, before the other game went on, when her eyes met his eyes, in seriousness, and in responsibility, and some sort of real truth was communicated and shared.

"Oh all right then," he pouted, sulked, slipped away. "But if I ever do get into trouble, then I'm glad I can fall back on that. Poor Paul, poor Paul, poor Paul, poor Paul . . ."

"If you want to be sloppy—and anyway there isn't anything so very special any longer about poor Paul. Because so many people are having it bad, they are having it worse all the time, and I can imagine a situation when you produce your trump card, poor Paul, mummy dead, father vamoosed to the Communists, brought up by mad uncle and his purported mistress, and everyone will just look at you, and be ever so tactful—because they'd had it worse. The Emperor Paul will have no clothes . . ."

"All right then, Martha, then if that's true but I'm not admitting it, then why should one try to be good, or kind, or anything . . ."

"Because you can ask that question—that's why."

"Well I'm not going to be!"

"That's your funeral."

The television set, its back to her, emitted noises of human beings in violent conflict. This machine was the real educator of the children of the nation. Francis, so much at school, watched it very little. Paul watched it four or five hours a day. Both had gone through phases with regard to it, the most interesting being this one: they had overheard, or been told, or had read, at any rate absorbed, the idea that they, "the inheritors of our future," were being fed a view of the world, life, that was all killing and violence. Both had used this idea to attack the adult world: self-consciously on stage, they had seen themselves as corrupt from birth. The adults, agreeing with them wholeheartedly and at once, had gone on to claim the same condition for themselves. Francis had

359

reacted by thinking about it: the process had taken him a step further into responsibility. Paul, younger than Francis, was still shrilly on a stage full of murder, arson and ugly sex. It seemed quite likely that he might stay there for the rest of his life. After all, a good many people did. . . . It was time to go down to supper. She was going to descend down the house, calling Paul, Patty, Mark, Graham, Jill, Gwen, etc., etc., in a calm competent voice, the voice of the middle-aged woman who has every string in her hands. She had become that person who once she hated and feared more than any other—the matron. Well, what alternative was there? But now she was there, in that place (but luckily one never stayed in any stage long, these caravanserais were only for limited visits, she could understand the source of that uneasiness. It was that thinking nine-tenths of one's time about other people, one acquired an insight into them that appalled even oneself. Power. Putting herself back fifteen years into Mrs. Van der Bylt's drawing-room, she was both the person who sat watching Mrs. Van, half amused, half wary, wholly protective of her own privacy while those small alert greyish-blue eyes watched and understood, and Mrs. Van, who looked at Martha and knew, She will do this, She might do this, If I do this then she will be saved from, or: If she burns her fingers, here, then, *tant pis*, she'll learn . . . Intolerable!

Martha called: "Paul! Supper!" She descended, knowing he would not reply; but would arrive fifteen minutes late for the meal, having made his point. Where the radiator for the central heating had been replaced last winter, the plaster used for easing the pipes into the wall had fallen out. She made a note, like a general putting a pin in a map, "wall behind radiator on Paul's staircase," and went past her own room, with a loud knock and a call: "Patty, supper!" A loud groan, humorous, answered her: "Oh my God, do I have to wake up? Never!" But Patty would be at the table, washed, bright, ready, in five minutes. "Mark, Graham, Francis . . . Lynda, do you want to change your mind . . ."

In the kitchen Francis was laying extra places. Phoebe had come in, with the colleagues. Francis was alight with pleasure. He adored people dropping in, people around, visitors, all the atmosphere of casual busy family life. And he adored it with the protective disbelief of a lover who is not loved—only now were Martha, Mark, understanding what Francis had suffered during the bad time, when his father was under a cloud, and he had had no friends. For that had been the

360

truth. One understood it, seeing him now, so delighted at—being normal. But for him it would never be normal. Friendship was a boon, a gift, something to be treasured, like love.

Looking at Francis now, one thought of love. He was sixteen. He had shot up into his adolescent bloom. He was still like Mark. Martha, who had loved Mark, looked at Francis and knew him: hiding the knowledge. He was a tallish brown boy, with an open rather flat face, and his father's brown eyes. He was also all Lynda, but this did not seem to be of the flesh. Lynda flickered and glimmered in her son in a glance, or a smile. Francis, sixteen years old and in the midst of adolescent self-garnering, all self and assertion, was at the same time never less himself. His parents flowed in and out of him, his flesh was incandescent, and Martha and Patty confided how well they understood that men loved boys—for did any girl, ever, have this moment of perversely beautiful flowering? The point was, its mortality; it was like looking at a crocus, perfect for a day; and all Francis's flesh which, before this moment and after it, must be solid, sensible, indeed, serviceable, was as wildly vulnerable as flowerflesh. And it was not as women that Martha, Patty, watched this creature, and could have wept, or worshipped—no; in them old males stirred and remembered, both fearing and wishing to pay homage. Not to Francis. Even when he was putting knives and forks on a table cloth, and setting plates, he was not Francis. He was so beautiful that Martha's throat started to ache. She sat herself quietly down and watched him: it would all be gone in six months. Meanwhile he was so happy in being ordinary, in being normal, in knowing that in five minutes friends and family would come in and they would all eat a long family dinner.

In came Phoebe's daughters. They were beautiful too. Fair, blue-eyed, pink-cheeked, charming, but there was no wild gleam in them. They were fourteen, fifteen, just taking shape, "setting" like jellies. Both looked at Francis and sighed for him. Not at all as Martha might, or Patty: pretty girls saw a handsome boy. To see the rest one had to be a conspirator with time. And when Nicky came in, who had passed through his poetic time and was ordinary again, the girls divided their attention between Nicky and Francis. These four sat at the foot of the table, in an enclave of youth. Not only Francis was stimulated by this family evening: Jill and Gwen found normality, or this approximation to it, a drug which made their eyes bright and their cheeks pink with happiness. For Phoebe and Arthur had also been suddenly transformed from vile criminals into admirable citizens, and their names, as often in the papers as they had been during the bad times, suggested a brand of heroic common sense. These children, blossoming, confessed by their happiness how very unhappy they had been, and had never confessed to being.

In came Phoebe with two Africans and a man from one of the committees. He was Jim Troyes, a middle-aged trade-unionist from Bradford. He admired Phoebe. The girls' attitude towards him said they were jealous of him. They suspected him, probably, of being her lover, but so far they were so happy to admire their mother that the only sign of it was the number of times they said they liked Jim.

When Graham came in, he looked to see if he could sit between the girls and continue his crucifixion, but there was no place for him. He sat between Phoebe, whom he vociferously admired, and Patty; who would spend the rest of the meal handling him, without his knowing it. Mark took the head of the table. Now everyone was there. Except Paul. A single chair stood speakingly empty. As Martha began serving soup, Paul appeared, oblivious of everyone, walked to this chair, sat in it, was alone in the midst of a multitude. People (unless something was done) would continuously examine him but without knowing that they did, while tension built up. He would suddenly assert himself, and there would be an explosion of some kind, which would enable him to make a dramatic exit.

Martha signalled to Mark. He made a grimace, and began, like a sheepdog isolating sheep from a flock, conversation which in a moment must include Paul and as it were defuse him.

It was a question of enabling Paul to appear a splendidly isolationist individual before he was impelled to do it for himself. As it happened the opportunity came fast. Soon everyone was talking about the demonstration that afternoon about Central Africa, and Mark asked Paul if he had been on it with the others. Paul said shrilly that he found demonstrations childish; the other young ones protested and criticised him. He maintained his position, was very rude. At last he subsided, and they were all able to get on with their food.

It would be a long meal if for no other reason than that Phoebe was here and able to answer questions about half a dozen subjects that interested them all. It was very pleasant to see her come into her own, after so many years in the shadow. Her tight face had softened: she was, after all, a good-looking woman. Jim Troyes sitting opposite her certainly thought so: he watched her and smiled with affection and admiration. Her pretty daughters were so pleased to be her daughters, and when the conversation lagged, pleaded ignorance on this or that subject, so that Phoebe might continue to appear as the one person present who always had every fact and figure at her fingertips, from the probable organisation of the next Aldermaston March, to what was now happening in peaceful and independent Kenya. The two Africans, who had been demonstrating that afternoon with the young ones, joked that "like all Phoebe's friends" they had just finished their obligatory terms of imprisonment for sedition and this was a good sign for their own independence. They invited Phoebe to visit when this event took place: when "we get our freedom." They were talking about freedom with a simplicity of approach which reminded the white people of the complications of their own attitudes: the subject of freedom was quickly dropped in the interests of general good feeling.

About now there were, one after another, three telephone calls, one from Margaret, who was in a condition of anxious tears, because a journalist had rung her up to find out why her son had refused to go on "her" committee; and two from journalists wanting to know if Mark would make a statement about why he was against reforming the law on homosexuality. He dealt with all the calls from another room, but he was annoyed, and this showed.

Graham became vociferous about the injustice of locking men up for their natural instincts, etc., and the Africans needed to be told why this cause was as important as others—for instance, seeing that colour prejudice was abolished in Britain.

But while certain political attitudes were taken for granted around this table, and the several thousand like it, others had the power to irritate or alarm. Attitudes about South Africa, and Central Africa, which ten years ago were held only by a small handful of people mostly on the left, were now taken for granted among a large enough number of people to merit the words "well-informed opinion holds that," but to say that colour prejudice here was a serious problem made everyone look embarrassed. These poor fellows were bound to be oversensitive, politely smiling faces said. Graham tried to change the subject, to introduce what he was interested in that evening, but Phoebe continued to listen while the two Africans politely tried to convince the young people that race prejudice in Britain was "nearly as bad" as in Africa. Francis said this couldn't be true because he had a coloured friend at school and everyone liked him. Phoebe said she thought there was something in what Matthew and Freddie said but ... Again Graham tried to catch her attention but in order to save bad feeling, Jim Troyes began talking about the press attitude towards homosexuals. He had been absolutely against homosexuals and approved of the press, until he had encountered Phoebe and her friends and discovered he was reactionary. Phoebe and Jim and Graham discussed Graham's committee; while Mark began to talk with Paul—he had been feeling ignored and showed signs of some kind of tantrum or demonstration. Patty explained to Jill and to Gwen how to cook a dish of beef without using any liquid. Jill and Gwen suddenly complained loudly that they knew nothing about cooking, their mother never had time to teach them. People were reminded how precarious was the peace between mother and daughters; that Phoebe found them difficult, and they found her unsympathetic. Phoebe broke off the discussion to listen, and then said she often cooked that particular dish, she didn't know why Jill and Gwen had to talk like deprived orphans. She was really annoyed.

"Yes, but you don't teach us, do you?" said Jill.

In order to prevent a quarrel, Patty began to talk about another recipe, about food, about marketing. In a moment the tableful of people was plunged into gourmandise—for at this particular time it was not possible for anyone to be uninterested in food and cooking, so far had this pendulum swung. Soon, the silence of their two guests from Africa who were listening to talk which (as the white people heard it as it were through their ears) suddenly sounded callous and greedy, and caused Phoebe to say that they mustn't think they thought of nothing but their stomachs in this country. Smiling politely, Matthew said that everywhere they went people talked about food. He wished that his own people were anywhere within sight of such standards.

For the third time the Africans had lowered the temperature of this meal, or seminar.

A safe subject was needed. There was only one safe subject and that was "the bomb," or the Aldermaston March, and now at last Graham was happy because he was wanting to get Phoebe onto the television to talk about this phenomenon.

The trouble was, although the first march had taken place only a few months before, the true facts of the situation had

364

already become absorbed into myth (even faster than public events usually do) and now it seemed like a kind of phoenix which had risen of its own accord out of nothing at all. It was this aspect which interested Graham, but as he approached it not only Phoebe but Patty politely refused to meet him there.

The fact was that for ten years, from the end of the last war, Phoebe from one political angle, and people like her, Patty from another, and people like her, had organised demonstrations, appeals, committees, etc., etc., about peace. They were Communist-oriented, or Labour-oriented; pacifist, liberal, independent; supported by this country or that, this bloc or that; they went doggedly on in atmospheres of suspicion, dislike and hostility in this country, and in America people lost their passports, went to prison, or were variously threatened. If Russia organised some kind of peace conference, then our government was likely to refuse visas for incoming delegates; if an organisation non-Communist organised one, the Russians would issue orders to all their satellites to conform with them in boycotting it. All this had gone on, ad nauseam: for years, people had been struggling to get "peace"(one item on a long agenda of good causes) away from an atmosphere where nothing would work or succeed or do anything but create bad feeling. And it went without saying that "the youth," Graham among them, had regarded all such activity as absurd in the extreme. When eight hundred people had marched out of Trafalgar Square on the Good Friday, it was no more than what had been happening for years under one auspice or other—Patty's, Phoebe's, what both stood for. Nothing more was expected by the organisers of this march than that, as usual, one hundred, or five hundred, or a thousand people would turn up, most of them known to one another, and disperse afterwards, while the newspapers commented sourly, if at all, and most of the inhabitants of these islands would know nothing whatsoever about it. Yet by the end of that particular Easter weekend several thousand people had been marching under the black-and-white banners, most of them young, and newspapers and television commented lengthily, and no one could have been more surprised than the organisers.

Why? What had happened? No one knew.

And this, the most interesting of the possible questions, had been allowed to slip away, partly in the delighted surprise of finding support where there had been none; partly because, one good cause exciting another, suddenly anyone with any sort of political experience was so much in demand and so very busy. It was now hard to imagine a climate where young people did not go off most weekends to demonstrate about this and that—yesterday Francis, Nick, Gwen and Jill had been marching for peace; today they had demonstrated for Africa. And practically everyone they met had been on that march which had made so many people brothers.

But. Now Graham wanted to do an hour-long programme called "Peace the Phoenix." For some reason both Phoebe and Patty got tetchy and kept relapsing into silences while they could be imagined counting ten. Graham went on, pressing them both. If they perhaps would write a programme together. Here Martha began laughing, Patty giggled, and Phoebe smiled sourly.

Jimmy Troyes said: "Ah, yes well, that would be quite a collaboration."

I really have no idea why you are being so absolutely absurd," stated Graham. And turned to Mark.

Mark's attitude was that when any "cause" at all has become safe, let alone popular, then that's when it can be counted as lost—what was happening in South Africa and in Rhodesia proved his point.

Graham said he was impossibly negative.

Mark had not gone on that march at first: he was not by nature a demonstrator. On the fourth day, as the columns of people neared Aldermaston, Phoebe had arrived in Radlett Street to demand Mark's presence—the thing was full of writers, artists, actors; "V.I.P.'s" as she put it, like the organiser she was, and thereby nearly put off for ever Mark's agreement to be there.

He said that there was "evidence for the belief" that the only guarantee for peace was that every country should be equipped with bombs of exactly equal power and capacity. It was in this rather inadequate sentence that there vanished into oblivion his brother's probable stand—the probable reason for his disgrace and his exile. Phoebe had forgotten that Mark might not look at the problem quite as she did, for she said: "Oh really, Mark, you can't possibly believe that!"

"Why not?"

"But it's such a negative way of looking at things!"

"Well then, I'd better give in—when one hears that word, it's time to put reason into the attic for the duration."

"Well, what do you believe?"

366

"Believe, believe? Why should I believe one thing rather than another?"

"What are you doing with those maps in the study then?"

"Those are facts. There is one basic fact: that there are more and more and more, and bigger and nastier bombs everywhere, all the time, more and nastier weapons. If you think a few thousand people marching back and forth over the countryside is going to change that—then good luck to you."

"If you won't come, can we send a photographer to take pictures of your study?"

"You're welcome, of course. How many people do you think will ever see them? How many people do you suppose will take any notice if they do see them?"

Martha and Mark had watched the early television reports of the march. Whatever else television was, it made it harder for "them" (in their aspect of concealers and distorters) to "get away with anything." It seemed that of television one was going to have to say what one said of the newspapers: it was the price one had to pay for democracy.

On the fourth day, right at the end, Mark had driven out to join the march. He was dressed in a formal suit, and carried a rolled-up umbrella. He could not stand sloppy clothes, could not bear masses of people marching under banners, hated slogan-chanting and police-baiting. However, there seemed no help for it. This march seemed yet another occasion for "defending the bad against the worse." Asked by a journalist why he was marching, he said it was because he believed in democracy; a reply regarded as so irrelevant that the journalist went on to somebody prepared to say something quotable.

There was nothing he could say that would not have been regarded as "negative."

He did not believe that this, or indeed anything, would halt the manufacture of weapons for war: too many people made money out of it, or wanted war. He did not believe that any government cared a damn about popular opinion, except insofar as it could be manoeuvred. He believed that within one decade, or two, or three, there would be some kind of war. He was entirely under false pretences on this march—until he began talking to others of his own generation, and found out how many agreed with him. It was better to be protesting at one's fate than not, many felt; and it was pleasant to see thousands of young people once more prepared to consider the conduct of the world their concern.

As a result of having been observed among those columns of people, and of being the relative of Francis, Gwen and Jill, Mark was considered "one of us," a member of the new progressive London. He meant well; his heart was in the right place; and so on; though if one didn't know him of course one had to believe him a reactionary.

Graham spent the rest of the meal defining Mark's exact degree of reaction: Stendhal, he thought, was nearest; or perhaps Alexander Blok?

Mark said he had never read Alexander Blok.

The two Africans confessed they had never read either. To study law was more useful that to study literature when one lacked freedom. The cycle had come around, and to forestall some more definitions of freedom, Patty pointed out that it was eleven.

Phoebe jumped up—she wanted to go down to the House of Commons to meet her ex-husband and to introduce him to Jim Troyes, who was interested in getting Arthur Coldridge's support for some new committee to do with shop stewards. Phoebe wanted Arthur's signature for a petition about freeing some prisoners in Northern Ireland. She had the petition on her: everyone signed it. Graham had his petition about homosexuals. He produced it for them to sign.

Graham went off to meet his current official passion, a young woman from Jamaica who sang in the newest club; and for the second night running said good night to the nymphets with a look of a man saying farewell to all poetry. He took Patty with him. The girls would stay the night: they went upstairs with Francis and Nicky. Paul went off with Mark to his study: Mark took opportunities when Paul was actually prepared to be friendly, even if it was because he felt excluded from the friendships of the people his own age, to try and interest him in his schoolwork. A lost cause. Everyone knew that once Paul had got into the study with Mark, had claimed Mark, he would lose interest and go off back to his own rooms where he would start playing a radio so loudly that someone or other would have to protest.

Martha went downstairs to Lynda.

Most nights they were together for a couple of hours— easier for Lynda, who slept so late, than for Martha.

This arrangement, or habit, had never been discussed, or planned—it came into being. Now they referred to it as "it" or "that."

It had begun during that period when Lynda had returned from hospital, and, without Dorothy, had started on her
368

efforts towards an ordinary life. Mark, then, had allowed himself to dream again of Lynda as his wife, of a real marriage.

How did Martha know?

Well, she had heard him. One night, lying in bed, she had listened to odd words, phrases, word sequences move through her mind. Her attention had been elsewhere, had returned to the words with the surprised knowledge: But that isn't the kind of thing I think: Good Lord, am I in love with Lynda? Shocked away, the phrases, words, stopped. Silence. Then, as the muscles of her mind relaxed, and an accepting dark came back, the words started. If she was in love with Lynda, then it was with a part of herself she had never even been introduced to—even caught a glimpse of. This was the language of a schoolgirl crush! This unknown person in Martha adored Lynda, worshipped her, wished to wrap her long soft hair around her hands, said, Poor little child, poor little girl, why don't you let me look after you?

Well! said Martha, who would have thought it? I'm a Lesbian, and a schoolgirl Lesbian at that. Listening to what she thought, for a while, was herself, she heard: "If you come upstairs, darling, I swear it, I promise, you can keep the door locked as long as . . . Let me be near you."

She understood that this was not herself, it was Mark. Making every kind of allowance for one's unconscious, it was past ordinary reason to take unto oneself attitudes that, after all, had been under one's nose as Mark's for years.

It wasn't her way of using words: that's how Mark thought.

Then: Perhaps I *think* that's what Mark is likely to be thinking?

But there was no way of proving anything, deciding anything—much better let the whole thing slide.

She switched off, firmly, turned her attention to ordinary practical problems. Next day, at breakfast, Mark used some of the words she had heard him use: he was confessing, with a kind of embarrassed desperation, that he was going to try to get Lynda back into his life, his room. "But if it makes it easier for her, I'll promise to keep this door locked until she feels . . ."

Very odd to hear this man talking, in his sad hot embarrassed voice, about his plans for Lynda, having heard his thoughts trickle impersonally, and without the colour of emotion, through one's head.

But then Lynda "became silly" again, to forestall his pressures on her.

Mark forgot about it.

Later she began to hear Paul. At first she tried not to. Good heavens, it wasn't far off eavesdropping, or reading other people's letters. Besides, hearing Paul was almost unbearable, like listening to a trapped animal thinking.

All his fantasies were of achieving power, in one form or another. In his daydreams he outbid, over-rode, undercut, triumphed, made them all look sharp, made them run, made them look out. He turned tables, and showed people up for what they were—interminably, night after night, when the radio stopped from upstairs, it was as if another had switched on.

But—after a while, questions. And she did not know how to answer them, let alone where to go for answers.

For instance: if a person is thinking, or at least letting fantasies, words, a linked pattern of notions run through his, her, head, which is what most people's thinking is, and this goes on for sixteen hours a day, and then of course in a different form in his, her, sleep, and then someone else, Martha for instance, overhears that odd phrase, that short trickle of words, then one has to ask: Why those words? Why not others? What Mark thought, what Paul thought, appeared in her mind as a small trickle of words. Was what she picked up words in its original form? Or did some mechanism exist which could pick up an idea, rather than words, from Paul's brain, Mark's, and translate it into words —like one of those simultaneous translators at a conference. Or like (or so they said was possible) a kind of computer that changed one language into another. Or perhaps it wasn't an idea to start with but an emotion. Who knew? Who could tell her? For although it seemed certain that the original impulse had been in words, since what she heard was recognisably Paul's or Mark's phrasing, it didn't do to say yes or no to that. It was conceivable after all that a hot wave of emotion in Paul hit Martha as Paul's emotion, no one else's; and this emotion got translated into Paul-like words.

It looked as if Martha picked up an idea, or emotion, a,b,c, because she was "tuned in" to a,b,c. For it was an interesting fact that while she might hear things that surprised her, or even shocked her because she was not expecting to hear (pick up) that thing at that moment, she had never picked up an idea, set of words, or an impulse that she might not have decided for herself was within Paul's, Mark's, range of behaviour. This could mean either that she knew them so well their behaviour could hold no surprises for her—possible; or that impulses, ideas, emotions in them which she did not expect from them, did not associate with them, got themselves translated into the nearest impulse, idea, emotion that Martha would accept. Was tuned in to.

And here she returned, and at such an odd and unlooked for place, to that rule, or law, current in Rosa Mellendip's circles: which was the paradox that one could never be told what one did not already know, though of course the "knowing" might be hidden from oneself.

In this realm one did not hear something, pick up something that one didn't know, or was prepared to accept, already. Which didn't mean at all that what one had already known wasn't something of a surprise. Perhaps it was more a question of remembering—that was a more accurate word, or idea.

And then—but the questions came fast. Why did she not hear Francis? As far as she knew, she had not. Or Lynda? Sometimes when in the same room with her, yes, but not casually and when not expecting it.

If emotion, as they said it was, was the conductor of such impulses, then that explained why Paul was the most often "on the air"—since he was more than anyone in the house a seething *olla podrida* of emotion. But then why Mark and not Francis—Mark was a simmering, locked-up man; Francis a simmering, locked-up boy. Neither was as violently emotional as Paul.

She knew Mark very well; she knew Francis less. She thought she knew Lynda as well as anyone . . . why, then—

So she brooded and puzzled and questioned and wished more than ever there were people to talk to, people to ask. Back came the other need, or almost a belief—she would walk into a room, or stop by a group of men digging in the street, or ask a girl serving butter behind a counter, and she, he, or they would reply: Of course, you'll find the answer to what you are asking *there* . . . there's a man who . . .

One night, going down to see if Lynda was all right, before she herself went to bed, she asked: "Lynda, do you ever overhear what people are thinking?"

Lynda turned, swift, delighted: "Oh," she exclaimed, "you do? I was waiting for you to . . ."

And Martha was already feeling extremely foolish. For what else had Lynda been saying all this time, in so many different ways. But Martha had not heard. She had not been *able* to hear. She had not had anything to hear with—there being no substitute for experience.

In short, the door had opened, as it tends to do, just under Martha's eyes, where it had been standing open for a long time now, unobserved, if she had only cared to look just there, had not looked in the wrong places.

But, having made that step, what then—another blank wall, another check.

Martha descended night after night, when the day's business was over, to talk to Lynda, during that part of the day when they could be alone and undisturbed.

They called it "working."

But they did not know what to call it, nor how to go about it.

Questions. It was a private, diffident pursuit of—but if they had known what to call it, then at least they would have known where to start. And they had to be secret—not because of any decision made or taken, but because circumstances ordained it.

Mark could not be upset—Mark found it all very upsetting.

The children must not be diverted from their proper education, must not be allowed to feel any more unusual than they were bound to be anyway.

The old cronies of the basement, Mrs. Mellendip and the rest, had dispersed with the going of Dorothy: though Lynda did sometimes see Rosa Mellendip, who at least did understand what they were talking about when they talked about what interested them. But Rosa was busy; she was rather successful in her career these days. And then, like all specialists, she tended rather to become impatient, or worse, tolerant, if they wished to speculate outside her field—fortunetelling by palms, cards, and horoscope.

Somewhere, and this was certain, there would be people whom they could talk to.

They chased hunches, gleams of insight, wrote letters to people who dropped remarks on television or in newspapers that seemed hopeful; wrote to authors; cross-questioned people they met who might say something which sounded like the promise of an unlocked door. They used their dreams, their slips of the tongue, their fantasies, but not at all as Dr. Lamb might have wished them to do, rather as maps or signposts for a country which lay just beyond or alongside, or within the landscape they could see and touch.

They ordered all kinds of periodicals which had to be

hidden from everybody, with names like *Destiny,* or *Star-time,* and examined them for those gleams of information which might appear in the most unlikely places. But here, in this region, already known, or at least partly known, through Rosa and the cronies of the old days, was something too easy, too complaisant. That door could so easily be opened into an area where people knew each other so very well, were very cosy, and all in an atmosphere of the initiated minority sharing truths denied to the outside world—repulsive; though one had to beware of losing opportunities to learn this and that, through finding anything distasteful.

And then there had been the business of Jimmy Wood. He now had published two very successful space-fiction novels. The plots of both these novels depended on the existence of people who had more senses than are considered normal. The last one had been about a conflict between a race who had inner vision and hearing, and a race that duplicated these capacities with machines. The machine race killed out the others, on the grounds that they were abnormal.

Martha, having read this with excitement, sidetracked Jimmy to the kitchen for a talk. There he sat, smiling as always, while she tried to get out of him where he got his ideas for the plots—a question which he seemed to find naive. "They were in the air," he said at last. And went on to say that "all of us" wrote about such ideas. He meant by "all of us" other space-fiction writers. He then went on to describe a new machine which he was working on that could stimulate or destroy areas of the brain, and not through anything crude like putting wires into the brain with electric charges, but by using frequencies of sound, or vibrations, which, said Jimmy, could be used with great sensitivity. Already he was within reach of aiming at an area of the brain the size of a pea . . .

Yes, said Martha, but supposing there were no machines. This race of people he had written about, for instance, had he ever himself experienced anything which might . . . But he was not listening. Not listening in the sense that he could not listen: his experience did not connect with what she said. He was not able to hear.

Mark often went with Jimmy Wood to a certain pub where science-fiction writers congregated. He found their company stimulating because the ideas in their books usually did not appear in the books of accepted and "literary" writers.

He would have been as polite as Jimmy was, however, if

Martha had asked if he went there because of any personal conviction or experience. Martha went with them to this pub. Twenty or so men, one or two women, discussed their craft. Martha kept approaching one after another, with questions kept tentative. Odd in itself that this had to be so: a man has written half a dozen books about people with this or that sense out of the normal; but he is embarrassed when asked if people might in fact have this or that sense. More than odd, when you thought about it ... But Martha had to come back and report to Lynda that she had drawn a blank. They drew blanks everywhere.

Yet in their own inner experience this was a time of possibility. It was as if doors kept opening in their brains just far enough to admit a new sensation, or a glimmer of something—and although they closed again, something was left behind. Just for Lynda and Martha, not for the other people they met and so anxiously, if carefully, questioned? Yet poetry, drama, old plays, everywhere, were full of hints and suggestions about what they looked for! During this period both read, or rather reread, poems, authors not read for years: they understood what it meant that "scales should fall from one's eyes"—scales had fallen. Where passages, lines, words had been obscured, or dark, or simply skipped over, suddenly there was light. What they wanted, looked for, searched for was everywhere, all around them, like a finer air shimmering in the flat air of every day. But to lay hands on it, to net it, that was different. It was as if the far-off sweetness experienced in a dream, that unearthly impossible sweetness, less the thing itself than the need or hunger for it, a question and answer sounding together on the same fine high note—as if that sweetness known all one's life, tantalisingly intangible, had come closer, a little closer, so that one continually sharply turned one's head after something just glimpsed out of the corner of an eye, or tried to sharpen one's senses to catch something just beyond them ...

They called it "working."

They might sit all night alone in Lynda's living room hardly saying a word, yet listening, trying to be receptive, to be alert. An idea might come out of it; or perhaps not. Or they might sound out this or that word, or phrase, or thought, by letting it lie on the air where they could get a sense of it, a feel, a taste; so that it might accumulate other sounds, words, ideas, like it. Sometimes they talked, trying not to talk too rationally or logically, merely letting talk flow, since in the spaces between words, sentences, something else might come in. They did not really know what they were doing, or how, really, they did it. Yet out of all this material gathered, they began to get a glimpses of a new sort of understanding.

They had no word for that either. Talking about it, or around it, they tended to slip back into talking about Lynda's being mad.

Perhaps it was because if society is so organised, or rather has so grown, that it will not admit what one knows to be true, will not admit it, that is, except as it comes out perverted, through madness, then it is through madness and its variants it must be sought after.

An essential fact was that if Lynda had not been mad, had not tested certain limits, then some of the things they discovered would have frightened them so badly they would not have been able to go on.

Three

The house continued, if not divided against itself, at least layered in atmospheres or climates. A slight reshuffle: Francis had moved upwards when he had left school; so now, from top to bottom it was Francis, Paul, Martha, Mark, Lynda.

A few weeks before A-levels, Francis came home and demanded "a top-level conference." This was his phrase (humorous) for such sessions, which might go on, often did, half the night. This time he wanted to know why they wanted him to take the exams. All the commonsensical reasons for doing so having been offered by Mark, Martha, Lynda, while he listened, not without an appearance of judicious thought, he said he proposed to leave school at once. None of them had needed degrees to live their lives by, he said; they all despised examinations and what they stood for; and anyway, he kept meeting people just down from university and who would want to be like that? And there was that ass Uncle Graham, he was the kind of thing universities produced at their best.

He went back to school to pack up his things and come home. They half believed it was all due to examination nerves, and he would take them after all: the teachers said he would pass satisfactorily.

But he came home. He was very moody; desperately gay, then silent. He kept dropping into his father's study, but they still could not talk easily; to Martha's room, where, having hung about as if hoping she might say something useful, he proceeded to entertain her with impersonations of his teachers and classmates. Then down to Lynda. He spent hours with her, wanted to take her out to theatres, restaurants; demanded she should buy new clothes. She wasn't doing justice to herself: everyone said how beautiful she was. Lynda became desperate too: he was treating her like a girl friend, and she couldn't understand why, when he had his own girl friends.

They none of them knew what to do. Having spent nights considering the illogicalities, inconsistencies and the general unsatisfactoriness of the position, the adults gave up: after all, you can't make a person study. Later of course they were able to see where all these deliberations had been at fault: they had been thinking of Francis as an isolated case. But he was only one of many thousands who decided the education they were offered was not for them. When a young person feeling himself to be alone and helpless fights pressures he feels are almost invincible, the fight is always oblique, desperate, ruthless. (Long ago Martha had made the same decision, had fought with cunning, ruthlessness, desperation, hardly knowing what it was she was doing, except that she was saying, No, no, I won't.)

Now, through Patty, Francis got himself a job backstage in a theatre where he proceeded to work very hard. He had always worked hard. Within a few weeks of leaving school he was earning (as he took pains to point out) what many men in these islands were expected to keep families on.

They continued to discuss his decision; talked their way into a kind of interim report, which went something like this. It was taken for granted by most people who came anywhere near that house that anything taught in school, except for a few minor techniques, like learning to read, write and use reference books, was a waste of time; that anything learned under the heading of history, or art, or literature, was particularly dangerous, since by definition it couldn't be true—was necessarily the product of derivative minds representing temporary academic attitudes congealed into temporarily rigid formulas. Anyone who wanted to learn anything could do so by himself in a library, or with a tutor in a few weeks, instead of the years demanded by schools and colleges. Education in modern societies was primarily an education in conformism. These beliefs, or attitudes, were so deeply theirs it was hardly necessary to state them. They were implicit. From time to time they had been set forth as warnings, or instructions, to Francis in words like these: Well, you've got to do it, so just get through with it somehow, get it over with, but don't take it seriously. In other words, from his family he had been asked to work hard, or at least adequately, while at the same time holding in his mind that what he worked at was unimportant if not dangerous. Saints had been asked to do no less. The school—semi-"progressive"—was as confusing. Like all the dozen or so schools of its kind, it both deplored the examination system and what that stood for; insisted that what it offered its pupils was much higher, better, wider and deeper than any study for examinations could be; yet, because of the "system" it was forced to spend as much time and effort on pushing its pupils through examinations as did any ordinary school.

These, then, were the lines of the "interim report"—filed and forgotten when they saw how wide a movement it was that Francis had belonged to, without knowing it.

Much later still, Francis came out with an incident that occurred when he was about thirteen, and which, he claimed, was a turning point for him. Mark could not remember it. Alas, parents so often cannot remember these moments which children carry with them like scars.

Francis had brought home from his new school (the semi-progressive one) some "mock" examination papers in history and English. Being Francis, he had not taken them to his father, or to Martha, to ask what they thought, but had left them lying on the kitchen table where Mark must see them at breakfast. Mark had taken one look at the English paper and demanded if this was meant as a joke—perhaps it was a parody of some kind? Francis had said nothing, had listened. He had done rather well in this particular paper. Mark had not gone on—apparently he found the paper so ridiculous it wasn't worth doing more than to say so. The history paper ("The Ancient World—Egypt, Crete, Greece, Rome") got the same treatment. Mark subscribed to a magazine that reported archaeological discovery: he told Francis not to waste time on school history. It was after this incident that Francis had dropped English and history as special subjects, and decided to do mathematics, chemistry and biology, areas where, he had hoped, facts could be eternal truths.

His coming home changed the house. The attic was large, accommodating not only Francis, but also Nicky, who stayed there most of the time: he didn't get on with his parents. Jill and Gwen might as well have moved in: they were still at school, but were doing badly—on principle, Phoebe claimed.

The attic vibrated with politics, chiefly Nicky's. He was "Committee of a Hundred" rather than Committee of Nuclear Disarmament. He was also an anarchist. He had not been in on the beginnings of the Committee of a Hundred, which were already swallowed in myth after only a few months. (The adults might well have claimed this little public event as support for their contempt for history: but what event does not get swallowed in lies and half-truths within weeks?)

It was debatable whether Nicky was political by temperament: he had been sucked into politics by chance. At a meeting in Trafalgar Square (despising politics, he had gone out of curiosity) he had been standing watching the proceedings with a friend when some fascists had started shouting and scuffling. The police, attracted to Nicky's tall lively presence, had taken hold of him, laid him on his back and assaulted him. Six of them had kicked him in the privates, punched him in the kidneys, and then bundled him into a van with his coat pulled down over his head in such a way that he would have suffocated, since he had fainted, if someone hadn't released him. In the police station he had protested his innocence. He was charged with assaulting the police. He had telephoned Mark, who had telephoned a lawyer, who had given the routine advice to plead guilty, because the magistrate always took the word of the police. Young and full of integrity, as he then was, Nicky had refused, and in the court next morning he had pleaded innocence, while a young policeman whom he had not seen before read a statement that he had been kicked and assaulted by Nicky. The magistrate had fined him fourteen pounds, while remarking that he was "a young man with an obvious propensity towards violence."

This experience had pitchforked him straight into aggressive politics. If he had not been middle-class, and brought up to see policemen as a kind of servant, the incident would have had no effect. He had already been arrested half a dozen times, and had done a short spell in prison for "sitting down" outside an American air base.

Francis, an old friend of Nicky's, was prepared to follow his lead in politics. But his early history made politics for him painfully serious: and it was known in the household that in private, he argued with Nicky, thought his political stand oversimplified, and some of Nicky's associates frivolous.

The girls were violently for the Committee of a Hundred. As Phoebe said: "Of course. What else? They've got to show how much they hate me somehow, and unless they become Tories what can they do?"

Gwen and Jill had both been arrested plentifully; but had never been charged with anything serious. Much to their chagrin. They complained it was because of their youth, or because their father was a member of Parliament. The truth was, probably, their particular brand of good looks, still a plump pink-and-white charm, deceived policemen, like everyone else, into believing they must be innocent of everything. Discriminated against, they worked extremely hard in groups whose main energies went into insulting Phoebe and her associates: for this new resurgence of the left, like every blossoming of the left before it, ran true to the rule that more time must be spent on fighting allies and comrades than the enemy. Phoebe, five or six years after being a criminally treacherous extremist, whose mail was at least half letters containing filth and threats, now discovered she was a milk-and-water opportunist and a coward.

At first she was humorous about this; then not so humorous—she went for a holiday to Nanny Butts. Returning from the holiday, she rang up Martha several times a day to complain about her daughters: she said she had headaches and nausea and could not sleep. Phoebe continued not to believe in "psychology"; she believed in a stiff upper lip. But she was having a breakdown nevertheless.

So was Margaret; but in her case the phrase was never used. As Mark had to explain, the upper classes have always accommodated a wide spectrum of eccentricity.

For a couple of years Margaret's house had continued a centre of agitation about legalising homosexuality. Her husband John had not been sent to prison, but a couple of his friends had been. He had been, people thought a nonpractising homosexual; but now, perhaps because he discovered so much sympathy for his condition, he had a couple of affairs, and even for a time thought of leaving Margaret.

She did not say what she thought about this. Her house continued full of charming people: she had never had any close friends.

Since one good cause leads to another, the people who began to campaign against capital punishment enlisted her, and soon it seemed as if every time one met Margaret, or went to her house, there was a new petition to sign, or committee to support. Sometimes she remarked, smiling, that she was an old Tory, she was an old die-hard; she had never seen herself as a crusader for causes. But it was not so much of a joke, after all. Secretly she did not understand how she had ever got herself into this position—she had married John, a pleasantly literary gentleman with a lot of interesting friends and a son with a reputation for being clever, and in no time at all she had become a pillar of progress with her name on a couple of dozen letterheads.

It was Graham's fault. Fault? Was it that she did not really believe in reforming the law on homosexuality, in abolishing capital punishment—and so on? Well yes, of course she did—though homosexuality had never come her way, or not to challenge her, before John; and while it did seem likely capital punishment was old-fashioned, it was not a cause she would have chosen to make a stand about. Well—had anyone forced her to choose it? Had anyone put a pistol to her head? No, of course not, but ... Why was it that Graham considered it his duty to broaden the mind of the nation in so many different ways? No, no, there was no reason at *all* why he shouldn't be a television personality; she was proud that she had welcomed television when so many of her class and kind, let alone all the intellectuals, had despised it. "Everybody" now went on television, and watched it. It was just that—well, what was it? Nothing that she could put her finger on, or be logical about. (Why did one have to be logical, consistent?) There was just too much of everything—too much, particularly, of Graham. He was always getting married—or nearly and changing his mind; getting publicly engaged; announcing new programmes which might or might not take shape; starting a new committee; organising a petition. Yes, yes, she was very fond of them, she was proud of him. He was a dear sweet boy. He was nearly thirty-five—*shouldn't he settle down?*

She wished ... she had no idea at all what she wished, or what she regretted. Perhaps she wanted an empty house and a silent telephone and a husband who was not like one of her own guests, an asset at a dinner table or on the lawn among roses but otherwise not much seen. By her, at least.

She departed for a long holiday to a small "unspoiled" village on the Costa del Sol where she developed a sympathetic relationship with a fisherman who in the summer took tourists for trips in his boat. He was about forty-five; he was handsome; he had a wife and a family; she discovered herself madly in love by the symptom that she was feeling that her entire life had been misspent. A long confused letter reached Mark; it was discussed between him and Martha. It sounded as if she wanted to be rescued. By Mark? But Mark was not sympathetic. He was angry; he was critical. Certainly she should never have asked Mark—but then, whom should she have asked and what did she want? Should Martha go? But with the young people, particularly Phoebe's daughters, not to mention Paul, in such a simmering state of emotion, she did not want to go. Who? Had Margaret no friends at all? It seemed not. Eventually Patty Samuels went. Margaret liked Patty; Patty admired Margaret. Patty found Margaret living in a room that cost about five shillings a day in the house of a widow and her married daughter; she was eating her meals at a little restaurant where she got a large meal for half a dozen shillings. The fisherman had gone off for an unexplained trip to Valencia. Margaret babbled a great deal about the simple life, and real values and so on. Patty was sympathetic, and listened for a couple of days. She realised that Margaret was indeed in a bad way; yet it was the kind of breakdown that could easily not be noticed. Margaret was a bit vague, she rambled rather; she was very dependent, but there was nothing startling to see.

Patty brought her home, and stayed with her for a few weeks, while giving it out that Margaret had caught a flu of some kind in Spain. John Patten again went off to stay with his aged mother. Margaret, who knew that her darling kind Patty must soon leave, kept visiting the house in Radlett Street, looking for love and the family and simple values.

She said to Patty that she adored her grandchildren; but for various reasons, Paul and the two girls and Francis were at that stage in their lives when they were least likely to adore her. She kept bribing them to go off on holidays, trips, visits to the theatre; was refused, and so she suffered. She suffered abominably, while Patty, staying with her, remained loud, calm, humorous and practical. Margaret was not told that the reason why Mark had so little time to see her, much less even than usual, was that Lynda was "being silly" again and that he was coping with it, without the aid of a nurse.

On the floor below Francis, Paul pursued his lonely course. Now, as always, the two had nothing to say to each other. They had been brought up together; yet in all those years it was doubtful whether they had spent half a dozen hours in each other's company for choice. They would sit through meals without noticing each other. If someone came into a room where both of them were, reading, or sitting, it was as if both were alone.

Paul, of course, talked about it, easily, volubly: Francis with difficulty. Paul said Francis was still jealous because he was a cuckoo in the nest. Francis said he didn't think Paul and he were on the same wavelength. The girls and Nicky discussed it all in depth and from time to time tried to involve the two boys with each other: which meant, inducing Francis to descend a floor to visit Paul. The two, very polite, exuding an embarrassed goodwill, ' sat as it were on stage, watched by other people for signs of the start of a psychological merger or liaison. . . . The fact is, people are very different from each other. They are much more different from each other than anyone likes to admit. Why is it so hard to admit? It is as if admitting it means admitting worse, some failure in humanity itself, the death or the delay of some hope for us all. It was noticeable that on these rare occasions when someone—usually Jill and Gwen—had tried yet again to make friends of Paul and Francis, and failed, that everyone was rather subdued, and tended to apologise profusely for small unimportant faults, while Paul and Francis went out of their way to pass each other bread or salt at the table and Paul made jokes about sibling rivalry. And when Paul acquired Zena, so very much on his wavelength, and was no longer painfully and reproachfully alone, with what relief did everyone on the top floor forget about the need, or the duty, to involve Paul.

He had left school. Three months before his O-levels, having done no work of any sort, he had suddenly begun to work frantically. His teacher had said in front of the whole class that with his, Paul's, brains, there should be nothing to stop him getting ten good O-levels. Paul had then insisted on taking ten O-levels. He had done fairly well on three, scraped through two, and failed the rest. Creditable on the whole, having done so little work; but then appeared the first evidence (or at least it was the first time they had noticed it) of that pattern which was peculiarly Paul's and would recur in one form or another. He had been let down, or so he felt. It was not his fault that he had done so badly. Not at all. Receiving the news that he had not got ten first-class O-levels, he sulked, had a tantrum, and then confronted his teacher with: "You didn't keep your promise." The sheer lunacy of this caused the teacher to interview Mark. The central fact here was that he, like all teachers in state schools, was so overworked that nothing much could be expected of him. He said: "He behaves as if I'd made a contract with him—something like that! Perhaps you could throw some light on . . ."

"He said it! He can't pretend now he didn't say it," Paul kept repeating. He would not go back to that school, or to any school. He seemed now to believe that he had only promised to stay on for the extra year past the leaving age of fifteen, because he had been promised ten good O-levels. The school suggested Paul could do with a psychiatrist.

Paul had done with several before, but in small doses. Dr. Lamb was once again consulted and Paul was interviewed, not by Dr. Lamb himself, now so high in the reaches of his profession that he was not available for bad risks, and Paul was that, but by a smaller reputation. But the opinion was that Paul, like Lynda, was simply not suited for therapy. He lacked the necessary basis for it.

What then was that basis? Translated into the language of ordinary living, they were back where they were before: Paul's absent sense of right and wrong.

He might not have one, but he certainly had something, perhaps a sense of self-preservation? He was always on the watch for what other people thought of right and wrong: was that not enough? On the whole, it was thought not.

Paul enquired when his therapy was to start; and was told that it wasn't going to. He said, first: "You aren't paying school fees for me. I don't see why you can't afford analysis." He said, next: "As far as I can make out, I'm too ill to be treated? How well do I have to be before they take me on?"

It became clear that Paul's *not* having therapy was going to be felt by him as yet another symptom of his abnormality: Mark therefore arranged for him to have some treatment with a less demanding therapist. Paul went twice, and returned saying she was a silly old twit, and he wasn't going to go again.

He did nothing for a time; stayed in his rooms, watched

383

the television, read a little, and fought with Martha, trailing her around the house to find opportunities of combat.

They usually occurred over food. He ate a great deal.

"Martha, would you say if I eat a lot it's because I'm eating reassurance?"

"Did one of them say that?"

"Two of them."

"Or perhaps you are greedy?"

"But that's not the kind of vice people have these days. You can be too fat—that's a vice. But eating too much isn't. I'm not at all fat. I'm very thin. Therefore I can eat myself silly and according to our ideas now, it's not a vice."

"Then do please have another helping."

"I have already had another helping. More, please . . ."

His rooms were even fuller of odd, or bizarre or beautiful or sinister, objects. Not so long ago his things, the cushions or bits of cloth or junk that had his stamp, his sheen, were like an exotic skin over the sober basis of bed, chairs, chests of the old house. But now the old furniture had been turned out, and that floor was all Paul's. He collected things from the markets and shops and nooks and corners of London the great junkhouse. They weren't stolen. He didn't steal these days. He could see no reason at all why he shouldn't; but other people did: he was positively magnanimous about seeing their point of view. He bartered and bargained and haggled; he spent days of resource and cunning to get that old chair, that rug, that table: he would not trouble over something easily got.

"Well, but I haven't stolen it, Martha—so why do you look like that?" He was sullen, or frantic: he was being law-abiding, he was abiding by their rules—so why did they, did she, always look like that?

For Martha knew quite well that he could not have got such an object for that price, unless the stall-holder or dealer or housewife—he knocked on people's doors in poor areas and tricked and charmed his way inside—was stunned, chloroformed, by that quality in him which was so excessive. In the game of haggling, bargaining, there are certain rules: they are unwritten, but they exist. None of them include Paul's knifelike need to have, to outwit, to do down. There is a pretence that this is what haggling and barter is about. In fact the basis is a kind of good humour. Somewhere behind this business of exchange which keeps objects of all kinds flowing through the cities is the recognition of human need which graces the barter of a corner of a sackful of potatoes for a fowl which has gone past laying. But all Paul knew was that there are rules which say you should not simply take.

"What are you going to do? Start a junkshop?"

"What's wrong with that if I did?"

"Nothing at all."

"But you'd like it better if I went to work in an office?"

"Why don't you start a junkshop?"

"Why should I pay rent for a place when I can use here? If you make this lovely pudding again tomorrow I'll give you my new print."

"I'll make it anyway if you want it."

But Martha's room became scattered with small jackdaw objects.

"Oh I know! You don't really like them! But you can have this cushion if you make me a black silk shirt."

"I'm sorry. I couldn't bring myself to—it's my generation. I won't make or wear a black shirt."

"God that's ridiculous. God that's sentimental."

"If you like. But you said that knowing what I was going to say. So I'm obliging you."

Here he got sullen, and flashed handsome sulking eyes, was betrayed. Games. The games you have to play. She played them. And one night overheard his fantasy: *If that silly twit Harry Singer says he didn't mean to let me have that cushion, I'll say it was stolen. The police would find it in Martha's room. She'd have to go to prison.*

He found Zena working in a shoeshop. She had run away from home, which was in Birmingham. She was eighteen years old and she lived in a "friend's" flat. The friend, Martha gathered, was an ex-lover of her mother's. Zena was Paul's female image, lithe, black-haired, black-eyed. They spent hours in his rooms playing games in front of a long mirror, winding bits of cloth around themselves, posing for imaginary photographers. Sometimes she slept there.

"Martha, I suppose you think we're having sex. You lot are so filthy-minded."

"I don't give a damn whether you have sex or not."

"Then why don't you? You are supposed to be looking after me, aren't you? Suppose Zena gets pregnant?"

"Then we'll deal with it when we come to it."

"There you are—you're filthy. We don't have sex. You wouldn't believe that, of course, and she lives with that dirty old man and he adores her but she never lets him touch her. She doesn't like being touched."

"Then that's all right then, isn't it?"

"You don't think so, do you? You'd like it better if we screwed each other day and night—you'd think that was normal, wouldn't you."

"Each to his taste," said Martha.

Paul's fantasy, overheard in small emotionless words trickling through her mind, so that it had the effect of a violently drawn cartoon with the words printed neatly in a small bubble over the action: *I'll tell Martha that Zena does sleep with the old pig. I'll say: Zena's got V.D. She's been using your towel. It doesn't matter, does it?*

Paul said at breakfast: "Zena's mother's lover has got filthy habits."

"Poor Zena."

"How do you know she hasn't picked something up off a towel—they share a bathroom?"

"Well, when she does, I expect we'll all know soon enough."

"Filthy. You're filthy." He was shrilly miserable, his eyes wide with hate: with hatred he watched the world outside. But with him, away from the world, safe, was Zena. At table they sat opposite each other, giving each other's faces small soft looks like kisses or the touches of a cat's paw. They wore jeans, bright sweaters, glossy black hair. In Paul's room they squatted opposite each other on the floor, adoring each other, not touching.

They descended the stairs side by side, hand in hand, their soft dark eyes staring in front of them, Paul and Zena, Zena and Paul. The others called them the Siamese Twins.

"You do realise, Paul," said earnest Jill, "that for both of you it's a narcissistic act?"

"Thank you," said Paul. "We know that. But love is always narcissistic. Look at most married couples—it's not that they've grown like each other. They were like each other to start with. That's why they chose each other, whether they knew it or not. But most of them are *ugly. Hideous.* They know they are *ugly* so they choose someone just as *ugly* so they can lie on their pillows staring at their own *ugly* faces. But we are beautiful. Zena and I are extremely beautiful."

"Oh listen to him!"

"It's true. And you can't keep your eyes off us. None of you. You stare at us all the time."

Below Paul and Zena—Martha. But of all the times in her life she had never been less Martha than now. Partly because of Lynda's being ill again; partly because of the young people, she was never alone, always tired; she was simply holding on. Never mind: everything passes.

Even her room was not hers: it was always bursting open under the pressure of some demand. The other rooms on this floor, James's old room, Francis's old room, now had occupants, usually Gwen and Jill, who after all couldn't actually sleep in Francis's room, even though it was where they spent most of their time. It was not that they lived here: they lived, as usual, with Phoebe, their mother. But Phoebe's breakdown caused them all to quarrel—or their quarrels caused the breakdown. Pleasanter here. Often, Arthur Coldridge's other family, the girls' half-sisters, came too. This floor seemed all young females, giggling, talking interminably in low tones, doing their hair and their faces—and popping in and out of Martha's room to take her clothes and her shoes, with the minimum of apology. This being one of the functions middle-aged women perform for young ones, she performed it—at first because she *ought,* and then in gratitude for what in fact was being done for her. After a year, or two years, with one's once cherished possessions, shoes, dresses, wraps, scent, always part of the setting for some young girl, all the delicious paraphernalia of attraction had ceased to be one's own. It was as if a shell or a skin had been peeled off, as if an aspect of one's self had floated away and become part of that timeless and fluid creature, A Young Girl, whose features were as little Gwen's or Jill's as they were hers.

And never again could she buy a scarf or a pair of earrings except as it were for some hierarchic figure whose function one temporarily had to fulfill, or for a character in a play. The rejuvenation a young girl gives her mother or an older woman is a setting-free into impersonality, a setting-free, also, from her personal past.

Every time Martha wished she could slap Gwen or tell Jill that she was a monster—she remembered Martha Quest. That girl, shrill, violent, cruel, cold, using any weapon fair or foul to survive, as she had had to do, as everyone's first task was to do, had been stripped off her, had gone away, was simply a character worn for a day or two, a week or two, a year, half a dozen years, by Gwen or Jill or anybody else who needed it.

There were lines written ready to be spoken; there was a play set like a duty.

Phoebe, apparently without any idea at all that she was behaving as if she had walked onto a stage and into the part of a mother with adolescent daughters, was speaking lines that Martha remembered word for word from Mrs. Quest. There were moments when Martha heard herself saying things which she no more felt, or felt personally, than things said by Phèdre or Lady Macbeth. "If you haven't any more consideration for . . ." "You wait till you get to my age and . . ." "When you have responsibilities of your own then . . ."

Arthur Coldridge, who had left the bosom of his Troy family at eighteen, quarrelling so badly with his mother that even now Margaret and he could hardly be polite to each other, had been aided in his flight by his first love, the wife of a Communist poet who had been killed in Spain. His first public act therefore had been as much sexual as political and it had ended his formal education. His views on morality (public) were liberal. But he told Gwen and Jill probably twice a week that they should finish their schooling and (he hoped) university, before "messing about" with sex, and that if they got in after ten o'clock at night he hoped Phoebe was being severe with them.

Some members of her generation found the lines harder to say well than others . . . yet Martha believed that "the children" were never more delighted, more enjoyably furious, than when listening to some resounding piece of traditional morality.

"God I hate you," Jill would shriek, as Martha intoned: "Of course you should never let a man kiss you on the first time you go out with him." "God you're so *sordid*," she moaned. But half an hour later she would be lying across Martha's bed to talk about clothes and love as if nothing whatsoever had happened.

And Paul would have been delighted if Mark or Martha had lectured him, had assumed the worst of his relations with Zena. Paul would descend to the basement to provoke Lynda into saying she disliked Zena, or that she thought Paul was lazy. Lynda, he felt, had a sense of morality, unlike Mark, who never gave advice, and unlike Martha, whose disapprobation could not be relied upon to be more than intermittent.

When Lynda shouted at him: "You're a self-indulgent little beast!" Paul glowed with fulfillment.

One ought to force oneself to recite the lines of this so ancient play, whether one believed in them or not? She came back and back to the same point, the only point of importance, she had to feel, about bringing up children, about being anywhere near children: from the moment the eyes of a tiny baby focussed and looked at you, so straight, and so seriously, and not a whit different from the look that person, when adult, would give, then it was as if one had to play games, marking time, until the baby grew into the eyes. It was not possible to take the games seriously. But of course it had all to be done right, to be played right ... yet it was all absolute nonsense. Yet Martha lay awake to worry, Should I be doing this, Should I be doing that; and Mark and Martha and Lynda met to worry, What do you think? Ought we to? But if we instead did ...

And yet when she had finished the cruel battle she had to fight with Paul (there was one thing everyone agreed about, including Paul himself, who said so, that he should never be allowed to get away with anything) then what was real was the moment when Paul suddenly caught her eyes with his, in the shared glance or acknowledgement, or amusement: *How ridiculous all this is.*

Then the games went on, and they resumed their roles, adolescent and grown-up, all doing what they had to do.

Exactly as it was with Jill and Gwen, the pretty adolescent girls. Between them and Martha there lay a cool understanding, a liking. But the games went on, the sulks and the looks and the banged doors and the complaints about their mother, the complaints about life.

Whichever game it was, over, then one or both would come into Martha's room, simple, straightforward, altogether delightful girls, and stay there for an hour or for the evening, and their eyes would have the straight intelligence of an infant's, or a mature person's ... until it was time to go on with working out or through a part of that other pattern, the need to feed and develop the adolescent.

It was as if veils of mist kept blowing across between them; as if steadily glowing lights, always there, moved towards and away from each other, but in a steady trust; while waves of turbulence came between, rocked and tossed violently for a while, then moved on, and the lights shone out again, communicating with each other.

The girls were coming to Martha, because their mother was ill.

The illness had been precipitated because Phoebe had agreed to marry Jim Troyes, and then the marriage had not happened. For a time things had gone well. Everyone was pleased that hardworking Phoebe was at last going to have some love and warmth in her life. Even some glamour—for Jim did not see Phoebe as dull or dutiful: on the contrary, his experience had been mostly local politics in various Northern provincial towns, and Phoebe was very different from the women he had worked with. For one thing, she was the ex-wife, still the friend, of the gallant crusader Arthur Coldridge. She was at home in London's political circles; much wider ones than strictly Labour. Indeed he was rather shocked that the political demarcations of his experience blurred here in London into what he could not help seeing as an indifference to principle. (When he left London it was always with the feeling that he was leaving moral danger.) And then, Phoebe was at home in the literary world —so he saw Mark Coldridge. She called by Christian name a dozen of Africa's new rulers, all of whom had been her friends. And yet this accomplished and many-sided woman needed him. He was altogether delighted with Phoebe, and prepared to be delighted with the little girls: his own children were grown-up. He was divorced.

It was the little girls who ended the thing; though it would be hard to say exactly how. Later of course they would be saying: God, I was so awful when I was a girl ... But it was bad luck for Phoebe that their period of awfulness coincided with Jim Troyes. First, they patronised him: they were dreadful little snobs. He brought Phoebe boxes of chocolates, but they were the wrong brand; he brought her large bunches of flowers, with which they made elaborate "arrangements" all over the flat; he bought tickets for the theatre, but not for the plays "everyone" was talking about. He did not at first realise he was being patronised; and when he did he took them to task, pleasantly and firmly, and they began to respect him.

Then they flirted with him. He was enchanted. These two pink-and-white little morsels with their honey-thick hair and their great blue eyes seemed deliciously touching. Poor fatherless girls, he thought; if they had had a proper father they wouldn't be behaving like this at all; and perhaps he was right. But every time Phoebe came into a room, it seemed that Jill was on the arm of a chair and that Jim was in the chair; or that Gwen sat at his feet staring up at him adoringly. And Jill took to kissing him good night and flinging her arms around his neck in a little-girl fashion that she must have got out of some film. Phoebe could not stand it. She privately thought Jill was sly and cruel. She was sixteen—not a little girl at all. Also, Phoebe had the benefit of Jill's diaries, left around for her to see, and she knew what Jill thought of Jim and of her, Phoebe.

But while she was angry, she was also self-distrustful: her own bleak but rigid honesty told her she was envious of her daughters. When she was young there hadn't been pretty clothes and make-up and she hadn't kissed a man till she was over twenty. She was genuinely glad for the girls now that they had such a good time, and that they could be pretty and free. But she resented it too.

She began losing her temper. She lost her poise, her confidence. She quarrelled with Jim over the girls. He went back to Bradford for a short holiday, and while he was there she wrote breaking the thing off. And as soon as she had done so Jill began taunting her because she "couldn't keep her man, poor old Mummy, she hasn't got what it takes."

This was where Phoebe had cracked: she did not know where to turn, whom to see. She went to her daughter's headmistress, who said the girls were both very lazy, but not much worse than most; yes, Jill seemed a perfectly normal little girl to her, girls at that age were difficult, etc. At the end of the interview Phoebe was feeling very guilty; the headmistress had spoken as if she, their mother, were lacking in sympathy for her daughters. Phoebe began lying awake at night to see where she had gone wrong with the girls. But she could not: unless it was that she should have married one of the people who had asked her? Yes, of course she should have married, for the girls' sake; but the fact was, she had loved Arthur Coldridge and no one had ever seemed half as good. Certainly not Jim Troyes, who himself regarded Arthur as a kind of hero.

Jill's diary, which for months she had ignored, since one didn't read other people's letters and private papers, until at last it had arrived on her dressing table, open at key passages, told her she was selfish and neurotic and cold: "a failure as a woman and as a mother."

She went to Martha, and to Mark, who said that she would "grow out of it." It was all very well for *them*, they made no pretence at an ordinary life, ordinary relationships; and now the girls were there most of the time, and she, Phoebe, might just as well have not tried to give them an ordinary decent life, any kind of crazy set-up would have done. But the sad truth was, she was delighted when the girls were in Radlett Street, for she had come to dread that moment when, going to the dressing table, or even the sink, or lying on her pillow, she would find Jill's diary, open at some deadly message which cut her so that she could hardly breathe for a time, had to lie down and rest.

She went to her doctor, who sent her to a psychotherapist. This was a woman. The relationship lasted for a couple of confused months. The central fact here was glaringly obvious, like the sun in the tropics: both women were stupid about people and their relationships with each other. Both were perfectionists, and managing, and dogmatic by nature. Mrs. Johns was a Freudian, and knew all about Phoebe from her first interview with her. Phoebe believed in self-control, doing one's duty, and behaving well even when others did not—she could not see what was wrong with this.

The thing is, no one ever gets to that point of moral confusion where one finds oneself sitting before a human being privileged to pronounce on one's state of being without having wondered and suffered and doubted. Phoebe knew well enough that she was a sadly rigid soul. But here she was, seated opposite another! Who was Mrs. Johns to pronounce on her, Phoebe? Phoebe kept wishing that Mrs. Johns would come to the point: there must be one, surely? For it was implicit in her manner that truths were there to be seen, but every time a truth or the intimation of one emerged, Phoebe thought it was suspect. For instance, Mrs. Johns seemed to think there was something odd about her long friendship with Arthur and his wife, Phoebe's successor. The way Phoebe saw it, her decision to maintain this relationship had been the hardest of her life: she had had to swallow pride and misery to do it; she would much rather have cut Arthur out of her life altogether. But then, there were the two girls, and it was hard on them to be deprived of a father. Sometimes she had thought that if she had not seen so much of Arthur, her husband (she thought of him as such—she had never had another, after all!), she might have found it easier to marry someone else. Had she been wrong? Mrs. Johns thought so. Phoebe was not prepared to agree.

Then there was the business of Phoebe's politics. Mrs. Johns said politics did not come into this, and Phoebe tried to give her the benefit of the doubt. But for Mrs. Johns politics was voting once every five years, and being tactful about other people being Labour; Phoebe supposed that being so ignorant about what went on in her own country did not matter to superior insights about mother-daughter relationships? Then it emerged that Phoebe's long career in politics was "masculine," she was competing with men; she wished to be one. Phoebe agreed at once that of course, had she been given the choice, she would have chosen to be a man, because they had so much easier a time of it—but

392

wouldn't every woman say the same, if she was honest? Mrs. Johns found this an admission of importance; but Phoebe could not see why. Yes of course having been brought up without a mother had been hard for her, yes of course it had been hard never having pretty clothes or being allowed to make up, yes of course she had felt unluckier than other girls. Of course. She waited for Mrs. Johns to come to the point, while she felt more and more ill, and did not sleep at all—she was convinced. She seemed to ache all over. But it didn't do to give in, to slacken, to indulge oneself. She put a good face on everything; and continued her usual busy life.

Why did she work so hard, asked Mrs. Johns?

Well, it's the kind of person I am, said Phoebe.

She despised people who didn't work hard, didn't she? No, Phoebe didn't think so: but she did go back again "to the beginning" which for her was the divorce with Arthur Coldridge, and wonder if she had been right to choose such hard work.

Because of course she could have earned a great deal of money; could have had a much easier life. But it had never even been a temptation: she was not interested in an easy life. Now it seemed that perhaps her daughters had suffered? Jill complained that "You always put your career before us!" It was true? She ought to have become a real career woman of some kind? The sort that earns a lot of money and is ambitious? "Neglected as I have been ..." an entry of Jill's might begin.

For years Phoebe had got up every morning at six, cleaned the flat, got breakfast for the girls and herself. Until they grew older and had understood that not everybody spent a couple of hours before the day started over breakfast, they had enjoyed that meal with their mother. She then took them to school, went to work. She shopped for the family during her lunch hour. In the afternoons arrangements were made for the girls to go somewhere, or for somebody to go to the flat with them. Phoebe came home to cook them supper, and see them into bed or to their homework, before she went out again to some committee meeting. She had lived like that for years. No holidays, except with the children; sometimes she had taken a weekend off to go down to Nanny Butts by herself while the girls went with their father. But she had seen they had pretty clothes, plenty of friends, and parties when other children did. She had always taken trouble over their food. She was an excellent cook.

About two months after starting with Mrs. Johns, she had to put off a session, because she was cooking a big dinner for some visiting Americans interested in Africa; it was a question of getting some American fund to give money to build schools in an area where there weren't any schools.

Next day, Mrs. Johns asked her about the dinner, and Phoebe described the food. She did not mention the object of the dinner, for Mrs. Johns would not have responded. Mrs. Johns then congratulated her on her new step towards fémininity. Phoebe asked what she meant: it appeared that Mrs. Johns saw the cooking of the dinner as a feminine pursuit and therefore good, by definition. Phoebe did not understand. At last she pointed out that she always had cooked well, had always enjoyed it. Mrs. Johns murmured encouragingly, "Good . . . that's really very good indeed."

Phoebe went home, in the grip of a suspicion that after all, it was simple: Mrs. Johns wasn't very bright; or, if she was, lived in some remote world where women didn't cook, do housework, bring up children, hold down jobs, mend the plumbing and the electricity and in their spare time make clothes and garden.

She made enquiries. It turned out Mrs. Johns had a husband who was a lecturer in physics, three children, a house, and one *au pair* girl. Mrs. Johns's life was very similar to Phoebe's, in fact; except that the *au pair* girl did most of the cooking.

Phoebe gave up trying to understand Mrs. Johns or psychotherapy.

Hearing that Phoebe proposed to "terminate the experience" Mrs. Johns said that Phoebe's trouble was, she didn't like to admit that she, Mrs. Johns, was brighter than she was.

Phoebe replied she didn't think Mrs. Johns *was* brighter than she was; but that wasn't the reason. She thought that they weren't getting on very well.

First she was hysterical about it, and wept. Then she was dry and humorous. But on the whole it hadn't done her much good—insights and "psychology" having failed her, she returned to her old self. The "breakdown" over, she was more Phoebe than ever. If only she had been able to hold the "breakdown," to explore it, develop it, use it; turning her back on it, she refused a chance to open and absorb. She became, instead, more rigid, more controlled.

The crisis with her daughters came to an end, or seemed to, when Jill turned up at her home after a week's absence at Mark's, and was told by Phoebe, in a hurry to go out to a conference, that if she didn't come home and stay home she, Phoebe, was going to get rid of the flat and get a smaller one: she saw no reason why she should run a large expensive flat for children who were never there. She had a week to make up her mind, said Phoebe, and departed.

When the diary arrived on her dressing table that evening, with passages underscored in red, Phoebe dropped the diary into the garbage can.

Jill moved all her things into Mark's house. Gwen followed her example. Then they heard that Phoebe had in fact put the flat up for sale; it was no game. They went home, sulking and tempestuous, to a mother who was not playing games: she was locked away from them in a disapproving determination that they should be "sensible." It was all dreadful: everyone knew it. When the girls came to visit Radlett Street, they were miserable, they complained that "our mother hates us." They felt hated. Phoebe felt hated. The three females hardly spoke to each other. From time to time one of them would ring up Radlett Street, or drop in, to ask for advice, wait for suggestions. It is built into us all that there must be solutions to problems. If Mark said this, of if Martha said that, then Phoebe would say or do this or that, and then Jill or Gwen could be or become that and this. There's a button somewhere, and you can push it—so we tend to think. But in fact things continued as they were.

And in Radlett Street Lynda worked her way through to the end of being silly.

It was Francis who had touched her off: but everyone, including Lynda, was concerned that he shouldn't suspect it. But after all, he wasn't a child now; he was almost a young man. Told that on the whole it would be better if he didn't go near his mother for a while, he nodded, talked of something else—and came back a couple of days later with the statement: "About Lynda; it was partly her fault for not telling me I was putting too much on her. But I don't think she ought to swing back to the other extreme. For her own sake, she ought to let me go down sometimes."

This message was transmitted to Lynda, a bedraggled slut who sat swaying on the floor with her back to Mark who guarded her, hour after hour. It reached her. After a while she said Francis should come down that evening. She then had a bath, dressed, did her hair, and sat waiting for him. It was afternoon; and Francis was upstairs watching time go past until evening. He came down, sat opposite her, said gently: "Hello, Lynda, how are you?"

"Not terribly well."

She smiled, pathetically. His smile was as painful. They talked a few minutes, then she asked him to go: "It's embarrassing for me, you see," she said.

He kissed her and went. He was crying. He had not seen Lynda before when she was badly ill. He locked himself up in his attic, and came down a couple of days later to confront Mark and Martha with a demand for a serious talk. He wanted to know the whole history of his mother's illness "right from the beginning."

Well, that wasn't so easy; but they did their best. There were a great many doctor's reports to show him. Again he listened, nodded, went off, and thought about it. Having thought, he came back, wanting to know if they didn't agree that it would be good if Lynda had to make the effort to dress and see him; regularly, let's say, every day.

It was extremely important to him: to them, it meant they suffered at the idea of *his* suffering if he saw Lynda looking like a sick witch, or worse. But again they transmitted the message to Lynda, who received it in an angry panic. She wanted to be left alone, left alone, left alone, she muttered, and growled and shouted. The shout was meant to reach the ears of Francis, and possibly it did. But he was dogged: he knew what he thought; he was convinced he was right. Lynda said no, not every day, but yes, she would try . . . so she got dressed, when Francis sent a message down, or rang her up. She put a smile on, and sat at the table waiting for him.

The point was, she was able to do it. In the past, it had been assumed by all of them that it was as if a variety of switch were turned, and then Lynda slid away from herself; then she had to suffer it out, and at some point, got better. They remembered that last time, sent off to a flat with a nurse, she had stayed there only a short while, had behaved quietly (a surprise to them all) and had come home much better than usual after such a time.

Throughout this spell, or bout, she had thought of Francis, intermittently, but responsibly.

As for him, it was during this time that he grew up. For a few days he had talked of leaving home, throwing up his job, going off somewhere, probably Australia, but he didn't go, he stuck it out. The change in him reached to the physical: there was nothing left of the wildly beautiful boy. He was a solidly built, quiet, contained young man, with steady brown eyes. He suggested patience, doggedness, strength. He was Mark all over again, but Mark said that he was much better and stronger than he had been at that age. The two, recognising likenesses, tried hard to talk, to be together: they knew they loved each other, but usually their attempts broke down in stiff politeness.

And Mark did not have much of a reserve, after spending what he did on Lynda. For, controlled and good she may have been with her son, but with her husband, she was abominable, she did not try at all.

For a time Martha thought Mark might very well crack himself: he thought so too. The three of them, Mark Martha, Lynda, were in a tight knot together of shared tension, all ordinary life suspended; for Martha was deep in it, though she hardly saw Lynda. Mark's attitude was that it was he who had decided Lynda should stay at home instead of going to hospital; and therefore it should be he, not Martha, who must take the strain. But it turned out that he couldn't manage by himself.

A week or so after Lynda's breakdown, Mark had come upstairs at four in the morning to wake Martha. He was almost sick with exhaustion, with holding himself in one piece while Lynda went to pieces. But it wasn't just an exhaustion, ordinary tiredness. He came to Martha for sex. Sex not for pleasure, nor for comfort, nor for fantasy, nor for friendship. It was for the explosion of an intolerable psychic tension. She was being used, if she cared to look at it like that, as a safety valve. He came to her as she had not ever seen him before: nothing in him now of Mark the white knight, Mark the friend, Mark the old lover. He was all a hard violent desperation, as if he were holding in himself a kind of charge or current that might shake him to bits if it got loose. And more of him was involved in this sex than ever before—or so it seemed. She did not know him.

They could not use her bedroom. Her daylight role as Martha the holder of the fort, housemother, friend of the young, meant among other things that she had no privacy. Her bedroom could be entered at any time. If she locked the door, people banged on it until it was opened. Paul and Francis allowed her some leeway—the girls none. Nor did she like going to his bedroom, which remained in spite of everything and after all these years the room where Mark was married to Lynda. It was no use his saying not; she heard what he thought, what he remembered.

They went to his study, which no one entered without

formality. On the walls multiplied the charts of the death factories, the poison factories, the factories that made instruments for the control of the mind: the maps of Hunger, Poverty, Riot and the rest; the atlases of poisoned air and poisoned earth and the places where bombs had been exploded under the sea, where atomic waste was sunk into the sea, where ships discharged filthy oil into the sea, where inland waters were dead or dying.

On the thick pile of a carpet in the room which had once been Mark's father's study the two lay behind locked doors, two bodies that exploded into each other, before Mark had to sleep a little, dress freshly, and go down to the basement again to be with his wife. A silent, desperate act of—survival? It seemed so. Mark said he was afraid. They lay in each other's arms, their faces running with tears of their shared tension, and rested, under the maps of the poisoned world, in a silent house. Somewhere upstairs, Paul or Francis might be playing music, late. Or Paul crept down with Zena to eat in the kitchen, alone. Or Lynda woke again: they heard her moving about below them, in a slow dragging sort of movement, while she muttered and sang and knocked things about.

"What are we doing it for? Lynda's just one woman."

"But what can any of us do?"

"I sit down there and I think, Lynda's just one woman."

"We can't think like that."

"I am thinking, like that—more and more. There's something we ought to be doing, something else, not just waiting for us all to be poisoned ... or perhaps I'm as crazy as she is, perhaps that's it."

"It won't last long. Nothing ever does."

"Sometimes it's as if ... I don't know how to explain it ... it's as if ... not that *she* is mad, but there's madness. A kind of wavelength of madness—and she hooks into it and out, when she wants. I could hook into it just as easily. Or it could hook into me—it's in the air."

"Or into me," said Martha. She lay, her head on his spent arm.

"Well, yes. Well—but what can I do? Go off to a prostitute? I couldn't do that. I never have."

Martha could have said, of course, "Oh, have it on me." Or: "You're making use of me!" Or: "Who do you think I am?" She could have made use of any of the remarks lying around suitable for such occasions. But she didn't feel them.

They passed through her mind, as it were showing themselves to her, to be rejected or not.

What she did feel, she couldn't tell Mark, because what help would it have been, either to him or to Lynda?

She was full of an irritable tension that was new to her. It had nothing to do with being "satisfied" or "unsatisfied." It had nothing much to do, she suspected, with sex. Day by day, or night by night, as Mark came up from the basement, when Lynda was briefly asleep, to take hold of Martha and link her in to his high energy, she became charged with a feverish electricity—if that was the word for it. She did not know what to do with it. She did not know what it was. She was desperate. But what was being created in her was not the never-to-be-sated "woman in love," "wife," "mistress," etc., etc. Sex ... what is sex? We keep using all these words, and what do they mean after all? The word sex has to do for so many different experiences, and like the word "energy," it is what you make of it. . . . Movement, she needed movement. She put on a dull coat and scarf over her head and walked through dark streets. London after midnight is not pleasant to walk in, if you are a woman. Even if you are not charged with an energy that makes you a centre for all the furtive prowlers looking for sex. The big cities of the world do not accommodate women walking at night: better forests, or a moor: less dangerous, less frightening. After midnight in a city a woman is a woman is a woman, even if masked in an old coat that had once belonged to Mrs. Van der Bylt, and an unbecoming headscarf.

She thought: If I were a man I'd go to a prostitute.

But Mark didn't.

She thought: Ought I to be angry with a man who puts me into this state? What state?

She telephoned Jack. "Martha! Believe me, I'm glad to hear your voice. Yes. When? Just a tick then, I'll see if . . ."

She waited. He sounded the same, a country boy all simple and straightforward enthusiasms. Yet he *didn't* sound the same. . . . Martha listened to the stillness while he checked with some woman, or looked in his engagement book and felt uneasy. Because why was she doing this at all?

He came back and asked: "Three o'clock would be better than two—is that all right?"

"Yes. Fine."

"Believe me, Martha, it's fine to hear you. I've thought of you often, do you believe me?"

"Yes ... of course." She felt *very* uneasy. It sounded as if he were checking something, finding out, or trying to?

"And our paths have never crossed all these years."

"I suppose they have without us knowing it."

"Yes, I'm sure they have! Martha, I'll be looking forward so much to the moment I see you—you do believe me, don't you?"

When the conversation was over, she nearly rang up to say it was a mistake, she was off to the South Pole—anything. She had been left tingling with a warning: *don't*.

Next night, she walked down a quiet middle-class street where only two or three windows still shone yellow in a strong white moonlight. Decorous little trees, like children allowed to stay up late, stood in patches of garden that defined individual front doors, each on its best behaviour, shining knocker, letter slit, bell. Each house, shored internally under paint and plaster by a thousand makeshifts, looked solidly desirable: behind them the canal lay quiet, discreetly reflecting moonlight. Elsewhere the moon rocked oceans in their beds, stuffed pillows full of uncomfortable dreams, made doctors double their dosage of sedatives for sad lunatics in hospitals, set dogs howling and drew fish up to goggle at the streaming white light.

Jack's door, black, had a wolf's head on it for a knocker, and a spyhole. Martha looked at a tiny globe, and knew that through it, somebody saw all of her. Nearly she walked away. The door opened. Jack, not a day older, a country boy in a green sweater that had a tear in the elbow, stood on bare feet on a thick carpet. Behind him was the hall, all solid thick expensive white paint and dark pile and an octagonal table mosaicked with coloured woods.

"Martha," he said, "I'm so very happy, I've been missing you, do you believe that?"

Brown eyes in a smooth brown face. He was waiting to see what she would do. Of course, he always had. She walked on, past the room where once the crazy youth had sat on guard. The door was open. It was—the word for it was "salon." She switched on the light and looked at a room which had been inspired by a room in a château: it was not English. It was elegant, formal, but also enticing—there was something sly about it.

"Do you like it? Do you like what I've done?"

The house was all like that, a surface of solid, indeed gloomy, formality; under it, something else. It was a fantasy house: rather, a house for the setting of fantasy. The room on the first floor hadn't changed. Stark with its oil heaters and darkened windows, the bed set for action, Martha said it reminded her of an engine room in a luxury ship. He looked at her carefully, suspiciously—he did not laugh. Then, he set himself an allowance of laughter, used it up, and sat crosslegged on the bed watching her.

Martha who knew she should not have come, yet did not go. Curiosity. Curiosity would kill the cat yet.

She kept thinking: My memory is playing me tricks, I'm remembering what it was like, all wrong—I must be. But she knew she was not. Jack had changed. He had changed fundamentally and vitally.

The years since she had come here to make love, she had spent above all in the exercise of holding on to what is permanent in people—while moods, phases, stages flow past: what else is the business of bringing up children? She had had an education in recognising a person's permanence. When she was here last, she could have sworn it, she was in contact with Jack, all of him in communication with what he was. But now, she kept reaching out, probing, waiting for Jack to talk, to talk to her. It was like being with Jimmy Wood—only insofar, of course, as this business of waiting for a resonance or an echo went; she kept addressing remarks to Jack, but Jack did not answer.

He sat on his bed, waiting. She sat on a rather nice old wooden chair by the heater. She sat holding a mug of cocoa, looking across bare boards to Jack. He was waiting for her to come and sit by him, but he wasn't going to suggest it. There was a feeling in the room of—waiting. More, a watchful, intent, urgent waiting. Jack watched, without seeming to, every move she made, seeing them as towards him, or away from him. She could feel his will encompassing her.

"Tell me about the house, Jack—you forget I don't know."

"I'd like to tell, you, I will. . . ."

"You are here by yourself?"

"You know how I want to live. I haven't changed."

"You want all your women under one roof?"

He nodded. Tears stood in his eyes. He had not meant them to be there, but he didn't blink them away: he held them for her inspection.

"Aren't you ill any longer?"

"No."

"Really? It's all gone?"

"Are you afraid I'll infect you?" He sounded wronged.

This startled her: he would never have said that once.

"No. I'm sure you wouldn't let anyone get anything—but you don't catch tuberculosis like that, do you?"

"No. I don't know. I'm cured. I've been cured for years. I have to be careful."

Joking, she said: "You mean, eating regularly and going to sleep early!"

He seemed to suffer, sat with bowed head. Softly he said:

"I am always waiting for trust. Believe me Martha, that's what I spend my life waiting for."

It was all discordant—off key. She got up, prepared to go. He had turned his head slightly so he could watch her without seeming to.

"I can see you are going, Martha. I'm sorry, believe me. But I would like you to let me tell you about the house. . . ."

She sat down. She could feel his will relax. He began speaking in a soft considered voice about how he had slowly paid for, acquired the house, done it up, but he did not say where the money had come from. He said: "I let that part of the house until I had the money to do it up and then . . . I want to tell you about that room you saw—you liked it, I could see you did. Well, I did that room for Jeanne. I never knew what to do with it. She is from the Loire. She came to London as an *au pair* girl. And her mother worked in one of those châteaux. When Jeanne was a girl she used to go up with her mother to help her work, she was a charwoman. Jeanne had always dreamed of a room like that. I made it for her."

"Did she live in it? Where did she live?"

He waited a little. Not looking at her, but missing nothing of any reaction she had, he went on: "She isn't here. She came here to visit. But that was her room—you understand me, Martha?"

"Yes. I do." And again talking to the old Jack, she said smiling: "Well if you decorate a room afresh for every woman you sleep with, then . . ."

But he was listening for something else: a theatrically humble smile appeared on his face, and he said: "Believe me Martha, there's nothing I wouldn't do, nothing, for any woman I love—you know that. But it's not what I want, that women should just come and go, I want any woman I have to stay with me forever, you know that."

He was looking at her direct now, willing her to come over to him. She did not want to, but she did. He sat on the

402

bottom of the bed. She remembered sitting there before; and he had sat where he was now. He could not suppress a smile of pleasure that she had come: and it was a smile of triumphant pleasure, like a small boy who had been allowed to get his way. He began talking, slowly, about the room and Jeanne. He was watching for every one of her reactions. He described Jeanne, slowly, with details of every asset, visible and invisible. Once he would have described a girl with a need to share his pleasure in her beauty. But now it was to rouse Martha. Knowing this, watching and listening, she was aroused. He went on to describe the exact use of various pieces of furniture in the room downstairs; and how Jeanne, at first reluctantly, then with pleasure, took part in this or that posture or pursuit on sofa, footstool or table.

Martha, manipulated and watching herself being manipulated, was waiting. She was waiting (as she realised afterwards) for the "real" Jack to come back, so that they could return to where they had left off. She was waiting for him to begin the slow ritual of rousing by atmosphere, eye, tension. But he went on talking about Jeanne, with breasts so and so, crotch so and so, armpits thus. And then about another girl, Olive. And slowly the geography of the house, in terms of sexual fantasy, was mapped. For instance there was a hexagonal room on the ground floor, with six alcoves or niches. He imagined that six naked girls ("all of them of their own accord, Martha, believe me, there'd be no pleasure in it otherwise") were chained in the alcoves. Then a specially trained Alsatian dog would lick the girls into sexual excitement. Meanwhile he stood watching: he would be fully dressed. Then, at last, he would undress, and, fondling the dog, he would allow the girls to beg for him. He imagined how they would scream and cry and plead. He might or might not comply. "I might just walk away smiling. Imagine it, Martha—me, quite naked, walking away with the dog, while they screamed and called me filthy names."

Time was going fast towards morning. He, no doubt, continued to live without reference to the clock. But she would have to be back home before morning. She slid into bed with Jack at that point when she understood that he had forgotten what he had been, that this was what he was.

Now she knew in what way he had changed. He had become cruel, hard, driving; all domination and hurt.

It was like being with a man she had not known before.

It was like an endurance test. On her side: *How much can I stand?* On his: *How much can I get her to stand?*

When it was nearly morning, she said she must go. He did not ask when she was coming back. Instead he talked, watching her with an almost theatrical cunning (so obvious that it confused her), of another girl, of how she liked this and that, and how she, this girl, had come to see that he, Jack, was right in insisting on her submission to this or that whim of his.

Before she left she asked: "Jack, do you ever make love the way you used—do you remember?"

He studied her in his new sideways sly way which was at the same time open, meant to be seen. He was trying to work out what she meant. He had forgotten.

"I've always liked it with you, Martha, you know that."

"Yes, but—you're different. Did you know that?"

In his new manner of mingled arrogance and humility he said: "There's always new things to learn."

"No I didn't mean ... oh well, perhaps I'm different too." She said this to be able to slide away from the subject. But now he was alerted and alarmed. "Oh no, you're not, believe me you're not!" He was genuinely upset at the idea that she might think she was different. This confused her again.

"Do you mean, you're different because you're older? I don't care about that. You don't know me if you think that matters to me. Oh, if only you'd trust me!"

He was almost weeping. That was genuine.

She left along the resurrected street as the sun came up red beyond the canal.

She had no idea at all what to think. Except for one thing, that Jack of ten years ago and Jack now were not the same person. But really not, literally not. What did that mean? She did not know.

And she knew that what had taken place with him, in his house, which was an elaborate stage or setting for fantasies of perverse sex, had nothing to do with the other electric tension she carried from Mark. Yet both were called "sex."

She had gone to Jack because of a restless drive she had got from Mark, who had brought it up from the basement, where Lynda was ill. But Jack was not on that wavelength. She was physically tired, physically satisfied. She also was alert and alive as a high-tension wire and might just as well have never gone to Jack.

So, then, it was of no use going to see Jack again. She decided she would not go. But she went. For one thing, if a woman goes to bed with a man then certain psychological rules start working, things have to play themselves out. A development or aspect of these rules was the process unrolling itself of his needing to see how far she would go, of her waiting to see how far she would go: it was an aspect of male-command-and-female-submission.

Besides, when she went away from him, it was always with the same thought: Where is Jack? She would think: I must be imagining that he is like this now. For she could remember so very clearly what he had been. Or she would think the opposite: I must be inventing what he was ten years ago. But she knew she hadn't invented it. Once he had been all a subtle physical intelligence. Now he had become stupid. Now his body was entirely a servant to a kind of cunning, which needed to get a woman under its will, in order to degrade her, but degrade her morally. It was an absolutely clear process, without ambiguity. He needed that his mind, his will, using the clumsiest of techniques for interesting, then arousing a woman, should bring her physically into a position where she had to submit to bullying. But the point was not the physical bullying at all—she could swear that was not what interested him. It was the breaking down that got her there which he needed. The need for this was what he had become.

One was able to watch while he used a kind of clumsy psychological technique to raise one's sexual and emotional temperature. The point was, other women must watch too: only a very stupid woman or an inexperienced one could remain unaware of what he was doing.

Or half aware; it was his clumsiness, the theatricalness of it, that was confusing. She could swear that all those years ago he had been neither theatrical nor cunning.

For all those years, while Martha had been in Mark's house, Jack had been here, creating a house which was like a perverted millionaire's brothel, and sitting like a spider while women came and went.

Also, of course, he had been ill. Very ill. His painfully thin body, which had always frightened him, had put him into bed for months in a sanatorium, and for months in the bare-boarded black-windowed room on the first floor of his house.

Jack said that she, Martha, had not changed at all. He needed to believe this. When he repeated and insisted that she had not, it was the only time that he was straightforward, nontheatrical, not playing games—with her, or with himself.

It was probable that some time while he had been ill the old Jack had simply died, or gone away, and this new person had walked in and taken possession.

Four

Easter Monday. Knightsbridge. Four, five abreast, they came past, under the black-and-white banners, the black-on-white posters, escorted by darkly uniformed policemen. Banners, pennants, symbols, pamphlets, broadsheets, badges, said what they said in white and black. For the rest, this crowd shambled along in variegated colour. They had been passing for three hours—impressive. From above, television helicopters had seen in England's hedgy landscape a road along which wound a moving column of little people five miles along, and had hovered low to make the most of this "national" phenomenon, just as reporters making estimates had put them high, at twelve thousand, rather than low, at six thousand, the ungenerous figure. The publicity people were making the most, rather than the least. Why? It would be easy to say "nothing succeeds like success"; unless of course one chose to remember the original aim of the march, which was not only to put an end to war conducted by means of nuclear weapons; but to put an end to nuclear weapons: to put an end to war.

Also, these impressive figures—more probably somewhere in the middle, at eight thousand, rather than twelve, or six—were not so impressive when one remembered that any Communist or a Labour Party May Day Parade might attract five, eight, ten thousand people; but these figures were usually lowered by unsympathetic editing to "a few hundred" if the marches were mentioned at all: which thought naturally led one to speculations about the nature not only of "news" but of facts.

For there was no doubt that to have been "on" a march unmentioned by the press or television was a very different experience from this one, where for the whole of the Easter holiday one could count on all newspapers and the television programmes "covering" the march.

Not only that; it was a different kind of a fact altogether, reading a column of print which began "The Aldermaston Marchers set out today in sun/fog/snow/rain, two/three/four/five thousand strong . . ." from seeing a picture of several thousand people under the magpie-coloured banners; as different again as from walking several miles in procession under this or that set of banners without seeing a word of it mentioned afterwards in a newspaper or photographed onto a television screen.

There were some among this crowd who had been walking across this or that part of the British Isles under banners for decades. Sometimes these walks, or excursions, had been public facts, like the hunger marches; some had remained almost private, like a nice ramble among friends.

From time to time, people in crowds feel impelled to express feelings of one sort or another by marching in company along roads to some goal, carrying devices and banners: the Crusaders (to stretch time a little) of course had no other means of locomotion but their own feet, or horses. But feelings about the use of nuclear energy for destruction were not expressed by rushing across continents in express trains, or circling the globe in jets, or even by driving an automobile across countries, but by putting one foot after another across earth. Strange, that. Suppose none of these people had read about those earlier marches, the Crusades? Or about the pilgrimages to holy places, on foot, across landscapes? Would they, we, still be putting one foot before the other across earth to say: Down with . . . or Ban the . . . or More money for . . . Well, yes, it seems more than likely. To move from one point to another on one's feet, as a means of expressing communal feeling about something or other, seems basic.

In other parts of Britain on that Easter Monday, groups of young people, mostly young men, were engaged in violently rushing from place to place, in gangs, either on motor bikes, or on their feet, but what they were for or against was not clearly stated or understood. They, too, were reported widely, given, in fact, as much or more space as peace marches—for homosexuality had dropped out of the spotlight of Morality, and had been succeeded by Teen-age Violence.

Most of the people on this march were teen-agers, probably three quarters. Some of them were violent. To move fast

407

along the march, from the back to the front, or to stand still and let it flow past one, was to feel oneself in a sort of river, sometimes quiet, sometimes tumultuous. In parts it ran fast —violent; people shouted slogans, and generated anger; the temperature was high. A few minutes later it ran quiet again. Those, by no means all teen-agers, who needed the high temperature were attracted to the parts of the column where the slogan-shouting and the aggressive singing took place. Others moved away to parts where people chatted, or sang indifferently. The fact was, the people on this march, united by the black-and-white banners, were extremely different from each other, had little in common except for the leaven of organisers.

This thought, like many others, was better kept quiet, or shared with a friend of one's own age. Martha leaned against a tree waiting for Lynda, who said she would be there. She waited, also, for Mark, who was bound to be at the end of the march. As usual he had nearly not come at all. The week before, by a coincidence, he had had two visits, one from an American, and one from a Hungarian, both under the impression that the well-known Marxist Mark Coldridge was a leading light in the anti-bomb movement. Mark had tried to refer them both to his brother Arthur, but as everyone knows, writers are more attractive as exemplars than politicians. Why? To answer that means to answer why writers are employed by universities to give lectures on "creative writing," when no creative writing ever comes out of this process. It means being able to answer why writers are asked to give lectures at all. It means, to understand why writers . . .

Why; how; where; when. Such questions are spawned by the hundred by social phenomena like the Aldermaston March and its spirit; which was something rather warm, generous, a little self-mocking, and very romantic.

Five thousand, or eight, or twelve thousand people amble across a damp soil at Eastertime to protest at the world's arsenals of poisonous weapons. But, as they joked frequently up and down the columns, every weekend in football stadiums all over the country hundreds of thousands of people paid out fortunes to watch teams of men kick a small ball around.

On the very first Aldermaston, a tall pretty girl had wheeled a pushchair with a baby in it, and carried a small square of postcard which said: Caroline Says No.

Did it matter a damn what Caroline said? Well, this

concourse of people paid tribute to the proposition that it did matter what Caroline said: against all reason and probability.

But if it mattered what Caroline said anywhere else, in Parliament for instance, would this march then be taking place? Very probably not, but who knew.

Such negative thoughts one has in England, leaning against a tree, watching five or twelve thousand people march past. In England, we are privileged. The Hungarian visitor was a Communist of forty-five or so, imprisoned and tortured under Horthy, then imprisoned and tortured by the Nazis, then imprisoned and tortured by that aspect of Communism now labelled Stalinism. He enjoyed a prominent position in the newly liberated Communist Hungary, and was full of infectious enthusiasm for the good qualities of the human race. When he lunched with Mark, he could eat nothing but boiled potatoes, since his stomach had been ruined long since by his various confinements, and had had to spend most of his time standing up, because his back, twisted in some bout of torture, hurt him when he sat too long. His demand was that Mark "on behalf of all lovers of liberty everywhere" should continue to march and demonstrate, not of course that these activities would have any effect at all on the arms race—he hoped that Mark would not think him so naive—but it was important that the youth of his country, Hungary, should see on newsreels and in newspapers that there were countries where people protested, were able to protest, that they had the right to protest. Freedom! Liberty! Democracy! For these, Mark should get onto his feet and walk from Aldermaston, to London under banners: what the banners actually said was almost irrelevant. Mark said yes; that was why he had been marching, though it was not a view which found much sympathy. At which his visitor had shaken his hand, called him comrade, and departed to some meal organised by the Arts Council.

The American, a young man of twenty-five, son of socialists, his father working as a clerk in a store because a Joe McCarthy committee had seen to it that he could no longer get work in a university, his mother in a mental hospital because of prolonged attention by the police, came to Mark saying that it was essential that Mark and people like him should march, because newsreels and reports of the marchers were making it easier for him "and the twenty people like him in the States" to get young people on to their feet

409

politically. "You are doing," said Brandon Stone, "more to undo what Joe McCarthy did than anything else that is happening anywhere." He had left to address a meeting of the New Socialists on American Poverty; but he knew it was a waste of time. For America was still, according to everyone except the American poor, not only wealthy but wealthy in such a way that there weren't any poor. To say anything different at that time was to earn tolerant or irritated smiles as for crankishness, or wilfully negative criticism.

Liberty. Freedom. Justice.

Caroline said no.

Mark was on the march, somewhere. Phoebe had telephoned the night before, indefatigably efficient organiser that she was, to enquire: Are you going to be there or *not?*

Well, I have been so far, haven't I?

Yes, but you are so *irritating.* I suppose you are going to be childish again? This sour note was due not to his perverse reasons for marching: she merely hoped he would keep his mouth shut, and not corrupt unspoiled people; but because "like all the other V.I.P.'s" he would *still* not march in the front where he could be seen.

What's the point of your coming at all, she cried, if no one knows it? In this way did she sum up the interesting question of the nature of fact: of how presentation alters an event. For if Mark Coldridge had been photographed by television cameras and newspapers then there is no doubt that he would have been more "there" than if merely mentioned in print; while marching even if "all the way" was as good as not marching at all since he didn't get either mentioned or photographed. And in fact, it could be said that being photographed, let's say on a plinth in Trafalgar Square, without having marched a foot, was to be more "there" than "marching all the way." That is, from the point of view of an organiser who, teased with "But Phoebe, I'm bearing witness," replied, "Who's interested in your conscience?"

Between people like Phoebe and Caroline, with her square of cardboard, there were, in fact, gulfs in outlook.

"I simply don't understand you, Mark—surely you're not still angry with the newspapers? They are all on our side this time."

Mark, looking at his study walls and ceiling and their lethal messages, while he telephoned, said: "Quite clearly it doesn't matter a damn whose side they are on. I was stupid to care then, and when the wind changes again I'll remember just what it's all worth." And, when Miles Tangin, now the producer of a television news programme, caught sight of Mark on the second day, and shook him by the hand, while his eyes grew damp with that emotion generated by the sight of thousands of people marching, Mark went out of his way to give him a great deal of good advice about his new novel. For Miles was marching "part of the way" with them.

Who was "they" this year, on this, the biggest of the Aldermaston marches? The phenomenon had reached its peak. But why? Who knew? Who knows how to chart such a curve? It had started unexpectedly, had grown on its own logic, had reached its height, would now decline. At the peak, this year, as at all similar peaks of political feeling, were thousands of people who had never before been near anything remotely political, and would soon drift off, to find, for one reason or another, anything remotely political rather distasteful. "Childish"—that word would be revived again when it always is, at the beginning of a time of reaction. Meanwhile the banners were those to be seen at any demonstration: C.N.D.... Peace ... Labour ... Communist ... Pacifist ... Trade Union ... Youth ... Young ... Jewish ... German ... French ... Trotskyite ... Anarchist ... And then the theatre groups, the bands, and the dancers and the singers.

But at the core, people from all over the world who agitated and protested and complained and fought. A Tory newspaperman muttered that if a bomb could be dropped on this lot, they'd have no more trouble for a decade. His view was in fact the same as Caroline's: it mattered if people, individuals, said no.

Heartening; except that to stand under a tree watching the columns pass it was to see on how small a number depended the belief in saying no.

Suppose one had had to stand here not being able to pick out this face, that face; suppose one did not know how twelve thousand melted to a couple of dozen when the heat came on? As it was, one looked for the faces—one here, one there, for the most part as ordinary, as unremarkable as Phoebe's.

Joss Cohen's, for instance. Having helped to organise a large mass movement "up North," he had been expelled by the Colonial government, and was now living in Britain, in Phoebe's flat, where he advised, aided, found money for Africans from many parts of Africa. He was now a stout man from behind whose spectacles his eyes gleamed as sensibly as ever. He had messages from Jasmine, in the process of being tried for treason in South Africa. They were cheerful messages, rather banally so. The words had been carefully chosen to be easily quotable in a newspaper and to give a good impression of "the cause." "Down with the Nats!" was one. Another: "Men and women of goodwill continue to fight!" But if Jasmine had been there, she would have been unnoticeable, a rather stolid woman in her good expensive clothes, and not anyone to look at twice. It was almost certain that she would be going to prison soon, and it was not likely to be a short sentence.

The core of the march was composed of such people. Yet to look at it it was as if socialism had decided to have a carnival. There was a wryness, a spirit of parody, or of sending oneself up, expressed in what looked like fancy dress, or carnival costume. Yet why, since what could be more practical than jeans and duffel coats, or Phoebe's blue plastic mac and blue headscarf, or Phoebe's daughters' fisherman's jackets? Perhaps it is that any large mass of people must have a look of charade if there is no common dress to wear? Mark, who rose every morning at six to polish his shoes, and shave, and brush his tweeds and his umbrella, to join the march at its start—wherever that was for the day—looked like a gentleman farmer, and raised cheers from the duffel-coated teen-agers. A group of young Tories wearing striped trousers, black coats and bowler hats, on principle, as they took pains to explain, raised another cheer, appreciatively ironical. There was no dress or form of behaviour that was not affectionately received; and perhaps the most telling incident of that march was when a Tory member of Parliament, annoyed with the march, stood by the columns in a wet field playing a portable gramophone and shouting insults at the marchers. But since one could not hear what he was playing (it was the national anthem), nor hear what he was shouting, he was taken to be an eccentric supporter, and cheered accordingly. Similarly, on the first march, in 1958, the man of peace in charge of Reading Cathedral pealed his bells as the marchers came in to express his hostility, but was assumed to be friendly and greeted by cheers. And a hostile bystander who shouted "I wish I could drop a bomb on all of you" was swept into the columns by some girls with long wet hair and rainy faces, and ended drinking tea under dripping trees in a field singing "When the Saints . . ." and so on.

But in the evenings, warming themselves with brandy in

Mark's study, Mark, Lynda, Martha (not the children, who were sleeping in school halls somewhere along the route) sat quietly together, three middle-aged people with nothing in their experiences of the world to help them to faith in the utility of Caroline's saying no. They sat in Mark's study and they looked at the walls. They looked at the walls, and they drank brandy and talked of the last war, which at no point had been within anybody's control, or indeed within anyone's imagination, before it happened. They thought that Caroline, walking sandalled with long hair down her back pushing a small baby in a chair, said no; and wondered if perhaps the spirit of the march, the wry gaiety, its gentle self-mockery, was perhaps a salute to the knowledge that no one wished to own; and despair being its own antidote, it was breeding from its nucleus something like a laugh.

When Mr. Quest lay dying, he looked around, in a moment of extra lucidity, at the creatures fussing around his bed, animals with clothes on who made strange noises with their mouths and noses to communicate and to express feelings, and he remarked, "A funny thing laughter, what's it for?" They did not understand him; so he kept quiet, again became an old man nearly dead, to be given medicines.

To leave Mark's study each morning early, so as to join the march wherever it had reached, was to leave a cold clear light for a carnival light.

A carnival, so some people said, critically or approvingly, of children. Well, one way of looking at this march was to remember that three-quarters of these people were children born either during the last war, or soon afterwards. One way of "doing" the march was in fact to talk to children. One might march, or amble, day after day, from Aldermaston with its great wire fences and its police dogs and its air of official righteousness and secrecy, on to Reading, most hideous of towns, from Reading on to riverside Staines, from Staines on to Chiswick, and so through London and its doomed streets, to Hyde Park and Trafalgar Square—talking to people under twenty-one. One might also set oneself to find out what place the last war had played in the beginnings of these people's lives. One found out that there was probably no person here whose conception, babyhood, childhood or youth had not been "disturbed" (to use the psychiatrist's phrase) by that war. One might also go on to make enquiries about the parents of these people, most of whom very likely had been fundamentally involved in the war before the last. There were very few people indeed in, or near, or associated with these columns of walking people whose lives did not have a great gulf in them into which all civilisation had vanished, temporarily at least. There was probably no one here whose life had, or could, be remotely like that one once described by Thomas as "being born under the elm tree, living, courting, marrying, dying, being buried under the elm tree."

These were people who had all been stripped. And their talk, when one got past the slogans and the temporary excitements of this big march and all the people, was extremely sensible. And rather sad. For one thing few believed that they had futures, in the sense that their grandparents would have defined a future. These were people who knew, before they were twenty, what their grandparents knew, perhaps, as they died.

They were also people prepared to protect their parents from unpleasant realities. For instance, for the whole of a marching or strolling afternoon, Martha had walked behind a group of students who were discussing the potions bubbling in the cauldrons of the laboratories of the world that will turn us all into sprites or toads. They were discussing their children, and how they might be geniuses or idiots; that they would almost certainly be mutants of some kind; and what their own attitude would be. A father of one of the girls came past, heard a scrap of the talk, exclaimed sharply that they were being very negative. At which the students politely engaged him in safe talk until he went on appeased, when they continued with their discussion. What kinds of mutant might be expected? How would one recognise one? What kind of capacity of brain, heart, imagination would be welcomed and what feared? Perhaps there were mutants already, for good or for bad, but one did not yet know it. After all, so much radioactive material was already loose in air and soil and water, it was likely that changes were in existence. And in which case . . . The talk went on until it was time to stop in a field for a meal. The girl's father appeared, and enquired in joke if she was still being so pessimistic. At which she had called him bourgeois, using the word correctly, meaning a person preferring safety, comfort, illusion, to the hazards and adventures of revolution. But in this case the revolution had gone inwards, was in the structure of life's substance.

This incident was typical. The discussions that went on up and down the columns were infinitely in advance of the slogans on the banners and placards; which might account

414

for the number of people who chanted slogans like "Ban the Bomb" and so on as if they found the syllables absurd. Of course it is not possible to have a political slogan that is anything but simple and therefore absurd. But there probably has never been a political demonstration where the content of people's talk was more divergent from the banners they walked under. In imagination they were exploring worlds of extraordinary possibilities, change, discovery, revolution; meanwhile they chanted Ban the Bomb and Down with ... and Hands off ...

When Mark came into view, he was at the very end of the march, surrounded by fifteen-year-olds blowing feather squeakers and wearing funny hats. The banner above them said: "The Moxton Young Socialists for Peace." With Mark was Jimmy Wood. His newest book was about a human mutant quite invisible to ordinary humanity because he was apparently and outwardly normal. Yet his capacities were superhuman. These children had read *The Man Two Doors Down*; they had never heard of Mark Coldridge. As the end of the march trailed into Hyde Park, the children were suggesting to Jimmy various capacities which humanity might find useful, if only they could be developed; Jimmy was seriously writing them down on the back of an envelope; Mark was waving at Martha and looking for Lynda.

A band stationed by the entrance was so loud it was necessary to stop talking till they were past "When the Saints ..."

In this area of Hyde Park was a sea of people, an ocean. The word went around that there were a hundred thousand people; two hundred thousand perhaps? No, that was too high, but as many people as would attend a good football match stood and sat on damp grass or were preparing to leave this stopping place: the head of the column had left as the tail came in.

And there was Lynda. She wore her pale shaggy coat, her pale hair was up in a knot, her pale face smiled. She sat on a shooting stick, and was trying to peel an orange into a paper handkerchief with heavily gloved fingers. She could not take off the gloves because of her bitten finger ends.

They joined her and stood watching the people, who were all engaged in watching each other for friends, relatives, comrades in arms from other countries.

They were all feeling that lightheadedness, a pleasant unreality that comes from watching large numbers of people moving apparently at random across space. Trees in new leaf seemed to move as the people moved, as one moved oneself; and overhead meandered great clouds. Lynda, Mark, Martha watched. In a great concourse of people one may watch Martha, Lynda, Mark pass and repass in front of one, variations on a theme.

For instance, Francis went past with young Nicky, and a strongly built vital girl with short yellow hair and dark eyes. Nicky, female, would be a Lynda; Francis would be his father—and how many different shapes had Martha already worn? A strongly built dark woman, middle-aged, with greying hair, on the arm of her husband, a tall thin rather stooped fair man, greying, his blue eyes remote and inwardly turned, had with them a roundish flat-faced girl with flat soft hair and straight gaze. Martha, Lynda, Mark. Three students went past, a tall rather stooping blonde girl with great grey eyes, and a stocky energetic blonde with her hand in that of a round smiling boy. A strongly built man, probably a journalist or writer of some kind, accompanied a roundly built, flat-faced, brown-eyed woman, possibly his wife; a blond tall boy, their son perhaps, was with them. Martha, Mark, Lynda.

They passed and repassed, on the thick spring grass, under rolling pearly clouds.

"Your mother is here," said Lynda.

"Checking her guest list no doubt," said Mark.

"For the last time," said Lynda. Last night Lynda, who was not very well, had said she must be here today because she felt this would be the biggest march, and she wanted to see it. The crowds were much larger than last year. Next year, Phoebe and others like her thought, they would be larger still. The obvious rightness of their point of view would bring out, year by year, larger and larger numbers of people wearing black-and-white badges, until from Land's End to John o' Groat's blossomed the symbol and swords would be beaten into ploughshares on the spot. Some thing like that.

But next year Margaret would not be here.

"I'm going home," said Lynda. "All these people. I feel in a swarm of bees."

Margaret approached across the grass. She did not really approve of the march, but so many of her friends were there, that she had taken out, by car, luncheon hampers to wherever they were likely to be, by lunchtime. Her food was, of course, very good. Behind her, smiling, came her husband John. The focus being off homosexuality and turned

416

elsewhere, John was on the whole a better husband to Margaret. In their circle they joked (it was Graham's joke first) that his father no longer felt obliged to prove himself. Margaret had just returned from a jaunt to Moscow where she had seen her truant son and been to many banquets: she had some Russian officials staying with her at the moment.

She observed her son, gentleman farmer, standing on two planted feet, his umbrella used as a stick; his wife, peeling an orange, and Martha, eating bits of Lynda's orange.

"A charming *ménage à trois*," she murmured, not so much cattily, but as it were attempting to define a position.

"Goodness, is that what we are?" asked Lynda.

"How should I know!" said Margaret.

"I should say sometimes yes and sometimes no," said Martha.

"I don't see that it matters what anyone says," said Mark.

"Oh, are you angry? I'm sorry," said Margaret. "Now you won't come to supper. And so many of your chums are coming."

"Unfortunately I can't," said Mark.

"My darling Russians are ever so interested in your book about me," said Margaret. "They are talking of translating it."

Mark did not say anything. Margaret smiled, nodded and turned to return to her guests. Behind her went John.

Phoebe came up, in her blue cellophane wrappings; she frowned.

"But dear Phoebe, it is such a success," said Lynda. "And so well organised."

"It would be if it wasn't for those lunatics."

There came to them, then, one of the lunatics, Francis. He gave his mother, as always, his wary glance for storm warnings; as always Lynda smiled, for him. He accepted a bit of orange.

"Really," said Phoebe, "why do you people *have* to, why do you spoil everything? I've had the police around again—what is the use of my making plans with the police if you people then change everything?"

"What you are saying is," said Francis, "why don't we let you run everything for us, because you know how to do it and we don't?"

"No, but . . . ."

"*Yes.* And I'm not even there, am I? Here I am, with the forces of law and order."

"Well, tell your Nicky to come and see me tonight, I really must discuss it with him."

"I'll *suggest* it. And he'll probably be in prison tonight."

Nicky had left the main march to go off and join in a Committee of a Hundred demonstration in front of the Soviet embassy. Phoebe approved, personally, of the demonstration; but knew that many of her committee would not. Her committee had formally dissociated themselves from this particular demonstration.

Several times a week, Phoebe rang up Francis to instruct Nicky; Francis remained polite.

"And have you seen Gwen?"

"She's with Nick."

"Oh for heaven's sake, if she gets arrested *again* then I suppose . . ." She stopped herself, while he waited for her to do so. He was smiling courteously.

"And I suppose Jill is here too?"

"Jill's just watching somewhere," he said gently.

Jill, some months before, had become pregnant by a visiting West Indian jazzman. She had refused to have an abortion until the last minute. Phoebe was urging her to have one. Jill had said, for about fifteen hours of every day, that Phoebe's wanting her, Jill, to have an abortion meant that Phoebe's support of Africans was all a sham. Secretly, said Jill, her mother must hate coloured people, otherwise she'd love her daughter to have a "a dear little black baby." This phrase nearly drove Phoebe wild with exasperation. When it got to three months or so, Phoebe said she thought it was too late now to get an abortion, and she would stand by Jill and help her with the baby. Then Jill decided to have an abortion after all; but it was nearly four months by the time she got into hospital, and she had had a bad time with it. Everyone had had a bad time.

Phoebe had been relying on Francis. A woman who never asked for help, because she did not believe it could be given, now without knowing it appealed for help continually, in voice, gesture, glance. Usually from Francis, that rock of good sense, Jill's friend.

"I'll keep an eye on her, don't worry," said Francis.

Her smile was stiff, pathetic. Relying on Francis was not all jam. When she had complained to him about Jill's behaviour, all he had said was: What were you like when you were seventeen? This had made Phoebe furious: it was unjust. Yes, she did see that for Francis the immorality of it (the carelessness, the indifference to the child's well-being) was

418

not the point: he was saying that everyone was difficult when they were seventeen. For him, quite clearly, *how* they were difficult was immaterial. Phoebe brooded again that she had been a virgin when she married Arthur, and had imagined herself to be principled and self-controlled.

Yet now she was depending on Francis, who treated her, so she muttered privately, as if she were just as bad and cruel as Jill. When he went off into the crowd, she trailed off after him, as if after a possible saviour. She looked as if she were tailing him: her rather reddened nose projecting past the edge of the blue plastic hood, her hands clutching papers and plans of all kinds.

Soon, Paul came past with the theatre group he had attached himself to. At first he did not see the three people to whom he referred, with his characteristic mixture of insolence and charm, as "my extended family." He was talking to a director from Hamburg, a man who listened to the boy with a smile that said he was being well entertained. Paul saw the three. Expressions passed rapidly across his face each one unmixed with what preceded or followed it. First, the look an animal has when it sees something possibly dangerous; next, a beam of pure spontaneous warm affection; next, a look meant to be observed by them, and by anyone else, of humorous tolerance for the absurd; finally, what he imagined to be a smile of worldly ease. Gently patting Zena to one side, with yet another smile, indulgent, gentle, he ran gracefully towards the three. Among the people he had left, some turned to note the writer Mark Coldridge; without appearing to, Paul watched to see who these were. "What, no orange for me?" he asked Lynda, who handed him a piece of orange, with a smile that said, though affectionately: You aren't fooling me. These two had recently become friends again; at least there was a truce.

"Yes I know," said Paul aloud. "But dependent entirely on my own resources as I am, having to make my own way in this wicked world as I do, you must expect me to use you."

"Oh not at all," said Mark.

Paul gave them all a smile both affectionate and impudent, and returned, running lightly, to rejoin his group. They saw how first he reassured Zena, with a look and a touch, before slipping in again beside the German celebrity.

They looked at each other, but muting what they felt, because from fifty yards away Paul craned back to see if he had gone too far. His face was apprehensive. They waved frantically. Delighted, he waved back.

On the whole, they were pleased with him.

Some months ago he had announced that "thanks to them he had no more education than the son of a workman" and that he supposed he had to educate himself since they would not.

He then set himself to acquire education, or rather information, as he acquired objects and trash from London's markets. He pursued people, or places that could inform him. Secretly he even watched television programmes that taught—but he did not like anyone to know this. Throughout the four days of the march he had been approaching people, not necessarily celebrities, who could give him something of what he wanted. The German director was at the moment in the news: Paul had announced before the weekend that he would become "a friend of his, you'll see." A friend of Francis's, a German boy, had recently stayed in the house for a week, and Paul had discovered he had a facility for languages: he had learned enough German to talk to the director. A part of this game was that Paul should not use Mark's name in any way; that is, not until Paul himself had made some kind of contact with whoever it was he pursued. This rule, like others, had been worked out from the beginning: another was that he should not have to pay for anything. The whole thing was to be done by charm.

The adults watched what was probably the birth of a con man; but after all, how much better that than some other futures they could only too easily imagine. And besides, there were other sides to Paul—Zena, for instance. She was now on the whole a liability to Paul, who was no longer shut in his floor of the house with his beautiful fabrics and his mirrors and his treasures. She stayed there when he was out, a silent, passive, beautiful little creature whom no one else could talk to. There she was, pale and listless, waiting for Paul. Her childhood had been so bad, or so it seemed, that she expected nothing from anyone; was surprised if anything was offered; assumed that it would be taken away again. Paul, she knew, would soon fly off or become impatient with her, as so many others had done before.

But Paul did not send her away. He was not unkind. He had even gone to "the old man," her mother's ex-lover, who was the chucker-out in a gambling club, and told him that if he did harm to Zena, he, Paul, would go to the police. The old man had thrown her out. Paul had taken her in. As he said: She practically lives here anyway, so what difference does it make? He went up to Birmingham where Zena's mother now was, to find out what went on: all Zena had said was that "Mum doesn't want me." This was half true. The mother had had a lot of children, and would probably go on having children: she was only just forty, and had Zena's numbed passivity. She spoke with a detached interest about Zena: as if the girl were not her daughter at all. Paul asked her if Zena couldn't come for weekends, or a holiday: "Zena is missing her family," he said. The passive mother had thought this was a good idea, but didn't say when Zena should come. Zena still felt she would not be welcome. Paul then took Zena to stay the weekend with her mother: this boy who cared apparently only for the beautiful, for success, for accomplishment, for comfort, bullied a wornout woman and her rather ill, or at least drinking, husband into being kind to Zena for a few days. He had even done the washing up and fed the small children.

But they all knew that one day, Paul would have to give up Zena: what else could he do?

Next to come past, with another theatre group, was Patty Cohen. She was with her current young man, another of the new working-class actors from the provinces. She did not look her best wearing a raincoat and a scarf: she looked like a healthy Jewish housewife. He was handsome, confidently working the vogue for his kind, with eyes on the lookout for every possible advantage. He spied Mark: they watched him edging her out of the column to come and greet the author. Patty was resisting—she even sent them a large good-natured shrug and a wink as if to say: Don't blame me for him!

Some weeks ago she had rung up to say that he was "going to be the last of the fighting cocks, I swear it." Apart from anything else, they were ruining her: it was not that any of them were deliberate spongers—but then, who is? The combination, as Patty said, of a warm-hearted mother figure who earned a good salary, and a young man with talent who was bound to earn too little, was simply *fatal*— she must put a stop to the whole thing. "When this brave boy flies away, then I must say no to the next."

Joking, she continued to assist them on their way, while she, it was obvious, was doing badly in other ways than financial. She had said that if she hadn't already had a breakdown she would be having one now—"but one gets tired of everything, including being neurotic." She said that ... she said a good deal, all amounting to the same thing, that she was bored with herself. The futility, the staleness, the harsh bright light of self-criticism that accompanies any stage of life where one is repeating outworn patterns of behaviour was aging her, staling her. Yet she could not stop. She had been unable to adopt a child: she was not eligible. Common sense told her that the authorities were right: what time would she have for a child, working all day? Yet children were what she wanted. She said that when she kicked the final young man out, then that would be the end of love and she could not face sleeping alone. Looking back over her life, which included so much hard work, for politics, for the theatre, she said there was nothing in it that was real save men, making love, sex.

She said this to Mark, one of the men, both Lynda and Martha being present. She had said it laughing; but she laughed all the time, and talked compulsively, asking continuously, Well, what do you think? What have you to say? Don't just sit there, tell me, what am I to do?

And so on.

She was doing this to all her settled friends, or as she said, "to anyone who has managed to share the same bed with anyone for longer than a year." She was making enemies; people were irritated by her, since, as usual, it appeared they were unable to see that she was rather ill.

She told Mark that he was an absolutely typical Englishman—that is, he was only able to stand a woman if she "was abroad, or dead, or married to someone else, or if he had seen her once like Beatrice from a distance"—and that if Lynda got well Mark would not be able to stand it; he'd run away.

"He'd probably fall madly in love with you, Martha, dreaming about you from afar, because of course you wouldn't be able to endure Mark's being in love with you, or at least wanting you to have and to hold; you're Mark's female equivalent."

All this had been at a supper table recently. Lynda, Martha, Mark and the young man, Derek from Leeds, had been in their different ways upset. The young man was fairly new in London and said he wasn't used to "the free and easy ways of the intellectuals."

"We aren't used to it either," said Lynda. "I'm not an intellectual."

"Oh sorry," he said, quickly; he was overapologetic. But then, she had been overangry. Feeling she had been, she said, with her special smile, "Oh never *mind*, please don't . . ."

In return she was engulfed in a great wave of his speciality, an easy sympathy. Lynda, always responsive to warm physical steadying, again smiled, her face turning to his like a sunflower. He smiled straight into her eyes; then remembered Patty, sardonically watching. He sat back in his chair, looked down at his plate.

For the onlookers it was like seeing a large stone flung into a small pool; overlarge waves had washed back and back.

This young man, now twenty-five, had used all the virtues one needs to get oneself out of the provinces into the talented city. He had been stubborn, patient, resourceful; had husbanded integrity and his talent. But, once arrived in London, he discovered that none of these was nearly as useful as a quality he had taken for granted, a straightforward human warmth, human response. He had of course read D. H. Lawrence as part of his self-education. Now he understood what D. H. Lawrence had been on about. He understood he was a Lawrentian hero.

It was not that he had ever consciously decided to move about in these circles like a battery of sexy-emotional sympathy; it was what he found was happening. Sometimes he would fiercely say to himself that London was corrupt: and he would remind himself of provincial virtues.

"I mean," chattered Patty, her shrewd gaze on her young man's safely lowered lids, "I simply can't imagine any one of you, I mean your kind of Englishman, Mark, actually living with your loved one and liking it—I don't mean just putting a good face on it, or being bitchy and spiteful in a long-suffering sort of way meant to be taken note of by poor wifie, or simply absenting themselves spiritually the way they do, but actually living with a woman all the way."

"I do," said Derek, speaking up stoutly for himself.

"Yes, love, but you are different, aren't you?"

At which point Francis had come in.

"And now shut up," said Mark to Patty.

"Not in front of the children," said Francis, smiling, his round boy's face ever-ready for hurt, looking with cautious enquiry at them all.

"And not in front of me," said Lynda.

"Oh for God's sake," said Patty, taking Francis into her camaraderie with a smile meant to be free and easy: "Francis isn't a little boy."

"Yes I am," said Francis, paling, setting a distance. "If you're on about what I think then I definitely am."

423

Patty did not sense his seriousness and was about to go on. She was kicked under the table by Derek. "Oh damn you," she said, leaning down to rub her ankle. "That's tact, is it."

"It's what you like, but shut up," Derek had said.

Later she rang to say she was sorry; she hadn't meant to upset anyone.

This having been the last time they had seen Patty, there was a tensing of the atmosphere as she came over the trampled grass with Derek.

He stood by Mark and began telling anecdotes about the day's walking.

"Come on, love," said Patty. "We'll never find our group again."

"In a minute."

He was watching a part of the crowd where people were forming up ready to march out of the big field. Soon a banner went up, rising into the air on sticks like a horse or a cow unfolding upwards onto its feet; and under it they saw Graham Patten, who would be coming past within a dozen feet.

"Oh do come on," said Patty, annoyed, realising why he stood there.

"You go ahead then, love," said he. "I'll catch you up."

Patty smiled with difficulty, then stood quietly to one side waiting. They were careful not to catch her eyes.

Graham saw them, and broke ranks to come over, including them all in his benevolent showman's smile. "Darling . . . darling . . ." he murmured, kissing Martha and Lynda, and nodding to Mark, who was his real object. He stood by Patty and moulded her bottom in his large hand in a way which dismissed her. Her value on the success scale was badly down, partly because her neurotically anxious state made her less useful to her employers; though they did not realise this, for they did not know the real reason why she was invaluable. It was partly too because the various young men, having used her and left, were malicious; and these young men had more "say" in setting tones, moods, indices, than anybody else.

To be with Graham anywhere was to know exactly where one stood in the success market: Patty not only looked annoyed, but went pale. She said to them later that night that she had had no idea until that moment had badly she had slipped. Now she did not suffer the amorously possessive but patronising hand as she should. She said, spurting anger:

"Oh for God's *sake*." All affability, Graham raised his eyebrows, took a step away from her, and dismissed her from his attention. He turned to Mark but found Derek beside him.

Derek was signalling sympathetic understanding towards Patty; but a humorous indulgence towards Graham.

Messages flashed between Graham and Derek: they were meeting for the first time.

"And what hair, too," said Graham, after a pause. ". . . what hair! . . ." As he said this, he looked, with a melancholy not at all forced, straight into the young man's eyes. Simultaneously he reached out a hand to fondle Patty's hair. She had a lot of it; it was in what might be described as winsome disarray, but after all, it was greying.

Patty was now too angry to protest; at the same time she shrewdly noted the interchange between her young man and Graham, dissecting Graham's multifunctional gesture. In fondling her hair after she had protested, he was insisting on his right to do so; also, he was putting her into the position where whether she protested again or not, she must look ridiculous. Also, he was telling her young man, that he, Graham had prior rights, that (very likely) he had had Patty at some time or another. Also, he was giving himself something to do while he recovered himself from the blow of seeing the young man. For, as the women looked at Derek from Leeds, their senses alerted by Graham's sudden and genuine gravity, they saw again that he was extraordinarily, marvellously, good-looking: a hero of the times, indeed. His hair, a glistening lively substance, like pale gold, worn rather long, showed ears all alert sensibility; his eyes were steadily intelligent; his mouth managed to combine the sensibility of a policeman's or prizefighter's with a look of being permanently damp with kisses.

In every mind suddenly danced images of love: ears, hands, buttocks, thighs and mouths whirled about them like leaves in a spring gale, and as the temperature rose, Graham, breathing fast, and laughing at himself, said: " 'I grow chilly and . . .' "

"And I," said Patty, "am *not* going to finish the quotation."

"Oh not yet darling, not yet, why should you? And I wouldn't either, in your place."

Graham continued to stand by them, or by Derek, while the columns unwound themselves out of the park. He had forgotten why he had come over, which was to get Mark to go on his programme.

He was about to rejoin the marchers, when he remembered, and said to Mark: "Have you thought it over?"

Mark said: "The thing is, I'm not short of money at the moment."

Graham, used to his stepbrother, did not look to see if he meant to be offensive: he knew he did not. Other people had found Mark offensive.

"I'll see all you darling people," said Graham, in his manner of sending up the things he was forced to say. After a swift involuntary swoop into the young man's eyes, he tore himself away and went off into the crowd. Derek looked after him: Graham's new television programme showed signs of being extra-successful.

Patty said: "And are all you darling people going home soon?"

"Yes," said Mark, "no speeches at any price."

"Then I'll come with you if . . ." She looked at her young man and said: "Perhaps you'd rather stay with the others."

His face lit into relief. "Thanks," he said. "Thanks . . ." He was already off across the grass when he remembered, turned, hastily gripped Patty in a kiss, and then ran lightly under the great damp trees to lose himself in the moving crowd.

"Oh *God*," said Patty aloud, in a sudden uncontrollable agony. "Oh God. Well, that's that, wouldn't you say?"

"On the whole yes," said Lynda.

"It looks like it," said Martha.

"Anyway," said Mark, "he's not good for anything that I can see, except . . ."

"Oh, yes, quite, precisely so, exactly," said Patty, laughing angrily. She wept, heaved with tears, blubbered, while they went with her across the grass in the other direction towards Marble Arch.

"I know I'm a fool," said Patty, gripping Mark, who was nearest, in such violence of grief that his raincoat was pulled down his arm. She staggered, had to be held up, her face was red and swollen, like a drunk woman's.

It was essential to get her home so she could lie down. Taxis for some reason were not about. They stood on the pavement waiting for one while Patty swore at herself and wept.

Lynda made a couple of cold and impatient remarks.

Mark said: "You sound like some kind of spinster, Lynda."

Lynda went very white; she reached for Martha's hand like a little girl. A taxi came up. Mark, anguished that he had been unkind to his beloved Lynda, said: "Lynda, you and Martha go on, I'll come in another with Patty."

"Oh," said Patty, "don't trouble about me, I'm just a fool and I deserve ..."

"Yes, yes," said Mark and bundled her into the taxi, getting in after her. "You two come on then," he said, and knocked on the glass for the driver to start.

Lynda and Martha stood, Lynda clutching Martha's hand, waiting.

Among the people crossing the road from the park came Jack. He was bending over, being attentive to, a young fresh-faced girl. As he reached the pavement, he saw Martha, hesitated, decided not to show he had seen her, and went past, attending to the girl, who looked Irish, like an old-fashioned gentleman.

Martha had not seen him for a long time.

She had discovered how he earned his money. He broke in girls for a brothel. But they were prepared in a certain way; for it was a certain kind of brothel.

Jack had described the methods to Martha, while she, stupidly, had exclaimed, Yes, but I don't see why ... why did you ... what is the point of ... Until she understood that this way of talking to her, which combined a rather offhand and insulting brutality about aims with a meticulous, patient and indeed humble care in "I would like you to believe me; please believe me, Martha, that ... what I want above all is trust ..." was in fact the technique used on the girls. And there was no need to ask why, how, what for, for she had only to watch her own reactions to see how it all worked.

It was essentially a process of degradation. But not a straightforward one. It would not have done, for instance, to take some girl and beat her up, or rape her, or force her into a brothel or into a compliance with this or that act. The girl had to be taken step by step along a road where she half understood and submitted to her own degradation. It was a process of psychological breaking down. When Jack described blow by blow how such and such an innocent girl (virgins were best) was led to voluntarily agreeing to stay in the brothel, this description was a breaking-down of Martha, insofar as she was prepared to listen and accept. Because it was calculated, measured, to affect Martha.

He would see or hear of some girl new in the neighbourhood, working in a laundry or shop. She was probably provincial, or from Ireland, or perhaps from the Continent. He would drop in to where she worked, was always formal, dignified, gravely interested. She usually remarked at this stage that she liked his manner, it was respectful: unlike most young men's. But during this stage he would drop in a couple of remarks or gestures quite out of character with this correctly formal person. He would suddenly belch a string of four-letter words; or goose her; it didn't matter what—the point was, whatever he did or said was quick, and instantly concealed again behind the grand-seigneur manner which (since he was a farmboy from the highveld) sat on him like a top hat on a farm labourer. There was something insultingly wrong about it—and purposefully so.

The girl would wonder if she had imagined the rude words, the gesture. If she referred to them, he might look surprised or shocked and say, "What do you mean?"

At some point he said something like: "I have a friend who would be interested to meet you." She would suggest a local café; he, his house. (But he would say my friend's house—or my flat—anything that was *not* the truth.) "Don't you trust me?" he would enquire in his melancholy resigned way when she demurred at coming to his house. She went, in the end. There she would find Jack dressed up as a Turk or perhaps an Arab. When she said: "Why, Jack, what are you doing in that costume?" he would reply: "I think you are mistaken. I am Abdulla"—something or other. She would giggle nervously; he would be gravely distant, suggesting she was bad-mannered. They would have Turkish coffee ("flown in from my homeland") or Turkish delight, or something of the kind. The whole purpose of this interview was to make the girl fall in with his charade. Which might vary. For instance, he would be his own younger brother. Or perhaps there might be someone else there: another girl induced to act as his sister; or one of the other men associated with the brothel pretending to be something that he obviously was not.

She would return, confused, to her work, thinking continually about the incident, half intrigued, half insulted and angry. He would not come in to see her immediately—not for some days. When he came he would not refer to the occasion until she did. She would say: "But Jack, why were

428

you pretending the other afternoon?" Or: "Was that really your sister?" Again, he would be gravely reproachful. Yet at some point (exactly as he had used the discordant language or gesture) he would, and with sudden vulgarity, say something like: "Oh, you can see through me, I like a girl you can't fool."

Even while she was smiling, flattered, very relieved that the farce was over, furious that he thought her stupid, he would have retreated back to his grand-opera dignity. He would leave her alone for a time. Not until he and whatever incident he had staged had become a memory that had more humiliation in it than pleasure would he again drop in to the shop or laundry or whatever it was. He would arrive in a state of moral indignation; at first playing a determination to preserve a wounded dignity, then (as if it were being forced out of him) reproaching her for not trusting him, for listening to gossip and so on. She, naturally, protested innocence. But in order to show she trusted him, she had to go to his house (or flat or room or friend's place) again. She went, feeling herself both falsely accused and deeply in the wrong. In Jack's house, she was taken to one of the ambiguously furnished rooms. Nothing very much was said: the atmosphere, however, was very strong. Something might be lying around—a riding whip, or a hangman's noose in nylon rope. "A friend of mine hanged himself last week—I was so fond of him." Meanwhile she was offered tea on a silver tea tray, brought in by a girl, or young man, pretending to be a servant. She would probably crack and leave at this point. But he would do nothing to stop her beyond saying: "You're going? I am so very very sorry. You do believe me, when I say how very sorry I am?" She might leave altogether, and push it out of her mind: rare, that. It would appear that there aren't so many strong-minded women; or perhaps it was that his original choices were good. She might leave the house, but find herself returning, full of incongruous emotion—she was in the wrong, she had behaved rudely. But this emotion would be in violent conflict with suspicion, unease, fear. Or she would get to the door and simply turn around and come back: "I'm sorry, Jack," she might say. "I don't want you to think I'm just silly."

She was now ready for the next stage. Over this Jack would spend a lot of thought, for it was enjoyable to choose just exactly that degree of "wrongness" for a particular girl. As he said: "You get a raw girl from Western Ireland, for instance, and if you can get her to neck just past her limit

429

under a crucifix, that would do the trick. Mind you, you have to choose the right size and style of crucifix."

It could be any such incident. For instance, there had been a girl who prided herself on her broad-mindedness and lack of convention. She had in the middle of a formal tea cried: "Where's your loo, Jack, I've simply got to spend a penny." With gravity he escorted her to the door of the lavatory, held it open for her, and then went in with her. As she hesitated he remarked, "I always know whether my girls really love me or not by whether they will show they are mine by letting me stay with them." This threw her into total confusion. First, she had not known she was "one of his girls." Or that love came into it, or was going to. She might ask him to leave the room; or hesitate, then squat down, smiling.

Soon, the girl would be wondering why she was not being kissed; for probably she had not been. He talked a great deal about his sex life, in vaguely horrifying terms, but he treated her formally except for the lightning flashes of filth or the sudden gesture. It would be the girl who would, out of nervousness or curiosity, make the first move. And at this point Jack went into a great emotional act of some kind, it didn't matter what. That he loved her "but not like that." Or he did love her sexually but realised she was the sort of girl who would not be satisfied with "just sex." Or he had five girls already, and would not be able sexually to meet her needs. She would then reassure him, and they got into bed, in his remarkable room, all black-and-white austerity in the middle of his house which was like a brothel. (It was not a brothel: the brothel was elsewhere; this was a breakdown area.) Again, she would be manipulated into accepting some posture or act or technique, it didn't matter what, which was just one degree beyond what she considered right. When the act was over, she would have been continually assured that this particular act was not only the essence of real sexuality, and that Jack was its exponent, and that her talent for it was extraordinary, but that it was considered beyond the pale by the conventional world (left undefined—but "them" as distinct from "us" was introduced at this point). She would have enjoyed an extreme of sexual pleasure; mixed or not, according to her disposition, with pain; but also mixed with moments of angry rebellion and humiliation which *she*, not he, had overcome.

Soon she would, to show she trusted Jack, sit in the room while he made love (usually quite differently from the way

430

he did it with her) or make love with him while some man
or girl watched.

After each such act, she would suffer violent reactions
against him, against what she had done. But he never approached her, persuaded her, forced her, except in ways
such as that he would appear outside the window of the shop
where she was working, looking pale, distressed, a tragic
ghost among men, and stand there for an hour, two hours,
sending her speaking looks. Then vanish without a word. If
she rang him up, or dropped in, she would hear: "I can't live
without you, you know that." Five minutes later, he would
say with a vulgarly casual laugh: "And you can't live without"—some vividly disgusting phrase, or one she would consider disgusting—"can you? Oh I know you."

After some months of this treatment, her will was broken,
she would do anything he asked, and she began to go on the
streets, but only in a very refined sort of way to start with.
To show that she trusted him. He would choose a man for
her, wait outside some room until the act was over, and take
her back home with him, thanking her humbly all the way.
He would not take the money at first. It was often she who
suggested the second act, because he would not: perhaps a
faint suggestion had been left that she had not done well, the
customer was not satisfied. In due course she moved into the
house, owned by Jack and a man from Glasgow. There were
several girls there. They catered for men and women whose
tastes were as much for psychological sadomasochism as for
the physical. In fact, the girls might come to Jack for a
"normal screw" because of the perverts that used the house.

Which was extremely profitable and had many highly
respected citizens as customers. Jack frequented public occasions of all kinds to find customers and new girls.

He did not keep the one he had found among the marchers—or it looked as if he hadn't. Outside Lyons, she went
away, leaving him alone. Now he glanced towards Martha,
and wondered whether to acknowledge that he had seen her.
But he had decided that she was without profit. That is, a
battle of wills had resulted in stalemate. Having understood
that her anger because "he was so stupid he didn't see that
she saw through every move he made" was in fact part of
the mechanism towards submission; she had said she would
make love so-and-so but not such and such. He had said she
was *unfeminine*—always a sure ploy with emancipated wom-
en. Characteristically, she was made to feel herself unfeminine for desiring to enjoy feminine satisfactions; everything

431

was stood on its head and became its opposite in Jack's house.

But he could only enjoy the process of *breaking down*.

The one thing she had never found out was how consciously he used these techniques, which were identical with those used in torture; and in certain armies, and some religious orders where the novice's will has to be broken: and in some brands of psychoanalysis? The common factor in all these is that a part or area of the person manipulated has to be made an accomplice of the person who manipulates.

Martha had learned that she would do well to be frightened—not of Jack. So they had separated, after a brief encounter.

He was examining Lynda carefully. He would be attracted by Lynda's look of illness, and by her country lady's clothes. Martha could see it was a toss-up whether he would come over. She wondered what sort of approach he was thinking about . . . a taxi came and she stopped it. He turned slightly to watch the two women get in. When Lynda was looking the other way he smiled a conspirator's smile at Martha; as it were saying: Get her for me. She managed a cool nod and smile, at which he could not prevent a small grimace of admiration, which was nevertheless mixed with annoyance: he would spend some minutes inventing humiliations for her. As the taxi turned a corner, he went back in search of fresh prey in the park, where hundreds of people still waited to leave. The head of the column must have reached Trafalgar Square long ago.

When Martha got back home, she found Mark had forgotten about people coming, and he had gone up to work. But Patty was upset, Lynda was upset: Mark and Martha would therefore have to cook dinner, organise an unknown number of baths, provide clothes for those who had got wet . . . in a frazzle of bad temper they did these things, while the unsightly image of Patty bewailing the end of love upstairs made it impossible for them to look at each other, two middle-aged people, with kindness, for they were in that condition where not only any possible present loves were made pathetic, but their past loves were nullified too. They could not believe that Mark, Martha, or indeed anybody else could have lain in young arms, rocked on their own heartbeats, and not been thinking all the time of—Patty upstairs.

But this, the most lamentable of middle-aged ills, has its antidote in the young with their immortal flesh; and as soon as the house was flooded with what seemed to be at least two dozen youngsters demanding baths and a lot to eat, even Patty came downstairs, sensible, and with a washed face and tidy hair.

After supper, they all went up to Mark's study: it had become a "tradition"—this had become true after the second of the marches, and while they all joked about a tradition three years old, nevertheless, to the study they went.

The study no longer looked anything like a room. Perhaps more like a medieval tent or pavilion decorated or hung with tapestries that had a theme: at any rate, there were no empty walls left. Not even a ceiling, which now had on it, printed in black ink, by Mark who got onto a stepladder to do it, dates and facts about space travel, such as: 16th September, 1959: *A rocket launched from the earth lands on the moon.* And this fact, or statement, would have fixed by it a star, or marker, in some colour—Mark used about a dozen of them, which connected it with one or several facts or statements in different parts of the room. For instance, the first moon rocket had (among other symbols) a mauve triangle by it; the mauve triangle occurred in other parts of the room, stuck by facts objective and subjective, one of them being a typed statement: "Night of September 14th. 1959: Lynda dreams that a great glaucous eye which is struggling to maintain life receives in it a dart, or arrow: rains of tears from the eye, flooding everything below in a dark stain." Another mauve triangle connected with an entry on the fourth wall: "According to the finding of Soviet scientists the moon is a breathing organism." And another: "Must be careful next week: full moon. Always sets me off." (Dorothy's handwriting.)

This particular area of the room had begun with some notes found among Dorothy's belongings after her death. There were boxes of papers, which included loose sheets, notebooks, etc. It seemed that these had begun with a sort of diary, but of the most routine domestic sort, and that Dorothy had used this to try and keep herself on an even keel, to balance herself into normality. "Must remember to order new light bulbs"—that sort of memorandum. These had developed into accounts of domestic transactions, first as an aid to exact memory, apparently to be used in possible controversies with firms, or even in legal cases, and then had become, in a soured frustration, a way of letting off steam, like letters to herself.

"3rd March, 1955. Men delivered telephone directories,

only for upstairs, not for us. Told them another set needed. They said would bring 'tomorrow.' 4th March. No directories. Rang exchange. They said no record of this number. I pointed out *this was not possible*. Said would look into it 5th March. No word from exchange. Asked Mark to exert authority. He offered me old directories. *This is not the point*. Rang exchange. Waited for connection for fifteen minutes. Got woman who had no record of previous call. Said would enquire. Would ring back. Did not. 6th March. Rang exchange. Was told I had been ringing the wrong department from the beginning. 'We have some new staff here.' Was given another number. Rang it: A Mr. Getnert said would ring back. Did not. 7th March. Wrote to Centre. 8th March. Acknowledgement of letter from Centre. 10th March. A man came around to investigate 'a complaint.' I asked for new telephone directories. He said he would look into it. 11th March. A man delivered a directory. Only A-D. Asked him for the other three. Said he had run out, would drop some in 'tomorrow.' 12th March. No directories. Rang the number that they said was the correct one. No record of any previous calls. Asked Mark to intervene. All right, but if that is being difficult why bother *to expect anything at all*. Are we paying for this service or aren't we? He offered me the three missing directories. Took them. 20th March. Telephoned for a taxi for Rosa late last night. Had not used that taxi rank for some time. Got telephone call from exchange saying complaints from the number I had been ringing, no longer taxi rank, but private house, a woman woken from early night. Exchange: Why don't I use up-to-date telephone directories? I told her why not. Said she would look into it."

This was one of the succinct entries. Some covered months.

When "the fifth wall" had begun, it was considered a joke, or in bad taste, or some private act of retribution on the part of Lynda towards poor Dorothy. But it was Mark who continued, doggedly, to adorn, or fill, the wall; and with seriousness, so that they had to consider, in seriousness, what he said: which was that this wall represented factor X; that absolutely obvious, out-in-the-open, there-for-anybody-to-see fact which nobody was seeing yet, the same whether it was a question of a rocket failing to get itself off a launching pad, or the breakdown of an electric iron the first time it is used, or a block of flats or cooling towers collapsing.

And, if they, "the children," were to say, "Yes, of course," without going on to consider its extensions and ramifications then, why did they, "the children," think that he, Mark, spent so much time on manipulating his damned room? For himself? Well, partly, it got one's mind clear, it helped to fit one fact with another, which, say what one liked, was the hardest possible thing to do—but no, he did it for them. He was supposed to be bringing them up, wasn't he? God knows he (and here he switched to the collective), *they*, he, and Lynda and Martha, weren't making so much of a job of it, but if he could not transfer to them *this,* what this room signified, in its potentialities for glory and horror, then he might just as well not have troubled to have them taught to read and write at all.

After supper, the first person up in the study was Paul, still in a flush, not merely of healthful effort, but of accomplishment, because he had won an invitation for Karl Holdt to visit him and to spend a week. This had been announced at supper, and everyone had cheered—half ironically of course, though Paul could never see why his achievements were greeted with this reservation. But underneath his pleasure was a worry: which was why he came fast to the "grown-ups"—Martha, Mark, Lynda, who sat in the big study chairs, among and under the diagrams and charts, drinking brandy, like travellers lingering together briefly before starting on a very dangerous journey.

He sat on the floor, and looked at them.

"You are upset," said Lynda, "because Karl Holdt says you can't bring Zena to Germany too?" Paul nodded. "And you want us to look after her while you are gone, but that isn't the point?"

"Well," he said, "I've only just understood ..." Here, suddenly, his eyes filled with tears. He had not meant them to—such weakness was for him the worst of self-betrayals. Aggressively, then, he brought out: "All right then, all right, but do you realise, Zena and I have been *together,* for over two years?"

"What did Herr Holdt say?" asked Martha.

"But ..."

"Well who else? You've been with him all day! And he's obviously made an impression!"

"What's the matter with him!"

"Nothing, who said there was?"

"Oh I thought—you're all so anti-German. I thought ... yes you *are,* you *are,* all of you, you keep pretending not to be ... I'd rather Karl Holdt than you—today has been one of the real days, it's been an important day," he said, leaning forward as if he were trying to impress this on them with his good looks. But his looks were dazzling. He was not quite eighteen, a boy, all physical, a glossy, beautiful boy. His charm took one's breath. It was not at all that light of beauty which had visited good-looking but after all quite ordinary Francis, though only briefly: no, it was built in, into aquiline features, dark liquid eyes, movements like an animal's. Yet he moved through London where a beautiful boy was a dozen times more in danger than even the most marvellous girl, quite safe because—he was not interested? He still maintained that he and Zena had never done more than kiss. He maintained it shrilly, as a point of self-esteem. He spent hours on his clothes, on his appearance; yet was shrilly contemptuous of people who found him attractive. And in moments like these, when trying to impress on others the importance of a stage of growth in his understanding, he both leaned forward all dark dissolving eyes and imperious charm, yet seemed to wish that he could dissolve or exorcise his beautiful self by an act of will—for otherwise who would take him seriously?

"Today I've seen something, not only about Zena."

"Well then, tell us." That was Lynda.

"You're the one I don't think I'd have to tell," said Paul, as if in remorse.

"Oh?"

"If you hadn't had a rich husband—well, money then—if there wasn't Martha, what would have happened to you?"

Lynda took in breath; and kept Mark, ready to comfort, or assuage, quiet with a nod.

"Of course I've thought," she said. "My guess is, I'd probably be in—Abandon Hope. Joke," she added. "I mean, I'd be sunk—destroyed. A wreck, cracked with drugs in some mental hospital. They'd say I was 'badly deteriorated' or . . ."

"All right," said Paul. For her voice had risen and shaken.

"I didn't mean to . . . Karl Holdt said—he was in a concentration camp as a boy, did you know?"

"We don't know him."

"Yes. Two years in the camp. The five in a displaced persons camp. He got out when he was eighteen—that's my age."

"Yes."

"He might have been my mother. I mean, if she hadn't been a woman and got to England . . ."

"Yes."

436

"When he saw I would like to bring Zena to Hamburg, he said, no, he was sorry."

A violence of grief was ready to shake tears out of Paul; he was red with keeping them in.

Lynda said: "What you are saying is, you know you can't look after Zena forever: and you don't think we will—and you think she'll . . . not be happy," she ended lamely.

"Thanks," he said, savage. "Happy—brilliant word. Without me . . . *she hasn't anything but me* . . . yes, but Karl was talking to me, he was being *kind*—he was explaining something, he said. All over the world there's a layer of people—like a stain in water—like a coloured seaweed—of people out of the concentration camps and the labour camps—those places. And what they know about life is so awful no ordinary people can stand them—so they keep quiet. They have to. Karl said, if they didn't shut up, ordinary people would lock them up again."

"Like Zena?" said Lynda.

"He said, we were corrupt. No, everybody. He said, we are all so corrupt, that we've got past seeing it. He said, the two world wars, particularly the Second World War, *your* war, had corrupted everybody . . . I said, but what will happen to Zena? He said, the worms are having fun."

"That's very German," said Mark with an instant distaste.

"What does that mean?" said Paul, cold. "My mother was German! She lived in Germany . . . German, Jewish . . ." He saw them struck and pressed on: "Well, go on then, tell me. I think your generation simply invented Jewishness for purposes of your own . . ." he was getting hysterical now, yet knew he had a point, and hammered on, his fists banging together—"Germany, Germany—but it's just across the Channel there, it's a couple of hundred miles away, and the rest of the world didn't stop them, so why Germany, Germany?"

"Don't get so . . . worked up," begged Lynda, "it'll start me off again."

"Yes," said Paul, bitter. "You can say that—but Zena can't. Karl said, 'Your young friend will likely come to drugs. She is the type.' R.I.P."

"All right," said Mark. "But you sound as if it's our fault. Do you realize that? If you go to Hamburg and we watch over Zena, that won't help—she knows perfectly well . . ." He stopped.

"All right, I know," said Paul, cold again. "You think that I want to leave her. But I don't. It's just that I . . ." Floods of tears suddenly. "Oh Christ," he said, "the others . . ." He jumped up and jammed a chair against the door, and when it wouldn't jam, stood with his back to it.

Mark came over, set him aside, stood on guard. Paul, in anguish, stood at the window with his back to them, fighting not to cry.

"He said it," said Paul at last, holding his voice steady. "He said: 'You have to understand, that there are people you can do nothing with—they are beyond ordinary life.' But I've been thinking, that's what I understood. . . ." He turned to face them. "There are, there must be, as many people who can't cope with ordinary life—as ordinary people. Well, just think of the people we know for a start . . . and that's what Karl meant by corruption, I saw it *after* he went off—he went off to some posh dinner. He meant, *corrupt*. Broken. Spoiled. Unable to cope. R.I.P."

Feet on the stairs. Jolly voices—here came the "children." Mark stood aside from the door. Paul said, lowering his voice and speaking fast, to get it all in: "I know what you think—I'll go to Munich and have a good time and too bad for Zena—but I'm not going to do it . . . do you hear me? I don't know how I'll manage, but I'll look after her. I'll do it somehow . . . or at any rate," he concluded, "if I go, I only go for two days, well three days, and she can stay here till I get back?"

"Well, she has before, hasn't she?"

The door opened, admitting the others.

Paul hastily removed his face to a darkened corner. In a moment, he was able to turn, smiling, a bit swollen, perhaps. *Crying is a funny thing: what's it for?*

He remained quiet for the rest of the evening, watching everyone curiously, and betraying his state of mind by this distance: for our fellow human beings only seem remarkable when in a heightened state oneself. Long afterwards he would refer to that night: You remember, the night I decided to hell with all of you. Or: Karl Holdt's night.

Patty came in, accompanied by her young man, who had decided he had been hasty: he was subdued, though the resentment felt by the young when forced into being targets of emotion they haven't bargained for showed in inadequately controlled glances and tones of voice. Also, he was curious about Patty, trying to sense his way to understanding the change in her. In the half a dozen hours, since he had gone off from Hyde Park, Patty had passed the point of no return: which did not mean she might not again succumb to

438

this, or another, youth. In her manner was already the irony which is the beginning of that ambiguous austerity where possessing no loves of the flesh, you possess them all, since there are no eyes, mouths, you have not kissed, having become all eyes, mouths, hands, kisses.

They were a dozen or so people in the little room, all in the mood of letdown that accompanies the end of an exalted public occasion. They were aware that for four days they had slept very little, eaten haphazardly if at all, had been wakefully energetic, had accomplished in every twenty-four hours five or six times what they did normally; and tomorrow they would re-enter the cage of habit. Last year, four youths who had joined the march "for a laugh" had gone off to enlist in the army a week later, because "they wanted to be taken out of themselves." At the supper table Francis had dismayed them by saying that he could see why: sometimes he thought he would do the same. He sounded serious. Jill was upset by this. Snuggling up to him she had said: "We won't let you go for a soldier. She said it with indulged petulance, "spoiled-child" style. But also as if she had the right to say it. So the older people noted. Francis did not, or so it seemed. It looked as if he thought he was humouring a young girl. Gwen and Jill, on either side of their cousin, no longer looked like rather smudged water-colour sketches of the same girl who was also the model for Phoebe, Marjorie or even unborn and unachieved variants of the same. Gwen was still a freshly plump girl. Jill was thin, rather beautifully haggard: a woman who looked adoringly at Francis.

Jimmy Wood had been there for supper; and had come upstairs to the study, one felt for the same reason that he had gone, just for one day, to the march: he was passing it, he had said, and it had come into his head to join in.

Jimmy sat on the floor beside Brandon, the American, who looked like a fresh-faced farmboy, and who, like Jimmy, smiled all the time. But Brandon's smile provoked comparisons with Jimmy's pink stretch, for his looked as if he were saying: "Don't hit me."

He had joked at supper that in his own country, an outsider because radical, he had never felt more of an outsider than this weekend, surrounded by radicals, who "believed—correct me if I'm wrong—that political protest is a question of stating a problem."

He had said it twice—but the words had sunk among the foam of chatter about people, food, the events of the day.

"You are ever so intellectual," Gwen said to him, and he had said quick and annoyed: "No, that's the whole point."

He now came back to it with: "Sir, I'd like to return to what I said."

Mark, a gentleman farmer, always disinclined for debate, or rather, disinclined since the death of the unconstituted committees, said: "Go ahead," but offered him a dollop of brandy as if dipping a child's dummy in soothing syrup.

Brandon saw this and said politely: "No, I would really like to—why do you fix your room up like this? Because the way it looks to me is, it's just stating the problem."

"It's hard enough to do that, surely?" said Mark, stiff. It was clear to his coevals that he was about to slide off, even go to bed, anything rather than this kind of talk.

Lynda said suddenly: "No, Mark, because he's saying something you think—it's just the language he's using."

"Thank you," said the boy to the woman, with the courtesy of his nation.

"All right," said Mark, "tell me."

"I thought I had—but that proves my point. I state something—I think it's achieved a change. Like the march—it's a statement. 'We don't want war.' End of statement. But nothing will have changed tomorrow when everyone goes back to work."

Groans of protest all around the room.

"Yes," said Francis. "But what else—we don't know what to do. If we did, we'd do it."

"But if this statement wasn't made, what could happen in its place?" persisted Brandon, smiling. "Do you see what I mean?"

As for Martha she realised that she was present at someone else's moment of insight: those rare moments when a door creaks open, light grows on a fact or object known to the point where one has not seen it for years. Brandon was in the grip of an attempt to convey such a moment. He leaned forward, his blue farmboy's eyes alight, vibrating with energy.

He said: "In the States I make a statement. The statement is: I want the right to be a political being. It's been knocked out of America by McCarthy, but I want the right. That's a statement. Perhaps it will breed other statements. Other people will say: I want the right to be political, to have my own views. Right! Do you get me?"

"No," said Mark seriously. He was trying.

Most of the others had already gone off into inattention: their glazed eyes showed it.

"I come here," said Brandon. "I make a statement: Things stink in the States. You're doing us and yourselves a disservice by ignoring it. That's a statement. It could breed other statements, people who say things stink, etc. But then what. Do you see?"

"Like breeds like," said Martha. An intellectually bred remark as far as she was concerned, for she was not feeling as he felt: he turned fast to see her, to catch the words, but because they had no understanding behind them, there was no spark. He agreed for the sake of politeness: "Yes. But more. It seems as if there's always just enough energy to state the fact, the problem. And not much more. The stating of it exhausts the possibilities. Do you get me? Do you follow?"

"Well," said Mark, "let's see. Suppose your statement did breed other statements and it again became possible to dissent in the States, would that disprove what you are saying?"

"Not if that was all. Not if the statement only bred statements of the same kind."

"Oh," said Lynda suddenly, "I get you. Oh yes, only too well. Oh *yes*. But then that means ..." Her eyes filled with tears; to hide it, she lit a cigarette.

"Yes," said Brandon excitedly. "*Yes*."

The others looked on. Emotion flickered between the two, and some of it leaked to Martha.

There was a slight opening in her mind. She said: "It's like Jimmy. He writes books about telepathy and so on—now it's mutants. But having made the statement that's it. He can't go that other step onwards ... Jimmy, do you realise how odd that is."

Jimmy turned his round spectacles to her, and she looked at his wet pink smile.

"The possibilities interest me," he said.

"Yes, but you take something for granted—where do the ideas come from?"

"Oh," he said, smiling, "that's easy—I'll show you if you like."

"Other space fiction," said Mark.

"Oh no," said Lynda, "it's everywhere—all around you if you can look, from the Bible to poetry to every edition of every newspaper or if it comes to that how one is oneself

..." The last words got lost, because they didn't have anything to hear them with.

"Do you get your plots from the Bible?" said Jill to Jimmy, teasing him.

"I don't know anything about the Bible," he said.

"Where?" said Martha.

"If you come out to factory sometime I'll show you."

"All right."

It nearly fizzled out there, in Jimmy. But Brandon took it up again:

"And there's this room," he said. "What makes you think that stating it doesn't exhaust what you can do?"

"Ah," said Mark suddenly, "now I do get you. Yes." His voice came to life and he looked at the young man with new interest. "Yes. But you see, that's as far as I know how to get."

"Thank you," said Brandon seriously. "Most people wouldn't have taken so much trouble to try and follow."

"Yes," said Mark, "but now *you* can't leave it there. I did have to do this—you know, set out a problem, get the shape of it. But now—what? I sit here by myself, and just take it in."

"And then?" asked Brandon seriously.

"Ah, that's what I am waiting for."

"Anybody else here?" asked Brandon.

"Me," said Francis. "I come here by myself."

"And I," said Paul.

"And I," said Martha.

"So far you're just stating the problem," said Brandon.

They were silent.

"Because there isn't so much time, is there," he pressed on gently, smiling.

"I don't know if it *is* just stating," said Lynda. "Because you assume that to think something is the end of that—a thought being self-contained, an end. Well it isn't."

He turned, smiling, to her. Now it was he who was outside.

"Yes," said Lynda. "Well, that's what one has to experience, I suppose."

And now the conversation had run out into the sands. Brandon was too interested in Lynda to set the currents going again. He leaned forward and looked at her: he respected her, he knew she said something important to her and therefore probably to him—but that the words she had used were dead for him.

"But," she said, "that is as bad—because whether the thought, or idea, is ended, in this room, which is how you see it; or goes out—changes other thoughts—the way *I* see it, it's still if you like 'stating a problem.' The only way that would be of some use would be not just throwing a pebble into a pool anyhow, so that ripples go out, but one doesn't know how, but knowing how to throw it so that the ripples go out exactly as one foresaw. Do you saw?" She was speaking rather breathlessly, and smoking hard, holding the cigarette between finger and thumb of hand gloved in apple-green silk. The exertions of the day had strained her: she looked haggard.

Brandon decided that she was a nut. They said she was a nutcase, he thought, and he leaned back, smiling politely.

Martha tried to explain Lynda to Brandon.

"It's like this march," she said. Brandon turned towards her, and so did the others. But her voice had gone dead for them: their attention was gone—she knew it by the way her voice fell muffled into a pool of politeness.

"When Phoebe and Patty and people like them did all that peace-marching and committee work all through the Cold War, the last thing they foresaw was the Aldermaston marches. That's what Lynda is saying, and it's the same whether it is an action, walking from one place to another, or a thought, or one of Mark's books. Mark writes a book. Then he watches what happens like one watches ripples from a bank after a water vole has dived in."

"You can watch a thought in your head," said Lynda. "You see the impulse that starts it. Then the thought trickles across your mind, strongly or weakly according to the strength of the first impulse. But the impulse needn't necessarily have bred that particular thought. Perhaps it could have bred another thought."

"What Lynda is saying," said Martha, "is that your statement 'I want freedom to say what I like as a political being' could breed similar statements or it could breed another McCarthy who says 'I won't let you say what you like.'"

They could hear that downstairs someone was arriving. Jill and Gwen exchanged glances. So short a time ago such glances had been loud, like histrionic sighs, had been meant to be observed, had said for the world to hear: Oh, our awful mother! Now they were private and signalled private collusions.

Gwen said aloud: "I'll go home. Can Jill stay?"

Jill was looking at Francis, who said affectionately to little Jill:

"Of course you can. Can't she, Martha?"

Phoebe came in on the crest of a wave of triumphant emotion which had begun days before, and culminated tonight in watching on television the biggest march of them all. It had been extremely well organised. The press, the television, the police, had been helpful.

Everyone she had met for days (and this meant people from all over the world) had been left-wing and assumed, as she did, that soon there would be a Labour government. After the final speeches in Trafalgar Square, she had gone off with a couple dozen people, most below forty, all Labour Party, all able, well informed, energetic. They had been talking about the future: there was no doubt that the Tories, after a disastrous decade in power, would soon be out; and here, among themselves, was the stuff of an efficient and progressive administration.

When she came into the study she was flushed, her eyes shone, she was drunk on pure spirits of hopeful confidence.

Between her and the people in the study who had been dropping political temperature for some hours there was no connection.

"Goodness," she said smiling, "you are a dozy-looking lot."

She wanted to know what they had been talking about. Brandon said: "Whether or not political action achieves anything."

"Well," said Phoebe drily, "you must all be very tired!"

"Any *change*" said Brandon, "whether or not things get *changed*."

"How very intellectual," she said. Because she was disappointed, because she was unwilling to lose the exultation she had been riding, she made it sound like a reprimand.

Jimmy Wood got up and said it was late and he had to be up early tomorrow.

Everyone got up from where they were sitting. Phoebe exclaimed that she did not want to break the party up.

In five minutes there was no young person left in the study, except Gwen, suddenly pale with exhaustion and standing by the door pointedly waiting to be taken home by her mother.

Phoebe got up and left.

Her voice could be heard saying: "I don't know why it is,

but I'm always made to feel like a wet blanket when I come anywhere near you."

Gwen's reply was inaudible.

Mark picked up off the floor a dropped leaflet, "Aldermaston to London, the Easter March," with the black-and-white symbol, and stuck it on a wall, connecting it by an orange sticker with other facts, one being the Defence Estimates for the United States in 1961—a figure so enormous that it was meaningless to the ordinary mind, like distance expressed in light-years.

PART FOUR

If you take a cell from the gut of a toad and transplant it into the toad's head, the gut cell has encoded in it all the information it needs to be a head cell.

A SCHOOLS' BROADCAST

From realm to realm man went, reaching his present reasoning, knowledgeable, robust state—forgetting earlier forms of intelligence. So, too, shall he pass beyond the current forms of perception. . . . There are a thousand other forms of Mind . . .

But he has fallen asleep. He will say: "I had forgotten my fulfillment, ignorant that sleep and fancy were the cause of my sufferings."

He says: "My sleeping experiences do not matter."

Come, leave such asses to their meadow.

Because of a necessity, man acquires organs. So, necessitous one, increase your need. . . .

THE MASTER RUMI OF BALKH, BORN A.D. 1207

Sufis believe that, expressed in one way, humanity is evolving towards a certain destiny. We are all taking part in that evolution. Organs come into being as a result of a need for specific organs. The human being's organism is producing a new complex of organs in response to such a need. In this age of the transcending of time and space, the complex of organs is concerned with the transcending of time and space. What ordinary people regard as sporadic and occasional bursts of telepathic and prophetic power are seen by the Sufi as nothing less than the first stirrings of these same organs. The difference between all evolution up to date and the present need for evolution is that for the past ten thousand years or so we have been given the possibility of a conscious evolution. So essential is this more rarefied evolution that our future depends on it.

THE SUFIS, IDRIES SHAH

One

Martha was suddenly not so busy. For one thing, she was no longer a conduit through which vast quantities of food from the markets of London reached the family table. For another, she was not a character in that adolescent morality play where adults have to speak through masks chosen to represent "Oppressor" or "Exemplar" or "Horrible Warning." When she was with Francis, Paul, Jill and the rest, she was able to feel herself, and to say what she would herself want to say; she communicated with Francis, Paul, Jill, and not with some anguished or raging usurper. In short, "the children" had grown up. Suddenly, it was as if friends were meeting after a long separation, when Francis, Paul, Jill and the rest dropped in to talk, or to have a meal with Mark, Martha, Lynda: there was a tenderly wry curiosity as to what "now that was all over" they were all *really* like. The wryness was a tribute to the now past (but necessary?) anguish. And also, partly, to that feeling of something having been got over, done with, worked through.

"We've done *that,* have we?" Martha, or Mark or Lynda might say to each other; and one of them would reply: "And now what's next?"

They did not know; but did know it would be a stage on in what had been completed in themselves as well as in the children. To have worked through, to have stood firm in, that storm which was the young ones' adolescence was, after all, to have been made free of one's own.

To have said patiently for years: I was like this, I did that, I felt that and this; Francis, Paul, Jill and the rest, they were me, I was what they are—well, for the opportunity to do this, the old ones owe a debt to the young. But this, of course, will not be understood (this particular variation of wry love) until the young ones come to that point where they must turn around and face towards their own past in their children. And so it is in this remarkable traffic between parents and children that there are as it were a whole series of postdated promissory notes in the currency of a contained and patient love that come due one after another when one least expects them: "So I've done that, have I? I've worked through that?" Or, if you like, it's as if those apparently dead plants, that look like blackened bits of twig clinging to dry rock in countries where the rains are infrequent, suddenly as the water fills them become a lively brilliant green.

Which is not at all to say that the lives of any one of the young ones ran smooth or conventionally—how could they? On the contrary, not one of them, or their friends, had any intentions of behaving as (so Margaret insisted on re-minding them) previous generations behaved. That is, they did not say: I want to be a soldier, a sailor, a ploughman, a thief, or even a bank manager or a civil servant. They had all become brilliant free lances each with a dozen talents. None cared, or so it seemed, about rewards or successes: none foresaw a solidly supported middle age, or, if they wished for that, did not work towards it.

They were driven, it was obvious, by precisely that same private passion, or need, which caused Lynda, or Martha, or Mark to ask: "We've done that, have we?" As if there was a generation where not an occasional person, but dozens of people, very many indeed, worked with that process of *being stripped*, being sharpened and sensitised, which uses the forms of ordinary life merely as tools, methods.

For instance, Francis. He supposed he was a man of the theatre; but a pattern continued: when he reached a mo-ment of success, he refused it, or drifted away from it. In the little theatre, where he had been earning his few pounds a week and conscientiously learning what he could, he had been offered, Graham Patten's influence assisting, a produc-tion of his own. He was to choose the play he wanted to do, choose the actors—make that step forward out of being nothing in particular. He was very young, of course—but as Graham said, "To have scaled the heights, as I did, at twenty-five, was an achievement, but now, when to be young is everything, it is the least one can expect." But while Francis did not exactly refuse, the production didn't come to anything. He wondered if perhaps London wasn't seeing too much Shakespeare; he asked if London really needed anoth-er production of Ibsen or Chekhov; he talked about a play written by a girl who was a friend of a friend: then Jill was sick, and he took her for a holiday, and while he was there he wrote some sketches, and some songs, for a new revue. He had already become involved with a show called "satirical" and was friendly with new talents, whose faces were known, through television, to millions of people. Francis had *almost* been one of them; or rather, the face and talents of "the clown," that childhood personality found in himself and brought out for this purpose, had been, briefly, commented on. He was offered a chance to be one of a team, working on a new television show. It was not that he ever said no, or sounded anything but enthusiastic. On the contrary, he did some writing for it and contributed some ideas. But when it came to the point, he was not there. He was with Jill. Or he was in Mark's study, correlating facts and figures, getting ideas, from the walls and ceiling of that room for use by his friends. Or he was talking to his father, or to Martha. He complained that he had not known he was satirical until the newspapers told him he was. He complained he felt entirely in a false position: he was experiencing, not only present annoyance, but past anguish; he was being forced to remember, to live through again, that part of his childhood when his father had been an enemy of the state. Now, it was with his father, and the two women with whom his father had shared that time, that he explored the present. He kept repeating, even while his face twisted up with the effort that went into making himself face what he remembered, even while he went pale, and sweated, that he was glad that had happened, he was glad he had learned what was possible. For, knowing what was possible (so he seemed to suggest), why bother with being a successful director at twenty-one, or even a satirist?

For some people the stripping process begins so young it is as if an announcement has been made: Don't trouble with anything else; this is what you have to do. The word "satire," used as it was being used, gave him first experience as an adult person of the senselessness of the processes which govern us: he had suffered the cruelty of them passively as a child; now he was trying to understand that paradox that in spite of (because of?) society's never having been more shrilly self-conscious than it is now, it is an organism which above all is unable to think, whose essential characteristic is the inability to diagnose its own condition. It is like one of those sea creatures who have tentacles or arms equipped with numbing poisons: anything new, whether hostile or helpful, must be stunned into immobility or at least wrapped around with poison or a cloud of distorting colour.

The process is the same under a variety of guises. There is a new phenomenon, or one conceived to be new: the creature, sullenly alerted, all fear, is concerned for only one thing, how to isolate it, how to remain unaffected. The process is accomplished, in this society, through words. A word or a phrase is found: Communism, traitor, espionage, homosexuality, teen-age violence—for instance. Or anger, or commitment, or satire. The organ (which is that part of the creature ostensibly supposed to function towards self-understanding, the press, the cinema, television, and the talk that goes on among people who influence society) finds a word for something that threatens.

Anarchy, irresponsibility, decadence, selfishness—into this box, behind this label, gets put every kind of behaviour by which the creature is made nervous, much to the surprise or the annoyance of the people so described, or labelled. Finally, the process becomes ridiculous even to the creature itself—quick, quick, a new word, a new label, "commitment," perhaps? "Mysticism?" Anything that will stop the process of thought for a time, anything to sterilise, or to make harmless: to partition off, to compartmentalise.

Francis, after days of the slow, involuted self-questioning by which he achieved his decisions, said he supposed he did not wish to be "a satirist." Which did not stop him writing for his friends. Just as his sliding into a decision not to direct the offered play did not stop him working on at the theatre, as conscientiously as he had been doing.

His centre, then, his growing point, was not where his ambition might conceivably be? Where then?

It was with Jill, whom he had begun by championing and helping, and ended by loving. He was, the family supposed, living at home, since he retained his rooms at the top of the house, and indeed was often in them. But his emotional life was with Jill. She lived in a large flat in a part of London that only four years ago had been sordid, but was already fashionable. Francis paid the rent for the flat. Jill would not take money from Phoebe, who, indeed, did not have any to give her. Jill no longer hated her mother, and had forgotten the years of what Phoebe remembered as cruel persecution. Jill was ready now to be friends. More: she longed for a mother. But Phoebe did not understand this; she saw Jill's way of life as a continuation of the adolescent girl's need to provoke her, Phoebe. Jill, shortly after the abortion nearly three years before, had got herself pregnant again by the same man, the jazzman from the West Indies. Asked by Phoebe and others why she had had the first abortion, she replied: "That was only to make everybody happy." Jill was bringing up the little girl, to whom she would refer, if there was any chance of Phoebe hearing it, as "my little pickaninny." She had had another baby since, no one knew whose. Francis said it was not his, but assisted Jill in bringing both children up.

Mark did not forgive his son for loving unreasonably—as he had done, and was still doing. That is to say, he would not accept what Francis was doing as something which he had to do: he continually argued against it. So that Francis would spend hours with his father talking about their work, about what united them most—their concern for the future; but when Mark mentioned Jill, the boy would excuse himself and leave. It was with the two women that he talked about Jill.

Lynda said: "But Francis, you're like your father. Look at me!" And she offered herself frankly for his inspection, with her pain-made face, her shabby greying hair, her burnt and rusty fingers.

"Yes, I think I am very like him."

"Yes. But the point is, can't you get through that one quickly?"

His smile acknowledged his understanding of this, their way of seeing him.

"How?"

"One can get stuck, one gets bogged down . . ."

"Are you, Lynda?"

"Yes. Unless I can move out—get out. Be independent. I must try."

Lynda said this to Martha, and to her son. But not to Mark: the dreams of these two so-long-married people were absolutely opposite.

"And if you can't?"

"Then I've been defeated."

"Really? As simply as that?"

"Yes, I think so."

"And you, Martha? What are you doing?"

"I'm paying off debts."

"Still! And now we're all grown-up?"

"I don't know what it is I'm waiting for—something."

For Martha, knowing that there was a step to be taken, had no idea where to look for it. It was under her nose, of course. It always is—the next step. But she couldn't see it.

"The thing is," she had insisted, still tried to insist, "we have to work through what we've been given—of course.

453

There's no way of getting around it. But don't spend your life at it."

"As my father is? You know that's what you are saying?"

Lynda said: "Jill's me—if you like, Jill was inevitable because you were landed with me for a mother; but that shouldn't be for all your life!"

"You start growing on your own account when you've worked through what you're landed with. Until then, you're paying off debts," said Martha.

He asked again: "Why do you want me to do so much better than my father? Why should I?"

This, it seemed, for the time being was where he wanted to take a stand. He had an extraordinary love for his father—all protective, as if Mark were his son. He seemed concerned, often, that his father should be saved from the nasty realities of life. Mark was not told, for instance about the difficulties of the ménage with Jill. It was Lynda who visited the flat, saw that Jill had clothes for the children, and some kind of family support. For Mark thought that Jill was "neurotic and inadequate" and Margaret Patten was always descending on the couple with advice.

"Francis! You can't marry her, she's your cousin."

"I didn't say I was going to marry her."

The truth was, he wanted to marry her, but Jill shared with Lynda a sad self-knowledge as to her incapacity for ordinary life, and did not wish to marry Francis. She did not love Francis, she said. Perhaps she would never love anyone. What was love? she asked. What she had seen of that quality people called love did not make her respect it, or them. But if Francis wanted to live with her, she had nothing against it.

"Well then," said Margaret, "why go on with it?"

"You mean you want me to marry and settle down, is that it, Granny?"

"There was a time when I looked forward to being a grandmother," said Margaret. "I *am* your grandmother, after all." She had recently made the jump from ex-beauty to elderly lady: tactfully (she believed) putting on an erect body and crisp white curls, like a uniform suitable for one's age. But there was something wrong: her movements were all sinuous, insinuating, and her great eyes were anxiously dependent, like a young woman's. She needed reassurance. She needed that other people should see her life as she herself did.

"You mean, Granny, that I should get married just *once,* and have let's see now, two children? Three? Four? And

454

have a house in the country and a house in town? And what else?"

"I don't see your point," she admitted, defiant. "I've not said my way of life is anything to be copied, have I?"

"Why not say it if that's what you feel? As a life goes, it's as good as may be. But it's not my life, is it?"

There appeared on the television a couple of weeks later a sketch: "She's as good as may be." It was written by Francis, and showed an elderly literary hostess who chased all the new young lions of London with the refrain: "I may not be good for much, but I'm good enough for you."

Margaret saw the show, and before it was over had telephoned Francis at the studios.

"Darling Francis, this is your Granny."

"Oh, hello Granny."

"I rang to ask you to dinner—no, not just you, darling, I can have you any time, but you and your clever young friends."

"Why not, I'll ask them."

Margaret then laid on the biggest smartest dinner party she could manage, serving up those "names" among the older generation of lions who had most volubly and maliciously criticised the young ones, with the young lions whose reputation for iconoclasm was greatest. It was all a great success: they liked each other, and their criticisms, malice and iconoclasm would thereafter be much modified. She had, in short, performed her function, which was to help along London's work in making a homogenous whole of literary and political and artistic society. As for Francis, he left immediately after dinner, to return to Jill, who he said had a headache—thus sticking to his point, and saying that hers was not important to him.

"Don't you want to get rich?" she would enquire. "All you clever new people seem to find it so easy?"

"Not in the least," Francis would reply. "Shouldn't you be after Paul, not me?"

"I'm sorry if you think I'm *after* anyone . . ."

Paul, not yet twenty, was well on his way to being rich. The third floor where he still lived was more than ever a repository for beautiful and strange objects which he might use briefly to sleep on, sit on, dress from, but which were always in the process of being bartered or sold. From this enterprise he had put in the bank about three hundred pounds. But he announced he was looking for ways to make some "real" money.

He was very much a part of the new young London, concerned, or so it seemed, more about clothes and furniture than anything at all. Clothes and furniture were Paul's meat and drink—so it seemed. A dress shop? Décor? He considered these, but settled for neither. Meanwhile he had met a girl at a party—very young, pretty, and newly in London. Her name was Molly Grinham and she wanted to be a singer. She sang well enough, with her looks and her quality of put-upon bravery which he told her was marketable. He was fond of her. He dressed her, changed her hair, organised singing lessons—or rather, voice production lessons, not the same thing—and gave her a new name, Sally—just that, suggesting an orphan child with big lost eyes. Her parents were grocers in Tunbridge Wells. Paul had just introduced her to a new pop group and it seemed she might be offered a job with them, when another intending impresario saw her and suggested a deal. There was no reason for Paul to lose his head: his rival had no more to offer than he had. But he lost it badly. He wrote her a letter full of reproach: our friendship, what I've done for you, etc. It included the sharp frightened phrase *"and in terms of our contract."* At no point had Paul suggested any return for what he was doing for her; for one thing, this was not how he felt, when he was at his best. But the girl, upset and frightened, showed the letter to her new admirer. This youth took the letter to a lawyer—one of the just-within-the-law dealers that were making a fortune in this new London. Paul got a vaguely threatening letter. He found a lawyer of his own: sharp, semi-shady lawyers licked their lips. The first Mark heard of it was when Paul came to ask for £200. If he, Paul, paid £200 into the hands of a certain lawyer, then "the matter would not be proceeded with." What "matter?" What had Paul done? But he was in a panic, a little boy again, petulant, vituperative, out of control. Mark saw his own lawyer. It appeared that Paul had in fact behaved stupidly. He had turned up outside Sally's flat in the middle of the night, shouting about betrayal, the police, goodness knows what. After kicking the door a bit, and bursting into tears, he had gone away. Mark said to Paul he was being black-mailed and should do nothing whatsoever. But the affair had gone beyond any sort of sense. Paul wanted £200. Paul felt that if he gave the lawyer £200, he, Paul, would be safe. Safe from what? Paul could not say. Besides, Paul "heard" that if Sally had £200 her new promoter could more easily get her a job with ... But, pointed out Mark, Sally would

456

not get anything like £200. It would more likely be £50, by the time the lawyers had taken their cuts. It was no good. Money is never anything but a fantasy currency: it doesn't exist. Never was this truth shown more clearly than in this affair of Paul's £200 which as he said afterwards "started him on his way." For one thing, he already had £300 in the bank. But that money was the result of some years of patient work; buying and selling with expertise. It wasn't fairy gold, like the £200 which never even reached the point of being figures on a cheque.

Mark, at last, said to Paul that if he wanted to throw £200 away, knowing that he was throwing £200 away, to line the pockets of crooks, then he, Mark, would give him £200. Paul dissolved into an effusion of gratitude. He rushed about, saying everywhere that he was saved, his uncle was saving him. Sally meanwhile was practically a prisoner in her flat, bereft of Paul who after all had done everything for her, had virtually created her. She reflected that she was the instrument for fleecing Paul of £200. By now she felt ashamed: her new protector was a nasty character, and the law and vague threats had become the air she breathed. She sneaked out of her flat in the middle of the night and rang Paul. The two had met secretly, in a Lyons Corner House. They wept together. She then returned to her protector to say that if he took £200 off Paul she would leave him. This cost her all her courage: she imagined prison, at least. That she had not signed any contracts was irrelevant to her: she was dealing, like Paul, in a very different currency. The youth magnanimously agreed to pay the lawyer's fees himself, but in return she should bind herself to him. She felt this was the least she could do. Paul therefore got a letter saying he need not pay the £200. Paul felt he had made £200.

Paul had two different sums of money, of two different kinds. One was £300, in a bank: he felt this to be connected somewhere with gold bars, something like that; the work he had put into getting it made it honest stuff. The other £200 was, so he felt, the "real" money he had been waiting to get his hands on.

It was in this way that Paul was made to understand money: its fantastic nature. During the few weeks after he had "made" that £200 he blossomed and burgeoned and went about as if he had laid hands on a map of hidden treasure.

With three other young men, he bought a hairdressing

shop in a dull suburb which was full of young people wanting to enjoy the benefits of new London. The point of this deal was that at no time did he, Paul, actually use money: that is, through a series of feints, delays, devices, he did not actually sign a cheque for the two hundred pounds which was what he contributed to the deal. Yet the sum existed—for when the shop was sold six months later for twice what they had paid, Paul's share was £400. Paid to him by cheque.

From absolutely nothing-at-all, or rather, some words, *two hundred pounds,* and how people saw Paul, felt Paul; another nothing-at-all, namely, a piece of paper with £400 written on it, had come into his possession, was his. . . . At this moment of enlightenment anything was possible: Paul might very well have taken off into the higher reaches of finance, become an adviser to governments on money—or turned to honest crookery.

But it was as if the act of being made free, suddenly, of how the finances of the entire world are in fact run, was enough for him.

He enjoyed many dreams of what was possible, but what he did was to use his £400, this time conventionally, by writing and signing cheques, to buy another hairdressing shop with his group of friends. They all had flair, taste, panache—at the end of a year after Paul's first £200, he had a £1,000. One thousand pounds, in fairy gold.

And now, for some weeks he sat like a hen on a golden egg, coddling it, then rolling it around under him, treading it, warming it. He spent hours talking to Mark, Martha, Lynda (she was once again a real friend whom he loved) about money. Or rather, they listened: not being part of this world of quick chances, quick profits, quick deals—fairy gold, where the last thing any sensible person did was to have an honest job and work.

"I don't know why you look like that, Martha—I don't break the law, do I? And Uncle doesn't like it either. Why not? And Lynda laughs at me—oh I know when people are laughing at me—I don't mind, I love Lynda, if she wants to laugh. But what would you rather I did, tell me that?"

Quite soon he bought half a house in an area which no one else had seen was "coming up." He furnished it improbably but beautifully with the stuff in his rooms. And now, after boasting for weeks about the steady income he was going to derive from this gold mine, paying tribute in what already seemed a way profoundly out of character to the

458

real stuff (gold bars and the rest), he installed in the top floor of the house—his old friend Zena. Whom he had never lost sight of, or ceased to help. She had left Radlett Street of her own accord, stealing away one night when Paul was away on some trip. Out of pride, Paul said. But he tracked her down and helped her into a room with some friends. Then she went into a mental hospital for a time. When she came out, it was back to Radlett Street. And so it went on: she was a brave girl, trying hard, and never quite able to manage without help. Which Paul gave her.

When he put her into his new house, he knew she would not pay rent, and that this "gold mine" would be so much less of one. And he promised her she could stay there: this meant he could not sell it for quick profit. In short, right at the heart of his preoccupation, his secret joy, his growing point, money, the romance of it, was what none of his elders and mentors had given him the credit of possessing—and he was good-naturedly derisive about it. "You thought I was going to turn into a sort of sordid old landlord, didn't you, Lynda? Didn't you, Martha? Oh, I know! Well, how do you know I won't after all!"

Into this house soon came another waif, a friend of Zena's, or perhaps a lover; somebody at any rate like Zena, not able to live normally. Very soon there lived partly at Paul's expense half a dozen young people who for one reason or another had no parents, or who did not get on with them, and who needed a home.

But Paul's capital was locked up. At which point he asked Mark to lend him some. "No, I don't want the money. I just want you to say I can have it. It comes to the same thing, doesn't it?"

Mark had a thousand pounds in trust, which he had never told Paul, from the sale of his father's goods when he vanished to Moscow. He gave Paul this money now. Paul received it with the quizzical tolerance due to likeable fools. Quite clearly, he could not conceive of anyone sensible having a thousand pounds, and letting it breed only five per cent. Three months later he came back to say he had trebled it, How, they wanted to know? Legally, they hoped! He received this with amusement. Ah, how old-fashioned they were. How absurd!

And he was buying another house. Fairy gold was not for Paul, except as a means, or as an enjoyment. Bricks, mortar, earth, antique furniture and pictures—this was how he spent his time. Incredibly handsome, with his flashing dark-eyed white-teethed good looks, beautifully dressed, amiable, alert, he was busy, busy, busy, all day; and in the evenings he went to parties and was seen with the newest pretty girl. He did not sleep with anybody, though, boy or girl. He liked it to be thought that he did. He would bring some sleek good-looking creature home, having made a remarkable exit from a party, and they would spend the night in a great four-posted bed picked up for ten shillings in a country market—they would spend it holding hands, or in each other's arms, tender, protective of each other's loneliness, but sexless.

A sign of the time: At a conference in London to discuss an esoteric interpretation of *Hamlet* half a hundred grown men and women talk for a whole day, Hamlet being forgotten in more urgent business, about "the youth" and in terms exactly identical with those used by a committee of middle-class social workers about slum dwellers, or a white farmers' meeting in Rhodesia about their black farm labourers. At no point during the day of sullen, resentful, or tolerant comment was there any suggestion of a reminder that the people they were talking about lived in the same houses, ate at the same tables, were, at least possibly, their own children.

Another sign of the time: Elizabeth, James Coldridge's daughter, having, after her affair with Graham, married an ambitious solicitor in Bristol and produced two children, had suddenly written a letter to Mark demanding the real name and address of his "City." She wished to live there. On being informed that "as he thought should be obvious" it was imaginary, she wrote to ask why he didn't arrange, or make, a similar one. "And in that case, just let me know and I'll help." Meanwhile she was leaving her husband, and proposed to assist drug addicts. For drug addiction had just succeeded to teen-age violence as that cause which should absorb every citizen.

This was by no means the first time Mark had had letters enquiring about this city—in Algeria perhaps? Arabia? He perhaps had contacts who might help the sincere enquirer?

On the whole, though, this book had become invisible—it was profoundly not of the time. So with the war book—the Second World War was "in" but only in its aspect of adventure, hair-raising escapes from prison, etc. Mark's novel was wrong in tone. He had written another which had caused annoyance. The play about Aaron and Rachel had finally died: warm-hearted protest was absolutely out. But the doomed brother and sister lingered with Mark, refused to die: brooding about them, about Sally-Sarah, about Martha's manuscript from Thomas, there had been born another person, a composite of all these people (but, Mark claimed, more Thomas's child than anyone); a boy who had not died in the concentration camps of the Second World War, had survived the dispossessed persons camps, and grown with just one idea in his mind, to get to Israel. There he became one of the generation who turned their backs on everything traditionally Jewish, the religion, the history, the talent for suffering. He was a soldier, that and nothing more, hating more than any other the creed of turning one's cheek, of patience, of tolerance, of endurance. His creed was, simply, to fight, to strike back hard when struck, for any reason at all. His life was an expression of one need: to struggle out of the dark blood sacrifice that was what Jewishness had meant to his parents. Yet he was a man seeking death, trained, equipped and waiting for it. He had become the mirror image of his parents and his ancestors; and his future, like theirs, was planned as death in a holocaust.

This novel was short, dry, and its conclusions were implicit, not stated. Mark's publisher had demurred about publishing it: it might be considered anti-Semitic. Paul was given it to read; for his mother, a still fertile ghost, was after all in the book. But he did not enjoy reading. He would watch television for hours, complaining that the programmes were moronic; he went critically to the pictures. But he read like a child of seven, word after word, and was glad when the drudgery of it all was over. He said to Mark he thought all this stuff about Jewishness was silly. He said that it "was obvious to everyone" that the Germans were Germans because of being locked up in the middle of Europe—that was their history and therefore that was being German. And Mark's book wrote of Jews locked up in the Middle East, Jews on the defensive, so why use words like Jew and German, he thought everyone was silly, he preferred watching television.

Francis read the book, but enquired as usual with his old patient endurance of anxiety: Would *they* like it? No, no, he was not suggesting that Mark ought to write books to be liked but ... and he hunched his shoulders as if taking on a burden and sharpened a defensive chin, as a small boy of eight or nine years old had done, reading what journalists said of his father.

The book was reviewed rather coolly: it was suggested for instance that Mr. Coldridge was not Jewish; he would do better to write about subjects he understood. It was also suggested that perhaps he was too lightweight a writer to take on such weighty subjects—for in the meantime Mark's book which he considered the nearest he had written to a pot-boiler had hit, belatedly and unexpectedly, exactly the mood of the time. *The Way of a Tory Hostess* had been reissued, made into television, serialised in a newspaper, and there was talk of it becoming a musical. Mark's secretary, then, was again very busy, and this happened not more than a few months after discovering that the children were grown-up and she had very little to do.

In these months, six or seven of them, she made an interesting discovery. For a long time she had been saying: When I'm not so busy I suppose I shall stop dreaming? By this she meant that when she was no longer under pressure, it would not be necessary for the invisible mentor to talk, explain, exhort, develop, through dreams, because she would have time and energy for other methods. What methods? But she did not know. The qualities she had developed during that long past period of fighting to drag herself out of a pit were presumably still there and could be called on; though she often marvelled at the memory of that time, could not believe it had really happened.

For years, while all her inner effort (not her's, her mentor's) had gone into dreams, she had charted that tempting, dangerous, glamorous territory lying just behind or interfused with this world where landscapes, shores, countries forbidden and countries marked Open, each with its distinctive airs and climates and inhabitants living and dead, with its gardens and its forests and seas and lakes, had come so close, so familiar, that a texture or flavour of dream might suffuse or interpenetrate a scene of ordinary life at a turn of a head or at a scent or a phrase or a smile from a person passed in the street who seemed as if she, he, might have stepped at that moment from a landscape visited only in sleep.

And sure enough, when the months of comparative leisure began, the dreaming lessened. But she did not know where else to look; for Lynda was not available for "working"; she was on an adventure of her own. Then, a period of new busyness began for Martha and she assumed that so would the dreams. But no, it turned out that after all for the time being she had done all she could there. She knew by the signs that show whenever we have finished with something, or with a person, a love, a country, a pattern of behaviour. There was a quality of resistance there. Entering (not *again!*

462

the dream's texture seemed to complain) a dream garden where she had been at home; or recognising the next instalment of a serial dream, there was a heaviness, a lack of flow. It was as if matter sulked, had become sullen, like a smile of welcome that has become mechanical. No, for the time being the road on was not there, through that country slippery with illusion and deliciously free from the logics of gravity of the ordinary body, where even pain seemed to hold an impatient longing that was its own promise.

There was no movement on in sleep, and her days were too busy for that process of patient waiting and watching that is essential for the netting of the rare birds, the infrequent visitors; she worked for Mark, and she worked with Lynda, in *her* adventure, which, poor Lynda, had to be yet another attempt at being ordinary, at being normal.

Years before Lynda had started to cook some meals, though as often as not went downstairs while other people ate them. Then, when the house was not so full of young people, and meals were less demanding, she cooked them and stayed for them. Soon she was ordering meals, and might even go out to buy food from the shops. She thought that perhaps she might even take over the running of the house.

This step forward she had achieved having given up drugs of all kinds, having thrown even the sleeping pills away. When the routine prescriptions arrived from her doctor, she gave them to Mark or to Martha to lock up with instructions not to give them to her "even if she cried for them."

Martha's task then had become a tactful withdrawal, allowing Lynda to become Mark's wife, or at least as much of a wife as was consistent with not bearing to be touched, for she still always went downstairs to sleep.

What Mark wanted does not need to be said: what Lynda attempted next, was to be ordinarily social. She said she would like to try a dinner party, to go out to the theatre, to accept Francis's and Paul's invitations to visit their London.

She made this demand almost impersonally: on behalf so to speak of her illness, or of an effort which they must applaud; just as she had announced in the past that she "was going to be silly" again and therefore would need a nurse or Mark's attendance.

The kitchen became a kitchen; was no longer the heart of the house. The dining room, unused for so long, was opened, and the long polished table cleared of the books and papers that had accumulated there. Linen was taken out of chests;

463

silver and china that had never been used by that married couple, Lynda and Mark, was got ready for use. An extra charwoman was engaged, and Lynda and Martha considered clothes.

Raw material: two women in their forties. Lynda's body was born for fashionable clothes; when stripped all bones and hollows, but thin, tall, pliable. Martha was shorter, more stocky. But she was in a thin phase again. She would do. Martha's greying hair, short, blondish, was dyed to a dull silver, as if she were choosing to go white: rather amusing really. And Lynda's dry mass of near grey hair was transformed into a sleek bronze mane.

Yes, they would both do. They stood in Paul's room, before Paul's great mirror, and looked at themselves as neither had done for a long time, using that special eye which is not focussed towards what a lover, a husband, friends may enjoy, or want you to wear, but outwards to fashion.

It was Paul who pointed out that Lynda had clothes put away dating back for three decades, and that to buy clothes was absurd. For already, in the early sixties, London had begun that extraordinary whirling dance, as if the fashions of fifty years had been flung up in the air together, like dead leaves in a wind, and it did not matter what anyone wore; or, if you like, it was like a newsreel cut to come together anyhow, picking out fashions of the twenties, the thirties, the forties, the Edwardians, the Victorians, at random, and without any logic but that inner desperation which was the real appetite of the time. Clothes parodied, reminisced, were like private fantasies; they mocked, peacocked, and joked; and Lynda and Martha handed half a hundred dresses to Paul, who told a dressmaker what to do with them.

Thus, though briefly, they became fashionable women.

Now all they needed was guests.

About guests and hosts: it is an interesting fact that there are very few of either. If one says to a man who one has heard has spent every evening for months with the current fashionable people, "I hear you're an 'in' person these days," he is almost bound to reply, "Me? Goodness no, I'm almost a hermit ..." For whatever forays he has made into fashionable haunts have been in search of information, like a detached sociologist; or in pursuit of a new mistress; or to save a friend's soul from perdition: Really, oughtn't you to be working rather than ... Forgive me, but admiring your talent as I do ... Which is why for nearly a decade foreigners made pilgrimages to London to share its brief moment of glitter and style, but seldom found it, for the half a thousand people who composed it were only spending their time agreeably with intimate friends.

Similarly, there are few real hostesses. Margaret arranged her life, her marriages, her houses, to accommodate people who, temporarily, had clinging about them that light which is generated by other people's envy: but she was angry with anyone who suggested this. "I never have had in my house anyone I didn't like and I hope I never will!"

For the half a dozen months, then, when the house in Radlett Street became a place where people were invited, it could be said that the Coldridges were among the very few real or deliberate hosts in London.

Their guests were (but the house became known as a place where one never knew who one was going to meet): Margaret's old friends, the literary warriors of the Cold War, already back "in" chiefly because of the cachet that now attached to possibly having been friendly with, or at least having known, or met, one of the famous spies; her new friends, the "wave" or "wind" or impulse from the late fifties; the pop singers and impresarios, the hairdressers and the restauranteurs—through Paul; the columnists and commentators from press and television, the semi-literary, semi-political figures—through Graham Patten; the solid stratum of left-wing politicians, through Phoebe, and Phoebe's ex-husband Arthur; with the organisers of this or that protest, march, relief fund, famine relief organisation ... all these people flowed together in and out of this house and the dozen or so houses like it, which had, like private extensions, the half-dozen restaurants, clubs, bars, which they frequented, had put up money for, and were run by friends.

Certain beliefs united them. One was that they were all absolutely unlike each other, since they came from various classes and one or two countries. This meant that they met with that curiosity held in check by well-exercised aggression that is the first requisite for falling in love. Another was that social history had begun in 1956, or 7, or 8 (the starred years that had given birth to this epoch), for already the new film makers, playwrights, cinema stars, editors who had risen on that wave dominated everything and the rapidness and ease of this ascent had created a mood of good-natured optimism about the future: it was extraordinary that this mood infected even people who had every reason to know better—Phoebe, for instance; the responsible left. Thirdly they tended to see the whole world, let alone all of Britain, through themselves, or behaved as if they did. It was a kind of self-hypnosis; as if the city were an enchanted wood, and anyone entering it lost his senses. The fact that outside these few thousand people London had not changed; let alone that outside London very little had changed, was forgotten as one stepped inside the magic wood.

Where, as in fairy stories, the most extraordinary contradictions lived side by side. Graham Patten, for instance, still a Marxist, and fond of saying that "everything is run by the dozen men who were in my year at Oxford and Cambridge." He said this with pride. As his father might have said, or as Mark's father might have said. Which did not prevent him and everybody else saluting the new classlessness, which meant that some talents from the provinces or from the lower classes had been attracted to London and had been absorbed—exactly as has always happened.

For what distinguished this stratum of a few thousand people was its uniformity: in approaching it, you had to become like everyone else. It was a sub-society working like one of those great drums where pebbles are jarred and shaken together to smooth and polish them into likeness; it was like homogenised milk.

Apparently it was a scene of debate, competition, violently clashing interests. Great business entities fought: but they worked together behind the scenes, and employed the same firms, or people. The newspapers that remained might call themselves right, left, or liberal, but the people who wrote for them were interchangeable, for these people wrote for them all at the same time, or in rapid succession. The same was true of television: the programmes had on them the labels of different companies, or institutions, but could not be told apart, for the same people organised and produced and wrote and acted in them. The same was true of the theatre. It was true of everything.

The rubbing-down process went so fast, everything went so fast, it was as if somewhere, invisibly, a time switch had been altered, for processes were speeded up that previously worked slowly through years. Once, for instance, a word, a phrase, or an idea might be "in the air" and then take five years or so to move through press, dinner tables, radio, book reviews, jokes. Now the opinion, the catch-phrase, the idea, might appear one week, and have blazed itself out by the next. Meanwhile hundreds of mouths proclaimed this new truth with the same solemn, soft, sincere gaze; for it was an opinion bound to reflect the highest credit on the beholder, everyone being at this time so impeccably highminded.

Indeed, inside the enchanted circle it was hard to believe that unpleasantness could exist anywhere else, let alone exist here ever again.

Oh how charming everything was! How urbane! How tolerant! What enchanting clothes people wore! What good cooks we were, what food we ate! How delightful that in any room were bound to be half a dozen black or coloured people, exactly the same as ourselves, and half a dozen working-class people, all as talented and as progressive, everyone effortlessly harmonious . . . which fact in itself seemed to proclaim the truth that soon, when the Labour Party got in, anybody at all, from Land's End to John o' Groat's, man, woman, Negro or docker, would have all the benefits of society that previously were associated with somebody like Mark Coldridge or like Graham Patten.

But it was Graham Patten, of all the personalities around London in that decade, who was most consistently its exemplar. As affable, as witty as ever, he was around not only "London" but the similar strata of New York, Berlin, Paris, Warsaw, all of which valued that quality so peculiarly his, of being the social equivalent of a piece of litmus paper, or a Geiger counter. Which is not to say that he was a chameleon—rather that, on achieving young manhood, he had foreseen the London which he was to personify, and had become that before London sensed its destiny. Other people, styles, modes, adapted to him. Since he was fifteen, he had been a dandy: it was not long before men everywhere became peacocks and cavaliers and dandies; "London" became socialist, which he remained. Following him, "London" became tenderly tolerant of absolutely everything. And, having understood that what he had once considered a failing was in fact his strength, he developed his versatility. He put on plays, directed them, acted in them; he advised other directors what to put on and criticised them when they erred. He wrote books, some witty and heartless, others sincere and forward-looking. He started a restaurant, where one of his mistresses cooked, called the Daisy Chain; and had money in many boutiques. His emotional life was as vivid, for besides having been married a couple of times, he was continually most painfully in love with the newest arrival in London, of whatever sex or colour.

But his real forte was television, for which he tended to apologise. "Yes, I know, but one must take it for what it *is*."

Yet it was here that he really touched the pulse of *now,* where he offered what no one else had ever done, or could, particularly in a programme which consisted of discussions with various of his friends, well known and associated with the arts. It was here, in this programme and the many variations of it, that there was reached the culmination of that attitude towards the arts born in the first half of the nineteenth century which was essentially a need to identify with the life of the artist. Hard to see how much better this particular need can be fed than to be able to watch, week after week, artists of every kind, writers, painters, musicians, and so on (or when the supply of these failed, "personalities" of one sort or another), sitting around in a make-believe drawing room, playing a charade which consists of pretending the cameras don't exist, but that they are a group of close friends living for free passionate liberal enquiry and that they have chosen just this moment to discuss their thoughts aloud. Here, people who had met half an hour before in the preliminary discussion about the programme, or under the make-up girls' hands (How do you? How do you?—in the mirror), called each other by their first names and discussed the most private details of their lives as if alone with intimates. They were like privileged children at a party where poor children looked through a window to marvel and envy. But the watching children no longer envied; on the contrary, it was a form of contempt, for it was they who paid for the party, and who chose these performers who would act out for them their fantasies; and if the performers were prepared to use their own lives (a form of sacrifice) in the acting of the fantasies—so much the better, and what did it matter?

For it was on television that had been created a continuous commentary or mirror of "real" life. To switch on the set when the day's viewing started, with one's mind slightly turned down, or in a bit of a fever, or very tired, and to watch, steadily, through the hours, as little figures, diminished people, dressed up like cowboys or like bus drivers or like Victorians, with this or that accent, in this or that setting, sometimes a hospital, sometimes an office or an aircraft, sometimes "real" or sometimes imaginary (that is to say, the product of somebody's, or some team's, imagination), it was exactly like what could be seen when one turned one's vision outwards again towards life: it was as if an extreme of variety had created a sameness, a nothingness, as if humanity had said yes to becoming a meaningless flicker of people dressed in varying kinds of clothes to kill each other ("real" and "imaginary") or play various kinds of sport, or discuss art, love, sex, ethics (in "plays" or in "life"), for after an hour or so, it was impossible to tell the difference between news, plays reality, imagination, truth, falsehood. If someone—from a year's exile in a place without television, let alone a visitor from Mars—had dropped in for an evening's "viewing," then he might well have believed that this steady stream of little pictures, all so consistent in tone or feel, were part of some continuous single programme written or at least "devised" by some boss director who had arranged, to break monotony, slight variations in costume, or setting (office, park, ballet, school, aircraft, war), and with a limited team of actors—for the same people had to play dozens of different roles.

It was all as bland and meaningless as steamed white bread; yet composed of the extremes of nastiness in a frenzy of dislocation, disconnection, as if one stood on a street corner and watched pass half a dozen variations of the human animal in a dozen different styles of dress and face, as little Amanda Coldridge (who would soon be Francis's legal stepdaughter) might experience a walk down the street to the shops, flick flick flick, the great lumbering many-dressed creatures walked or ran or talked their way past among a clatter and a roar of metal objects while a four-legged furry creature higher than she was that smelled strong and rank ran between their legs and lifted one of its own to spurt out a yellowish smelly liquid on a corner of damp brick. A minute child with enormous dark eyes fringed by curling black lashes in a face of brown cream (she was all shades of delicious brown set off in a white dress and white shoes) hung tight on the hand of a fair-haired blue-eyed roses-and-milk English girl who pushed a pram with her other hand; and people passing flicked their eyes down at her, then up at her mother, eyes suddenly narrowed or sharp or commenting, or bent to smile with all their lips and teeth offered to her, flick flick flick, they passed by; and it was the same inside at home, when Amanda sat in the great chair opposite that part of the wall where pictures flicked past all day. Her mother sat near nursing the new baby. "Mummy, Mummy, Mummy," she cried, "look at me, take notice of me, smother or throw away that baby that I love so much," and Jill said: "Look at that lovely horse on the telly, darling," as she swung the new baby from one large sweet breast to the other. Then in came Francis who was not her daddy. "No, he's not your daddy, Frankie's your daddy," and Francis came over, swung her up, and held her with a great spurt of tender love that enclosed them safe, safe, while they sat together watching the little pictures flick past. "Goodness," said Jill, "he's in form tonight," as Arthur Coldridge, cut-and-thrusting, bending forward in the energy of argument, came and went among the pictures on the screen. "Who's that?" "That's my daddy." "My daddy?" "No, my daddy, the bastard." Or, as a face appeared whose mouth twisted and moved and combatted: "Phoebe Coldridge, one of the candidates for . . ." "Goodness, look at *her*," said Jill; and Francis-not-her-daddy who loved her said quickly: "I think she's doing it rather well." "Oh, she always does, the old cow," and as the baby started crowing or laughing somewhere in the room behind the great chair, "Oh God, turn that damned machine off," and Amanda sets up a wail, "No, no, no, I want, I want to . . ." "Oh leave it then, I've got to make her supper anyway. Are you staying for supper, Francis?" "No, I've got to be back at the theatre." "See you then." "See you, love." Off goes Francis the man who comes and goes, he's gone, flick, but in comes, flick, a tall lady who smells like sweets and jam, she's-your-granny-Lynda, and she drops chocolates, bottles of fruit syrup, frozen chickens, flowers, just like the adverts on the telly, in a heap on a table and then off she goes, flick. "Where's my granny, Mummy?" "She's gone home, darling." Flick, flick, faces, people, animals, dressed, undressed, carrying cauliflowers or drinking milk out of mugs with telly pictures on them or killing each other with guns or kissing, the same faces over and over again, as if at an enormous fancy dress party the hostess had asked all the guests to put on the same mask at the door, just very slightly different, so that one twisted in a grimace can be either LAUGHTER or TEARS or I LOVE YOU or DIE, flick, flick, like the faces of the people who for that short period before Lynda cracked up again came to luncheons and dinners and teas at Radlett Street, ghosts tossed up like foam on the top of a wave, charming, urbane, friendly intelligent ghosts, so beautifully dressed, so marvellously equipped for a life of good talking and good living and good thinking.

Food, food, food—and clothes. Clothes and furniture. Make-up and clothes and food and the decoration of houses.

Fifteen, ten, seven years before, people like Martha had patrolled London which was full of damped-down, deprived, graceless people and watched for a gleam of colour, or flash of taste, or panache, or flair; had dreamed of just that one

restaurant where real food was served, of clothes even half
as good as one could imagine—and wondered to what extent
this hunger had been responsible for "London" in the sixties,
which thought, or so it seemed, of nothing, ever, but food
and clothes.

Discussing food, clothes, art, and politics, the three hosts
blended with their guests and were in no way astonishing to
anyone but themselves. Lynda, particularly, was the success.
She was accepted as normal by people who, if they had
heard of her at all, knew of her as a painful half-secret.

"You see, Lynda, you've been such a dark horse, but I've
told them, you're just a little nutty sometimes, you shouldn't
mind, because everyone is, these days." That was Paul,
smoothing her way.

But even if being nuts from time to time is a part of
everyone's life these days it was odd that these highly talented and insightful people were able to take Lynda entirely
on the level she chose to present. She was a tall, rather
silent, smiling woman, who wore extravagantly beautiful
clothes and, invariably, long coloured gloves (very smart,
that), and if she departed from her own party for half an
hour, to make a telephone call, that was what she was doing;
and her look of wide strain ... well, she had drunk too
much, very likely. Yes, certainly Lynda must drink. But
then, who didn't?

On one or two occasions, she did not crack so much as
fray slightly, and became rather scatty and pattering in
speech; but, covering up, Mark and Martha discovered that
there was no need to cover up. A discovery not without
importance.

The fact was that Lynda, "totally incapable of ordinary
life," was judged by her guests who were by definition the
most sensitive and talented available as like everyone else.

And mad? But certainly not!

"You say that Lynda sometimes has breakdowns?"

Extraordinary. But this thought does lead one on to the
next ... who, then, is mad? (Banal, of course, but all the
same, not without its uses as well as its hazards.) Lynda, for
a start and for a certainty. Martha? Well, there is evidence
for supposing ... Mark? Certainly *not*, he was an artist.
Graham Patten? Good God no, or at least, if he is, who
isn't? Francis, Paul? It was too early to say. Jill? But having
illegitimate children, and practically on principle, is not cer-
tifiable. Margaret? Her husband John? No, no, this train of
thought won't do. Much better use the humility of the

471

psychiatrists (which they display here and nowhere else) when they say that someone who can't cope with ordinary life can be considered as, perhaps, not as balanced as one might wish. Back we come to Lynda. Lynda, certainly, comes under this head. Martha? Jill . . .

How about Dr. Lamb or Mrs. Johns?

No, it will be seen that this particular quest for definition doesn't get one far. Particularly as . . . the fact is, for the six months when Lynda was a hostess, and a real one, with no more than reasonable help from Martha and her husband, with guests around her day and night, and putting all the energy one has to into having her hair done, her shoes fitted, her stockings matched and her menus just perfect, Lynda, who was as mad as they come, and showing more strain with every day that passed, did not strike anyone as more than engagingly "different."

Her gloves, for instance: they charmed everyone. When asked why she wore them, she said it was because she bit her nails until they bled. "Lynda's gloves" became a kind of family joke—among dozens of people.

Lynda, asked why she didn't have any affairs, replied that she couldn't have an affair because she never took her gloves off: the remark was found the very essence of *camp*.

Meanwhile, her two comrades, her husband and Martha, were sitting it out. Martha enjoyed it all—more or less. But it was destructive of that part of herself she cared most about. To eat and drink half the night, getting to bed at three or four; then, to get up late so as to attend to one's clothes and help Lynda about food and charwomen; to talk and talk and talk; to meet a dozen new people every day, each one more delightful and intelligent than the next—it was utterly exhausting. Martha could not understand how it was anybody could live like this for long; but after all, many people did. She was more exhausted than Lynda, who seemed to be running on a battery of fine nervous energy unknown to Martha. She was more exhausted than Mark, who was simmering quickly but steadily on a low fuel of patience.

Sign of the time: A London dealer who bought on behalf of American universities wrote to Mark among many others to ask if he had manuscripts of any of his books. Mark replied that he destroyed first or second drafts, and that in any case he typed. The dealer, having begged for an interview, came to say that "in the interests of literature" Mark should not destroy early drafts, because "when students

472

came to write theses about you, how would they know what to think about your work?" Further, Mark should not use a typewriter "if he could help it," because good prices were only paid for handwritten work. Author X, having earned £341 for a highly praised novel, which he had written straight onto the typewriter, and, needing money badly to write another, took three months off to write out the novel again in longhand, with all kinds of erasures, additions, notes, etc.—this work of art he sold for £900 to an American university. Paul was very angry with Mark for not allowing Paul to do the same with all Mark's early books. "Everyone did it," as he said. No, of *course* Paul did not want to get the benefit; he knew a young painter who desperately needed money: if Mark would let this young man make a fancy-free version of, let's say, *A City*, then Mark could feel he was doing good: after all, they never even checked about handwriting. Or how about an imaginary diary? It would be worth a fortune; he, Paul, would guarantee at least £10,000 for it. Well, if Mark was so rich he didn't care about throwing away £10,000, just like that, what about all the poor starving people in wherever you cared to name. Paul knew just the man to write an imaginary diary—he had already done one for the novelist so-and-so.

Sign of the time: The young man who was the narrator of Mark's book, *The Way of a Tory Hostess*, had gone off to fight in the Spanish Civil War. Now, no matter what Mark could say, he was taken to be a veteran of the Spanish Civil War. He was in America at that time, he said; he was not interested in politics then, he protested—but it was no use. His disclaimers were put down to modesty, and then (after all, he was such an old Tory!) to the fact that he had fought on the wrong side and was trying to cover it up. The ending of his book then, was hypocrisy.

Then he got a letter from the *Daily Y* begging for his reminiscences about Franco's armies. A publisher offered him several thousand. At the same time, spies being so well fancied, he was offered large sums for his personal memories of those spies which got away ten years before, all of whom he had obviously known, since he had known his brother.

This was the year when he worked out that if he had written his memoirs of his service for Franco, his reminiscences of Burgess, Maclean and the rest, and allowed Paul to organise the fair copies of his books, he might have made something like thirty thousand pounds for that six months, which was all due, of course, to his engaging in that occupation essential for authors, being currency in the literary world.

But, being so occupied, he was not able to do anything else; any future work, any present work, all past works but one, had become absorbed, not into the book *The Way of a Tory Hostess,* but into the personality of a romantic revolutionary (left or right wing, it didn't matter) of the Spanish barricades.

There is probably nothing one can do about this except, as some writers seem to have discovered, to write novels and call them autobiography.

It has literally become impossible for anyone to read a work of fiction except in terms of the author's life. Since they have learned to read at all, the "lives" of artists, the experiences of artists, the opinions of artists, have been offered side by side with the work of artists, which has become infinitely less important. Plays, novels, stories, poems, are "taught" in schools, in terms of the author's lives. So and so was gregarious; such and such was mad; X was deaf; Y was a lady; Z was a man; Shakespeare was a homosexual ("Suns of the world can stain if heaven's sun staineth—" what *else* could that mean?) and modern writer XYZ has been married and divorced four times.

Faced with a highly educated young woman who leans forward to ask "Mr. Coldridge when you were in Spain did you . . . ?" it is a waste of time to reply: "I was never in Spain," because a slight shade of annoyance will cross her face with the thought: I wonder why he feels he has to say that; what a prima donna! And she will continue: "But when you were in Spain did you . . ."

"It is not the slightest use Mr. Coldridge saying this is not autobiographical; everyone knows that Margaret Coldridge was hostess to everyone who . . ."

"The autobiographical element here has been well absorbed into . . ."

"Of course most novels are a mixture of autobiography and imagination . . ."

So far has the process gone that one may be quite sure that if a group of friends wrote a book, or put some related pieces together, and published a work anonymously, in the hope that perhaps there might be someone left who could be persuaded to consider whether there are other ways of looking at a book (or even at a life), then the reviews would say something like "It is impossible to see why the authors, whose identities are transparently obvious from the context, should resort to such a ..." and would continue to discuss the book in terms of parallels between the material and facts known or imagined about the authors' lives.

This habit of dealing with books, however, operates only with *serious* writers, never, for instance, with a Jimmy Wood. He had just published a story called *The Force Dealers*, whose "storyline" as that a certain type of human being had learned to "plug in" to the energies of other beings, and live off them like a species of vampire. Some of the people who were thus being bled of energy knew about it, but others did not. Those who knew tried to warn those who didn't. The vampires did all they could to keep their victims passively in their power. A war developed between the vampire people and the warners. As more and more of humanity became involved in mutual destruction, it was as if the war was a sort of psychological Trojan Horse, whose function was to channel off energy to feed another planet— since planets were beings, rather than swirls of fire or lumps of earth and stone. This flight of fancy sold thirty thousand copies in the first month, and was bought for a film for £20,000. But when Jimmy attended dinners in Radlett Street, no one had heard of him.

"You are a writer, Mark says?"

"Oh, just space fiction."

Lynda cracked up again. This time it wasn't fast and obvious: she fought all the way. It was defeat for them all. For Mark had not, this time, allowed himself to suggest holidays together, or that his wife might come upstairs to him.

And Martha had been there, in the background, never offering help unless Lynda wanted it, never imposing herself. For Mark and Martha, it had been an exercise in watchful self-effacement. The personal had not been imposed on Lynda. Rather, *they* had not imposed the personal on her.

But it was this that in fact had reached her, was "upsetting" her—through Jill and the children.

It was obvious to Lynda that Jill needed Phoebe; and that Phoebe suffered over Jill. Saying this to either was a waste of time. Lynda had therefore placed herself like that person in the game who slides out of the ring leaving people on either side holding each other's hands when they think they are holding hers. She bought presents which she allowed Jill to think came from Phoebe, and messages from Jill (invented) were transferred to Phoebe. Meanwhile she worried over Francis; believed that he should be shielded from his need to immolate himself in service to the sad girl and her infants.

Lynda began long hopeless weeping fits. Everything was her fault. She rang up Phoebe to say she was sorry, she had done more harm than good.

Phoebe rang up Radlett Street to ask if Lynda had cracked up again.

Interestingly, neither Mark nor Martha had seen this: for weeping and a sorrowing concern for all humanity, but most particularly Jill and Francis and Phoebe, had not been how Lynda had ever started being ill before.

Then Lynda announced she was ill, and she suggested Martha should see her through it, since Mark wanted to work again.

She knew she was ill because suddenly she did not care at all that her efforts had achieved nothing; one week she had lain awake all night, and wept continuously, but almost from one moment to the next, she did not care.

She tried to care that probably she had done harm.

Phoebe, receiving affectionate messages from Jill, Jill getting presents from Phoebe, waited for the other to take some step. But nothing happened.

Phoebe decided not to bother Jill, who had her own life to lead: she described this to herself as *behaving well*. She was very lonely. Gwen had gone off to share a flat with some girls. All quite normal and in order. Phoebe said: "Young people should try their wings," and did not say that she hadn't heard a word of Gwen for months.

Since above all one should behave well, Phoebe never allowed herself to say that Gwen had left home on that day Mary, Arthur's wife, rang up to say that this marriage was probably going to break up. Gwen had taken the news (given by Phoebe without prejudice, her voice neutral, for above all one should behave well) with rising colour and eyes going wild, as if she were being hit with her hands tied behind her back. Phoebe knew exactly how her daughter was feeling, but did not want to say so, did not want to criticise Arthur. Then Gwen went very white, and vomited.

Arthur had thought briefly of leaving Mary to marry Joyce, one of the devoted women admirers. Mary had thought briefly of marrying Phil, a charming lecturer from Cambridge—philosophy. Both Arthur and Mary had come to see Phoebe, separately of course. Phoebe had sat very quiet, listening. With Mary, her supplanter, she had provided

476

variations of the theme: You should do what you think best. But with Arthur, she was suddenly out of control, and got up and went slapping and banging around the room like a windmill with broken sails until at last she turned to him, choking and green and said: "Oh get out."

Next day he wrote a letter to say he supposed he had been insensitive, but he thought of her as his closest friend. The letter she wrote back, but did not allow herself to post, contained years of protest, misery, reproach. When Arthur had left her to marry Mary, sweet, pretty, gentle little Mary (without a brain in her head, Phoebe thought privately though never said, since one should behave well), Phoebe had felt pain. When Arthur left Mary, or thought of it, was when Phoebe felt betrayed. The letter she did not post included the words: If you were going to get tired of her so easily then why bother to leave me at all and land me with all the misery over the girls.

She had never before suggested that she was suffering over her responsibility for the girls. After thought, she decided not to say it now. When Arthur rang up a month or so later, to say he and Mary were staying together "for the sake of the children," Phoebe behaved well. Even to the extent of not telling him that Gwen had left home in a final repudiation of them both. Besides, she suspected, wearily, or if you like, bitterly (though she did not admit a right to be bitter), that soon Gwen would be back, in and out of Arthur's house, while she still kept away from her, Phoebe. Hadn't it always been like that?

Arthur, very busy, as usual, devoted himself to politics; Mary allowed the affair with her lover to continue for some time; then her children, vulnerably adolescent, reclaimed her. These children began visiting Phoebe, making sad jokes about extended families. Phoebe, surprised, realised after a time that they liked her; with gratitude that made her weep (to her own surprise) one night, great floods of tears, she understood they needed her. She then, with both her own girls gone and neither wishing to see her, devoted herself to Arthur's and Mary's children. Gwen visited (Phoebe had been right) Mary and her father, who were "getting on" at all costs under these watchful and disbelieving eyes. But it was Phoebe who had been hurt more by the (passing) rift in this marriage than either of them. She had been more than hurt. It finished something for her—her feeling of worth as a woman; more, her belief in the possibility of a worth in any of these marriages, loves, liaisons all so dingily precarious.

Arthur Coldridge had stabbed her to the heart twice, the second time more dreadfully than the first: and no one but she understood it.

Phoebe, who had always behaved well, who had never allowed herself a jealous look or a word or a petty thought, now, when with Arthur on some political trip, and he made a large harmless male joke with a girl, or flirted, or basked a little—now Phoebe went pale, tightened her lips, was catty or looked away from the scene.

She thought: to think I used to lie awake at nights for years and years, crying my eyes out about Arthur ... if I'd known he was going to leave her too! And her liberal views about censorship, morals, individual liberty, tightened. She felt that she had always believed that people when young made far too much fuss about love and that sort of thing, and that they ought to be protected from themselves until they reached the age of knowing better. Yet she did not dare say this to Gwen, on the very rare occasions she saw her; and all she would say to Francis, when he came to see her, was: Look after yourself, my dear, you must look after yourself. For she thought Jill did not deserve his devotion.

She reflected that there were many things now she was not saying aloud, and wondered if her integrity was less. She was perhaps demoralised by the now nearly thirteen-year-old stretch when the government was everything she hated, and the party which was her moral framework frayed by what seemed a perpetual opposition? This long exile from what in her youth she had believed was what her lifework ought to be had made her corrupt?

Hundreds of people like her were making this a point of conscience: she knew this, for she travelled a great deal in the course of her work. The business of "selling out," of "being bought," was being discussed continually among the journeymen of the party, when other matters were done with. Late at night, men and women sat around, usually in a poorer kind of house, like those of the people they believed that they fought for, and the talk would come back, back, to the razor-edge days of just before the First World War, when Revolution was imminent; and the General Strike, which was *nearly* a Revolution; and Ramsay MacDonald and the coalition governments; and every campaign or turning point seemed to have a fatality of weakness built into it: there were always men who "sold out," chose the handful of ribbons or money. Yet while their minds moved along the path of those years ("The History of the Labour Movement") there were big gaps: the First World War, the Second World War, as if these periods were outside politics, as if the business of national survival cancelled everything else.

Recently, there had been the almost thirteen years in opposition. The party was reft, split, full of groups and divisions and hostilities. Any group in opposition is like this: it is inevitable. But Phoebe was less affected than many in the movement: she belonged to that section of the party—not over at the extreme left where Arthur was, but where the left merged with the centre, which was, she believed, the hope of them all. It was just here, where she belonged, that growth and development was visible: it was where people joined, supported, argued, published books. There was a ferment lively enough to change the whole nation! That is, would be if "the people" would soon enough vote out the Tories and vote them in. Thirteen years had been too long to watch impotently while everything went from bad to worse. For if one kind of demoralisation was feared, watched for, discussed (that of "selling out" or drifting away) another was actual and visible, a central fact which screamed and shouted to be seen. For if people like Phoebe could not put their faith in "the people" there was nowhere to put it. Yet what "the people" supported during those years was a government more corrupt and ineffectual than any in the history of this country. There had never been one with such a record of broken promises, bad faith, indifference. It was during that time Britain's bondage to America (begun in the Cold War while the nation's eyes were fixed, hypnotised, on Russia) was confirmed and built into an economic keystone; those years saw Britain's abject role in the arms race laid down; during those years occurred painfully ludicrous excursions into nineteenth-century colonial warfare—Kenya, Cyprus, Suez. Internally, the country ran down even further than it had during the war: the schools, hospitals, services, slumped into out-dated incompetence; old people died in impoverished neglect; science and technology were poor relations of the great money spender and breeder, war; nothing was right anywhere; and yet "the Tory press"—a phrase used by Phoebe exactly as she had always used it—would begin editorials: "Once this country of ours was divided into two nations, rich and poor. Those bad old days are over and ..." A sort of built-in imbecility, a blindness, persisted: as if it were impossible for anybody to see what was actually happening. And yet still the "people" did not

479

vote out the Conservatives. As the by-elections and the council elections and the rural elections came and went, the popularity of the government fluctuated; but these fluctuations seemed to have nothing to do with what the government actually did, or what promises it broke, what opportunities it missed, nothing to do with good or bad government.

It was here that people like Phoebe took punishment, where it did them real damage: for if they could not believe in "the people" what could they trust in? The Conservatives never pretended in believe in "the people." So their cynicism proclaimed. But the Labour Party, the Labour movement, was, could be nothing else, of the people—who, or so it seemed, did not care what lies they were told, how often they were betrayed, or how the country slid into a slough of incompetence. One must have belief! One must believe in wells of strength and integrity in the people: one must hold fast to knowing that the people, "given a chance," will believe and trust. At the heart of the Labour movement, where its strength is, is this weakness, or at least an ambiguity.

For this "History of the Labour Movement" (let's say 1910 to 1965, for argument's sake) which leaves out the two world wars also, tends to leave out the other great surges of mass feeling, Communism and Fascism. The fact is, anybody who has been tempered at all by the politics of the last fifty years is in a state of mortal funk because of "the people" and what they (we) are capable of. The history of the twentieth century as far as we've got with it is of sudden eruptions of violent mass feeling, like red-hot lava, that destroy everything in its path—First World War, Fascism, Communism, Second World War. There isn't an administrator or politician anywhere that isn't playing whatever hand he holds with one terrified eye always on the next emanation from "the people"—yet he appears to hide it even from himself.

Phoebe might look at a sheet of paper on which the figures were written, the billions and billions and billions and billions of pounds spent on war, on preparations for war, on weapons that within a year become obsolete (but had fulfilled their purpose, which was to create and use money), on the machines which (if anything went wrong and things were always going wrong) would poison air, seas, soil, people; she would spend hours calculating, figuring, marvelling, over such formulas, as mysterious as those used for distances expressed in light-years, and, thinking that the minutest fraction of that sum would educate the people of the world, would feed the hungry, she would still mutter to herself like an incantation: When the people put us in, then . . .

And she sharpened her conscience, examined her own state of integrity, of readiness for office. She had not sold out! She had had plenty of opportunities! When the devil is laying bait for your soul he does not whisper: You are wasting your opportunities on that work; I'll pay you ten times as much! He says: What you have that is irreplaceable is your integrity! Oh, no, no, I know I could never buy that. It's priceless. What are you getting paid now? £3,000? Well, I'll offer you £4,000 (the cost of living is going up) and all I want is your fine feeling for values, for what is real . . .

Phoebe and her friends were experts on scenting out variations of this bait, on visualising themselves in five years' time, if they left their strait path. Goodness, look at the history of their party!

When Phoebe looked at the in-fighting and the gossip-swapping and the sheer nasty-minded malice of those late days at the end of the Tories' thirteen years, and could not prevent herself wondering *When we get in, how on earth are we going to pull together as a team?*—then she remembered the dozen or so responsible jobs she had turned down; she thought of the high crusading temper of Arthur Coldridge, stomping the country to purvey the truth instead of bringing light and integrity to the upper reaches of the Tory press; she thought of the hard-working, devoted, quietly faithful journeymen of the Labour movement up and down Britain, and she thought: *When we get in . . .*

This was a time when everything conspired to confirm the advisability of behaving well, of having behaved well. For instance, her standing as a candidate in a random by-election. She knew that in another kind of party, someone like herself with thirty years of hard work and expert knowledge behind her would expect, and get, a safe seat. She was put in to fight in a marginal constituency: it was taken for granted that Phoebe Coldridge would be ready to sweat it out in a hard campaign, knowing she would lose, for the sake of the party. But she got in, against everyone's expectations. And she would make a good member of Parliament, she knew that; yet she had not asked for it, nor ever expected it.

And there was the business of "her" Africans, so many of whom filled government posts in countries where they had been five, ten years before exiled, jailed, forced underground (by, of course, the Tories: any lapses in this direction by her party she softened as minor faults), and now she, Phoebe, visited, a welcome guest, and the more welcome for understanding where welcome must end. Cool, friendly, ready with advice when asked for it, she accepted invitations to official teas from men she had fed, given money, found lodgings; for whom she had organised legal advice, and got abortions for their girl friends. Of course: in helping people whose cause was just, she had never imagined rewards or punishments. She contrasted her own conduct for instance with the exile Joss Cohen, whose quality of sardonic dedication she found unappealing (once a Communist always a Communist!) and who now was suffering from (Martha's joke, funny she could suppose, if she tried—but once a Communist always a Communist) "withdrawal symptoms." Joss, unwillingly in England for years, having been deported from his territory for sedition and associated misdemeanours, was now able to return to Africa, and did so—frequently. He always returned from this area or that, for another spell in Phoebe's office, rather silent about his visits. It turned out that he had not understood that the half a hundred white people like himself who had made the African cause all their own were as much of an embarrassment to Africans, once in power, as returned heroes are to governments after a war. He had imagined goodness knows what futures for himself, as journeyman, or adviser, or in the government of this or that African territory: and in approaching men whose comrade he had been in times of trouble, he had done so exactly as if they had not in the meantime become prime ministers and cabinet ministers, while he remained rather dubious material, of the kind any government, anywhere, must suspect.

His heart had been broken. To use that phrase which is used when the forward direction of a person's life is blocked. And he could not believe it! To Phoebe, listening with discretion, he would describe how ringing up old friend X he was answered by a member of the old Colonial Civil Service, who had imprisoned not only himself, but old friend X and who was now serving X as if the African cause had always been his own: "I am very sorry—what did you say your name was? Mr. X is too busy at the moment—perhaps you'd care to write?"

Phoebe smiled: she could not help it. Joss could not smile: that is what comes of—*not behaving well*, which is how Phoebe saw it.

"Phoebe," he said, "all right then—but how would you feel if, let's say for argument's sake, Aneurin Bevan had ever been Prime Minister and you telephoned him to have a glass of beer or a nosh-up and the Home Secretary of the previous Tory government who for some reason had become his personal secretary said: 'He's too busy to see you'?"

And at her smile, this time meant for his perusal, he cried out, "Don't tell me you wouldn't be shocked?"

Phoebe privately taking her stand on "the people," said, dryly, that she did not think he, Joss (who had spent twenty years dramatically in politics), was suited to ordinary bread-and-butter politics—and for her money, no other kind mattered. She said, further, that if he wanted to be useful, he could start combatting race prejudice in Brixton or Liverpool or Notting Hill Gate; he didn't have to go to Africa; she said finally that if people went into politics for any other reason but the desire to serve, she had no time for them.

In the last few months before that election when the Labour Party at last got back in, Phoebe, like some others, was rather like dough that had been left too long to rise beside the fire. She had "never had time" for people who did not face facts; she prided herself on being able to see them, and face them no matter how bad. Yet, whole areas of fact were being blotted out, or at least softened a little.

For instance, the Labour Party had never in the past got in except at times of acute crisis whose severity prevented them from doing anything of what they wanted or had promised the electorate: it was clear that this was such a time of crisis.

And again: the country had no idea at all of the state things were in—"Tory propaganda" had seen to that; before anything could be done, the people who were voting them in for, she suspected, wrong reasons would have to be educated into the right ones—which always took time.

And again: the whole of the Labour Party did not consist of people like herself, forward-looking, modern in outlook, scientifically oriented, sober, cool, and, for the most part, young, ten or fifteen years younger than Phoebe, who herself was much younger than most Tory members of Parliament. No: and when the party became government, it was not only people like Phoebe who would govern—far from it; many of them were worse than Tories, she thought.

And again, the temper or the mood of "the people" seemed to her particularly unsuited for a Labour administration: no one cared about anything but enjoying themselves or making money: the young people were all absolutely demoralised—by the long Tory government, of course. Look at Francis, who said he didn't care whether the reds or the Tories were in, they were alike. And look at Paul—but Paul seemed to her particularly deplorable. Look at her daughters! Both talked about the processes of government worse than irresponsibly. Look at—who could you look at among the youth with one reasonable idea in his, or her, head?

Phoebe found herself softening what she thought about the youth: she chose words, temporised. But ought she to? Was she being corrupt in this?

The young people she knew were irresponsible, *but when the Labour Party got in . . .* She had dreams of new armies of young people with red banners in their hands and sober common sense in their hearts. She drove around Britain on a long electioneering trip with Arthur and Mary, and she had never felt closer to her husband (that was how she still thought of him, she could not help what Mrs. Johns's diagnosis might be), and when they stopped the car outside a school, one of the dreadful slum schools which officially did not exist, or a "college" that wasn't fit for pigs, wasn't a college at all, she knew, for she knew him so well, that he was thinking, as she was, with a great heart-swelling warmth of emotion that included not only these children, but all the children of the British Isles: "Just wait—when we get in, we'll change all this . . . when the people put us back in, then . . ."

Two

Martha, who had not attended Lynda during one of her bad times, asked Mark how she ought to behave. He supposed that the thing was to be as sensible as possible.

Sense: yes, yes, of course. After all, when is it not a good thing to be sensible?

But there were those who said that Mark's continuing marriage with Lynda was not sensible; others who complained that for a busy man with responsibilities (to art, letters, literature and so on) to spend months at a time with a mad woman instead of depositing her in a place set up to deal with madness was not sensible. Dismissing these, as Mark did, and descending to a particular, one might ask if Mark had forgotten how he had been driven upstairs by Lynda's nonsense to as it were earth himself in Martha? She probed. Mark now used these words of that time: "I wouldn't have been able to do that and stay sane if you hadn't stood by me." What it amounted to was Mark hadn't forgotten: he didn't want to think about it. (The same thing? Perhaps it was?) He didn't want, or hadn't been able, to let go of ordinariness to sink himself into Lynda. And, not letting go of ordinariness, holding on to sense, had not been able to ask: What is it? Why? What is driving me now? But if Martha wished to let go, sink herself, then that was her business. He said that he had done Lynda no good, so his example wasn't much use, was it? In short, he was busy, was in some new phase of his own. A book, he kept saying it was; but it didn't seem to be a book or even the plans for one. He had dropped out of social life again. He had stopped frequenting the pubs where the "science-fiction" writers gathered. He spent a great deal of time at the factory; and was engaged in some kind of battle with Jimmy Wood, for brisk telephone calls were being exchanged.

"I should have thought that ..."

"Well in that case why ..."

Lynda said: "Mark's up to something—oh yes, he is!" This was on a day when she was being sensible. That is, one could talk to her as one talked to anybody, even if she was distraught and ill. Another day she might be out of reach, and did not hear, or heard only what she chose. Yet all this was odder than it looked. After all, she hadn't cracked into being silly until the guests had all gone, and the time was right. And now, presumably, that person who had licensed another to be "silly" was there, somewhere behind the wide, strained eyes that Lynda held before Martha like a shield on which was written: *No, no, I'm not to be reached!* Even: *No, there's no one here at all.*

Her flat wore the same aspect of guile, or doublefacedness. It was still solidly beautiful. As Lynda had once said, or complained: "Really, it is a kind of Ideal Antique Flat, as if Christie's or Sotheby's had done it." And they built to last when those tables and chairs and cupboards had been made: all Lynda's and Dorothy's ill treatment of them had done very little harm. Martha went back inside an old thought with: A week of painting, and mending and doing up—and no one would be able to guess the horrors and miseries that have gone on here.

No; if someone walked into that place for the first time they would be charmed, put at ease, by the serenity of the furniture and the thickness of the rugs and carpets; only to be seized by an uneasiness that didn't at once explain itself.

For instance, around the walls there was a clear space or runway, as if there were a second invisible wall against which a table, chairs, bookcases, were arranged, a yard or so inside the visible wall. And again, all around the walls to the height of about five feet the paper had an irregularly smudged and rusty look, which turned out to be bloodstains from Lynda's bitten finger ends. And yet again, a pair of shoes apparently left forgotten on a chair, if you examined them carefully, took on the significance of a travelling gypsy's or an Indian's sign to friends or tribesman: one shoe would be set at an exact right angle to the other. Or one of poor Dorothy's embroidered cushions that had *God is Love* on it was put in juxtaposition to a theatre advertisement showing a conventionalised hell. And so on: after a few moments, what had seemed a perfectly normal set of rooms became a place to get out of as fast as possible—either that, or a place to study, to make sense of, to sink oneself into.

Lynda wore an old flannel dressing gown, which she had put on like working clothes or a uniform. It was tied neatly at the waist with a cord, and turned up at the wrists as one does to scrub a floor or do the washing up. Her mass of shining auburn hair that had coarse grey pushing up into it was tied behind her head in a ribbon. Thus had she prepared herself for the task or challenge of being ill.

She moved around the space between the two walls visible and invisible, with her back to the room. She moved slowly, staring, directing the pressure of her gaze up and down and around the area of wall she faced; and she pressed her palms against it in a desperate urgent way, as if doing this would cause it to fall outwards and let her step out of the room over rubble and brick. Or the movement of her hands had a testing feel: How solid is it? Or: What is it really made of—are you sure it isn't *soft?* Or she would turn her back to it, and face into the room, and, keeping herself in a straight line from head to buttocks, bump herself against it in short regular bursts of thud, thud, thud, thud; and this movement seemed to say: I must go on doing this, must go on with some kind of activity, until it creates enough energy to let me turn myself about and go on. After a short recuperative time of such almost-resting, or meditative movement, she would turn herself about and continue on her progress around the wall, feeling, pressing, banging—around and around and around. When she reached the window, across which the curtains had been pulled, making a tall wide pasture of deep green velvet, she sensed her way across with subtler gentler touches of her fingers; and during these parts of her journey one had to ask if—since this was a window, an opening—her pressing and pushings at the wall did mean: Can I get out? How strong are you? For perhaps they meant something quite different.

Martha sat in a comfortable chair in the middle of the room, watching; and Lynda, ignoring Martha, worked her way around. Yet it seemed to Martha that while Lynda seemed to be ignoring her, might even try to walk right through her if she had been in the way of her circular progress, she was really waiting for her to say something, or do something; for in her posture, the set of her head, even in her furtively directed glances was the suggestion of a defiance held in check, but kept ready: *I'm not going to do what you say!* But Martha had no idea what was expected of her: what Lynda's experience made her expect. When Lynda fell off to sleep, which she did in a huddle near the wall, like a prisoner dying against an obdurate barrier behind which she has been shut, Martha went up to Mark. It was nearly two days after this bout or fit had started: Martha had napped, slept in the chair; as far as she knew, Lynda had not. Mark was in his study, not working, but lying in a deep chair trying to absorb what the walls said. (There was a new wall, hinged, with the facts and figures about mental hospitals, asylums, patients, mad people, people incapacitated, in the countries of the world.) He also had the appearance of listening to what was going on in the basement, or following it in his mind.

"When Lynda goes around and around the walls, what do you do?"

"There isn't much to be done. I keep reminding her—You aren't locked in, Lynda, you can walk out anytime you like."

"Oh, I haven't been saying anything at all."

"Well, keep her in touch with reality—that sort of thing?"

"I suppose so."

When Martha had bathed, and eaten, she returned to the basement and found Lynda sitting on the floor, like a child, humming to herself, and swaying back and forth. She looked contented; or at least gone far enough inside herself not to care about the outside world. She saw Martha and shot her a look of hatred. It was theatrical. Then she got up and began her progress around the room, shooting her angrily enquiring glances towards Martha.

Martha tested: "Lynda, you aren't locked in, you can walk out anytime you want—there's the door."

This had an astonishingly large effect—though Martha had half expected it. Lynda moved faster, using her fists in a series of short violent bangs on the walls, looking at Martha all the time. It was very theatrical. Somewhere in Lynda someone watched what she did, so that the look of challenging defiance at Martha was—funny? No; yet Martha needed to laugh—hysterical gusts of laughter were suppressed. Lynda moved faster, waiting for Martha to say it again. Martha kept quiet: Lynda's movements became wild and angry and her eyes widened in prepared fury. "Lynda: those are ordinary walls. This is where you live. You can walk out anytime you like."

And now Lynda whirled around on Martha, picking up a heavy Victorian leather chair and holding it over Martha's head. It was incredible that she had the strength: yet she held it there, grinding her teeth at Martha, until, when Martha did not move, but confronted Lynda with a smile kept as cool as she could make it, she put down the chair, muttered to herself, and shook her head, which looked as if she were saying: *You can't hear what I'm saying, because I don't want you to*—and then continued her progress around the walls. Faster than she had; muttering angrily, darting her theatrically furious glances, playing the role: Leave me alone: you aren't there.

So Martha said nothing. Lynda wanted Martha to be "reasonable" so that Lynda could then defy her? Or, Lynda wanted Martha, or somebody, to be there, but didn't want them to be anything, say anything—merely wanted to be left alone? At any rate, for a day, then two days, Lynda continued, around and around, while Martha stayed in the chair. Lynda did not sleep during that time and after a while, since Martha did not say "Those are your walls, they aren't a prison cell," she began moving more slowly; then might stand for an hour or so, hardly conscious of Martha, her head resting on her fists that rested on the wall. Yet her eyes were open. She had gone completely inside herself, and never looked at Martha, yet once Martha dozed off, and found that Lynda was crouching beside her staring into her face, the way a child stares for the first time at a frog or an ant, or some new creature. Then she found Lynda had pushed a cushion against her head to stop it slipping. And once Lynda said, in a perfectly normal voice: "It's cold in here, shall we have the heating on?"

Yet she did not eat, or drink, nor did she need, or so it seemed, to sit down, or to lie down and sleep. Another day passed. There was a small crisis that could have been worse when Lynda returned from a visit to the bathroom with some pills laid out on her palm. She did not look at Martha, yet she laid them down on a table in a row, like prettily coloured little toys, or sweets, and made as if to take them. Her desire to challenge Martha into starting up and forbidding her to take them was so strong that Martha had really to fight to keep quiet. But she did keep quiet. Then Lynda swept the pills, without taking any, into the palm of one hand with the edge of her other hand and dropped them into a saucer. There they stayed, untaken, as if Lynda said: Look, you see, I'm *not* taking them.

And now Martha was unable to stop herself worrying about Lynda's not eating, not drinking. She was always too thin: now she was a branch of bones over which an old dressing gown was tied, and the skull grew strong while eyes, cheeks, sank into it. Martha made some light food in the kitchen and brought in a tray, and, without speaking, put it on a table. At once Lynda went into her posture of defiance, she sparked angry eyes at Martha, muttering inaudibly.

"If you don't drink something, you are going to be ill," said Martha; at which Lynda picked up the tray and flung it on the floor. She then continued on her way around the walls. Martha got out cleaning things and began to clean up broken crockery, spilt eggs, milk. Lynda watched, in her way of observing everything while appearing not to do so. Then she came from the wall to the carpet, knelt down, and lapped milk that lay in a half-broken saucer. She watched Martha as she did so. Martha felt an extraordinarily strong compulsion to do the same. Yet she realised it was no impulse of Lynda's that had brought her to lap like an animal on the floor: she had worked it out; she had known what she was doing. Now Martha, kneeling on the floor beside Lynda, worked out what *she* should do: she realised that her "if-I-do-this-she-will-do-that" was the counterpart of Lynda's calculation. There was a danger here. What sort of a danger? Being "reasonable," "sensible," was always wrong—or so it seemed: it was that which had turned out to be dangerous, ending in threateningly wielded chairs and thrown traysful of crockery. Thinking: This is dangerous, to me, not to Lynda, she nevertheless poured an inch of milk that lay in the bulge of an overturned glass jug into a plate, held this to her mouth (she did not go down on her hands and knees to the floor to drink), and drank symbolically, not quite lapping. And now Lynda sat up, from her all-fours position, and watched, smiling. It was a sour smile. Triumphant? No, she was acknowledging something, admitting something? Martha had no idea. Then Lynda got to her feet, went into her kitchen, and came back a moment later with a large glass jug filled with water and a glass. She poured water, unsteadily, spilling a lot, into a glass, and drank it. The unsteadiness, speaking of weakness due to not eating, not sleeping, alarmed Martha, but now she made herself keep quiet. Lynda drank glass after glass of water, without looking at Martha, with an air of someone in a desperate hurry to get on with her real business of checking, or challenging, or acknowledging, or holding up, the walls. Which she proceeded to do.

It was stifling inside this large low room, with its burning lights because of the drawn curtains, and the heat full on. But Lynda would not hear when Martha suggested opening the window. There was a strong smell of sweat. Lynda sweated badly. Lynda ought to bathe; Lynda ought to sleep; Lynda ought to eat: Lynda ought, ought, ought, ought ... Time passed. Upstairs, presumably Mark sat in his study, "working," or trying to make what was on the walls into a pattern of sense. Outside in the street life went on. Indeed, the sounds of workmen lifting the road to mend drains or gas or electricity or telephones could be heard: there was a drill at work somewhere close. All around and above, London worked, ate, slept, talked, went to parties, but here it was like being under water, or shut away, or looking at ordinary life from another dimension.

Martha found she was longing for movement: she said to herself that she was an active person, not made to sit day after day, controlling movement, controlling words. Her limbs were restless and longed to be in use. Then she understood that with part of her she wanted to join Lynda in her journey around the walls: she did not want to go out of the flat at all. Of course not—how could she ever have thought anything so irrelevant as that it was possible to go out of the flat. How could Lynda go out, as she was, skinned and flayed, exposing herself to a world that would judge her "sensibly"? And how could Martha go out, since she was part of Lynda? In one moment she, too, would get up and progress around those walls, around and around and around.

To sit here, an observer, while Lynda worked on this task of hers, was callous? Ought she to join Lynda as she had (almost) lapping from a saucer like a cat or a dog? *Almost* ... she hadn't actually done it.

She could not bear to sit still another moment. She got up, holding what felt like a potential explosion of energy, and, having cleared a space on the carpet still stained by spilt milk, slowly did physical exercises, taking no notice at all of Lynda.

To move, to use one's muscles, after long sitting, long inactivity, what a joy, what a gift, what a blessing! She went on slowly, enjoyably, stretching and bending and reaching, working out the restlessness from her body. And Lynda leaned against the wall and watched. Not at all aggressively, not at all needing to defy or to challenge; nor saying, Leave me alone; or, You can't reach me.

When Martha had finished the exercises, she said to Lynda, "I'm going upstairs to bathe—I'll be gone some time." For she had thought it out: in all these years of Lynda's being in hospitals or having to be guarded by nurses or by Mark, she had never hurt anyone, had not even much hurt herself. There had been things thrown, a fight or two, a broken window. They said she was violent; she said of herself that she was violent when being silly. Yet the fact was, she did not do hurt—no one had been hurt. Martha spent a long time in the bath; changed her clothes, ate. She even slept for an hour or so. She came down again to find Lynda sitting in the middle of the carpet. Lynda did not look at Martha, but got up and went to the bathroom and bathed. Slowly and messily; water could be heard sloshing about; and things were thrown. Lynda was singing and muttering. Snatches of songs, bits of conversations, a yell of gutter laughter. It was filthy, disgusting; but the obscenities had a rapid, repetitive, almost ritual sound to them. Lynda, like women in the street shouting envious obscenities at a famous whore, or a film star; or like Mrs. Quest talking to herself. had decided to visit that particular region of the human mind; and, like Mrs. Quest, had decided not to stay there. She came out of the bathroom like a good clean child in another dressing gown, this time a dark pink cotton, and her hair was washed and newly tied. She returned to sit on the carpet. She and Martha looked at each other and this look said, on Martha's side: Lynda, are you ready to become normal again? And on Lynda's side: No, not yet, I don't want to.

And now Lynda sat swaying, and singing little songs to herself, nursery rhymes and children's songs, while Martha cleaned up the swamps in the bathroom and washed Lynda's sweat-soaked gown. Then she came and sat down. Time passed: days and nights. They did not sleep. Or they slept in snatches, but it was not a real healthful sleep. Lynda drank water. She would not eat. But Martha observed her dabbing at some crumbs on the kitchen shelf, and so brought down packets of biscuits from the other kitchen upstairs. Mark came from his study to meet her there. She noted that she now observed him, not with hostility, but critically, from a distance where she also observed an abstracted-looking woman in a faded blue cotton overall and fingers stained with nicotine to the knuckles, who moved in a climate of stale air and smoke. A shaved, clean, strong man, with intelligent eyes, put arms around this woman, and enquired: "Are you all right?"

She listened carefully: What he said sounded extraordinary, every word had a weight to it which compelled attention—she had never heard them before, certainly never thought about them. She understood suddenly that when Lynda muttered, protecting her words from Martha, it was because she was listening to them, to how they sounded; and knew that if Martha handled them, used them, it would be destructive of their real sense. She had not answered Mark, and now she saw alarm on his face. In this alert, clear state she was in, this look, alarm, like other emotions, or reactions, was printed on his features as clear and fresh as if she saw alarm, concern, for the first time in her life. But she had to speak, and finding a normal smile and the right words, she said: "Yes, I'm all right and I think she will be soon." As she spoke, what she said seemed ridiculous: the sounds the human race made when communicating among itself, they were absurd: why did these creatures put up with them? For the fact was, if Mark and she, this lean woman vibrant with a nervous tension that derived from some finer, or at least more potent, air had not said one word during this encounter, they would have communicated well enough: Mark knew she was all right, in spite of her exhaustion, and the way the flesh was going off her frame of bones: he had known as soon as he had set eyes on her—the rest was a formality paid to custom.

He kissed her. Lips, a slit in the flesh of a face, were

492

pressed against a thin tissue of flesh that saved them from pressing a double row of teeth which had lumps of metal in them. Then these lips moved to touch her own slit through which she was equipped to insert food or liquid, or make sounds. A kiss. That part of Martha which observed this remarkable ritual was filled with a protective compassion for these two ridiculous little creatures—as if invisible arms, vast, peaceful, maternal, were stretched around them both, and rocked them like water.

The observer and Martha went downstairs with biscuits and a slab of fruit cake. Yes, she had indeed gone a long way inside of Lynda's country. Yet she was—sane? In control, certainly. And not afraid. She was curious, and angry with herself that she had not done this before—good God, this door (like so many others, she must suppose) had been standing here, ready for her to walk in any time she wished. And she had not, she had not.

Lynda ate some biscuits. She drank water. She had a bath. How long after the first? How long had Martha and Lynda been at work? They could not be bothered to calculate. They did not sleep. Martha believed she had forgotten how to sleep. She regarded, with incredulity, that world where people lay down to sleep at regular intervals—but she had been here before. When? Many years ago. Where? Yes, it was on a boat, a ship. She could feel the swing and the sway of the vessel and smell salt air. On the boat she had felt this: how extraordinary that people could voluntarily, indeed eagerly, throw away their precious lives in sleep.

She knew very well this area of the human mind where the machinery of ordinary life seemed more than absurd, seemed a frightening trap. And she knew it from before the boat. When? Where: her mind seemed to be a thin light texture through which other textures, feelings, sensations kept passing. Oh, it had been long before the voyage to England. . . . Suddenly Martha was in a room she had forgotten, looking at enormous people, giants, engaged in . . . yes, she had been a child, she had felt this as a tiny child, looking at grown-up people, as they sat around a table, dressed in clothes that made them seem like her dolls, talking and smiling to each other with put-on false smiles and looks. For they did not mean what they said. They were afraid of each other, or at least had to placate each other: the small child had called this activity "lies." She had watched (how old? Small enough for a knee to seem large and dangerous, like a horse's trampling legs) and judged these

493

giants as cowards and liars, engaged—incredibly—in meaningless activities and rituals of dressing and undressing and eating and talking, and their fear of each other, their wariness, was so great that two of them could not meet without going stiffly on guard and stretching their mouths and making movements which said: I won't hurt you if you won't hurt me; look, I'm so nice and kind, don't hurt me. Martha had seen all this, understood it, had even said to herself in an anguish of fear that she would be swallowed up: Don't let yourself be sucked in, remember, remember, *remember*—but she had not remembered, she had been sucked in, she had become a liar and coward like the rest.

Martha, now, wept, bitterly, at the wasted years. And Lynda, sitting on the floor, looked up and smiled her a knowledgeable smile—which Martha now understood very well. It was not sour; it was not even critical. It was sad. Martha cried; and Lynda sat quiet until she had finished crying. Then Lynda said, "Yes—but how to get out, get out, get *out* . . ." And she began again on her circumambulation.

Martha was sitting there saying to herself, exactly as she had when she was—how old? remember, *remember*, don't forget, when you go back to ordinary life, don't forget. But she was also frightened. For she had said this before, awake; and had been poisoned and hypnotised; and what was to stop it happening again? She sat watching Lynda. Now she understood very well what it was Lynda was doing. When she pressed, assessed, gauged those walls, it was the walls of her own mind that she was exploring. She was asking: Why can't I get out? What is this thing that holds me in? Why is it so strong *when I can imagine, and indeed half remember, what is outside?* Why is it that inside this room I am half asleep, doped, poisoned, and like a person in a nightmare screaming for help but no sounds come out of a straining throat?

Lynda moved around and around because she had said to herself once, long ago perhaps—perhaps when she was a child?—Remember, don't let yourself go to sleep; and if you go on always, testing the walls for weakness, for a thin place, one day, you will simply step outside, free.

It will be as if the walls, in that one place, have crumbled and gone. And the room will seem like a horrible little cell that an animal fouled.

Lynda was sitting on the floor, swaying. Back and forth, and from side to side. From side to side and . . . on and on. She crooned or sang, then was silent. Then said, aloud, a word, and listened to it. Martha listened too. Lynda said:

"Bread," and listened. Martha listened and the word reverberated with inner messages, each one precious, as if the
word itself contained little depth charges that went off in the
mind: bread, bread. Bread. Or Lynda said: "Wine," and
listened.

The words kept dropping into the listening space that was
Martha's mind. She knew that if a person were to take one
word, and listen: or a pebble or a jewel and look at it; the
word, the stone, would give up, in the end, its own meaning
and the meaning of everything. But she had known that
before, and had let it slide away. . . . Her limbs, her body
kept twitching with restlessness. She was being swept by
small storms, waves of—what? It was a current that made
her limbs want to jerk and dance. Lynda sat swaying, back
and forth, around and around, and it seemed as if Lynda's
sitting there, moving, made a force, an energy, which got
into Martha and prickled along her limbs and made her
want to dance, to move, to . . . do something, she could not
remember what.

She understood that it was this that had sent Mark up to
Martha, to make love. What an extraordinary phrase that
was, "make love." Love, love . . . Martha sat listening, while
the word "love" exploded and bred, and thought of the act
in which she had engaged so very many times and with
different people: she could see Martha, in different shapes,
and sizes, according to the time, her limbs moving and
enlaced with this man, that man, always the same way, or so
it looked from where she was now, but subjectively, putting
herself back inside the act, it was not possible to use the
same words for what she had felt. Mark, when he had come
upstairs, possessed by the same explosive force which
gripped her now, and had made love, made sex, made
something, had used a very different energy from what Jack
had used, all that time ago when he had used their two
bodies like conductors of conduits for the force which
moved them and lifted them to—she could not remember
where, only that if she did not find a way of getting back
there, it would be a self-betrayal. And there was Thomas:
oh yes, but that was not a name she could use even now
without an emotion shooting across her like a flame from a
flame thrower . . . she was sitting and muttering as she had
years before: We don't understand the first thing about what
goes on, not the first thing. "Make love," "Make sex,"
"orgasms," "climaxes"—it was all nonsense, words, sounds,
invented by half-animals who understood nothing at all.

495

Great forces as impersonal as thunder or lightning or sunlight or the movement of the oceans being contracted and heaped and rolled in their beds by the moon, swept through bodies, and now she knew quite well why Mark had come blindly upstairs to the nearest friendly body, being in the grip of this force—or *a* force, one of them. Not sex. Not necessarily. Not unless one chose to make it so.

Jack had once said: "The thousand volts." He had been talking of hate. "The thousand volts of hatred." A thousand volts of love? A thousand volts of—compassion? Of charity?

When she, Martha, had gone to Jack, as Mark had come to her, to earth this force; and found that Jack had, in the intervening years, become possessed, had succumbed (to what? She didn't know—unless one chose to use shorthand words like evil, to be done with thinking about it), then she had simply, because she had had to, found that place in herself where the force could be dammed, contained, held. She had had to. But she had forgotten since that time that she had learned to do this because she had had to learn it.

Mark, "plugged in" to Lynda, had come to Martha; Martha, "plugged in" to Mark, had gone to Jack. But Jack had moved away, taken a step sideways as it were (any such term would have to do) into a fresh field, onto a different ground. There were plenty of ways one could describe it, or think about it. One was: Jack had allowed himself to be taken over by a low and degraded form of mind, almost like a medieval imp or entity. In the Middle Ages they would have said he was possessed. It was as good a description as any. Or one could say: Jack had become a sadist ... good, fine! And what then? This was about as much use as saying that he was possessed. It was a description.

But the point was (her point) with this new Jack (or the old Jack's shadow side, turned outwards?) she was able to separate off in herself various strands or levels or layers simply because he had gone off into an extreme, and she was therefore forced to define, as an act of self-protection. There was woman coming to man for sex, and her reactions, which were expected, known, understood. There was woman experiencing this new thing, sadism, masochism— succumbing to it then holding it off, refusing it, looking at it. And, different from either, an impersonal current which she brought from Mark, who had it from Lynda, who had it from . . . the impersonal sea.

But she had known very well that bringing this current to Jack, who was now plugged in (a term that did as well as another) to hate, as he had once years before feared he could be, she was in danger. She had known she was in danger. The impersonal sea could become the thousand volts of hate as easily as it could become love—much more easily, human beings being what they are.

She had left because she had to leave. Having to leave, she had learned to contain what Mark brought from Lynda and what she experienced first as a drive to move—a need for any kind of movement at all, whether dancing, or walking, or exercising; and this before she had thought (and acted) "sex—who, though? Yes, Jack." Leaving Jack, returning to Mark, she contained. She had forgotten that she had learned to contain. Yet, forgetting, forgetting again and again, life brings one back to points in oneself, to that place where the check is, over and over and over again in different ways, saying without words: This is a place where you could learn if you wanted to. Are you going to learn this time or not? No? Very well then, I'll wait for you. If you're not ready now, too bad! I'll find ways of bringing you back to it again. When you are ready, then . . .

Martha sat still in her chair, feeling herself shake, almost shake apart with the force of whatever power it was that was being generated in that room, and made herself remember what she had learned through leaving Jack. Essentially, it was keeping still, holding, waiting. She sat still; and instead of letting her limbs, or even her imagination—the same thing?—move her around the walls, crave for movement, sway like Lynda, back and forth, and around and around, instead of spilling, or using, this energy in any way whatsoever, she let it accumulate—yes, that was it, of course, she had learned that too, and had forgotten it—you must let it build up . . .

Her head became very clear, very light, receptive, a softly lit bubble above the violence of a body whose limbs wanted to move, to jerk, even to dance; whose sex was alert, ready to flare up, and demand; and whose waves of—what?—came and went, running and ebbing as from another invisible sea of power. If she sat quite still, or walked steadily up and down, the space in her head remained steady, or lightening and darkening in a pulse, like the irregular pulse of the sea. She had known this lightness and clarity before—yes, walking through London, long ago. And then too, it had been the reward of not-eating, not-sleeping, using her body as an engine to get her out of the small dim prison of every day. But how could she have allowed herself to forget and not have spent every moment of her time since trying to regain it, to get back here where at least one could begin to see the way out, and forward?

Martha sat, or gently walked; she was listening, receptive, waiting. And Lynda sat on the carpet, swaying, sometimes humming or crooning, nursery songs mostly, and sometimes silent. The two took no notice of each other at all.

Martha could easily hear what Lynda was thinking. Being more sensitive now, by far, than normally, she heard better: normally she could hear an odd phrase, or a key word, or a sentence or two, summarising what was going on in somebody's head; now it was not far off being inside Lynda's head, for the jumble of connected words and phrases linked together by past experience, which is how we "think," most of the time (a mechanical association of notions, like strings of sausages), this stream ran through her mind beside her own stream, or sometimes displaced it. Lynda was thinking not of the present, but of what her life would have been if she had not got ill—had not (Martha heard the words) "been so silly as to tell what I know." Lynda was thinking, not violently, or even with grief, but dispassionately, how she would have liked to grow up quietly in the country, with brothers and sisters, and a simple relationship with parents, and then to marry a farmer, or a gardener, and have a large family. It was a fantasy so plain and wholesome, like Nanny Butts's butter cake, so divorced from anything that happened now, that it had the effect of making Lynda seem capricious and spoiled, as if she had said: "I want to live in a marzipan house." And then her thoughts ran on Mark: if only Mark had not sent her to the doctor, if only Mark had trusted her—and then, earlier than that, if only her father had not made her see the doctor, and if only she, Lynda, had not said what she knew, if only she had known enough then to keep quiet.

Behind these rivulets of words was a great chaos of sound. Martha could just hear it. She thought, or wondered: is it in Lynda's head or in mine? And, with a shock of impatience against her own obtuseness (for surely she had been here often enough not to have to ask, or wonder); well, of course, it is not a question of "Lynda's mind" or "Martha's mind"; it is the human mind, or part of it, and Lynda, Martha, can choose to plug in or not. Which she had known, had known well—this business of charting the new territory meant a continual painful effort of discovery, of trying to understand, to link, to make sense, and then falling back

498

again, "forgetting"; and then an effort forward again—a baby trying to walk, that was what she was; but surely there was no need for it, it was inefficient, for obviously it was not possible that Lynda, Martha, were the only two people who tried to make maps of these territories. It must be a question of looking for, and finding, the right guides.

It was as if a million radio sets ran simultaneously, and her mind plugged itself in fast to one after another, so that words, phrases, songs, sounds, came into audition and then faded. The jumble and confusion were worse when she allowed the current that pumped through her to get out of control, to rise and jerk and flood; the sea of sound become more manageable as she held herself quiet and contained. Yet even so, it was all she could do to hold on; Martha rode the current, a small boat on a fast river, or a tiny aircraft in a storm, her own body bucking and rolling under her; and words, shrieks, gunfire, explosions, sentences, came in, faded, or stayed. When something stayed then it, they, might develop or grow loud and accumulate around it other words, sounds, phrases, of the same kind or texture, like a bit of metal attracting to it particles of substances of a certain nature, so that a word, "bread," proliferated into the phrase "bread of life," burst into a pure high song like a thrush, from the Ninth Symphony, then jangled into banality with "you can't have bread with one meat ball," gave snatches of recipes for loaves as they were once made on a hearth, leered, jeered, threatened, on a wavelength of mockery, until suddenly—while Martha understood (again) how the words, phrases, sounds, came in from that sound-length in an exact relation to some mood or impulse in herself (as faint and as fleeting as you like)—she realised that she was being taken over; she was taken over because she had allowed herself to become frightened. Her whole body, organism, vibrated, shook, was being shattered to bits, by the force with which the sea of sound entered her. Her head was a jar, a bedlam; but, as she was about to cry out, scream, let go of control, perhaps bang her rioting head against the walls, she looked at Lynda sitting quiet on her part of the carpet, and remembered that some days before, during Lynda's long progress around and around the walls, she had remarked: "I must get through the sound barrier. Here is the sound barrier. I must get through it." As Martha remembered Lynda saying this, Lynda said, "You can, but it's difficult. If you let it take over, then it is hard to make it go away again. Be careful." These words threw Martha first into a panic; then, as she flung herself down on the floor beside Lynda, thinking that it was not possible to "get through" and that she was doomed forever to be shattered by sounds as powerful as pneumatic drills at work inside her brain, her whole person (apparently on the point of explosion and shaking and trembling) resisted the invasion, clenched itself in self-defence, and held, contained, gripped tight, calmed. Martha dropped off to sleep suddenly, totally, but probably not for more than a few moments, the space of some heartbeats. When she woke, or came to, her body was rested and her mind back at that point where it was soft and clear and listening, with the ocean of sound a low retreating booming noise safely far away.

She rested, face down on the carpet, eyes closed, her mind empty, as if she rocked on long waves inside a reef beyond which crashed the roaring sea.

Resting, refusing to admit the sea of sound, she saw that the small moving pictures ran before her eyes. Was it then that when in this heightened condition one was closer to, or vulnerable to, that more perceptive or intelligent place in oneself that (who?) could communicate through sound, or through the small moving pictures, or, if one was in a phase of sleeping well and alertly, dreams? Was it that something that needed, that *had to* get itself communicated, simply found, like water, the easiest channel through the lump of incomprehension which was Martha in her daylight or normal condition?

Lynda said: "I keep trying to find people who know but I haven't yet. But they must be somewhere."

She was humming lightly to herself. *How many miles to Babylon? Three score miles and ten. Can I get there by candlelight? Yes, and back again.* These lines seemed full of information, just beyond Martha's reach, but which she would one day be able to grasp. Meanwhile, before her eyes were displayed gardens rising vertically in receding banks till the plumes of fountains moved among moving white cloud; and water fell, trickled, ran, splashed, sang. She smelled sun on wet foliage.

Now Martha saw Lynda in a pale shaggy coat sitting in a kind of tearoom or self-service place, opposite a fattish, smiling Indian gentleman.

"I can see you with an Indian in a restaurant," said Martha.

"Oh? Yes, that's right. It must be the flower guru, you know, he was here. I heard of him through all those books, you know. I met him in a Lyons. He kept sitting there smiling and saying God is Love. And I kept saying yes I'm sure that's true—because I don't feel people like us have the right to talk about God, Martha."

Martha, watching this scene and not wanting it to be shaken away by her speaking, said nothing.

"He gave me a large pink rose and he said, This is Love. So I put it in my frock."

"No you didn't, you sat holding it in your hand," said Martha, speaking in a fast monotone, to keep the scene steady.

"Oh, did I? I thought I—then I said, I don't know anything about love. Other people have to look after me. I've never known how to love anybody. I loved my child but I couldn't look after him. I can't even love my husband. I've made him miserable for years and years because I can't bear him to touch me. Then he said the Great Mother had perhaps chosen me as one of her daughters who had been freed of the tyrannies of the flesh—lust, he said. I said nuts to that. I said if I could go to bed with my husband and let him be happy I'd feel I'd make a step forward to love. He said I was a victim of Western thinking. I said if God is a rose, then God is sex, East, West, home's best. He sat there smiling and smiling, knowing quite well in his heart that I'd see it his way as I matured—like Dr. Lamb. So I got up and left."

"You handed him back the rose," said Martha.

"Did I? Was it then when I . . . ?"

Martha laughed: it was sad and funny, the soft round smiling Indian man, while Lynda stood there tall and smiling politely, holding her great pale fur around her with one hand, clutching the pink rose. Then she suddenly leaned forward to hand it to him, not meaning to, but feeling she ought to be polite, like a little girl.

Lynda walked out of the restaurant, and the scene switched off.

"Machines," remarked Lynda.

"Yes. But how many?"

"What we want, I suppose . . ."

Martha was certainly a radio: so was Lynda. Martha was a television set, only, unlike a television set, not bound by time. She was a camera: you could take pictures of any object or person with your eyes, and bring it out afterwards to examine it—that is, depending on how you had concentrated when you looked at it. What else?

Lynda said: "In that first hospital where Dorothy was ill first she had a friend. She was Hortense. Hortense knew what moods the doctors were in by the colours in the air around them. The doctor before Dr. Lamb was very bad, he was always an awful dirty yellow colour, like fog, or bad breath, and when he was angry it got streaked with red."

"I saw red," said Martha. "It was when I was angry."

"Well, so she used to scream when he came near, she said she felt suffocated. So he put the machines on her head. After she'd had the machines a few times, she didn't see colours any more. And I used to see pictures, before the machines on my head."

"I wonder what colour Dr. Lamb would be?"

"Oh, I don't want to know. Grey. Cold. A bright cold grey—there was a nurse in that hospital, and she was always a sooty black, so said Hortense, for feet around her the air was sooty black, except when she was giving injections—she'd stand there smiling, and the black started to have flames through it, like fires in hell, but the thing is, we've got it all wrong, we say, men invent machines, but we make machines to do what we can do ourselves. If we didn't have the machines and someone told us, You don't need machines, it's in your minds, you don't need computers, there are human computers, perhaps we'd never have to make the machines. What do we need machines for? To dig ditches and make roads, but our brains could be rockets and space probes, if they can be radios and television sets."

All this in a fast low voice, a murmur, while she swayed back and forth from side to side. It was the monotone self-absorbed murmur of madness, for she did not really care if Martha answered her or not. Or perhaps the even monotonous tone was a way of keeping herself on an even keel, as Martha did not speak or she maintained her voice on a level so as not to jar away the pictures. Or perhaps the murmur was a way of saying to Martha: Don't interrupt, this way of talking is a way of thinking, I find out what I think when I talk.

But if Lynda had spoken thus before a nurse in a mental hospital, before a psychiatrist, they would have said: "Mrs. Coldridge is badly confused today."

Martha said: "But if the human brain could be a space probe or a moon-walker or a radar, it could also be a bomb or a disintegrator, and people would use it to destroy, they aren't fitted."

Martha lay face down, eyes closed, watching gardens,

fantastic gardens, beautiful gardens . . . never had she imagined such gardens, she wanted to cry because of their beauty: Nurse, nurse, I'm seeing such lovely gardens!

"Are you, dear? You're a bit hallucinated—just take this pill and go to sleep."

Lynda said: "Like a man who has lost a hand, he uses a machine-hand instead. But you must be careful, Martha, careful, you mustn't say what you know, they'll lock you up, they want machines, they don't want people . . . but you can do it. Once I thought I could do it, but I can't. I am ruined, you see. My mind was ruined by all the drugs, my mind is no good now, and then there was that electric-shock machine they put on my head when I was a girl, ever since then I'm not what I was. I pretend to myself I am sometimes but I'm not, but you could do it, you can find out, I am sure there are people somewhere who know."

The word "drug" had snagged on Martha's attention. She thought: if drugs could cause the clarity, heighten it, make the pictures deeper, open the door to . . . Her feet had taken her off the floor and into the bathroom. Lynda's drugs were in bottles ranged from end to end along a four-foot shelf. If she took . . . She was gripped by arms from behind, and pills, already in her hand, fell into the bath. But she had half expected Lynda to follow her; had even invited it, relied on it: as a child provokes a parent into showing attention. Lynda pushed Martha away, and got onto her knees to pick up the sweetlike pills that had fallen to the floor. These she flung into the bath too, turned the taps on, and washed them all away. Then without looking at Martha she went back to her place on the floor. Martha returned to lie beside her.

Lynda said: "You only did that because you were afraid when I said you had to do it, had to get out. You know it will be very hard, and so you thought, If I take drugs I'll have an excuse not to try, because I'll be ruined—that's what you were thinking."

Martha was tired. Yet she was restless. She wanted to go out and walk, as she had not walked since those months when she first came to this city. She must walk: but when she pulled aside the curtain and looked out it was the dead time of the night, about two in the morning.

"I'm going to walk when it's light," she announced, and plunged down on the floor again, dropping off to sleep, saying to herself, Wake me at nine.

Her sleep was drenched with a golden light, like the clear light immediately after a storm, when the sun comes out, and sky, leaves, earth, clouds shine and glitter, and the few last drops from the flying depleted cloud explode in tiny splashes of gold. Her dreams had been all of happiness: that far high hunger, yearning, which is so intense that it is soaked with the quality of beauty that it longs for, so that longing and what is longed for merge into a sharp sweet pain. To wake from such a sleep, which is all a light, a delight, and a promise, to such a day ... Martha woke with a sob: she was weeping because she had to wake, and saw Lynda seated with her face to the wall, swaying back and forth, back and forth, so that her forehead bumped regularly against the wall, like a child dispelling tension. Martha remembered that in her dream, beside her in a sweet golden light, had walked Lynda, a smiling girl, and they went towards a man whose face was all strong confidence and welcome. This was Mark. Martha, awake, saw a dirty, sour-smelling bedraggled hag who sat and banged her forehead against a wall that was rusty with tiny bloodstains. The light was showing in strong outline around the curtains. It was nine o'clock.

She got up off the floor to go out, and Lynda said: "It's awful looking at outside. Don't. You'll be sorry."

It was a fine day outside, but she could not go in the dress that she wore, which was crumpled and foul. She bathed quickly, and could not find a dress. She did not want to go upstairs now, for she was afraid of disturbing Mark, who would say: Are you all right? Shall I come with you? She put Lynda's coat over a petticoat, and let herself out quietly.

The day was fresh and the world newly painted. She stood on a pavement looking at a sky where soft white clouds were lit with sunlight. She wanted to cry because it was so beautiful. How long since she had looked, but really looked, at the sky, so beautiful even if it was held up by tall buildings? She stood gazing up, up, until her eyes seemed absorbed in the crystalline substance of the sky with its blocks of clouds like snowbanks, she seemed to be streaming out through her eyes into the skies, but then sounds came into her, they were vibrations of feet on pavement, and she looked down again at an extraordinarily hideous creature who stood watching her, out of eyes that were like coloured lumps of gelatin that had fringes of hair about them and bands of hair above them, and which half protruded from a bumpy shape of pinkish putty, or doughlike substance. The slit under the bump that had two air holes in it was stretched in a grimace that said: What are you doing? What is up there? Am I going to miss something if I don't stare too? When the creature saw she was looking at it, the grimace twisted, and dirty teeth showed in the slit, and this was as if an animal pleaded with puckered muzzle and half-bared teeth and a raised paw because it might be beaten, but the pleading held a menace too, if the animal thought of biting before it was attacked. This creature was exposed only in the region of the face, for all the rest was covered in a varying kinds of substance, from the top of the head, which had a sort of brownish shell on it, to the feet, which were inside hard cases, of a shiny material. The body was encased in a thick hairy stuff which had openings through which the head and feet emerged, and various vents, slits, pouches contrived in it for the natural functions or to carry artifacts and tools.

It was only by the bumpy plane of pinkish tissue, surrounded and tufted with hair, in which the eyes were situated, that this creature wished to be judged, or through which it was exposed.

It smelled awful, in a strong reek which it seemed to carry with it as it moved. The creature said something, but did not particularly expect to be answered, for when Martha walked on, the slit loosened from its stretched position and fell into a loose pout, and it moved away by putting forward one after another the two appendages below its body in a shambling balance. As it went, a four-footed creature covered with a fell of long black hair moved out from behind a parapet of brick, and lowering its hind part, it defecated among the feet of more of the two-appendaged creatures who approached. For all along the paths where they went, there were heaps of excrement, and the posts that held lamps and the corners of buildings were all soaked with strong-smelling urine.

Martha looked up back at the sky, shutting out the street, and walked fast. The sky, oh the sky! and the trees in the square, whose branches moving in gentle air sent her messages of such joy, such peace, till she cried, Oh trees, I love you, and sky I love you! and the cloud up there, so absurd, so sweet, so softly, whitely, deliciously lolloping up there in blue air, she wished to take it in her arms and kiss it. Oh Lord! she prayed, Let me keep this, let me not lose it, oh, how could I have borne it all these years, all this life, being dead and asleep and not seeing, seeing nothing; for now everything was so much there, present, existing in an effulgence of delight, offering themselves to her, till she felt they were extensions of her and she of them, or at least, their joy and hers sang together, so that she felt they might almost cry out, Martha! Martha! for happiness, because she was seeing them, feeling them again after so long an absence from them. She walked, she walked, looking, gazing, her eyes becoming cloud, trees, sky and the warm salutation of sunlight on the flank of a high glowing wall. Until, suddenly, the small voice of the tutor said in her inner ear: *"And only man is vile?"* And she let her eyes fall again—and wished to run back under cover, to get into shelter, fast, anywhere where she did not have to look at these beings all around her. What an extraordinary race, or near-race of half, uncompleted creatures. There they were, all soft like pale slugs, or dark slugs, with their limp flabby flesh, with hair sprouting from it, and the things like hooves on their feet, and wads or fells of hair on the tops of their heads. There they were all around her, with their roundish bony heads, that had flaps of flesh sticking out on either side, then the protuberance in the middle, with the air vents in it, and the eyes, tinted-jelly eyes which had a swivelling movement that gave them a life of their own, so that they were like creatures on their own account, minuscule twin animals living in the flesh of the face, but these organs, the eyes, had a look which contradicted their function, which was to see, to observe, for as she passed pair after pair of eyes, they all looked half drugged, or half asleep, dull, as if the creatures had been hypnotised or poisoned, for these people walked in their fouled and disgusting streets full of ordure and bits of refuse and paper as if they were not conscious of their existence here, were somewhere else: and they were somewhere else, for only one in a hundred of these semi-animals could have said, "I am here, now, and conscious that I am here, now, noticing what is around me"; for each was occupied in imagining how it, he, she, was triumphing in an altercation with the landlord or the grocer or a colleague, or how it was making love, or how its child had done this, or how it would soon eat something. It was painful in a way she had never known pain, an affliction of shameful grief, to walk here today, among her own kind, looking at them as they were, seeing them, us, the human race, as visitors from a space ship might see them, if he dropped into London or into another city to report. "This particular planet is inhabited thickly by defectively evolved animals who . . ."

For their eyes were half useless—many wore bits of corrective glass over these spoiled or ill-grown organs; their ears were defective—many wore machines to help them hear even as much as the sounds made by their fellows; and their mouths were full of metal and foreign substances to assist teeth that were rotting, if not equipped entirely with artificial teeth since their own had been removed; and their guts were full of drugs because they could not defecate normally; and their nervous systems were numbed by the drugs they took to alleviate the damage done by the din they had chosen to live in, the fear and anxiety and tension of their lives. And they stank. They smelled abominable, awful, even under the sweet or pungent chemicals they used to hide their smell. They lived in an air which was like a thick soup of petrol and fumes and stink of sweat and bad air from lungs full of the smoke they used as a narcotic, and filthy air from their bowels.

But the most frightening thing about them was this: that they walked and moved and went about their lives in a condition of sleepwalking: they were not aware of themselves, of other people, of what went on around them. Not even the young ones, though they seemed better than the old: a group of these might stand together looking at others passing; they stood with the masses of the pelt hanging around their faces, and the slits in their faces stretched in the sounds they made to communicate, or as they emitted a series of loud noisy breaths which was a way of indicating surprise or a need to release tension. But even these did not listen to what the others said, or only in relation to the sounds they made themselves: each seemed locked in an invisible cage which prevented him from experiencing his fellows' thoughts, or lives, or needs. They were essentially isolated, shut in, enclosed inside their hideously defective bodies, behind their dreaming drugged eyes, above all, inside a net of wants and needs that made it impossible for them to think of anything else.

She walked, walked, fast, wanting to get away, till she came towards a sheet or expanse of gleaming substance and saw approaching her a creature wrapped in the fur of an animal, short pale fur on its head, its eyes wide and horrified as if in flight from something, or looking for somewhere to hide itself. This, she realised after a moment, was herself, Martha, who so lately had been dissolving in joy at the sight of a sunlit cloud above an airy mass of leaf.

She fled down Oxford Street, looking at the narrow strip of blue air above it, in which hung an explosion of golden light, and imagined how the space traveller, speeding away from the revolving bubble of golden gasses, might say, formulating the words of a report in his mind: The third globe of solid substance out from the central swirl of brilliant light which holds circling around it in a kind of flat spiral formation an assortment of such lumps or balls of varying kinds of solid or gaseous matter, is the globe, or ball, on which the creatures described above under Section II-B-iii live. At no point did they appear to notice any member of our team: their faculties of attention and comparison are either atrophied or as yet undeveloped to an extent which enabled us to work and live among them for as long as was needed, without doing more than using their clothes and their system of communication (partly sound: oral) and concealing from them the fact that our sight, hearing (etc.) are a thousand times more developed than theirs. They are so susceptible to flattery that anything may be done with them; provided they are not allowed to suspect their inferiority. For they are so vain that they would certainly kill or imprison or maim any being they suspect of being better endowed than themselves.

There was a harsh jiggling going on in her head. She was picking it up from somewhere? No, it was music coming from a shop. She went into the great shop, feeling herself drown in the filthy air, and pushed through a seething mass of creatures who were engaged in the process of acquiring objects in a noise and vibration of movement at which Martha's stomach wanted to churn. She climbed into a place on a stairway from where she could look down. Beneath, a crammed space of every kind of thing, object, artifact, and people, people, people—these, the inhabitants of one of the rich countries of the world, the favoured of humanity who never stopped reading, talking, thinking, working at health, beauty, elegance, were engaged in buying what was needed to acquire or maintain these qualities—and look at them! If you gazed down into that sea, to find a face that was not drugged with anxiety or day-dreaming; not absorbed in fantasy, not distorted by anger, or worry, or greed, then you must look, and look ... Where was one person who was healthy, did not wear glasses, hearing aids, false teeth, who slept well, who did not take half a dozen kinds of drugs, who did not attend doctors, psychiatrists? This was one of the favoured countries of the world, a country which others envied, and these were the favoured of this country. Suppose one closed the door of this emporium for a day and put in a team of researchers to find among these several thousand people to ten who were, simply, whole; whose organs were normal; and who slept well and who did not take drugs.

508

Ten? Supposing these researchers looked for ten who were in control of the amount they ate, and the smoke they drew into their lungs and the alcohol they numbed themselves with and how they used themselves sexually. Would they find ten?

Now Martha remembered that Lynda had said she would feel like this, had warned her: she wanted to get back to Lynda. She struggled down through a mass of people onto the pavement, and pushed through them along the pavement. She had no money with her, she would have to walk. She fled through this species, her own, wishing only to hide herself, to conceal herself, her own ugliness, to hide what she thought.

She rushed past trees, and the sunlight of the square: yes, the price you paid for being awake, for being received into that grace, was this, that when you walked among your kind you had to see them, and yourself, as they, we are. She did not want it again, not so soon—she was running back to the basement, fast, fast.

In the rooms under the heavy house, in the basement, the lights burned behind drawn curtains, and Lynda sat exactly where Martha had left her, banging her head against the wall.

Martha threw off the animal pelt she had used as a disguise, and lay on her back on the floor. The ceiling light, hanging low, threw an orange glow, flecked with yellow, up into a wide disc on the ceiling. The glow of orange, the dots of yellow, seemed held, or enclosed, in a wash of white light, more imagined than seen, yet there, and growing into visibility as she stared. And now, imminent behind the white, was a blueish shade, as if the ground of orange, yellow, white were blue, a luminous soft blue, a bell of soft glowing blueish light, always there, but not looked at, or taken in unless one lay on a floor, honed down by fasting and lack of sleep and walking in a world full of the drugged cripples who were one's fellow human beings—oh, she could not bear to go out again, she would not, even if walking among the defective half-animals meant also to walk through trees, clouds, flowers, and light which were like presences from another world whose existence just behind this one made her want to cry out with longing, with hunger. She would stay here in the basement with Lynda. She would never move out. She and Lynda would live down here and Mark would hand them food and supplies through the door, which was like a trapdoor into a submarine or a lower part of a ship. And here they would live. Why should they need to go out, they had radio sets, their own built-in television, radar, time machines ... she giggled. She heard the sound disconnected from herself, like a bubble coming up through water. It was a variety of laughter. Laughter was the noises made by the species in the street when they needed to fit together two forms of fact or information that were different from each other, of different substances from each other; for their brains were so compartmented that their organisms were always being thrown off balance by having to take in, or at least to handle, two or three different kinds of fact at once, for which they were inadequately adapted. That was laughter: a kind of balancing mechanism, a shock absorber. But giggling was a retreat away from a fact which needed to be faced.

Lynda giggled a great deal when she was at her worst. She even said herself that it was a bad sign when she started to giggle. Now Martha lay and giggled. She did not wish to stop. She lay behind a barrier, which was the act of giggling.

A shock of alarm or warning reached the outer defences; but this alarm was not one she chose to listen to. Or not now. She was thinking: Better mad, if the price for not being mad is to be a lump of lethargy that will use any kind of stratagem so as to remain a lump, remain nonperceptive and heavy.

She would lie on the floor and watch the magic lantern slides ... she shut her eyes, saw the glow of light through her lids from the ceiling, and waited for the pictures. But her lids stayed dark. Why? Why at some times pictures, but not at others? Why the sound-length sometimes, and not others? Why some people at some times in their lives? Why some people with one or more of these capacities who were not afraid to develop them, while others hastily suppressed or hid or ran away into dark corners with them? Why did some people have to hurt others who had these capacities, while some people helped and developed?

The first intimations of this capacity had been in childhood, just before sleep or on awakening: a faint flash of colour, a couple of pictures perhaps, or a fragment of music, or some words, or her name called as if in warning or reminder: *Remember, remember*. Well, a great many people experienced this, but being well-ordered, well-trained, docile, obedient people, they heard the doctors or the priests say—whatever the current dogma ordered, and that was that: they were prepared to bury the evidence of their own senses,

510

they ran away. And, like any neglected faculty, it fell into disuse, it atrophied.

Later, she had had experiences when she had been very tired, or slightly ill, or under strain, or when making love, but only with Jack.

And then, during the battle for her memory, something had opened, changed—for that was when the pictures, sounds, had become more than flashes or intimations or an occasional thing, but something that might happen often. But not controlled ... suppose one could learn to control ... *how?*

Where were the people who knew? It couldn't be possible that everyone in the world had been frightened into obedience.

No. For one thing, there was Rosa Mellendip, a perfectly sensible woman, if bound by her packs of cards and her tea leaves. Yes, but that was not where what was needed could be found. That world was cosy, self-satisfied, stagnant, the mirror and shadowside of the orthodox scientific world which was also cosy, self-satisfied, stagnant. One was a rationalism which once had been useful, a patterning of habit-thoughts already outdated by what was happening on its own outposts. The other, formed by coming into existence in opposition to "science," and then having to maintain itself as a humoured and tolerated minority, had the same quality of lifelessness.

Elsewhere was the sense of sharp change, of old thought breaking up, of flow and of movement; in life, that is—in what one experienced, in where one learned. There was a prickling challenging liveliness, a vitality at work. But not in the backwaters of "rationalism" which was the official culture, and not in the mirror of the official culture. Mrs. Mellendip—now a rich woman (using her money well and wisely as a good businesswoman should, and as charitable and kind as anybody else) and indeed rather respectable; for "everyone" now had their fortunes told—from her office in Kensington advised some of the largest businesses in the country about how to harmonise their activities with those of the stars. There was nothing shady or dubious or to be hidden about her now; she had come into her own, for as she said in her homely way that yet managed to suggest depths of wisdom: "What goes up must come down." Very true indeed, but it was the apotheosis of Rosa Mellendip as a respectable woman that signalled the end of the two worlds, conformist/rational and nonconformist/eccentric; for one can be certain that when a formerly rejected movement or strand in society becomes tolerated by what fought it, both are about to be depth-charged from somewhere else.

But the prickling liveliness, as if the substance of ordinary life were being drenched or bombarded by a particularly vivid type of atom—that feeling she, her world, conveyed no more than did, let's say, Graham Patten, whose programmes on "the occult" on television (very popular) always managed to suggest a sixth-form debate between prize pupils, one on the "literary" side (*There are more things in heaven and earth*) and one "doing" science.

And it was precisely this quality at work everywhere, the lively yeast, which made Martha hold on to that prime thing she had learned in her life, had been made to learn over and over again, so that she knew it as one does know things that have become part of one's substance, to be acted from because the knowledge is oneself: it was that if she was feeling something, in this particular way, with the authenticity, the irresistibility, of the growing point, then she was not alone, others were feeling the same, since the growing point was never, could never be, just Martha's, could not be only the property or territory of one individual. No, if she experienced and was asking questions, then others like her were experiencing and asking questions: others looked for her as she looked for them. Somewhere near there were people to whom she might say "television," "radio," "radar," "time machine," "camera"—or whatever other shorthand phrases were suitable—and these people would not reply: "You're hallucinated/sick/imagining it."

Nor would they say, as in Rosa Mellendip's country: "Of course, *we* know that," there being no more to say about it, since everything was being said: nor, as in Jimmy Wood's territory, would they look at you in surprise at the suggestion there might be a connection between what people wrote and what they thought was possible.

Yet it was Jimmy Wood who had put up a small signpost. He had said to Martha that if she came out to the factory, he would show her where he got plots for his tales. She had imagined that he would perhaps ask her to apply her eye to a microscope to look at animalculae in the violent battle for growth and survival which is what a smear of blood or bits of tissue became as the eye descends like a diver to that dimension; or to look through a telescope to see the stars circling, dividing, eating each other, exploding, dancing, singing—animalculae to somebody perhaps. But that hadn't happened.

In the storeroom of the factory, among shelves full of devices and contraptions which Jimmy said were machines that hadn't come off yet but would perhaps when he got a hunch about them, were books which one might have expected to find on Rosa Mellendip's shelves, but never here.

There were books on Rosicrucianism and the old alchemists; Buddhist books and the dozen or so varieties of Yoga; here were Zoroastrianism and esoteric Christianity; tracts on the I Ching; Zen, witchcraft, magic, astrology and vampirism; scholarly treatises on Sufism; the works of the Christian mystics. Here, in short, was a kind of potted library representing everything rejected by official culture and scholarship.

It appeared that Jimmy's unfortunate wife (now living a widow's existence with her sisters, though Jimmy from time to time went to see her, saying that they should live together, since as far as he was concerned they got on perfectly well), had taken some years ago to astrology, just about the same time as Jimmy had chanced to read some science fiction and decided he could do as well. To write was clearly not beyond an ordinary person's capacity, since here, working beside him, was Mark Coldridge; as for the matter, he knew more science than the authors of these books. Plots came plentifully to mind. Most of them, however, had already been used, as he discovered when he efficiently read his way through enormous quantities of science fiction. It was clearly not a question of discovering new plots, but of developing old ideas differently. An article on Yoga in his wife's copy of *Destiny* led him to a bookship specialising in such literature; and what he found there solved his problems. For, since he had not had a literary education, professed himself insensitive to style and taste, he was not put off by old-fashioned or flowery or clumsy language, and was able to extract ideas or information where these existed. From this sort of material he was led to old alchemical material, mostly untranslated and lying unused on the shelves of museums or universities, which he found full of surprises and usefulness.

And now here Martha had come against—as it seemed, many times before with Jimmy—that barrier of incomprehension which still she could not measure. There he sat, in this dusty little storeroom behind the efficient streamlined modern office, a scientific genius, Mark still insisted, better than any computer, said Mark, since you could feed dozens of facts and figures into him and out would come an answer as if buttons had been pushed; he was an inventor of machines, and as good as a library of scientific information; but when Martha said to him, "But Jimmy, how then do you see all this ..." she couldn't finish her question. The point was, you have to expect a question to hit home somewhere in a person before you can ask it. His round pinkish face, on his round (probably) pinkish body, presented to Martha his unvarying pink-rubber smile, and the surface of round staring spectacles. And no, he was not embarrassed. Embarrassment is not even a human characteristic: an intelligent cat or a dog, discussed insensitively by human in its presence, will show the distress that is embarrassment.

Jimmy did not mind being asked questions, did not mind being probed, would probably have spent as long as Martha wanted explaining to her any problem she needed to have explained. But it was of no use saying to Jimmy things like: What effect does this material, these ideas, have on you, the inner Jimmy Wood? Do you think that at some point three, four hundred years ago, science threw out a very important baby with the bath water? What do you think of those capacities you write about called telepathy, second sight, levitation, and the rest? Do you wish to develop such capacities, if it were possible? What do you think of ... For when she got anywhere near such questions, he looked carefully at her, to see what it was she wanted, and then answered by reaching out and handing her a book in which these beliefs or phenomena were described, or prescribed, or recommended. Or he handed her with an eager smile which said: *I am trying hard to meet your request,* a copy of his latest novel.

It is only when one meets the extreme, or pure type of something or some person, that one can begin to understand the things, people, in between, of the impure, or halfway type: in Jack, Martha had known and had at least begun to understand the existence of such people, a person who functioned, understood *was* in his body, his animal being. That was where he lived, had his centre.

And in Jimmy she met somebody who lived, had his being—where? Easy to say, his mind. As easy to say "body" for Jack—shorthand again, clumsy words for what we don't understand. The word "mind" covers, for instance, intuition: which in itself can include variations and extremes. The word "mind" wouldn't do; yet it was as if Jimmy had been born with one of the compartments of the human mind developed to its furthest possibility, but this was at the cost of everything else. Mark said "in joke" that he was a human computer. Good, fine, very helpful; till you remembered that the essential fact about a computer is that it is programmed by human beings. Martha said, defeated by definitions and attempts at them: He's got a screw loose. Lynda said: He's not all there. His wife said: He gives me the creeps, I can't help it, I know I'm wicked.

Martha asked him if she might borrow these shelves full of books. She put them into laundry baskets, the baskets into a car, and drove them home. There she again went through that process of ripping the heart, the pith, out of a subject, when she was ready for that subject. She stayed in her room with the books; took the car down to the book-selling streets of London and bought more books; got hold of all the books that sounded as if they might give out, from wherever she thought they might be

She had emerged with two main conclusions. One was that all these different faiths, or sets of ideas, were talking about the same processes, the same psychological truths. She was reading different languages, or dialects, describing the same thing. This was true of all of them from the poems of St. John of the Cross to states of mind described in the U-panishads. The second was that it was surely a remarkable fact that her education, the education of everyone of her generation (and of how many generations back?), had been so set, programmed, that not a word of any of this information had been able to come through to her except in odd fragments, phrases, notions, each one soaked in, redolent of, "dottiness," "eccentricity," shadiness, unpleasantness.

This second conclusion was interestingly reminiscent. For instance, before even approaching this material she had to fight off the distaste, a reluctance, implanted in her by her environment. Certain terminologies were more distasteful than others. Some phrases and words held so strong a charge of the "distaste-factor" (to coin a term) that she had to stop herself giggling, or beginning to apologise for herself to invisible critics. Words like "prana," "aura," "astral" were particularly powerful—yet they were easily translatable into others from different systems which did not produce distaste (a form of fear). These reactions were identical with those she had experienced in politics. Just as once she had found herself in the state of mind labelled "right-wing," hating and fearing the labels and attitudes "left-wing"; and then switching to "left," while the targets for what she hated and feared switched; so that ever since she had been able to put herself, at will, into these attitudes; so now she kept moving in and out of mental positions (but they were emotional, or emotionally reached, guarded, maintained) and looking from one outlook into or at another. The mechanisms were always exactly the same, whether political, religious, psychological, philosophic. Dragons guarded the entrances and exits of each layer in the spectrum of belief, or opinion; and the dragons were always the same dragon, no matter what names they went under. The dragon was fear; fear of what other people might think; fear of being different; fear of being isolated; fear of the herd we belong to; fear of that section of the herd we belong to.

She had been afraid to approach this mass of material—which, when she had at last dealt with it, had given up so much more than she had expected. (For one thing, a reminder of how easily we are made afraid.) Everywhere in it were gleams of life, the authentic note or throb of vitality, the unmistakable pulse. Yet, while all of it had the same message, or central statement, using different styles, sets of words, terms, historical associations, disciplines, nowhere was the door which Martha knew must be somewhere. Or rather, there were too many doors.

And so felt Lynda, whom she had asked to read these books. Lynda said that "she'd done all that" in the early days with Rosa Mellendip: she didn't see the use of it, it wasn't for her.

When Mark was asked, he took half a dozen of the books, read them at least partially, brought them back to Martha in that closed-in reluctant state that says as clear as words, I'm impervious to this; and said: "Yes, but what's the point even if any of it were true"—for he was already preoccupied, if you like, obsessed, with the immediate future of humanity, and was spending his time in his study with his charts, his figures, his maps, the pages torn from Dorothy's diary, and Thomas's manuscript.

"When the bones of our people's ancestors rot beneath the waters that will fill this place; and the spirits are drowned, their mouths filled with water and no longer able to guard and cherish the tribe who feed them in death so that they may be kept alive—then will the tribe be taken in lorries to a high dry place hundreds of miles from here, the white police and the black police guarding them. That will be the death of this tribe when the ancestors and the children are separated by water. Afterwards fire will come across the high ground to the new village and destroy it. Many will be burned. Many will have no heart to live after that night. The new village built by the white men will be a place of death. So will our people die." *Thomas's note to this:* "The old man, brother of the Chief's wife, spoke last night. He was in some kind of trance. It was after a beer dance. He said that he foresaw a flood or some kind of inundation in this part of the valley. These savages believe the spirits of the dead are fed by thoughts of the living: the spirits in return protect their own, by warning them against dangers and so on. There is a tree near a rock a mile from here: this is a sacred place. The medicine man puts beer and kaffir corn there when the moon changes. Last full moon a herd of eland came to this place and knocked over the crocks; their hoofprints in the beer-wet earth hardened. The wind blew the corn into the prints. Dew sprouted the corn. The spoor of the animals under the sacred tree were marked in green. Green on dry ground. A sign: the harvest will be good this season." Across this diagonally in red pencil: *I'll scratch your back and you scratch mine.*

Note by Mark, "This was written nearly ten years before the Kariba dam was finished and the valley flooded."

When Martha did not look at Lynda, but lay listening, the regular thud-thudding of her head on the wall, the irregular breathing which accompanied her rapid mutter, made quite a different kind of message than what Martha heard when she listened to the low muttering by itself. But Martha knew that the thudding, like the sound made by women pounding grain, was for Lynda not sound so much as the sensation in her head as she banged it: and most of the muttering too was for Lynda herself. The way Lynda was experiencing this was that everything, thudding, breathing, and the low talking, was private—all except for an odd loud, or louder, word which she put in with the intention of communicating with Martha, which sometimes Martha understood and sometimes not. Like "mad," repeated in a crescendo—mad, mad, Mad, *mad,* MAD—which Martha understood perfectly. Yet while Lynda meant just this occasional word as her bridge across to Martha, Martha was, whether looking at Lynda or listening, able to understand Lynda, what Lynda was at that moment, by everything, a whole, the sight, sound, smell, the *feeling* of Lynda.

Lynda was inside herself, trying to be private, because she was arguing with someone.

She was defending herself against someone, something:

517

Martha realised, suddenly, that Lynda always lived in a world of sound, or near it, threatened by it. Trying to imagine this, Martha felt terror. Good God!—to come even for a while close to that sea of sound, close enough for it to threaten an invasion, was enough to frighten her. But Lynda was often inundated by it: sometimes she lived under the ocean of sound for days and days. And not only Lynda—how many people?

There were people whose machinery had gone wrong, and they were like radio sets which, instead of being tuned in to one programme, were tuned in to a dozen simultaneously. *And they didn't know how to switch them off*. Even to imagine the hell of it was enough to make one want to run, to cover one's ears. Martha couldn't run. She knew that sometime she must take risks and explore. Because she had not even begun to ask the questions. She did not know what questions to ask. Before knowing she would have to take risks.

She lay, listening with her ordinary ears to ordinary sounds. Lynda's mutter, her breathing, then her own breathing, became extraordinarily loud; then she heard sounds from the street outside as if they were in the room, footsteps, voices, a drill at work breaking up the street. Even the regular sliding rasp of her dress sleeve moving with her breath on the carpet became like an iron file on her nerves—then the outside sound went, deadened. The inner sea of sound came up, loudened: and as she came near it, or allowed it to come up into her, there came the enemy she remembered from so long ago, a need to laugh, to cry, to shout, a welter of emotion shaken out of her by stretched nerves. Yes—hysteria. This country, the country, or sea, of sound, the wavelength where the voices babble and rage and sing and laugh, and music and war sounds and the bird song and every conceivable sound go on together, was approached, at least for her, or at least at this time, through hysteria. Very well then, she would be hysterical. She held herself tight, exactly as if she were about to switch on strong volts of electricity, while she listened hard and did not care that she would be hysterical—for who was her companion after all? Poor Lynda who would not be frightened. Martha was crying out—sobbing, grovelling; she was being wracked by emotion. Then one of the voices detached itself and came close into her inner ear: it was loud, or it was soft; it was jaunty, or it was intimately jeering, but its abiding quality was an antagonism, a dislike of Martha: and Martha was

518

crying out against it—she needed to apologise, to beg for forgiveness, she needed to please and to buy absolution: she was grovelling on the carpet, weeping, while the voice uttered accusations of hatred.

Lynda had come from the wall and was kneeling by her, looking down. Leaning over Martha was a creature all bone, with yellowish-smelling flesh, with great anxious globes of water tinted blue stuck in its face. Lynda was saying: "Don't, Martha, don't, don't, don't, Martha," like a stuck gramophone.

But for a moment Martha could not stop. Then she saw Lynda scramble off to the door, to the hatch between this and the upper world. She was going to fetch Mark. Now Martha sat up, snapping off the connection to the sea of sound. She was shaking all over, as if she were machinery built to carry voltage, but a bit of machinery had jarred loose. She said: "Lynda, it's all right."

Lynda came back and said: "Are you sure?" With a peremptory nod, she said: "You mustn't do that, Martha. I can't bear it." And she sat down again in her place by the wall. Martha was angry: but she understood that yes, of course it was reasonable, Lynda was not as strong as she was. If she, Martha, were going to find out about the sound-ocean, then she must be alone, by herself.

Lynda said: "You mustn't get locked up, Martha. I can't do it, but you can. And when you do it, you'll do it for me too."

This message was perfectly intelligible to Martha. She nodded. Of course: Those who could had a responsibility for those who could not. She would do it for Lynda. But—first things first. Now she must be normal, because Lynda must not be upset by her losing control. It was a question of finding some place somewhere in which she could be alone, and not upset people. But later, when Lynda was willing to be better again.

For once she asked, or stated, among the muttering words: "Shall we stop now, Martha? Yes, I think so—soon. Not just yet"—and on she went with her private conversation, or argument.

Lynda's antagonist, as Martha suddenly understood, having just had a small taste of him, it, her, before having to come back and be responsible, was the same as the jeering disliking enemy who—it was clear now—was not personal to Martha, but must be in a lot of people. Everyone? Everyone of this particular culture? One had to meet him, it, her,

519

confront him, come to terms, or outflank him? There was a way around him? Or not? Who was he? Why? These were the questions she would put to herself—when she was able to. But not now. First she must wait for Lynda.

With her mind set ahead, to that time when she could explore on her own account, she listened to Lynda; postponing, as it were, herself, she tried to hear, to make sense of Lynda's monologue. It was as if the louder isolated words were being thrown at her as clues, or hints. "Mad" was one. "Doctor" another. "Scapegoat" . . . "frightened" . . . "alone" . . . until it was like that game where one is given a dozen words and invited to make a story around them. She listened. Suddenly she began to understand; she realised this was one of the moments in one's life after a period of days, or hours, or months, or years, of handling in one's mind, brooding about, wrestling with, material—then suddenly it all begins to click into place, to make sense.

Instead of passively idling, like an engine, while the current of Lynda's talk went by, she became a part of it, and the clues or signals clicked into place: she understood what it was that Lynda was saying, what she had been saying, trying to say, poor Lynda, for years.

For one thing, it occurred to Martha that the words or the atmosphere pervading them were not of Lynda now, but of a girl. A young girl. A young girl inside this smelly bedraggled female argued with—the antagonist. Was it possible that Lynda had been forced to confront that antagonist in her (in everyone) too soon, or alone, and had never defeated him? Was it possible that one could be worsted in that battle and be forever like Lynda "ill," "unfit for ordinary life" because of having to confront that buried self-hater when one was not strong enough?

All these years that Martha had been here, in this house, part of Lynda's life, and her marriage, and her child, she had been a clod, and a lump, not understanding the first thing about Lynda, which was—that she need never have been ill at all. She looked at this poor damaged creature, with the great eyes that, like Thomas's once, were full of depths of light into which one could lean, like pools, or clouds or trees; and was invaded by great washes of understanding, insight, knowledge; ideas came in one after another so fast she could not keep up.

What had happened to Lynda was something like this: Her father was a young man in the London after the First World War, when to be young was to have value, and for the same reason as now—when life is threatened, the young acquire the glamour of pathos and are licensed for enjoyment. In gay party-going London, he had married Lynda's pretty mother. For years they had been poor, as all their kind were, after that war, and they had a child, Lynda, who was the showpiece for the marriage, which was not a success. They "adored" her; and did not separate or divorce for her sake. Lynda had acquired before she could talk that sharpness, the acuteness, of the child with parents at loggerheads who are putting on a front, and quarrel over a teapot rather than over the central difference, because quarrelling over a teapot is safe. Lynda's antenna for atmospheres and tensions and what was behind words was her first-developed organ. The marriage, uncomfortably continuing, had settled into a pattern where Lynda's mother spent a lot of time with her parents, country people: "It is nice for a child to grow up in the country." Lynda had been a country girl and ridden horses and when her parents met watched them, all her senses alert for storm signals. She knew exactly what they were thinking about each other. When she was eleven her mother died. Lynda preferred to live with her grandparents rather than with her father in London; but her father wished to be a good father, and wanted to make a home for his daughter. He fell in love with a woman in every respect suitable for a second marriage, a First World War widow, charming, kindly, intelligent. But she had been afraid of marrying a man with a daughter, or had felt she ought to be, or at any rate had made too much of it, for Lynda had felt herself an obstacle to her father's happiness. They spent a holiday together in Somerset, the three of them. Lynda said at the end of it that the new woman did not like her. She had told her father so, and her father was angry. He knew that his proposed wife *did* like Lynda; she had said she did and she was not an untruthful woman. But Lynda knew exactly what the woman was thinking: that she was spoiled and "difficult."

Lynda said that it didn't matter, she would go on living with her granny and her grandpa. "They like me," said she, "and I'll be grown up soon anyway." This had been said reasonably: Lynda had felt it to be reasonable. But her father had been angry, for he thought what she said was an accusation. A great scene of tears, confrontations, angers. Lynda was fourteen—a difficult age, as everyone agreed. It was not true that Rosemary did not like her. They would all go for another holiday, this time in France, and really get to know each other. And so they went for a holiday to France. Lynda was at first very silent and well behaved. Then she became hysterical and cried out that she knew Rosemary hated her and wished her dead: she had heard her thinking so. This remark had sent her father into an angry panic. What did she mean, she had heard her thinking so, was she mad? And so on. Rosemary was frightened away altogether.

For Lynda this was a time of great confusion about herself. She had been alone most of her childhood. At school she had had a friend or two, but was by nature solitary, and she had always known what people were thinking—she said this to the doctors who were called in. Didn't everyone? For Lynda had not known that everyone could not hear what other people thought. She had assumed that people did. She had not known herself to be abnormal. Now she was told by one doctor after another that she was not well: she was suffering from hallucinations. She began to stand up for herself, to insist she was not lying, she was not imagining: then she began screaming and fighting. The doctor hated her, she said: she could hear what he was thinking. The doctor was not Dr. Lamb, but an earlier version of him, much less worldly-wise and sophisticated, using methods quite different from anything used by Dr. Lamb over a decade later. Lynda had been taken off to an expensive private mental home, and there treated with electric shocks. She had had half a dozen of them and they were discontinued. Then she had a course of insulin. Lynda was much improved, the doctor said. For Lynda had become cooperative. When told she was ill, she kept quiet. She had observed in the hospital that patients wishing to leave did as they were told and kept quiet about symptoms. So she tried to do the same. Yet from time to time she had outbreaks of violence—once when another patient was being dunked forcibly in and out of an ice bath, and she was trying to prevent this from happening. And once when they threatened her with the electric shock machine for being disobedient.

Lynda was discharged back to a father doing his best not to resent having lost a wife because of his sick daughter; and ready to help Lynda to be normal. For a couple of years Lynda had fought a silent battle for "reality." She thought she was worse when they said she was better. For one thing, the voices, once friendly and helpful, were now dreadful. It was as if she had an enemy who hated her in her head, who said she was wicked and bad and disobedient and cruel to her father. Before it had been as if she had had a friend close to her who had "told her things and kept her company." But now she tried to behave well because of this cruel tormentor in her head. She kept quiet, paid a great deal of attention to her clothes (for she noted that "they" took this as a good sign), was beautiful and lived in a state of terror.

Then she had met Mark. She supposed she loved Mark; for, listening to what he thought, she knew he was a good man. But she tormented herself because he did not know what she was like; she did not dare tell him about herself. And, worse than anything, since she had had the electric-shock treatment, she had had periods of feeling dazed, of feeling shaky and out of control. And so she married Mark and left her father, who had handed her bound and helpless to the doctors, where she had struggled and fought and been bludgeoned into silence by drugs and injections, held down by nurses and dragged screaming to have electric shocks.

She clung to Mark, "Oh save me, save me!" but when he made love to her felt she was being assaulted, until, cracking again under the attacks of her inner enemy, who said she was cruel and unkind to Mark, she found haven in the mental hospital with Dr. Lamb who had been able to send away the voices for long periods at a time with blessed drugs that kept her permanently in a state where she did not have to know that she was a freak.

And so: Lynda need never have been ill.

This fact, which was obvious when you came to it, had not been seen by the people closest to her, Mark, Martha; even when Martha had had in her possession some of the facts which made it obvious. There is something in the human mind which makes it possible for one compartment to hold Fact A which matches with Fact B in another compartment; but the two facts can exist side by side for years, decades, centuries, without coming together. It is at least possible that the most fruitful way of describing the human brain is this: "It is a machine which works in division; it is composed of parts which function in compartments locked off from each other." Or: "Your right hand does not know what your left hand is doing."

The civilised human race knew that its primitive members (for instance, Bushmen) used all kinds of senses not used by itself, or not admitted: hunches, telepathy, "visions," etc. It knew that past civilisations, some of them very highly developed, used these senses and capacities. It knew that members of its own kind claimed at certain times to experience these capacities. But it was apparently incapable of putting these facts together to suggest the possibility that they were calling people mad who merely possessed certain faculties in embryo.

Suppose Lynda had been a fifteen-year-old in a society where "hearing voices" was not sick, but a capacity some people had; a great many people, if they did not suppress it. Suppose she had met someone who could have suggested to her that when she heard her future stepmother saying she hated her, wanted to kill her, it could have been a bad mood, the kind of bad-tempered impulse anyone may have and then afterwards forget. This person might have asked Lynda, who was a reasonable girl wanting to be reasonable: "Would you like to be judged by your fantasies, Lynda? *Think*—are you what you imagine when you are at your worst?" Or suppose the doctor had been one of the doctors who are biding their time; who, knowing quite well what the truth is, have to hide their knowledge because of the prejudice of the profession they belong to; he could have supported her, consoled and advised her father, and—suggested she should keep quiet if she didn't want to be locked up.

But she had had no such luck; had been made a psychological cripple before she was twenty.

Like hundreds of thousands of others; probably millions. There will be no way of knowing how many. These crippled, destroyed people will become another of our statistics, like the "roughly" forty million dead of the Second World War, or the *x* million who die when there is a famine, though they could be kept alive on what goes into the dustbins of America or Britain.

Soon, probably in the next decade, the truth would have to be admitted. It would be admitted with bad grace, be glossed over, softened. And just as we now say, "They burned and drowned witches for a couple of centuries out of a primitive and ignorant terror," soon we will be saying, "When they stopped torturing and killing witches, they locked people with certain capacities into lunatic asylums and told them they were freaks, and forced them into conformity by varieties of torture which included electric shocks, solitary confinement, ice baths, and forcible feeding. They used every kind of degradation, moral and physical. As the methods of society for control and manipulation became more refined, it was discovered that the extremities of physical violence were less effective than drugs which deprived the victims of their moral stamina and ability to fight back; and more effective than the drugs were techniques of persuasion

and brainwashing. By these means the members of the population with capacities above normal (those people now considered to be in the main line of evolution) were systematically destroyed, either by fear, so that their development was
inhibited from the start (the majority), or by classing them
with the congenitally defective . . ."

Sometime quite soon Dr. Lamb would say: "Yes, it seems
we made a mistake." Dr. Lamb? Probably someone in the
heart of that profession. There is a sound principle that the
place to look for the reaction to anything is at the heart of
that thing. Meanwhile, it is wise to keep out of the way.

Lynda, lying sobbing on the floor. "No, doctor, no, doctor, no, I'm not, it's not true, you are, how do you know you
aren't, nobody said you could, you aren't God, why do you
say that when it's not true, no, I'm not cruel, I'm not a
murderer, I'm not wicked, I think terrible thoughts, doctor,
oh I'm wicked, I want to kill people, I want to hurt people,
please don't give me that injection, please, please, don't,
doctor, my mind gets silly and fuzzy, please don't, yes, yes,
give me, give me, give me my pills, please, please, please . . .
oh yes, punish me, I'm wicked, I want to kill you, I want to
kill everybody, yes, punish me . . ." And on and on in a
scream, if a toneless whisper of a scream can be a scream—
a formalised scream then, Lynda remembering, or living
again, or using a ritual to forestall repetition: "No, no, no,
no, I'm not, you're wrong . . . yes, I'm wicked . . . Martha,
shall we stop now?"

Lynda rolled over on her back and went to sleep where
she lay. So did Martha.

When they woke they bathed, dressed, ate, and supported
each other to the hairdresser, since their sense of reality,
that is, their sense of how to conform to the outside world,
was still weak.

Nearly a month had been spent in the basement. The
ordinary world was extraordinary: lovely or grotesque, everything shone out in recognition to their newly washed
eyes.

They wished to surprise Mark by their return to humanity
but he was not in the study.

Lynda's hair, in a graceful chignon, was coloured straw-
berry-roan. Her eyes, enormous now, were enhanced by
silver, jade green, ash-grey salves. Her make-up made the
most of the prominent facial bones of her skull. The weeks
of near starvation had rendered her breastless and removed
her buttocks, but in a twenties dress that had been her

mother's, of sage-green chiffon whose skirt descended to her knee on one side—the right—and to her ankle on the other, in a diagonal of jagged points, like the serrated edge of a leaf, and with a foot-long cigarette holder in pale silver that matched her elbow-length silver-grey gloves, she looked both extremely fashionable, and beautiful in an intriguingly damaged way.

Martha's hair was light brown, cut as was the new mode since she had been immolated in the basement, in a short glossy helmet shape. A look of health had always, she felt, suited her; and her face was tinted a very faint rose with a hint of apricot. Her eyes were emphatic with gummed-on eyelashes an inch and a half long, in mink colour, and her eye paint was pale cinnamon and black. Making the most of every minute of her being excessively thin, with great hollows about her collarbones and hips, she wore an Edwardian blouse with a boned collar in cream net, and a trailing garnet-coloured skirt in taffeta, so tight she could only stand or sit gingerly on the edge of chairs: the waist was twenty inches. This had belonged to Margaret's elder sister. She had to stuff her bra with rolled stockings in order to achieve the authentic low nursing bosom.

While waiting for Mark, they drank his best brandy, and studied various new dispositions of the material on his walls, mostly to do with the spread of mental illness and the lack of facilities for dealing with it. The leaves from Dorothy's diaries had been moved to the areas near the ceiling from whence, it seemed, rockets and space ships took off to chart stars and/or study the possibilities of how to kill and damage as many human beings as possible. By standing on a chair Martha read: "Again rang the Gas Board. Said they would send a man. Time spent on getting a connection: twelve minutes. Told them to ring before coming. Nobody came. *Next day:* Rang to ask when man coming. Time to get through, eight minutes. Girl said she did not know: once she had reported work, out of her hands. I had to go out. Was out two hours: man came while away. Lynda asleep—not well. Rang Gas Board. Girl said she would remind. Asked them to telephone first. *Next day:* Man came nine o'clock. Looked at freezing cabinet door. Said he would report it. Went. *Next day:* rang Gas Board. Girl said would enquire. Afternoon another man came. Said would inform makers of fridge, not their responsibility. Would take two weeks. *Three weeks later:* Rang Gas Board to ask. (Their line engaged, took *twenty minutes!*) Girl said once firm informed out of her hands. Suggested I ring firm. Rang firm. Could not get anybody. Said branch that sent men around in Ealing. Would remind. Asked them to ring before coming. *Two days later:* Man came when Lynda and I out. Rang Gas Board and firm. *Five days later:* Man came from firm. Said would supply new door to freezing cabinet. Cost 30/-. Asked why should pay for new door to cabinet, shouldn't have broken, only three years old. He said, off record, this design obsolete, no good, fridge redesigned. Suggested I buy a new one. I said no. He said he would bring new door when ordered. *Ten days later:* Came with door: wrong size. Suggested I should run fridge without door to freezing cabinet: would work without, but more expensive to run. I said no, must have door. *Two days later:* Came with door. *Next day:* Door wrongly done. Fell off, and cracked. Rang firm. No record of transaction. Tried firm's branch. Said young man transferred to branch Acton. Told them. Said would send a man . . ."

This fragment was stuck next to an account of some rocket in the States that had failed to leave a launching pad.

There was one epic, poor Dorothy's masterpiece, which was fifty-odd pages of single-spaced foolscap detailing the matter of the new cooker that had been delivered with a defective door, and which involved the visits of twenty-odd men, three months of time and a near-explosion when a mechanic switched on something that a previous mechanic had just connected wrongly. . . .

There was accumulated mail.

A letter said the house was going to be compulsorily purchased for demolition, or redevelopment.

Another from Maisie said:

My dear Matty! Remember your old pal? Yes, it's me! Life is much the same. But I'm at Gokwe now. Did you hear—I was *married?* What do you know! Well, when you're married you wish you weren't married and you forget all your loneliness when you had no one to hold and cherish. Are you all right these days? This is to say my Rita is coming to visit England. Can she stay with you? *If inconvenient, do not hesitate to say so.* She is a good girl if I say it myself. She is looking forward very much to meeting you. I often tell her about the old days and all the good times we had when we were young.

Well, that's all for now.

Maisie Canfield
(His name is Dennis, Denny for short.)

There were also some sheets of paper on Mark's desk headed Memorandum to Myself. But he had only got so far with it:

"It is now clear that in the next decade or two it will be a question of the human race's survival—but survival from certain hazards not at the moment envisaged, since the coming catastrophe is as little foreseen in the form which it will actually take as the previous wars. We can assume that governments will react as in the past; and that it will be the responsibility of individuals to forecast, plan, make provision for . . ."

That was as far as he had got. Soon Paul came in, agreeably surprised to see them—Uncle Mark had asked him to keep an eye on them for him, as he had gone off on some urgent trip, to Scotland he thought.

They both looked absolutely enchanting: had they been at health farms? No? They really must allow him to take them both out to dinner that very moment.

Paul was just the person Martha wanted to see: if she was to achieve some weeks in privacy to be as eccentric as she pleased, without benefit of society's watchdogs, then she needed someone with a house, or a flat.

He took them to Café Royal—dressed like that, said he, they could go nowhere else: they would be a sensation. They looked as if they were characters from two different novels; Lynda, he thought, had a look of *Women in Love*, while Martha looked like a New Woman from Bernard Shaw.

Three

Among Martha's contemporaries there was no single person or group of people to whom she could say: Give me privacy to explore my own being: promise not to summon doctors and psychiatrists, policemen. Who then were these younger people to whom she could say, and so easily, just that?

Paul's house was now full. (So was another of his—also partly owned, as was this.)

There were about twenty people in it, mostly single though there was a married couple with two children in the basement. He had been an alcoholic, from time to time still was, and this made it hard for him to keep jobs. He earned his living as a carpenter, since his real career, which was to be an architect, had foundered in alcoholism. He paid Paul no rent, but looked after the house. His name was Briggs; he had the careful watchful manner of those who have an inner enemy on a tight chain; and his face (pleasant, friendly, though permanently tinged with a reminiscent flush, like a sunset sky) changed not at all when she told him her requirements. Paul had of course already asked that she should be left alone. He thought she wished to experiment with drugs, and offered the remark that he was sorry drugs had not been "the scene" when alcohol had beguiled him. She said no, she was not interested in drugs; but he nodded as if to say: Quite right, one had to be careful what one admits. This turned out to be the passport under which she was able to travel in this house: person after person came to her to say that they had smoked marihuana, hash; or taken LSD or mescalin; or took them sometimes; or proposed to try these things out when circumstances were favourable; or had friends who did. She was given a great deal of friendly advice, and offers of help. The people who were on the same floor and beneath (she was at the top of the house) were naturally of greatest interest. Under her were two young women with jobs in market research. Both had breakdowns from time to time, when they looked after each other, under the care of a doctor who kept them supplied with sedatives. One was Rose, one was Molly; they both looked drained, tired: they were people who found even the ordinary processes of life too much to manage; they did manage, but with nothing much left over. They said to Martha that if she wanted anything she must knock on the floor three times, but otherwise she would be left alone. It turned out that she did once, on a peak of terror because of the self-hater, knock on the floor, but luckily they were not in. She did not see them again until she went to thank them as she left.

Sharing a room in the young women's flat was a sad and polite couple, a boy and a girl. But it turned out they were married. She had been pregnant at school. This boy had married her: he loved her, he said, and would be happy to bring up the child. This baby was born into a bed-sitting room in Islington. It never stopped crying. The boy one night hit the baby. It died a week later. A welfare worker and a doctor hushed the thing up. The boy became a Roman Catholic. The girl was again pregnant (from intention, not by accident) and they were both pleased: they loved children, they kept explaining to everyone. They were not yet twenty years old. He worked as a packer in a chemical firm. During Martha's progress through the Stations of the Cross towards the end of her stay in this house, he came into the room and was satisfied by what she said about her inner processes that she must be a convert like himself. She had to be careful to substitute the name of God for the Devil, who in fact accompanied her on her journey; so much value there is in one word. That God hated, tormented, and punished her so seemed to him a sign of grace: that the Devil might frighten him into an offer to call a priest.

In the large room across the landing lived Zena. Paul had paid for lessons in voice production. She sang sometimes in a club or at a private party. Not very well: it was herself she cleverly produced and marketed; herself that other people needed so much she did not have to do more than be there, on offer. Her effaced obliterated quality, her frightened sexuality, a brave passivity, was so much to a current taste that she was known to "everyone." She was in fact a type of courtesan. Many gentlemen prepared to pay highly for their pleasures paid to accompany her to parties, to be seen publicly with this girl who was the Victim incarnate. She might even sleep with them, but without any pretence of enjoyment. Her attitude was: If you enjoy what so wearies me, then please, I should be delighted . . . Given presents of money or jewels she spent or used or gave away, or left lying about, or lost. She did not care. Caring about absolutely nothing, she drifted, smiling her sweet lost smile. This room was her private refuge, her own room. No one came here but Paul. Several times during Martha's stay in the house she came in late at night with a cup of coffee. "Paul asked me to see if you were all right, Martha? Good—I'll go then."

Also across the landing was Bob Parrinder, who was altogether more prepared to be involved. He was about twenty-seven, tall, and very thin . . . but it is easier to say that if Lynda were male, she would look like him, if he were female, he would look like Lynda. He had had three years or so in the hands of psychiatrists, and had decided to give them up at the price of being very ill from time to time, when one of his girls looked after him. In between, he earned his living on the fringes of the film industry in a variety of ways. He had an immediately arresting personali-

530

ty, and a good deal of authority: people were attracted to him. He gave advice, help, took responsibility, had girls one after the other. He was a type very common indeed in this half-hidden, or rather hiding, stratum of London. He was a sort of self-appointed prophet or mentor who attracted all kinds of people, not all of them weak-minded, as hangers-on and disciples. To Martha, who said only that she wished for a time of "retreat"—she chose the word since his bias was towards Christianity—he offered a very great deal of advice about the inner life, but said that his girl, Olive, would be only too pleased to do her shopping and keep an eye on her while he was out working. Olive, a beautiful dark girl with a baby not his, had that look of ecstatic self-immolation which such young men tend to evoke in certain young women: but it was too excessive to last, Martha thought, and already showed signs of wearing off. To wash Bob's socks was one thing; to serve Martha, very naturally, another, even if Bob did command it. She said the baby took a lot of her time, and if Martha wanted anything, she should simply knock.

In fact it was all very satisfactory, and Martha was able to shut herself into a large room which, because she had asked Paul for it, had a thick carpet on the floor to deaden sound. There was a large brass four-poster bed; Paul wanted so much money for this that he could not sell it. He was keeping it: the value was bound to rise. There were some chairs and a good fake Queen Anne writing desk which Paul maintained would shortly be worth a good deal: when the antiques were all bought up, their copies (if old enough) would have value; and, no doubt, and in due course, *their* copies would . . .

She had about three months. Not very long, but Maisie's Rita was due to arrive. There was no saying how long Rita would be in London; and since it is always later than one thinks, and the house in Radlett Street did not seem to need her much, she might as well do it now.

Lynda was well: she was occupied with Francis and Jill and various new complications. Poor Mark was quarrelling finally with Jimmy Wood. Mark was all hot tempestuous rages and violence, interspersed with locked inward-growing misery. He had discovered that Jimmy had for the last ten years been supplying machines, designed by himself, whose function was to destroy parts of the human brain by electric charges. These machines were developments on those already in use for legitimate purposes. Jimmy's had all kinds of interesting possibilities, and he was selling them to the re-

531

search institutes and departments of hospitals where they were being used at the moment on animals. He had also perfected (on request) a development of this machine to be used by governments, to destroy the brains of people they felt to be dangerous, and who were weak, helpless, or unknown, and could vanish without protest, or much protest, being aroused. Jimmy had already sold a dozen or so of these, but under arrangements and conditions which had made it hard for Mark, always bored with paperwork, to trace them in the books. Jimmy was on the point of selling (the difficulty was that people did not seem to believe it would have a use—but war departments are always more forward-looking than any other section of an official apparatus) a machine, or device, for stimulating, artificially, the capacities of telepathy, "second sight," etc. All kinds of hints found by him in old manuscripts or dubious "esoteric" books had gone into the creation of this device; but the trouble was, as he was only too prepared to point out, "there seemed to be evidence for suggesting" that brains stimulated in such ways (Jimmy was afraid the machine was still very clumsy) might very well be destroyed. So what it amounted to was that interested governments, or departments, must have a large supply of expendable human material, and material that was will-less, or treated to be will-less, for these extensions of humankind's machinery would "burn out" very fast and must be constantly replaced. Jimmy visualised a bank of people, housed probably in some kind of barracks or building, well fed and cared for, of course, with every amenity of sport and entertainment, whose sole function would be, when needed, to be taken into the room of a certain building and to be treated by this, Jimmy's machine, when, for a short space of time, they would be able to act as a variety of radio, or telephone. Asked what was the point, first by an unnamed war department, and then by Mark—why bother with human beings when there were machines?—Jimmy showed all the agitation of an organism frustrated in its functioning. Surely situations could be envisaged very easily where it would be more convenient to have a human being with such capacities rather than a machine? For instance, imagine a group of people spying in foreign territory—to have such a person with them would be invaluable! Of course, that this person might very well be as good as a zombie could (in circumstances) be a handicap, but the whole project was still in the experimental stage. He, Jimmy Wood, was prevented by laws of all kinds from doing research, but everyone knew that in wartime, or even in peacetime with the inmates of some mental hospitals, certain kinds of research could go on. Jimmy, talking in a soft, agitated way (for hours and hours, while Mark listened), wove what sounded like the basis for another of his space-fiction novels. (The unnamed gentleman from the not-to-be mentioned war department had said, in joke, that he thought Mr. Wood was taking space fiction for fact. But he had asked to be kept posted of developments.)

In short, for years now, Jimmy had been engaged in activities which Mark was bound to find abhorrent; and had been engaging in them openly, had not tried to deceive Mark at all. For instance, walking around the factory, he might say: "This is for Project 25A—you know, I told you." Or, in the ledgers, Mark would see entries: Research on 25A.

The talk about this went on for days and days. Mark sat in the office where, for years and years now, he had sat, feeding Jimmy Wood with his fuel, talk, and talked now (feeling ill, angry, self-reproachful, etc., but being as calm as possible), trying to, as he said to Martha, "get inside Jimmy's skin." The point was, Jimmy never met Mark on his ground—which was, Mark supposed, if he was entitled to the word at all, an ethical one. Asked about project this-and-that, device that-and-this, Jimmy would talk, expound, go on in his jerky, soft, informative way until stopped—or switched off. Asked if Jimmy thought it was a good thing for human beings to be made zombies, or treated in this or that way, without (presumably) being asked, he might reply: "But if you stimulate that area—look on the model, Mark, there—it seems likely that function will superimpose on function X—do you see, Mark?"

All this was still going on when Martha kissed Mark goodbye (but only temporarily, for she would certainly drop into Radlett Street from time to time) and left for her period of "retreat."

Very extraordinary indeed was the human mind. Mark, a man of integrity if there was ever one, had worked for nearly twenty years with a man whose actions (he did not have beliefs) contradicted everything Mark held dear; but, *for some reason*, Mark had not thought that this was so, or had not—what? Troubled? Cared? If Jimmy Wood was arrested tomorrow on charges of almost pathological indifference to any ordinary ideas of decency, then Mark would be (or should be) arrested with him. But of course Jimmy would not be arrested, nor suffer in any way at all, because he was merely "contributing to human knowledge." All the same, if the case were to be put to Mark as a hypothetical one, with himself in it, but masked, he would hate and despise himself. But for twenty years he had gone along with it, had not "put two and two together."

Martha, living cheek by jowl with Lynda for years, and in what she had imagined to be the closest sympathy with her, had not seen what was screaming out to be seen—though Lynda had so little belief in its being seen by anyone, even Martha, that its manifestation was mostly in moments of self-defence seen by others (and even herself) as aggressive violence; could only communicate it through "gibberish" to be deciphered by someone (Martha) who at last had reached the same place in experience.

It was at least interesting that these discoveries, hers in connection with Lynda, Mark's in connection with Jimmy Wood, and the reflections they gave rise to, coincided with Martha's determination to challenge her own mind.

Alone in the empty room, high over noisy streets that were full of humanity, yet held in a carpeted space where no one would come if she did not call them, she—was extremely afraid. She had not expected it. Quite one thing to say: Yes of course it's dangerous, very risky, etc.; another to actually go into danger.

And she did not really know how to do it, except that she knew from the past that if she did not eat, slept very little, kept alert, she sharpened and fined down. But both times in the past had been unplanned, she had not intended anything.

Now she stopped eating, though she drank tea and coffee, and stopped sleeping, and walked up and down, up and down, on the heavy carpet which protected Molly and Rose under her feet from annoyance.

She knew there were areas she was likely to have to go through: there would be the stratum of sound, for instance. She was more than likely to become hysterical: she had in the past. There were rewards—oh yes, she remembered there were, though not clearly at all, except as a fact. Looking back on that time when she was first in London, and then again on the recent time with Lynda, what she remembered was an intensity of packed experience—which she longed to have again. But there was nothing in particular that she expected.

She walked, she walked, she walked up and down, smoking, drinking coffee, waking herself as she drifted off to sleep.

She was thinking of poor Lynda—washes of soft pity came with it. She thought of Mark, poor Mark alone in his house without his friend Martha, and without Lynda who (though he did not know it) he was going to lose altogether very soon—Lynda was leaving him. Oh poor Mark. How cruel she, Martha, was; how unkind to do this, to say: Mark, it's your bad luck you have nothing but eccentric women, but I'm off for a brief trip into a totally uncharted interior! No, she had not said that, she had concealed and softened. All the same, how could she treat Mark so—and how appallingly had she always treated poor Mark! How coldly, how finally, all those years ago, had she dismissed him from her life, from love, poor Mark who had had such a bad time with Lynda, poor Mark who had so little warmth in his life and who had been sent off by her, Martha, into a series of minor love affairs which bored him . . . it was all her fault! She was callous and . . .

As she entered the country of sound she encountered head-on and violently the self-hater . . . yes of course she had half expected it, was even hoping to; but oh, how powerful an enemy he was, how dreadfully compelling, how hard to fight. The days passed. Someone observing Martha would have seen a woman lying on the floor, beating her head on it, weeping, crying, complaining, calling out to a large variety of deities, official and unofficial; accusing an unknown assailant of cruelty and of callousness; lying prone on the floor for a few moments, apparently asleep, then jumping up as if galvanised by conscience or command into some kind of frenzied but absurd activity, such as sweeping the floor, or energetically washing up coffee cups in the kitchen, or even doing violent exercises, while tears streamed down her face and she muttered and argued . . . not a sight to instruct or to edify. A sight, rather, to frighten, or upset: but this would depend on who came in. This turned out to be a man not yet met by her who lived on the second floor and who had heard she was "on a trip" and had come to see if she was all right. Martha found to her surprise that she was not so far gone that she did not instantly pull herself together and converse with calm and with sense. She said it was LSD—anything for a quiet life, as she muttered to herself—and that she was well used to it. Off he went, and she resumed.

She was completely in the grip of this self-hating person, or aspect of herself. Remorse? No, it was more that her whole life was being turned inside out, so that she looked at it in reverse, and there was nothing anywhere in it that was good; it was all dark, all cruel, all callous, all "bad." Oh she was bad, oh she was wicked, oh how very evil and bad and wicked she was.

Time passed.

It was the most banal and ordinary of considerations that saved her—she had been here for two weeks, and she was squandering precious time. After all, for a human being in this our society of the 1960's, to achieve three months of perfect solitude without interference was so rare . . . and here she was squandering it. Because, right ahead of her (and she now saw how very lucky that was) was Rita's visit, for which she must be normal and competent.

It could not be said that she was able to defeat the self-hater all at once, or completely—no. He, she (it?), was too strong. But push him aside she did, for periods, writing as she did so on sheets of paper that she had arranged for this purpose on a table in a corner of the room.

The self-hater. This is where Lynda was defeated. She is never free of this.

Beside this entry were a whole forest of underlinings, exclamation marks, and signs of all kinds that Martha put there in a sort of despair: they were there to remind her, afterwards, that this series of words said so very little of what she wanted to say, were a thin scratching on a rock, a pathetic shorthand, for what she knew. For the complexity of what was going on (later she said it was as if she had crammed a dozen years of intensive living into a few weeks) and the speed at which she was learning were such that she was all the time in the grip of an anguished fear she would forget, forget, forget all this she was learning. For she remembered that one did forget—oh yes, one forgot appallingly. This was the third time, for instance, that she was charting the country of sound (although this time she was accompanied by the self-hater) and she only remembered when she was doing it what she had learned before.

However, defective though her experiments were, terrified though she was, totally inadequate in every way for what she was trying to do, she *was* encountering previously known states of mind (regions, boxes, areas, wavelengths, countries, places), and in them were recognisable features. So this was not all chaos, it was not just a jumble: one could, in fact, make some kind of sense of all this by using one's ordinary faculties of memory, judgement, comparison, understanding. In short, one could use one's common sense here, in this uncommon area, just as one could in ordinary life.

And, using one's common sense . . .

But, looking at Martha from outside (a woman lying crying on the carpet, or sitting in an intense thought which knotted her muscles), it might be hard to credit her with the calmness of mind which she was in fact using . . . better perhaps to skip the detailed blow-by-blow account of this "work" which Martha was doing, and to rely on her notes.

Which of course must be inadequate; but then so would an attempt at a description.

The woman lying on the carpet crying: which would be more subjective, to see her thus, describe her thus, or to describe the contents of her thought?

The woman scribbling with agonised speed, to get everything down fast before it flew by: more subjective to describe her knotted pose, her clenched face, or to transcribe the notes?

Better, perhaps, the notes, like small signposts, or footmarks, for other people who may or may not find them useful.

The first entry after the one about the self-hater was: *Why couldn't Lynda get out from under? I can make him weaken, I can fight him off. Strong emotions, thoughts, can make a kind of groove in the brain, and if you do that you can't get out of it? I am scared. Suppose I can never send away?*

But soon sheets and sheets of paper were scrawled and scribbled over as the notes and remarks accumulated, were put down so fast that she did not have time to make them more legible.

You've got to be alert enough to catch a thought as it is born. That is how to distinguish. There are different qualities in thoughts. (The word "qualities" was ringed around and boxed and made to stand out in Martha's attempt to remember it, to emphasise it.) *Very slight differences in quality. One should be able to learn how to tell an overheard thought or words from the self-hater, for instance.*

Yes. Into a mind comes different qualities of . . . Hearing a thought of Lynda is different. How? No emotion. Remember this, remember it. Words trickling through your head with no emotion: that's likely to be overheard, someone else's thought. There is emotion in the self-hater. Go away, go away, oh please God go away, I can't bear it, just imagine, people live all their lives with you in their heads, poor, poor, poor Lynda, how does she bear it, a life sentence in hell. Go away.

537

Suddenly, yes, today's been Jack. This is where Jack was defeated. His body got taken over. His body is fine. Body is neutral. Something to use. Body can't be bad. A bad low cunning mind uses his body. His body says, I don't want to be cruel. If his body wanted to be cruel, then what he does anyway would be enough. (This underlined and scored and emphasised.) *It is his mind likes hurting. A nasty little mind, like boys pulling wings off flies.*

For two days Martha jibbed. She would not go on. She was being brought face to face with certain aspects of her own character—to do with sadism, masochism, the pleasure in hurting. Physically. But going on in this way seemed to be the price of going on at all—the jeering, hating, mocking tormentor in her head sulked, and like a schoolchild said: Oh if you won't play I'm going to go ... and went, or was silent. Martha, crying, weeping, in an agony of shame and reluctance to remember, at last went on.

She wrote: *For days now ... very well then, now I know. Next time I read that a man has strangled and raped a child, I know. Or why the death penalty was once public and is still desired by most of the British public. DON'T FORGET THAT YOU KNOW.*

She wrote: *Three days on, I think. The tortured and the Torturer. Am being both. Am not just the pain-maker. Pictures on the television set: smoke from a gas chamber in concentration camp. Then first separate but becoming the same, the ragged bit of refuse (me) pushed into the gas chamber and the uniformed woman (me) who pushed.*

Very economical this editor in my brain. He cuts film beautifully ...

On the screen half a dozen personalities, symbolised. For instance, one of them Carroll's old knitting sheep. Beside it, clumsy trampling horny bull. The bull of Bashon. (Very funny, you make very bad puns. No, no, no, of course, some of them are brilliant.) Bash-on. Ha ha.

Must be days later. Suddenly understood. He (who?) is showing me characteristics (mine) and their opposites (mine). I am so dense. It was perfectly obvious a week ago, if only I'd got it. And now remember it.

For some time now Martha was stuck. What was happening was something like this. She would discover herself uttering sloganlike phrases, or feeling emotions, which were the opposite of what she, the sane and rational Martha, believed. For instance, she would find herself using the languages of anti-Semitism, first the sly subtle approaches to anti-Semitism, which then worsened, so that for a few hours she was sounding like Goebbels. In a panic she floundered about in a total loss of her own personality. For she would retrieve from her own depths a phrase or an idea which embodied what she thought, but it would at once be swallowed up by its shadow. This plunged her into a violent state of fright and shame. Then she saw this was more like an embarrassment, almost a social embarrassment, as if she were being caught out in a social gaffe, which she was afraid of people discovering. She became ashamed (really ashamed) of her own triviality. Before this could be understood, and worked through, she was switched off into a hatred against black people. Then, fast, she watched herself using the languages and emotions of hatred of black people for white people, and of white people for black; of Germans and of Jews, and of Arabs and of the English—etc., etc., until her chattering mind and the "television set" was like a hate programme arranged for the pleasure of some international lunatic.

Why is it that it takes so long for me to understand something perfectly obvious? I'm so stupid. Of course: I am switched in to Hating, which is the underside of all this lovely liberalism. But just because we are all such lovely liberals it doesn't mean . . . well why does he (who?) tell me that? Don't I know it already? . . . Why, I don't . . . it's because I keep forgetting I can't say, reasonable, civilised, etc., etc. Thinking that I am. I am what the human race is. I am "The Germans are the mirror and catalyst of Europe" and also: "Dirty Hun, Filthy Nazi."

Oh God, I'm so tired. I'm so tired. How many volts all the time?

Shrieking self-pity and hysteria.

Is this what all those books call "the pairs of opposites?"

Love, hate, black, white, good, bad, man, woman.

Somewhere here in came Bob Parrinder. Martha was lying crying on the floor. His pretty girl friend stood behind in the door, with her baby in her arms. She wore tight faded jeans, brown sweater, a mass of long drowning hair. He smiled. Martha looked up at this immensely tall tall tall man whose head was near the ceiling. She sat up, and it lowered.

He was sympathetic. His eyes were hungry to share. He was here, Martha understood, because of some argument or tiff or something with his girl—if he came to her, Martha, commanded her in some way, it would prove something to the girl? The girl, Martha thought, wasn't really a very nice girl. (Ten minutes, or ten hours, ago she had abolished words like nice, nasty.) Martha did not like the slow, stupid, obstinate face. She did not like the young man's usurping of authority either, but she thought: Underneath all that nonsense, he is nice, he's a person.

Martha, sitting with her legs stretched out, her arms behind her, resting her weight on her palms, said to him: Do you know what it is you are really wanting?

The man now kneeled by her, became a very thin, gently smiling man with soft-falling fair hair. But she knew he wanted to dominate and control.

"Are you sure," he said, "that you oughtn't to have a rest or something?"

"Yes, I am," said Martha crossly.

"Well, if you are sure . . ."

"Do you know what it is you really want?" enquired Martha. For now it seemed extremely urgent that she should tell him, that he should understand, and that he should by this be saved from his own varieties of foolish behaviour. She could do this by simply *telling* him. (Just as if what she had been learning, basically, was not that one has to experience to understand.)

"No, you tell me," he said, smiling.

"You want someone to boss you. To dominate you."

His mouth fell in out of his smile and became determined not to show annoyance.

"I don't think so."

"I know so."

At the door the indolent girl crossed her legs differently, and laughed, so as to demonstrate her agreement.

"That is *quite* true, I think, Bob," she said, in purest Kensington.

"It is not at *all* true."

"Yes," said Martha. "All you young block leaders, you simply can't wait to hand yourselves and your disciples over to the nearest guru or gauleiter. Blind leading the blind."

"I am sure you'd feel better for a cup of soup or something. Olive, how about some of that soup we made for lunch?"

"Do you want some soup?" Olive asked Martha.

The baby began to complain. Olive parked him on one beautiful hip, and joggled the hip. It looked like a kind of dance—a one-sided or crippled shimmy. Her breasts swayed and marched, one, two, one, two.

Martha fell back on the floor and laughed. She laughed, and laughed.

Stopping laughing, she noted that Bob waited, smiling, to be told why she laughed. Behind his head, a ceiling moulding looked like a square halo. She laughed again.

"Do you know what a halo is?" she enquired. For she had understood in exactly that moment what a halo was. "Certain people have haloes. They have white light or yellow light around their heads. Instead of dirty-breath green or angry red or efficiency grey."

"That's interesting," he smiled.

The baby began to half laugh, half cry the way babies do when they are being jollied along by mother or somebody and they feel obliged to laugh but really they are angry and would like to have been allowed to hit, or bite, or scratch. A sobbing laugh. A laughing sob.

"I don't want to be rude," said Martha, with extreme, and indeed finicky, politeness, "but I haven't got all that much time, because Rita is coming soon. She's Maisie's daughter. No, of course, you wouldn't know Maisie. And I've got to get through this lot without putting myself into a loony bin—time's running out."

"Ah," he said, "I do see." He unfolded his legs upwards under him and again became a beanstalk reaching to the ceiling.

Martha saw that he would go off, quarrel with the girl, who would not bring her soup (now she saw this she was sorry, her stomach raged with hunger), and that they would not, or not soon, come back. They felt that she, Martha, was probably in need of help; they did not want to break their own code of social behaviour by calling doctor or police or the carpenter from downstairs who would, or might, do this: so it would be simplest if they did not come back to see Martha too soon. Blessed are the cowards and the indolent: what a lot of trouble they save.

The interruption into the room's activity changed it. The hater retreated a bit.

I'm in Bosch country. I know where Bosch got his pictures. Good Lord, look at that . . .

Is it always here? (There?) Where. I can see why those books say you should not get too interested in this. You could spend your life just watching television.

Bosch country. If I could paint, and I painted this, I would be a forger. Are forgers people who plug into Bosch country?

541

Why am I so stupid. Have understood. If I didn't know better and I plugged in to hater by accident, I'd stay a hater. Did Hitler plug in to hater by accident? (For instance.) A nation can get plugged in to—something or other? A nation can get plugged in through one man, or group of men, in to—whatever it might be. Here is Martha. I'm plugged in to hate Jew, hate black, hate white, hate German, hate American, hate. Now not plugged. Might be plugged again in ten minutes' time.

This is Dali landscape. I'm plugged in to Dali mind. If I could draw, paint, then I'd paint this, Dali picture. Why does only Dali plug in to Dali country? No, Dali and me. Therefore Dali and—plenty of others. But nurse says, delusions. If ignorant, does not think is Dali country. Thinks: That's a silly picture. If educated, knows, thinks: I am a copycat. Or, that must be a Dali picture I haven't seen? (Perhaps it is.)

He couldn't have painted so many. Why not?

Plagiarism. (Think about this after when time.) Mark writes something. Then it's floating in the air. Someone can plug in. A City in the Dessert is photostatted in the photosphere! (Oh, very funny. Ha. You only deserve half a laugh for that one.)

> *One of them is rather weak,*
> *And one of them is very meek.*
> *And one of them is just a horse.*
> *And one of them is rather coarse.*
> *One of them would like to strangle.*
> *Hurt and tear and bite and mangle.*
> *And one of them is rather crude.*
> *And one of them is just a prude.*
> *And one of them . . .*

For God's sake stop, sobbed Martha, clutching her ears as this awful da-da-da-da-da ground into her eardrums.

Lying face down, nose in a thick plush of carpet which smelled faintly of dust, the sea of sound came down, swallowed her.

Almost.

> *One of them is rather bright.*
> *One of them just must be right.*
> *One of them is . . .*

Eyes shut, she watched the pictures pass in front of her eyes that went with the jigging rhymes, like a child's picture book with verses. "One of them is rather meek" was Lewis Carroll's shawled and knitting sheep.

542

And sometimes you are very kind,
But often you are cruel, you'll find . . .
God I'm so stupid. Obvious. Me. What makes up me.

Martha, kneeling by the low table, scribbled and scribbled notes, words—memoranda to herself for later—but listened to the jigging rhymes and kept shutting her eyes so as to miss as little as possible of the television programme.

Martha, a breathing individuality of faceted green, reflecting sky, house, pavement, cloud, man, woman and dog, a gaunt wretched woman in an old towelling bathrobe, watched the facets of her personality march past—watched, and scribbled, *remember.*

For God's sake. Don't forget. Or you'll have to do it again. ·

It's later than you think.
Girls and boys come out to play.
The moon is shining as bright as day . . .
I am the creation of my own mind.
I am the creation of my own mind.
I am . . .

Words, words, words, words. If the words come, the reality will afterwards?

Paul came in. She was asleep on the floor. Incredibly handsome as usual; beautiful, in clothes that managed to combine elegance with a half-laugh at it, he sat on the edge of his four-poster bed, looking quizzically at Martha.

She snapped into common sense, in the habit of alarm: here was one of the "children"—she was not being responsible.

"It's only me," he said.

She lay back again. He lit a cigarette and gave it to her.

"You aren't looking your best," he remarked. "However, I suppose you know what you are doing."

She had been slipping into a region of terror: a one new to her. She was relieved that he had come; and that his coming steadied her.

She sat up, made him tea, talked: all with the aim of testing out to what an extent she could present normality to him. Inside her head the world of sound, conducted like an orchestra by the self-hater, rang, hammered, drilled. Soon, being with Paul subdued it.

Because it did, she was able to send back with him to Mark a message that yes, she would be able to come to the restaurant tonight. Margaret was very upset about the house being bought by the Council; she intended plans, campaigns—

at least a family conference. She had already pulled several strings.

Asked if he was to be at this dinner, Paul said gracefully: "Well, I'm not entitled to it, am I? It's not my house."

This was not a plea, or a complaint, or from bitchiness. He felt this. After all, he had *this* house—half of it; and half of another like it.

Was Francis to be there? He had been asked, but said he was sure the grown-ups would do everything for the best.

Martha put on a suit, made herself up, and saw in the mirror that no one could possibly guess that she was, by any yardstick this society used, a raving lunatic. The self-hater had become, logically enough, the Devil, and commented, or exclaimed or jeered, or criticised her every move, thought, memory. Her will went into not succumbing, while at the same time, she listened, trying to be neither frightened nor resentful. She was going to take the Devil to the restaurant, and it was necessary that no one should guess this. That Paul had not was a good omen.

The restaurant was one of the small expensive ones, French, doing good classic food. The décor was modestly pretty, and reminded one of French provincial hotels.

The guests: Mark. He was silent, sombre, occupied with his own thoughts.

Martha. She was accompanied by the Devil.

Lynda, silent, looking rather ill: she had had now definitely decided to leave Mark and "to be a real person without props." Extending her activities she had found she was not as strong as she had thought. She had had a week on sedatives and was badly set back. In short, she was very frightened about her future.

Margaret. She was full of angry unhappiness.

Her husband, John, who was tight. He had been drinking a lot recently, having fallen in love with the newsagent's assistant in Marleybridge, which passion he was fighting with alcohol.

Phoebe, now a sub-minister with various responsibilities in the new government. Everything the government did went from bad to worse, as if the whole world (she felt) conspired against it, and she, too, was angry. Also extremely tired, being overworked. She, having not had a proper meal for days, had had a sherry while waiting and was a bit tipsy.

Arthur, who had not been given any job in this government, because he was too left-wing. He was in exactly the same position he had always been in: nothing of what he

544

believed, or stood for or had ever campaigned for, was being attempted by this, his Labour government, so he did not feel he had been challenged. He was still waiting, a vigorous handsome man of nearly sixty, for the future to begin.

His wife, Mary, who had fallen in love this week with a charming boy, the carpenter who was putting new shelves into the bathroom. Understanding by this that she was now definitely middle-aged, she had rushed out in a psychological *crise,* had bought herself a grandmother's woollen dress, and was wearing it. Her Arthur had said he did not think the dress suited her—she reflected that this clever man had never understood her, nor "anything to do with the emotions." This thought was enshrined in the small dry smile on a pretty face smudged by long crying. It stayed there unaltered until the theme of *The Youth* was introduced.

Elizabeth, who had spent the afternoon with Mark, to set up an ideal community "somewhere in a new free country." She had been drinking brandy all afternoon and was tight: and sizzling with frustration. She simply could *not* understand Mark, who had described a perfect city and was not prepared to make one. She had burst into tears several times that afternoon and had been very rude. Mark, realising that she was in the middle of a breakdown, had rung Dr. Lamb, who was going to see her tomorrow. She kept her hungry eyes on Mark.

This was a family conference.

They were here because of Margaret. First they ordered food, while she held her fire.

One order of pâté *maison,* one of pâté *campagne,* two of *moules,* two of melon, two of artichoke, one avocado pear. They were all drinking muscadet except Arthur, who was drinking Scotch.

Margaret said it was a disgrace that the house should be taken over, even if it was (as she had heard was likely) to be used, with minor alterations, for administration. She had a petition ready and they must all sign it. She produced from her bag a petition, and a selection of others, one on behalf of Fidel Castro's exiles in America, one on behalf of some prisoners in South Africa, one for Oxfam, and a letter to the *Times* about some writers sentenced to imprisonment in the Soviet Union. At which Phoebe, without speech, produced some petitions from her handbag. She had the South African one, and the letter to the *Times;* but also a draft letter about political imprisonment and torture in Portugal, and a state-

545

ment or affirmation, designed for the *New Statesman,* about the behaviour of the police.

They all signed all of Phoebe's, except for Margaret, who would not sign the complaint about the police—the government's recent report (Tory) made it clear that their behaviour was impeccable and complaints against them the work of troublemakers. They all signed all of Margaret's, with the exception of the petition about Fidel Castro's victims, which was signed only by Elizabeth.

There now remained the question of the house. Margaret cried out to Mark that he sat there, he did not seem to mind, but after all, he lived in the house, didn't he? He said, briefly, that he doubted very much that it mattered whether one lived in this house or that—the future was likely to be too barbaric for that. Appealed to, Lynda came back from a long way off, smiled and said she was sure Mark was right. Margaret obviously had not meant to appeal to Martha publicly, as she certainly would privately, but now she did.

Martha, listening with one ear to the Devil's angry sneer about her callousness, eating avocado pear while the world burned, said it was not her house. This was as outrageous in its way as Paul's saying the same thing. The family looked at her, Mark's mistress (?) or at least his companion, with reproach held in check.

She said: "My usefulness is over, isn't it? I'm not contributing anything now."

In her ear the Devil sneered: *If you ever did.*

Mark shot her a warning look: Discuss it with me, not in front of the others.

"Don't any of you care?" said Margaret.

"Of course we care," said Lynda absently. "It's always been a lovely house."

"Well, where are you all going to live?" asked Margaret.

Here Lynda's, Mark's and Martha's eyes enmeshed: this contact was a comfort to them. The three were infinitely apart from each other, and grieved that they were. A sense of imminent partings was strong.

The others, seeing this instinctive affirmation of a continuing need, did not press.

Now it was time to order again.

Margaret had *canard.* Phoebe had *filet en croûte.* Martha had *boeuf Stroganoff.* Mary said she would skip that course, but ordered *boeuf* to please them. John had *coq au vin.* Mark had *poulet.* Arthur ordered grilled salmon. Lynda ordered, but did not eat, salmon.

"What about the children?" asked Margaret. "Why aren't they here?"

"Elizabeth's here," said Mark, trying to be kind.

Elizabeth said with bitterness that she had never had a home and it looked as if she never would.

Lynda, appealed to about Francis, said it seemed as if he proposed to continue living with Jill.

Phoebe said: "Then more fool him."

Martha, appealed to about Paul, said that they all forgot Paul was a houseowner himself, even though he was not much over twenty.

"He'll probably be putting us all up," said Margaret, bitter, bitter, her eyes full of brilliant tears.

"What about your children?" said Phoebe to Arthur and Mary.

"Oh *them*," said Mary, bitter. "Selfish little beasts. I can't wait till they get to our age, and see how they do, they really are . . ."

Scene of the time: A room full of middle-aged people, eating hard, preoccupied half the time about weight problems, always on diets of one sort or another, most of them smoking, a lethal habit as they were told at the top of every publicity voice there was, most of them on sleeping pills and sedatives, all of them drinkers and some of them drunk— talking about the youth.

The young took drugs. They were irresponsible. They were selfish. They were dirty. They were self-indulgent. They had no interest at all in politics—that was Phoebe, who kept demanding: If they'd only go out and canvass for the party, they'd have a purpose in life and they wouldn't need to take drugs.

Margaret, Phoebe, Arthur, Mary, found themselves in perfect agreement on this theme, and while the plates were being cleared, started drafting a letter to *The Observer* about why the youth were not interested in politics: Margaret said it was because they had not suffered when children, they had had it too easy. Arthur agreed.

During the coffee, this draft was completed, and then Lynda asked Mark if they could go home. At once Mark said yes, infinitely relieved. Martha was only too ready to go.

"But we haven't settled anything," Margaret kept saying, pathetic, bewildered, looking from one to the other of this trio, Mark, Martha, Lynda, while she held a silver and turquoise pencil over the draft letter.

Elizabeth, ill, had to come with them.

Martha asked to be dropped back at Paul's house.

Lynda said to her: "One would think that if there was a Devil there'd be a God."

Martha said: "I don't know how you stick it, going on all the time. I'd kill myself."

Lynda said: "You can get used to anything."

Mark said to Martha: "When are you coming back?"

"Well, how about in six weeks?"

"Couldn't you make it sooner, there are things . . ." He meant Elizabeth, sitting beside him, her profile turned to him. In the half-dark of the car's interior, her slightly parted lips, her calm rounded forehead gave her the look of a venturing girl. Perhaps that was how she saw herself at that moment. But she was well over thirty, and in the light, looked more.

Lynda said: "Elizabeth, have you left your husband and children?"

"Of course not," said Elizabeth, indignant. "I've decided to find some place where they can really *live*, that's all. I just like the sound of Mark's city, that's all."

"I'll make it a month," said Martha.

Lynda said: "Mark wants you sooner than that."

"Oh no," said Mark hastily, "please, Martha, not if . . ."

"If I loved somebody, really really loved somebody, I wouldn't leave him, not for one moment!" said Elizabeth.

"All right, three weeks," said Martha.

Inside her head, during this exchange, titan battles had taken place: she wanted very much to stop now. Oh how tired she was, how confused, how frightened . . . she felt she had the best possible excuse to say to Paul, Thanks, but that's enough, for the time being at any rate—and go back home.

What home? It wouldn't be here, within a few months.

Besides, three weeks of absolute privacy, good Lord, what sort of a fool would throw that away, not knowing when the next chance would come?

With half her need she stayed in imagination with Mark in his home, poor Mark who would now spend a night trying to hold together his crazy niece Elizabeth, and who had no friend there to help him. With the rest of her she was being driven to return to her retreat as fast as she could.

Inside her room she checked her body, the instrument, the receiving device. She had eaten a lot; she had drunk enough.

548

It would take twenty-four hours at least to get herself back into a sensitive state.

Sensitive to what?

One always assumed that . . . the point was, she knew nothing, and was taking such risks: she might very well end up in the hands of Dr. Lamb—why not? *It can't happen to me!* Everyone says that, all the time. It could happen to her. It was happening to her. If she now went into Dr. Lamb's room and said these and these and such and such are my symptoms—that would be that.

Luckily she knew better.

But she did not know the first things about what really was going on in this machine, mechanism, system, organism. Who did? Did anyone? Not Dr. Lamb!

If she didn't understand she could describe, she could record. Above all, she could remember.

Time out from the Devil had lessened him after all, as she saw when she was able to compare the mental furniture of the room with what it had been before she went out.

She was able to hold him back, hold back her collapse into tears and screaming self-pity for a while. Meanwhile, like a baby who has drawn a deep breath for a yell of temper, but is holding out for a greater effect, she knelt by the table and scribbled notes fast, fast, before—as she knew she must—she would collapse into self-abasement.

Works like this. Thought comes into mind. If conscious, thought is in words. If not, if ordinary association-thought, then it isn't words. Words are when one stands back to look. This first word then sprouts into other words and ideas like a flash of lightning. No, like water suddenly lifting limp branch off sea bottom. Words proliferate so fast you can't catch them. A word: then an idea suggested by that word (Who suggested the word?) You think: My idea? Whose? Make the first word or phrase or idea stay still so you can look at it. Then you can ask: Is that an overheard thought? Whose? Why? Or is it something fed by the invisible mentor. If you stop thought, make it go out of mind altogether, it can retreat and make its way back in sound. This sound can get louder. It can use different voices, known and unknown. If known probably you associate that thought with that person. That thought can also come from the corner of a room or another part of your body or a chair or something. Mind is also a ventriloquist. Devil for instance before I went to dinner—from corners of the room.

Essential be conscious the moment thought comes into mind otherwise it is a lost thought.

Here we go again: If you don't know something you can't know it/ You can only learn something you already begin to know/ "I can't tell you something you don't know."

And again: Every attitude, emotion, thought, has its opposite held in balance out of sight but there all the time. Push any one of them to an extreme, and boomps-a-daisy, over you go into its opposite.

I am good and kind and intelligent. I am bad and cruel and stupid.

All right, all right, all right. You just keep off a minute.

The young man in Virginia Woolf's story who was mad. He heard the birds talking in ancient Greek.

Onomatopoeia. Think about it!

An emotion. Fear for instance. You can see how it converts into a thought—if you are quick enough.

A body is a machine for the conversion of one kind of energy into another.

Here Martha succumbed again to the Devil.

Hell (one of them?) is hot. It has a harsh light. There is a sticky clinging feel to it. MOST IMPORTANT OF ALL it has a beat. Both regular and irregular. Like a mad clock, like the way paraffin lamps flare up before going out, but it flares with a regular irregularity. A wild hysterical sort of beat yet regular. Yet at the same time small and unimportant. A harshness of black and white. A sticky feel. Light without shadow. Monsters. First you see just people, you and I. Then you see, they, we, are deformed, our faces twisted with greed and anger. Man from grocery, a portly slow-moving man, high-coloured in face. In hell he leers—you see that he has dog-teeth, fangs, is subhuman. Faces like embryos, half-formed. A gallery of faces of people. Devils. Ordinary people. Faces are blanks which can take masks, good or bad. Hate, envy, greed, fear, slide over people's faces so fast you can only just catch them.

It was at that stage that Martha was conducted through the Stations of the Cross by the Devil. She knew nothing of this ritual, had never been instructed in it, nor had known well enough to affect her people who performed it. Yet it was as if she knew it, knew its meaning. From the moment when Pontius Pilate washed his hands to the time when she, Martha, who was also the Devil, prepared to be bound on the Cross, because of the frightfulness of her crimes, she was as it were whipped through the ritual by the hating scourging tongue of the Devil who was her self, her hating, self-hating self. Yet though she was not able to refuse obedience to this ritual, she was quite able to protect herself from the boy who visited her during it: the boy who had killed without meaning to the baby he had said he would protect and who was now doing penance for the sin he had committed. He was a slight fair boy, who looked much younger than his nineteen years. He looked like an earnest schoolboy. He sat on the edge of the big four-poster bed, wringing his hands together and weeping, while he explained to Martha how God was punishing him out of love; and how if Martha was being punished, it was out of the love of God. When he had gone—he had to get up pretty early to be at his packing work at the chemical firm in Tottenham—Martha continued taking instruction from the Fiend, until the play was played out. "But I've done that, I've finished with that," she said crossly to the Devil, refusing further instruction, and lay down to sleep for a while.

Martha was now unable to leave Hell. So she thought. Exhausted, she would say "Enough," and lie down to sleep in Hell. In sleep the most dreadful nightmares followed her. But she remembered that when she was a child there had been a long period when she had been frightened to sleep because of nightmares, and had used all kinds of tricks and techniques to outwit them. She remembered these now, used them. It occurred to her that she thought she was finally lost, was cast forever into this sea, but all the same she could say, I'm tired, I will sleep—and did. Or, asleep, say: I am in Hell, wake up, and did. Or performed the rituals before sleep that could ward off nightmares which she had learned through necessity as a child.

This thought lessened the grip of the Devil and of Hell.

But did not send them away: she was still curious.

If all these subhuman creatures are aspects of me, then I'm a gallery of freaks and nature's rejects.

See above. Fool. Don't you ever learn. These things are there. Always. I can choose to be them or not. I can collect them the way dust gets collected on a magnetically treated duster. Or not.

In Hell the light is on all the time.

In prison cells and in the torture cells and in the locked wards of mental hospitals light burns always.

Man understands the Devil very well. The Devil has taught him all he knows.

All dark or all light. Monsters and sadists create these conditions. Monsters and sadists live in them.

The face of Bob Parrinder. He hasn't grown into his own face yet. He is a self-important little boss. His face like a landscape before sun rises. Shadows and light will fill it. If I held the mask of self-importance in front of him, as last night when he said, Oh yes of course, I understand all that, he'd die with shame. Olive's face: what she is.

Mr. Briggs the Carpenter says: A letter for you, Mrs. Hesse. His face like a cauliflower going yellow and rotten at fringes. Underneath tired and very frightened.

Paul's face: Sally-Sarah's little Paul, when he sucked his thumb and put his face on his mum's silk breast.

For a week Martha wrote nothing. She was too far gone in Hell. Yet not so far that she didn't watch the days pass: five days, four days left, and so on. Inside her head hammered the enemy: or, voices might come from a wall or a chair. (Not accidentally, she began to see; she directed this, but did not yet know how. But there was no time to learn how.) She had wished to return to the house in Radlett Street in a shape of competence, but would have to do so still undermined by the Devil. At this stage she believed she would never lose him—that, like poor Lynda, she would carry him with her for always. She thought that the last few weeks had taken her right over the edge into a permanent stage of being plugged in to the sea of sound; and that its main, persistent, hammering, never-sleeping voice was the Devil's, the voice of the self-punisher.

She bathed. Drank tea. Ate toast. She tidied the room, which looked as if a cyclone had been through it. She dressed and examined herself.

She was again much too thin. She looked haggard. However, there were three weeks before Maisie's daughter arrived and in the meantime doubtless Mark and Lynda would put up with her. She would go to the hairdresser's tomorrow ... Thinking these practical thoughts, Hell retreated a step or two.

She collected all her notes and scribbles together and before bundling them into a box for future examination she wrote:

"1. This sort of thing is not only very dangerous, but extremely inefficient. There must be other ways of doing it. And not drugs either. I've sent myself over the edge.

"2. If a dictator wishes to control a party, or a country; if a hierarchy of priests wish to control their flock; if any

power-seeker anywhere wants to create a manipulated group
—he, she, has to embody the self-hater. It is as easy as
that. *And it is very easy to do.*

"3. I've been turned inside out like a glove or a dress.
I've been like the negative of a photograph. Or a mirror
image. I've seen the underneath of myself. Which isn't me—
any more than my surface is me. I am the watcher, the
listener . . .

"FINALLY: THE CENTRAL FACT. IF AT ANY TIME AT ALL I
HAD GONE TO A DOCTOR OR TO A PSYCHIATRIST, THAT WOULD
HAVE BEEN THAT. I'M OVER THE EDGE. BUT EVEN IF I STAY
HERE I CAN MANAGE (LIKE LYNDA). WHY? BECAUSE I KNOW
JUST THAT SMALL AMOUNT ABOUT IT NOT TO LET MYSELF BE
STAMPEDED. IF AT ANY MOMENT I'D GIVEN IN DURING THIS
SESSION I'D HAVE BEEN SWEPT AWAY. WITHOUT KNOWING
WHAT I KNOW, THROUGH LYNDA, I'D NOT HAVE BEEN ABLE TO
HOLD ON. THROUGH HINTS AND SUGGESTIONS IN ALL THE
BOOKS, THROUGH MY OWN EXPERIENCE, THROUGH LYNDA—
BUT WITHOUT THESE, A DOCTOR OR A PSYCHIATRIST WOULD
HAVE NEEDED ONLY TO USE THE LANGUAGE OF THE SELF-
HATER AND THAT WOULD HAVE BEEN THAT. FINIS, MARTHA!
BRING OUT YOUR MACHINES. BRING OUT YOUR DRUGS! YES,
YES, YOU KNOW BEST DOCTOR, I'LL DO WHAT YOU SAY: I'M
TOO SCARED NOT TO.

"Classic definition of paranoia: 'A feeling of being slighted
. . . favours the secret nurturing of ideas of great power . . .
such an individual may come into conflict with the law,
either as a direct actionist (e.g. murder) or as a petitioner
(lawsuits), a development which he regards as the natural
outcome of his great but unrecognised importance, and of
the envy and malice of an indifferent world . . . an impressive facade of reasonableness, earnestness and "normality"
may cloak this psychopathology to an alarming degree.' "

The house was empty. Lynda had left a note that she was
staying with Jill and Francis. Jill believed she was pregnant
again, she did not know by whom. Mark's message said he
had taken Elizabeth to Nanny Butts: the doctors said a few
weeks of rest on the drugs prescribed would probably send
her back to her husband and children in a reasonable frame
of mind.

There was a letter from Maisie, giving the date of Rita's
arrival in about a month's time.

On Mark's desk was the Memorandum to Myself, now
rather longer.

". . . it will be the responsibility of individuals to forecast,

553

plan, make provision for contingencies whose outlines are already visible.

"1. We are all hypnotised by the idea of Armageddon, the flash brighter than a million suns, the apocalyptic convulsion, the two-minute war, instant death. Populace more than government; but governments as well. Everyone is stunned by an approaching annihilation like an animal dazzled by an approaching car.

"2. This prevents preparation, psychological and physical, for what is likely. Which will be local catastrophic occurrences—the poisoning of a country, or of an area; the death of part of the world; the contamination of an area for a certain period of time. These events will be the development of

"3. What is already happening. A bomber carrying nuclear warheads crashes in Spain. All kinds of denials, evasions are made. It can be taken as an axiom that all governments everywhere lie—it is inevitable. Naive people think that conspiracies are seven men around a table in a Machiavellian plot: a conspiracy is an atmosphere, or a frame of mind in which people are impelled to do things, perhaps those things that they could never do as individuals, or couldn't do at other times when the atmosphere is different. Ever since the last war governments have stockpiled every conceivable weapon of attack and defence, and there have been innumerable accidents, mostly minor ones, or threats of accidents—but the populace have never heard of them, nor would they find out except by accident, or by a member of the 'conspiracy' (government department, commission, factory, etc.) not being sufficiently brainwashed into secrecy and spilling the beans, or when something happens like a bomber crashing carrying radioactive live warheads. *What will happen is a development of what is already happening and what has been accelerating, out of control, since 1914 and the green light for mass extermination.* Areas of the world are already being poisoned, contaminated, threatened, etc. In five years, ten, fifteen, twenty, something 'unforeseeable' will happen, such as that a mysterious disease will decimate a country, emanating from a factory which manufactures disease, or that a container full of some poison or destructive material sunk in the seabed in an (indestructible) container will be washed up or explode or release its contents, or that in a moment of extreme crisis between countries one side will by accident, in a fit of

554

hysteria, release weapons which will totally destroy its opponent or even itself—something like that.

"4. It can be taken absolutely as an axiom that the populace will not be told the truth, nine-tenths because the governments concerned won't know what is the truth, will be as much in the dark as anybody else, and one-tenth out of panic, greed, hysteria, *fear of their own citizenry*.

"5. Therefore groups of people aware of this situation should set themselves to . . ."

Here the Memorandum broke off.

Martha rang Lynda.

Who said that Jill said she wouldn't have an abortion again "just to please all of you." Francis had said that she must do as she wanted.

The point was, said Lynda, where was everybody going to live? There were Francis, Jill, the children. Gwen had moved in with her sister. There were two new campers or squatters. One was Nicky Anderson from the old Aldermaston days. He had had a bad breakdown after a spell in prison. He had been told that he was paranoid. This had seemed convincing at the time—the "classic" definition of paranoia could scarcely fail to convince an unprepared person—and in any case he was very weakened by one thing and another. Then, coming out of the doctor's hands into those of his old friend Francis, it occurred to him that after all there wasn't a revolutionary or reformer in history who could not have been dismissed or discouraged by such methods. It had not been easy to maintain this rallying towards self-esteem except with Francis's help, and he had asked if he could stay with the couple. He had a girl friend who had been kind to him when ill, having been ill herself. His parents had cast him off (or so he felt—they would welcome him back into the bosom of the family as a penitent paranoiac, but not otherwise) and he said he wished to live with this girl. She had moved in too. He had no money, so she had been keeping him. There seemed no signs of this couple leaving Francis and Jill's flat.

"They are really all so very *sad*," said Lynda. "But I suppose their teeth have been set on edge. And my teeth have been set on edge. Perhaps my poor papa's teeth were set on edge too? He used to go on about that war all the time . . . But it's not only Jill now, it's Gwen. Gwen has a job as a bunny because she says she is sick of sex. And Jill won't sleep with Francis, she says she hates sex. And she says that something comes over her when she's with some man in a

555

pub, and then because she doesn't have a contraceptive, she gets pregnant."

"Poor Francis," said Martha.

"And poor Mark," said Lynda. "I'm a wicked woman, I know that."

"Lynda, are you sure you haven't been doing too much?"

"How could I ever, ever, *ever* do too much—after all the misery I've inflicted on everyone?"

Martha went to fetch Lynda, to get her to come home and rest: she recognised only too clearly the person who was speaking through Lynda.

Lynda did come, but said it would only be for a short time. If she was going to crack up altogether by staying out in the world, working, then she would. She was not going to live her life out on the terms that either Mark or Martha must look after her. She was violent, weepy, self-punishing.

Martha's Devil-haunted head rang with echoes from Lynda.

Soon, however, she noted that because she was very busy, very worried over Lynda, her own Devil retreated. From being too terrified to listen too closely, in case she provoked him into worse, frightened to use or think words, phrases, that might "bring him on" (like an attack of malaria!), she became careless of him. Soon, the Devil, once histrionic, flamboyant, accusing, violent, had become a silly little nagging voice, which became swallowed in the sea of sound—was just one little voice among many. And soon, the thing was all over—finished. Her mind was her own.

She was as sane as the next one.

But before Rita's arrival, there appeared the Maynards, in the form of a letter which Martha even now could not help seeing as a summons instructing her to meet them for lunch next day at such and such a restaurant in Chelsea. The letter was from a hotel: food for thought here, since the Maynards had so many relatives in England. And the choice of the restaurant too; for it was one of the half-dozen "in" restaurants of swinging London.

She had of course heard from time to time of the Maynards, but not much more than that Judge Maynard had retired, and that Binkie Maynard, who had remained married to his war widow, was an alcoholic, or not far from one, and was running an important government department.

Facts: (1) They must be well over seventy by now. (2) There could be only one reason for wanting to see her—

556

Rita. (3) Whatever they had heard of her way of life, they were bound to disapprove of it.

The restaurant was called Charlie's and Johnny's Eataria—Charlie's for short. When Martha went in, she saw the Maynards, two very old people sitting at a not very good table. They looked through her, not recognising her. The thing was, she was making the most of her post-retreat thinness, and wore a "wand" of white linen, with chestnut hair, and dark glasses.

She went up to them, greeted them, sat down, putting on a pretence of ease to cover up their look of—not merely surprise—but affront, which, Martha could see, was due not so much to her, personally, as to a London which produced so prodigally unpleasant phenomena.

They were indeed old, and seemed more so in this scene set for youth, or for people who wanted to appear young, or who wanted to feed themselves on the aromas of youth. They were attended by a charming little waiter, probably Italian, wearing a strawberry-coloured cavalier's muslin shirt, with ruffles, and a minuscule striped cotton apron with frills half concealing, half displaying what tight white pants were designed to emphasise. All the waiters had pretty little bums, glossy urchin hair, the look of well-used tarts in a good house.

The food had names like "Bobby's Own Stew," "Our Own Bread," "Salade Nikki-oise," "Tommy's Pie," and was very good, when it came.

The Maynards, two shrunken old people with their strong dark faces gone to bone, in clothes which they could have worn in London of fifty years ago, looked out from their corner and made nothing of what they saw.

They ate steak and cheese and drank claret, and said very little to Martha, beyond asking her questions like "Do you travel a lot?" and "I hear you've been having some good weather?" In short, they needed help to begin—which fact, naturally, flung Martha into disorder, since it was difficult for her to believe that this was possible.

She should revive "Matty" perhaps, hard though this was, after such a long time? But striking a note or two of "scattiness," of wilful humour, she was met by long sorrowful stares—not of criticism, but of noncomprehension.

"Of course," said Mrs. Maynard, petulant, "when everything is for the youth, one feels one ought to go off into a corner and die."

Martha saw that she, a middle-aged woman, was being seen by them as "youth."

She therefore made a great deal of small talk, and thought that ... she was wishing she could put her arms around them both, her old enemies. Yes, here they were, who had had such a very powerful influence on her that, looking back, she could say that of all her educators these had been the most valuable. He, Mr. Maynard, had done her the inestimable service of putting strongly before her, so that she could not possibly mistake it, that most deadly of weapons against what every young person (for a time at least) needs, wants, longs for: he had shown her disbelief, in the shape of an accomplished and withering irony: he had toughened her against ridicule. She, Mrs. Maynard, had shown her power at its ugliest, when it is indirect, subtle, hidden, since she who wielded it knew so perfectly that she must always be in the right and never doubted herself.

Ah, but what a very good job had the drunken cook made of the Maynards, stripped, stripped down to a sullen old age with nothing left of all their years of power. Indeed, one could not easily imagine how much more bitterly and painfully things might have been arranged for them.

Mrs. Maynard had always governed, intrigued, managed, by virtue of Government House, and powerful relatives in England. But now Government House was the enemy for her, must be, although she hated the government in her country, which was composed only of the second and third generations of Zambesians, whom she despised, found raw, crude, unfit for responsibility. They had no touch of "home" about them; yet "home" (England) was what both Maynards had repudiated decades ago—and what, revisiting it now, had changed so that they could find nothing in it to admire or like. When their country (theirs when it was run by yahoos unfit and unable to govern even themselves?) had cut itself off from their country (which was being run by unscrupulous socialist agitators who knew nothing about the blacks); when, looking around the continent of Africa (their home) they could not see one state anywhere, white or black, run in the way they believed states ought to be run—then they had thought (but only briefly and weakly) that perhaps somewhere in England (Devon perhaps, there were cousins there) they might find a sympathetic soil. Therefore had they come to visit with a half-brother, Richie Maynard, large farmer in Devon, and at the first weekend, a granddaughter had arrived from one of the new universities with a West Indian boy friend with whom (or so it appeared) she had spent the night.

Mr. Maynard had taxed the half-brother, who had replied that "his policy was, a tight rein made for a short run"; the gal would get tired of it and settle down with someone of her own colour, and luckily Peregrine (the son), father of the girl, "had the sense to see it."

This was putting a coloured boy from a slum in Trinidad on the same plane as once, fifty years ago, he, Mr. Maynard, had been put for Myra. Black sheep from some remote colony, he had courted Myra, who had been given a long rein. . . . They were going back home next week, they told Martha.

"The thing is," said Mrs. Maynard, with a hint of her old trumpet power, "people have no idea at all about service now, they care only for themselves. I have been seeing my grandnieces and nephews. They take no thought for the future at all."

Now Martha found herself watching Mr. Maynard, who was tasting claret as if it, too, could not be what it had been: she was waiting for what, after all, she had always relied on from him, an unfailing urbanity, his need to deflate.

He had subsided back into his chair, head lowered, jowls on his chest, his hand about his claret glass.

"We are neither of us," said Mrs. Maynard decisively, "as young as we once were—my husband has to be careful of his heart, for instance."

"Oh it's not bad, not bad at all," he said angrily.

"No, but all the same, my dear . . ." Her eyes were on his wine glass, and he sat back and allowed the little waiter to trip away with it and the half-empty wine bottle poised in a wicker basket.

"I have a touch of arthritis," she said, taking Martha into her confidence. "But I don't do much these days—I garden. Gardening is my exercise."

The meal was nearly over.

"How is Maisie—do you see her at all?" asked Martha.

The two old people's eyes met in a look.

"She is quite deplorable," said Mrs. Maynard. "But one would not expect anything else from her."

"Yes, yes, yes," muttered Mr. Maynard.

Guiltily? It sounded like it; Martha was not sure.

"And Rita?"

"My husband sees her sometimes but she does not appear to care for me," said Mrs. Maynard.

"Well, my dear Myra," protested Mr. Maynard, blowing out his cheeks, puffing, protecting some delightful private secret.

"*Yes*," she said. "But I hear she is coming to stay with you?"

"In a couple of days," said Martha.

"Well, we have been thinking of coming Home for some time and we thought . . ."

The look she gave Martha was all appeal. *Unfair!* an old Martha judged it. What right had she? But it was no use: Mrs. Maynard leaned forward with her old command, her white hair falling in wisps about her face, yet her flashing dark eyes and trembling lips made her all gallant, reckless girl.

She was plunging a ringed hand about in her handbag. Wads of notes appeared.

"We were wondering. Perhaps you could persuade her. A finishing school?"

A waiter raised eyebrows at a heap of five-pound notes, and brushed crumbs away from around it, in a delightful little play. Out went Mrs. Maynard's hand to weight the pile until he had finished.

"But how old is Rita?" asked Martha.

"That is *not* the point. She had no idea. None at all. And her accent . . ." Mrs. Maynard's voice, which not even fifty years of colonial vowels had been able to incriminate, rang out.

Martha was silent. She looked to Mr. Maynard for help.

"Does Rita know?" she asked, when the old man said nothing.

"Goodness knows what she knows!" said Mrs. Maynard, with a look of pathetically brave accusation at her husband. Again he blew up his cheeks and let them deflate, pop, pop, pop through his lips. His wife disdained the old man's trick, stared him out.

He reached out his hand for his glass.

"Brandy," he said to Nikki, or Colin or Bobby, whoever it was now standing with another, a twin, against the wall. Both watched the scene with a frankly humorous interest.

"Sure, sure!" cried one; and *"Mais certain*ment!" the other, materialising brandy bottle and glasses.

"Me too," said Martha, allying herself with him; while

560

she, Mrs. Maynard, as always in the right, said: "If you want another heart attack."

"Alcohol opens the arteries," he said firmly, putting back his head and swallowing the lot. Bobby, or Ivor, refilled his glass.

"Or if she won't go to finishing school," said Mrs. Maynard, "you could perhaps ..." She pushed a ream or so of money towards Martha.

Martha said: "But what does *she* want?"

"Ah," said Mr. Maynard, "now you've hit it. But Myra won't see ..."

"I see everything," said she. "But we all of us have to do things we don't like sometimes. But whatever *she* sees fit to do or not, something must be done about her. Her clothes, for instance."

Here she darted a look at Martha's clothes, remembered how unsuitable she had invariably thought them, and then that it was Martha or nothing.

"The life's she's been leading, dreadful, dreadful, dreadful," she cried. "Dancing every night, and she's mad about boys, dreadful."

"Myra, she's well over twenty, well over," said her husband.

Tears washed down Mrs. Maynard's old face. Nikki, or Colin, standing by with the cognac, went tck, tck with his tongue, and shook his head and sighed in sympathy as he smiled at her with a charm which made her sit up and straighten and glare back.

"Well I really don't *know*," said he, in B.B.C. English. Then, in cockney, "Reely, Hai don't *knaow*. Some people ..."

He went off affronted.

"The most extraordinary people," said Mrs. Maynard, "and they're everywhere you go."

"How long have you been here?" asked Martha.

"Two weeks. It's more than enough. This country is ..." And now, at last, she said what she thought.

"What is going on here? I mean it isn't just the clothes, I suppose when I was a gal I wore clothes too. Gals will be gals, but one does feel that ... and ... and ... and ..." This went on for some minutes and ended with: "And to think you were going to invade us. *You* invade *us*."

"And still might," said Mr. Maynard to Martha.

"I somehow doubt it," said Martha.

They looked at her suspiciously: she had perhaps

changed? All three decided on diplomacy, and Mr. Maynard said quickly: "But we're out of all that. I'm retired, you know."

"And it's not only here, it's everywhere," said Mrs. Maynard, her lips trembling.

"Go on, have some brandy, do you good, Myra," said her husband. He looked around for a waiter, but saw two pointedly turned backs.

"No," she said, and looked for her things, to put an end to the possibility of brandy.

"The bill please," said Martha to one of the turned backs. He nodded, cold: his charm, his real self, having been refused, he proposed to go on sulking.

Martha pushed the heap of notes back to Mrs. Maynard.

"No, keep it. Keep it for her."

"We can leave it to her in our will," said Mr. Maynard.

"Yes, but let us hope that it won't be of benefit to her just yet," said Mrs. Maynard.

"I'm sure she'll find something to spend it on," said Mr. Maynard, defying his wife, who glared at him through tears.

They left the restaurant.

Outside Mrs. Maynard said to Martha: "Perhaps you'd like to let us know how Rita does get along?" This was an appeal she hated to make; it came out peremptory, but her eyes pleaded and sorrowed.

"Yes of course I will," said Martha, intending to.

Mrs. Maynard nodded at her husband and they turned themselves about and faced the pavements. An orange-coloured London sun poured down a hot glitter into the gulf between the buildings all of which sold clothes, food, jewels, furniture, every item of which had the stamp of the moment, which was not to take itself seriously. The old people kept their eyes straight in front of them, as they went away among throngs of youth who were either wittily dressed boys and girls who had the world for their bargain counter; or tasteless exhibitionists with overdeveloped naked thighs, yards of false hair, faces hidden behind dark glasses, or whiskers, or beards—anything that concealed. According to how you looked at it.

The two ex-consuls did not look at all: they fled past as if anything they saw must undo them.

Martha watched them out of sight, and went home with her handbag forced open because of all the money in it. Counted, it turned out there were £800 ready for Rita (Maynard's) education.

Four

To sit in a house which is going to be pulled down, left derelict, manipulated in some way or another, is the oddest of the forms of patience. Through here, where one's femur makes a plane with the door handle, will run a shelf? The line from head to left ankle will be that of a dividing wall? Or, floors rising and falling as they do, one walks with one's feet on air twenty-six inches below this floor (ceiling) existing now which will vanish into dust and bits of lath and plaster.

Particularly dust.

A feverish transience. This had characterised the eighteen months since Rita Gale's (Canfield's?) arrival here; more than ever, and just as Martha remembered feeling before (again, again, again), her life was like a railway platform which served trains departing fast in every direction.

As she sat now on a summer's afternoon doing final accounts for Mark she could hear people moving in and moving out all over the house.

The flat in North London having been bought by speculators, Francis and Jill were moving in here with their flock. Three children. Gwen. Gwen's boy friend. Nick. Nick's girl friend. An ex-boy friend of hers. The ex-boy friend's girl friend's baby—she having taken an overdose of drugs and died. Jill was pregnant again. This time by Francis. Lynda had said to him: Unless you want to be the father of at least twenty children, none of your own (since Jill like a Victorian woman would probably produce yearly until the menopause), you had better be one of the men she doesn't enjoy sleeping with. Francis had considered this, as was his way, first battering his mother with a kind of anguished ribaldry and anger, but then concluding that, her choice of words apart, there was a good deal in what she said. The two were thinking of getting married. Particularly as Jill had announced that she liked making love with Francis more than anyone and she might yet get around to seeing that there was something to be said for the activity. She had never before, she said, had sex with a *friend*.

While this house was compulsorily purchased, or almost, the formalities were all likely to drag out, as they do, for some months, and the Francis-Jill household thought that they might as well make use of this space of time before it became an office for the Rates or the Town Planning or before it was demolished altogether.

They all assumed that when they must move on, they would move on together, like a caravan, almost certainly accumulating items of humanity as they went. In short they, like Paul, providing places, havens, and homes for the sad, forlorn, sick, rejected, were also focuses, or growing places, for people who probably would not come to much before a very late maturity but who then . . . but it was much too early to say.

Paul and Francis, oil and water, never meeting for pleasure or liking or for the sake of their childhood under this roof, met now often because they were considering buying a farm somewhere on which their friends might live, self-supporting and without more reference to society than was essential. Neither used the word "socialism" or "community" or "kibbutz" or "collective."

Francis was to have a share of the money from this house, about £5,000. Paul would provide most of the money. Living for the shine of money, for the making of it, the manipulating of it, the pleasure of it, he was nevertheless ready to risk the lot now. He would not live on the farm himself; the city was his place; but he proposed to sell his share in one of the houses, another house all his, a boutique and a barber's. After all, said Paul, he had a gift for money; Francis had none—he didn't see that it mattered: he had no doubt he would be where he was now in five years: probably richer.

Downstairs Lynda was packing to move into a flat with her new friend, Sandra, who babied and bossed Lynda as poor Dorothy had done. Sandra, a large sighing blonde, all good-natured freckles, who might very well wear her hair in short plaits with baby bows at the ends if in the mood, was, as Dr. Lamb told Mark, "very disturbed when she was, but quite adequate for normal purposes." Adequate or disturbed, Mark disliked her extremely, and everyone found her an embarrassment: she not only believed in flying saucers from other planets—after all, nearly everyone did—but corresponded telepathically with a demon lover who was captain

564

of one of them. She comforted Lynda that she was not to worry. Algavious (she called him Al for short) would take off her, Lynda, with her, Sandra, when it was time.

Lynda had had another very bad time. She had left Mark and the house to move into the room in Paul's house, to see if she could be self-sufficient. (Mark had taken it very badly—which misery coincided with the arrival of Rita.) There Lynda had found not solitude, but many friends. And, since she longed to make up for a life which she saw as totally selfish, and misspent, she was soon busy with Olive's baby, Bob's personality clashes, Molly's and Rose's breakdowns. She cracked, not under the strain of solitude, but because she wore herself out. Then, by misfortune, she became involved with a crisis of Paul's. This house he half owned with a young businessman of good family and orthodox habits who had flitted into smart young London but then had flitted out again. This excursion had involved him with Paul. He had imagined the house was being let on ordinary business lines. He discovered that half the inhabitants lived there rent-free, others paid very little. He was disturbed by the atmosphere of the place when he dropped in one afternoon. For one thing, he found Lynda in a bad spell, sitting on the floor banging her head against the wall and singing to herself. He diagnosed drugs, and got into a panic because of the police. Paul, on being challenged, said that Lynda was his stepmother. Further, he said that if the house was not earning much in rents, it had doubled in value—so what was he, Percy Dodlington, complaining about? Percy threatened the law. Paul lost his head and wrote a letter: Our friendship ... trust ... in terms of our contract ... will sue if ... as he had alas so often before. Lynda then found herself in the middle of a row that threatened to reach the courts. Paul found her in bed, weeping that she ruined everyone, she was useless, she ought to be dead. Martha was away seeing Nanny Butts about looking after the three babies (Harold Butts had died) and Mark was off on an organisational trip with Rita. Paul took Lynda to Dr. Lamb. Dr. Lamb arranged for her to go into a fine new wing of an old hospital and there Lynda had been very sick indeed. The doctor this time was of the new nondidactic flexible school who refuse to use any of the old jargon, but who supplied her with a drug which he said was new and wonderful. Lynda took it eagerly: she wanted only to get back to trying to be normal, and this drug, said Dr. Bentin, would do it. She began having new symptoms which terrified her. Asked what they were, she said she kept "seeing things." She was soothed and comforted; it seemed this drug didn't suit her, they said, but another new one would. The symptoms continued.

Around about then Martha came back from visiting Nanny Butts, who said that while there was nothing she would like better than to take on the three dear little babies, she felt she was really getting too old, being well over seventy now: might she suggest her niece Pauline, a very good girl. (Pauline moved into the flat in North London and became nurse to the three infants and the girl friend of Gwen's boyfriend, Gwen and he having separated.) Lynda was in a large room painted a shiny mustard colour that made Martha queasy, and was watching television with half a hundred patients and nurses. She was curt and listless with Martha. Martha asked if she could see her alone: Lynda came, with bad grace, to sit on her bed, with the white-sheeting curtains drawn—privacy. Lynda towards Martha was as if two totally different attitudes had been stirred together to that point where they nearly coalesced, like the "marble pudding" of childhood. She alternatively snubbed her, shrank, blocked herself off, and immediately afterwards, or at the same time, seemed to yearn and beg for help and for forgiveness.

The doctor had told Martha that Lynda was hallucinating badly.

Martha reminded Lynda of their joint experiences. The Lynda who remembered them was either not there, or was frightened to admit she was there.

Lynda had had, for the space of several days, a series of visions or pictures (on the inner television set) and the dreams like stills from the visions. These showed landscapes that were all known to Lynda, like the country around Nanny Butts's cottage, and around Margaret's house, and from her childhood. They looked as if a kind of frozen dew had covered everything so that at first glance she had cried out, "England has been poisoned, it looks like a poisoned mouse lying dead in a corner." For everything had appeared as a faintly phosphorescent or begemmed stillness. They had given her larger doses, had taken her off to a small room for a couple of days of deep sleep. But when the sleep had worn off, she began dreaming again. England was poisoned, she cried; some enemy was injecting England with a deathly glittering dew.

Young Dr. Bentin had been very kind; had explained that what she was doing was to project her own loathing of herself, her self-hatred, outwards onto her country. Lynda had been very ready to accept this, God knew she loathed herself: she knew she was useless, debased, fit for nothing.

They lessened the drugs; she had another few days of the hallucinations; this time, she kept quiet, remembering the past.

But she had decided she wanted to stay in hospital. She had met Sandra, who (Lynda knew this very well) was dependent on Lynda, while giving the appearance of looking after her; Sandra, without Lynda, could expect nothing but a room alone somewhere: she had no money, children who had grown up and did not like her. It was a most common story.

Lynda wished to stay in the hospital, with Sandra as friend and companion. But a new dispensation had set in: no one was encouraged to stay in hospitals if they could go out. Lynda and Sandra begged and asked and tricked, played every game they knew, to stay in, but without taking drugs. But no, Dr. Bentin gave them a time limit, four weeks, to leave: he would see that the supplies of drugs were adequate. It was an absolute clash.

Lynda did not want to come back to Radlett Street. She felt as if she was beginning again on an old cycle. Over fifteen years ago she had "come home" with Dorothy and prescriptions for drugs—different drugs, it was true. She did not believe she would ever get herself free of these that she was taking now. Besides, she did not want to "see things" again. Hearing them was bad enough. Therefore, for the whole of an afternoon with Martha she listened, while hanging her head, turning herself away, sighing in dramatic exasperation, and Martha pointed out that "seeing things" did not have to be frightening . . . had Lynda entirely forgotten? No, Lynda had not; for she would, while sulking or grinding her teeth at Martha, suddenly reach out a dirty hand and stroke Martha's timidly, as if to say: Take no notice, here I am; as a cat puts out a paw saying, Have you forgotten me?

And when Martha said: "You've simply gone under for a bit, that's all," she nodded quickly up and down, while her eyes filled with tears. But a moment later she shot Martha a melodramatic sideways hating look.

Lynda had come home, with Sandra, to the basement, less than six months after she had left it to learn independence.

She was now packing to move out again.

When asked how she was, she said: "I'm perfectly all right, thank you!" with a small trembling toss of the head.

But to Martha it seemed as if Lynda had at last been defeated. She did not talk now at all of doing without the drugs; she did not say "I know what I know" and "You have to keep silent" or make any of her small gestures of self-respect. She went once a week, as Sandra did, to see Dr. Bentin or an associate, and just as she and Dorothy had done, the two made a tight defensive alliance which no one could penetrate. The taking of medicines, sedatives, pep pills and sleeping pills regulated their days and nights.

Across the landing in Mark's bedroom, Rita was packing for him: they were off to North Africa in a few days. Martha had been listening (as she added pennies to pennies, shillings to shillings, pounds to pounds and—as this was money to do with the new Coldridge-Esse Perkins Scheme—hundreds of pounds to hundreds of pounds) while Rita sang, over and over again in a cradle-rocking croon: "Pack your bags and *get* Ferreira, pack your bags and *go*." But there had been silence for some time; from which Martha concluded they were making love. As Rita said, often enough: "Can you blame him! I mean, when you think his wife was never a true wife to him!"

Before Rita arrived Martha had dreamed—she couldn't make head or tail of it, though it was extremely vivid—that she went into Mark's bedroom and found Maisie naked, sitting up in bed by Mark, who was asleep. This was the Maisie of before the war, a fresh plump girl with tendrils of gold hair on a lush neck. "Martha," said this young corn goddess, "your trouble is, you've never given Mark what he wanted." "I know that, Maisie," dream-Martha had meekly replied. "But don't you see, I had to hold things together—don't you see that?" "Well, it's lucky you've got me, isn't it?" had said Maisie, lying on frilled pink pillows (in the most appalling taste) and extending a majestic white arm to curve around Mark. "Yes, thank you very much," had said dream-Martha. And woke, full of the wild painful grieving that only a dream can contain, full of memories of Thomas.

At the airport, what had walked through the barriers at Customs was a tall strong dark girl with short black hair in curls. The straight dark eyes, the strong black brows, of the Maynards gave Rita an arresting uncomfortable beauty. She was altogether too recisive in style for the taste of the sixties, which was for dollies, kittens, babies, schoolgirls, kewpies, space girls, little things of one sort and another. So Paul had told her the very first evening. "You'd better let me take you in hand," he said; to which she had replied: "Why?"

And indeed, why? And what was upsetting Mrs. Maynard? If Rita's clothes were wrong for London, then it was because they were painfully conventional, and too long, and had no fantasy. Her voice was heavily accented, but then it was bound to be. She wasn't at all elegant in any way—but when had the Maynards ever been that? In short, Martha found herself again brooding (exactly as she had when she was a girl) about the private standards the Maynards must set themselves and which no one else could be expected to share, and which had nothing at all to do with beauty, or kindness, or charm, or intelligence, and which, for the Maynards, were the only excellence that mattered. It was not conceivably possible that the Maynards were hoping to turn Rita into a lady?

Were they criticising her for not being one? It was only when Martha actually saw Rita that she realised how strong must be that obsession which she privately referred to as "the Blood of the Maynards." For getting on for twenty-five years, what dreams had been dreamed, what hopes encouraged, what lacks and needs felt, to make of Rita someone who needed urgent improvement?

She solved Martha's problem about how to greet a person she had not seen since babyhood by putting down her suitcase and flinging her arms around Martha's neck and kissing her. Almost she might have murmured: "At last, I've come home!" On the drive back to the house she talked—giving news after a long separation. She walked into the house with a look of such delighted fulfilment that it was impossible to tell her so soon it was probably going to be pulled down. And indeed, when she did hear this news, it was clear that it would be Rita who would suffer most about its death.

Mark was there for her first meal at the house, but he was self-absorbed in misery at that time, for he had just heard that Lynda planned to leave him. He hardly spoke, and it did not seem that Rita had taken much account of him.

Paul came in that evening, as handsome and as poised as usual, and after she had said: "Why?" the following dialogue took place.

"Because you won't do as you are."

"Do for what?"

"You could be absolutely super, I mean it!"

She looked at him. Onto her face slowly came a look of

569

purest frankest most confiding sexual confidence, like a page or two from a *True Love Confessions* magazine. He blushed, became pettish, and said spitefully: "You're quite sexy, I suppose."

"Thank you," said Rita, laughing heartily; for as she told Martha afterwards, she had not met anyone like him before.

"Well, if you won't change your hair and get some clothes *I'm* not going to take you out," said Paul.

Delicacy prevented her from saying that if he didn't, experience told her there would always be those who would.

He misunderstood her smiling silence, and pressed on: "I'll take you to see Madeleine tomorrow: she'll cut your hair."

Madeleine was London's second-most-fashionable hair-dresser, and a personal chum.

He now observed that she was embarrassed—but for him. It was not that he had not encountered before this a kindly embarrassment in a girl—he often did. But in Rita it was stunningly open, like a reproach from Demeter, or a young Boadicea.

He stood before her, as it were crying out: But I'm the epitome of what every sensible girl could want!

And she stood smiling her: You're very handsome but . . .

The two continued thus all evening, but in the end, rather kindly, she did agree to be taken shopping by him—no, not tomorrow because she was busy, "but soon, I promise."

Francis and Jill came to meet her; and invited her to visit them. She went. She had become part of the family. Mark said: She's welcome to it, but it's as if she were coming home?

Yes, it was; and in her manner, all the time, whatever she said or did, or whether she chatted away to Martha or to Mark or patronised Paul, there was a secret delighted confidence, as if she wore a magic talisman which she knew could not fail her.

Martha thought at first that her manner, the warm quick ease of it, was simply Maisie's being given—so to speak—its head, room to grow in sympathetic surroundings. For being brought up in that awful little mining town could have been no joke. And there was no doubt that her nature was all Maisie's, if her looks were all Maynard.

But Martha was wrong. She did not understand how wrong for some time, though she even tried something she always avoided (it was like eavesdropping or reading someone's letters!). She tried to overhear what Rita was thinking.

570

It was difficult: she was simply not on Rita's wavelength. And when she did manage to catch some phrases they sounded like dialogue from an old-fashioned romantic novel, all to do with "being found," "coming into her own," "her secret destiny" and so on.

At last it all came out, very late one night over cocoa and biscuits and cigarettes, in the kitchen.

Rita had been brought up by her granny until she was ten, in the town that had begun as a mining camp and which had kept the flavour of one when it became one of the colony's "towns"—five thousand white inhabitants every one of whom she knew by sight or by name, and a hundred thousand black inhabitants, whom she never saw at all. Everything revolved around the mine and the only entertainments were bars and the cinema. Here Rita went to school and saw her mother only occasionally. Then Maisie had made an extended visit. Presumably the good times were at last wearing thin, or she had discovered she loved her daughter. But she had stayed, and then married an engineer from the mine, and they had all four, granny, Rita, Maisie and the new husband, lived in the tiny tin-roofed shanty house where the view was the mining machinery across a sandy road, and a small garden full of zinnias and canna lilies. Then the granny had died; what this had meant to Rita was clear enough from her face as she told it. The marriage was neither successful nor particularly bad. Maisie drank a lot but was good-natured if slatternly. The engineer was given to drunken bouts, but he was kind to Rita, while nagging at Maisie for being fat and so lazy. There was a large picture of Maisie on Rita's dressing table: she had had an eye infection, had neglected it, and now wore a pink eyeshade permanently over one eye. Also, she had had a slight stroke, and her mouth dragged slightly, giving her a peevish sour look. But Rita had not spent much time after she was eleven in the mining town; for one day the Maynards appeared and had offered to pay to send Rita to boarding school with the nuns in the city. Maisie had made no objection. Rita then had been for eight years at the convent, had spent holidays with her mother, and even one holiday with the Maynards. But she couldn't stand Mrs. Maynard, she said: once was enough.

She was popular and social, did well enough at school not to attract attention, read enormous quantities of love magazines, was taken out often by Mr. Maynard to tea or to the pictures—and about the age of fifteen had understood the obvious fact that Mr. Maynard must be her father. She had always felt (she told Martha) that her real father was not the airman McGrew. Maisie when drunk sighed and wept and talked of the men she remembered and for a time it sounded to Rita as if "a red Communist from Greece" had been her father. "*In vino veritas*—as they say," said Rita; for her mother had once sworn that cross her heart and tell no lies, it wasn't Andrew.

And when Rita had made the step into a discovery, for she had only to look into the mirror to see the truth, and had said to Maisie: "I'm surprised Mrs. Maynard doesn't mind!"—all Maisie had said was: "Blood is thicker than water!"

And it had been left at that.

For years then, Maisie had been paid for, been taken out, been given treats and clothes by Mr. Maynard, her father—so she had felt it. And she would not again visit the house out of delicacy, for she did not wish to wound Mrs. Maynard. She was fond of Mr. Maynard, a dear old sweet man, she said he was. It seemed she imagined the uncontrollable passion of an elderly man saying goodbye to his youth, and herself its lucky fruit. Lucky it had been: her inheritance was the Maynards, and what they stood for, or had stood for. One day a letter, or a message, or a lawyer's announcement would arrive, a door would open, a road would become clear—and there she would be. And here she was, with her mother's old friend Martha, and this house was her future.

She did mention Binkie once: he was a bit silly, she thought. Not at all the kind of son for the Maynards. He did not get on with them. It must be terribly hard for them. Of course, men did drink, she knew that—being brought up in a mining town had taught her everything. But there was drinking and drinking. And his wife—did you ever meet her, Martha? Well, she's one of those civil-service types, you know, and really, those two boys of hers—she, Rita, had been out with one of them once, and that was enough. But she didn't like speaking ill of people.

So she went on: Maisie's daughter would not like to say straight out, "I'm not surprised that he prefers me, the daughter of his joy, to an idiot like Binkie and Binkie's unsatisfactory stepchildren," but that she fully understood and supported his preference was clear from her happy smile as she told how he, Mr. Maynard, always took her out, but never them, always remembered her birthday, and never let a Christmas go by. At which point Martha produced £800 in five-pound notes, to be spent as she wished. Tears filled her eyes: not surprised tears, of course not; she was one, she knew, to whom the good things would naturally come. "Oh he's so kind Martha, if you only knew how kind he was!"

Martha postponed the truth with the thought: Well, I'm sure it doesn't matter if I tell her later.

"He's always so kind to everyone. Caroline—you don't mind my mentioning her? Well, I saw her at school sometimes, but we weren't *really* friends, you know, they are civil-service types really, it's not my style. But one afternoon he took me and Caroline out together and then sometimes we saw each other like pals—sort of. He's good to her too. But not as much as to me. He visits their house a lot. He spends as much time there as he does at his own home. But I think for a person with a kind heart like him, a house without children must be a sad place. It often makes me sad when I think of him, the way he feels for Caroline and me. But if I say it myself, Martha, I know I'm his favourite. You can't help feeling these things."

To the middle-aged who have been dedicated to propositions like "The Truth will make you free" and so on, come very interesting moments, such as being confronted with Rita. It was not that Maisie's daughter would be shocked to hear that Mr. Maynard, now over seventy, still pursued his lifelong liaison with Mrs. Talbot, even when she was an ancient lady confined to bed with a nurse permanently in attendance—she was a bit dotty now, people said. Or that Mr. Maynard would have sentimental emotions on two counts for Caroline, Martha's daughter, his old mistress's daughter's stepchild. Of course not. She'd find it all very touching. Probably it was, too; probably it was Martha who was at fault. (She remembered being made to feel like this by Maisie, who would be incapable of doubting that the heart is always better than a nasty critical carping head.) And what did it matter that it was Binkie and not Mr. Maynard who had fathered Rita who almost certainly, like the old Maynards themselves, would be bound to believe that the Blood was the thing? And besides, who else had ever found Mr. Maynard sweet and kind? And besides, blood or no blood, who would want Binkie as a father if she could have Judge Maynard? Thus did the truth not so much go down with trumpets before Rita, as slink away, with something like an embarrassed smile. Martha was able to feel she ought to be shedding a tear or two for Mrs. Maynard, thus

573

cheated so finally out of a granddaughter—but whose fault was it?

What mattered was Rita, who was quite profoundly all right, though for what Martha could not stop wondering: where was this child of good fortune going to find anything to match her expectations?

Meanwhile, she took over the house without being asked: she felt, it seemed, that if a house was there to be run, then obviously it was her place to run it. She attended to those letters of Mark's which he and Martha found most irksome—for like many authors, he was expected to run a kind of private advice bureau on personal problems. Mark refused to touch them: Martha would sweat and suffer because what could one ever say to people who believed that a few words on a piece of paper could solve such tangles of misery? Rita had no such ridiculous inhibitions: she knew by instinct that what unhappy people needed was for someone to pay attention to them, and she wrote pages and pages of admirable advice to anyone who asked for it. ("You say you feel depressed when you think of your wasted life? That does no good! You must keep your chin up and think of others!") She also enjoyed London, but in her own way, which announced to some observers that she regarded all this as a prelude to a destiny. She got on with an extraordinary number of varied people, since Maisie's daughter would be bound to know that Graham Patten's unkind wit was due, like the old miner Saul Baines's grouchiness, to life's wounds. "People like that often have a sad heart, when all is said and done." Lynda, whom she was taken to visit, was "just like the wife of the postmaster at Gokwe, she has to go off into the loonybin sometimes when things get too much for her, like in the Christmas rush."

She went about with Paul. He was in love with her. She treated him with maternal firmness. He announced to everyone that he would marry Rita, who was exactly right for him. He took her to parties, to theatres, to all the new films, and she enjoyed them all: she was incapable of being bored. More, he took her out before she had decided that his taste in clothes was very good, and when she was still wearing her own. Not to mention her own hair. Taken to Madeleine, the genius with the scissors, by Paul, who said that at least she might *try*, she had said no, she would not have her hair straightened. Sensation! There was probably not one girl in London, apart from Rita, who had short curly hair: much worse than being crippled or ugly. Sitting in front of a mirror clutching her curls (to be fashionable and, indeed, almost compulsory a couple of years later) she had demanded why it was that at the dinner the night before there had been seven women aged between seventeen and seventy all with exactly the same haircut, "Madeleine's cut." Madeleine replied that "a hairstyle, like a fashion, must evolve logically from the style before." "Yes, but I like to be myself," said Rita.

At this act of rebellion Madeleine had brooded, while her scissors as it were meditated among Rita's curls. Then she had summoned a young man from the end of the *salon*. "Carlos," she had said decisively, "from now on you will be doing Miss er—what did you say your name was?—hair."

Rita then found herself before another mirror, with Carlos, his scissors poised to start work on "Just do what I've got now only better—after all, it stands to reason you'd do better than they do in Gokwe!" His scissors remained immobilised for minutes, while he struggled with himself, at last crying out that it was impossible for him to cut out of the current style—his scissors simply would *not* bring themselves to do it. Therefore, every time Rita entered a room, shocked or intrigued eyes turned to look at her curly head, and she instantly earned a reputation for great strength of character. "Yes," she said modestly, "but then I'm a Zambesian, we are independent by nature, though I can see that in London everybody has to be like everybody else, I mean, you're all brought up like that, aren't you?" This kind of thing caused furores of annoyance, but she was well able to deal with it. Politics were not, as she said, her concern, though she had given the colour question her attention early on in life. It was a pity that the blacks and the whites couldn't get to know each other as people, because then they would be bound to like each other, people did, when they really knew each other, didn't they? Sometimes she did feel like smacking certain people's bottoms for them, she wasn't going to say whose, but where there was a will there was a way, and she was sure good would come out in the end.

On the basis that she was very original, she and Paul were invited everywhere. At last he proposed, formally, on an occasion prepared for and worked up to. She refused, saying that her heart belonged to another.

Paul took this very badly: probably nothing worse had happened to him since his mother had died. He put a good face on it, but was rather ill, and went away by himself to recover. Yet Rita's refusal, and its manner, did in fact hold its own cure.

The thing was that Paul had been living for years in a sexual or romantic mirage. Many men do, and this is due entirely to women's kind hearts (or their cowardice, what you will) because they can so seldom bring themselves to say: No, no, you're ugly; you're unsubtle; you snore; you've bad breath; you can't make love; or I don't like the way you talk about your wife. Now Paul was very handsome. Sex, above all in this London (and he'd never known another) where everyone was young and everyone made love or sex, was something that he had known he must do, or at least appear to do. (The girl with whom he spent, still, most of his time and to whom he always returned was Zena, whom he never took out, but in whose arms he might spend chaste nights.) Otherwise a thousand women had been to bed with him once, but had discovered they loved their husbands or former lovers; or had just that week decided on monogamy or a regular love, or were unfortunately not feeling well, or felt towards him like a sister. Or if they knew other women who had been to bed with him would not go to bed with him at all—no, no, it was not that he wasn't as attractive as twenty sheiks rolled into one, but appearances were deceptive and gossip a liar—actually they were virgins.

Rita said to him: "But Paul, you and I wouldn't be suited, you see, because I wouldn't marry a man who didn't like a lot of kissing and cuddling."

"But how do you know what I like?" said Paul. "You won't go to bed with me!"

"Oh now don't be so silly, Paul. Why do you put on an act with me? I feel really hurt about that, I do, honestly."

"But I don't see why you say that."

"Oh Paul, do stop it. Your trouble is, you aren't being realistic, I mean, it's silly, isn't it? Because nothing but unhappiness will come of it. No, what you have to do is to find a nice warmhearted girl—older than you would be a good idea, but she shouldn't be too keen on that kind of thing, I mean, a lot of girls aren't, they just pretend to be, because they want people to think well of them. But you aren't passionate, Paul, you see. You are affectionate, you've got a warm heart, but you aren't a passionate person. So that's what you have to do. You want to find a girl who wants a man to be very kind so that she can be kind back, but she shouldn't want to make love much, because you wouldn't like that, not really."

Paul having departed, Rita was without an escort: it was only now that it became evident that this was how she had seen him. Poor Paul had been made use of: girls made use of him. Also, he had been a shield, for Rita did not accept any of the young men who now presented themselves. She was much at home, a daughter in the house, helpful to Martha and to Mark. Or she might ring up Lynda in Paul's house, and invite herself to tea: there, she offered to run errands, liking, as she said, to be of use. Meanwhile they— the older women—watched, without much verbal comment, that marvellous phenomenon, the singleminded ruthlessness of the female in full confident pursuit, though so far were aims of self-knowledge on parallel lines that she was all passivity, secret sighing tears, and dramatic loss of weight. (Needing to lose weight, she was all the better for it.)

Nor must it be thought that Mark was oblivious. On the contrary. He said that the girl had a crush on him and it was very flattering to a man of his age. He might say this in Martha's bed, for she was comforting him for the loss of Lynda—though he was still trying to persuade himself she would come back; and he was comforting her because she was depressed, knowing that her life was about to blow itself into a new shape, with no idea at all how or when.

But it got on his nerves, he said, having those lovelorn eyes fixed on him day and night; couldn't the hussy be got out of the place somehow? He needed all his energy for his schemes for the future, and one of these days that girl'd find herself raped; he was only flesh and blood after all, and if one more time he found her draped all over his bed in a nightie darning his socks, he wouldn't answer for the consequences. So they joked.

Graham Patten was telephoned. He, in the grip of a fearsome passion for his first wife (they were about to marry each other again), said he could not assist personally, but would see what could be done to widen her interests. Rita then entered Graham's territory for a while. After a couple of weeks he telephoned to say that he knew earthwomen were *in*, but the trouble was, peasants were always politically so reactionary, and he had his reputation as a Marxist to protect.

What had happened was this. It goes without saying that all fashionable parties at that time were stocked entirely with progressives concerned with the state of affairs in Zambesia. A young woman had darted up to Rita and exclaimed that she, Rita, ought to be ashamed of herself but that "history would soon have its revenge." Rita had instantly replied, on a reflex action, with a whole series of statements full of flaming moralistic fervour and uplift, like Jefferson, or Wilberforce. At which the young woman had embraced her as a freedom fighter and invited her to speak on a platform next weekend. Rita said no, but was talked into it: she was a girl who could not withstand being told she was irresponsible. On a platform of the Free Zambesia movement, Rita then delivered herself of a lot more rhetorical statements to do with freedom and liberty to an audience warmly welcoming this precious creature, a white liberal. Only slowly did it dawn on them that she was in fact a firm supporter of the rebel regime in Zambesia. Confusion all around, and apologies from both sides—proving Rita's point that people could like each other ... the trouble was that the education of the young Free Zambesians had not included the information that—to simplify—a young Nazi in 1938, say, would not have said: "I am a brutal racist who will lay Europe in ruins and end freedom in our time." On the contrary, he would have sounded—like Jefferson. As for Rita, she had heard the young white Zambesians stating their position in high moral and idealistic terms and had been attracted by the sentiments. These she reproduced, on request. This experience more than ever determined her to eschew politics, particularly as the Free Zambesians rang up Graham Patten to complain about his friends ... he forgave Rita on condition she wouldn't do it again. This led to the next, and crucial, incident. Rita was at a party attended by the essence of the screen and stage (vintage 1958 matured) and, attacked yet again as a Fascist, she saw that the young woman who was doing the attacking was in fact a young man. She began to mutter something defensive about the bottoms of both sides black and white needing to be smacked, received an unintelligible reply, and went off by herself to sit in a corner and observe the scene. First she saw that there were practically no women present at all, appearances to the contrary notwithstanding. Then she saw that the guests were in fact the casts of the plays she had seen the night before and the night before that—*Romeo and Juliet* and *Othello*, both with all-male casts. The theatres and the actors being world-famous, that she was finding the scene before her eyes repulsive upset her—though she did not wish to be old-fashioned. She looked for Graham, who, comfortingly, was in love with a woman, even if confusingly—but he and his wife had quarrelled and had left the party separately, sulking.

She was rescued by a man (she examined him carefully to make sure he was not merely dressed as one) who asked her to go and have some coffee and cheer up—"he wasn't political either." Rita, well out of her depth and tending towards tears, felt that this was probably a hero (since heroes were kind) and she confided to him all her moral dubieties. He was extremely witty. Rita knew that he was being witty, and enjoyed it, but on one occasion said: "Please make your jokes more slowly, it's not that I don't get them, it's just that people aren't so sophisticated where I come from." So he did. He took her to supper where Graham and his ex-mistress but one were paying out his ex-and-future wife and her present lover by being seen together where she (the wife) was bound to be—this restaurant was always the scene of these marital tiffs. Rita told her new friend that for her part when she got married, she intended it to be for good. He said that in his opinion she was quite right. Rita then went home with this consolingly integritous man to his flat, where she soon found herself altogether at sea. It was clear that they were going to make love, for he said that they were; and indeed they got into bed at last, where he made a great many more witty remarks, all to do with bottoms and bosoms, and his inclination towards one, but not the other. Finally having said that it was entirely his misfortune but alas she had too much of both, he played to her some Bach on his record player, and in the morning when they woke up, a brisk girl secretary was bringing them breakfast in bed, quite undiscomposed by seeing Rita there. When her host had gone to the bathroom, Rita got out of bed to look at herself in the mirror (for as she said to Martha later, she could hardly believe this was happening to her); she saw ranged in a row beside the bed four riding whips graded in sizes. It was not that Rita was ignorant about dear old London; after all, she had been around in it for months now (though more in pop and boutique and television circles where as she said she thought things were more old-fashioned) but she found it very hard to connect whips with herself. "I kept thinking: but I don't like horses. I don't like horsy men." Finally, as the secretary entered with the *Times*, and the announcement that Mr. Bravington Poles-Warren would soon be out of the bath, Rita understood that she was sitting naked on a gilt chair in front of the mirror, and the secretary was briskly putting away whips as if filing papers. It occurred to Rita that the whips had been put out to impress the secretary: there had been no suggestions that she, Rita, was to be, or should have been, whipped. She examined the secretary—who seemed a perfectly ordinary girl. But perhaps she was just a poor girl who needed to earn a large salary to support a widowed mother or something like that. Rita thought of her companion of the night before, and kept saying to herself, over and over again, That poor thing, he must have had an unhappy childhood and be wearing a brave smile over a sad heart; but after she had bathed, he took her down to find a taxi, and insisted on taking her into the sweet shop immediately below where he lived, and, saying good morning darling, good morning Petronella, good morning sweet, good morning George, to the salespeople, he bought Rita an enormous box of Continental chocolates. Once again Rita understood this was not for her benefit, but a sort of showing off to the salespeople.

Suddenly Rita cracked, having preserved the most gentle and good-humoured tact throughout a trying night and morning. She said in front of everyone in the shop: "You're only buying me those because you want everyone to know that I spent last night with you. How many girls have you brought in here beaten black and blue? Well, if you think real men have to beat girls, then you'd better meet one." At which she strode out, all hot tears.

At home she said to Mark that she didn't think Graham's friends were very nice: she was broad-minded she hoped.

She wept. She was very low. She put her arms around Martha's neck like a small girl and said she didn't know why it was but she just want to cry and cry. Found by Mark on his bed putting buttons on his shirts, in wan tearful beauty and pale blue georgette, she told him the whole story, and, one thing leading to another . . .

Martha, adding pennies to pennies, hundreds of pounds to hundreds of pounds, was thinking as she half listened to what was almost certainly a love-silence from next door: I wonder if Rita has remembered that she probably won't be able to buy disposable nappies in . . . But they weren't yet absolutely certain where they were going: it was some small village on the edge of a semi-desert.

Mark's Memorandum to Myself (still unfinished) continued:

"6. Therefore, groups of people aware of this situation should set themselves to make flexible preparations based on the fact that within 2 years, probably ten, or fifteen, one, two, or three areas of the world, *almost certainly heavily populated ones* (see maps **B** and **Ba** and Dorothy's notes), will become uninhabitable, permanently or temporarily.

"7. Any preparations made will have to take into account the inevitable hostility of governments, expressed subtly rather than openly. This means that any organisation will have to be scientifically self-sufficient. But this is again an age of mercenaries—we can hire what we need.

"8. Locations must be found in parts of the world less vulnerable to contamination by wind, rain, etc. and prepared for large numbers of people.

"9. Preparations should probably also be military. If there is one thing certain it is that everyone will be in a state of panic, as rumours, counter-rumours, denials by authority, multiply while catastrophes occur, nearly occur, half occur. Muddle will be the keynote.

"10. The first thing, then, is to get money.

"11. In order to do this we need . . ."

The fund had started with the promise of Mark's share of the £5,000 from the sale of this house. Rita offered what was left of £800. Martha who had continued to spend little and earn well all these years, contributed £2,000, reflecting, as citizens do on these occasions, that such a large sum to her would buy a few postage stamps for the organisation. It was all very heart-warming, but hardly enough to set up machinery which Mark saw rescuing large groups of people from death and disaster. It was enough, however, to hire scientific advice, which turned out to be Jimmy Wood's. Mark had severed connection with him by simply withdrawing from the factory: someone else had bought it, and Jimmy remained in charge. Mark had told Jimmy why he could no longer work with him. Jimmy had said that he was sorry. A week later he had turned up at the Radlett Street house as if nothing had happened to say that he had a very exciting idea for a new device which . . . What had happened was that his new partner, or employer, had not yet understood that Jimmy would not work unless fed by talk, so Jimmy was coming to Mark to get talk. It was only then that Mark really understood, really believed, that there are people who cannot be judged morally. They are not responsible for their actions. Jimmy being much around, he was asked for advice—but the problem was, one could not ask Jimmy's advice on this or that problem to do with germ warfare, fallout, air pollution, etc., etc., except in the vaguest of terms. Because anyone had only to say to Jimmy: I hear that you are involved with some crack-brained seditious scheme for . . . and if this person talked enough, Jimmy would talk back—he couldn't help doing this. Mark therefore postulated an imaginary novel which involved certain hazards: Jimmy was infinitely obliging with his advice.

Now Jimmy was also a bit of a literary celebrity in his own way: he was one day in a pub talking about a new book of his own to a couple of journalists, when he chanced to mention Mark Coldridge, saying that Mark planned a new novel about such and such. Mark, asked by one of these journalists about the new book, thought, Why not? It's a good enough screen while one makes enquiries and works things out. It sounds, said this friendly young man (for journalists had infinitely changed since the bad old days: invasions of privacy, bad manners, bullying of any kind had long since been forgotten, were altogether obsolete, under the new dispensation of the Press Council), as if it might be a sequel to *A City in the Desert.* True, said Mark, it might very well be. "And has it got a name?" Mark replied (but after all it is not everyone who can make up good jokes on the spur of the moment) " 'Son of the City.' " " 'The Sun City'?" "Yes, why not?"

A paragraph appeared in a gossip column, and that was that. Not quite. Weeks later Mark got an agitated letter from a certain Wilhelm Esse Perkins, an American industrialist, who had read this paragraph (he was much addicted to London and English culture and always followed its newspapers) while on a business weekend in Peru. He wished to meet Mark, and was quite prepared to fly over to London to meet him, if that was agreeable. It appeared that something in that paragraph had "gone right home." At any rate, Mr. Perkins had bought a copy of *A City in the Desert* as soon as he returned to New York, and even before finishing reading it—but Mark must not think he was by nature an impulsive man—had decided that Mark was the man to help him build an ideal city on the lines laid down in Mark's book. He had always been a believer in an enlightened despotism, he said. He saw his task as providing money, and Mark's as planning and building this city. They would then create some kind of committee or trust (elected from suitable interested people, but the details could always be worked out later) whose function it would be to choose an enlightened despot. They would advertise for applicants for this post in a normal manner, go about it all quite openly and without pulling their punches, and above all, taking their time, because clearly, that the despot should be the right man for the job was a key point.

All this Mr. Perkins had told Mark within half an hour of arriving in London, which he did a day after getting Mark's letter saying he looked forward to meeting Mr. Perkins when next—etc.

But why was Wilhelm Esse Perkins so anxious to rashly risk all his money on such philanthropies? It was simple: he was in the grip of a sudden conversion of the type which was to be so common in the seventies. What had touched it off was that he had chanced to read a secret and confidential report (kept from the owners by the chemists they employed) on the results of certain chemical research in a factory where he had his shares. God forbid that it should be thought that Mark's modest little factory (with a capital of £15,000) or that the products of that factory (some machines for hospitals, a few devices for the manipulation and rearrangement or obliteration of human or animal brains) should be compared with the fortune and activities of Mr. Perkins, who was many many times a millionaire and the products of whose laboratories influenced the health of continents; but what had happened to Mark had happened to Mr. Perkins—that they should discover this only after actually being drawn together (like being attracted to like) caused neither more surprise than is common when such things occur in life. Mark began by seeing Mr. Perkins as a man afflicted by a sudden case of inappropriate morality (for so do other people's attempts towards truth always strike us) but soon saw (it was Rita who kept exclaiming in awe at the amount of money he had) that after all, this man might be the solution to his problem. The trouble was (when they first met, at least) there seemed to be not one aim shared by them; they had in common only a cause for remorse. However, as they talked and they talked, it was always in Mark's study, so persuasive in any discussions that took place there; and it became evident that their aims were not so far apart after all. Mr. Perkins would have to shed his visions of the city beautiful, since the future was not likely to include one; Mark would have to accept a benevolent dictator—it occurred to him that he had already: he was quite prepared to spend the rest of his life (which he felt would be short) on this scheme. What Mr. Perkins needed was *to do good:* the nature of the good to be done was pretty irrelevant to him when one got down to it. What Mark needed was money.

The time Mark spent with Mr. Perkins in his study had resulted in a large tract of unfortunately very dry sand being acquired in Tunisia. They did not own it; at least not yet; but they had permission to build on it. They were at cross-purposes with the government, who saw them as particularly devious holiday speculators; for why anyone would want to build a holiday resort in a desert was not immediately clear. An army of spies and informers and information-mongers of all kinds were busy with finding out what the Coldridge-Perkins company was really up to: nobody believed them when they said what they were doing.

Which, admittedly, was mostly to talk; at least, at the moment. Mark was once again back in another version of the unconstituted committee.

And, in three days' time, Mark and Rita would take off for a village of a few hundred souls in North Africa where, soon, Patty Samuels and John Patten would join them. Both had decided to devote themselves to this work. They and Willy Perkins would in the next few months set up an office and organisation in London; and another in America; while Mark and Rita brought their new baby into the world well out of England (the divorce with Lynda would not be through for some months) and engaged suitable natives (people who lived in, or were familiar with, the local terrain) and generally acclimatised themselves to what in their plans was called Point A. Point B, probably on the west coast of Ireland, was to be developed next. A Point C was envisaged.

A great deal of money would shortly be available: the person who inherited Martha's position—Patty Samuels?—would be adding millions of pounds to millions of pounds. But of course by then the thing would be so large that it would need battalions of lawyers and accountants: already Willy Perkins had bought himself a couple of first-quality lawyers in New York who were doing nothing else but envisage difficulties.

This afternoon and evening, one of the last probably for Martha in Coldridge territory, was likely to prove an apex of complication and emotional cross-purposing.

Weeks ago, when John Patten had told his wife that he felt he could contribute usefully to the new scheme, Margaret had said that of course he must not worry about her. She meant it. She would miss his courteous attendance on the fringes of her social life; but living side by side as they had for years, trying to be kind about each other's needs

584

which they could not meet, made both unhappy. He said he would leave the house for her to use as she liked: for his part he did not expect to be much in England.

Now an elderly, almost an old man, who for so long had impressed everyone with his damped-down carefulness that they had forgotten he must once have had something to damp down, he had come to life suddenly in a late burst of energy, was learning Arabic, had shed fifteen years. Margaret's reaction to learning that she would be living alone was to shed fifteen years, buy herself new clothes and have the house repainted. The two forgave each other for being so pleased to separate.

Margaret had said: We'll have a big send-off party for all of you. This was generous, for she did not approve of or share the new enthusiasm. But, having committed herself to a party, she took to lying awake at night to brood about the sad fortunes of her family—for who was she to ask?

Mark and—who? Margaret could not stand Rita, but saw that there ought to be a marriage for the baby's sake. She had never liked Lynda, but wondered if Lynda ought to be asked with Rita. This annoyed Mark, because of *course* Lynda should be asked.

And who, after all, was Margaret to disapprove? (She conceded this quickly before someone, probably Francis, had time to point it out.) When Oscar Enroyde came to England he would stay with his current wife at Margaret's; and she and John and Oscar and whoever it was found the rewards of being civilised worth any pain or embarrassment. Very well then, Lynda and Rita would both come, and so would Martha. There was Sandra . . . no, that was asking too much, there Margaret would draw the line. Dorothy had been bad; Sandra was awful. So Lynda was asked without her friend and replied that without her she would not go. Mark then complained to Margaret who extended the invitation to Sandra: but it was no good, neither would come.

Francis was asked with Jill, but Margaret had added that she hoped "not more than half the menagerie at most" would find time to come. Francis had returned the answer that they were moving that day "as it happened" and the menagerie would be too busy to come. Later it turned out that there would be a great party in Margaret's room to which at least a hundred young people had been invited.

Margaret, hearing about this, had rung up Francis in tearful accusation. Francis had said he quite agreed two

585

parties were absurd: he could perhaps bring his friends out to her house?

So there were going to be two parties.

Yesterday Margaret had telephoned to say that they must not expect too much—hers would be a small informal gathering: quite clearly no one really wanted to come to her party at all.

It was natural she should be feeling irritable and sad: the word went out that "everyone" had to go to her party even if only for an hour.

The first carload to leave was Mark, Rita, Paul, Jill. Rita, six months pregnant, was in magenta chiffon. Paul had chosen the dress. Paul chose all her clothes. She looked gorgeous, they all said; and she did.

Lynda came up from the basement to say—it was clear she had hoped to say it more publicly—that she would not come. She found Martha in her bedroom.

Martha let her adjust her manner from the one which had been prepared to what she hoped would be at least an attempt at Lynda at her best. But Lynda was tired with packing, and had not slept. She had come up unkempt, fingers torn and raw, and had found only Martha, with whom she needn't bother to be defiant about Sandra, but to whom she had already said everything she wanted to say.

She sat down and watched Martha put on a rather dull dress of the kind that is "suitable" for a variety of occasions.

So Martha wasn't at her best either.

In the mirror Martha saw Lynda's face at an angle to hers: it was looking past her out at the sycamore tree.

Lynda said: "Do you know what you are going to do yet?"

She sounded perfectly sensible. A black cat, the old black cat's successor, stalked around the corner of the door and got up onto her lap.

"Not yet."

Lynda and she had already had this conversation: they were making some sort of small talk now.

"I suppose you hate Sandra like everyone else, so it's no use asking you to stay with us while you are at a loose end."

"I don't mind being at a loose end."

Well over fifteen years ago Martha had arrived in London without an idea of what she was going to do, and everything had followed quite naturally.

She had said to Lynda: "I stepped into the dark then. I'll
586

do it again now. Why not? Doing it then I landed with you lot. I could have done worse."

"Not much," Lynda had said, and had giggled.

Remembering this conversation Lynda started giggling, and Martha laughed too.

"Mark wants me to go and help him with his refugee camps," said Lynda.

"Yes, I know. And me too. Perhaps I'll go—after all, I suppose it would be useful."

"Not really."

"Who knows?"

"I do," said Lynda seriously. But, as Martha looked away from the mirror, and straight at Lynda, to meet this, Lynda stood up, hastily, with a quick frowning evasive look, scooped up a cigarette from Martha's box, and said: "I'm sorry if Margaret is going to be hurt about my not coming, but she'll have so many people she won't notice."

She went downstairs.

From her door (soon to be whose door?) Martha shouted upstairs: "Francis, Francis, are you ready?"

"Coming."

But he did not come. So she went downstairs to wait in Margaret's room for him, and for the others—Phoebe and Gwen were going with them.

In Margaret's room a nice-faced boy and a pretty dark girl put out great flasks of wine coloured gold, red and pink for tonight's party.

She had not seen them before. Had they moved in too?

If so, where were they going to find room to ... but it was no longer her business. She had lost the capacity to care. Oh yes, she really was on her way out and away. No longer was this house her responsibility; she contributed nothing, held nothing together—the holding operation was long over.

A pang? Only a mild one.

She would not mind going.

She would not mind—what would it be? Living in a bed-sitting room again? A small hotel?

No, all that was no problem, did not trouble her. Her secret preoccupation was (she might have shared it with Lynda once, but not now) that she had made no step forward at all since that last "bout" or "session" just before Rita's coming all those months ago. She had gone thick and opaque again. Her dreams, faithful monitors, kept her informed of what was going on, but that was a dull enough record. Her other senses were strictly utilitarian and there were no surprises anywhere.

And people too were thick and opaque; and it was not easy to be with them. She could look at them and think: I know that's not what you are, I know that—what are you then? This couple at the end of the room, for instance, arranging glasses in rows beside the wine flasks, the fair open-faced boy, and the pretty girl—well, that was what they were, there weren't any currents running.

Still, she had learned that one thing, that most important thing, which was that one simply had to go on, take one step after another: this process in itself held the keys. And it was this process which would, as it had in the past, be bound to lead her around to that point where—asking continuously, softly, under one's breath, Where, What is is it? How? What's next? Where is the man or woman who—she would find herself back with herself. Of course. But there are times, there are indeed times, when to put one foot soberly after another seems harder than to wrestle with devils or challenge dangers—which in retrospect seemed tame enough. She had forgotten, then? Yes, her memory of the last time had blunted. She remembered everything except—how frightened she had been. Well, that was a mistake, a danger in itself. She was forgetting, she had forgotten, one always forgot . . .

Into the room came Francis, rather larger than he had been, a generously built, round-faced, ruffle-haired young man who carried a weight of responsibility and showed it.

"Martha," he said, "I'm ready if you are." To the unknown pair he said easily: "I'll be back in at eight. You could get that rice cooked up with stock and put on some soup. And could you please go and see that the babies are all right in about half an hour? Leslie's got to leave then, and Claire says she's fed up with baby-minding."

They accepted this instructions; and he escorted Martha down to the car, where Gwen was, with Phoebe. Mother and daughter began conversing, with the best of good intentions: this carload arrived at the house in silence.

It was immediately clear that a very large party was in progress.

From the darkening house light glimmered intimately onto lawns where a crowd strolled among the roses who said they were there only by their scent. As the party passed through the house to catch the last hour of dusk, every room was bright and crammed with people.

A hot bright noisy jostling house; but on the slopes to the river were hushed voices and faces turned towards the sky.

If one is a hostess—then that is what one is. Margaret's first generous impulse had envisaged a splendour of a party for her son and his new plan. But this guest list had dwindled in the old irritations and checks. At the idea of a small party every instinct went into insubordination.

There must be two or three hundred people here, and of a most extraordinary variety. Groups of strangers kept passing each other; and the most frequently used words were: "Who is that, do you know?" The least numerous guests were those for whom the impulse had first sprung. The "family" were hardly there, or came and went away early.

The Arts, as had been the case for many years now, predominated; particularly the theatre in all its forms, with the cinema and the television. There were some ballet dancers, a couple of choreographers, a new soprano from Wales.

Graham sat in a corner with an Indian film director, a Polish film director, a Russian poet, and an American poet. The apparent stars of the party, however, were not these, but a couple of veterans of the peace movement who had just returned from North Vietnam: their expenses had been paid by the *Daily X*, whose editor was Miles Tangin. They were in discussion with a couple of young men, relations of Oscar Enroyde, who had ended their stint of fighting in Vietnam, one wounded in the hip, one whole. Graham, while conducting the conversation in his group, looked across towards this one, planning how to get them onto a television programme to continue or repeat this discussion (amicable) for the benefit of the public.

In another room Rosa Mellendip was in conversation with one of her clients, a man who ran a chain of holiday camps around the Mediterranean. She, with her vital face, white hair, and a strong-minded white suit like a uniform of service, dominated a room (full of people hoping to catch her eye for free advice, as they used to do for psychoanalysts) and made this very rich and able man (self-made, still on the way up) appear like a suppliant.

But it was not here that the practised Margaret-watchers were looking for auguries.

On a low stone wall by a sunk garden Martha found Mark sitting, and she sat by him. Rita was flirting maternally with Paul some yards away. Gwen was telling a young American who did not wish to fight in Vietnam that there was plenty of room for him and his friends in Radlett Street. Phoebe was explaining to John Patten that he was evading his responsibilities by going to North Africa; he ought to be canvassing for the Labour Party by-election due in this area next month.

Margaret was sitting under a large oak tree beside a couple of bishops and a mini-Royal with her ex-commoner husband. With them was Oscar Enroyde, and an associate from this side of the Atlantic, a key man in the Associated Federation of Industries of the British Isles. There were a couple of other discreetly powerful looking people, among them Hilary Marsh, now retired from the Foreign Office, but with a mild job as adviser to industrialists about certain tricky international problems.

A dozen or so paces away, this group were only just visible, and their voices were a pleasant murmur.

"Well," said Mark, "there it is."

"I'm afraid so," said Martha.

Many years ago, in one of the unconstituted committees—which? ah, yes, it had been when "everyone" was a Communist—Britain's version of a Fascist phase had been competently forecast. There it was now on the wings, ready to come on, gentlemanly, bland, vicious. There it was: big business, backed by the landowning landlording Church (its face, however, would be chummy, slangy, modern, tolerant) and Royalty, solidly and narrowly traditional (its face easy-going, goodfellow, amiable) and all taking orders from America—not of course directly, anything open and straightforward being inimical to the spirit of these ancient partners, but indirectly, through groups of international bankers and vaguely named and constituted advisers.

As they watched, Graham Patten emerged from the house: he stood on the terrace with the light behind him to survey the disposition of the garden, then descended into a dark patch to emerge in the half-light of Margaret's group. He joined them. They caught the phrase (he was talking to a bishop known for his progressive theological outlook): ". . . and if you could join in the dialogue then I'm sure . . ." After him, from the house, wafted a cloud of poets and writers and artists and pop singers which settled on the dewy grass around those so solidly shod feet.

"I wouldn't be at all surprised," said Martha.

"I'm afraid so," said Mark.

Here a purple billow materialised from the dark, and Rita inserted herself between them, kissing and hugging them as she sat down. "I'll go home with Paul," she said. "You don't want to come yet, do you?"

On her knees rested the unknown baby, and she held strong young arms carefully around the bulge.

"Oh I've had enough," said Mark. He got up. Martha watched Francis collecting his carload, Mark collecting his. They had forgotten her? No, Francis ran across to ask if she wanted to come yet. Martha said she would get a lift back in later. She walked up and down the long lawns that were springy and wet under great trees, while one after another people moved past her into the house. The stars came out.

Now the voices and the sound of movement were gone, and the stream could be heard running quietly under its banks. The air was full of the scent of water and of flowers.

She walked, quiet, while the house began to reverberate: a band had started up. She walked beside the river while the music thudded, feeling herself as a heavy impervious insensitive lump that, like a planet doomed always to be dark on one side, had vision in front only, a myopic searchlight blind except for the tiny three-dimensional path open immediately before her eyes in which the outline of a tree, a rose, emerged, then submerged in dark. She thought, with the dove's voices of her solitude: Where? But *where*. How? Who? No, but *where*, where ... Then silence and the birth of a repetition: *Where?* Here. Here?

Here, where else, you fool, you poor fool, where else has it been, ever ...

APPENDIX

Appendix

R.A.F. MAN "VICTIM OF PORTON NERVE GAS"

(Report in *The Observer*, August 11, 1968)

The Ministry of Defence has admitted that a former R.A.F. flight-lieutenant, Mr. William Cockayne, aged 50, was a victim of nerve gas exposure, while serving as an armaments officer at Porton Down.

The admission came last week in a letter to Mr. James Dickens, MP for Lewisham West.

It says: "While at Porton he reported sick twice to the small hospital there. On the first occasion, on 5 August 1953, he was suffering from myosis [contraction of the pupils] caused by a mild exposure to a nerve agent. He was treated for this with codeine and there was no recurrence of the complaint.

"Almost certainly this mild exposure occurred as a result of a field experiment to assess the vulnerability of tanks, which records show took place on 5th August 1953. It was not unknown for members of the Porton staff at the time to suffer mild myosis as a result of small accidental exposures to agents; recovery was normally complete within a few hours without any treatment at all."

Mr. Dickens is now pressing the Ministry of Social Security to allow a nerve gas specialist to make a fresh examination. Mr. Cockayne has spent 14 years trying to establish the cause of a series of nervous breakdowns. He has tried three times to commit suicide.

He served in the secret weapons department at the chemical and microbiological establishments at Porton from 1952 to 1954. In 1952 Churchill called for a special department to be set up at Porton to develop a gas weapons system. The department did not, according to Cockayne, come under the Ministry or the Services, but was answerable only to 10 Downing Street.

595

"The problem was to develop a weapon that would cover as large an area as possible," he claims. "A crop-spraying device from an aircraft covers only a very limited area. I had nothing to do with tanks at Porton. That was the Army's job."

Cockayne's explanation of how the accident happened is that, one evening in the middle of a mess party, he agreed to escort a scientist from the mess to his laboratory.

"The scientist was a bit drunk. When we got to the lab, he opened one of the jars, unscrewed the glass cap—it was still sealed with a rubber top—and said. 'Here's the filthy stuff,' or some such words, 'there's enough here to wipe out Salisbury. Go on, take a sniff.'

"Like a fool I did. An involuntary action I suppose. The next thing I knew was that I'd collapsed on the path to the squash courts and had to crawl back to my billet."

Although there is at present no evidence that the exposure to gas, however it happened, was the cause of the breakdown which followed it, Cockayne has been a sick man virtually ever since, plagued by irrational attacks of depression (a symptom of nerve-gas poisoning).

Several doctors have examined him without being able to identify any specific cause for his condition. At one time he was treated as an alcoholic.

His problem has been to persuade people to take seriously what seemed, on the face of it, to be a sick man's fantasy.

The Ministry letter says: "There is no record that when he resigned from the R.A.F. in 1954 be made any complaint about his health having suffered from nerve-gas poisoning. Nor is there any evidence that he suffered any lasting ill-effects from the mild dose of nerve-gas poisoning in 1953."

> *Various documents, private and official, dated between 1995 and 2000, in the possession of Amanda, Francis Coldridge's stepdaughter, destroyed by her before the Northern National Area (formerly North China) was overrun by the Mongolian National Area.*

I. APPEAL

It is requested that survivors from Destroyed Area II (British Isles) should write down as much as they can remember, *as they personally experienced them*, of the events leading up to the catastrophe, the weeks of the crisis, and their subsequent escape. It is of course generally realised that the destruction of historical material and artifacts from which history can be recreated has been very great, since so many of the world's great museums, libraries and archives are either destroyed, or contaminated and unreachable being temporarily or permanently sealed. People everywhere have been magnificently cooperative and generous with their time. But the available material for the recording of the last thirty years is scant and scattered. *It is emphasised:* what is needed is personal recollection, in the greatest possible detail, with names, dates, places. This material should be handed in, or posted to, the embassies of the Mongolian National Area in any city throughout the world.

Signed: [illegible]
For the Preserver of Historical Studies,
Mongolian National Area

II.

From X30 (Francis Coldridge, working as Deputy Head of the Reconstitution and Rehabilitation Area, near Nairobi), to X32 (Amanda, nee Coldridge, wife of Mao Yuan, working as a clerk in the temporary administration), enclosing Document I (above). [In the following letters codes were used for all names of places, persons, also dates. Names have been replaced where they are likely to be familiar to the reader.]

Dearest Amanda,

These documents seem to be everywhere: to my knowledge all over Africa and I *gather* over North and South America. In America they are as from the Mexican Central Government. I am sending them in case you have not seen them. For if not you soon will. I *gather* that there is no official contact between your third of China and the Mongolian National Area, between you and the Southern National Area—nor between these two areas. In short, the joke that China is repeating previous epochs in a pattern of warlords ruling territories with rapidly changing frontiers is true? Also that all written material exchanges through the mediation of people planted in various armies—since there is little movement except by the military? See therefore that our people in your National Area, and in the Southern National Area, and in the Mongolian National Area (*these above all*), are

597

warned that this appeal is a method of extracting names and information with a view to immobilising or exterminating us. The older people will hardly need a warning—but the younger people? Is it any less true, even after the experience of the last decades, that the human race cannot learn from experience?

See that the following information is spread *and absorbed*. The mass of the human race has never had a memory. History, the activities of historians, has always been a sort of substitute memory, an approximation to actual events. In some epochs this false memory has been nearer to events; in others very far—*sometimes by design*. Previous deliberate creations have been for instance when the officials of the young Christian Church destroyed or sufficiently distorted the facts of what the first Christians were really teaching; and such records as there are of the activities of the Inquisition (most particularly the official reasons for the destruction of the Albigensians); and the suppression of witchcraft. At such times "history" becomes a deliberate distortion instead of, as it usually is, the dirty smoke left in the air after the fire of events. The real facts are committed to memory and passed on verbally; or written down and concealed for the information of the few. The deliberate creation of false history is taking place now on your borders in the National Area of Mongolia; in Mexico; in Brazil; and in Kenya (the new ruling points of the world) because of what emerged into ordinary human knowledge—that is, the consciousness of the man in the street, before and in the time of the Destruction. It is our function to guard against what might happen; and what may easily happen is that inside half a century, if what is left of the human race has not yet again committed hara-kiri, there will be no true record of the events of the Epoch of Destruction, except in certain carefully chosen, prepared and preserved human minds for careful transmission to similar minds. You know the Memories, and we are looking for one or two safe places for the preservation of written material—we have not yet found the latter. The purpose of this letter is to ask you to see that our people in your care understand these facts; and that whatever they personally know or remember is carefully committed to one of the Memories, but *never* to paper unless there is no doubt of the authenticity of the request.

And now, as my personal contribution to the record, I am writing down what I know to be truth.

I begin with the moment when we and our friends left London to live in the country.

Towards the end of the sixties, about thirty of us left London for Wiltshire: our friends, or Paul Coldridge's friends, or friends of these. We had nothing in common, not even an expressed desire to "live simply" or "drop out"—or any of the other reasons why similar groups or movements of young people left conventional society to set up communities of one kind or another. When we did it, we did not have motives, or reasons, or rationalisations: we did it because it seemed sensible. Now, looking back, I am struck at how it happened. For one thing, not so many years later it was these people and their friends and families who were among the not so very many who escaped. (How many do *you* think? I've just seen the amended figures. All figures so far released by the Controls have been very wrong, even by my personal experience—half or less what I (and Check) think are likely. From this I estimate that very many people must have already been destroyed as unrehabilitable.)

Now I wonder about things that were not important then, trying to isolate what might be significant. One is that of our people (at the most five or six hundred when our "community" was at its height) very few would have been chosen by currently acceptable yardsticks as "good human material"— to use the phrase so much in use by authority during the last phase. Few were anywhere near what would be classed as "average" or "normal" or even "desirable." Of course, as that decade went on, and the general madness deepened, even they were using such terms more carefully; but it is certain that the people who were attracted to us were by definition those who were "eccentric" or slightly ill, or damaged, or simply unable to cope with the demands of that society. For one reason or another all were unwilling or unable to live according to the norms of the time—which were the more savagely defended as norms as society got crazier and crazier.

I repeat: these are thoughts I have now, the last I or any of us had then. On the contrary, what was remarkable about us was that we were not self-conscious. This was perhaps because so many of us had had contact with psychiatry in one or another of its forms: it was perhaps an overviolent reaction. And most of us had had some kind of contact with politics: our teeth had been set on edge. Whatever the reason, it was not until the middle of the seventies that we realised, because of other people's interest in us, that our chief characteristic was that we had no ideology, plan, constitution, or philosophy. We had grown as a community. People had started to live together. Others joined us. We moved to the country because it was cheaper and easier to live there with the children. Typical of how someone might join us was the way Martha came to visit us, offered to stay and housekeep while I and your mother took you children for a holiday, and then moved down from London altogether to help in the nursery school. (Incidentally, if you have not already received this information in material sent off a year ago, I believe Martha to be alive: she was certainly alive fairly recently. She is on an island somewhere, but would not give whereabouts *for fear of being rescued*. I've heard her several times, but receiving was bad.)

To begin with we had a farm of about a hundred acres, with some farm buildings. These we made habitable, and we grew vegetables and fruit and kept some cows. Some of us had money. Others had none. Some worked very hard; others did not. Yet there was no feeling of mine or thine, or resentment because some were less useful than others. (Not at the beginning, nor for some time: this is because we hadn't formulated anything, hardly understood what was happening.) We did not all live in one place either, for we soon expanded. For instance, when Nanny Butts died we took over their cottage and land, and Gwen and her husband, who had always wanted to garden, continued his work: growing plants for sale and advising on gardens. Other places were bought. Yet a feeling of community remained even when we lived apart. This was not expressed in any formal way, with meetings or discussions. Not to begin with: later there was a monthly discussion, but it didn't bind anyone to anything. I repeat: this did not then strike us as extraordinary. Now I wonder about it. In all the histories of the many utopias or ideal communities has there been one without any kind of religious, political or theoretical basis? I don't think so. And they all grew, prospered or faded—conformed to the laws of change. So did ours, of course. If we hadn't had the sharp shock of having to move when we did, I'm pretty sure we would have come to grief—split by quarrelling, then disintegrated. But of that later. It has been asked since (as they asked on that unfortunate television programme) "How do you account for this harmony?" I don't know. Perhaps it was that no one was ever asked for anything: they offered. But now I put forward what I wouldn't have been capable of thinking then;

nor have said publicly if I had thought it: I believe that unconsciously we knew what was going to happen, that a shadow of foreknowledge was in us; and that this put ordinary laws out of action, or at least forestalled them. And that this shadow from the future was in everyone, affected anyone: accounted for the fantastic character of that decade. But some people it quietened and sobered; made them grow fast, developed them.

But let's put aside this possibility. Here is another thought. I once read of an "ideal community" set up by some Viennese doctor in the early days of psychoanalysis. This group outlawed jealousy, property feeling, and envy—by, as it were, an act of communal will. When this small community fell apart, it was said that it was because the couples who composed it began to marry for the sake of the children. "We could survive sexual jealousy but not property feeling about the children." Now, this could have been said about our people too. That is, if our "family" had been set up on such lines, we might have said: We were threatened with discord and disintegration at the time we had the most small children. But supposing our formulation had been: We are pacifist and outlaw violence. We might then have said: Our danger time was when we were threatened by violence, and had to form a private militia to guard ourselves.

This is why I don't want to say that a spirit of irritable dissension set in at that time when people began asking us questions about our philosophic or religious basis, and we began to wonder what *did* hold us together.

I make this point because theories about the rise, existence and collapse of utopian communities have always been prolific; and when the human race has recovered enough energy for such luxuries, will doubtless again be prolific.

For a couple of years at the beginning it was a time when we were all very busy and very happy. (Personally very happy: your sister was born, our fifth child, and your cousin, Gwen's second child, and your mother was finding that kind of simple work around the farm very much to her taste.) But our hard work and our pleasure did rather blind us to what was going on outside. I have said that we were overreacting. We went on doing this—as Martha warned us. So did my father, either by letters, or when he visited us. They said we were naive, and foolish not to be prepared. But we were so happy to be out of London. When we visited it, we came back saying it was awful: it was increasingly frightening and awful; so we stayed away from it. Then things began to change in the towns and villages of the countryside. How? Well, it means conveying an atmosphere! At first it was an atmosphere. I can only suggest that a Memory should try and "gather" an atmosphere—first let's say from 1970, then from 1975—and try and transmit a feeling of the change. Looking back I see that ever since I was born, to my knowledge—and the old people say before that—there has been an obsession with dates, decades, periods, times. It is because the "flavour" of living changed so much from decade to decade, even from year to year. And it kept speeding up. We felt as if we were in the grip of some frightful acceleration. But it is just this I don't know how to convey. You must pick it up. And perhaps it will be hard for you: you and the other children say those years were all bliss and you remember them as a sort of pre-eating-of-the-apple Golden Age.

In 1969 and 1970 there was a worsening of the economic crisis, masked (as by then had become the norm) by large loans from international bodies whose insistence on "stability" led to the national government of the early seventies. This crisis did not affect us immediately: not economically. The people affected were those already affected, the working people, old people, everyone on fixed and low incomes. But what did affect us, what affected everyone immediately, was the tightening of the atmosphere away from the "everything goes" of the sixties. The new government stood for order, self-discipline, formal religion, conformity, authority. In America the new age of "piety and iron" (foretold by a Dr. Spock on being sentenced for unconformity in 1968) began in 1969. In Britain it got into its stride a couple of years later. This was a government which got the British to swallow what no government before had ever dared suggest, or—rather—admit. For what had previously been considered unfortunate necessities, to be played down and apologised for, now became civil and national virtues. As early as the fifties the regimentation of human beings by tapping telephones, opening letters, informal spying of all kinds had been established. In the seventies these were taken for granted, even approved of. (Anything that conduced to the expansion of business and "the recovery of the nation" was good; everything that did not, was bad: these devices were supposed to help an atmosphere of discipline and order and were good.) Also good was the most sinister development of all: the docketing of every kind of information on citizens, not by government and police, but by business firms (on centralised computers), which information was used by police and government. It was a logical development in a society where the needs of industry came before anything else.

But it was a government full of paradox. It stood for a national campaign against corruption and decadence; but in practice this meant the forms of behaviour which had been approved of in the late fifties and the sixties—that is, there was a swing towards puritanism, first of all in sex, followed by a reaction against the obsessions with food, clothes, furniture and so on. (This was partly out of fear, because of the threatening resentment expressed by the half of the world that was not hungry or starving.) It was not that we thought less about food, décor, clothes and so on: a newspaper might campaign for "simplicity and sacrifice," but changing one's style would involve heavy expenditure in money and time. But while we were paying all this attention to surface problems, the basic structure of the economy remained unchanged: it had done since it was consolidated after the Second World War in a balance where it received continuous handouts from international funds (really American) in return for being an obedient part of the American military machine. The working classes were sullen and rebellious. But they worked, on the whole: every pressure of public opinion, backed by police and army, was used to make them work longer hours and for less money.

I see that what I have written is misleading: the last part of what I've written describes any "Fascist" regime anywhere—this was what its enemies called it. But this time of bland, insular conformity, with its nasty amalgam of church, royalty, industry, the respectable arts, and the formerly unrespectable arts (every variety of "pop"), together with official science and official medicine, was also an age of anarchy which grew worse every month. It was as if while a ship was sinking, captain and officers stood to attention on the bridge saluting the flag, while the crew and the passengers danced and drank and rioted, though from time to time they went into a drunken parody of a salute to please the po-faced self-hypnotised officers. But how to convey the atmosphere? Tell a Memory to try and "catch" one of those "appeals" on television when a symposium consisting of a duke, a senior partner from a national chain store, a visiting banker from Switzerland, a general from the Second World War, and a representative from the Federation of Trade Unions "talked to the nation" on national recovery. After-

603

wards banks of pop singers and popular idols of all kinds would stand to attention to sing "Land of Hope and Glory" and "Jerusalem." Outside in the streets was a curfew because of the rioting over something like the cancellation of a football match or because it was a very hot day, or because a street fight had started between the private armed guards of two big businessmen. For this combination of a smiling, deprecating, velvet-gloved "establishment" with a continually erupting violence was the "feeling" or "air" of that time before the Catastrophe, like a man making a speech about civic virtues to a well-dressed audience; but he turns to reach for a glass of water on the platform table, and he has exposed a monkey's flamingly indecent bottom.

But I'm writing all this from the view you get of things afterwards: capsuled, speeded up, less frightening, because understood. We understood only very slowly what was happening, because we stayed on the farms, and we were people who did not want to be interested in politics.

The very first symptom of the general collapse was an old one: *nothing worked*. I remember my father's study (your grandfather Mark) just before the house was vacated: he stripped the material from the walls, except for one thing. (The contents of this study, its facts, its arrangement, has been projected: the key is in the possession of 7X40 who ought to have arrived by now—she started four months ago from Mombasa.) This thing was a model of a space rocket, a miracle of precision engineering, and pioneering precision engineering at that: it killed the astronauts in it because of the failure of minor electrical equipment on the level of an ordinary household's room switch. This fact, or event, ended my father's summing up of *his* time. I see no reason to disagree with it.

Things did not work. That a car for which £2,000 had been paid went dull in colour because of poor quality paint; that it might take two days to buy a screw which could fit a newly acquired bit of household equipment; that a newly laid road went into ruts three months after it was opened; that the service one got was not what one had paid for—it seemed that nothing could be done about such things, and soon they were pressed into service as signs of national integrity. We believed we preferred to suffer hardship and inconvenience to further the interests of the nation. We on our farms and in our villages began early to do without the unnecessary, though this was never decided as a policy. Our lives were simple, though they did not have to be, since there were sources of money: we did not "choose poverty." It was that quite soon machinery and gadgets became more trouble than they were worth; and the ordinary organisation of life became so complicated, because everything was so inefficient, that our life was simplified.

I think this was really what most people were feeling: an electrician splicing a wire unconsciously cursed it out of a kind of hatred for what it stood for; it soon broke and burned out fuses and wiring. He did not know what he had done. Similarly there was a steady increase in all kinds of accidents everywhere. It was like an emotional Ludditism: an unconscious "no" to how we were expected to live. Unconscious, unrecognised, unofficial—for if you said to the electrician, or the mechanic whose carelessness caused the air crash, or the men whose mistakes had caused the fire in the factory, "Are you trying to ruin our national recovery?" they would one and all have replied, "Of course not," and believed it.

Half believed it. I think it was the same kind of phenomenon as happened under Hitler with some Germans; they called it "an inner immigration." It was a kind of noncooperation, a suspension of ordinary living. Something of the same kind went on under certain Communist rulers, a slump into a muddle where everything was allowed to go wrong, but no one ever decided this or even allowed themselves to understand it. However that may be, the most striking ingredient of the early seventies was that nothing worked, everything fell apart—that is, from the point of view of ordinary living, where one caught busses and trains and pasted letters. Or rather, things would work with extreme and inhuman efficiency in small areas, which did not connect with other areas: a machine or an institution could work brilliantly, but only in isolation. The next machine or a sister institution could be unholy anarchy. Meanwhile the government talked of nothing but national this and that, British that and this, but using the grandiose language of Imperialism, or the emotional language of wartime.

Meanwhile we lived quietly, unaffected on the whole, like the similar communities or groups all over the country. So we would have remained if it were not that your grandmother (your mother's mother) was prominent in this government; and that my father was well known because of his Rescue schemes, and people were always confusing what we stood for. A kind of relative (by marriage), a Graham Patten (he was killed in the Catastrophe, presumably in a government shelter), suggested to his wife (she was for a couple of years Assistant Minister of Arts in the national government) that there should be a programme on television about us. His wife had inherited his television programme when he became a government official. This was a kind of friendliness, really: they "meant well." We did not much like the idea, but we seemed to ourselves irrational. After all, we knew our friends to be happy, when very few people were. It was suggested to us we were being selfish in keeping ourselves to ourselves: we should share our formula. We agreed, and then were sorry. The programme itself was embarrassing, rather silly. The point was that by then no one was able to believe in the possibility of something unorganised, unregimented, undoctrinaire: this we had not foreseen. So the programme emphasised all the points that to us were not important—that there was no constitution, no legal agreements; that some of us had money and others not, and so on. The programme was called "An Essay in Primitive Communism," was an hour and a half long, and occupied a monthly "slot" reserved for programmes with a very high moral and cultural tone. For us it was a disaster. Martha and others had warned us not to let them use the word "Communism." In the seventies the word was as loaded as it had been in the fifties, but loaded vaguely. In the fifties it had meant, quite simply, the Soviet Union, and had associations of treachery and espionage. Twenty years later it meant anything that wasn't good—a kind of portmanteau word of unpleasant and frightening associations that were never defined. Well, after that we were stuck with the word. There were two bad results, one immediate, one lasting. First, we were overrun by gangs who had come down from Birmingham. They smashed a lot of windows, burned down a thatched shed, stole two cars—nothing worse. Little enough considering the sort of damage done later in such raiding parties "for laughs." And now we were exposed to neighbours as possibly dangerous eccentrics and never after lost the attentions of the police. But the real damage was done among ourselves. For the first time there was a bad atmosphere. Suddenly people were sitting around in "discussion groups" and "forums" and "debates" theorising about us and about other ways of living. Some people left. One wrote an article in a local newspaper, "How I was taken for a ride by the Reds"—yet five minutes before he left he was in tears and saying: I know I'll never be so happy again. Officials started to investigate. Nothing much to begin with: inspectors from the Ministry of Education to find out how we were indoctrinating the children. There was nothing to find out, but they didn't believe it and kept dropping in unannounced: by then it was taken absolutely for granted by everyone that it was the state and not the parents who had the last word about how children should be brought up. Welfare workers were very attentive. Quite a number of us had been in the hands of welfare workers and psychiatrists at some time or another (well, of course this was true of every kind of person) and we found that long-outlived records were being opened up and re-examined. For instance, there was a couple whose first child had died probably as a result of the brutality of the husband—who was eighteen at the time. But since then they had had two children and did quite well except that he got bad depressions when he was convinced that "they would catch up with him." A conscientious welfare worker began visiting the family. He became obsessed that he would have to go to prison. The two cracked, and fled to a Catholic institution like criminals claiming sanctuary in the Middle Ages. They left no address—doubtless thinking they were making things easier for us. But of course we were thereafter plagued by officials looking for them.

This was the time Nicky and his family left us. (They all died in the Catastrophe.) His dossier had him as a professional troublemaker. (The Businessman's Pool of Consumers' and Employees' Cross-References, centrally computered.) The police were trying to find out if he was using the farm as base for agitation in the factories at Reading where there was a lot of industrial trouble. The questions of the police started off self-questioning about politics: *Ought* we to be living like this while Britain burned?

So much quarrelling was engendered that we all agreed to try and return to the pre-programme times. Things would blow over, we decided, if we refused to let ourselves be provoked into statements of principle. Well, they did, but only partly, and it was the end of our time of innocence.

For one thing, we did as so many other organisations, or rich families, or clubs did: we arranged for our own protection. We formed our own militia from among the young men. (In secrecy, of course—we had never before been secretive about anything.) It was by then a choice of protecting oneself, or being protected by the police. The police had remained "unarmed" because British police always had been—but were equipped with a large variety of weapons like tear-gas pistols, "humane" anti-riot guns, etc. Being protected by the police was complicated. By then they were all in the pay of some criminal syndicate. Not directly, of course. In the countryside it worked like this: the big farmers, separately or in groups, paid money into the funds of the crime syndicates. This was not known as protection money, but then the syndicates weren't criminal. The funds would be called something like Guardians of British Liberty, and the syndicates were integrated with ordinary industry; all were linked with the networks of the Mafia and the old Ku Klux Klan on the pattern that had operated in America for years. But of course, on the humble level of an English county, all it meant was that rich farmers (who protected less rich farmers), in return for subsidies to funds, got their farms protected by the police, who were paid by one group or another. These warring groups might very well be subsidiaries of a central organisation: but by then crime was pretty well centralised everywhere. In the cities it worked similarly: areas, or districts, were under the patronage of some personage, usually a very respectable one, who worked with the police to protect the district. That this protection was probably against the bullyboys of the patron of an adjoining area who was his business associate and possibly even a personal friend of course doesn't make sense: it made sense when the getting and spending of money was what mattered. For everyone paid protection money in some form to somebody. Our people paid money to the police, but it was to be left alone by them while we looked after ourselves.

But I must try and describe the violence of that time: it was a development of the type of the violence of the sixties. Its essential quality was a pointlessness, a senselessness, as when in the sixties groups of football fans smashed train compartments for fun, or street gangs wrecked telephone booths, or adolescent boys raced down a dark street smashing milk bottles against curbs or motor cars.

For a long time before that in the United States it had not been safe to walk in the big cities at night: sometimes in certain areas not in the day. For years they had moved about by the grace of paternal or brutal police; or under the protection of some gang. (It was in the mid-seventies that it came out for how long the United States had been run by an only partly concealed conspiracy linking crime, the military machine, the industries to do with war, and government.) Whether he chose to be protected by the bullymen of the gangster groups, or by the police, or by the deliberate choice of a living area that was safe and respectable and inside

608

which he lived as once the Jews had lived in ghettos, in America the citizen had long since become used to an organised barbarism. This state of affairs spread to Britain. The difficulty was, it spread slowly, and subtly: nothing was ever called by its right name; and there was always a good patriotic reason for every one of the liberties we gave up. I'm apologising! One generation apologising to the next for "the mess we've made" became a sad joke at the end.

I remember a ridiculous scene. I was visiting your great-grandmother Margaret (she died in the Catastrophe) at a time when your grandfather Mark was trying to get me to join his Rescue schemes. We were met at the station by a chauffeur engaged because he knew karate, and during the afternoon the man from the next estate came over to say gangs from South London were on the prowl in our area, and we should let loose the guard dogs. My great-grandmother burst into tears and apologised to my grandfather for the "mess they had made." My grandfather was very moved. He apologised to me for the delinquency of his generation. I imagined myself to be the innocent recipient of the contrition of History itself—then I realised you were in the room, forced to remain in the house to play because there were so many kidnappers about, and it was time I began polishing up my lines for delivery to you.

But who did all this rioting or fighting for fighting's sake?

Sometimes it was gangs of young men linked with a street or a factory, who might decide to go off in cars or even running in a pack like wolves to smash up some other place. Or it was men and women together—but these usually rioted around their own living area. Sometimes it was students. Sometimes it was the semi-organised militia employed by a big farm or industry, who decided for an evening or a weekend that attack was more enjoyable than defence. But the fighting and rioting tended now to be between students and students, workers and workers, one area of streets against another, one group of strong men against another; not between public and police, who were becoming more like referees, or who might even fight against each other as members of opposing gangs.

Apart from the raiding and rioting expeditions for fun, the fighting tended to go on under high-flown slogans. They were mostly patriotic and the reverse, for these had absorbed many of the party-political divisions. But fighting did go on between "Fascists" and "socialists"; though less and less as time went on. This was not because there were less left-wing and right-wing people; but because the labels were used so cleverly by groups of *agents provocateurs* in street fighting that the old banners of the socialist and Communist demonstrations were tarnished. Once everyone had known more or less what the word "socialist" meant. Now, for lots of people, it meant the gang who smashed up Lord's cricket ground last week. The fighting was more like one of the old Westerns, between goodies and baddies. From the early seventies onwards individuals or groups or even whole cities might suddenly succumb to a condition like a child's "promising to be good." A university would suddenly "pledge solidarity with" or "obedience to" or "support for" the country. This was like the waves of self-immolating fervour that happened under Stalin. But nearly always when this happened, there would be a minority in the factory or institution, or an opposing factory or trade union, who would "choose independence." They would be (according to their opponents) "talking the trade-union jargon of the thirties." This last, under the national government, became the equivalent of saying that the group or trade union concerned was seditious, anti-British, dangerous, and deserved punishment. Some group would administer the punishment while the police watched. There were race riots too, but not as bad as people had feared: black and white people beat each other up, as part of the general disorder. The government tended to be lenient about the fighting. But it severely punished offences against property—the waves of casual smashing and burning and looting which grew more frequent and more violent. Such a wave might start in one city (usually in summer, for summer was increasingly for violence all over the world) with burnings and smashings and theft, and sweep across the country, this process taking a month. Then things might be quiet for a bit, while the nation followed on television and in the newspapers the stories of how inciters and ringleaders were being caught and punished. Our systems of punishment reverted: there were higher sentences for theft and damage to property than for assault or murder. Throughout this time there was agitation for the reintroduction of hanging, of severer conditions in prison, of beating. The cat was reintroduced for property offences; hanging for assault against certain categories of people, the police and members of the government, for instance. Citizens took things into their own hands when they disagreed with the sentences of the courts. There were odd hangings made to look like suicide, quiet beatings up, and so on.

And I am ashamed to say that throughout the growth of this we did our best to ignore it. Yet I also defiantly assert that it would have made no difference if we hadn't! I didn't start seriously thinking until Nicky left us. I suppose my state of mind was something like: Things are going from bad to worse, but then they always have. Nicky left and both I and your mother were upset. We had been close, all of us, since our teens. We had been close even when we disagreed politically. That was before we left London. On the farm he was not interested in politics. I swear that he hardly read the newspapers. Of course very few of us did. But when he went back into London with his family he went back too into active politics. It was a repetition of his first introduction to politics, as if he were saying: You say I'm an agitator! Very well, that's what I shall be! But the first time it happened he was fifteen, and even then he used to make jokes about it, about the way he became political. Now he was over thirty. I went to see him in London, but could not talk to him: he was a fanatic. Later he wrote me a letter. It was quite unlike him. Its tone was, if I can try a crazy sort of description, as if he were roaring with laughter while he was telling me about an accident in which his family had been killed. The letter said that he had made a bet with a friend that he could start a riot or demonstration in any highly educated audience (such as a university) by the simple means of describing how the banking system worked, or a mortgage, or an insurance company, or even reading them portions out of that old socialist book *The Ragged-Trousered Philanthropists*.

It would have to be a middle-class audience. His point was that the education of middle-class people was always a blank about the mechanics of their own country—increasingly so under this government. A working-class audience would say something like: Teach your grandmother to suck eggs. The educated audience would riot not because of their anger at suddenly exposed wrongs, but because of their anger at having been made fools of: this moment in such a person's life was always explosive. Having made the bet he proved it, in Sussex, Essex, and Reading. Then he was charged with assaulting the police with violence and given five years. I went to see him. I couldn't recognise him. He was like the teacher's pet in a class, the good boy. He talked of earning remission of sentence by good behaviour; had already earned privileges. He said he deserved his sentence, was "grateful to the magistrate."

I went home and realised I was thinking about him as if he were drugged or poisoned. Not because of this conversion to conformity. It was because of the suddenness of it. I began thinking about what was really going on. Yes, of course I should have done it before. But when I did at last sit down and say to myself that I had been lazy and blind—I realised that in fact I did know quite a lot about it already. This sudden change in a person wasn't new. Things like that kept happening. An old friend would suddenly send a crazy letter full of untrue accusations: a week later you'd meet him—he'd literally forgotten about it, or behaved as if he'd had a boil lanced, a boil full of general hatred, but it was bad luck you got the discharge. Someone you'd never met would write you a violent accusation that you'd ruined his life. You'd never know why. A woman whom you knew to be kind and honourable you'd hear had stolen something and gone around blaming somebody else, or had started a slander campaign against somebody or other. And in public life too, it was a time of abject apologies, and new starts after false ones. The government would dramatically issue an order for someone's expulsion, or the disbanding of an organisation— this without warning, or explanation to the public, and in the name of democracy. A month later it would be acknowledged that there had been a mistake.

People kept taking leave of their senses—and then returning to them, astonished. This is why I thought Nicky's conversion to being a prize pupil of the police, and a model prisoner grateful for what was being done for him, wouldn't last. And it didn't. He broke out of prison and went into hiding somewhere. I never saw him again.

I began reading and studying, trying to understand what was happening. I went into London and studied the files in newspaper offices. I saw that in what in the old days had been called "informed opinion" our condition had been stated for years. We *were* poisoned. Our nervous systems were shot to pieces—mainly from the noise we had to endure from traffic and (most particularly) aircraft; the air we breathed was foul, and full of toxic substances; we were ill because of the drugs we filled ourselves with—aspirin, for instance, which people took like sweets or cigarettes—and purgatives of all kinds and sedatives and sleeping drugs. Our food was poisoned by preservatives and the toxic substances we used on crops, and the atomic wastes dumped in the sea.

The air was increasingly filled with radioactive substances—already in the sixties they stopped giving milk to schoolchildren in certain parts of the United States because the poorly fed among them couldn't tolerate the level of radioactivity in it.

All these facts had been known and had been discussed. Sometimes there would be an agitation or a protest, and then it died down. The authorities would always deny danger and disclaim responsibility. They said there was no danger. They were in good faith. Any one of these things taken separately was tolerable, we could have stood it. But put them all together, and the fact was—we were slowly driving ourselves mad. The human race had driven itself mad, and these sudden outbreaks of senseless violence in individuals and communities were the early symptoms. In moving out of the city away from some of the noise (though not the worst—aircraft), and by growing food less contaminated than what could be bought, we had done the right thing for the children. The people on our farms were quieter, healthier, happier, less neurotic than most, and that in spite of the fact that so many had started badly as rejects from conventional society—but that wasn't saying much; for the atmosphere was affecting us too. Suddenly we had to face outbreaks of savagery among ourselves. This was among our private militia: logically enough. There were hysterical crises in the women, soon over, but frightening while they lasted, with suicide threats and threats that they intended to kill the children (what was the point of bringing up children to live decently and honestly when it was clear that our little enclave of quiet and simplicity would soon be destroyed—and by internal pressures as much as by external ones). Then some babies were born deformed—all about the same time, in the space of about eighteen months. Our doctor said it was a coincidence. A number of us got a kind of mononucleosis (a blood disorder) and got rid of it only with difficulty. There was a sharp increase in migraine. Marriages that had been happy broke up . . . mine among them.

But I was back in a very early childhood atmosphere: the facts were known, but no one knew what to do. There was no need to look for extraordinary reasons for the riotings and the illness and the hysteria and so on: the reasons were all there, out in the open, had been for years; but people couldn't add two and two together, or if they could, were numbed by despair.

And so, for a time, was I, because of your mother. To

613

start with, our marriage wasn't one: it was a kind of despairing alliance against what we called "the mess our parents had made of everything." Later we were happy, when we left London. And then your mother suddenly fell violently in love with a newcomer to our community and went to live with him. It happened overnight—literally; she met him one afternoon and left me next morning. We couldn't even talk about it: she had become a stranger to me. The children, you, were left with me, that is, in my cottage. Jill had taken leave of her senses, as other people had, were doing, would do.

More and more, because a continually greater strain was being put on us. But I think now it was more than that: it was the instinctive knowledge I mentioned before, a kind of despair because of the future. The very near future.

I went through a crisis of my own about then. I could have gone over the edge into—whatever the general illness was. Because I was so close I think I understood it. The sudden fits of silliness, of taking leave of oneself, of rioting and so on, were a way of saying: I can't manage, it's too much, I can't be responsible. A man in a mental hospital will have a fit of violence and destroy his bed and his bedding and his locker. Why? He's learned he can't destroy the doctor, or the nurse or the superintendent. And anyway, what for? Long ago he learned it was useless to think of beating up the teacher or the old woman in the basement. What did he want to kill? His father? His mother? His sister? It doesn't matter. Long ago he became filled with an enormous sorrow, he knows that somewhere he lost a birthright, he diverged from himself, he will forever be shut out from some sweet truth that once he sucked in like air through his pores. He'd really like to kill himself, but he daren't. He mutters sullenly: They'd punish me for that too, I know them, they'd be waiting for me just over the frontier . . .

I was alone and miserable. I loved your mother and there she was, close to me, on the same farm, across a farmyard with her new lover. And it was literally as if she did not see me. She'd say, Hello Francis, how are you? with a charming smile. But only if I went right up to her and made her acknowledge I was still there, and the children were still there. Above all I knew the misery you children felt when your mother treated you as importunate strangers. I had known that myself.

But above all I was tormented by our helplessness—I mean, the helplessness of us all. I saw the human race, or at

614

least, my countrymen (I wasn't able to care a damn about "the world," other countries, the way our family always has), as people who had had a spell put on them by a magician. I felt myself as a solitary sane person among maniacs. I spent months like this. My work for the farms and the community was done by friends, and I shut myself away except for you children.

During this time I went for long walks. I walked over Wiltshire and Somerset. It wasn't easy. It already wasn't easy to walk as one wanted. A move to make us all carry identity cards had been rejected by a people still able to say *no* (a ray of hope which a lot of us felt too strongly) but one was continually challenged by policemen, guards, people in and out of uniform, continually coming to fences or boundaries beyond which one couldn't go. Also, one had to dodge any group of people, particularly young men; for it was as if the act of being together in a crowd was enough to spark off the aggression—usually suddenly and without warning.

All that part of England was more or less army property. It was the seat of a dozen military establishments of various kinds. Of course Salisbury Plain, which once held the sacred places of England, had long since been in the hands of the army. Quietly, more and more of Britain had passed into military hands. There were more and more research stations to do with warfare by gas and chemicals and disease. There were more and more nuclear stations for manufacture and research. There were more army exercises and training. Yet there was less protest about them. They were less noticeable. A new research institute would be part of a hospital or university and its purpose disguised. An army exercise would be unnoticed because fewer but more specialised people took part. The skies were full of all kinds of highly secret weapons, but few people ever looked at the sky and when they did these objects were taken to be flying saucers or space ships from other planets—much to the relief of the authorities.

At this time rumours proliferated, and so did denials of rumours. Nobody and everybody believed the rumours—which were as fantastic as you can possibly imagine (but not as fantastic as the truth) and nobody and everybody believed the denials. People had ceased to care. Or had become a different sort of creature, able to believe and disbelieve at the same time. Flying saucers and visitors from space, both benign and malignant; armies which landed and took off in transparent space ships (which was why they were so hard to see), swarms of animals which were supposed to be in hiding waiting to take over the earth; civilisations of fantastic advancement and beauty which were prospering on the inner surface of the earth (hollow, like a Halloween pumpkin)—anything and everything was both true and untrue. Our government, behaving as usual as if they were sane men governing the sane, were always issuing solemn or indignant denials and explanations to a populace sullen, or roaring with laughter, or rioting, or committing arson. This is not to say the government did not believe what it was saying. Government usually does. This government was more than usually in the dark about its own actions, partly because after all it was only a deputy or servant of the international banking system, and partly because so much of its function was taken over by obscure technicians whose names will never be known. For already was established that stratification which is the principle of the world we live in now: a horizontal, almost nationless organisation—though then, as now, this did not prevent feverish and virulent nationalisms. As one small example: I know (check Key) that chemists in research institutes in Britain, Russia and the United States were exchanging information in code for their own private edification and in the interests of science, and this when such behaviour, if found out, would have probably got them life sentences. (Death sentences in Russia and the States.) But who was to find out? Huge, expensive espionage organisations looked for spies. They found spies, in great numbers. But under their noses, all the time, went on this quiet kind of exchange between men who could not be made to think in the old way. So when a government issued this or that statement, with all the authority of the ranked battalions, the eagles, the trumpets—it may or may not have been made in good faith. But it didn't matter, because things had gone too far towards the edge.

On the edge there, during the last handful of years it was ... I forget that you shared it. But you were a child, and you could say, even at the end: We were happy. It was a Golden Age. You told me that was true even when we moved, split, went into a solitary half-hidden sort of life. The world can be jittering as if it has the St. Vitus dance, but one can still, by choosing a good house, a stretch of sea below a window, and a large sloping field, create for loved children a Golden Age. We shut the world away from you, in spite of the visiting inspectors, the welfare officers, the policemen; in spite of the aeroplanes that screamed overhead and split our nerves; in spite of everything. But now, when I look back from the high, silent, comparatively pure air of this country which is still half empty, I know I was more than a bit mad too. Despair was my illness.

At the height of my bad time two things happened—in the same week. One was a letter from my father, saying he was getting old and tired. He was not yet sixty, but he wanted me to take over his work for the Rescue organisation. And Martha came to see me to say my mother, then in a mental hospital near ———, most particularly wanted me to go and talk to her. Martha gave some indications of what she wanted me to hear: I reacted violently. The truth was, I had had enough of the fantastic. I wanted to shut it out. We, all had to put up with planetary visitors and green men and herds of lurking watching animals (they were visualised as a kind of werewolf) but I didn't want any more of it. I remember I said to Martha that I had no time for women's-magazine occultism. She said, drily, that "it might be the worse for me." We were irritated with each other, and were careful to be tactful. I said I'd visit my mother, but I wouldn't listen to any "fortunetelling." Martha said: "Please listen to Lynda. Please listen, at least." I promised I would and went off to visit my father in your great-grandmother's house: this was the occasion of the "remorse of generations scene" I described before.

My father had Rita and his new family with him. His children were about the same age as mine. This made me sad: on my mother's account. I knew she would not need this sadness, but this did not prevent me from feeling it. My father offered to take out all our people to one of his camps. He had three going in various parts of North Africa. He said he thought there was no point in staying in Britain: it no longer stood for anything a civilised man could care for. Margaret was angry. She was absolutely behind the government, she was still active although over eighty by then. She said he was unpatriotic. She talked as if he were personally responsible for the large numbers of people leaving the country. . . .

(In parentheses: More people left Britain in those years than ever had happened before, for Canada, Australia, New Zealand, various parts of Africa. It is these people who, taking with them so much furniture and Englishry of all kinds, have set up everywhere communities with names like "Little England," "Newest England," "England Again," which are more English than England ever was. I saw a village three hundred miles from Nairobi last week which Nanny Butts could have walked into and hardly known the difference. And parts of Africa once bitterly antagonistic to Britain now indulge in a sentimental nostalgia for an England that never was, and a breed of administrators that never were. There is, now England has gone, an archetype of England; and an English civil servant, as Kipling might have dreamed him up in a sanguine moment, all high incorruptible integrity coupled with the most sensitive tenderness for other people's feelings.)

But that weekend of quarrelling and tears ... my father argued with his mother, as always. Both put pressure on me, one to go, one to stay. And now I have to confess that I nearly returned to our friends and advised them to go. The Rescue schemes had become becalmed. They were part of international government. The Red Cross, Unesco, the United Nations, used them. The skirmishes that broke out continually in the Middle East kept the camps full of the homeless and the hungry, but while my father and his associates had been pleased to be of use, it was not what my father had wanted to do. Which I was never able to get him to define. If he wanted to assist the destitute, then that was what he was doing; but I suppose he wanted to rescue more than people. Something like the transplanted "Little England" and "England Again" communities but on a much larger scale, and widened perhaps to include the European spirit—whatever that was. But he was dreaming of something vague and marvellous, I am sure of it. Anyway, we were not getting on that weekend; it wasn't easy to talk. However, I was tempted by a farm of several thousand still undeveloped acres in Libya which he said we could use.

While we were talking, Lynda telephoned from her hospital, begging him to come back again and talk to her. It came out that he had been to see her that morning. Then I understood his mood—dry and edgy and sad. Rita was urging him to go back and see Lynda: she's a kind woman, if not exactly brilliant. But he was angry with Lynda: she had been warning him of all kinds of imminent disasters. She had said she proposed to warn me too. I was not happy, and neither was he that the only way we could be in sympathy was when we were being irritated by Lynda. I remember his words: "She expresses with extreme clarity the landscape of her paranoia." He told me he thought she was much worse. He said he thought Martha was a bad influence on her. This last was a new trend in him, and it upset me. For the years

618

of my childhood I had felt intermittently bitter about that triangle, my father, my mother, Martha. Then later I came to take pride in it, because of its kindliness and its generosity. That evening I understood that my father was allowing himself to be angry with Martha because even now he loved my mother so much he could not bear to criticise her for anything. Rita saw too and she said to him: "But you say Martha's been a good friend to Lynda." My father continued: he was very unhappy. Rita went to bed, in silent criticism of him. My great-grandmother went to bed. I went to bed and left him there alone. It was an awful evening. Yet that night I decided to put pressure on us to go out to Libya. I nearly decided not to go and see my mother until all the arrangements were made. You see how close I was to taking all of us into a certain or almost certain death, for bubonic plague killed most of the people on that farm a few years later.

Next morning I woke, having decided in my sleep to see my mother before anything else. I went back to the farm, picked up Martha, and we went together. Lynda left her hospital; and we took rooms in a hotel in ——. It was the most remarkable few days of my life. I was, of course, in a remarkable mood, after months of solitary misery, and in despair because of what I could see happening even among the people I loved most.

What I have written up to now is probably more of personal interest to you than of general use. Nothing in it implicates anyone much. I'll send it by Route C. If it arrives before the second half, expect that in Route G. When you've seen and taken in what is there, and had it absorbed by a Memory, then burn it.

I end with my love and . . .

[Here followed various messages to people from the old community who had found their way to the Northern National Area.]

III.

Second Part of Francis Coldridge's letter to his stepdaughter, enclosing Documents IV, V and VI.

Following the death of her friend Sandra Hill my mother was badly ill and found herself in a mental hospital she had not been in before, at 4B under a Dr. YN2 now working in the Argentine with a Dr. YR14. (Check Key.) She described this man as "the person I had been trying to find for forty years." He had been looking for someone like her, defined as "a patient of good intelligence who had undergone a wide range of deleterious treatments but who retained enough balance to be objective." She quoted this with humour. They began working together under the guise of his giving her psychotherapy. I'd forgotten you probably won't know what that was. Lynda did collect a lot of representative material and collated it: the last I heard of it, it had reached Delhi. Therapy, or analysis, was a process which was supposed to release suppressed or unconscious drives in neurotic people. A doctor or similar person involved himself with patients in a kind of symbiosis. There might be any result. The commonest was that the patient became dependent on the doctor and was unable to free himself from the doctor, or, later, from an authority figure. This was the easiest to see. Another, also common, but less easy to see because no one had thought of looking for it, was that doctors became dependent on their patients: as it were, fed on them. A doctor of a certain type who treated a group of patients over years created and then became part of a kind of psychic group where everyone was dependent on everyone else. You will remember that it was not admitted that there could be any kind of interaction between people but a verbal one (the use of words or the withholding of words)—an interesting contradiction when you think of the premise of this kind of therapy. No research had been done on involuntary hypnosis or telepathy, in this type of situation. As for the idea that a doctor in the role of a leader of a flock might be a kind of scapegoat or shock absorber for a collective of varying individual psychologies, it had not yet dawned. Research on this is going in Delhi officially and unofficially—both at the Institute.

Anyway, Dr. YN2 was able to use this pretext to spend a great deal of time with my mother, and later with others as well. This was a bad hospital. That is, it was one of the many which consisted of groups of old-fashioned unmodernisable buildings, and full of hopelessly damaged people. But it had a modern wing. They soon found another twenty or so people who could be described by the definition I've quoted. But only five had the essential qualification that they could be trusted to be discreet even when in a mental crisis of some sort. Thus was this unit created. Later they found another half-dozen hospitals (check Key) where doctors independently of each other were working on the same lines, the beginnings of a diagnosis of the hitherto not understood disease schizophrenia. All these doctors had lines out to places or people whose medical knowledge included what had been called "mystical" or "esoteric." These continued to work under cover until the Catastrophe. Unfortunately a good deal of this work was destroyed, although we did try to save it. Some was dismissed (when we tried to release it) by doctors who were too conditioned to see anything outside the current orthodoxy; others became interested, but were frightened of their colleagues: this was probably the most conservative and hierarchic profession in Britain. To quote my mother: "Since the birth of modern science, any person with a conventional education has been sent into a state of abject apology, has been made to recant, by the simple device of telling him he is superstitious. This word has done in our time what previous generations needed the Inquisition to do ... this word, and ridicule." I found this in notes for a book she planned to write, but unfortunately they got lost in the Catastrophe.

Nevertheless, towards the end, doctors everywhere were on the edge of the truth. What is extraordinary now is that they couldn't see what was staring them in the face. But they were badly handicapped by their "scientific method" evolved centuries before, useful for some things, but useless for others. Yet it had become sacred, surrounded by religious emotions: they were not able to jettison it.

Also, they suffered from the same problem as a modern-minded Pope convinced that the time had come to make his flock accept birth control. Millions of women and their mothers had accepted unlimited child-bearing to please God and the Virgin Mary. It would had taken a brave man to face telling them that their sufferings and sacrifices were outdated because of the new encyclical.

It would have taken a brave man to stand up and make the simple announcement that millions of people with nothing much wrong with them had undergone every kind of torture and maltreatment—but *voilà?* the profession had suddenly seen the light.

The shock had to be cushioned.

Meanwhile, people were quietly working in various places over the British Isles; and typically for that time, while mostly aware of each other, and even helping each other, were unorganised and unaffiliated, and using without ever formulating them the old concepts which will always be revived in times of dogmatism and persecution: silence, secrecy, cunning.

This was about as far as I got on the first night of the days I spent with my mother and Martha in the White Hart Hotel at ——. Though of course I'm now putting in things that I learned later, that happened later. We talked about it over dinner, and afterwards drank brandy together. I left the two old ladies fairly early on the pretext that they needed an early night. The truth was, I wanted to think about it all. Two old ladies—I am seeing myself as I was then. I'm nearly as old now as they were that night.

I went to bed calmly considering the information they had given me. I woke up in a state of angry shock, furious with them and with myself, as if they had been trying to trick me, and I had been gullible. I stayed in my hotel room that day. I sent a message by the maid I did not want to see them. I was in an uncomfortable state physically and mentally: as if some irritant had been stirred into a liquid, my normal self being the liquid, and now everything was in a rejecting angry ferment. They did not come near me: on purpose, of course, as we afterwards discussed. They had expected this reaction, having experienced it, or variations of it.

On the next night I went to their rooms sulky. They were patient.

We drank whisky while they "invited me to consider" the reactions of any government, any body in authority anywhere (remembering my own experience of politics, political methods and atmospheres), on learning that a significant proportion of the population had various kinds of extrasensory powers—not as a theoretical possibility but as a fact. We discussed this, almost as a game. It became a very amusing one. There was no government then (as now) which believed it could govern without a complicated structure of controls. Information was given or withheld from citizens who on really vital issues did not know what was being given or withheld. The movements of people were controlled. The passport, for instance, was granted not as a right but as a reward for good behaviour as defined by that government. There were vast interlocking systems of spies and counterspies—in our country alone there were seven espionage organisations a good part of whose energy was devoted to spying on each other. Ever since the Second World War we had been told how much of our money we could spend on travelling and where, and the conditions under which it was possible to travel were more and more officialised. Letters were opened, telephones tapped, dossiers proliferated. Imagine, then, the possible dent in this structure made by a group of people with ordinary telepathic powers—very well, such thoughts are familiar to you, but I'm writing down, for the benefit of researchers, the reactions of someone only twenty-five years ago, on first considering these very obvious—to you—facts. To imagine the possibilities of ordinary telepathy—I remember it entertained us during dinner. Through coffee and brandy I remember we left government and thought of industry, which locks up processes for fear rival firms might use its methods; we thought of the centralised computers on which all our vital facts were recorded—accurately or not as luck or the case might be. We thought of the stock exchange and the race tracks and the lotteries—which of course is where most people begin and end. We thought of the secret scientific processes that go on in laboratories.

By the end of the evening I was in a condition of euphoria. I don't remember another like it. All my life I had watched the powers of government grow, the liberties of ordinary people lessen; I had felt the slow tightening of control in every department of life. The air got steadily darker, more oppressive, claustrophobic. This government we were under whose standards were all to do with money, the making of it, the spending of it, the control of it, but whose slogans were all of service and self-sacrifice, had created an authoritarianism that governed as much as atmosphere as by law—and here we sat laughing, imagining how in human beings themselves were growing (faster every day, accelerated perhaps by the radiations and poisons we were subjecting ourselves to) powers which could make all this machinery useless, out of date, obsolete. I remember the evening ended on the thought that all existing forms of government were as irrelevant as dinosaurs: government by concealment, lies, trickery, even stupidity was—dead. The old right of the individual human conscience which must know better than any authority, secular or religious, had been restored, but on a higher level, and in a new form which was untouchable by any legal formulas. We quoted to each other Blake's "What now exists was once only imagined"—and did not, for once, choose to remember the dark side of the human imagination.

I went to bed in good humour, full of optimism. I woke up as I had done the day before, sullen and raging, like a trapped animal. I was amazed at my reaction. I reminded myself of the day before, but that did not help today. I hated my mother and I hated Martha, in waves of a pure resentful hatred that seemed to come out of the air, flow over me, and fade out leaving behind my usual wry affection for them. The last two evenings seemed like excursions into mania and yet I couldn't see them as fantasy, or "imagination," or speculation, because both old ladies had said, had repeated, that this is what they had asked me to talk about. But it was only when I cajoled or manipulated my own mind into saying "Well, it's an agreeable sort of game" that I was able to push aside the hatred, and go on with what I wanted to do—think about it all quietly. For I knew what the hate was. I had spent so much of my time fighting; to run our community was hard enough, because of the increasingly authoritarian pressures from outside; and behind me was always my early childhood, which even now I can't remember without pain. But I knew very well what it was Lynda and Martha wanted. And I didn't want to have to fight, and expose myself and take risks—yes, I'm sure you are smiling, as you look back at what has happened. But I was hating them for reminding me that there was still fighting to be done, and I knew that was why.

Through the afternoon I sat by a window looking out over a soft English meadow with elm trees standing above an invisible river. On the table where the maid had put the tea tray was a newspaper with its usual load of savagery, violence and horror. There was no connection between that soft English scene and the newspaper: or none that I could make. But sitting there I reminded myself that the euphoric talk of the night before had begun with their asking me to consider how a contemporary government would react on finding out that a number of its citizens had mental capacities which for a start (and considering nothing else) made all "official secrecy" obsolete. They had not asked me to enjoy an adolescent hour or so of imagining the overthrow and discomforture of authority. Well, I sat and considered. And what I was able to foresee frightened me.

Again I went to dinner with them sulking. They teased me. We discussed my psychological reactions of the day before, and of that day, and the reasons for them. My mother pointed out to me that accepting the evidence of her own senses against a climate of orthodoxy had cost her her health and, for long periods at a stretch, her sanity. It had taken her most of a lifetime. Martha said that in her case it had taken a decade of private experimenting without any-

624

thing to guide her but hunches and a naturally tough constitution. But she thought she had been lucky not to damage herself permanently.

I had been subjected to "dangerous thoughts" for only three days . . . I saw they were apologising. They were tender. They were humorously appealing—there wasn't much time, there wasn't time, they kept repeating. Time for what? But I didn't "catch" this plea for attention to what they really wanted to say. We went on talking on the lines of the previous evening instead, considering previous periods of history when governments, churches, or courts might have suppressed certain evidence and why. (Again, these ideas will be commonplace to you: I am reminding you that in the mid-seventies they came as a shock to an "educated" person.) We spent time on the suppression of witchcraft in England. The old ladies had interesting things to say about it. (Check Key.) We drifted off again into a long fantasy about what would happen if any street in London were taken—it should be a fairly short one, where people knew each other at least by sight—and a rumour was spread that in such and such a house lived people who could hear what others thought, could see through walls, "knew" where lies were told. I remember we talked about this as if it were a novel my father might have written, if he had not given up writing novels. We concluded it would not be long before this household found they had to move, if they were not locked up on some pretext—probably for creating public unrest and disorder.

I understood that my mentors were quite pleased the conversation had got onto these lines when my mother asked if I thought that they (herself, her associates) were wrong to work in secrecy. I agreed after difficulty that they were right; knowing that without the slow process of the last three days, when I was told things bit by bit, while my whole organism reacted against it, I would have immediately made statements about irresponsibility, about sharing information for progress, and so on.

That night, they told me that a certain scientist working on orthodox lines on ESP had been approached by his government, which wished to employ potential telepaths in espionage. And it was in the early sixties that the Russians were already talking about the use of astronauts with telepathic powers—legitimate, but what government was likely to stop at that?

They told me that "all of us"—meaning not only the

doctors and people working quietly in the hospitals, but friends outside—regarded their work, their experiments on themselves, as a kind of trust vested in them on behalf of mankind. No vow or promises or oaths were asked for or given: but it was assumed among them that the nature of authority in our time was such that it could not be trusted with such a temptation. Not only for their own sakes, but to protect others (people who perhaps did not know their own potentialities) from danger, they must keep quiet, work in silence, secrecy and trust, to protect a developing human capacity from the wrong sort of attention.

It was an appeal for my secrecy. So I understood it. I remember that I would have been childishly pleased if they had asked for promises, vows, that kind of thing. They asked me to consider that every kind of secret cult or group, let alone institutions like armies, law courts, religions, asked for oaths and promises: betrayal is implicit in formal oaths. Promises had value only between friends, when they did not need to be made at all: an oath that was worth anything had already been proved unnecessary.

I went to bed exalted: I woke like an animal stung by wasps. Now I expected the reaction and was able to study it. My mind watched my emotions rage, as happens when one falls into a fit of being in love, or disliking someone, against one's will.

Towards the hour of dusk over the water meadows I regained my common sense and began thinking about what might seem to you the most interesting thing of all—that I had asked no questions, not even the ones that screamed out to be asked. I had been informed, with details, that in my own country, under my own nose, groups of people amounting by now to several dozen had been seriously experimenting for years in what used to be known as the "occult." Had they come up with anything interesting, I might have asked; particularly as no week passed then without forecasts of Armageddons or freshly minted Paradises.

I hadn't asked because it was as if my brain had been numbed or jammed with an excess of new information: each meeting with my mother and Martha was a switchback ride through new information and my own emotions.

That night at dinner I asked the obvious question, and was answered simply by my mother: Well, yes, for one thing, it looks as if this country is going to have some kind of accident—probably fairly soon, but we don't know when.

We discussed this for the rest of the evening. I remember

626

(with interest, to put it mildly) my state of mind. I thought: Well, of course, it was bound to happen somewhere, sometime. And: Everyone has been unconsciously expecting something of the sort. And: Right, well in that case one ought to . . .

My mother, as far as she knew, was the first to have this premonition, in the shape of a "vision." Then others had had it too. The trouble was while the "visions," or the dreams, were consistent with each other, the time was hard to pinpoint. "This region of the mind knows nothing about our scale of time." It looked as if the catastrophe would involve radioactivity. The country would be uninhabitable for some time. There would be great loss of life.

I went to bed making vague plans for my friends and family; and woke up in the morning in a state that wasn't (like the previous three mornings) a sullen anger; but of astonishment at myself. I could not believe what I had been told. It is simple to write that. I don't mean that I thought Lynda and Martha were lying, or that they were misguided. I mean, specifically, that while I accepted what they said, I couldn't take it in. Nine-tenths of me, at least, did not believe in it, *because it had not heard what Lynda had said, and what I replied*. I was helped by remembering Dostoevsky's account of the man who was to be hanged next morning. He slept well, and dreamed with enjoyment. He ate breakfast and was taken to the scaffold watching the sky, the streets about him, as if he had all the time in the world. He felt as if he had plenty of time. And when he was reprieved, all his resolutions on the way to the scaffold to live differently, to maintain this sense that time was a treasurehouse and every minute precious—were forgotten. He returned at once to humanity's usual somnolent condition.

Several of the persons that made up his personality had never heard the news that he was to be hanged. Probably they would still be "enjoying themselves" as the trap fell.

As an interesting psychological fact I tell you that throughout the day after I heard from Lynda—whom I trusted and believed—that my country had at best a handful of years to live, I was considering (which I had been doing for some weeks now) how to buy a cottage across the lane from us as an extension for the infants' nursery, and what local sales it would be useful to attend so as to furnish it cheaply.

At the same time I was thinking of what I had heard, trying to "take it in."

Well, I didn't take it in for some time. I kept saying to myself: What you look at now will, fairly soon, be as dead as the corpse of a poisoned mouse—Lynda's phrase. Meanwhile I was happily admiring tree, sky, the flowers in old Butts's garden, when I went to visit my cousin Gwen and her children. I found myself discussing the breeding of a new stock of cows on one of our farms. I remember how I spent a whole morning putting a splint on a puppy's front paw: then suddenly I found myself crying. At least part of me had "taken it in." It began to hit slowly, as the news seeped through to all parts of me.

It was this problem that I took back. I and Martha; who had told me that four people among us had been working quietly, and were ready to help in the task of telling our friends what was likely to happen in a way that would forestall panic, or the kind of derision that is a cousin to panic and stops people thinking.

We didn't use any of the currently acceptable methods, like calling a meeting, or sending out a circular. For this kind of thing was not in the spirit of "movement" which wasn't one; and which people "joined" by liking one of us, and settling somewhere close and sharing a house. After a period of not knowing what to do, we behaved as we would for any other problem, and simply began talking to friends. I don't know what I expected, or was afraid of. Some sort of rushing about, perhaps, or an angry rebellion at Fate. But nothing happened. Quite soon we were talking about a probable contamination of our country, what to do, how to save people. But there were a lot of cults and movements active during the last days; a lot of "prophecies" and forecasts, some accurate, some not, were in the air. When you came to talk to people, you found a great many confidently expected some form of disaster, but were not doing anything about it. Well, what could one do? That is, if one was trying to get more people to listen than just one's friends.

And there were the authorities to consider. It really is hard to convey a "feel" of those authorities. Now everything is so stratified and codified and hard—necessary, of course, when half the world is wasteland and there are so many millions of the homeless, contaminated and hungry to handle. We have an administration which is in fact exactly the same from country to country, though the national divisions are so sharp and hostile. The administration is privileged and comparatively free. The hordes of human refuse have nothing but what charity can do for them. But we do all know

628

more or less where we are. Then the government, or any kind of authority, had to be handled like a hysterical person, or a mentally feeble one. It was touchy. It took umbrage. It bestowed favours and withdrew them. It had to be placated and flattered. An extraordinary time! The one thing we could not expect from it was consistency or ordinary common sense.

And with the authorities (even worse than with oneself and one's friends) one would be up against that reaction I had experienced when I was wondering how to buy a new cottage economically and furnish it cheaply, the morning after I had heard of the coming disaster. This psychological reaction would be of necessity a hundred times worse in an authority, a body of people, than in individuals or small groups. And besides, we couldn't say anything more definite than: It looks as if this disaster will take place in between five and ten years' time; that it will be pretty bad; but that nearer the time accuracy will be greater because some of what people have "gathered" indicates that a good many will listen and escape with their families.

Practically and immediately: we wanted to see that on the west coast of Ireland there were places where people might go when the time came. The west because the prevailing winds are from west to east. We bought a holiday place for the children and a family moved in to caretake while we looked for other places.

And now started a ludicrous and frustrating time. We couldn't get people to move, to do anything but talk. We were helped by chance. It was to do with the buying of the first house in Ireland. There had been a rift between Paul and ourselves. Not a serious rift, more a weakening of sympathy. He might visit us for a weekend, and we would meet in London. But we joked that we had drifted apart. I told him if he spent more time with us, he wouldn't feel estranged. But his life was in Fashionable London, seeing dozens of people a week. He had married a childhood sweetheart, who was then a sort of prostitute, model sixties and seventies. Not really a prostitute: sex was not the essence of what they offered or what was wanted from them. Girls like Zena were prized for their *style*, a highly dramatised and self-conscious "I am a lost soul" quality. They drifted listlessly, displaying their psychological wounds like medals, or as if saying: This is what you made of me. But I bear you no grudge. Please hit me again! (You'll see I didn't like her—that antipathy is alive still! And for a woman who is dead . . . Paul died with her. He died trying to get her out of the contaminated areas, but she wouldn't go.) When married they lived in two different halves of the same house and I don't think they met oftener than before they married. Of course they didn't have children! Paul took her out to big parties or theatre nights: there were photographs in the papers: Mr. and Mrs. Paul Coldridge. They were fantastically handsome, like a pair of gorgeous butterflies mounted side by side on a twig. When he came to see us (always without her) he'd say that our simplicity was what he longed for; but after two or three days he'd always go back to London. He was very rich.

He had joined my father and Willy Perkins in the Coldridge–Esse Perkins rescue enterprises very early. But public philanthropy and getting rich went hand in hand. He kept giving it away: it flooded back to him. I've never known anyone as generous. He'd give money to everyone he even heard of who needed it. He'd give away hundred to friends of ours when he came for the weekend, particularly if they had children.

And suddenly I got a letter from him which was—mad. It was a mad letter. I took it to Martha. She said to take no notice, something triggered it off in him, always had. It would pass. Meanwhile I should go and see him. Before I could leave for London there was another letter. He accused us of making off with funds, cooking books, goodness knows what. Buying the house in Ireland was "behind his back." We had betrayed him. In London I telephoned him: he was shrilly abusive. I was served with a summons in the hotel. The thing had become crazier still. Paul was wanting to be re-paid half the original sum of money he had given us when we started. From this had been deducted arbitrary sums for staying with us "one dozen days in 1971" and "sums for fresh fruit and cream during 1973." That kind of thing. The point was that the sum he wanted was nothing to him, it was £5,000 by the time his deductions had been made. "£374.19.6 for repainting my old friend Jack Sumerson's house in 1970." Mad. I saw a lawyer though I knew what he'd say. If the thing was allowed to get into court it would be one of the cases where everyone concerned would look a fool. We had never accounted for his money separately—or anybody's, for that matter. It wasn't in the spirit of the thing. People put money in, and that was it. Before returning to Wiltshire I managed to see him. He was not himself, but he wasn't the person who had instructed a lawyer to send me that insane document. He was low, and sulky, and looked as people do when they've had a bad headache for days. I realised this was another example of that phenomenon—someone taking leave of their senses for an hour, a day, or a week. I knew he would recover. He did. He came down to Wiltshire full of apologies and consternation. Meanwhile it was in all the newspapers. Paul was a highminded philanthropist given to whimsically impulsive generosity, which had been abused by his pack of seedily eccentric relations. We were presented as some kind of sinister secret society which believed in the imminent end of the world, and which spread alarm and despondency for undefined private ends. We were supposed to take money from victims to line our own pockets. Reporters came down, and detectives. All this was fairly routine mud-slinging, nothing new or even surprising about it. It was run-of-the-mill too because charges were vague and could not be answered; accusations were levelled, withdrawn, re-levelled, changed. All this created an atmosphere of unpleasantness and distrust.

It would have been easier if we had some label, some guise. What drove the investigators into a frenzy of suspicion was that we had none. We went through unpleasant weeks. It was a war of nerves. I recognised it from childhood experiences during the long-forgotten Cold War. The intention was to frighten us. Government in Britain in times of stress has always been by threat. And not even threat of prison or physical ill treatment—social ostracism, social disapproval, has been enough. What they wanted of us was some sort of recantation on the model of so many recent ones. We should publicly promise to be good, as it were, abjure former evil thoughts, that kind of thing. We did not. Suddenly government issued an order for our dispersal. We had not expected this. For one thing, legally it would have taxed them to discover who "we" were. We hardly knew ourselves. How would they define it? While we were still absorbing this, and its implications—the order was signed by Phoebe Coldridge, your grandmother—it was as arbitrarily withdrawn.

Then we decided to move. The decision was made "by feel," as it were, without even formal discussions. The detectives who by then attended our every occasion were even more baffled, because from the way their minds worked, no decision had been taken. It was like birds migrating. We didn't stay together—that is, within an area. There was nothing to stay together for. So many other groups of people

631

had "opted out," as the old phrase was, and were living quietly together in various places: if someone went away from us, they left individuals, not a way of life. Living simply is living simply, it is a matter of temperament. Half a hundred people went off to other places where they had friends, in this way spreading the information that an accident of some sort was expected. And, quietly, groups and families moved off to the west coasts and lived there as before, without fuss or making demands or drawing attention to themselves. By the time we moved you were twelve or thirteen years old, so you will remember as well as I do how we lived and how we prepared. I attach the names of all the people I can still remember who survive and where they are now as far as I know, excluding those who are with you in the Northern National Area. I will ask the people in Delhi to send you the material put together by Lynda from the work done by her and her group and by the associated groups.

The names are divided into (a) Those people who were with us for any reason at all, including those who came at the last moment because of our offers to look after and save anyone who came to our places on the coasts. Of course I don't have all the names, there was much too much confusion at the end. (b) The small number with capacities of ESP who were divided among the others in such a way that every group would have some sort of specially qualified help. These names are not to be kept written down, only to be remembered. (c) Those who left Britain before the accident to warn people in other countries of possible repercussions. (d) Those who we think might still be in sealed-off Britain, either in a shelter (as you know, this is considered impossible) or on one of the islands.

My greetings to your husband. I was invited to the Mongolian National Area last year as a fraternal guest to their Pan-Asian Conference. I made excuses in case this would prejudice my chances of being invited by your government to the Conference on Pan-Europe and Russia. Any chance, do you think? I'd like to meet your husband. My love to you and to the children . . .

IV.
Public Statement on the Notice of Disbandment and Dispersal served on the Community on the White Boar

Farm and Environs. Signed by Phoebe Coldridge as Minister.

We have taken this step in the interests of the community as a whole and for the preservation of democracy. This is a singularly unpleasant cult which divides families, purports to provide a "healthy" way of life while inculcating principles inimical to those held by the majority of the people in this country, and, as we have become satisfied, financially disreputable. We have therefore ordered its dispersal.

V.

Portion of a letter from Paul Coldridge to Phoebe.

. . . you're putting me in such a position! I am wondering how much of this is my fault? The lawyers got hold of the wrong end of the stick. I was ill that week, or I'd never have let them go ahead. A detective visited me yesterday. I was asked if I would give evidence against them if it came to court. I said no, of course not. Surely you'd never expect . . . [a line crossed out] Jill is [three lines crossed out] happier than I've seen her *ever*. I *know* it's not your way of life, nor is it mine. Yes I do agree when people say it is affected of them. When I was down last time I felt they got increasingly *away* from the problems of ordinary people. But I have friends there. I'm a kind of father figure to some of them. Yes, I suppose that is funny. I feel it is dangerous to say to you, Phoebe (I *can't* believe this is *happening!*), that I put money into this right in the beginning and as far as I was concerned Francis was free to use it. The lawyers misunderstood. Francis is very competent. I mean the *last* thing I'd want *anybody* to think is that he'd been capable of misusing funds! Yes I suppose he is high-handed sometimes, but then look at the responsibility. Everybody puts things on to him and then they criticise when they go wrong—an old story, *isn't it*, Phoebe? Please, please, I do beg you, is there anything now you can do to . . .

VI.

Letter from Phoebe to Paul, the envelope marked "private and confidential," the letter delivered by hand.

633

The order has been rescinded, as you'll probably have seen by now. I acted on the advice of my officials. Of course what you say in your letter has made a difference. I hope I do not have to ask you not to let your letter or this letter become public? I shall issue another statement to the papers and let it be understood that we would be glad if the thing was dropped. My personal feeling is that these so-called simple-life places should be forbidden. I can see the attraction, of course—who can't? But it's a very selfish way of living. It withdraws much-needed skilled labour. If some of the riffraff and troublemakers would only go off and occupy themselves on the farms—but no, it has to be people who could give something to the country if they didn't think they had better things to do. With our poor country in the state it is and every hand needed at the wheel, I'm not surprised public opinion is so hostile to these people. The fact that my daughters have chosen that way of life has nothing to do with it. I hope I can be trusted at my age to separate public and personal feelings. I may say that while Gwen is kind enough to see me occasionally, I haven't so much as had a postcard from Jill for years. Nor does Francis honour me with his confidence. I do not see my grandchildren. And how are you? Why didn't you ask for an interview and come and see me rather than writing. (Pleasanter and safer!!) If you people had ever troubled to keep in touch, to explain, then this unfortunate incident would not have happened. Unfortunate for this poor government, but I don't suppose any of you care about that. I hear your efforts on behalf of the Coldridge bandwagon are well thought of.

> Yours affectionately,
> Phoebe

VII.
Portion of a letter from Martha Hesse addressed to Francis Coldridge. It was written in an old school exercise book. When it came into Francis's hands he wrapped it in Top Strength Barrier Paper and wrote on the outside: "From the contaminated island of Faris, off the northwest coast of Scotland: Dangerous Material."

Is it you I am writing to, Francis? I hope so. I shall die soon and that's why I feel I should write things down. Memories might have become precious. To what an extent they have the young ones will find when they leave here. I know you have gathered where we are. I have gathered where you are. I have often heard you. You have had a hard time? I've heard your father. He is very unhappy. I've tried to talk to him—but I was never very good. I've imagined once or twice talking to you? But I've been afraid to say too much, in case it was picked up by the wrong people: will it surprise you to hear that no group of people cast away on an island have been less anxious to be rescued?

If this letter is to you, dear Francis, then I need to start only at that moment when the last panic began. You'll know the rest.

I lost touch with you the last three weeks. It was three years before I gathered you had got safely away with your party. My trouble was I lost Lynda. We had planned that each unit concerned with rescue should keep with them a first-class "listener," a first-class "seer." Ours was Lynda (who was both by then). We didn't begin to foresee how great the confusion would be. For one thing, there was our decision that so many of us had links with mental hospitals was a mistake and that this should be changed: it made no difference at all. (That was in 1977, if you remember.) In the hysteria of the end, they were hauling in anybody and everybody and locking them up on the grounds that they were crazy. Lynda had been living out of hospital for some time but they arrested her and put her into a closed wing of a hospital. They called these arrests "taking people into custody for their own protection." The paradox was that those who were already in the hospitals were free to move as they liked just as usual. The ones they scooped up at the end were not. So during the last weeks some of our best were locked up and didn't get out till the very last minute. If at all. They were of no help when we needed them most. They were the last to reach the embarkation points. I heard Lynda had got out but I did not see her again.

At the end when I was standing on the pierhead looking back over the past six months I was thinking how very differently we should have done it. (Six months because of our knowledge that we would have four to six months' warning of the event.) Our plan that when we knew definitely, from four to six months before, we should simply stand up announce and warn and take the consequences, was ill prepared. Our mistake was not to have expected the mass hysteria. I suppose it was because everybody had been so jittery and violent for so long that we couldn't believe things

635

would get even worse? We had not foreseen that the whole country would be rocking with rumours of impending disaster. Many people who had potentiality who had never developed it (would probably even be angry or frightened if they knew they had it) were "picking up" fragments of the future. And Britain was only part of it. There were as many rumours about the inundation of New York and New Jersey, the partial inundation of Virginia—surprisingly accurate. But the general effect was of a thousand voices crying Woe!—ours among them; and when people are frightened, they are cruel and stupid. That's all. I suppose, if you're expecting a bad time when people are bound to be frightened, the most important thing is to guard against the panic and the cruelty.

We were too reasonable. We put advertisements in newspapers that would take them; made as it were casual warnings in the course of television appearances; and we called meetings. A meeting in the Caxton Hall coincided with one of the evenings when the streets were full of "dancers." They were like the hordes afflicted with St. Vitus's dance of long ago. We sat waiting for people to come into the hall. Then half a dozen people reeled in, giggling, said they knew they were doomed but they didn't care, and reeled out again. They were middle-aged people: drunk women, drunk men. Or perhaps they weren't drunk: it was hard to see when people were. But that was the way things were happening at the end. It was as if people were damned. As if they didn't care what happened. At any rate, on that last morning before our party was picked up off the beach we understood that nearly everyone that came had personal contact with one of us: they had responded because of a personal trust or liking. Was that true for your party as well, I wonder? Of course a lot did come at the last moment because we had left leaflets about with addresses. And some came up and said things like: I've come because I felt this was the right place. And people brought children that they had rounded up from where they were wandering frightened on the streets. A black man came up to me with his ten-year-old son and said, Look after him. He went back, to try and rescue more people. I don't know what happened to him. And of course a lot of people had left before the disaster because we had been saying: If events take place which make you think our forecast of a disaster about such and such a date is true, then go as fast as you can.

Would you believe that for some days our group was not sure what form the accident had taken?

We were in the northeast helping our people to move west with as many as would go with them. The government denied the rumours about the gas leaks. People were saying that gas from the North Sea supplies were escaping due to vandalism and lying over a large area of northeast England, held there by a ceiling of warm air. Others said that radioactive missiles carried by the Russian submarine which had been missing for some weeks had sunk, releasing its poisons, in the North Sea. We still don't know if there was anything in this! But when we left, the beaches were piled with stinking fish, the birds were dropping dead from the sky, and for miles inland there was a creeping death that spread from the sea's edge. The authorities were issuing statements, then withdrawing them. The Russians did the same. I suppose we can conclude that nobody knew the truth at that time? Anyway, that part of Britain was sealed off first, and no one could go in or out except the decontamination squads. And by that time we were already at our embarkation points on the coasts. The announcement then came, and was contradicted, that a wing of the research station at Porton had caught fire, and that in the confusion, some sort of nerve gas had been released and was affecting everyone. We should be calm, report to the nearest hospital. For all I know this might have been true, and not another of those rumours that swept through the country like fire or a storm. On the same morning that there was a rumour that an accident had occurred at Aldermaston, and that half the country was already doomed, it coincided with an announcement on radio that a Chinese aeroplane had crashed in Oxfordshire. A pilot "choosing freedom" had got into a warplane full of particularly lethal nuclear devices destined for delivery to the guerrilla armies in Brazil. His crash landing did for Britain. This announcement was not made by a representative of government. All officialdom had descended to the underground warproof shelters.

Some of them are there still—so I really believe, Francis. I know it sounds absurd. While I know (have seen) that at regular intervals the squads visit Britain to see if it is yet fit for the work of rehabilitation and restoration, I know that there is no map or plan of all the underground shelters that exist in a thick net all over Britain. The whereabouts of some are known, but others not. This is the price that is being paid for the abnormal secrecy, the paranoid envy, among the different branches of the armed services who would not trust each other with such information. It is conceivable that more than fifteen years after the event survivors still live like moles in their concrete runnels, not daring to come up. I think this is so. I've seen a lot of "pictures." But perhaps these are old ones, not recent, I don't know.

At the end, the announcement of what had happened was made for the most part over private radio stations, set up for this purpose. Those people who were not dead or dying or expecting to die were told to make their way to the western coasts and wait there. For no aircraft would dare to land inside infected Britain.

On our particular station at the coast, we had gathered every kind of scientific gadget and medicine, with people trained to use them. We had money and barterable objects of all sorts. We also had concentrated foodstuffs and quantities of warm clothing and blankets and furs. For in this last and most "sophisticated" of wars it remained more than ever true that the first casualty in time of war is warmth.

We stood with these things stacked up around us and watched waves of aircraft coming in from every part of the sky. They landed where they could, took off loads of people to points in Canada, Newfoundland and the West Indies, and came back again. Ships converged towards us from the horizons. It seemed as if all the world was at its skilled and brave and resourceful rescue work after yet another foreseeable and preventable horror.

There was no particular reason why our party left at the moment it did. I was reminded, as we stood there with our babies and our bundles, of a story told me about the Second World War. A man was on the "unsinkable" battleship *Repulse* when it was sunk by Japanese warplanes within a few minutes. He was an officer. He stood at the foot of the stairway which was already perpendicular from the slant of the ship. Men went past and up, very fast, but disciplined, knowing the ship had only a few minutes to live and that those at the end of the queues waiting to go up the stairs would die. My friend stood there watching. A fellow officer went past him and said: "Aren't you coming?" This moved him into joining the stream of men. It had been some sort of sense of honour, or even good manners, that had kept him standing there letting others pass while every second meant life or death.

For us it was not a question of seconds, or minutes, or hours, or even days. We knew that with a strong wind blowing from the coast eastwards, we would be safe for a time.

We waited in a body for some hours, surrounded by weeping, beseeching people; and by people who were sober and sensible; and by people dying because they had been too late in leaving; and by children who had become separated from their parents, and were alone.

Our party moved together down onto a small boat of the kind that was used to take people on pleasure trips around a coast. There were about a hundred of us, with the children, and a very great deal of baggage. At the end we hastily discarded the baggage which had the instruments and medicines in it: we thought we would soon be across the Atlantic and in safe hands, and would not need these things.

The sea was calm enough. When we were out of sight of land the wind changed and the seas rose and we were in a bad storm. We believed that when the storm was over we would be picked up by one of the big vessels that were everywhere in that part of the Atlantic. But the boat was not designed for more than travelling from port to port in sheltered waters. It did very well for a day, then the engines went. We were driven northwards by the storm for nearly a week. We did not think the boat would survive, the seas were so high. Several people died: from cold, from the insane rolling and pitching, and from seasickness. We were crashed onto the coast of this island early one morning in the hissing whistling dark of a storm. The boat was held by rocks at an angle which had us huddled together like maggots in the corner of a matchbox. When it was light we saw it was low tide and that the sands began at the boat's prow. More people had died. We rolled the bodies down off the slanting deck into the sea: later they were washed up and we had to bury them. We staggered ashore on a chilly morning with the sun hidden behind a veil of angry reddish cloud.

There were seventy-three of us left. We were on an island which had been inhabited not long before. A dozen or so stone cottages remained, in quite good repair. There were sheep on the island, and some cattle. Both were very wild. We spent the first day getting our things off the boat when the tides made that possible. We thought the boat would break up, but it did not. It was jammed tight in the rocks. The island is about fifty miles long by twelve. We think it is off the west coast of Ireland. We do not know its name.

First, the problems of physical survival.

Warmth has remained the worst. We had good warm

clothes and blankets—fifteen years ago. We have husbanded our sheep, and have made good sheepskin clothes; but fuel is always short. The island is covered by a low scrubby vegetation which makes poor fuel. We use dried seaweed and driftwood. But we burn fires for warmth only in the worst of winter cold, and as a result we are hardy. Some of the old people died of cold in the first winters.

Or perhaps it was from the radiation. We lost another thirty people from undiagnosed diseases in the first three years. One of them was our doctor. They were all to do with bleeding—bleeding from the mouth, nose, eyes, anus, vagina, ears. Or skin became as if leprous and flesh fell away. Or people got dreadful headaches like migraine, but they didn't go away like migraine. So they couldn't stand it and killed themselves. From the start the people who got ill went away from the healthy to the other end of the island where they built huts of stone and lived out their time together.

A few went mad. But our experience did not make it easy for us to say that anyone was mad. We had to tie up one woman who tried to kill others. We tied her with ropes. Then she became sane and we released her. For the years till she died we had to tie her like an animal for weeks at a time and feed her like a baby. When she felt it coming on she would come and ask to be tied. We do not know what this disease is. Lynda would know, or someone like her with experience of mental hospitals.

Food has not been a problem. We luckily had seeds with us. One of us brought seeds "just in case." They were the best thing we had, except for the warm clothes. We kill and eat the sheep, also the cattle, but sparingly. We have milk for the children. We catch fish. We have tamed and bred a variety of duck.

We have built many more stone houses, in three separate places. We use clay mixed with some sand and crushed gulls' eggs for mortar.

We have sometimes joked that a tourist of twenty years ago looking for the unspoiled life might spend days with us before noticing that perhaps there was something odd about us after all! We have all the necessities. But how long before the bad time was it possible for there to be a community without a dog, a cat, a donkey; without goats, horses, mules; without a canary in a cage, without tobacco, or sweets or sugar or tea or coffee?

Perhaps our hypothetical visitor in love with the unspoiled life might swallow all this, but what would he make of there being no radio, no motor car, no bicycle, no motor bike, no typewriter. I suppose there must have been communities without electricity for lighting, stoves and refrigerators? But none, I am sure, without oil. We use candles made from sheep fat for lighting, and soap made of fat and sand.

We have one lack which we regard as unlucky: after all, there might very well have been bees, but we have never found any. Some of us older ones crave for sweetness; the younger ones know "sweet" from the taste of parsnips and beetroot, a taste among many. They suck bits of salt-encrusted rock. We explain to them the food on a modern table, machines, mass-produced clothes, traffic, skyscrapers and methods of war. We talk about libraries, recite poems and tell them stories from the countries of the world, describe orchestras, operas, ballet, a formal ball. They listen, gravely, taking it all in, knowing one day they will have to fit themselves to such things. Meanwhile they wear sheepskins or garments made out of old blankets; they have oxhide hand-cobbled shoes; their food is what stone-age men ate. And it is cooked on open hearths in aluminum cooking pots taken from the boat, prepared with the implements of a modern kitchen.

It is these children I want to tell you about.

When we arrived we had half a dozen babies, infants, two of them without parents, a dozen growing children, half parentless, some young adults who soon coupled off, as well as the middle-aged or old. Even the babies we came with are nearly grown up: they are pairing off. They are seventeen, eighteen, and they take the bad taste out of one's mouth that is still there from the grown-up babies of our dead civilisation. Or perhaps it isn't dead—and it all goes on. If so, dear Francis, then perhaps these children would be better off if they stayed here? Considering the small total number of people we landed with, we have given birth to a lot of children. And none of them have died. They are very healthy. Or we think they are. *We don't know.* Remember that we have no way of interpreting some of our facts. We have no Geiger counters, no methods at all of measuring fallout or possible pollution of sea and land. We haven't got so much as a rain gauge or a thermometer or a barometer; we only know that some insects like wet, others dry, clouds have certain habits, and birds migrate at certain seasons. Just as we see that among insects and birds and fish there are an awful lot of abnormalities. That is, it's how we older ones see it. The young ones look at it differently: that kind of bird is sometimes like this and sometimes like that. When a new baby is born we stand and wait for the first glimpse of it, and when it comes in the shape of the old print it is as if we had hauled something alive and safe out of the holocaust. We have had no surprises so far. That is, no physical shocks: limbs, eyes, noses have been in the right place.

I saw yesterday a girl of sixteen expecting her first baby kneel on a stretch of sand to look at a washed-up fish. The fish was as it were double—no, not a Siamese-twin fish. It was one fish enclosed in another fish, the enclosing shape being of a finer subtler transparency, and it was hard to say whether the imprisoned fish was dying because of being shut in the embracing fish, or whether the delicate outer fish found its inner burden too much for it and so was dying.

But for all we know such fish may now be the ordinary inhabitants of other oceans where they flourish and only have to die if they stray into our cold northern waters ... You think I'm joking perhaps? Remember that when we began our stay here Britain's air and waters were newly poisoned, and the seas around her coasts. Remember that the disasters along the American eastern seaboard were new. We did not know how badly the world had hurt itself. We still don't know. We have only our senses to rely on. And among us are only mediocre seers and listeners. At first when we listened in (and this was true for months and months after the disaster) it was to a screeching wailing howling bedlam of sound as if all humanity begged for mercy and help. And it is still too easy to plug into this band now. We had no idea, still don't know, if the event in Britain had triggered off more wars elsewhere, and if perhaps there were now more than two sick areas. We did not know if we could trust the air that blew over us, the seas that surrounded us. For weeks, for months, we were cramped in a state of only just controlled terror, with each breath a possible murderer—saved from panic only because we had so much to do to keep ourselves fed and warmed.

There are small streams on the island. We watched them for the state of their fish and their birds. We kept watch on the sea. Nothing happened. Yet we knew that while the winds blew nearly always from southwest and west towards east and northeast across the British Isles, it would not be long before the winds must mix whatever radioactivity there was into everybody's breath. We all watched our health, minute to minute, the health of our children, the new births. Many people died—then these first deaths stopped, so we believed that they were from the actual immersion in the atmosphere at the time of the explosions.

While they were still dying, we saw one day that all the coast on the west and southwest was heaped with dead and dying fish and seals. We did not allow one drop of seawater to touch any one of us after that, nor did we eat fish or touch seaweed or go near the edges of the sea until one day some children watching from a point that looked over the western sea came running to say that some seals were playing there.

During that year we hit the depths of our fear, a lowering depression which made it hard for us not to simply walk into that deadly sea and let ourselves drown there. But it was also during that year when we became aware of a sweet high loveliness somewhere, like a flute played only just within hearing. We all felt it. We talked about it, thinking it was a sign that we must be dying. It was as if all the air was washed with a bright promise. Of what? Love? Joy? It was as if the face of the world's horror could be turned around to show the smile of an angel. It was during this year that many of us walking alone or in groups along the cliffs or beside the inland streams met and talked to people who were not of our company, nor like any people we had known—though some of us had dreamed of them. It was as if the veil between this world and another had worn so thin that earth people and people from the sun could walk together and be companions. When this time which so terrible and so marvellous had gone by some of us began to wonder if we had suffered from a mass hallucination. But we knew we had not. It was from that time, because of what we were told, that we took heart and held on to our belief in a future for our race.

And, from that time, we put aside thoughts of being rescued. We knew that there wasn't much prospect of it, but now we actively did not want it. We knew that aircraft flew over Britain to see if that silent charnel house was coming to life again—how? Trees putting out shapes of leaf and fruit no one has ever seen? Toads the size of bulldogs? Dwarf or giant children born from despairing poisoned matings as Britain died? Crystals breeding from the sides of mountains and moving like men? We sometimes saw these aircraft flying across the sky to the south. We knew that ships passed not far off: we saw their smoke.

But there was no reason why anyone should come to our island. On maps it would probably be marked as once inhabited and now deserted. Quite possibly the stone huts we found dated from some outpost in the last war. If an aeroplane did fly over it, they wouldn't see anything unless they most particularly looked, and flew low to do it. Smoke comes from our chimneys for three months in the depths of the cold when there is usually a low thin cloud. Our cooking is done communally and economically once a day. We wear sheepskins and move among whitish-grey rocks on a greyish earth. If a man were to be seen in a patch of green oats or among the vegetables, he would look like a stone or a sheep.

If we wished to be rescued I dare say we could be: we could burn all our reserves of fuel to make smoke signals. Or I could talk definitely instead of vaguely to a man with whom I have a clear connection in Canada. He's a trapper, and his life not far off ours. I suppose that's why I can pick him up easily. But we have decided to bring our children up away from what is going on in the world. We regard every year as a year of grace, which will make them stronger and keep them safe and away from the people who would like to harm them. Also we were told that there would be people ready to look after them when we were rescued.

Some of them are very vulnerable: that is, if the world is still as it was?

You'll remember that half a century ago now, when you were a child, a novel was written about some children born all the same time with above-normal capacities? Where this author made a mistake was, imagining children being born the same as each other, with the same powers, communicating through exactly the same channels.

Our children, particularly those born later, grow more and more diverse. If an organism is shocked by a dose of sudden radiation (as they used to bombard atoms in the laboratories with neutrons to change their structure) then perhaps it may become ill and bleed, turn idiot, or develop in any one of a number of unknown ways?

Three of our little ones are idiots. Or we think they are. They look normal enough, and they sleep and eat well. But they don't talk, at six years old. Yet it seems that they communicate with each other. They go off together quietly, sit in the sun, play with pebbles or with flowers and are content—in silence. When the time comes for them to rejoin their own families they do, without complaint. But it seems that their families—all of us—are strangers to them. They don't much want to be with us. They aren't deaf, or dumb—

644

they know words. We think they are subnormal, but who can tell?

Then there are some who "hear" as none of us or any of those we worked with—even Lynda—could. When they were tiny they often seemed to be listening to music. Once or twice I caught a fragment through them. They would lie and smile, listening. Later they tuned in to the noises of terror and misery that are so loud now, and they cried, frightened. Later they began asking for explanations. It was then we realised that before the catastrophes all human children were introduced as soon as they understood anything at all to the fact that they were born into a world of murderous animals. But they were broken in gently, corrupted bit by bit. But our children can't understand. It is not true that small children want to hurt each other, that they naturally behave as grown-up people do. They have to be taught to do it. Or the children here do not. It is so rare for them to hurt or fight that one small boy who was "born different" (their phrase) was always off by himself away from the others because they would not let him behave as he wanted. He grew up with grown-ups: we see him as a throwback. The children regarded him as some sort of unfortunate born with the need to quarrel as if he might have had a harelip.

Another group of children, when they were tiny, used to shut their eyes tight and laugh, and did not want to open them again. They were watching the pictures on their lids. This capacity faded as they grew older, but not entirely. Between the years of six or seven and twelve or so, these capacities seem to go into abeyance. But they come back, if not discouraged. I wonder how many small children in the old days had this capacity but lost it because they were laughed out of it or punished for "telling lies"?

The children who "see" and the children who "hear" tend to stay in their separate groups when they are very small. Later they come together and share what they have. Some have both, but one thing tends to be stronger than another.

I merely record these things. I am not explaining or defining. It is possible that everything I say about these children is true only for this time on this island. It is a place with a rare fine air, a "high" air, if I can use that word. Sometimes it seems that inside ordinary light shimmers another kind of brilliance, but very subtle and delicate. And the texture of our lives, eating, sleeping, being together, has a note in it that can't be quite caught, as if we were all of us a half-tone or a bridging chord in some symphony being played out of earshot with icebergs and forests and mountains for instruments. There is a transparency, a crystalline gleam.

It is the children who have it, who are sensitive to it—being with them means we have to be quick and sensitive ourselves, as far as we can be . . . yet these children were for some time brought up with not even books or means to learn writing.

But when they do leave here and come back to ordinary life, they will have learned enough reading and writing, because of acquisitions we made about four years ago, not to seem ill equipped with ordinarily educated people—if they still exist.

I said the boat was rammed between rocks. It began to break up in the winter storms. As it broke, we took off the machinery and the timbers. There were three men with us who knew how to build a small boat out of the big one. But it was very simple, good for not much more than rowing around the coast. In a spell of fine weather that looked as if it would last two men went southeast to where we saw clouds rising out of the sea, as if over a piece of land. While they were gone we had a fire burning day and night on a high place to guide them back: they had no instruments, these were all broken. They found an island. They think it is about eighty or a hundred miles away. Again, it had been inhabited, but this time it looked as if people had fled from it at the time of the catastrophes, for there were all kinds of furniture and goods in the houses. The name of this island is Huig—we have never heard of it. There was a tiny shop, which was also a post office. In it were pencils and paper. There were magazines too, and some books, but the books were not worth bringing back. They did not touch things like sugar and jam and tea, for fear of contamination. There were radios in some of the houses, but they did not work. Bicycles, a motor bike, a typewriter—in the end they decided against all these, for there were no supplies for them. In the end they brought back only some plates and cutlery, some potatoes that had gone wild, for we had never had potatoes, a great lack; and some chickens which were wild but were healthy. There were a few clothes, like jackets and sweaters, but not much clothing had been left.

These they filled the boat with and set off back northwest, on a flat blue sea. It did not stay flat. They came streaking back with a hard wind behind their tiny sail which had not been made for more than a light breeze. They only just managed to land on our beach near where we had the fire burning. They, and we, had had our hour or two when we thought they would be swept past our island and out towards the Arctic. We have talked about trying again one summer in good weather, and perhaps using Huig as a base for a further expedition. But we haven't yet.

So we have taught the children (not the three who may be sub-, or super-, normal) to read and write. They are arts that seem useless to them. We tell them they must learn for when they return to ordinary life. They ask what they can get by reading. Remember that magazines came back on the boat from Huig, which, although we were excited when we saw them, we wanted to hide from the children: we were ashamed. And the children were polite about them. I've left what we call "the new children" until the end. There are seven of them, and they are between four and five. We didn't see at once that they were extraordinary. On the contrary, they are superlatively ordinary, if I can put it like that. They spoke, walked, played, as normal children do. They all both "see" and "hear." These being qualities we understand, we can recognise them: but what qualities do they have which we don't know anything about? There are three girls and four boys. One little boy is black, the first child of the child that was left in my care on that day when we were waiting to be rescued. One is brown, we think perhaps Moorish or Arab, or with something of the sort in his heredity: one of his parents is Portuguese. There are three flaxen-haired babes and two brown-eyed with light brown hair.

Well, what distinguishes them from the others? There's nothing you can measure or count, but we all feel it, and particularly the other children. For one thing, they are grown up—no, not physically of course, but mentally, emotionally. One talks to them as if they were adult—no, not that; one talks to them as if they are superior to us ... which they are. They all carry with them a gentle strong authority. They don't have to be shielded from the knowledge of what the human race is in this century—they know it. I don't know how they know it. It is as if—can I put it like this?—they are beings who include that history in themselves and who have transcended it. They include us in a comprehension we can't begin to imagine. These seven children are our—but we have no word for it. The nearest to it is that they are our guardians. They guard us.

I think of these people, babies in appearance, out in the world and—I can't bear it. They tell us not to be afraid. They say that in three years' time Britain will be opened again, will begin to revive. The islands around the coast will be searched. We, this community, will be taken off and to America. From there we will disperse. The seven will not stay in one place, but will be scattered over the world. I will be dead by then.

We are vague about the exact date, but it is the summer of 1997 now. Next winter will be severe and will take me off. Therefore I am writing down what I can remember and what I think is important. Joseph, the black child, will come to your settlement near Nairobi, and you will look after him. So he says. He says more like them are being born now in hidden places in the world, and one day all the human race will be like them. People like you and me are a sort of experimental model and Nature has had enough of us.

Well, my dear Francis—after all these years, I am able to send you this marvellous child ... he will tell you everything much better than I can.

If you are in contact with Amanda will you please send her my ...

VIII.

From M'tuba Selinge, Head of the 3rd Reconstitution and Rehabilitation Centre, Nairobi, to his Deputy Head, Francis Coldridge.

Dear Francis,

Among a new batch of fifty reconstituees just arrived from Little England (Los Angeles) are five survivors from an island off Scotland (*Incredible!*) Also some discovered in caves in the Lake District when the squads went in last year. These latter are not rehabilitable. I have put them in Closed Camp 7. Among the five is an eight-year-old who calls himself Joseph. Surname Batts. Father black, mother white. He has been classed ¾ Negroid (on appearance). His parents are in Little England (L.A.) undergoing First Degree Testing. He has asked to be directed to you. It seems on the island was a woman, Martha Hesse, (now dead), who was a relation of yours. She befriended this child. The parents have consented to Release from Family. Anyway, it is unlikely they will be released from First Degree Testing for at least four years. There seems to have been some sort of administrative ball-up at base *again. This child was given permission to leave clearing base within three months of his arrival!* God only knows what they think they are doing. Dr. Kalinde has examined him.

He classes him subnormal to the 7th, and unfit for academic education. But fit for 3rd-grade work. Perhaps you could find work on the vegetable farm?

Yours, M'tuba.

How about chess tomorrow night, nine o'clock ... we've been sent a case of Bristol sherry from Brazil!

IX.
Notes found in Mark Coldridge's papers after his death.

What sort of irresponsibility is it that takes people whose job is quite something else into administration? Last week I found among a shipload of rubbish from Tel Aviv dumped on the quays of Alexandria an old copy of my first book written when I was a boy in my early twenties. In it was everything I needed to have foretold all that has happened since I lost my senses—and became an administrator. This outburst is because yesterday I totalled the amounts that have passed through our hands in thirty years: £1,900,000,-000. Nineteen hundred million pounds. Of course such sums are meaningless. This was true before the World Crisis. All the same I cannot help dreaming of that perfect city, a small exquisite city with gardens and fountains that one might build somewhere with that money. This although cities have become like people, refuse to be shovelled into the nearest incinerator.

I sit in a valley filled with tents and army huts already refilled since the epidemic of Asian flu that emptied it three months ago.

Suppose I and Willy Perkins had refused all this international money that took us prisoner almost from the beginning ... but we did plan to make in the world refuges for those people who would be homeless because of easily foreseeable disasters. It's what I've done. It could only have been a question of scale. But somewhere in my mind must have been a premonition of the coming death of England, and a need to save and protect—all folly, and hubris. Stupidity. Right at the end I was still thinking. All right, we'll whisk them off, we'll keep them safe, we'll warm them and feed them, and afterwards we'll ... take them back and put them

649

gently down again on their own soil! Loving a country is like loving a person, it's all moonshine and anguish. What is it one loves? If you say, It's history, that means the gallantry and endurance of some men and women. Or, the look and the smell of it ... but the world is full of exiles who revive for themselves the taste of their own air or the feel of their own sunlight from wind or sun in countries that are alien. Or you can say: My forbears walked on that soil, and try and make it a truth for your own feet: but that soil and what they saw went long ago. Yet the word England, England, makes me ache, makes me stretch out my arms. They'll read Shakespeare and have poetry recitals. They'll try to recreate Harold Butts's garden. All those sweet fields and good people gone, and I keep thinking, How can they have been saved, how; meanwhile that murder is twenty years old and I sit here in a valley of tents in a hot dusty moonlight with thirty thousand people to see fed and clothed and most of them are under thirty years old. I'm over eighty years old, and I should let it go now, I should be able to let it all go. I can't. I ache and I rage and I anguish. Nothing has been done right, and I don't know who I can tell it to. Lynda is dead, Martha is dead, and my son has not forgiven me for not forgiving *him* when he would not give up what I thought was an eccentric bit of amateurishness with his compost-loving health-farm friends. When I flew to see him last year in Nairobi he was polite. Oh yes, he was very kind. We do the same kind of work, he and I, I among tents full of the survivors from the cataclysms of the Middle East, he among mud huts populated with survivors from Britain.

He says: "I have hope for the future of the world."

I said: "Please convince me." I know my manner was wrong. I could hear my own voice, dry and critical.

We played chess all night and drank cognac. "Cleared by the Commission for Pure Foodstuffs." Farce. All food, all products, all humanity is passed, is cleared, is classified and subclassified into grades of purity—while the world's air and the world's soil is rampant with poison and quite soon there won't be norms any more for plants or people or even for the cats and dogs in our houses. We live among sports and freaks and the living dead, governed by bureaucrats stratified on a world scale into 119 divisions. I am one of them. Mark Coldridge, Administrator, Class 13.

As administrator I eat First Category Food and drink "cognac" from vineyards whose vines have all been replanted in the last five years. There are fashions again. World Centre—Brazil. Well, they always did have a flair ... farce, farce, farce. My son has hope for the future of the world. He says there is hope in the world, a good thing happening, a new start. He sounds like an old socialist tract. He says that soon England will be replanted and there will be the start of a new history.

He flew over the British Isles on one of the early reconnaissance flights. He lies when he tells me what he saw. Just as I lie when people ask, What did you see when you flew over the devastated areas of the Middle East. All those old cities, the olive trees, the vines, the fields, all gone, fusing the civilisations under them into seas of glass, so that looking down under a violent angry sun it was as if one looked at an icy sea where a world had been drowned and frozen.

We said Nineveh and Tyre, and Sodom and Gomorrah, and Rome, Carthage, Balkh, and Cordova—but that never meant anything. A desert which was a graveyard becomes a place where cities are not built. That is all. We live on the edge, or in the fertile seams of the Sahara and the Gobi and the Arabian deserts that once held gardens and cities and orchards. We say, There were once civilisations here.

Soon new people (with two heads and fifty fingers—I can't help it, I've been in the clinic all afternoon among the monstrous children) will live on the edge of the new desert and start boring through a crust of glass to pilfer new objects to fill the world's new museums. I've heard that people are creeping back to live in the great dead buildings along where the Thames ran once. They say it is silted up from its source to the sea with weed like a giant seaweed.

And what next? Oh how full the world is now of brotherly love and concern! How we all sacrifice ourselves for the poor children! If one hundredth of all this love and money had been spent *before* to teach something as simple as that if you light a fuse a bomb will go off, then—

For two decades the world has had no wars, no prisoners, no armies. Only the armies of the rescue workers.

We have no enemy. The human race is united at last. We used to joke a long time ago that we would not stop fighting till someone invented an enemy on one of the planets—oh what a joke that has turned out to be. One that will keep us all busily looking into each other's faces for marks of *difference*—I suppose it is a step forward.

We are all brothers now, except for those who might turn out not to be.

But suppose we had noticed *before* the disasters that we

651

had no enemy? Even then our armies were mercenary armies—no government could conscript for the last of our "small" wars. Called differently (everything went under false names), mercenary armies fought over issues whose names changed every month. The mercenaries were the death-loving of the world who knew they loved death before humanity's acts proved we all did. They were officered by men whose occupation had gone—men from Britain's public schools, from America's officers' schools, from Russia's military schools. A nastier race of savages has never been seen anywhere, but we put up with them because the rest of us were left in peace from the absurd game of playing enemies. The enemy was Russia. Then when it was discovered that America and Russia were allied (had been secretly allied long before the world knew it), the enemy became China. China had split into warring provinces long before, but we had to have an enemy, so the war against Communism (or against capitalism) was fought with all of mankind's wealth, and with psychopaths and sadists and those who wanted to die before they had to. And the rest of us crept about minding our own business; and I and some other fools played God saving handfuls of the homeless and starving while we allowed our governments to make certain the death of whole nations.

Last night I dreamed of Lynda. My son dreams of her, he says. He says she isn't dead. I'm not going to ask what he means. I can't stand that nasty mixture of irony and St. John of the Cross and the *Arabian Nights* that they all (Lynda, Martha, Francis) went in for. He says Martha is alive. He says he "feels" she is. I'm not going to ask why or how or where. If they find the thought of forgiving ghosts a help, then why not. I can't talk to him.

Who can I talk to, who can share what I feel?

My young wife? But of course she is not, that is an old man's vanity. She is a woman of sixty who spends her time tending children who have lost their parents, her own children being dead. Mine, of course, but never mine as—is it very terrible to feel like that? I suppose one ought to be able to help what one feels. I'll burn this, throw it away. What I've felt has always been absurd. Lynda, and then Lynda, and then Lynda. Lynda and England. And now it is still Lynda and England and Francis, but he says his mother talks to him and that he believes in the glorious future of humanity.

Rita's children died of bubonic plague *in the same week*

that Lynda did. In the camp outside Addis Ababa they came to tell me that the plague was there *again.* We had believed it over. I went down to see the first victims. That being my third ordeal by plague I had become hard. As I walked back through the lines of tents where everyone was silently waiting—praying, no doubt—Lynda started up from behind a lorry. This time he was a Yemeni Arab, twenty years old, with her face, her wide blue eyes, her smile.

I gave him some money to fetch me something from the village.

The holocausts of the flesh in our lifetime have made it hard to believe that there can be any conversation between the shape of a face and the spirit. To walk through that camp piled in twenty places with the plague victims—can anyone believe after that that any God would care to inhabit such self-mutilated flesh?

The boy came back with some cigarettes and my change. I joked so that I could see Lynda's smile. He went outside and sat in the moonlight by a wall. The shadow he threw was purple on pale sand. Next morning he was not there. I had not asked his name. With twenty thousand in the camp I did not try to find out. Next week, I walked past a pit ready for the day's intake of plague victims and saw him stacked with the others. My children were there too.

Thirty years of living with Rita, whom I was never sorry I married, all that could not mean to me what that boy's smile meant that night when he squatted down by the mud wall—because of Lynda, who is dead. And so I used to torment myself that Martha, who brought up the children and kept my house and was reliable and good, did not mean to me what it meant when Lynda was well and came upstairs to sit with us a little before going down again to that awful sick hole under our feet.

All this is crazy, I know that.

I don't see any point in writing any more—what point has there ever been? To whom? What for?

I write every night when the camp is quiet and Rita has gone to bed but I don't know who or who to. Lynda, I suppose, or Martha.

X.

OFFICIAL, *attached to private enclosures. From Mao Yuan (Amanda's husband) to Francis Coldridge, Nairobi.*

We have extended your visa to include your employee Joseph Batts. You will appreciate that as he originates from Contaminated Area B he will have to be confined in quarantine for the regulation month before being permitted to enter. It will be in order for him to inspect parks and gardens within the limits of seven miles from the city. No aliens are allowed outside that limit. It will be in order for him to attend courses on gardening. I take it that your statement that he is ten years old is a misprint?

Yours, etc.

Author's Notes

This is the fifth and last volume of the series *Children of Violence*. The first was *Martha Quest*, 1952; the second, *A Proper Marriage*, 1954; the third, *A Ripple from the Storm*, 1958; the fourth, *Landlocked*, 1965. Volumes one and two were published first in America in 1964; volumes three and four in 1966.

When I started writing this series Zambia was Northern Rhodesia and Rhodesia was Southern Rhodesia. (I lived for twenty-five years in Rhodesia before being made a prohibited immigrant.) I used the name "Zambesia" for the white-dominated colony described in this series because I did not want it to be thought that what I described was peculiar to Southern Rhodesia. My Zambesia is a composite of various white-dominated parts of Africa and, as I've since discovered, some of the characteristics of its white people are those of any ruling minority whatever their colour, and some are those of white people anywhere—in Britain for instance. But Zambesia is not meant to be Zambia, which was born in 1964 out of the old Colonial Office territory Northern Rhodesia.

This book is what the Germans call a *Bildungsroman*. We don't have a word for it. This kind of novel has been out of fashion for some time. This does not mean that there is anything wrong with this kind of novel.

Finally ... this is a time when publishing firms are bought and sold like pounds of sugar; are tiny parts of huge empires. One of my publishers was sold on the stock exchange as part of a package deal; and the first the men and women working for it knew of it was when the information came over on the ticker tape. This sort of thing doesn't conduce towards good publishing; and has ended the old way when authors had personal friendships with their publishers for a lifetime. But, tucked away in this edifice of moguls, of

655

publishing men who change firms every three or four years, of agents whose function these days seems to be setting up films with a high artistic content, of accountants and paperback men and publicity experts and ... and ... and ... there are individuals who make up for it all. One is Robert Gottlieb of New York, who is a publisher of the old kind. Another is Juliet O'Hea of Curtis Brown, who has been my agent for nearly twenty years. Juliet stands by her authors when she dislikes their politics, is sad about their lack of religion, and considers that they would be more usefully occupied in writing something else than novel series which drag on for a couple of decades. She backs us when we aren't writing profitably and are not behaving profitably either ... in short, she's a gem of an agent. Juliet, my grateful thanks.

DORIS LESSING

ABOUT THE AUTHOR

DORIS LESSING was born of British parents in Persia in 1919, and moved, with her family, to Southern Rhodesia when she was five years old. She went to England in 1949, and has lived there ever since. She has written more than a dozen books—novels, stories, reportage, poems and plays.

READ THE WOMEN WHO TAKE STANDS AND ACT ON THEM

THE NAMES THAT SPELL
GREAT LITERATURE

Choose from today's most renowned world authors—every one an important addition to your personal library.

Hermann Hesse

☐	13956	MAGISTER LUDI	$2.95
☐	13523	DEMIAN	$2.25
☐	11978	THE JOURNEY TO THE EAST	$1.95
☐	12529	SIDDHARTHA	$2.25
☐	12758	BENEATH THE WHEEL	$2.25
☐	12509	NARCISSUS AND GOLDMUND	$2.50
☐	13174	STEPPENWOLF	$2.25
☐	11510	ROSSHALDE	$1.95

Alexander Solzhenitsyn

☐	10111	THE FIRST CIRCLE	$2.50
☐	13441	ONE DAY IN THE LIFE OF IVAN DENISOVICH	$2.50
☐	2997	AUGUST 1914	$2.50
☐	13720	CANCER WARD	$3.95

Jerzy Kosinski

☐	12465	STEPS	$2.25
☐	13619	THE PAINTED BIRD	$2.50
☐	2613	COCKPIT	$2.25
☐	11899	BLIND DATE	$2.50
☐	13843	BEING THERE	$2.50

Doris Lessing

☐	13433	THE SUMMER BEFORE THE DARK	$2.95
☐	13675	THE GOLDEN NOTEBOOK	$3.95
☐	13967	THE FOUR-GATED CITY	$3.95
☐	11717	BRIEFING FOR A DESCENT INTO HELL	$2.25

André Schwarz-Bart

☐	12510	THE LAST OF THE JUST	$2.95

Buy them at your local bookstore or use this handy coupon for ordering:

Bantam Books, Inc., Dept. EDG, 414 East Golf Road, Des Plaines, Ill. 60016

Please send me the books I have checked above. I am enclosing $_____
(please add $1.00 to cover postage and handling). Send check or money order
—no cash or C.O.D.'s please.

Mr/Mrs/Miss _____

Address _____

City _____ State/Zip _____

EDG—3/80

Please allow four to six weeks for delivery. This offer expires 9/80.

READ TOMORROW'S LITERATURE—TODAY

The best of today's writing bound for tomorrow's classics.

Bantam Book Catalog

Here's your up-to-the-minute listing of over 1,400 titles by your favorite authors.

This illustrated, large format catalog gives a description of each title. For your convenience, it is divided into categories in fiction and non-fiction—gothics, science fiction, westerns, mysteries, cookbooks, mysticism and occult, biographies, history, family living, health, psychology, art.

So don't delay—take advantage of this special opportunity to increase your reading pleasure.

Just send us your name and address and 50¢ (to help defray postage and handling costs).